The Black Rose Series

By

LM Morgan

VOLUME 1

When Darkness Falls – A Prequel to the
Black Rose series
Pg.5

Book 1 - Embracing the Darkness
Pg.29

Book 2 - A Slave to the Darkness
Pg.321

ISBN - 9798478896744

An important message from the author.

Before you read this book, please be ready to delve into a dark and taboo world of demons and angels who can and will do as they please. This series, especially the first novel, will immerse you in a world filled with dark places and even darker beings. They are not human, and do not act the way you and I act or think the way you and I think. Please be ready for some controversial themes and for me to push the boundaries.

I tell you this not just because there are adult scenes or a few taboo subjects, but because I mean it, and would hate to give you any false expectations about happy endings and softly, softly romance. This series is not for everyone, and I know that, so please decide if you're ready before diving in.

If you're on the fence or have heard the rumours of the depravities and darkness that await you, please assume they are all true. I can understand how some readers were upset and discouraged by the thought of some of the darker themes, but urge you to trust me…

PLEASE NOTE

This story depicts explicit sexual relationships between consenting adults, including romantic suspense, elements of forced consent, instances of domestic violence and incest. This series is very dark, and may not be suitable for those under the age of eighteen.

Cover art by LM Morgan
Cover photograph courtesy of Deposit Photos

When Darkness Falls

A short prequel to the Black Rose series

By

LM Morgan

Christiana

1115 A.D.

"What's he into this month?" the demon and fallen angel, Leviathan, asked his fellow minion of Hell, Beelzebub. His scruffy friend shrugged.

"Virgins?" was his attempt at an answer, but even the usually so astute demon didn't seem so sure. "Go with that. Either way, just get something sorted, otherwise we'll both be in his bad books, and we can't have that. Not with All Hallow's Eve coming up."

Leviathan grinned and rubbed his hands together. He loved this time of year, when they all took the opportunity to quite literally raise some hell. Everything was already neatly arranged. All he had to do was lure in their guests when the time came and the three of them would certainly host a party worthy of their fierce and unstoppable ruler's reputation.

Together, the pair of demons then scoured the small village they'd teleported into for a suitable female, which given it was only the twelfth century Britain was relatively easy, but their master also had certain requirements he expected to be met. Beelzebub was right. Their almighty Dark Prince sure did have a penchant for virgins at the moment. He liked them older than many men of this time took their brides, but they had to be fully intact where it counted. Lucifer also wasn't interested in girls. He wanted women. Busty ladies with soft skin and a sweet innocence he could corrupt and exploit. He'd bend them to his every whim before taking their virtue away without a care for the consequences, only for his own enjoyment.

Leviathan had seen him in action and knew without ever having to ask the women in question that his wooing methods weren't only effective, but how once a suitable young woman found herself in his sights, he was downright impossible to refuse. Lucifer's needs came first, as always, but then Leviathan and the other demons knew it would be their turn to have some fun. He and Beelzebub got their share of conquests alongside their powerful leader and knew this time would be no exception. They were an unconquerable team. Together, the three of them had built a netherworld full of sinners' souls to be proud of, and he'd agreed to take command of Lucifer's new army until he found and trained a suitable protégé.

However, there were parts of himself he was still learning to control since his descent into darkness. Leviathan had been transformed from angel to demon in a heartbeat, and in doing so, he had accepted not only an evil fate but also a wealth of dark power. Among his gifts, he'd inherited an empire of his own to possess and command. The underwater parts of the Earth were his, whether he'd wanted them or not. He had a connection to water he couldn't deny or ignore and over the centuries had steadily altered himself to become another creature entirely. There was a monster that lived within him that demanded regular satisfaction. It needed satiating, and there was only one way to do it.

Because of the immense urges to commit sin he tackled every day, plus the energy he drew from being master of the Earth's oceans, Leviathan often recruited his new followers from the numerous vessels that littered his seas. His almighty power would expand tenfold whenever he hit the water's edge, and he would sense every life held within its powerful grasp. Leviathan could choose which soul to save and which to claim as easily as selecting a ripe apple from a tree. He owned each and every life beholden to the whims of the tide. He alone decided who lived and who perished, and the rush of taking those final breaths was one Leviathan had never dreamed he might crave. As an angel, he'd watched over the seas, cast away storms, and protected those explorers searching for distant lands. As a demon, Leviathan was now full of dark power and was happy only when those same oceans were full of the dead. Their fear empowered him. Their calls for help were like sonnets ringing blissfully in his ears, and the looks on their faces as they accepted their death was the most beautiful sight he'd ever beheld. There was something truly evocative about death and destruction, carnage and chaos, and Leviathan indulged not only to satisfy the monster but also the man.

"Excuse me, miss. Might I bother you for a cup of water and a handful of hay for my steed?" he asked the young woman tending to a small flock of sheep behind a low rock wall. He dismounted, tipped his hat, and even gave a small bow for added flounce. When he looked back up to meet her gaze, Leviathan smiled so sweetly he was confident he saw her blush. She was positively delectable, and he quickly decided that if Lucifer didn't want this girl, he'd have her for himself. She was a truly natural beauty, and her thick woollen dress did nothing to hide the womanly curve of her breast and waist underneath.

"You'll have to speak with my father, mister. He's at the farmhouse tending to the lambs," she answered, her voice lilting with soft inflections that told Leviathan he was in the West Country. He'd stopped paying attention of late, simply repeating the same cycle of lust, sex, greed, and death no matter where he went. This town, just like this farmhouse and his gentlemanly routine, was all the same as before, and would be the same again the next time.

"Then I shall ask if he could use my help in return for some nourishment for my horse, and perhaps even be so bold as to ask for a chance to spend some more time with you, miss," he answered, grinning down at the young woman again. "What's your name?"

"Christiana," she told him, and Leviathan had to force himself not to laugh at her so virtuous name.

"Christiana," he repeated, and then took off for the small house. The monster within him stirred when he spotted a wide river in the distance. Thoughts of taking Christiana for a walk down by the water's edge filled his head. He imagined himself spreading her legs and diving inside of her, enjoying every moan and cry for more until they were both satisfied, before then luring her into the water to clean off. There, Leviathan's monstrous alter ego would take what Christiana hadn't offered, but he wouldn't give her the choice. Her soul would then belong to him, and he would make her his plaything amidst the other concubines he frequented in his private dungeons of Hell.

Leviathan shook away the craving. His master got first refusal, as always. Everything he did was in service to the almighty being who'd not only given him purpose and a life to lead in the netherworld, but a title and a home at his side. They were brothers, not by birth, but by bond. Lucifer had dared stand against their group of leaders—the High Council of Angels—and lost, but in doing so he had also gained an incredibly new power none of the others had ever counted on. He wasn't lost in the darkness. Instead, he drew power from it. Lucifer had taken on his involuntary position as Hell's ruler without any refusal and over time he had become a force not a single one of the angels in Heaven could reckon with.

Leviathan remembered easily how he and Beelzebub had felt their doubts creep into their once so steadfast loyalty to the light at different times, but they'd both known it the moment each of them had turned. Leviathan's had been like a strike of lightening to his chest, surging within him with such force it couldn't be denied. He'd closed his eyes and fallen, before letting the leader of the High Council of Angels or any of the others have the pleasure of pushing him over the edge. It'd been liberating, and the dark power had welcomed him before, then filling the voids left behind without him having to ask for it. His heart had blackened before he'd even hit the ground, and when he'd opened his eyes, Lucifer had been peering down at him with a surprised smile.

"We aren't hiring help, son. There's barely enough crops to feed ourselves, let alone another mouth," the farmer barked as Leviathan approached, but he continued on towards him with a non-threatening smile.

"I hear you have fresh lambs, sir? I'd like to offer my assistance, but require no food for my belly, only a graze at your glade for my horse wouldn't go amiss?" he asked, and the man seemed surprised. He looked Leviathan up and down and simply nodded. The old man seemed exhausted and could evidently do with the help. This was going to be a piece of cake, he was sure. "I'm Leofwin," Leviathan told him, having chosen a common name for that era as an alias, and the farmer shook his outstretched hand.

"Benedict," he answered with a craggy smile. Leviathan couldn't read minds, but he could tell from his touch that Benedict and his family were good people. The lightness within him wasn't caused by fear of God, but because of his good deeds in life. Part of him might've felt guilty for wanting to use the man's daughter to appease the urges of his Dark Prince, if it weren't for Leviathan's now unyielding evil core. Guilt was an emotion long since lost to him, like many others.

Together they tended to the sheep and made swift progress gathering the day's crops. Benedict seemed surprised with Leviathan's strength and skill, but also grateful for the assistance. Despite his earlier denial, he later insisted their guest stay and eat with his family. Leviathan accepted with a gracious smile and sat down with the group as they each tucked into a hearty bowl of stew and homemade bread that had been cooked by the farmer's wife, Mary.

After dinner, Leviathan went to see that his horse was well, which was all for show, of course, but his ploy worked a treat, and soon Christiana was beside him in the pasture.

"He's beautiful," she whispered as she stroked the steed's black mane.

"Shadow, like the swift and unending darkness. He's a whisper on the wind, an echo in the night, just like me," Leviathan answered poetically, and then he watched her eyes widen. She was clearly succumbing to his lure, and he easily spotted the flush of her cheeks and panting of breath.

"You speak so differently to anyone I've met before, Leofwin. Are you from another place?" she asked, and he nodded.

"A place very different from here. I'd love to tell you all about it." She smiled so shyly, as if she'd never spoken so personally with a man before, but instead of finding it endearing, her morality almost sickened him.

"Different how?" she asked, and Leviathan smiled. He considered what Christiana might do if he answered her honestly. Would she let his master take the innocence from her and then effectively own her body and soul? Would she run away in fright? The unknown was a thrill for him, and yet Leviathan said nothing of the depravities Lucifer had planned for girls like her. He wouldn't warn her against allowing a monster between her thighs, because once his Dark Prince was done, he himself would take his turn, and what a delight it would be to show her his underwater world.

"We work hard, like you and your family, but we also play hard, too. Have you ever let yourself go, Christiana? Have you ever said farewell to what inhibits you and just let yourself be free?" She shook her head no and looked down at the ground with such virtuousness he had to fight his laughter. She was a virgin, he had no doubt, and Leviathan pinched her chin between his thumb and forefinger, pulling her gaze up to meet his. "Don't shy away. Don't ever hide your face, for it is truly beautiful. The world deserves to know this face, to enjoy and admire it."

Christiana positively glowed with his compliment, and Leviathan knew she was already well on her way to being quite smitten with him. What a silly girl she was being fooled by nothing more than fake smiles and false promises. He wanted so badly to take everything from her. To use and abuse her kind hearted spirit and leave her for dead. First and foremost, though, he had a job to do. "Can you get away tomorrow? Come and meet my friends and I down by the old alehouse. We're staying there while we pass through on our way west, but I want to see you again. I have a surprise I'd like to give you…"

"A surprise?" she asked, beaming. She was entering a lion's den if she came, but he had to tempt and tease her. Free will meant her actions had to be the result of her own decision, but he was sure going to make it as hard as possible for beautiful little Christiana to refuse.

"A nobleman travels with us. He's rich beyond measure and likes to entertain as often as we can arrange it. We've invited some people to our temporary home tomorrow evening, and I'd like you to come as my guest, if you'd like to?" he put on his best imitation of a gentleman and had to contain the satisfied growl that threatened to emanate from within when she nodded her head yes.

***

Christiana took flight as soon as the lamp was put out the following evening, and she then found the old alehouse with ease. Inside were more than just a small group of people who were already supping wine and mead, talking loudly, and clearly enjoying their evening. The mood was jovial, and she took a deep breath. She'd never sneaked off before and knew her parents would be furious with her if she was caught, but how it was worth it if she could end the night with a stolen kiss from the man who'd come to her farm the day before. Leofwin had been a breath of fresh air. A call for freedom she hadn't known she'd yearned for. She was excited to see him again after spending all day thinking about him.

"Are you going to come in or are you just going to stand there and stare at everyone?" a deep, alluring voice asked her from the shadows. Christiana felt her cheeks blush hotly. She turned to find the man who'd spoken but found nothing but the darkness.

"Who is it? Who spoke just now?" she called, and then gasped when a face appeared out of the shadows. The man was stunning. He was chiselled and handsome in a manner that spoke of aristocracy and wealth, but there was a danger to him. It was the very same danger she'd been so drawn to with Leofwin, and Christiana bit her bottom lip as she contemplated the things these men of the world must do with the women they met on their travels. Things she had only ever dreamed about.

"Well, here we are, aren't you just the most sublime treat? My man has done well," he said, and she trembled as his deep voice washed over her. "Did you enjoy his company? Did my aide help you tap into a need so buried deep you didn't know you had it?"

"Yes," Christiana replied, and surprised herself by her honesty, but it was as if the man had read her mind. "Is he inside?" she asked hopefully, but he shook his head.

"He doesn't want you," he replied, making her heart sink. "At least not in your current condition." His eyes dipped to her waist and back up again.

She paled and immediately felt foolish. Christiana regretted sneaking out already and stared back at the man incredulously. How did he know a thing about her? He couldn't possibly know she'd yet to bed a man, or could he? She was so inexperienced in such matters it wouldn't shock her to discover that her innocence was visibly noticeable to a member of the opposite sex wise in such things, and she took a tentative step back. "I can help you. I'll show you what he likes and what he needs from a woman. When we've finished, you'll be ready to love him properly, but he won't want you while you're still so inexperienced. Leofwin likes women, not girls."

Christiana shook her head. Her mother had told her never to give up her innocence so readily, and only for true love. She wasn't about to hand herself over to the stranger standing before her, regardless of how gorgeous and alluring he was. There was something grand and powerful in him, though, and despite her attraction to Leofwin, she wanted to find out more about the strange man standing in front of her.

He smiled, as if he somehow knew of her fascination with him and stepped closer.

"Who are you?" she whispered but didn't step away as he closed the gap.

"My name's Luke, and I might be an angel in disguise, or your worst nightmare. Do you care to find out which one?" he asked, his words sending a shiver down her spine. A million voices in her head were telling her to say no and walk away, but there was this one voice that was somehow more powerful than the others, and it was saying the opposite. She'd been cooped up on that farm her entire life, sheltered and controlled by her parents to such an extent that she'd missed out on everything—friends, lovers, and adventure. Christiana wanted Luke to kiss her, to teach her things, and make her feel something she'd been missing her whole life. She wanted him to show her how to be a good lover for Leofwin. To be a woman like he wanted. Rather than feel torn, she somehow knew that this was right. Leofwin didn't want her while she was still a virgin and she'd heard stories of men her friends had bedded that had a similar view of the untouched girls who'd tried to lure them into marriage. They didn't have the patience to teach them how to be a good lover and so had turned them away in preference of those who knew what they were doing and did it well.

"Yes," she finally breathed in response, and Luke grinned so wickedly it made her heart lurch into her throat.

***

Lucifer stared down at his prize and inspected the gift his good and loyal subject had procured for him. Christiana was indeed pure, innocent, and untouched, just as he'd hoped she would be. There had been countless others before her, and Lucifer knew there'd be many after, but for tonight she belonged to him and he watched her with hunger in his eyes. There had been numerous times over his long and sinful existence when the Prince of Darkness had craved different things to entertain him. He'd not only embraced the most depraved and unusual of sexual appetites, but he'd also downright encouraged and developed the very premise of some of them. Lucifer had hunted his prey, fucked, and then murdered them for sport. He'd partaken in lovers from across the world, and sometimes with those he knew were off-limits, but hadn't cared in the slightest. He had turned white witches and followers against their angelic masters and had then mocked those who fell on their knees before him and begged for mercy. Guilt wasn't an emotion that plagued him like it did so many humans. He was free from the binds that'd once shackled him to the rules and heavenly commandments and hadn't cared to miss them even once.

The one snag was that the moon bound Lucifer to Hell. Thanks to an almighty magic even he couldn't fathom, he could only visit during either a full moon or on All Hallow's Eve. But when free to roam the Earth, he would often bring with him a plague of darkness that infected everyone who encountered him. The devout of soul and freest from sin were often the most susceptible to his lure, and what a prize it was to ensnare a reverend's daughter, or even better, their wife. He would possess them, drive them insane, and occasionally whisper thoughts in their ear of murder and revenge, and then watch as they slay the ones who loved them too much to kill them first. Lucifer claimed each of their souls, every one too tainted with darkness to be welcome in Heaven, and then he'd simply throw them into the abyss far below and use their essence to strengthen his own reign.

Going by his alias was a necessary burden. Thanks to the bible his old leaders had insisted bear his true name to warn others of his lure. He wanted nothing more than to have a woman scream his real name as he brought her to climax, but the human alias would do, he supposed.

Christiana whimpered slightly when he crushed her body into his, but her flushed cheeks gave her away, as did the thoughts running wild in her head. As the all-powerful ruler of Hell, Lucifer had many powers, and one was his ability to read people's thoughts. Not a single creature he'd met had been immune to his invasion, and Lucifer thought nothing of prying into their deepest, darkest thoughts while he was there.

She had come tonight with the intention of meeting with and seducing Leviathan, but Lucifer had found her first and he intended to prey upon each and every doubt she was riddled with from within. Her mother had raised a good and sweet young woman, but she hadn't instilled in her the strength she needed to fight the lure of the unknown, and her quizzical mind had led her to this place filled with monsters of the netherworld. Using barely any effort at all, Lucifer had used his power to call to her desires from feet away, and she'd succumbed in seconds. Her thoughts of Leviathan were already gone from her mind and Lucifer marvelled yet again at how quickly she'd given herself to him instead. Leviathan would have his turn, but tonight Christiana belonged to him, and Lucifer was ready to take everything she had to offer him.

"I want you, Angel," he moaned. Her eyes lit up at this pet name, when actually he'd used it ironically, but he didn't care. Whatever worked was worth it, even if he had needed to utter a heavenly title to get her closer to the edge. Lucifer kissed Christiana's lips and then neck, plunging his head down to her heaving chest as he slid away some of the layers she'd wrapped herself in. Christiana let out nothing but almost silent sighs, as though afraid of expressing herself, and Lucifer knew she'd soon be screaming his name without a care in the world. "Come with me," he told her, and then led her around the back of the old alehouse to his private quarters.

With the full moon having only just risen, Christiana was his first conquest during the short respite from Hell, and he was eager to have her naked beneath him as soon as possible. Lucifer craved his release, and so decided to forgo any lengthy foreplay. He led her over to the bedside, where he left her to watch while he lit some candles and then removed his heavy coat. Regardless of her innocence, Christiana watched him, eager to see more. She was ready for him and let him strip her naked without shying away even once.

"Who are you?" she whimpered as his hands stroked at the yet untouched folds of her core, and she hissed when his mouth lapped at each nipple in turn. "I want to know you, Luke."

He tried to ignore her questions, but she seemed insistent and, while he was growing impatient, Lucifer decided to play the game a little longer. He pulled his away from her delicious skin and regarded her as he stepped back and removed the last of his clothes.

Standing on show before him, Christiana instinctively put a hand over the exposed flesh at the tops of her thighs and sat down on the bed behind, but she couldn't hide her interest at finally seeing a man without his clothing. When Lucifer unveiled his rock-hard and ready to be sated rod from his shorts, she turned a shade of red he positively adored and that flush of heat went all the way from her cheeks to her thighs.

"I'm the man who's going to show you the time of your life, Angel. I'll take care of your every need and make sure you remember tonight for the rest of your life," he assured her, surprising himself that he hadn't replied with more lies. It didn't matter. Christiana fell for his promises hook, line, and sinker. She pushed herself back on the bed and opened her legs, revealing the sweetest sight any red-blooded man could ever dream of. "Do you want me to show you?" he teased, and then trailed kisses up her thigh as he joined her on the bed.

"Yes, yes," she groaned, arching her back when he slid his tongue over the already swollen bud at the apex of her thighs. Her legs shook as he kneaded the nerve endings with his mouth and he knew from her thoughts that she'd never so much as flicked it before, so had no idea she could feel so good by simply fondling the small bead.

Lucifer decided to be selfish. He stopped after just a couple of minutes spent playing with it. He wanted to be the one to come first, but knew once he was inside of her, the delicate human would beat him time and again before he finally got his release. There was no rushing to achieve release where he was concerned. Lucifer could have a quick fuck with any woman, but to fully get his satisfaction took hours, and that was why he'd become so fussy about who he took to his bed with him, or rather, what. He'd had men and women, young and old, but knew he was attracted to those he either couldn't have, or those he could control and bend to his every whim. Virgins were his current obsession and most of all, he enjoyed having the power to both give and take from them in the same moment, while they didn't know better than to deny him.

He climbed between Christiana's thighs and spread her legs wider, opening her up to him and his impressive length. Teasing the opening, he glided inside just enough to moisten the tip and he felt her tense up. This simply wouldn't do.

"Relax, Angel. Give yourself to me," he whispered, and peered down at her through hooded eyes.

"I don't think I can. Maybe I'm not ready?" she replied, and Lucifer had to close his eyes. He could sense how they were swirling with blackness, his power coming to the surface that'd been called forth by both his need to move things along, as well as the rage building from within at his prey's hesitation.

He kissed her, acting out a scenario he'd had to imbue numerous times before, and he hated it. Lucifer's lips coaxed her body into submission, filling her with explosive passion while he played his part as the doting lover well, displaying a need for her that had her body reacting within seconds.

"You're ready, Angel. I can feel it," he groaned against her lips, diving in with his tongue to silence her response. *And you've already given me my yes,* the voice in his mind reminded him. The darkness within swelled, urging him onwards. It was time.

Lucifer could feel her wetness coating his still perfectly positioned cock and, without another word, he plunged inside. The small snap that then emanated from within her made him shudder, and, like a drug addict, he let the high wash over him. Lucifer remained perfectly still, impaling her on him while also stretching her to accommodate his size. Christiana writhed in a bid to ease the sting she felt, and he could hear the pain as it registered in her mind. It only added to his gratification. Her movement was fruitless, though. It actually helped bury him deeper, and soon she'd taken all of him. "Your body is flawless, Christiana. See how I fit so perfectly? Can you feel how your womanly parts want to grasp me tightly from within?" Lucifer was lost in the moment and wanted to slap himself for becoming so poetic, but it truly was a moment to cherish. He knew he'd remember Christiana fondly, just like all the others.

He leaned up and back, resting on his knees while still inside of her, and withdrew just enough so that he could see her lost innocence splayed against his skin. The red wasn't bright, but a deep and dull crimson. The strands had woven into her body along with her soul upon creation, and now they belonged to him. There would be no wiping his conquest clean or giving her a chance to rest, either. He needed his next high.

Lucifer had been charmed by Christiana's readiness to give a tremendous part of herself to him, but not enough to walk away now that the deed was done. A good, god-fearing man would've withdrawn and left her soul untainted further, but he certainly wasn't that man. His adoration for their poignant moment didn't stretch as far as leaving her untouched by his darkness, and his carnal need took over. Lucifer began sliding back in and out with slow, deep plunges, all the while strumming against Christiana's clit with his thumb to help her remain at his ultimate command. Her deliciously tight core flooded. The prim and proper farm girl was ready and waiting, willing to give him more, and Lucifer took it all from her without hesitation.

***

Luke was an animal. He was predatory and intense in the fiercest way, but also so incredibly beguiling that Christiana was mesmerised. His body rippled with power, as though the world turned only for him, which was an absurd thought, but she was lost in him and so didn't care for the strange and sordid thoughts running through her mind. He moved in and out of her with incredible poise and a sexually skilled body and seemed to take her without a care for anyone or anything but them, so Christiana cherished every single moment. She felt special, privileged to be spending the night with the man who seemed more than just an outsider. It wouldn't surprise her to discover he was royalty, and to have been chosen to share his bed was certainly something she knew she'd remember forever.

As he moved back and forth atop her on the bed, so too did the huge beast at his waist that'd buried itself deep within her. She flushed hot and cold again, her nipples taut with the icy chill of the autumnal air, while between her thighs burned hotter than the sun. The pain was easing already, and thanks to the hand strumming against the tender bead above her opening, Christiana felt a need building she'd never felt before. It was as if a knot inside of her was being kneaded, untangled, and spread open for Luke to take away and leave her anew. He thrust in and out, hitting places she didn't know she had inside, but her body welcomed him. She clenched and tightened, which only made him move faster and harder to combat her uncontrollable constriction.

Christiana let out a whimper and, in her shock, she bit down on her lip to silence her outbursts, but Luke simply grinned down at her. His eyes were somehow both brighter and darker at the same time and he licked his lips as he watched her, smirking again when he plunged deep inside and an unsolicited moan escaped her mouth.

"Can you feel it? Do you know what I'm creating inside of you?" he moaned, slowing down slightly. She shook her head. Christiana knew babies came from doing this act with a man and felt a wave of panic rise from within her. She had to wonder, was he trying to give her an illegitimate child?

Luke laughed, as though he'd read her mind, and Christiana guessed her expression had given away her fears of falling pregnant with a bastard child. "No, Angel. I cannot give you a child, so do not fear," he told her, and she was sure she caught sight of what looked like regret in his stare, but it was gone again so quickly she didn't dwell on it. The friction was still building between them, and she was desperate to know what he was talking about now that her mind was back in the moment.

"What are you making, Luke? What is this feeling you're giving me, this ache in my belly?" she asked, arching her back when he leaned down to capture a nipple in his mouth. Christiana's breath hitched when a strange spasm from deep inside of her clenched in a way that spoke of claiming him, rather than pushing against the thrusting cock Luke continued plunging into her. She moaned again.

With his mouth on her breast and one hand still between her thighs, a fluttering began in her belly and Christiana squealed. She didn't try to silence herself this time, but instead gave in to the pleasurable cascade claiming her once so unused body. It built up, a crescendo of tingling energy that brought pleasure in its wake, the likes she'd never known before, and she was sad when it subsided.

"Good girl, Angel. That was called an orgasm, and I have plenty more where they came from, if you'd like?" Luke asked, kissing his way up her chest to her neck and lips. She was roaring with heat, still coming down from a burst of pure passion she hadn't known she was capable of, but knew she absolutely wanted more.

"Yes, Luke. I want more. Take whatever you want from me. I'm yours," she groaned, desperate for that release again, and she wasn't against begging if he demanded it. His relentless rhythm started again in answer to her pleas, and Christiana wrapped her legs behind his waist, lifting her hips up to meet his as he pummelled against her soaking body.

***

Christiana was putty in his hands. Clay to be moulded and sculpted at his will, but he didn't want her that way. There was no future in this rendezvous, only the here and now, and Lucifer carried on his deep and heavy thrusting in search of his own high. He'd given her an orgasm worthy of the record books and knew more would follow before he found his release, so carried on working her supple body like the ripe peach she was.

Lucifer flipped her over and took her from every angle he desired, and all the while, Christiana gave him total command of her body without question. She gave into her pleasure and became the perfect concubine, but that wasn't what he wanted, either. She'd given him his prize. Now he sought satisfaction—and that was all. The girl would make a great follower for Leviathan to savour slowly at his leisure, and the Dark Prince grinned to himself as his friend's thoughts washed over him from a few rooms away.

Leviathan had enjoyed Christiana's company and was now wondering if the screams he'd heard were hers or another's that Lucifer had taken with him to bed. He was horny as hell but wouldn't take another. Leviathan wanted Christiana and he would wait. Little did the ancient demon know, but by the time the sun rose the next morning, the pretty little cunt would be so well used that he'd have to wait days for her to take him without wincing. Lucifer would make sure to leave his mark on her too, in one form or another. He hadn't decided how yet.

Christiana's impending orgasm brought Lucifer back to the present, and he couldn't resist slowing, watching as she struggled to tell him of her need for release. He delighted in her cravings and turned her back over so that she was facing him. The flush in her cheeks gave away her exhaustion, but the building climax in her core demanded attention, and instinctively she ground into him with her eager pussy. Oh, how quickly she'd become a woman in his care. Some lessons couldn't be taught because they were instinctually there, waiting to be unleashed, and Christiana was no different to any of the others.

Lucifer decided he wanted a taste this time and slid off the end of the bed. He took Christiana with him, enveloping her clit with his mouth when her hips reached the edge of the hard mattress. He leaned down onto his knees and went to work. Two fingers quickly joined the action, and then a third. But it was when he pressed his thumb inside her back opening that she cried out in shock and awe that such a strange act could give her pleasure, too. Christiana's mind was alive, contemplating what he might be doing and why, and how it could possibly be so good. But she wasn't guessing long, as her body soon radiated again with an epic release and she writhed against his hold like the whore he knew had been hiding beneath the layers of self-doubt and fear of the unknown. Once they let go of their inhibitions, every woman he'd known was a wanton sexpot, and he loved watching them unravel thanks to his touch.

Lucifer stood, leaving the still throbbing girl empty for just a moment. He then lifted her legs up against his torso and pushed himself back inside. Christiana whimpered softly, evidently unable to form words, but her soaked heat welcomed his huge length back inside and he began pounding her, hard. This time, he was relentless, feral, and wild with his need.

The almighty Devil then reared his head back and stared up into the heavens.

Fuck you, he mouthed, as he emptied his dark seed into the once so sweet and innocent girl before him. The ground shook, but he clung on, pouring his evil essence into her so welcoming body. Before she could even begin to wonder what was happening, a final orgasm ripped through Christiana, rendering her completely useless to thought or reason. Lucifer knew she'd barely remember the seismic event caused by his explosive climax and would undoubtedly put anything she did remember down to hallucinations caused by the intensity of her own release, so didn't bother trying to cover his tracks with a story.

Lucifer then simply pulled out and covered the exhausted Christiana with a blanket. She fell asleep almost instantly, which was preferable to those silly fools who tried to entice him into bed again to snuggle with them. He'd gotten what he'd come for and was set to head to the next location where Beelzebub had his second prize at the ready. His moment of harmony and satisfaction, thanks to Christiana's kind gift, was just that—a moment.

Lucifer bid her goodbye with a kiss to the temple and then washed up, got dressed, and teleported away without a word to the sleeping bundle he'd left behind.

***

Leviathan waited until it was almost sunrise before he went inside. He'd sensed Lucifer's departure hours before but had opted to let Christiana sleep rather than send her packing too soon after her night of many firsts. Jealousy wasn't in his nature and, in fact, he'd found it incredibly sexy listening to her screams the night before. Knowing that his master had taken her innocence and replaced it with a carnal need only those daring enough to embrace it could answer was a huge turn on. A human man would never satisfy her in the way she had been last night, but he could, and would, show her how to express her newfound sexuality with ease and enjoyment for them both.

"Christiana, it's almost morning," he whispered against her ear. Leviathan could smell the sex and sweat all over her, along with the lingering evil that corrupted her body and soul from within. It made him want her more, and her sleepy moans did nothing to silence the monster that stirred inside.

"Morning? I need to go!" she then cried, forcing herself awake and jumping out of bed, seemingly forgetting that she was naked. Leviathan didn't avert his eyes. He simply smiled and handed over her dress. "Oh, Leofwin. Thank you for bringing me to him," she said as she tied the threads of her corset back together and pulled on her socks and shoes. "He said you'd be happy with me, are you?"

"Oh yes," Leviathan replied, and he couldn't help from smiling as Christiana winced when she sat down against the chair. "I'm incredibly pleased with you. And you should be proud of yourself. He said you were a rare beauty, more delicious than anyone he's ever known," he lied, but Christiana didn't seem to care. She absorbed the compliment and sighed wistfully.

Leviathan knew the look she wore well. Lucifer had given as well as taken from her the night before and he also guessed from her words that Christiana's thoughts of him had given her attraction away. Lucifer had, therefore, done what he did best. He'd exploited her fears and hopes for more with *Leofwin*. She'd perhaps wondered if she'd be enough to satisfy him in bed, being a virgin and all, and the almighty leader of Hell had lured her into his bed, promising that the only way to please her beau was to rid herself of those doubts and insecurities by giving herself to him first. Leviathan also wondered if Lucifer had promised Christiana that she could practice on him and liberate herself of her blasted innocence in the process. What a kind and gracious man Luke would've seemed to the unsuspecting young fool, and she'd undoubtedly played right into his hands.

Lucifer and Leviathan had acted out this same routine time and again, and just like all the other instances, he played along in the aftermath. Christiana was his reward for a job well done and now that she'd given into her dark desires, nothing would be off limits without the right encouragement. Leviathan looked forward to their time together, even if he had to play the role of gentleman a little longer first.

"Will you walk me home?" Christiana's soft voice pulled him from his reverie, and he nodded. He offered her his arm and together they walked the mile or so to her family's farm. Her father and mother would have no idea she'd sneaked out, or that she'd lost her virginity the night before. For all their sakes, Leviathan and his demonic comrades had helped ensure the secret was kept. He wanted to take a piece of Christiana's soul for his own, after all, so it was in his best interests to keep her sins from being discovered. To safeguard her secrecy, he'd sent one of their dark witches to watch over the house and make sure that her parents stayed asleep while she was gone. A heavy slumber had taken them both and it wouldn't be lifted until she was safely back in her bed, but before she could be allowed more rest, Leviathan wanted something from her.

"Let's wait here a moment, Christiana," he said, and rested against a small cobble wall. She stopped and turned, looking into his face with such delusional faith he wanted to slap her, but instead he kissed the lips that still reeked of Him.

"I want to please you, but I'm not ready again. Is there a way I can show you how true I am to you? How I let your master have me so I could know how to accept you inside of me?" she asked when he pulled away and Leviathan had to force the smile away that'd slyly crept upon his lips.

"Did he give you pleasure with his mouth?" he asked and caught the red flush that hit her cheeks and told him yes before she even nodded with affirmation. "And did he show you how to please him with your mouth in return?"

"No," she replied, licking her lips. "Can you show me?"

She didn't have to ask him twice. Leviathan took off his thick coat and placed it on the ground for Christiana to kneel on. He then indicated for her to position herself before him. She looked so sweet and innocent as she fell to her knees and seemed to consider it so chivalrous that he'd braved the cold to protect her legs and clothes from the chill, when in fact he wouldn't have felt the temperature regardless of the time of year. Demons weren't slaves to the elements, but he'd gladly let her be beholden to him for yet another seemingly kind gesture if it got him what he wanted.

Leviathan unbuckled his belt and released his hard-on. Christiana's eyes widened. "Are all men so large? It's as if God himself has carved you both from stone. You're chiselled and perfect rather than born with imperfections like us mere mortals," she mumbled, and Leviathan was struck by just how right she was. Angels weren't born of a womb like humans. They'd been created in the abyss between time and space, in a place where they weren't children who were nurtured into adulthood but had sprung forth into existence millennia ago as grown men and women. They'd developed brotherly bonds over the years and had ruled Heaven using instincts given to them by an almighty unseen force. But throughout it all, they had never been given guidance from their maker—hence why some had fallen while others had thrived in the light.

"Leofwin?" her soft voice lured him back to her again along with the small hand that stroked his ready length with unsure sweeps up and down.

"Lick your lips, beautiful Christiana. Open wide and let me in. I'll do the rest," he told her, and like the good and willing lover she'd become overnight, she complied. Leviathan was slow at first, dipping in and out of her mouth with just the tip as she coated him with her saliva, and then he plunged a little deeper. She followed his lead as he tilted her head back and grabbed a handful of her hair, fisting it as he found his rhythm. "That's it, you're amazing," he encouraged her when she seemed to be struggling with the speed he was driving into her with and Christiana immediately relaxed. She gagged when he came, but drank every drop of him down, not that he gave her a choice. Leviathan pressed his cock into the back of her mouth and released, using her throat's tense tightening to help milk him.

When he'd finished, he gently pulled away, tucking himself back into his trousers while she wiped her mouth clean. Leviathan couldn't deny it'd felt so good to relieve some of the pressure building within him, and with a gentle hand, he helped her stand.

"Was it good?" she asked, and positively beamed when he told her yes.

Leviathan then lead the way in peaceful silence. He walked her to the door, kissed her cheek, and bid Christiana goodnight before disappearing into the darkness.

***

The next morning, Christiana slept late and had to rush her chores to get them finished in time for lunch. She didn't say a word to her mother or father about why she was so exhausted but delighted in keeping the secret night of pleasure to herself. She knew she ought to feel guilty, but somehow didn't. She even smiled to herself many times as images of her night came springing to the forefront of her mind.

Christiana noticed the extra bowl at the table when she began plating up the soup her mother had made that lunchtime, and she had to contain her surprise when Leofwin stepped over the threshold with her father. The two men were talking casually, like old friends catching up, and even her mother seemed enthralled by their strange yet helpful visitor. She ushered them both to the table and served them, before insisting her daughter take the seat beside their handsome guest.

"We cannot thank you enough, Leofwin. The lambs are healthy and well, bulked up and ready for the winter, and together we've ploughed fields these old bones weren't sure they could get done in time. How can I ever repay you?" Benedict asked him, and Leofwin bowed his head graciously.

"No thanks or payment is necessary, my good man. These wonderful meals and the company of your fine wife and daughter are all a man like me needs. Knowing they have a roof over their heads and food in their bellies, prepared to face another wintertime, is a privilege any man worth his salt should cherish," he answered, and both Christiana and her mother sighed dreamily.

She was smitten with him, there was no doubt about it, and even her mother seemed ready to pick out wedding gowns, judging by her wistful gaze. Christiana didn't have the heart to tell her he was leaving with his group of men again soon and almost hated the thought of it herself, too. The farm, and her world, would be empty when he left. She was glad he'd come back to spend a day with them again, even if it was spent tending to the land and livestock with her father rather than with her.

"Speaking of, why don't you enjoy the last of the sunshine and take a walk together this afternoon?" Mary asked, and she ignored her husband's overprotective stare. "Christiana needs to deliver a basket of wool to the tailor's wife for me, and I was thinking that perhaps you might accompany her on the long walk?"

"It'd be an honour, good lady," Leofwin replied with a smile. When her father turned away to grab a bread roll, he winked at Christiana. She melted beneath that stare and suddenly felt incredibly eager to get her usually long and boring walk to the village underway.

***

Leviathan took Christiana's hand in his the moment they were out of sight of the farmhouse and her father's protective gaze. Benedict had warned him to remain a proper gentleman around his only daughter, and Leviathan had played the role of the honest and god-fearing man with such ease it'd been child's play. He'd won him over in a heartbeat and there was a part of him that'd even enjoyed his elaborate deceit. Taking Christiana's body in whatever way would pleasure him most would be a sublime indulgence but doing it right under the watchful eyes of her parents would make it an even sweeter sin. They trusted him and had welcomed him into their home and lives, when in reality they were inviting one of the very monsters they had tried so hard to fight throughout their hardworking lives. Men like Benedict knew what was lurking out in the darkness and did well to both fear and respect it. He'd protected his family from pillaging travellers and villains aplenty, but when pure evil had wandered into his yard, he'd unwittingly welcomed it right on in. Their land, cattle, and crops would be tainted by his touch, but again, Leviathan didn't care.

"Let's stop here a moment," he said, and then yanked the sweet young thing into his embrace. Christiana followed his lead and went along without a word of hesitation or even a playful refusal. She clearly trusted him to keep her safe and what a foolish little thing she was.

Leviathan sheltered them beneath a huge oak tree and pressed her into the trunk with his mammoth frame, while helping himself to a taste of her lips, neck, and the tiny sliver of her exposed breast.

"Your lips feel wonderful against my skin," she groaned, thrusting her hands into his hair. The coy virgin from before was gone and in her place stood a woman who knew how it felt to reach a wondrous climax, and she evidently craved more. "I want to feel your body against mine, Leofwin. And I want to pleasure you in return."

"As do I, but surely you aren't ready?" he replied with a smile he hid against her skin, letting her take the lead. Christiana flung herself against him with reckless abandon and lifted her skirt, revealing her nakedness beneath. She was so brave, and her wantonness was such a turn-on that Leviathan couldn't resist. His hands explored her swollen core, still tender from the night before, and while he wanted to delve inside, he knew she wouldn't last long if he took her in this sorry state. Stopping halfway to ease her soreness was not something he liked the sound of, so he decided to do something he hadn't done in years—make an exception.

Leviathan ran his hand over her shawl, searching for the ideal implement he could use to help with his deception. When he found the brooch she'd used to secure her wrap around her shoulders, he quickly pricked his finger on the tip of the protruding needle and hissed angrily.

"What is it?" Christiana replied, and she blanched when he showed her the bloodied fingertip. All he needed to do was convince her to drink from him and she'd not only succumb to his lure easier, but her body would also heal at his command. She'd be ready for him without the need to wait or take things easy, and Leviathan was more than ready to have her.

"It's just a scratch, my darling, nothing to worry about. Perhaps a kiss will make it heal all the faster?" he asked as he placed the bloody finger to her lips. She seemed surprised at his strange request, but did as he asked, and kissed it better.

Leviathan grinned and pulled the already healed wound from her lips. His blood remained behind, just a drop or two against her soft pink lips, but he couldn't deny it was a sight to behold. The primeval demon kissed the blood away from her parted mouth and dived in with his tongue. He could sense that she was already under his spell from the small amount she'd ingested. Christiana's body began to heal at his command, the soreness easing immediately, along with the scratch Lucifer had left for him to find on her inner thigh. His leader always left a mark of one kind or another, and this time had chosen to leave his conquest with an 'L' scratched into her flesh. It would never completely heal, though, and Leviathan grinned to himself. Christiana really did have no idea who she was dealing with, and part of him pitied her. He also wanted her so entirely it consumed him, and couldn't resist spurring on her infatuation, using the control he now had on her mind at the same time as her body reacted to his ownership.

"I'm ready. I want you," she whispered against his lips, lifting her skirts higher around her hips to give him full access to her core. Leviathan unbuckled his trousers and let them fall to his feet, and then pulled at Christiana's thighs so that they wrapped around his waist.

"Are you sure?" he had to ask, thanks to the laws his kind had about free will, but while positioning the tip of his heavy erection by her opening at the ready.

"Yes," she groaned against him. Christiana's breath hitched as he plunged inside, and she yelped but didn't try to pull away. She was so tight, clenching and yet opening up for him with each thrust all at the same time, but her cries of pleasure told him she was ready to take a proper pounding. Lucifer had well and truly broken her in. Leviathan focussed on his climax and the enjoyment he felt in taking his sweet, kind young woman so carnally. He soon felt his pleasure building inside of him, ready to be unleashed, and pummelled her hard, delighting in her moans as she accepted him so willingly.

Christiana came quickly, and she screamed his name as her body throbbed with its release. She was beautiful and had Leviathan in awe as he watched her unravel, but the demon didn't stop. Unlike his master, he didn't have to pursue his pleasure for hours to find his satisfaction. He was close behind her and emptied his climactic release deep within his conquest while also unleashing a deep growl that emanated from somewhere between his lungs and his black heart.

The ancient being knew he was claiming this girl more than he'd intended to. He wanted her in ways he hadn't desired another being for hundreds of years, and yet he did nothing to stop himself from falling over that precipice with her.

Christiana closed her eyes and rested her head against the tree trunk behind, while Leviathan took the opportunity to properly own her, once and for all. He lifted her right arm and inspected the soft, pale flesh he found there.

After a gentle kiss against the delicate skin, he then traced his fingertip across it in two straight lines that crossed at the bottom. The inverted cross he'd drawn was their new symbol that would mark a follower as a demon's personal belonging, and Leviathan chose to give her his mark so that no other demon would ever touch her than him. Christiana could be in a room filled with Lucifer's dark minions, but none would harm or try to seduce her now that she belonged to him. And he smiled to himself. He then quickly controlled her mind to forget the sting of the mark on her arm, and the red symbol faded away within seconds, but he still sensed it.

Leviathan then placed a hand over her heart. He called to the ancient essence that resided deep within her and felt the shift of her soul as its allegiance altered from light to dark. She was now and forevermore bound for Hell. Only his own will could release her from the binds that shackled her soul to him, and he adored the extra power his new acquisition had given him.

Christiana was his to command and Leviathan groaned as he peered down at where they'd fit together so wonderfully. He was still nestled deep within her and her body remained tight, ready, and waiting for his next commandment. The wondrous moment did nothing to sway his desire to blacken her soul further. In fact, Leviathan was hard again and ready for more action in a heartbeat. He began moving inside of her while tracing his hands across her thighs and to her clit. The friction and motion against her swollen nub brought Christiana back from her controlled reverie, and her eyes shot open. "I love being this for you, Leofwin. I love you," she whimpered, and shuddered as a second orgasm claimed her.

"I love you, too," he lied, pouring his dark seed inside of her again. Regardless of their new deepened connection, Leviathan knew he wasn't in this for the long haul. Their secret love affair was only temporary, and he knew that before long he'd have moved onto the next sweet girl and her eager pussy. Christiana was a worthy follower, but still a being far inferior to him. He withdrew from her soaked core and dropped her skirts, not bothering to clean her up. He wanted her thighs to remain slick with his seed. He wanted her dripping with it as she walked, but it seemed young Christiana had other ideas.

She skipped away and had rounded a corner before he could finish buckling his belt, and when he tracked her down, Leviathan gawped.

"Join me," Christiana begged him as she waded into the river he somehow hadn't sensed was even there. When she reached waist-depth, she stopped, cleansing herself in the rush of the clear water, and all he could do was watch her in astonishment.

The sunlight sparkled and set the young woman aglow. It seemed it was her turn to seduce him, and instinctively, he stepped closer. As soon as the water hit his skin, Leviathan was transformed. Christiana was looking away, out into the distance with a smile, which was good as it meant she hadn't noticed him suddenly disintegrate into a million black particles.

Leviathan was in the water with her, but as part of its makeup rather than as a separate entity. He was nothing but a haze in the rapidly darkening water, and as that shadowy blur, he surrounded her. Christiana had no idea that her lover was no longer man, but a monster, and when she felt a soft grip that clutched her ankles, she considered it nothing more than a piece of weed billowing in the current. It was only when he transfigured further and yanked her under that she thought to scream, but it was no use.

Leviathan surrounded her and he captured every flailing limb in his powerful grasp. The last remnants of air left Christiana's lungs, and he filled the gaps with his watery form, revelling in the sensation as her body jolted with the last beats of her heart. Leviathan then watched as the life drained from her eyes, then he teleported away and let the current wash her body downstream to be discovered.

He'd wanted longer to enjoy her, but it seemed there were periods when fate forced his hand, and this time the monster had been sated sooner rather than later.

Leviathan heard her screams and felt her torment as she joined his legion of the newly dead in the catacombs of Hell's dark castle. Christiana was terrified to discover that the myths were true, and that she had been delivered to Hell for her sins in life.

The monster wasn't finished with her simply because Christiana had taken her last breath, though. If anything, he would enjoy having an eternity to bend and break her even more. Her whimpers gave him strength, while her pain brought him comfort. No matter what he once had been, this was who he now was, and Leviathan wasn't saddened that he'd taken another life. In fact, he was downright overjoyed.

The end…

Embracing the Darkness

Book #1 in the Black Rose series

By
LM Morgan

2021 Revised Edition

CHAPTER ONE

Dark eyes had watched Cate's every move since the day she was born. She had no idea of her fate, or of her maker's impatience at having to wait for her. But he waited. Waited for the day that she would be ready, able and—most importantly—willing, to join him. Only then could Cate's true nature be revealed, and only then could she possess the power and the ability to really be a part of his world. Only then could she begin embracing the darkness within and reach her full potential at last.

***

"What the hell am I doing here?" Cate whispered into the cold night air. She'd woken to find herself hidden in the shadows of a tall, dark, sinister looking building in the centre of town that she'd never even seen before, and this was not the first time. She had no idea how or why she'd suddenly begun sleepwalking, but for the third night in a row, she had gone to bed and jolted awake, standing in the middle of town dressed only in her pyjamas, and shivering violently as she came to.

Cate pressed herself into the wall, panicking and feeling desperate to be back home in her bed. She looked around, but found nothing familiar in the shadows, and no sign of home. So, she just began running in the same direction she had the previous nights'—heading towards the closest light she could see on the horizon. She peeked back towards the shadows and felt as though there were eyes on her. It had to be her mind playing tricks, but she was sure she could even make out the dark figure of a person standing near to where she'd awoken. The shadow soon disappeared though, and she pressed on, making her way towards the main road and back to her home without so much as another glance back.

Everything about those episodes freaked her out, but Cate refused to speak about them to anyone, not even her mother. She was in denial. Talking about them would just make it real, and even more terrifying. At just eighteen years old, Cate Rose's life so far had been otherwise uneventful. Well, until the strange sleepwalking sessions had begun a few nights' before.

Her mother, Ella, hadn't heard a thing each time, but Cate wondered if her regular nightcap helped her remain oblivious to the comings and goings after lights-out in the Rose household. Cate knew her mother was very much alone but had remained strong when it came to their quiet and sometimes lonely life. It had always been just the two of them. They were comfortable and 'normal', and Cate was a strong and independent young woman. She enjoyed having her freedom, and so earned her own money on the side by working shifts at the local pub.

She looked a lot like her mother, strikingly so. Her long, dark brown curls and bright green eyes were the same. Everyone had always commented how she was the image of Ella, and Cate had always been able to see it herself, too. She was the same height, slim build, and even had the exact same curvy, hourglass figure as her. Cate often wondered what traits or looks she might've gotten from her father, but she couldn't see anyone else in herself at all. Ella hardly ever spoke of the mysterious sperm-donor, but when Cate had finally pushed her one night, she seemed ashamed to admit that it'd been a one-night-stand with a boy she'd met during her slightly rebellious younger years. He'd reportedly been at a party she'd gone to on Halloween, and the pair of them had met whilst dancing in the sea of goths and punks. Luke, or so he'd told her his name was, had literally crashed into Ella as they both danced with their friends, sending her flying. He'd then supposedly apologised and offered her a hand to dance, and she had been smitten with him instantly. Ella had then told Cate how it wasn't long until they sneaked off to an upstairs room to be alone together.

"He was just so gorgeous, a real life bad-boy," she'd said, her eyes glazing over at the memory. "One word and I was putty in his hands. We only went up to talk in privacy, honestly, but one thing led to another, and I ended up sleeping with him. The next day, I woke up, and he was gone, and I never saw him again. I tried to find him but have never managed to track him down. A few weeks later I realised I'd skipped my period, and voila!" she had then said, giving her daughter a hug before eagerly changing the subject.

Cate wanted to understand it but hadn't been able to. In fact, she'd never been interested in boys, so couldn't understand the appeal of a one-night-stand. There was just no spark, no lust, or desire for them. If anything, she was so utterly bored by their fixations on computer games, cars, and sports, and so she just switched off whenever she was around them. Her indifference to the opposite sex seemed quite clear, and she'd often found herself wondering if she might be gay.

During her mid-teens, Cate had started hanging around with a small group of girls her age, and most of them seemed uninterested in the boys at their school as well, so it'd suited her perfectly. At eighteen, Cate had put her theory to the test and finally had her first kiss with her best friend, a girl named Dylan. They'd met at school and gotten closer over the years until finally sharing the drunken kiss, and while it'd been nice, Cate still couldn't find that passion within that others described. For some reason, it was as though an unspoken voice deep inside of her chimed in resistance to her ever getting close to anyone—as though she was holding out for someone life changing. She and Dylan were close, but Cate knew things would never go any further. She trusted Dylan completely, so it wasn't that she was shy, but for some reason, Cate would always back off if things turned into more than mere flirtation. Nothing had ever felt completely right, and she worried she might never figure it out. Cate had quickly realised that even her relationship with Dylan was nothing more than a deep and lasting friendship. She enjoyed their closeness but wondered if perhaps she was just struggling so much with her sexuality that she had misinterpreted her feelings for her friend. Deep down, she knew Dylan was no fool. She knew Cate wasn't serious about experimenting with her but seemed to be enjoying having that closeness to someone, anyone. Rather than put a stop to their intimate connection, she kept up the pretence as well.

The night after her third strange awakening in the shadows, their group of friends all decided to camp out in an old field close to town. Cate wasn't sure at first. If she were honest, she was worried about finding herself outside the strange building again after another sleepwalking episode but couldn't bring herself to tell any of her friends about her nightly strolls, or her fears, as to why they were happening. She'd even tried to find her own way to confront those fears but couldn't find the creepy old church during the day, no matter how hard she'd tried.

After being badgered by her best friend all day, she eventually went along with the camping idea. Dylan had fluttered her eyelashes and pleaded with her, and in the end, she couldn't say no. They always had a blast, and Cate had no doubt that night would be any different. Their group of friends would regularly hang out together at each other's houses, or at the local beach, where they could enjoy their privacy once the sun went down. Even in the winter months, they'd build a fire or huddle between the wooden huts that straddled the beachfront. Nothing stopped them from having their fun. In their small hometown on the southeast coast of England, the rest of the world would fall away when their group got together. Cate felt at peace with Dylan and the others. She was light and carefree, as though nothing else existed or mattered, and knew she'd needed it.

She often watched her friends and wondered about them, who they were in the recesses of their souls, or what surprises they might be hiding. Cate wondered about a lot of things, mostly their secrets and which lies they'd told throughout their lives. She wanted to get inside their heads and learn their truths, and while Dylan was Cate's best friend and her closest ally, she still wondered what went on beneath the everyday façade she instinctively knew everyone wore—even her.

Cate watched Dylan as she tended to the campfire, and for some reason felt compelled to really take her in. She was a curvaceous girl, and her short height accentuated those curves effortlessly. Dylan always wore her ash-blonde, shoulder length hair up in a constant ponytail and had her hazel eyes hidden behind thickly rimmed, stylish glasses—even though she didn't need them. She had a prowess about her every move that made almost everyone stop and take notice. Although not conventionally gorgeous, she radiated mischievousness and knew how to use her sexuality to her advantage.

Dylan was warm and kind as well, and Cate had been drawn to her from the first moment they'd met at school years ago. She'd been having a hard time with the dreaded long distance running, and one day had decided to skip their PE class, opting instead for hiding out in the girls' toilets to wait for the bell that signalled the next lesson. There, she'd found Dylan, hiding out as well. They'd got chatting to pass the time and had liked one another instantly. From that day on, they'd become the best of friends, and she'd been there for Cate in ways no one else had ever been.

It didn't matter if she hid secrets from her or wanted her in ways Cate couldn't reciprocate. She felt it in their bones that they were connected and would be forever.

CHAPTER TWO

The group of girls pitched their tents in the field and sat around a fire in the centre. They then chatted long into the night and shared a few bottles of a vodka-based fruit drink Angelica—the diva, and without question the leader of their group—had picked up on her way over. The others were giggling loudly without a care in the world, but for some reason Cate couldn't relax. She was tired and wanted to get some rest, but was worried about the sleepwalking, and the whole thing made her feel uneasy. To top it all off, the entire time they were sat around the fire, she was convinced someone was watching her. Memories of the figure in the shadows were now haunting her, and she just couldn't shake it. There was also a strange feeling in the pit of Cate's stomach, almost like something was calling to her, telling her to follow its beacon. It was strange, as though she was needed elsewhere, and the whole thing scared her. Her entire life, she'd struggled with peculiar urges she couldn't explain, ones that sometimes scared her. Night terrors had plagued her childhood, and then for years she'd sworn to having seen shadows moving in the periphery of her vision. She'd given up on channelling the urges via art or by trying to pen stories based on her experiences, as all she seemed able to create were sick and disturbing images or scenarios. Since meeting Dylan and the other girls, the nightmares had eased dramatically. It was as though the distraction somehow kept her innermost oddities at bay. At least until her sleepwalking sessions had started a few weeks after her eighteenth birthday, of course. Still uneasy, Cate grabbed her mobile phone and sent a text message to her mother, checking in with her. She was panicking in case the strange feeling was some kind of omen that things weren't right back at home, but thankfully she got back a quick reply within a few minutes.

I'm fine, have fun with your friends xxx

It was a short response, but probably just meant Ella was pre-occupied or chilled out at home with a glass of wine. Cate imagined her curled up on the sofa watching one of her favourite soap operas and smiled before sending back a smiley-faced emoticon.

Hours later, the other girls were all fast asleep, but Cate still couldn't shake her strange urge to leave. She just lay in her tent, wide-awake, listening to the sounds of the night all around them. Their small town was more than safe, so she knew not to be afraid, but still, she couldn't settle. Just after two o'clock in the morning, she'd had enough. Cate dressed as quietly as possible in her jeans and hoodie jumper, matched with her black boots and scarf, and then she left the small tent. Her roomie for the night stirred, but didn't wake up, and Cate was glad. She didn't want Dylan to worry, but also needed some time alone, and so headed off towards the nearby town for a walk and to try and clear her head.

As soon as she left the field, she felt different almost immediately. It was as though something really was pulling her towards the outskirts of the small town. There was a powerful urge that compelled her onwards despite the dark, cold night, and it was one that could not be ignored. Cate headed through the empty streets, taking in the shadows around her, and she wondered if the strange urge was the same thing that'd pulled her out of her bed the past three nights as well. This time, though, she was fully awake and aware of her surroundings, and the adrenaline kept her pushing on towards the strange beacon. The rational part of her brain thought it was odd that she wasn't scared, but her urge to follow the calling spurred her on. She eventually headed off the street and down a back alley, and was completely unsure where she was even going, but somehow knew she had to go there. Something inside her yearned for the answers she sensed she'd get once she arrived at her destination. Cate had no idea how she knew that, but every fibre of her being told her she had to trust it and follow her impulses.

She soon found herself at a run-down building that looked almost like an old church. Cate soon realised it was the same building she had found herself outside three times previous and was sure of it when she found what appeared to be the same spot she'd woken in the night before. The windows of the old building were smashed, and the brickwork was battered and covered in graffiti, but there was a hint of light inside. She couldn't help but go in, curiosity getting the better of her. It was where she needed to be, where her body had been trying to drag her night after night, she just knew it. As she got closer to the source of the light, the feelings inside her intensified, and her whole body tingled with anticipation. Her thoughts were running wild, and she forced herself to stop and take a breath.

"How could I just leave my friends and wander off like this?" she wondered aloud, speaking in just a quiet whisper to herself as she leaned against the dusty wall amidst the shadows. It was so dangerous to be out in the middle of the night all alone, and she almost turned back. Her inner struggle was beginning to overwhelm her, yet everything inside implored her to carry on. She knew she was so close to learning the truth. The how's and why's behind her nightly jaunts. Her body was urging her to continue with her pursuit of the strange beacon, and her mind eventually obeyed. She knew she had to find answers, even if she didn't like what she found.

The sound of women chatting quietly greeted her ears as Cate rounded a corner, and inside she discovered a group of four women sitting huddled around a small lantern in the centre of a large, dark room. It was mostly empty inside, apart from an old altar in one corner, but it'd clearly seen better days. The women all looked up at her and smiled as she entered, beckoning her to join them when she came further into the large room. She went to speak, but one of the women, a petite lady Cate guessed to be around forty years old with black hair styled in a bob, held her index finger to her lips to shush her.

"Welcome, Cate," she said, as her eyes skimmed over the girl standing before her. "We've been trying to reach you for days. It took us a while to get through their protective circle tonight, but I'm glad we managed it in the end." The woman positively beamed, eyeing her warmly and with clear affection in her dark brown eyes. She then shuffled sideways so their new guest could join her and the other women around the small bit of heat that came from the lantern.

Cate was shocked and confused by what she'd found, and yet she stepped closer still. The women all grinned as though they really had been expecting her, but she couldn't understand what the woman had meant by her comment. She sat down in the now vacant spot on the floor and looked at her in obvious bemusement.

"How do you know me?" she eventually asked and took a wary look around.

"I'm afraid I've gotten this all the wrong way around. You see, we haven't had to do this before," the woman replied with an almost shy laugh. "Let me explain. My name is Alma. I'm a dark witch, and these ladies all form part of my coven." She looked around the circle and Cate followed her gaze. Despite thinking they were clearly all insane, she smiled politely and leaned forward to shake hands with each of the women as they introduced themselves. Opposite Alma there was a woman named Sara, a muscularly built woman with long blonde hair and dark blue eyes that twinkled warmly in the dark light as she greeted her. Next to her was another black-haired girl called Amy. She had light blue eyes that somehow shone in the dark church, but she seemed colder, more distant than the other two. Cate found herself eager to move on from her intimidating gaze, and quickly greeted the fourth and final woman, a red-haired and seemingly much younger girl called Nancy.

After the introductions, Cate was still none the wiser. With the formalities over, she looked back at the woman beside her, and was unsure how best to ask her for clarification on the one word she'd spoken that was still at the forefront of her mind—*witch*. "You must be wondering what the hell I'm talking about?" Alma asked after a few moments and laughed at what seemed to be an inside joke, but then carried on before Cate could answer. "We were sent here to get you so that your progenitor can come and take you home, my dear."

Cate gasped and felt incredibly confused. After all, she'd never heard of such old-fashioned words being used in everyday life, nor had her mother said a word about Cate's father being more sperm-donor than long-lost relative. Ella had always maintained that she hadn't seen him since the night she was conceived, so had never been able to tell him that his daughter even existed, but never in a way that spoke of such distant overseeing.

She opened her mouth to tell Alma that she must be mistaken, but no words seemed to find her lips, so the strange woman continued with her even weirder story. "You see, he can only visit your world when the moon is in the right phases with the Earth. He's been trying to sire an heir for quite some time, and you're his first and only successful progeny at present. Your master has waited eighteen years for you to come of age so that he can take you home and teach you all about your powers and true heritage, Cate. Today is that day, and it's a truly wonderful occasion, for all of us."

Cate's mind went into overdrive; it was all just too much. She couldn't even fathom what crazy games these women were playing with her, or why. She wanted to get out of there, but found herself rooted to her spot, unable to move her body for some bizarre reason, and soon began to panic.

"What the hell?" Cate blurted out, making the other witches laugh, but Alma remained straight-faced. "This doesn't make any sense at all! Who exactly are you talking about? I don't get it. And what's all this stuff about the moons and siring heirs? Yuk. Who exactly is this guy?"

"That would be me," a deep voice from the other side of the room called over to them, and its ominous sound silenced her rambled speech in an instant. There was power behind that voice. Scary and intimidating power. Cate tried to see through the darkness but could only just about make out an outline of a tall man over in the shadows. He moved slowly towards them, and as he came closer, the witches bowed their heads to him and she heard them mutter the word, *majesty*, in greeting.

Cate felt her body release from its strange paralysing hold, and she eventually stood to greet him, hoping to get some answers at last. As she watched the man approach, she quickly realised just how utterly scared she was of him—terrified to her very core, in fact. Cate could feel the air around her buzz with some kind of omnipotent power, and she felt him drawing her in. It was as if she was opening up to him on some otherworldly level, and the sensation freaked her out. As he reached her, the man outstretched his hand, and Cate instinctively took it. They shook formally, and her whole body went crazy with that same invading sensation. It was as if her senses all came alive at once. His touch was both intense and powerful, and it overwhelmed her.

"I'm your maker. I'm pleased to meet you at long last." The man smiled and stared down into Cate's eyes, seemingly taking her in easily despite the darkness that enveloped them. "I know that you are known here as Cate, but the name I had wanted you to be given was actually Hecate, in homage to the fabled dark goddess. In Greek mythology, she was associated with being the goddess of fire, witchcraft, and the moon. It would've been perfect for you. But, despite my attempts to sway her, it seems your mother wasn't too keen on it in the end," he informed her with a small laugh, and then he suddenly pulled Cate into a tight hug.

In his arms, she still felt scared, yet somehow safe. She could sense his power, but still didn't understand any part of the situation at all. Either it was all some crazy and elaborate hoax, or it was for real, but one thing was for sure, Cate knew things were never going to be the same again. Who exactly was this guy, and why did he refer to himself as her maker?

"You made me?" she asked, feeling as though the rest of the world had fallen away around them. He was all that mattered. His power and presence the only thing she needed.

"Yes," the peculiar man told her, smiling down at her affectionately.

"What does that mean? And who exactly *are* you?" she then added hesitantly.

He pulled away from their embrace and cupped Cate's face in his hands, drawing her gaze to his as he contemplated his response.

She had a moment to really look at him then, to take him in as he stared down at her. He was handsome. Cate guessed he was in his mid-forties, with dark blond hair and deep blue eyes that were somehow almost black in the dark church. He had a rugged look but there was also a softness to him. Cate saw it when he looked into her eyes, but he soon hid it away again behind his stoic features.

"I'm the being that gave you life, just like you must imagine, and yet so much more. You belong to me, Cate. I own you," he whispered, and seemed to revel in her surprised gasp. "Oh, and I'm the Devil," he finally added with a sinister grin.

CHAPTER THREE

Cate's head was spinning, and the witch's words were almost starting to make sense, but she couldn't bring herself to believe them. She was still incredibly confused and wondered what on Earth he was playing at telling her such an outrageous story. Cate thought about her friends back at the campsite and wondered what Alma had meant when she'd referred to them and their circle that she'd been inside in that field.

That was the moment she realised the strange man could read her mind. He spoke to her as though she'd asked the questions aloud and didn't even offer a flicker of an apologetic expression that he'd been caught eavesdropping on her private thoughts.

"I know you think you can trust them, but don't. They're a coven of white witches, Cate. They've been keeping tabs on you for a while now, just like Alma and her dark coven. They've tried to hide you from me for years and used their power to try to keep you away tonight so that I couldn't call you to my side. That's why Dylan befriended you in the first place," he told her, without a care for her pain at finding out the truth about her supposed best friend. Cate's breath caught in her throat, and a small sob forced its way out of her. Had Dylan had been lying to her all along? Cate had to wonder if she'd really been serious about her friendship at all, or had their entire relationship all been simply to keep her under their scrutiny?

"I don't believe so," he answered her thoughts again, and his words pulled Cate out of her sad reverie. "By all accounts, she was only ever meant to be your friend, to get close to you and gain your trust. But I think she got too close and started developing a real friendship with you, just as you did with her. I know you'll miss your friends, but the life you have waiting for you at my side will be so much more plentiful than you could've ever imagined. You won't even think about that white witch once you're home with me, where you truly belong," he informed her with a grin. "And besides, we don't consort with white witches, anyway. You'll soon forget all about her, my love," he seemed to add as an afterthought.

The dark witches then rose from their places on the floor and encircled the two of them.

"It's time, your majesty," Alma said quietly, and he nodded.

"Will you come with me, Cate?" her master asked, while staring into her eyes and holding her close again. She couldn't truly fathom where it was he meant, but she assumed he was talking of Hell and despite being terrified, Cate knew she had to go with him.

Her strange past suddenly all made sense, and she wanted a piece of what he was so willing to offer her. They'd only just met, but she knew then that the strange beacon and urges she'd felt the past few nights were all thanks to him. She was drawn to him entirely and had to know if what he and the witches had told her could possibly be true. Curiosity got the better of her. The promise of a life by his side stretched out before her, and Cate quickly made up her mind. What was the worst that could happen…

"Yes," she replied, and she drank in her master's smile. She then relished in the warmth he shared as he held her tight, pulling her to him. Cate had never known a man's affection, and knew she might truly be going crazy, but that this might also be the closest she'd get to it if his words were true. She knew he was powerful and scary, but already trusted that he'd take care of her like he'd promised. He watched her for a moment, and then leaned in close to speak softly in her ear, evidently pleased with her so easily obtained compliance.

"This is going to feel weird at first. You'll feel as if you cannot breathe, but you just need to remember that you're an almighty being—far more powerful than any human. Your power is there for the taking; you only need to open yourself up to embody it. There's no need to take a single breath to survive in Hell, and in fact, there's no oxygen at all down there. You are my heiress and will be henceforth known as the Dark Princess. There's such greatness and potential within you, and I cannot wait to spend eternity with you by my side," he told her, and with that, the world around them whizzed away. She felt like she was being squeezed for a second or two, all the while being pulled downwards, and the odd sensation made her want to cry out, but Cate kept her cool. It only lasted a few seconds, and then it was thankfully over.

She felt the floor solidify again beneath her feet, and as he'd warned her, Cate's chest suddenly tightened. She began to panic and felt as though she were being suffocated. The heat was intense all around, and her vision blurred for a few seconds, making her panic even more, and yet her conscious mind reined her back in. She slowed her frenzied thoughts and remembered what he had told her, all the while coming to terms with the realisation that it really was no hoax or crazy and elaborate lie. They truly had just teleported into Hell.

Cate closed her eyes and thought about the breath in her lungs, telling herself that somehow, she needn't do it to survive. She slowed her body's cries for air and focussed instead on regaining her composure. After just a few minutes, she stood tall and stared in awe as the full reality of what'd just happened dawned on her. She even wondered if it could truly be real, or if she was seeing things, lying beside Dylan in that cold tent while her mind was somehow vividly dreaming away.

"Yes, my darling, it's all very real. Welcome home," he said, responding to her thoughts again.

Cate looked up at their ruler and was finally able to see him fully in the red-tinged light. He took her aback. The Devil was so commanding and had so much power and presence, but of course he did. The almighty master of Hell was everything he had ever been portrayed to be—powerful and fierce, yet alluring and seductive. Cate knew she had a lot to learn before she would truly feel a part of this world, but honestly, she couldn't wait to get started.

It wasn't long until she was given a tour of the nether kingdom that was to become her home. She had no idea of her place in it yet and didn't feel comfortable taking on her title of Dark Princess until she felt she deserved it. He might not have been a presence during her life, but she was certain there were expectations of how their relationship would go now that she'd come down into the fiery depths with him. She was his one and only heiress by the sound of it, and Cate wanted to do Satan proud.

She tried not to look lost as Alma led the way. In many ways, Hell reminded her very much of Earth, apart from the red skies and intense heat, and she took it all in with a smile. She even thought to herself how the portrayals in books and on television back up on Earth was close to the truth, and she was full of admiration at how they'd created an entire civilisation there. In the centre of the gigantic city stood a huge castle overlooking the entire realm. It was vast, oppressive and gothic, yet beautiful, and was surrounded by many buildings and gardens that opened out onto walkways. The setup was similar to a human city and its streets, but without the cars or lights to provide a backdrop.

She was informed that many different beings lived in the city and walked those streets, although she suspected none of them were mortal. Cate let her mind wander and began to imagine where the human souls might be kept. She thought of torture dungeons and fiery pits somewhere in the depths below, but knew those things were most likely very real, and didn't want to ask the question aloud in fear she might be right. She didn't need to know about those things in too greater detail just yet, and she certainly didn't want to see them.

Inside the dark castle itself, Cate was given a tour. After seeing the lavish palace in all its glory, she was shown around her family's private chambers last of all. They were huge, and the living area took up an entire wing in the fortress that loomed over the city. Their wing was her master's main residence and evidently hers now, too. It was spacious, comfortable, and private, with access only granted to their dark minions via direct order from Satan himself. She found it odd at first that he wanted her to live with him there and offered to take a room in the opposite wing where the level one demons lived, but he wouldn't hear of it.

The deep and meaningful conversations would surely come, but for starters Cate felt like nothing more than a treasured guest. She was referred to only as his progeny—like some sort of property he'd left in the hands of another all these years. It didn't feel good being treated like an object rather than a person, but Cate was so starved of male attention that she never once argued. She didn't want to admit it to herself, or to him, but there were some clear daddy issues that were impending her ability to make the right decisions. Like how she'd come with him without so much as a second thought. A decision she knew might come back to bite her.

The Devil did tell her how he'd lived alone for thousands of years but was ready to share his world with another at last. Despite his many underlings, he seemed lonely. Cate took his desire for her to remain close by as nothing more than his need to fill that void in some way, and so took his offer with a gracious smile, and said nothing more about living elsewhere in the castle.

She adored her new home, and there was absolutely nothing old-fashioned about the way the palace was inside. It was smartly furnished with heavy wooden units and beds, while dark, sultry art adorned the walls. In Cate's bedroom, ornate mirrors covered the entire wall on one side, and it made her already huge room look even larger. She also had a large window that looked out over the black and red hazed skyline and wondered how it was this had all come to be. Her questions went unanswered for now though, and she embraced the changes with an open mind, rather than dwell on the details.

Cate was given many gorgeous clothes and jewels to wear, and she was informed to let Alma know if there was anything else she wanted. Nothing was too much and would be procured for her without question. But there wasn't a single possession she was missing, just one thing. Cate missed her mother. She knew she'd chosen a life in hell over a human existence with Ella that night in the church, but she hadn't realised at the time that she would be expected to stay away indefinitely. Time would tell, but she hoped she might be able to go and see her soon.

As time went by, Cate soon settled into the strange new world she was apparently heiress to and had the space to roam freely once she found her bearings there. Everyone she came across addressed her as the Dark Princess, and they seemed fearful of saying or doing the wrong thing with her, regardless of her insisting they needn't worry. The witches were so eager to please her that she wanted for nothing, and it was an odd transition from being an everyday human girl to a privileged princess being waited on hand and foot. The only exception was that she couldn't have any food, as for some reason, it was impossible to make or teleport down. It would rot within seconds and was hardly appetising in that state. She didn't really want to think about the reasons why anything full of life perished in seconds, but found that she didn't get hungry, anyway. It was just a force of habit to have a cup of tea or a snack as she studied or chatted with her new friends, and it was one she endeavoured to kick.

There were the darkest of beings around Satan all the time, and she couldn't deny it took her a while to grow comfortable in their presence. Witches, demons, and other such things she had yet to learn about surrounded them, and many still terrified the naïve young woman. Cate could tell that each demon or creature was different, as if it was a sense rather than a physical element that gave them away, and she soon learned many things about herself and her master, thanks to his eagerness for her to truly be a part of his reign.

Satan told her about how the underworld came to be, and that he was once an angel up in Heaven. He and the others were brothers-of-sorts, only without a mother or father. They were created by a higher power, and then left to fend for themselves. He told her how they'd quickly put together a hierarchy of angels like the demonic structure he'd created in Hell, in which the strongest reigned supreme. A group of the oldest and most powerful upper-level angels quickly emerged, and they now made up the High Council of Angels, rather than Heaven having one ruler.

The concept of God, according to Satan, was quite unlike the one almighty presence that many humans chose to believe in. There was not one divine being, but the combined say-so of the High Council of Angels, who overlooked mankind from their light realm. They made decisions and commandments for the humans' wellbeing, and the continuance of their heavenly decrees, and grew stronger with every passing year.

He eventually sat Cate down and told her how it was he'd come to be ruler of Hell, and she listened, enthralled by his gloomy tale.

"One day, millennia ago, I had disagreed with their plans for one time too many. My outspokenness that day had come after a spree of disrespectful behaviour, all because I'd found my own mind and wanted to make my own decisions. The council accused me of trying to take over, and they made the unanimous decision to cast me out of Heaven. But, they hadn't wanted to send me to their newly created Earth, so the angels fashioned another realm," Satan told her, and his eyes turned black as they often did when he was angry or tense. "It was a place where nothing thrived and was truly a hellish pit for me to be banished to. I lived here alone for hundreds of years and hated the imposed solace at first. I saw it as a prison, but then over time I grew to love it, and felt at home in the darkness and the decay. I created the dark castle using summoning powers I drew from the realm itself, and before long, I was commanding my own desolate world with ease. Then, the people of Earth started to evolve, and commit sin. Their souls were thus unwelcomed in Heaven, and needed to go somewhere, so Hell was the obvious choice. I quickly found myself accompanied in my exile by the decrepit souls of sinners, each of whom later became either my allies or our playthings."

Cate sat with him for hours, utterly engrossed in his story. Before long, she learned how two more angels had also fallen from Heaven, too. They'd been cast out thanks to their supposedly sinful deeds, and they'd joined Sataniel's side in the darkness. They were Leviathan and Beelzebub, his closest friends, and still like brothers to him. The pair had readily joined him and quickly became his two most trusted and powerful demons, and the first to be ranked in his highest level of the demonic class system. Those others along the way that were deemed to be of strong enough character or high calibre were then chosen by the Devil to join his ranks, and he'd given the chosen few a higher command in his armies, which began the hierarchy of Hell. That very system then became the chain of command that still held up the pillars of his reign today, and Cate was fascinated to hear all about it.

She knew he was reading her thoughts while he spoke, listening in on her inner reactions to the tales he wove, but didn't care. Being around her omnipotent creator and having him lavish attention on her was wondrous, and she didn't regret her decision to leave her human life behind.

To finish off her lengthy lesson, Satan told her how he'd wanted a child for many years. He'd seen how the High Council of Angels could do it with the child, Jesus, and tried for nearly two millennia without success. It was only when he changed tact that his plan had worked, and eventually his first heir was created, Cate.

"Neither demon nor human, but my progeny nonetheless, you were finally born. You're truly a precious gem to me, Cate. I'll never let anything happen to you," he said, and she lapped up his adoration. It was strange, but she trusted that his words were true. She felt his power and presence flowing through her in her every waking moment now that she had come of age and accepted him as her ruler, and it seemed to empower her more and more as the darkness consumed her willing soul.

It wasn't long until Cate was happy and comfortable in Hell with her new and unusual band of demonic friends. She soon felt every inch the Dark Princess in her new home and before long she barely even thought of her old life, or those she'd left behind.

The weeks, months, and eventually years whizzed by, but Cate didn't age at all, and she knew she wouldn't grow older either. She realised very quickly that this was what her master had meant all that time ago in the old church, and that once she came of age, she would stay that way forever.

CHAPTER FOUR

It took Cate a while to get used to her new life, but even after she was familiar with the netherworld, and the changes she'd made to be part of it, she still had little desire for more than friendship in others. She guessed her master wouldn't allow anything to happen anyway and had quickly realised his protectiveness knew no bounds when it came to her safety and care. There were times he'd left her terrified following the forceful delivery of his orders regarding her care. He'd made it perfectly clear that whatever happened would be his decision, rather than hers. Satan had told her early on that she was not to lose her virginity until he had given her permission to do so, and that it would be with a partner he'd deemed worthy. She hated the very idea of giving that part of herself away at his command and found it a strange concept to get her head around. Still not wanting to rock the boat, she didn't argue out of fear he might punish her the way she'd seen him discipline the various other beings she'd witnessed at his mercy—or rather, lack of it. Cate quickly decided she'd rather remain untouched and in their almighty master's good graces, than begging him for sympathy she already knew he was incapable of having. She just hoped that when the time came, she'd be able to come to terms with a possible forced marriage at the behest of her dark master.

At times, Hell could be lonely, though. Many years had passed since she'd accepted her fate, and Cate missed her friends and family on Earth. She'd grown close with one of the witches, Sara, over the years, and was glad to have a true friend in her new life. Sara was a kind witch and had a fun-loving nature that Cate couldn't help but be drawn to. She reminded her of Dylan in many ways. Sara had been one of the witches that'd welcomed her that night in the church, and Cate had liked her immediately. She had a wicked sense of humour and eyes that twinkled as she played jokes and lured Cate in on her pranks and games, reminding her to have fun and act her age sometimes. Sara was Cate's new best friend, and she was so glad to have someone she could confide her fears and worries to. She still thought about Dylan but knew that her days as her best friend were well and truly over. She even resented her for not telling her about the white coven and their intentions. Cate could've handled the truth, she was sure of it, but guessed she still would've chosen the other team, regardless. Their friendship was evidently doomed from the start, and Cate had to admit it was better she left all thoughts of Dylan in the past where they belonged.

Despite those few regrets and the pain she felt if she let herself think of her mother, she flourished. Cate mastered her demonic powers well. One of which allowed her to teleport quickly from place to place, and eventually she even managed to pass from Hell to Earth and back again with relative ease. She was not restricted like her master, being equal part human and darkness. The combination meant she could go between the two worlds any time she wanted to, well, whenever *he* allowed her to.

She enjoyed going to Earth and was eventually allowed to visit Ella. First, though, she had to master another one of her powers—to alter her appearance and age herself physically at will. Cate could make herself look older or younger as she wanted, which allowed her to look the part when she finally visited her mother eight years after disappearing that night in the church. She fed Ella elaborate lies about running off with a boy she'd met and fallen madly in love with. She spun lie after lie, telling her how they'd married and moved to London, where she was now happy and successful. Her mother seemed to believe the story, but Cate knew she was still hurting from her disappearing the way she had. Ella simply couldn't hide her disappointment, even though she seemed happy to know that her daughter was okay.

Cate had also learned another power during her time away that meant she could heal her body's ailments almost instantly, but it didn't help ease her guilty conscience that day. In fact, she still hadn't had to use it yet, but she guessed that power might well come in handy in the future.

***

When she was officially thirty years old, Satan succeeded in creating another heir. His methods for passing on his power were still unclear, but either way, a little boy was born who held the dark flame. The witches and warlocks working for their evil master watched over the baby, just as they had with Cate, and the news brought with it a wondrous sense of pride for them. All they had to do was wait until he came of age, and then he would be invited to join them in Hell, just as she had. Cate was so excited that she had someone else to share her world with and held no jealousy towards him at all. She knew that when the time came, they would both revel in the powerful lives Satan had provided for them, and knew she'd enjoy having someone around to spend eternity alongside.

Shortly before the new heir, Devin, turned eighteen years old, their master came to Cate and told her what he expected her to do.

"I want you to go to Earth and watch over him. Befriend him. Mould him so that when the time comes, he's ready to join us," he ordered.

It was a shock to finally be given such a command though, and Cate had to hide her surprise at being sent away. She'd been kept cooped up and alone for so long. Had walked the long halls of the dark castle at length, having nothing better to do than simply be.

Be ready for the orders when they came. Be ready to serve. To do whatever her master commanded without question.

However, her initial instinct was to imagine she must've done something wrong. Part of her wanted to beg him for mercy, guessing she'd displeased him in some way. His demeanour towards her was no different than usual though, and she had a hard time understanding his motives. Plus of course, he wasn't the type to allow for follow up questions.

Cate still went to express her uncertainty at being given such an incredible task but saw her master's eyes start to darken in his anger at her even thinking it. She'd halted her foolish thoughts before they could become a spoken question, but her master was clearly furious at her hesitation, and she was too terrified to speak against his decision to send her away. Cate forced herself to recover, and agreed to his follow his order, despite the fear still niggling in her gut.

"Of course, he won't come of age for a while. Shouldn't I wait and greet him when the time comes instead?" she finally replied, hoping to buy herself more time.

It was odd. Now that her freedom was in her grasp, she didn't want to go, and couldn't be sure how she would manage being away from home again.

He was clearly reading her thoughts, and frowned, but didn't address her fears.

"No, you're to go now, Cate. I want you to alter yourself to look younger, and you will join his school. You're not to tell him anything of our realm, or his place in it, but you can be his confidant in many other ways," he went on. "Do you remember how you had nightmares and were plagued with dark thoughts that terrified you as a teen? Wouldn't it have been nice to have someone to confide those fears in, someone who understood? You can be that person for him. You can let him know that it's okay to let the darkness in."

He was right, and Cate knew it. She would've given anything to have a trusted ally back then. Satan smiled to himself, as though already pleased by her receding reluctance. He looked down at her and grinned, taking her face in his hands, just like he had the night she'd first met him. Cate smiled back, silently accepting the order via her thoughts.

Plans were made the very next day. Alma and the other witches oversaw putting everything together promptly, while also ensuring that it was safe for Cate to live on Earth again. The wise high priestess also tried to raise her concerns with the Dark Prince that it was too soon for her to leave, but he wouldn't hear of it.

"It's for her sake, and mine," he said quietly, before dismissing the witch and returning to his chambers. She didn't have the guts to ask him why, and respected him too much to dwell on it, so she simply strengthened her vow to serve him as best she could.

Alma adored her infernal majesty—in ways she couldn't even begin to express—and showed him so through her unending service and unyielding loyalty. She wasn't about to stop now.

Cate was sent straight up to Earth just a few days later, and, looking like a fresh-faced teenager again, was enrolled at Highgate College in Devin's hometown.

"Here we go again," she whispered to her coven of comrades as they walked into the college and headed off to her first class.

CHAPTER FIVE

Alma and Sara enrolled at the college alongside Cate, both having used their magic to alter their appearance to look younger as well, of course. They immediately took their places by Cate's side and helped her to become part of the popular crowd. She didn't want to be the queen-bee type, but a well-rounded student who was liked and respected, and quickly became the head-girl type that other girls looked up to and aspired to.

Cate could also sense that there must be an allure the others felt towards her new power, as for some reason, the boys suddenly wanted to know her too. Some went as far to proclaim their affection for her on the first day, and she was shocked at how candid they were about wanting to be with her. Times certainly had changed since she was a teenager. Some of the boys stared, some downright babbled incoherently, and others simply whispered about the new girl while waiting patiently for the gossip. She figured it was safe to say her arrival had caused quite a stir.

There were no white witches around Satan's new heir this time around, thanks to the dark watchers having remained extra vigilant during Devin's upbringing, and the trio soon relaxed into their new identities with ease. They dressed casually, acting their supposed ages, but always wore skater-style black dresses with biker jackets, or skinny jeans with boots and slogan t-shirts—pulling off the preppy yet gothic style look they all looked gorgeous in.

Like everyone else, Devin noticed Cate on the first day, but unlike some, he played it cool. He too was one of the popular boys, and their paths crossed quickly when their groups of friends began mingling in the lunchroom. Cate had to smile at Sara as she snuggled up to Devin's best friend, Jonah, who was already her new boyfriend. She'd made quick work of merging their groups, but it helped that he happened to be the chief warlock of the dark coven that'd surrounded Devin for many years. They all knew it was just a ploy to get his group of friends closer to Cate's, but it was fun watching them mess around so freely.

Cate wished she could have a frivolous fling like that too. But in reality, she still felt nothing for anyone—male or female. It wasn't as if she was jealous of what Sara and Jonah looked to have, and she didn't resent her master for enforcing her years of continued celibacy. But, as she watched them fawn all over one another, Cate wondered what she was missing.

Rather than dwell, she focussed instead on the matter at hand. She leaned in and whispered in Alma's ear, who giggled, having perfected their teenage girly routine well. Alma also knew this sort of thing would play on the boys' softer sides and help Cate capture their attention.

It worked perfectly. Cate caught Devin's eye across the busy table and shot him a cute grin that she made sure wasn't flirtatious, but friendly. She couldn't deny though, he was gorgeous, and was the first boy she'd found even remotely attractive in years. Devin was tall and he was dressed casually in jeans and a band logo t-shirt, but what surprised her most was that even at a young age, he oozed desirability. Cate could feel herself being drawn to him and had to fight the flush beginning to form in her cheeks. Within seconds of meeting his gaze, she'd forgotten all about her indifference to men, and realised at once what all the fuss was about.

It terrified her to feel this way about Devin, though. Their dark coven all knew he was the next begotten heir of Hell and not the betrothed lover she'd awaited all these years. Could she even go as far to call him family, given their shared heritage? But Satan had always insisted his heirs were created by his power, not his seed. He's always kept her guessing, never once having provided a straight answer. And as infuriating as it was, Cate had never been able to do anything other than accept it. When ruled by an iron fist, she had given in without a second thought. What he said and commanded was gospel—end of discussion, no matter how cryptic he could often be.

In a world where witches were her friends and the Devil was the closest thing she had to family, Cate couldn't bring herself to care what Devin was or wasn't. What she kept coming back to was the fact that Satan hadn't given her permission to be more than a friend to him, and she knew she had to fight her feelings until he commanded her otherwise. She reminded herself that she was only there to gain his trust so that when the time came, he'd be sure to follow her back to Hell with their sire.

Friends. Devin needed someone he could trust and nothing more.

Cate then, accidentally-on-purpose, reached for a ketchup bottle on the tabletop at the same time as Devin so that their hands touched, just for a split second. All she'd wanted to do was get his attention on her for a moment longer, but the spark that travelled between them severed any doubts she'd had about her sudden attraction to the opposite sex. Cate wanted him, and bad. Those feelings she hadn't experienced all her life about boys kicked in all at once, and judging by the heat behind Devin's eyes, he'd reacted the exact same way towards her as well.

Cate gave him a coy grin and sat back, doing her best to pretend she hadn't noticed the spine-tingling sparks that'd just transferred between them. When in fact, it had permeated every inch of her being, and she suddenly felt more alive than ever before. The trip to Earth wasn't turning out as bad as she'd once thought, or so it seemed.

Devin leaned back in his chair with a sigh, all thoughts of ketchup seemingly gone, and Cate hoped he might be feeling the same way she was. The intensity of their connection seemed amazing, yet terrifying at the same time, and she looked to Alma for some advice, but got nothing other than a shrug from her magical friend.

After that first meeting, Cate couldn't take her eyes off him. Their groups hung around together most days, thanks to Sara and Jonah's blossoming fake romance, and Cate continued to play it cool. She decided to let Devin come to her rather than making the first move, just in case he thought she was coming onto him, and also because she was terrified he might actually like her back.

The next few weeks went by in a blur, but Cate kept a close eye on her charge and slowly but surely edged her way into his life. She was so focussed on Devin that she had to rely on the witches' help to ensure she kept up her grades and got to her classes on time. They worked their magic and ensured she received good marks, as well as always being on time for classes and her other commitments at school. The pretence was just as important as their mission to watch over Devin alongside Jonah's coven, and together they made sure that he always remained under their watchful eyes.

One weekend a couple of weeks into the new term, a girl in their class threw a party while her parents were out of town. Unlike Cate, she really was the queen-bee type, and loved throwing parties and being the centre of attention wherever possible. She'd evidently had her eye on Devin for a long time as well, so Cate and her coven had kept a close watch on her too. Brandy had been heard moaning about he didn't even seem interested in girls though, and Cate had to force herself not to laugh. The silly girl took offence that he'd never looked her way, and according to her everybody wanted her, so she bragged to everyone how she was determined to get his attention that night at her party.

As soon as Devin walked into the house, though, he went off in search for Cate. He didn't know what it was about her, but he just couldn't seem to stay away, despite having been too shy to make a move yet. He couldn't figure it out, but just had to get closer to her. A deep yearning within pulled him in her direction whenever she was near, and it'd happened whilst at school as well. Something about her just screamed to him, and he knew she had to be his. Brandy tried to intercept him a few times, but Devin just ignored her as he wandered around, catching glimpses of Cate and her friends from afar, but he was unable to get near enough to talk to her. He'd decided tonight was the night, though. He had to get closer. Devin knew he had to figure out his attraction to her at last, and most importantly, make her his.

Cate also sensed every time Devin was in the same room as her, but she kept up with her friends as they floated back and forth between the spiked bowl of punch in the kitchen and the makeshift dance floor in the living room. Each one of them were playing their parts, enjoying themselves and getting drunk quickly on the strong alcohol. However, Alma had disappeared on her, which was unlike the usually so cautious overseer. When she eventually reappeared, she had a smile on her face the likes Cate hadn't seen in a long time, and she had to wonder if their infernal master had put it there.

"He's given you his permission," Alma whispered in her ear, and Cate grabbed her by the shoulders, peering into her face intently.

"What?" she demanded, and Alma's smile widened.

"He hoped your connection would lead you both to something more, but there was no way of knowing until after the pair of you met. He said for you to detach yourself from all sordid fears and simply follow your heart. Do not give in to human misconceptions regarding the right or wrong but go with what you feel is right for you. The pair of you have his blessing, and as long as you don't tell him the truth about his place beside you at Satan's table, you can stay here until Devin comes of age."

Cate shrieked with happiness and hugged Alma. This was perfect news, and while they were far from anything remotely serious, it was wonderful to discover that she had their master's permission to at least give a relationship a try.

With the help of Jonah, Devin finally found his way over the rest of the group. The warlock had torn through the crowd, practically running across the room to grab Sara in his arms and deliver her a passionate kiss. Devin was hot on his heels and pushed in closer thanks to the busy throng. He ended up so close behind Cate that she had to calm her hurried breath. His presence was so intense she trembled with desire, the likes she'd never known before.

He played it cool and leaned past her to grab a drink, but having his torso spread across her was almost too much for Cate to handle. The sparks were flying again, and it was enough to make her shudder in sweet anticipation there and then. She turned to look at him, and their faces were so close she could feel his panting breath on her face. He felt it too.

"Hey," she managed, desperate to move things along, but had to force herself to be patient.

"Hey, Cate," he replied nonchalantly, but she could tell he was trying far too hard to keep calm. She could see through the façade and wondered for a moment if her desperate attempts to fool him were so obvious as well.

"Yeah," she replied, aiming for casualness as well, but she ended up sounding more like a shy girl. She mentally kicked herself up the arse and spurred herself on. "You all right?" she added with a smile and had said it more as a statement than a question.

"You want to go get some air?" he then asked, and she nodded, smiling wider. He mirrored her smile, and his light blue eyes sparkled as it reached them. Cate was already head over heels for this boy, and mentally thanked their master for allowing her the opportunity to act on her new and all-consuming impulses.

She then followed Devin towards the back garden, where it was quieter, and felt grateful for the few moments of comfortable silence they shared as the pair filtered through the crowd. It gave her the chance to take a breath and plan her next move. She hoped for privacy and was glad when they discovered that the only other people out the garden were other couples that were making out and groping each other on the deck chairs or the flattened sun loungers.

The still nervous pair found a spot on the low wall and perched there side-by-side. She leaned in and they stared into each other's eyes for a long time, neither seeming able to speak. Devin's eyes were the colour of the sea in the summertime, and they made Cate think of her old home with nostalgia and fond memories. She couldn't help but smile to herself, thinking back to all the fun times she'd had there with her friends and family, regardless of how things had ended so abruptly between them.

Eventually, she knew she would have to make the first move. Knowledge and age were on her side, even if he wasn't aware of it yet. She chatted about everything and nothing and then asked Devin about his family. He was, of course, an only child with just a mother around. There was also the long-lost father who'd never been in the picture. Cate wondered how Satan had managed to finally do it, but couldn't figure out the logistics behind it all, so gave up trying. She focussed back on the boy sitting next to her, and truly felt as though they were kindred spirits—the same and yet different in their own ways.

"My mum never really speaks about my dad, but I think it's because she's ashamed. I get the impression he was a one-night stand," he told her, and shrugged. Cate knew that story all too well and put her hand on his thigh in comfort.

"One day you'll know the truth, I'm sure," she replied, and he seemed genuinely eased by her kind words. Cate liked spending time with Devin, and enjoyed getting to know him better, even in the short timeframe. She then decided that enough was enough, and she did what she thought most teenage girls would do—she asked him out.

"Would you like to be my boyfriend, Devin?" she asked, confidently, yet with a hesitant approach that wasn't her pretending at all. She really was afraid he might say no and humiliate her. He seemed taken aback by her forwardness at first but smiled and nodded.

"Yeah, sure," he said with a shrug, trying to keep his cool demeanour in place, but she could tell he was jumping for joy inside.

After that night, the pair of them couldn't keep away from one another and they spent every day getting to know each other better. Even just walking down the street together left the two of them feeling like the only two people in the world that mattered, and it was wonderful after spending her entire life without that kind of connection before. Cate quickly knew she loved Devin. She adored him with every inch of herself, and their first kiss a while later was an explosive combination of hormones, desire, and insistent need for one another. It was perfect, and she was happier than she could've ever hoped for.

It wasn't long until they were the most popular couple at school. All the others wanted to be like them, and their single classmates strived to find their own version of that amazing connection they both oozed with. They were powerful and spurred on others to follow their lead without even realising what they were doing. It was an unexpected new ability Cate hadn't counted on, yet she could feel her dominance seeping into those around them, and she relished the power it gave her.

To be adored by all her friends and peers, as well as their teachers, gave her strength, confidence, and a prowess Alma and Sara told Cate was befitting of her high status as Satan's eldest heiress. She could feel her power growing every day and cherished it. Devin seemed to bring out the best in her, and he also helped her to realise that beneath her layers of uncertainty and guilt, she also had the strength to lead. Cate discovered that with Devin at her side, she could encourage everyone around her to want to follow her example, and they didn't seem to know they were doing it. She and the witches could sense her influence affecting their human schoolmates, making them confident and, in turn, her more powerful. She had a new dark prowess emanating from her now that somehow infected those around her that seemed susceptible to it, and Cate revelled in having a following of sorts for her own.

The formidable couple were also stronger together and made each other more powerful with each passing day. Devin's power hadn't come to him yet, but it would, and when that happened, Cate was certain he'd be a formidable heir to Satan's throne, just like her.

Cate was open with him about her past as much as she could, and in return Devin shared his insecurities and lack of past sexual experience. It didn't matter to her, as she had a similar story, though. The details were inconsequential, and all that mattered was that someday they'd be each other's firsts. She would wait as long as it took for him to feel ready, even if it was another decade. Time meant nothing when you had an infinite future ahead, but she refused to take a single day of it for granted.

Much to Cate's happiness, she was given a message via Alma a few weeks later. Her master was pleased with her progress and urged her to carry on with her chosen course. The dark witch had been summoned back to Hell to give him an update and had returned to urge Cate to obey his command. She was eager to, but strangely, Cate missed him. In a way, she hoped he might visit her during the next full moon to update her himself. She knew Satan had to sense her desire for his company, but for some reason he continually stayed away. Thankfully the messages relayed via Alma were always positive, so she didn't take it to heart. He'd left Cate and the witches to carry out their mission without much input from him, and while she didn't know why, she guessed he needed the time alone.

***

When Cate and Devin were older, they decided to make love for the first time. Both had waited as long as they could bear. Kissing and fondling, while amazing and climactic, were just not enough for either one of them anymore. He was old enough to know what he wanted, and Cate knew with absolute certainty that she was finally ready for more. Devin's mum was rather strict but, of course, Cate's fake parents—a witch and warlock named Carrie and Jude—were more than happy for them to spend the night at their house in secret. And so, Devin lied to his mother, and said he was staying at Jonah's house, while Cate ensured they had the place to themselves.

When Devin came to her home a little later that night, he and Cate were both nervous at first. They knew what they wanted to happen, but their inexperience quickly showed.

"Are you sure you want this, Devin?" she asked, and knew she needed him to tell her yes before they could go any further. The ancient laws had to be followed, or at least that was what Alma had drilled into her before letting her pursue an initial night of passion with her new beau.

"Yes, I want you. I need you so much," he replied, and then led her up to the bedroom. They kissed and warmed each other up, and together they explored each other in ways no one had ever done before. "You're so beautiful, Cate. I love you," he murmured between his kisses.

"I love you, too," she moaned, and gave him everything she'd kept locked away for what felt like forever. They were insatiable for each other. Every touch was like a drug, leaving both needing the high over and over again. Their bodies were a perfect fit for each other, and she didn't regret a moment of their first night together. They both knew for sure what they'd wondered all along—they were meant for each other, now and always.

CHAPTER SIX

After their first night together, Cate and Devin couldn't keep their hands off each other. Every spare moment they had, the pair of them could be found making out or sneaking off to be alone together. They were quickly the centre of each other's world, and with the help of the witches and warlocks, somehow managed to continue their perfect record of attendance and grades. The pair remained the college's hottest and most popular couple, and always had their groups of friends in tow. Throughout all of it, Devin still couldn't believe how strongly he felt for Cate after his aversion to girls before. His urge to love and worship her was like nothing he'd ever felt before, and it scared him just how much he needed her. He was honest and told her all about how she'd break his heart if she ever left, and Cate always gave him the same heartfelt answer—that she wouldn't leave his side.

One night, she took him to a concert to see one of her favourite rock bands perform, Forever Darkness. Devin loved seeing her so excited, and the thrill and energy of the crowd permeated them both, heightening their desire for one another even as the warm-up band performed. The pair then pushed to the front of the crowd, where a bouncer immediately escorted them around the back to meet the headliners before they started their performance. What Devin didn't know was that the entire band and their entourage were demons, and they could sense Cate and Devin's true dark flame beneath their human exteriors. They all knew, of course, not to say anything to Devin and give the game away, but each greeted the two of them warmly, seeming grateful that they'd taken an interest in their music.

The lead singer, a demon named Berith, gave Cate a tight hug. He then took the opportunity to whisper in her ear what a huge honour it was that they'd come to his gig, and she knew he meant it. They were royalty, after all, and the title she hadn't felt all that comfortable with before was suddenly a welcome addition to her rapidly expanding prowess. She grinned back and revelled in the demon's attention, while Devin's jaw dropped at the sight of them chatting away like old friends.

It was already a fantastic night out for the young couple but was made even better when they then watched the rest of the gig from the side of the stage as personal guests of the band. Cate loved the attention and soaked up the energy from the crowd as she danced with Devin amidst the spare guitars and roadie equipment. Berith looked over and give her the odd wink as he sang, and she lapped up his attention as much as their demonic onlookers. The ancient demon was alluring in his own way though and had long dark hair and a thick beard that very much suited his rock-and-roll look, while his soulful voice wooed the crowd. Cate watched in awe as his mesmerising words encouraged sin and tempted the humans in the crowd to blaspheme and fight, and it was abundantly clear they had absolutely no idea that he was doing anything.

***

As more time passed, the powerful couple continued to excel at everything they put their minds to and breezed through their final university exams with their friends at their sides. As they approached Devin's twenty-first birthday, Cate sensed he was finally coming of age. He'd been a bit behind her, but she didn't care. She loved their little bubble and knew the time would soon come that their master would reveal his identity to him. She was both excited and scared for when the day finally came. Cate worried Devin wouldn't understand or accept her once he knew the truth, or that he might say no to going back to Hell with their sire. Devin didn't seem plagued with nightmares or vivid imagery like she'd been as a child and teen, and apart from their affection, she wasn't sure she'd become enough of a confidant to him. She guessed only time would tell, but truly hoped he'd see sense, just like she'd done all those years before.

Cate was officially now nearly fifty years old. It seemed crazy to think that but of course she had aged herself to keep in tow with Devin so hadn't felt it. Actually, she didn't feel that old in the slightest. She had remained a child all these years thanks to having been swept off into the netherworld and not having had the chance to grow up, only to then reliver those years over. Would Devin be the same? He would soon come of age, then Cate hoped they would learn and grow together. That they would both grow up. Perhaps they could even have a family of their own. If their master let them of course.

One week after his birthday, Devin woke suddenly in the middle of the night and shook Cate awake.

"Something isn't right. I have a strange sensation in my gut, like I'm needed somewhere but I can't explain it," he told her with a wide-eyed expression. She knew straight away what it was, and that she had to encourage him to follow those urges.

"It's fine, let's just take a walk and see where we end up, okay?" she replied, and despite the late hour, Devin nodded. He seemed to trust her implicitly, and she hoped he would continue to do so even after he'd discovered where it was she was luring him to.

They left Cate's house and walked silently beneath the full moon. She considered taking him via his house so he could say goodbye to his mother, but knew it wasn't possible without giving away what was waiting for them at the source of his inner beacon, so stayed quiet. They followed Devin's lead until they came upon an old church, just like Cate had done before. She urged him to keep going, and only stopped to kiss him quickly before they went inside. One last time, just in case. She pinned Devin to the wall, deepening their kiss and relishing in his touch, before forcing herself to pull away and silently usher him inside. He grinned, drawing her back to him for more kisses, but Cate pulled away. She shook her head. She couldn't push her luck or keep their master waiting.

They then made their way inside and wandered through the maze of dark corridors. She could hardly see through the intense darkness but knew the way as if by heart. When they eventually found their way into the large main room, Devin was surprised to find his friends there waiting for him, all sat in a circle around a small fire.

Déjà-vu, Cate thought with a smile.

"Hey. What's going on guys?" Devin asked, and each of his friends offered him kind smiles, but let Jonah greet him with an answer.

"Hey pal, come and sit down. We've got a surprise for you, but you just have to wait a few minutes," he said, and grinned at them both excitedly. Jonah indicated for the two of them to join the group on the floor and slid sideways to make room.

Devin was confused but did as he was asked and sat in the circle with Cate by his side. No one spoke again, but it didn't matter, because it wasn't long before their almighty master appeared in the doorway.

Satan approached and he smiled down at Cate but said nothing to her. She felt her heart and mind flood with both anticipation and fear in his presence, but she tried her best to hide it from Devin, who just looked puzzled and slightly scared of their new arrival. He still couldn't understand why no one was saying anything to him, but she knew he'd be able to sense Satan's strange power, just as she had done.

He peered intently at Devin, who quickly stood to greet the stranger following a nudge from Jonah, and he offered him a hand to shake. The shrouded man shook it, but neither spoke as they took each other in for a few seconds. Devin had no idea that his master was reading every thought and memory he'd ever had in that small touch, or that he was impressed by what he saw.

"May I have a moment?" was all he said after a few seconds, and off they went to a dark corner of the old church. Devin wasn't sure to make of it all, and he rested a hip against the old altar when the pair of them came to a stop. Despite the changes in his confidence over the last few years, he was unsure of himself in the strange man's presence and fidgeted with his jacket as he waited for him to speak.

Cate and the others stayed in the centre of the room, sat around the fire in wait for their leader's next order. They talked quietly while their master and his youngest heir had their discussion in the corner, and the small group was eager to get the formalities over with so they could return home. Cate just hoped Devin would embrace his new life in Hell alongside his dark friends. She was nervous though and had to stop herself from looking over at them while they talked just out of earshot.

After what felt like forever, the two men came back over. Devin barely even looked at her as she rose to greet them, but it was their omnipotent leader who came straight to her. He gathered Cate in a strong hug and then whispered in her ear, having read her thoughts, and sensed her worry.

"Devin's fine. Don't worry. We're going home momentarily," he told her. "I'm so proud of you."

Damn, that was exactly what she'd needed to hear.

Satan pulled back from their embrace slightly to lock eyes with hers, and Cate shuddered as his power coursed through her at his request. She had almost forgotten how much being in his company could be so immense but was pleased to hear him say the words and felt amazing thanks to his few choice words that lifted her spirits tremendously.

Satan held her gaze for a long while, and she knew he was looking deep into her soul, luring out her innermost thoughts and desires. He took in all the memories she had to offer of her time with Devin, and she could sense him digging around inside her mind and soul. Cate opened herself up to her scary master, and he sent a wave of affection and love back to her in return, randomly allowing himself a rare and wonderful sharing of his own emotion he hadn't ever done before. When he finally shut it off and pulled away, Cate gasped. Their exchange had been wonderful. She'd never felt such a connection with him before, or with anyone else, and she wanted more, but it seemed he was done with the affectionate pleasantries.

Satan then took Devin's hand in his, while the rest prepared themselves to teleport back home. After a quick speech about Hell, which sounded a lot like the same explanation he'd given Cate before taking her the first time, she felt the familiar whooshing, pulling feeling she'd become accustomed to after her teleportation training. When they reached their destination—the gates that led into the dark city and up to their large castle home—Cate caught her breath instantly and then helped Devin to steady himself.

"You don't need it," she told him as he gasped for air and choked on his empty lungs. It took him a few moments, but it wasn't long until he eventually grasped the concept and stopped his body's desperate attempts to take a breath.

Devin slowed his panicked panting and steadied himself. He stood tall at last, and she was immensely pleased with him. Once he was level-headed again, Cate finally had a much-needed opportunity to figure him and his mood out. She was aware they'd not had the chance to talk since their big reveal but hesitated when it came to asking him if he was okay. The Dark Princess peered up at her lover affectionately. She knew her worry had to be etched clearly on her face because Devin reached out and put one palm on her cheek, his thumb gently stroking up and down over her red lips and chin as he stared into her eyes. The little moment of tender connection was enough to re-assure Cate, and she smiled up at him.

"I'll be fine. I guess I'm gonna have to get used to being in love with the Dark Princess of Hell. Aren't we competitors for the throne though?" he asked her, and then chuckled to himself. "Yeah, as if he's ever stepping down."

"Not a chance," she replied with a smile. "We're bonded by our dark flame, just like any other demon or dark being. Two heirs together as one. No need for competition."

Cate had to wonder what Satan had told him in that corner of the church before and hoped he hadn't changed his mind about who was his first heir.

Devin could tell she was fretting and held her close before linking his hand in hers.

"We're to share everything, Cate. Together, as prince and princess…" he added, and the pair then followed their entourage up through the city steps to the castle, while all she could do was gape at him in awe.

In the months that followed their return to Hell, Devin learned all about his place beneath His Infernal Majesty, and about their powers. He'd laughed hard when Cate told him how old she technically was, and then referred to himself as her toy-boy for a while, until a threat of celibacy from her let him know she was not one to be messed with. She even withheld her affection from him for a while until she calmed down and relinquished her stubborn mood but knew she couldn't stay mad at him for long. The pair were still perfectly comfortable together and desired one another incredibly, now more than ever. They got to know each other inside and out during their free time, and Cate found it was freeing to finally be able to open up to Devin about her real self.

Their omnipotent ruler was always busy with his reign. He seemed content to leave them alone to explore themselves and each other as much as they wanted, much to the smitten couple's delight. They'd formed such a formidable duo on Earth and Satan encouraged that love to blossom now that they were back in their true home. Devin and Cate made love for hours during their alone time, and let their sexual curiosities and fantasies flow freely, while revelling in each other's willing openness. Cate confided everything to him, and even told him all about her dabbling during her youth, but that it was never real, and she knew that now thanks to him. He had to admit though, he found it extremely sexy, and begged her to bring a playmate into their bed for just a little bit of fun, but Cate didn't want to share him, and pouted playfully in response.

"You wish. And anyway, you wouldn't even know how to handle two of us," she teased him one night. A cheeky grin then curled at her lips before she jumped off the bed and ran for the bathroom in a bid to get away from the slap he tried to administer to her naked bum cheek, and she giggled uncontrollably every step of the way.

***

Many years soon passed by in the blink of an eye. The power-couple spent every day together between Devin's on-going lessons in power control and enhancement. The pair never aged physically but gained more and more understanding of themselves and each other as the time passed. They truly were the ultimate duo, and even in Hell, everyone around them admired, respected, and followed their lead without question. It was empowering to be continually proving their master right and being rewarded with more power was a prize worth working hard for. Cate did everything she could to serve her dark overlord, and never once shied away from her prestigious role beneath him like she once had. Nowadays, she downright demanded their evil minions addressed her as such, and she was sure she made Satan smile on many an occasion as he watched her bloom.

One night, Cate was summoned to his chambers alone. She was still a little nervous around her powerful sire, but she would never disobey, and followed the summoning without question. She wanted to please him and make him proud, but also remained aware to keep herself in check and to ensure she didn't to let him down or disrespect him in any way while vying for more power of her own.

Somehow, Devin had seemingly developed a far more relaxed relationship with their ruler than she had, and Cate wasn't sure how he'd managed it. He seemed to effortlessly be able to carry out his orders without batting an eye, and even addressed him more casually than she ever seemed comfortable enough to. The two powerful men seemed a lot surer of themselves and their relationship than Cate had ever felt, and she often panicked that deep down she might be weaker than her beau.

When Cate followed her leader through an open door into one of his private chambers, she gasped when she saw who was kneeling at their feet.

"Dylan?" she called out, and panic flared in her gut. She started to go to her old friend but was stopped in her tracks by Satan's stern expression. He was regarding her with apparent interest, and she knew he must have been reading her every thought and reaction to finding Dylan there in Hell with them. He was testing her.

"This white witch was discovered trying to sneak into our realm," he told Cate with a dark look that told her she wasn't there for a social visit. "She claims she wanted to see you. She's here to save you from my evil clutches."

Cate's face dropped. She knew Dylan would be punished severely for coming to Hell and would beg for death following what he would no doubt put her through for having dared try. Despite those fears for Dylan's safety, she still felt glad to see her old friend after all the years since she'd left her behind in that field, and it was good to know she cared after all. Cate could tell her master was waiting to see what she'd made of the remarks Dylan had made about his 'evil clutches,' and she tried to put together a suitable answer.

She hesitated for a moment, and was unsure how best to proceed, but then quickly composed herself. Deep down, she knew exactly what he expected of her. Although seeing Dylan again after all their years apart was a welcome sight, Cate knew she had to do what he demanded. She had to give him some recompense. Satan wanted vengeance.

It was time to choose sides, once and for all, and while she felt bad for Dylan, she'd known what a risk it was coming here, and so had to have known what might happen if she was caught.

"Well, witch," she said maliciously. "You can see there's no need for your concern. You're not welcome here or needed. I know how you tried to keep me from my true fate when I was younger, and that you were never really my friend," Cate added, with as much indifference as she could muster. She knew her master could read her inner turmoil, but that he'd also see she was trying to overcome her doubts. Part of her even began to worry if perhaps she was trying too hard. Was she fooling him? She couldn't even be sure she was fooling herself.

"What do you propose we do with her?" he asked, beckoning Cate closer, and she went over and stood by his side. There, she finally had the chance to take in the awful sight before her. Dylan was chained down, kneeling before him by force, and every inch of skin Cate could see was bloody and bruised. Her shirt and jeans were tattered and streaked with blood, but she was conscious and still fighting the hold he had on her. Dylan tried to look up at Cate, but a flick of Satan's hand sent an invisible blow down onto her head, forcing her even lower in the crouch. Cate couldn't help but flinch.

"We could throw her in a fiery pit?" she suggested, but a disappointed look told her he expected a far more elaborate choice of punishment. "Or, how about we beat the crap out of her and send her back up to Earth, as a lesson to the other white witches?" she tried, and he seemed a little more impressed with that suggestion, but not much.

"Almost there, my dear," he said, and in a surprising show of affection, he stroked her face gently. A snap of his fingers then transported the three of them to one of his torture chambers. Another click, and Dylan's chains were released.

She stood and stared him right in the eye. Hatred and fear mashed her features into an almost unrecognisable guise that Cate could hardly bear to see. Her eyes were puffy, and her darker than usual blonde hair stuck to her bloody cheek lankly. She stood her ground despite his ominous glare, however she shook uncontrollably, which gave away her terror. "You choose first," he commanded Cate, and looked over at the table of weapons and other terrible implements that ran along one wall. She walked over to it, looking the awful items over for a moment before she eventually grabbed a pair of handcuffs. She didn't want to be the first one to inflict pain on her old friend and took Dylan by the arm. She dragged her over to a lonely cot that was on the other side of the room and shackled her with her arms up over her head on the bare mattress.

"Please don't do this, Cate," Dylan begged. "You know what they'll do to me."

Cate felt her stomach drop, and guilt welled up inside of her, but her own fear pushed it away again. If she didn't do it, she had the sneaking suspicion she'd be the next one shackled to that bed, and she had to put her own safety first. She stared the witch right in the eye and stifled a sorry sob but spoke her response without so much as flinching.

"I never asked you for anything, Dylan. Especially this. I don't know what you were thinking of coming here. But you underestimate me if you think for a second I'm that same naïve little girl you once knew. The girl you once had so fooled. I won't do you any favours," she told her. Without another word to her old friend, Cate stood back up and walked back over to join her master again.

She caught his eye and felt his pleasure with her creep under her skin. He'd opened up that strange link between them again, and it contented her to sense his emotions through the bond she couldn't believe she'd ever questioned. Her body sang with his approval, and she wanted more. It made her ready and willing to commit more sin for him, and she guessed it was perhaps his point. This was still so new, and Cate couldn't understand it, but she felt as though their bond was getting stronger and stronger. Things were finally falling into place, and she wasn't going to let anything come between them.

"You may leave us now," he suddenly said, releasing her from his hold, and it left her empty. He snapped his fingers again, and in a second Cate was back in her room. She hated that she hadn't had the chance to question his decision to dismiss her or do more to earn further chances to bask in his emotive affection. In a way she somehow both despised and adored, she hated how unsatisfying her part to play in Dylan's torture had been.

Devin was asleep on the bed, and her frustration quickly turned to desire, so she decided to let him know. She stripped quickly and jumped on the bed, waking him up with a start. One look at her naked body was enough of an invitation for him, and rather than question her, he threw the covers off and tossed his briefs to the floor.

Cate pounced. She threw herself onto her lover with such urgency she came after just a few strokes of him inside her, but it wasn't nearly enough. Her body needed her release more than even she understood, and Devin answered her desperate call without breaking a sweat. The strange energy Satan had shared with her still resonated inside, and it somehow spurred her on in search of satisfaction that was always just out of reach.

Devin knew something was up, but she didn't give him the opportunity to ask what.

When the pair finished the last of their climaxes, they lay exhausted on the bed, revelling in their shared afterglow. Satan then chose to teleport into their chambers at that very moment. Devin jumped up in surprise and grabbed the nearest bed sheet to cover himself, but Cate couldn't reach anything in time. She could feel her master's gaze all over her and despite not needing the attention, she lapped it up as she threw her black dress over her otherwise naked flesh.

Devin noticed, but didn't dare say anything despite his confusion, and she had to wonder if their relationship was as strong as she'd thought if he wasn't willing to tell her off or demand another man take his eyes off her, even if it was their all-powerful ruler and master.

"Now that the pair of you are finished. Hecate, I thought you might like to see how well we got on with the witch?"

Devin looked at each of them and was clearly baffled to hear that something had gone on he wasn't aware of.

"What witch?" he asked, but she didn't get the chance to answer him. Cate caught their master's expectant stare and knew he was quickly growing impatient at having to wait for her.

"Later, gorgeous," she said quickly, giving him a wink as she went over to their master and took his hand.

A blink of an eye later and they were back in the dungeon with Dylan, and her previous high was replaced by a vat of hot guilt that almost brought her to her knees. The witch was still handcuffed to the cot, and her body was severely beaten and disfigured. Cate pitied her and stifled a gag at the sight of Dylan's dirty body. Two demons stood over her, both of whom seemed utterly pleased with themselves and their work. She guessed what they must've been doing to her and looked away. Her master wouldn't be happy with her for showing her distaste, but she simply couldn't look at Dylan any longer.

"I think she's had enough now, don't you?" she asked him, not meeting his gaze. "I'm sure she and the other witches will get the message when she goes back like that," she added, and continued to stare at the ground. He wasn't impressed, Cate knew, but nodded and ordered the demons to take Dylan back to Earth and dump her outside a white church.

Cate hoped she'd be discovered quickly, and that she'd get some help there. It was common knowledge, though, that their demonic minions wouldn't be able to take her directly to her coven. Whenever demons or any other beings from Hell were on Earth, they couldn't cross over into a white church's protective barrier. It was as if an invisible line was drawn around the holy place and they could not cross over it. The same, of course, went for the Satanic churches with the angels or white witches. They couldn't cross over into their hallowed ground, either. Cate then wondered what Dylan had done to get through the barrier, and still didn't understand why she'd even wanted to try and get to her after all this time.

"She committed a sin," Satan answered her silent query. Cate was still shocked every time he read her like that, and constantly kicked herself for forgetting that no thought was ever truly safe from his prying. "Nothing too juicy. She convinced a married man to commit adultery with her and then performed a dark spell. It tarred her just enough to cross our threshold and sneak in through our portals, which I shall endeavour to strengthen. So silly the things *they* deem so evil," he added, and pointed upwards with one finger.

She paled at how far Dylan had gone to find her, and yet all she'd done in return was leave her to be tortured and beaten while she got her kicks with her new boyfriend. She hated how much she'd failed her old friend and wanted desperately to be alone. Satan chuckled to himself, as though he found her guilt amusing, and then he led Cate away without a word.

CHAPTER SEVEN

"I want you both to go up to Earth and oversee one of my companies," Satan informed Cate and Devin later that same day. "It's based in the centre of London, where you will remain until further notice. You will use Black Rose Industries to take over smaller ones and help them grow, but only if the owners sign their lives away for the privilege, so to speak. The basic principle is expansion of our ideas, commandments, and unholy decrees, etcetera." He waved his hand as if he couldn't be bothered to go on but knew they both understood him clearly. Cate nodded and was surprised that he'd used their surnames to create the business title, and Satan gave her a knowing smile. He'd clearly been reading her thoughts again.

"World domination and all that?" Devin said, chuckling to himself, and Cate giggled.

"Absolutely, my boy. One little bit at a time." He smiled and nodded his head. In a blink, they felt the familiar pull as they were dismissed and sent to Earth at their master's command.

The pair were quickly delivered to a huge penthouse flat overlooking the centre of the vast city, where a tall demon named Belias welcomed them. He bowed and addressed them with their formal titles as Dark Prince and Princess, and Cate still couldn't get enough of it when they did that. Devin was even newer to that sort of treatment, and looked quite uncomfortable when being greeted that way, whereas she was coming around to it more and more as time went on.

"Welcome to your new home," Belias continued. "Let me give you the tour." They followed him around the huge home and found room after room, all fully decorated and furnished in dark reds and blacks. *Of course,* Cate thought with a smile. The place had their master's influence all over it, and she wondered if he'd used it as a base the times he'd come to Earth. She imagined wild parties full of sinners and depraved sexual acts, and very much doubted her musings were far from the truth at all.

"I'm gonna like it here," she whispered to Devin with a sly grin as they both took it all in. He beamed back and nodded, taking her hand in his.

Devin swung her around, dancing their way through the penthouse as they finished with their tour, and the pair were excited to get started with their next Earthly adventure.

The next few days were completely taken up with shopping for new clothes and getting everything they'd need to look the part in the hectic business world. They both aged themselves up to around thirty years old so they could fit their roles better, and also did it so they'd be more respected than if they stayed at the comfortable early twenties look they both usually maintained. The business had evidently been run from afar until their arrival, which helped them to slide right into their chosen positions once the day came. They were to assume the identities of Mr and Mrs Black—young entrepreneurs and successful business moguls that'd thus far run the business from Düsseldorf, in Germany. They were to say they'd decided to move back home to London so they could expand the business, which would explain the numerous takeovers they had lined up ahead of them. There were no board of directors or shareholders to answer to. The business was their baby to take control of and run as they wanted, and Cate loved having been given the opportunity to show their Dark Prince what they could do in his name. If they did encounter any trouble, almost all the senior staff were demons, warlocks, or witches, and would help the pair out as per their duty, but they hoped it wouldn't come to that. Both heirs of Satan were looking forward to getting their teeth into the challenges that awaited them and were more than ready to get started.

Each morning, Cate had a demonic assistant who came to choose her clothes and do her hair and makeup. She wanted to look good every day and, as per her master's orders, she was now the face of the company, so needed to look the part. The Dark Princess was perfect at it and went from strength to strength in her new role. She wooed clients and oversaw all meetings and take-overs effortlessly, while luring in other prospective clients at every available opportunity. They were easy targets and seemed to revel in her warm, tender allure. To many it felt like she was doing them a kindness, as otherwise they'd undoubtedly try and fail in this cutthroat world, so she made it an easy decision to sign away their businesses, and souls, in order to take their places in her promised favour.

She was used to being sought after by their clients, but was new to running a business, and relied on her employees to ensure things went smoothly. All those she supervised in the Black Rose head office seemed to adore Cate, whether male or female, and did anything she wanted, no matter what that might be. She loved it and lapped up the attention while growing in confidence and prowess every day.

On the other half of the power-couple sat a tycoon, more commanding than she'd ever known. Devin was the decision maker and firm hand of the company, and he charmed their clientele in other ways. He maintained a strong and powerful presence, and the human staff members were always scared, yet highly respectful to him. He soon discovered how whenever he asked any of them to do something, they all jumped to it right away. They were eager to please him, and he revelled in his new-found power alongside his pretend wife. The women were seemingly drawn to his driven demeanour, and many of them swooned over Devin constantly. They delighted in his powerful, bad-boy attitude, and he played on it effortlessly while lapping up the attention without a care in the world.

The couple later decided to start holding elaborate parties at their penthouse, which of course were invitation-only events. The employees and clients working with them were known to fall at their feet if they thought it would get them an invitation to the highly sought-after affairs, and both Cate and Devin enjoyed having such control over their personal minions.

Often it was nothing but a cocktail party, and sometimes they took the themes a little darker and decided on orgies or BDSM themed masquerades. Cate had also been known to arrange for ancient rituals and spells to be carried out at a secret rendezvous, and they were never empty despite their dark premise. The parties almost always involved depravities and luring innocent humans into committing sin. It was in their nature, and neither denied their calling. The humans involved were let in only if they took a vow of secrecy beforehand, and then they could relish in their rewards for signing their lives away to the dark couple, or the attending upper-level demons. So very many men and women ended up selling their souls for fame and fortune, and it wasn't long until business was booming. She and Devin enjoyed every second of their new lives, and it felt good being in control and so commanding at last.

The dark pair's love affair knew no bounds. They were so in love and in sync with each other that nothing came between them or made either of their eyes wander. They both enjoyed being back up on Earth together again and liked having some time away from the stifling reign of their dark overlord. Their master visited Earth many times when the moons were right and he could come up from Hell, however he usually went off in search of women for him to have some fun with first, but afterwards would head to the penthouse. They'd often throw a party in his honour, to which only upper-level demons, witches, and warlocks could attend, along with their choice of human partner. If the time was right, Satan could sometimes stay for two or three days, and the party often went on the entire time of his visit.

One night, during his annual Halloween visit, he instigated an orgy. With his loyal demons' help, they lured an entire crowd of women to the penthouse, and the vast living room was transformed into a huge area full of soft black cushions and red sheets. It reminded Cate of a gigantic bed for them all to share and was grander than any sexually themed soirée she'd thrown in the past. There were no holds barred, but their master was guest of honour, and he climbed in first. The human women were on him in a heartbeat, and the mood was quickly fuelled by the sight and sounds of their arousal. Next, the high-ranking demons brought their human playthings onto the huge bed, while Cate and Devin watched on from the sidelines. They joined the group soon after and were more than ready for it after having felt the sexual ambiance fill the room, as well as understanding their master's expectations of them.

The pair stripped and began their pursuit of each other's climax as the whole room vibrated with a frenzied energy around them. It was amazing. Cate could hear the women climaxing loudly at Satan's touch, but rather than distract her, the sound fuelled her on. Devin sat before her, and his amazing body was beautiful. His cock was so hard for her, but as he lay back onto the huge, silky floor, she chose not to jump right on.

"Mine," she said, and smiled up at him before she sucked the tip of his hardness into her mouth. He groaned and grabbed her hair, urging her down further onto his throbbing length with a cheeky grin, but she didn't fight his hold. When in the throes of passion, they were limitless, and afforded each other many opportunities to dominate one another equally. She obliged him and licked and sucked until he came into her mouth. Once finished, he sat up and pulled her round and onto her back with one swift move. Devin wasted no time. He yanked Cate's hips towards him and spread her thighs with his strong hands, peering down at his prize while she writhed unashamedly.

"Mine," he said, and licked his lips as he leaned down to devour her. Cate groaned with intense pleasure as he slipped two fingers inside her already soaked core and pushed down on her g-spot, and then cried out as an orgasm quickly rippled through her. That was when she sensed someone's gaze on her. It wasn't unusual during an orgy to have the odd voyeur, but this felt different somehow. Opening her own eyes instinctively at the feeling, her gaze suddenly locked with a set of intense blue eyes that didn't belong to Devin. They belonged to their master. He held it just for a second, but the electricity in his stare was enough to make her senses stir. She instinctually knew he'd been watching her, and the grin on his lips made Cate blush.

Devin kept going between her trembling thighs, but Cate couldn't concentrate on anything other than what Satan was doing in the opposite corner. He looked back across at her, and it felt as if he had silently commanded her to keep the eye contact, because she was suddenly unable to look away. He then winked as another climax coursed through her, and she throbbed beneath Devin's amazing touch. Her back arched, and she cried out with pleasure, and the intense pulse that flowed through her rendered her powerless for a few seconds while she regained her strength. By the time she could compose herself and get back up into a sitting position, a quick glance at their master showed her he was already busy with another human lover. He was thrusting into her as she cried out in pleasure for him, but he wasn't paying attention to the woman on her knees before him. Satan looked over at his Dark Princess again. His eyes looked black, and he was smiling to himself, clearly amused, and Cate tried to convince herself it was because of the concubine beneath him rather than their accidental interaction.

It was only another second before Devin leaned over and broke Cate's concentration with a kiss on her shoulder. She turned to face him and kissed him back, before guiding his hard cock inside her. She needed the distraction from the strange feelings that were now corrupting her mind, and he innocently gave her it, not knowing how preoccupied her thoughts were.

The lovers moved in time with each other, and Cate welcomed Devin's powerful thrusts. She needed him to take all coherent thought away and urged him to bury himself even deeper inside of her. The years they'd had to perfect these moves did nothing to take away from their passion or desire for each other, and she stared into his eyes as they came together. She didn't risk another look at Satan and his horde of conquests but focussed instead on Devin and the way he'd made her feel. Cate loved him with everything she had and tried to convince herself she'd imagined the strange back and forth with their sire from before. She guessed he'd used every one of his omnipotent tricks to keep the women in his throng ready and willing to please him and was sure she must've sensed his magnetism as well. That had to be it.

When the party was over and the sun began to rise, their master took a moment to talk with them before he headed back home to Hell. He looked his usual calm and powerful self, and was remarkably kempt, despite having made his way through a few dozen women that night. He'd kept his short beard and had shaved his hair this time, making him look even younger than Cate had ever seen him before. His deep blue eyes took them both in for a moment before he spoke, and she knew he was reading them. She couldn't hide her desire-driven angst, and Satan barely hid his dark grin as he read Cate's thoughts on the strange subject that had her emotions so fraught.

"I've another heir on the way," he told them with a smile. "The mother's due to deliver in the next few weeks," he added, and Cate wasn't sure whether to congratulate him or be worried that he'd chosen to create yet another heir. As it stood, she and Devin weren't vying for his throne, but if there were more of them, she was sure things could get ugly quickly if they decided it ought to go to one of them instead.

"That's great. Where are they?" Cate asked, and she tried to be excited about it.

"The USA, New York City," their master replied, seemingly ignoring her uncertainty. "She won't know of me, or the pair of you, until she comes of age, just the same as before. But she will be watched over by the witches until that time comes, of course."

"She?" Devin murmured, and Satan nodded. Not another word was spoken aloud, and Cate guessed their master didn't feel the need to explain himself. He simply kissed her on the cheek, patted Devin's shoulder, and disappeared down into the darkness below.

***

The business continued to be a success, and as the time passed, Cate and Devin's wealth and power grew immeasurably. They had to alter their look to ensure they'd aged a little more, but of course, they both kept looking as good as possible. When the time came around again that their master decided to come and see the pair of them on Earth, his next heiress, named Serena, was six months old. Alma had given the pair regular updates, but like he'd warned, they hadn't been allowed to see her. When the moon was full, Satan went to see the child, and was gone just a few hours rather than for the majority of his Earthly visit like normal. He returned to the penthouse and took his two eldest heirs to one side.

"Things are going to change," he said, watching them both intently. "For all of us."

Neither of them was sure what change he meant but didn't get much chance to ask before Devin was ushered away by Sara, and Cate was left alone with their master. "I've decided that you're no longer going to be with Devin. He will now marry Serena when she comes of age," he informed her, without any care or compassion at the gut-wrenching loss she felt at his words.

Cate's stomach dropped at the thought of being taken away from the life she'd loved and the future she'd planned by Devin's side. It terrified her to imagine him with another, and in that moment, she despised the baby girl across the world for having taken him from her. They'd been together for fifteen years. She'd never been with anyone else but him and loved him with all her heart. Cate stared back at Satan in shock and didn't understand how it could be over because he'd said so. She opened her mouth to ask him, but then felt the familiar pull that told her they were teleporting away—back to Hell, and without Devin.

When they arrived, she was still speechless, but so many questions filled her head, and she couldn't hide them from Satan's prying power. She felt scared and had to wonder if this meant he was displeased with her, or whether he was planning on giving her to someone else. The sheer thought of being handed over like some prize or bargaining tool sickened her. Cate had to know the truth behind her master's change of heart.

"Please tell me why," she pleaded, but he wasn't interested in her pleas. He'd seen and heard it all before, and she gripped her tense stomach.

"Stop over-thinking it, Cate. All will be made clear very soon," he answered curtly, before taking her hand and leading her towards their wing of the castle. "Take her to her room," he ordered Alma, who was waiting just inside the door for them, and she curtseyed. "Make sure she stays there," he added before teleporting away, and the iciness in his voice made Cate panic. She had to have done something wrong and was going to be punished, but she had no idea what she'd done to deserve his wrath.

"What did I do?" she pleaded with the witch as they walked slowly towards her room.

"It's not what you did or didn't do, it's who you are that's the problem. I can't answer your questions, but he will, and I'm not sure you're going to understand them," Alma answered, and Cate felt as if her whole body went cold, which was quite some feat being that they were in Hell. The high priestess then half guided, half pushed Cate forward, and she headed into her room in a daze.

I suppose you can't live forever and not have to mix things up every once in a while, Cate eventually thought, and she did everything she could to try and calm herself down. She was still confused and tried to go over everything that'd happened again.

Their sire had insisted upon them both that she was destined to be with Devin and how he'd chosen them as his heirs. He'd told her himself how they were destined to have a family and carry on their strong line from the first conceived successors of Hell. It pained her to realise how that fate now belonged to Serena, and it worried her that she might now be heading to her room for a life of celibacy until someone else came along that Satan deemed worthy. Or perhaps he was done with her completely, and she'd be discarded, forgotten, unwanted, and unloved.

Cate's stomached churned at the concept, and she thought she might be sick. If that were the case, she just hoped he'd be merciful and give her a quick death. But then again, it was the Devil she was dealing with, and he wasn't famed for his compassion. In fact, it was quite the opposite.

CHAPTER EIGHT

Alma didn't say another word. She simply locked the door and left Cate alone with her thoughts. The Dark Princess slumped down onto the bed and realised her current overriding emotion had changed from one of shock to anger. Annoyance rose up in her over the lack of information she'd been given following her master's destructive news, and she screamed into her pillow. She then lay back on her black sheets, staring up at the ceiling thoughtfully while she tried to figure out what was going to happen next, but genuinely had no clue. There was no guessing what was coming next, and a cold chill swept down her spine again as the deafening silence echoed the thundering in her ears.

She wasn't left alone too long, however, and a quiet knock at the door startled her. The lock turned and the large wooden door opened, allowing a man to enter, before it locked behind him again. He was spectacular looking, and Cate watched him in fascination. Her visitor was tall and slim, like Devin, but with more defined muscles that rippled in his arms and chest under his t-shirt. His chiselled features, piercing deep blue eyes and dark-blond hair framed him wonderfully, and Cate perked up straight away.

"Can I help you?" she asked, and he let out a gruff laugh that made her blush.

"I'm sure you can, Hecate," he said, startling her with the use of her pseudonym. She knew that voice, though, and it took her a moment to place it.

"Is that really you?" she asked and was getting more confused. As if he'd willed it, she then began to see through the changes in him. Satan did indeed have the same features she knew so well, but he was now much, much younger. Her Infernal Master had discarded the rough-looking beard in favour of a fresh-faced look and had slimmed himself down, as well as having altered his age. Satan now resembled the twenty-year-olds Cate and Devin had associated with back on Earth, and his dark prowess and bad-boy demeanour only added to his sexiness.

"Yes, I've decided to change my look. What do you think?" he asked her with a cocky grin. He'd known every thought that'd gone through her head since walking through that door, and she guessed he wanted to hear her say the words out loud.

"Well, you're gorgeous, of course. But what's all this for?" she asked and was still naïvely confused by his alterations. Cate slid down to the edge of the bed, where she stood to greet him, but Satan didn't answer. He stepped closer and took her in his arms, and she wondered for a minute if they were about to travel back to Earth, but when they didn't move, she hesitantly glanced up to search his face for answers. He softened his features and allowed that strange back and forth of emotions and electricity to travel between them again, flooding her with a wonderfully sensual wave of adoration and desire.

"This is called *expression*, Hecate. It allows me to share a part of myself with someone that I don't normally allow others to experience, or even let show at all. You're the first being in over a thousand years that I've felt close enough to do it with," he told her, being honest at last.

Her head swam. The overflow from him was making her dizzy, and the strength of his words both scared and intrigued her.

"What's going on, master?" she asked hesitantly, looking up into his eyes, and Satan groaned.

"Don't call me that anymore, Cate," he whispered in return. For the first time since she'd known him, he sounded desperate, and she caught him looking down into her face and staring at her lips.

"Why?" she managed to ask, while mesmerised and taken aback by the strange vulnerability he was showing her.

"Because from now on, I want you and I to be lovers, equals," he replied, and then let out a deep, raspy laugh. Cate was still woozy from his *expression*, and now that he'd finally revealed his reasons, it made her gasp with shock. She was taken aback and had no idea what to say in response. Yes, she'd felt the connection change between them recently, but it wasn't real. It couldn't have been, otherwise why had he sent her away? Why would he command her to be with Devin if he wanted her for his own? None of it added up.

Satan sensed her hesitation, and she felt his hold on her tighten slightly, as though he was unwilling to let her go.

"We can't," she told him quietly, fearing his reaction. "I'm in love with Devin. I thought you saw me as your child, someone you nurtured and helped blossom into adulthood? Perhaps you don't understand your feelings towards me?" she asked and knew straight away that he wasn't happy with her response. He hadn't really been anything more than a mentor to her, but she'd never considered him a potential lover either. Hell, he wasn't even a real person, but it all still felt so wrong.

The *expression* stopped immediately, but he remained where he was, holding her tightly, and their faces were just inches apart. Satan's eyes turned black as he regarded her for a few seconds, and Cate wondered if he might lash out at her. Instead, he kissed her. His deep and powerful show of forceful persuasion surprised her into submission, and he held his would-be lover even tighter.

Cate felt him luring her in. She knew there was even a part of herself that wanted him back, but she couldn't let it take over. She didn't know if what she was feeling was real, or just another order for her to follow from her dark master, and that realisation made her angry. After pulling back, he stared down at her, and then threw her down onto the bed with just a tiny push.

"No one says no to me, Cate. Not even you. I may have afforded you certain liberties in the past, but not anymore, not with this issue," he told her. His eyes seemed to grow even darker and his demeanour more ominous as he stood over her. Cate pushed herself backwards on her elbows, but knew there was nowhere to go, and certainly nowhere she could run. One thought kept running through her mind, a conversation she'd overheard one day between two level one demons, and she hated it. *It doesn't matter what we want. He comes first, and his needs overrule any of ours. What Satan wants, Satan gets. He can and will do as he pleases.*

He climbed onto the soft down and crawled over to Cate and kissed her again. She swooned and couldn't help but kiss him back, succumbing to him involuntarily, but she was torn between the various rights and wrongs swirling around inside her head. She wanted him to open the *expression* link again to help her understand his desire, but he didn't. He kept himself deliberately closed off for some reason, despite her silent pleas. She realised then that perhaps she'd hurt him with her arguments, refusals, and hesitations—both spoken and silent.

Cate truly did not want to disappoint her master, but she somehow knew that she didn't want to be with him the way he wanted—at least not without having some time to think it over first. He'd made her life so incredibly fulfilled since he'd come to her in the church that night, but all they'd had since was a relationship more like a student and her teacher than potential lovers.

She didn't know when his feelings towards her had changed and found herself wondering if maybe it was that night at the penthouse when she'd caught him watching her. Or was it before that?

Regardless of her frenzied thoughts, he continued his pursuit, and kissed her again. Cate's head swam while her lips tingled from his kiss, and her body screamed out for him to continue. It didn't matter that her heart and body were feuding internally. She knew she didn't want it to happen, and her heart soon won the battle.

He knew, of course, and reacted almost instantly to her thoughts. He kneeled over her and stared down with black eyes. Rage and pain were clear on his otherwise gorgeous face, and Satan hesitated just for a moment, as if not sure how to go about dealing with her.

"Please," Cate quickly begged, hoping to divert his attention away from the punishment she was sure he was deliberating over.

"So, it's a no?" Satan eventually asked, and there was no emotion in his tone, while his face remained completely unreadable. The younger look of his was a little alien to Cate, and she had no idea how to read him. It felt as though he was a stranger to her again. But that had to be the point, she wondered. He wanted her to see him differently and had obviously chosen a look he thought she'd like, one that might help sway her decision in his favour. Evidently, he wasn't impressed that it'd backfired.

Cate knew she'd been flirtatious with him. She'd let her thoughts wander and her head be turned, but that was when she'd thought it was nothing more than harmless desire. Wanting what you couldn't have was alluring, but now? She was terrified of what her master apparently wanted to offer her.

"It's a no," she mumbled from beneath him, and couldn't meet his dark gaze. Satan climbed backwards and without another word stood up from the bed, reaching out for Cate's hand. She was confused but took his offer and let him help her stand.

She looked up into his cold eyes pleadingly, unsure of what to say, but all words were lost to her. It felt as though she'd lost the two most important men in her life on the same day, and the thought of being left alone and miserable made her shudder. She wanted to beg him for forgiveness, and perhaps even give him the yes he desired, but knew it wouldn't be sincere, and that he'd know it. The way she felt now, she'd never be happy at his side. Could she force herself to lie to him, or to herself? The answer had to be no.

Before she could even try and fight the tense air between them, the familiar dizziness washed over her that told Cate they were teleporting away. She hoped they were going back up to Earth and back to Devin, but no. When the pair came to a stop, her heart almost skipped a beat, and she began trembling despite the heat.

They were in a deep, fiery pit. Dark red flames licked her body, burning her skin and singeing her hair. There was no way out, and the walls all around her were just inches away from her either side of her body, threatening to scorch her skin if she touched them.

Her master stood a few inches away, seemingly unaffected by the flames, while she was already blistering from just the proximity. Satan smiled maliciously down at her and kissed the backs of her hands.

"I might respect your answer, but it doesn't mean I have to accept it. I'll think give you some time to think about what you really want," was all he said before he disappeared, leaving her all alone in that terrible place with nothing but her thoughts and the flames for company.

***

Cate couldn't bear it all alone in the sweltering fiery prison. She had no concept of how many days or weeks she spent there, but she knew her master was punishing her severely for her foolish resistance of his advances. She guessed she'd only be released when he was done seething over her refusal and knew it might be a while. It wasn't in his nature to forgive and forget.

The walls and floor burned constantly with flames and running lava, and there was nowhere for her to rest or sit, so she was stuck standing in the constant blaze. The flames caused her just as much pain as any burn would, but because of the power given to Cate by the same man who'd imprisoned her, she would heal instantly, and it'd begin all over again. She figured she might find the irony funny if it weren't so painful.

Tears dried instantly on her cheeks the moment they were shed, and she prayed for death to come and take her, but it refused her. It was too much. Cate knew she was too weak to take any more, and she cried out, calling for her almighty master and begging him to return for her, but he didn't listen.

After what felt like forever, she knew she was broken. Cate let out a bloodcurdling scream and fell to her knees. The once so tough Dark Princess no longer even had the strength to stand up, and while she cried out when the hot rock burned her legs to the bone, she simply hung her head in agonising defeat and let them tear away more and more of her burning flesh. She tried to summon the witches, warlocks, and every demon she could think of, but none of them came to her aid. They knew far better than to defy their Dark Prince's orders.

When he eventually returned, she could fight him no longer. She looked up into Satan's cold, black eyes as he stared down at her, and silently begged him to take her away from this awful place.

"I'm sorry, please," she moaned. "Please…"

He put a hand on her shoulder and obliged her pathetic plea. Satan returned Cate to her bedroom, where she was left alone for now. She was filthy. Her clothes were so badly burned that she stripped and tossed them straight in the bin rather than try to salvage them. She then took a long shower and pulled on a heavy black dress that shrouded her entirely, and the dark look matched her gloomy mood. After a few minutes of uncontrollable tears, she tried the door, but wasn't surprised when she found it locked. Cate didn't know when her master would come to her, or how things would go when he did, but she had to assume he still hadn't changed his mind regarding his plans for them.

She fell onto the bed, exhausted, and slept for what felt like days, and thought maybe it even was. When Cate stirred, Satan was sat on the bed beside her, watching her intently. She could sense his intense gaze on her, but not the *expression* she still so desperately hoped for. She wanted to know how he was feeling towards her, and what he wanted now that she'd seen out her punishment. Cate was also anxious to know how best to approach her master and make him understand her reasons for saying no and to explain what she wanted but didn't know where to begin.

She wasn't even so sure what she did want any more. "Thank you for bringing me home," she eventually whispered. The fresh young face peering down at her was unreadable. He was still gorgeous, despite his awful behaviour, and was equally as lethal, as she still couldn't read him.

"Did you have time to reflect down in your pit, my love?" he asked, and a sly grin curled at the corners of his mouth as he spoke. His evil pleasure showed on his face as he took in her painful memories of that terrible place, and she hated him for enjoying her misery.

"Yes, I think we both know I had more than enough time to think things over," Cate replied dryly. Satan shrugged and let out a small laugh and then carried on.

"So, is it a yes now?" he said, leaning in to get closer to her. He seemed so insistent on having her full submission, and she thought it odd he was so desperate for her to willingly accept his barbaric methods at wooing her.

Cate realised then, in a moment of clarity, that free will was all that was stopping him from simply taking her by force. He needed her to say yes, otherwise she would never truly be his to possess. Her revelation stopped his advance, and he pulled back quickly. Satan's eyes darkened and bore into hers, and he laughed, although nothing was funny about the way Cate felt under his sinister scrutiny.

"Got me," he whispered and grabbed her hand.

"No, please," she cried out as her master pulled her away from her room. Cate was teleported away against her will again and materialised on her knees before her sire in a cold, dark abyss. She was crying and begging her master, pleading with him not to hurt her anymore, but Satan was cold and distant again as he towered over her. He looked through her as though she was of no care to him at all, and her pleas made no dent in his icy exterior.

A masked demon dressed all in black then approached and looked to his master for confirmation. A swift nod was all he needed, and then Cate was dragged across the jagged rock floor by an invisible force. When she reached the demon's side, she was bound by her wrists with thick rope and pulled up off the floor to hang there by them. Her shoulders throbbed and her wrists ached already, and Cate bowed her head in defeat. Her will broke with every moment that passed, and she knew she couldn't bear another sentence of lengthy torture. Satan approached and lifted her gaze to his by gripping her chin and turning her head up so she looked him in the eye.

"Let's see how you feel after another year of torment, darling," he told her. "We have all the time in the world to play these games, and you have no idea what other treats I have up my sleeve. You're right, Cate. I do get what I want, and whether it's wrong or right doesn't matter to me. In fact, the more I have to chase, the better the prize will be when it's mine."

Cate didn't get the chance to respond. With a smile, he teleported away, and she just sobbed as he disappeared, leaving her to her misery. She cried out uncontrollably when the first lash of a whip slashed open her clothes and drew a streak of blood from the skin on her back. Cate begged the demon to stop but knew that he wouldn't listen. He couldn't defy his master's orders any more than she could, and knew he'd suffer a similar torture if he dared try.

Hours, days, and eventually months passed by in a dark and painful blur. The demon whipped her unrelentingly day and night, but time mattered little during her isolation. She couldn't sleep, and her healing powers hindered her from numbing to the pain of each whip. Cate once again prayed for death to come for her, but of course, it never did. She felt utterly broken and powerless and knew without a doubt that there was no fight left in her at all.

Her feelings for Devin had completely diminished over the time since she'd been taken away from him, and she was exceptionally aware of how alone she felt. Tears splashed down her cheeks, and would come and go as the torment continued, but would soon dry up again, as she knew all too well.

"Please, stop this!" she cried out over and over, begging for her master's mercy again. The sudden slash of her ropes then sent Cate falling into a broken heap on the floor, and she watched as the binds magically disappeared moments later. She curled into a ball and looked around the dark pit but didn't see Satan anywhere. Just as she began to wonder why the torture had stopped, she was then teleported away.

Cate closed her eyes as she was pulled between time and space involuntarily. She hoped she'd look up and find herself at home when she arrived wherever her master was sending her, but unfortunately, he didn't intend to release her from her torment quite yet. She instead found herself in an enclosed cell, surrounded by torture implements and weapons, just like the one Dylan had been in such a long time before.

"Let's really put your powers to the test, Prrrrincessss," said an ugly warlock behind her, his tongue rolling the sound of her title in disgust. Cate's instincts kicked in, and she leapt to her feet and tried to run away, pulling on the cage's door handle, but there was nowhere for her to run. She was trapped. The sniggering behind her made her turn, and the disgusting man delighted in informing Cate there was no hope for escape.

"Do your worst," she told him, and knew her fight was over. She was finally defeated. "I'm pretty much dead inside anyway," she added, and he shoved her into the metal frame. Without another word, the warlock then grabbed her right hand, proceeding to break each finger with a loud crack.

After many more days of torture at the hands of the vile man, Cate knew there was no use fighting Satan's feeling towards her anymore. Free will meant nothing if she had to endure countless beatings and torture to keep hold of it. She hoped he could hear her words, or even just her thoughts, and she whimpered as loud as she could between the beatings her hideous tormentor administered.

"Yes. It's a yes," she cried out with the last of her strength, and Cate then lost consciousness. She gave up, and it was the last thought she had before everything went black.

CHAPTER NINE

When she finally awoke, Cate was lying naked in a deep bath somewhere in the depths of the dark castle. She'd been immersed in some sort of thick, gooey, black liquid that had no smell, but felt strangely nice against her sore skin. She could feel it healing her body, drawing out the death that'd tried to creep in during her torturous imprisonment. Her evil master sat by the side of the bath, watching her come around with interest and a sly smile.

"You fought hard, my love," he said, seeming pleased with her in a way she couldn't even begin to understand. Cate looked away. She couldn't bear to look at him, much less share in his pleasure following her submission. "Tell me again," he demanded, and grabbed her chin, turning her back round to face him. Satan drew her attention without a care for her pain, and her empty gaze met his. Cate then swallowed hard, struggling to fight the tears she felt hovering only barely beneath the surface of her stubborn expression.

"Yes," she said quietly, looking him in the eye. She was fighting back the sobs that threatened to expose her broken soul and hated him regardless of having given into his desire for her. He smiled and touched her cheek lightly; seemingly uncaring that she was so damaged thanks to his aggressive methods of persuasion.

"Good. You need to stay here for a while to heal first, but then we'll be together," he told her with a smile, and then disappeared without another word. The realisation then dawned on her what she'd agreed to give him, and tears flowed uncontrollably within seconds.

Alma and a couple of young witches tended to her, keeping her under their watchful gazes, but none of them seemed able to soothe her broken soul. They encouraged Cate to rest, but she had no other choice—her body was too much of a mess to fight the sleep. Her mind was even worse. The memories of her torture haunted her dreams, but she was too exhausted and couldn't pull herself out of them. Her master would often appear in her mind, but as a Halloween style mask—silly and bright red with horns and a pitchfork. But he would then grow larger and turn darker before sucking her in and devouring her. Other times, the image would take the form of the last warlock and deliver her beatings or break her bones. When Cate would finally wake up, she'd be dripping with sweat and sob uncontrollably, before falling back into an exhausted sleep again.

When she was finally healed, Cate was taken to Satan's private chambers. The witches who'd cared for her teleported in alongside the Dark Princess, and not even one dared say a word to either encourage her to remain strong or give her their sympathy. She guessed they'd been warned against it and knew their master would know the moment any of them were disloyal to their omnipotent ruler. Ever since she'd said yes, Cate felt Satan's presence inside her even stronger than before, although she hadn't seen him since the black goo bath. Her thoughts were not her own, and she knew she couldn't hide anything from him. He crept in everywhere, haunting her day and night, and Cate thought she might go crazy.

She barely even registered the soft hands that guided and moved her body. The witches undressed her and then led Cate over to the gigantic bed, urging her to lay in wait for her master. She looked up at Alma before she left, and her face was warm, but tense. Even Satan's high priestess seemed too scared to say a word, and she and the other two witches exited silently before locking the doors behind them.

Cate lay still on the bed, shivering despite the heat. She closed her eyes, clearing her mind as much as she could. She knew she had to give herself to him, that there was no going back now, but she was truly terrified. It was one thing being the Devil's progeny with a future and fate decided for her by her almighty master, but it was another thing becoming his lover and the sole focus of his dark attention. His affection could be intense and overwhelming, and the thought of having more than just the usual fleeting fondness scared the hell out of her.

She felt his presence before she saw or heard Satan come into the room a few minutes later, and opened her eyes, taking in her dark master as he loomed over her. He undressed slowly, removing his black shirt and jeans, while taking his time to look her up and down before he climbed his way towards her on the bed. His body was fantastic, just the right amount of strong, toned muscles she might enjoy looking at if these were different circumstances, and his deep blue eyes bore into hers with such intensity she quickly lost herself in them. His cock was huge and hard as steel, ready for her, and he finally allowed the *expression* link to open between them. In that moment, he gave her a rush of emotion, lust, power, and finally—love. It overwhelmed her, but it was also exactly what she needed to go on.

Satan climbed on top of Cate and slid between her trembling thighs. The tip of his length rested lightly on her navel as he kissed her, and her only conscious thought was how it was a good thing she didn't need to breathe.

The kisses he planted on her lips were so intense and deep he would've cut off her air supply within minutes.

She gave in to him completely and slid her arms around his back to grip his shoulders tightly, allowing him to kiss her deeper and more intensely with his authoritative tongue. He relished in her, flicking his tongue expertly between her lips, down onto her neck, and then to her breasts. Cate tried to fight the pleasure welling within her at his touch, but her body was defying her, and she writhed beneath him as he took her nipples between his teeth one at a time and bit down gently, sending painful pleasure signals throughout her core.

His hands then opened Cate's thighs wider and lifted her hips to meet his eager mouth. Satan groaned as he tasted her, delving two fingers inside her open cleft. She gushed as he rubbed her g-spot while sucking her throbbing nerve-endings expertly, and she came for him within minutes as he relentlessly pursued her.

Cate then called out incoherently as he climbed up and thrust his stiff hard-on inside her, and a second orgasm rippled through her almost instantly when he began thrusting deeper inside. As the last climax faded, she couldn't help the small sob that escaped her lips, but he ignored it. Her infernal ruler reached down and grabbed his prize, pulling Cate up onto his lap so he could kiss her while moving her up and down fast and hard onto his greedy length.

"See, you should've just said yes a long time ago, Hecate," he said while thrusting up inside her. "Can you feel how right this is? Can you see now how perfect I am for this body?" he asked as he ran his fingers down her spine.

She knew he was right, but still couldn't fight the sense that it was still so wrong. Her body welcomed him and wanted him inside, yet her mind still resisted. It didn't matter what he said. She wasn't ready to let down her walls and let him in quite yet. Satan eyed her ominously, and could tell she was still torn, but still pushed her on to orgasm after orgasm until he was finally ready for his own climax. He grabbed Cate tight and pulled her close, staring into her bright green eyes, and into her soul. "I hope you're ready for this," he whispered, and then the walls of the room started to shake violently. The bed beneath them vibrated and rose up from the floor a few inches, and Cate's body shuddered with her final release as he plunged deep inside her and came. He then lifted her face and kissed her, staying firmly rooted inside her while the walls seemed as though they might collapse around them thanks to the strange shockwave of power that'd emanated from him in that final crescendo of pleasure.

The moment over, they rested together in peaceful silence for a while, neither one asleep, but there were no words to express what'd just happened between them. The floodgates were well and truly open though, and she felt his *expression* coming thick and fast through their strange but still so strong connection. In her head, Cate was still unclear about what she wanted. As much as their lovemaking had been wonderful, she was still angry and incredibly frightened. She agreed now that they *could* be together the way he wanted but didn't know where to begin to try and talk to him about how she truly felt. She was still so defeated from the torture, and humiliated by his conquest, so she stayed quiet while her mind ran riot processing all the strange ups and downs she was trying desperately to get her head around.

It felt strange. Her adoration for him was still ever present, but now it seemed to be growing, changing. He'd come to her one night so long ago and told her he was family, and yet somehow all of that had changed. The man she'd readily accepted as a master had changed, and what he'd wanted from her had altered dramatically. The almighty being laid next to her had decided he wanted something other than an heir, and he'd evidently been willing to do whatever it took to make Cate change her mind.

She wanted to hate him but couldn't. Affection for Satan as a lover crept into her once so steadfast resolve, and she knew he'd almost succeeded in seducing her mind as well as her body. She'd resisted him for so long and had done everything she could to push him away. However, he'd still wanted her, and had made love to her so powerfully and incredibly once he'd claimed his prize. She knew she might never be the same again. It didn't make her happy to realise no man might ever compare to the ancient being who now shared her bed, but for some reason, she wasn't saddened by it either.

Taking in his chambers, she saw the mess and debris that littered the vast space following their intense lovemaking session. A snap of his fingers would sort that out no problem, she had no doubt about it, and Cate wished she could be repaired just as easily.

Satan watched her, listening in on her thoughts as she worked things out in her head. This time around, he decided to stay silent while she figured everything out, even though her unease angered him. He'd hoped she'd come around by now but knew Cate would get there in her own time; he would just have to force himself to be patient. The Prince of Darkness decided to let his actions speak louder than his words, and he pulled Cate close so that he could kiss and make love to her again. She obliged him, and it was a delight to read her thoughts and discover how much she was enjoying his touch, regardless of how much he'd had to break her to make her his finally so willing concubine.

***

The pair rested together for a while, and Satan was the one to eventually break the silence. He had been holding Cate in his tight embrace under the satin sheets of his huge bed for a long while, and he'd let his *expression* flow to her the entire time. Keeping her close while she wordlessly arranged her scattered thoughts was a necessary step in helping Cate recover, and he, too, had been considering how different everything would be from then on.

"I've been thinking. We need to figure out what you're going to scream when I make you come, Cate," he said, releasing her before leaning up onto one elbow with a bold grin. Cate smiled and nodded.

"What do you have in mind, master?" she asked and smiled. After the hours spent in his tactile care, she now felt stronger and more comfortable in his arms than she thought she would've been. Cate guessed she'd forgotten how good it felt to be held so preciously and soaked up every ounce of strength and emotion he seemed to want to share with her.

"Master's far too prim and proper, darling," he replied playfully. "After what we just did, there is absolutely no need for formalities anymore, and you most certainly won't ever be regarded as my heir ever again," he added and then laughed, thinking on it for a moment. "I know…you, and only you, can call me Lucifer," he told her, and Cate smiled.

"Wow, really? No one has called you that in centuries," she asked, remembering the history lessons the witches had given her when she first came to Hell with him. He had reportedly been so angry when the angels had cast him out of Heaven that when Hell started filling up and his minions would call him by the name, the Council had chosen for him, Satan didn't like it. He wanted to be above everyone—respected and feared. It was how he became more powerful. As time passed by, and with every soul that was sent his way, he grew stronger, but even more so if they remained terrified of him. Eventually, no one dared say his real name in Hell, and even on Earth, for fear of his wrath. All his demons, witches, and warlocks addressed him formally on pain of torturous death. He had readily adopted the names of Satan or the Devil to heighten his prowess and control over the realm and continued to strike fear into the hearts of any who dared speak of him with his ancient title.

"Well then, Lucifer it is," Cate replied with a smile. "I suppose that's okay with me," she added playfully, but she was overjoyed. It made her feel special to know she was the only one allowed to address him so informally, and had to admit, it was a worthy gift for her compliance. She liked it and enjoyed knowing she'd earned the right to his heightened favour after everything they'd been through together.

***

The new couple hid themselves away for months, making love and mending the connection Lucifer had destroyed to break her will, as well as simply enjoying their new love affair. Cate came to realise that he cared for her so much that her resistance had hurt him deeply. He opened up tremendously during their time in isolation together, and she wished he'd just been honest with her all along.

"I've never opened up to anyone before, Cate," he explained. "And when I finally did, you told me no. You told me it didn't feel right. That you thought it was wrong, when everything inside me was screaming that we were meant to be. I kinda went crazy, and I knew that if I couldn't have you, I didn't want anyone to," he told her one night as they lay in a hot bath together. Lucifer was behind her in the deep suds, and Cate turned her head back to meet his gaze, utterly shocked by his admission. "I wanted you so badly, and nearly let myself force you. I just wanted to make you see how wrong you were about us. But, I knew you'd have to come around in your own time, otherwise we could never be together in the way I truly wanted. Even after you nearly killed yourself trying to defy me, I could still sense your hesitation, but I decided to be patient and let you figure it out in your own way."

Cate smiled but couldn't help the sadness from creeping in when she thought about the terrifying way he'd swayed her resolve.

"And although I did come around eventually, I still can't believe you did all those things to me," she told him honestly, and her face fell. It still hurt, and she couldn't hide it, but a part of him didn't want her to conceal her emotions. They were his burden to bear, too, and she knew he would— forever. Despite Lucifer having gotten his own way in the end, it'd pained him having had to hurt his true love so severely to get what he wanted from her.

"I'll spend eternity making up for it, my love," he promised, kissing her softly. "Without the drastic measures, though, I might have never gotten you to see sense. I hope one day you'll understand that."

Cate had to admit he was right. Given the chance, she would've pushed him away and continued saying no forever, even if it'd meant losing Devin, and probably everything she'd built over the years with their master. Although it pained her to admit he had been right to push her. She would never tell him that, though. Saying yes had already taken everything from her, and an added admission of defeat would be one too many burdens for her to bear.

CHAPTER TEN

Eventually, the time came that the witches and demons around them needed Lucifer to tend to his business. They both knew that things would be a bit strange for everyone at first, especially Devin, and Cate wasn't looking forward to seeing him again after all their time apart. Lucifer seemed understanding, but insisted she remain strong, and went off to convene the Dark High Council. She was alone for the first time since she'd said yes to him and wasn't sure what to do with herself.

She teleported back to her bedroom and checked that her door was unlocked, just in case, before getting showered and dressed. Cate then stood looking at her naked form in the bedroom mirror for a few minutes. She took in her perfectly healed body but could somehow sense every scar and scorch mark as though it were still there. Despite her awful memories, she chose to think of them as some kind of invisible shield—armour to protect herself from ever being hurt or broken like that again. Lucifer would lead and she would follow without question from then on. There was no doubting that, but she'd never let her guard down again. Cate was determined never to see the inside of those terrible pits or torture chambers if she could help it, but she would never forget, or get complacent with him ever again.

She also had to mentally prepare herself to face his council, and part of her knew she was stalling. Cate dressed all in black, her preferred choice of colour nowadays, and pulled a black metal ring from her jewellery case. It had a bright green stone in the centre, and it matched the hue of her eyes exactly. The girl who'd been given the ring by her master was a very different person to the woman who stood reflected back at her in the mirror. Nothing would ever be the same, regardless of whether she wanted it to be or not, and Cate finally accepted her fate. There really was no going back. No matter what, Lucifer was her future, not Devin.

Cate thought about the man she'd once loved with every fibre of her being. It'd been over three years since Lucifer had taken her away from him at the penthouse, and she didn't know if he'd been told what was going on, or if he would even care anymore. Lucifer's new heiress, Serena, wouldn't come of age for another fifteen years, and Cate hated he didn't have a new lover to take his mind off her betrayal. Devin could've spent every day pining for her for all she knew. She had a lot of making up to do, Cate was sure.

She walked out the large doors and down the corridor, headed to the main meeting room of the castle. Lucifer's council room was a huge suite where all her master's top minions and advisors normally met to discuss important issues with him in privacy. Cate had never been there unannounced before and had certainly never been present when their ruler had convened his Dark High Council. Those meetings were usually strictly off-limits to anyone outside the council, but now the important issue they were due to discuss was her, and Lucifer had insisted she attend. An ancient demon named Lilith was waiting at the doors that led to the main council room, and she intercepted her as she reached the chamber. Lilith's face was stern and as unfeeling as ever, but she reached for Cate's hand before they entered in what she would assume was a gentle way, if it were anyone else. The powerful demon drew her gaze and smiled uncharacteristically.

"Are you okay?" she asked, taking Cate aback with her moment of apparent care. They'd never been close, and Cate didn't trust her. Lilith was aggressively loyal to Lucifer, even against her, and she loved him more than any other being under his rule. The ancient demon did his bidding without question and always strived to gratify her dark master in whatever way he asked of her. Lilith had earned his respect throughout the years, and her coveted place as second in command of his underworld army. Nothing she said or did was about anyone but her master, or herself.

"Yes, I'm fine, thank you, Lilith," Cate replied, smiling over at the dark haired demon. She was a short and slim framed woman, but Cate knew that beneath the human looking exterior, she was both incredibly strong and viciously cunning. Lilith was the leader of a council that convened to test and trial potential new demons as they tried to move up the levels that made up the hierarchy of demons below the royal family. She'd seen Lilith in action as she tested the souls who wanted to become new demons. Torturing them into submission or delivering dark punishments seemed like a hobby of hers, and there were many who tried and failed beneath her tutelage. Without batting an eye, Cate had watched her issue terrible orders for the wannabe demons to carry out for them to even be considered for the honour. Only the exceptional evil would eventually carry on to complete their initiations and challenges under her watchful eye.

"Good," Lilith replied, looking back at her with a fake smile. "Because if you're happy, then he's happy, and you know how important that is to all of us." She reached out for the door handle. "I suggest you don't defy him again," she added, and opened the large door, ushering the seething Dark Princess inside.

The council members all looked up as the pair of them entered, and

Lucifer ushered for Cate to sit by his left side at the huge table. Lilith went to his other side and bowed graciously to her master as she took her seat.

"Some of you know already, and some of you do not. I've only discussed this with those absolutely necessary before tonight," Lucifer addressed them all, looking up and down the long table as he spoke. "Hecate is no longer going to live with Devin on Earth. He is now betrothed to Serena and is waiting patiently for her to come of age while he continues to run Black Rose Industries under my command. When such time comes, he will go to her, just like Cate did with him, and become her teacher and lover."

He paused for a moment to ensure he had their undivided attention. "Cate is now my *inamorata*, my lover," he added, looking over at her with a satisfied smile. Lucifer then slid his hand over her thigh, sending wonderful tingles throughout her entire body, and she felt her cheeks burn. "From thus forth, she is no longer to be addressed as or regarded as my heiress. Anyone that does not treat her as my future Queen will be dealt with accordingly."

The room was so silent even Cate could hear the cogs turning behind the primeval demons' intense stares, but Lucifer seemed oblivious to their shocked expressions. "Those who are caught not following this order will be punished, however I see fit. Perhaps, for example, I might dump said traitor in one of my many dark pits for all eternity with their eyes gouged from their sockets and their disrespectful tongues liberated from their mouths." He took a deep breath, relishing in the vivid imagery of the punishment. "Do I make myself perfectly clear?" Lucifer asked sternly, the rhetorical question more of an order to his small crowd of minions.

He then looked around the table to all the highest and most regarded members of his chain of command, and they each nodded in agreement. He took the time to look each and every one of them in the eye, reading their thoughts as they stared over at Cate or down at their hands, and none but Lilith dared to fully meet his gaze. She smiled at her Dark Prince and silently agreed to follow his plans without question, much to his pleasure, as usual. "Even you, Asmodeus?" Lucifer then asked a few moments later. He peered down the table at a demon sat third on his right with his face half covered by a dark cloak. "Your thoughts give you away, old friend".

"No, sire, not at all. I, I, I…" Asmodeus stuttered while trying desperately to be heard by his master, and Lucifer was glad to know he'd taken his threat seriously. "I just pondered that perhaps it is not the right match for the pair of you to have a proper marriage, and by that I mean having any children together, nothing at all to question the relationship itself. Your majesty's, please forgive my foolishness." The demon bowed his head and hoped that Lucifer was happy with his explanation. He stared at Asmodeus darkly for a moment before leaving the demon alone and addressing the group once more.

"And what about the angels in Heaven who are still as I once was?"

Lucifer asked the question rhetorically again. "The many spirits who then went on to give birth to thousands more celestial beings. And let's not forget Adam and Eve, who then parented the entire goddamn human race," he added, and Cate could sense that Lucifer was getting angry, but he regained his composure again quickly. "Cate and I are going to be married. After that, we have all eternity to try and make a family together," he informed them, and it was clear that was the end of the matter. Lucifer pulled her closer is if to prove his words were true, but all she could think of was what he'd said about them being married. While terrifying, it was also a wondrous thought to become a Queen at last. Not to inherit the throne if and when he decided, but to be crowned and beheld as ruler of Hell by his side. That she certainly could do.

Cate was gladly excused from the council meeting soon after Lucifer's speech, and she went for a walk around the castle to clear her head. She was already so much clearer on everything that he now wanted from her and had slowly come around to the idea of willingly giving him all that he desired. She supposed the whole marriage thing wasn't such a big deal. They'd already made the ultimate promise to love each other faithfully and were committed to being together forever after all. Becoming his eternal bride would put Cate at ease even further. She'd know then for sure that he would not simply change his mind again like he'd done with hers and Devin's relationship. A proper union and the higher status that came with his hand would hopefully give her more power, control and a say in her own life in the long run as well, and she welcomed the upcoming change in Hell's leadership.

Cate wanted more than anything to be loved, respected, and happy. She also wanted to be trusted to make her own decisions and not to have to follow Lucifer's orders all the time but have her own valid opinions as well. Becoming Queen of Hell was right. Cate could feel it. She was also excited about the prospect of children. It'd never occurred to her before that they could ever try and have a family together.

That evening, as Cate undressed for bed, Lucifer teleported directly into her bedroom, and immediately went down on one knee before her.

"Darling. I know I let my intentions slip prematurely earlier, but I meant every word," he said as he took her hand and pulled a huge, black diamond encrusted ring from his pocket. "Will you be my wife?" Lucifer then asked, and Cate smiled, allowing him to slide the ring onto her finger.

"Yes," was all she could manage to respond, but it was the only word he needed to hear.

***

Up on Earth, Devin worked at his desk late into the evening, again. He'd had nothing else to occupy him other than Black Rose Industries during the last few years while he was waiting for Serena to come of age, but the monotony of the world bored him. He'd thrown himself into running the company as efficiently and successfully as possible since Cate had gone back home with their master and had done it well.

He thought back to that night. The witch, Sara, had taken him aside and informed him of Satan's new plans for his lover. She didn't even bother to sugar-coat the fact that Devin and Cate were no longer destined to be together.

"Cate has gone, and you must not try to find her. You're to wait here for Serena to grow older, and then you will go to her. You'll be for her what Cate was once for you—a friend, lover, and bridge between the world she knows now and the dark world she must embrace when the time comes," Sara had told him hastily. "Cate is a friend to you now, and nothing more. There will be more changes soon, but they are your master's orders to command, not mine. In the meantime, you are forbidden from returning to Hell until he is ready to see you, Devin. I've been ordered to inform you to carry on your life here until further notice. Jonah will stay, and he'll take you to New York for Serena when the time is right."

She had then teleported away without a word of sympathy or understanding for the horrendous loss he'd just suffered, and Devin hadn't seen the witch since. It'd felt as though someone had ripped out his heart that night, and he'd felt the anger pour out of him as he wept openly for his lost love. They'd been so perfect together, so in sync, and he couldn't imagine his life without her by his side. Jonah had sensed his rage at their ruler's betrayal and had tried to calm his friend in the fear of him being punished by Satan for speaking ill of him.

"Our whole bloody union was *his* plan all along, and now suddenly he's just changed his mind?" Devin had bellowed in his fury, feeling both enraged and offended.

"He's not just your leader, don't ever forget that. He's your master and King first, Devin," Jonah had told him following his outburst. "He can, and will, do as he choose, and you'd do well never to forget that."

Now, it was three years later, and Devin no longer felt the strong love-bond he'd once had with Cate. He could sense her power within him like an awareness rather than a formidable desire. It'd become nothing more than a small flame somewhere deep within him that linked them, but no deeper love, and no sexual need—not anymore.

He was completely indifferent to the women around him, both demonic and human again as well. Having been ordered to wait for Serena had bought about that familiar abstinence he'd had instilled in him before meeting Cate all those years ago, and he both understood and resented it. Devin felt as though he'd been forgotten about up on Earth. His master didn't visit anymore, and there'd been no further orders from him for far too many years.

Eventually, and out of the blue, he felt the familiar beacon as it called to him, and he was summoned back to Hell. He travelled there immediately and went straight into the castle, where he knelt before his master as he sat on his black throne. Devin immediately saw the age difference in him to the last time he had seen him up in the penthouse. He had to be twenty years younger looking than the familiar guise he'd always worn before, and it was a surprise to see him with a different look.

"Welcome back," Satan said, with an edge of warmth to his tone that began to ease Devin's anger towards him in an instant. He then beckoned for him to come forward, hugging him tightly when he did so.

"Thank you, master. It's good to be home. How might I serve you?" Devin replied, being careful to remain respectful, but still he hoped he might hear some news of his old flame.

"You need do nothing but listen, for I have some incredibly happy news," Satan told him, and smiled when Cate came in and joined the two of them. Devin's immediate reaction was to question the coldness behind her eyes, as if she were only half the soul she'd once been. There was a strange detachment there he couldn't understand, and when she smiled, those beautiful green eyes no longer lit up like they once had. "Cate is no longer my progeny, she's going to be my bride," Satan told him, and Devin couldn't hide the gasp that escaped him as his mouth dropped open in shock.

"And I suppose I was the last to know because it took you such a long time to win her round?" he mumbled, and Cate shrunk back at his dismissive tone. "Or perhaps she wanted this all along?" Devin added and shook his head at Cate in distaste. Hatred trickled out of every pore, and she was dumfounded by his assumption that she'd somehow instigated this entire plan to elevate herself into a position of power rather than share it with him. "Maybe next time you break my heart, you'll be a little gentler, Hecate. Perhaps for pity's sake, you'll go as far to pretend for a moment that you actually care about anyone other than yourself."

She guessed he wanted to think the worst of her and decided to let him. It was much safer for Devin if he hated her rather than blame Lucifer for how things had changed so drastically between them. Despite his awful words, she didn't want him to end up with the same punishment she'd endured and knew her fiancé was capable of far worse if he were provoked enough.

"Perhaps…" she mumbled in reply, before walking away so he couldn't see the tears falling from her sad eyes.

CHAPTER ELEVEN

The world around them shuddered and shook violently as Lucifer climaxed inside his lover, and she wondered if the castle might fall around them if they weren't careful. Cate trembled as the last of her many orgasms coursed through her body, sending wonderful messages throughout her entire core. By the time everything came to a halt, she was limp and exhausted in Lucifer's arms, yet exultant and relaxed. He lay her down and covered her with the black satin sheet, then clicked his fingers—repairing the damaged bed and surrounding furniture immediately. Cate lay back and wondered to herself if the whole of Hell shook when he came. If so, the beings around them surely knew when they were making love. Even if it were only the castle that knew, she'd still find it embarrassing. Lucifer laughed as he lay down beside her, reading Cate's thoughts again.

"No, I'm pretty sure it's just whatever room we're in at the time, darling," he answered her. "It only happens strongly down here, but on Earth it's more like a deep vibration. A bit like a blast of power that comes from me and anything in the immediate vicinity gets a beating, or an orgasm in your case," he added with a wink.

She smiled but nodded. "Oh yes."

He then simply held her closer and savoured the feeling of having the woman he loved so much wrapped tightly in his arms, and Cate soon drifted off to sleep in his warm embrace.

***

Lucifer left her alone after watching her sleep for a few minutes, which was his normal routine. He never needed sleep, so would often just wait for her to drift off before getting dressed and going off to his chambers, or to convene his council and use the time to see to any issues that might require his attention. He was always needed. Eternally busy, but he couldn't deny his top priority these days was to make plenty of time to be with his future Queen.

He thought back to when she was just a baby. The existence of a child bearing his flame had altered history, and he'd known right away that she was special to him. It was inevitable that Cate would change his entire existence dramatically. It was as though from the moment she was born he'd known things would never be the same for him again but had accepted it regardless. At first, he'd thought it was just an extra special bond he shared with her as his first successful heir. After such a long time trying, she was his most coveted prize, but in time Lucifer's growing feelings had taken his affection in a wholly different direction.

That night in the church was the first time he'd been with Cate in the flesh her entire life, which had been a necessity thanks to the white witches' involvement. To this day, he still couldn't understand how they'd discovered her and gotten so close and knew he might never find out. His witches had played their parts along the way, though. They'd kept her safe and made sure her mother had enough money and security to keep a roof over their heads and food in Cate's belly. He'd even ensured that Ella hadn't ever married nor had any serious relationships after giving birth to her unholy child. It wasn't because he'd wanted her for himself. In fact, he felt nothing at all for her. Like all the others, Ella had been a means to an end, an incubator and carer for the precious cargo he'd hoped to create with each full moon.

He'd kept possible stepfathers away simply so that Cate wouldn't be influenced or affected by having a male father figure in her life. Lucifer had wanted her weak and clueless when it came to men. Pliable to his every desire, and the epitome of the phrase, 'having Daddy issues.' Even back then, jealousy had stirred in him at the thought of another man loving her as his own. It was a wonder to him how he'd been so oblivious to his attraction to her for so long.

Now, though, Lucifer faced a different future than the one he'd planned for Cate all those years before. He'd focussed his efforts in nurturing her mentally and ensuring she learned everything there was to know about him and her new home as soon as she'd come with him to Hell. Lucifer had even been forgiving that Cate had so many questions and hesitations rolling around in her mind when the time came for her to go and watch over Devin.

She'd continually forgotten back then that he knew everything, but part of him liked it how she wasn't always on her guard with her thoughts and feelings in his presence. Cate regularly let her mind wander, and Lucifer had enjoyed watching as her thoughts and memories played out in her mind. He'd found himself enthralled by the flow of her feelings, ups and downs through her unmasked responses to the new, strange world around her. Lucifer had especially enjoyed the way Cate had felt about him back when she'd first come of age. She had been so excited to discover what she truly was, and so eager to please her new master that she was acquiescent to his every request. The perfect underling to mentor and groom.

Since the successful creation of a second heir, the plan had always been to bring Devin home once he came of age. His identity would be revealed just as he'd done with Cate—by summoning the teen to a Satanic church and informing him of his true heritage, before asking him to come home with him. He'd made the decision to send Cate to Earth early to meet Devin simply because he couldn't stop himself desiring her. It'd always been his plan that they'd be together. They were to become a superior couple that Lucifer believed would deliver his realm many more powerful heirs over the years. Their offspring would grow and become an eternal family, and by mixing his power with humans, he'd hoped his incredible bloodline might then finally be allowed to rule up on Earth, as well as in Hell. He'd imagined them all going back and forth and taking over, piece by piece. Lucifer had even envisioned a world in which the saints were cast out into the cold and their churches burned to the ground, while the Satanic churches rose from their ashes. Any oppressors would then be punished and submitted to an eternity of torture at the hands of his demonic minions. It was a dark and ominous future that he'd wanted so very badly, bad enough to push away his personal desires to try and procure it.

And so, for his own peace of mind and the preservation of his dreams for the future, he'd sent her away. Lucifer had known Cate wasn't capable of handling his affections, so he had pushed her. He was sure he would've taken her for himself back then, and for that, she was not ready. That still so timid young woman and her fragile mind would've never been able to handle him. Lucifer couldn't be sure Cate could handle it all now, but there was no going back. He'd already waited as long as he could bear and couldn't change things even if he wanted to.

His plan had worked for a while, though. With her gone, Lucifer finally had time to focus fully on his realm, where he felt her presence deep within him, as normal, but didn't hear her thoughts or feel the intensity of her prowess like he did when she was in Hell with him. It'd calmed him having her at arm's length.

It all changed again when Cate and Devin made love that first time, though. Lucifer had felt it, almost as if he were there—as if he were the one experiencing her first time through his son's eyes. He was somehow in Devin's thoughts, watching through his mind's eye. Lucifer had been working incessantly and had tried to rest his frenzied mind that night but had found himself dreaming. It'd seemed so real. He was there, watching Cate make love to him, and he felt every thrust as though he were the one doing it to her.

When Lucifer had come back to himself, his right-hand demon, Lilith had come to him worried. She'd told him that he'd been missing for several hours and none of them could sense or find him in Hell or on Earth. He knew then that he must've gone into Devin's body for real, and not as a dream. It wasn't via possession, but more like a morphing of their consciousness. Lucifer didn't believe Devin even realised it'd happened and had decided to keep it to himself at first. He later explained the strange phenomenon to his high priestess, Alma, who urged him never to do it again. She was worried he could get stuck in someone else's consciousness next time if he didn't know how to control the power properly. She'd also promised to find out as much as she could about the combining of two beings' minds, though, appeasing Lucifer's curiosity on the matter for the time being.

After that night, he'd tried to occupy himself with either torturing the poor souls in his realm or concocting new means of endless pain and suffering with his demonic council. He shut his two progenies' out from his mind and left them at the edge of his thoughts. That was until the witches informed him that the full moon approached and Devin had come of age on Earth.

Once Lucifer opened his mind to them again, he became fully aware of their bond and adoration for one another. Devin was completely besotted with Cate, and she loved him with every fibre of her being too. His son was finally ready to come home, and despite him feeling a touch of jealousy for their bond, Lucifer decided it was time to go and retrieve the two lovers.

He went up to Earth right away, and the rush of emotion they sent his way were hard to ignore. When he'd got the signal from Jonah that Devin was at the church, Lucifer teleported towards the beacon and arrived there instantly, but didn't go right to them. He watched from the shadows as the pair sat down in the circle of warlocks. He was truly proud of Cate in that moment—she really was his ultimate treasure. He didn't know how she did it, but she drew his attention instantly, however Cate was not his intended focus that night.

Lucifer had instead walked right over and introduced himself to Devin. He read his thoughts before ushering him over to a dark corner so that they could talk and knew the boy was nervous. His mind was racing, but it was also open and ready to accept his new fate. They spoke for a few minutes, and Lucifer outlined his real heritage while giving him the same speech as he'd given Cate on her same night of revelations.

"Now, any questions?" Satan had then asked with a grin. Devin had been utterly dumbfounded. His mind had raced, and his thoughts were all over the place, but he'd seemed to handle it well, and had shaken his head. "Good. So, how do you feel about coming home with us to Hell?" he'd then asked him, and Devin had nodded, much to Lucifer's delight.

"Yes," he'd added, seeming unable to say much more.

"That's all I need." Lucifer had then led Devin back over to the group. He could tell Cate was worried about how things had gone, and she even wondered if Devin might reject her now. What a fool she was to believe anyone who loved her could ever forget her so easily.

Lucifer hadn't been able to stop himself from gathering her up in his arms, and he told her how proud he was. He knew she needed him to reassure her that Devin was okay, but he'd also felt envious. However, then, there was something else, something unexpected in their embrace. Lucifer had sensed how Cate was somehow enjoying his closeness a little more than she should've been, as well. He'd been able to hear her heart pounding harder while in his tight grip, and her body responded to him in a way he hadn't expected.

He had been overcome with his emotion for her in that moment and knew then that he wanted her to feel his love. For the first time in far too long, Lucifer had allowed his *expression* to open for her. He'd let her into that tiny part of himself that felt passion and affection, and she'd soaked it up. Her thoughts had become dizzy with his offering, but Cate had relished his warmth, and lapped it up gratefully.

Lucifer had needed to force himself to release her, except by her hand. He'd then taken Devin's in his other hand and, after a quick explanation about the atmosphere down in Hell, they'd finally left for home.

As time had then gone on, Lucifer had continued to push his desire for Cate aside. Allowing the couple time to enjoy their new-found vigour and accentuate their power had been a necessary torment. He'd instructed the witches to teach them while he busied himself elsewhere again. No number of women satisfied him, though. No number of deviant, sadistic debaucheries with his usual lovers had made even a dent in his insatiable need or his unquenchable thirst for the forbidden fruit. He'd craved Cate. Lucifer had known it to his core but had endeavoured to push those feelings away for as long as it took to hopefully quash them. She hadn't helped him though, especially when brazenly showing off her naked, just-fucked body without a care when he'd visited them to take her back to the white witch's cell.

He was more to blame than she and knew full well that they were both still naked when he'd made his entrance, but Lucifer hadn't stopped himself. Curiosity had gotten the better of him. Cate had been so beautiful. Still rosy-cheeked and glistening with sweat from their passionate lovemaking session, the view had done nothing but feed his strange addiction to the tormenting pleasure of her. The cravings that the sight of her naked body had stirred in Lucifer had overcome him, and he knew then and there that they could no longer be overlooked. Following that night, he'd wrestled with himself and his desires, and had soon decided to send them both back to Earth.

Once they'd gone, he hadn't cared for the quiet. Lucifer had summoned witch after witch, demon after demon, and ordered them to work harder and longer to help fill his time. It'd been no use though, and one Halloween when he went to Earth for three days during a full blood-moon, some good news had struck him dumb with inspiration. His suspicions had been right, and Lucifer received confirmation of a pregnancy with one of the human females he'd visited a few months before. Another female progeny of his was indeed growing inside the human woman and would be born just a few months later.

The idea that Devin could be with the younger heiress was entirely feasible. He and Cate still weren't married, and if he tore them apart in time, Satan could then have her all to himself. That seed of doubt had then grown incredibly, no matter how much he had tried to push it away. The orgy he'd then instigated the following evening was all for her—Cate. The women that came along were nothing more than a distraction and a ploy to tempt her gaze and attention away from Devin. All he'd needed was a second, and he'd know whether she felt that tiny seed of doubt, too. He'd hoped there was that small wonder of *what else?* And indeed, he'd gotten it. Leaving again had been hard on him, but the moon demanded it, and he was as ever its unwilling slave.

Lucifer had always hated not having the freedom to come and go on Earth as he pleased. For thousands of years, he couldn't go at all until his dark witches finally found the loophole with the lunar phases. For some divine reason, when the moon was full, he could go to Earth and roam freely until it started to wane again. Every year on All Hallow's Eve he also had from midnight to midnight should he wish to visit. When he'd tried to teleport up years before, Lucifer hadn't considered such things, and had evidently gone at the wrong time in the lunar phase. Within minutes, the fallen angel had started having violent headaches and begun losing his powers. He would then have nosebleeds and a consuming weakness of his usually intensely strong muscles before eventually passing out. Luckily, he'd always ensured that at least one of his demonic council members went with him. Their job was to see to it that Lucifer was brought straight back to Hell once those reactions started, or else he wasn't sure what might happen if he'd stayed. The longest he'd been able to stand it on Earth was a mere two hours per visit during those trials. He'd then given up for a long time, despite his desire to roam freely from Hell, and when the witches had worked the lunar loophole out for him, he'd welcomed the news. He'd tested the theory during the next full moon and had remained there for a full two days without any reaction at all. Lucifer had caused nothing short of chaos and mayhem during his first visits, with his demonic comrades Leviathan and Beelzebub at his side, as they corrupted and tainted the then sparsely populated world.

He thought how the times had changed, and how he'd changed. It was so strange to him to no longer be only thinking about only himself, but suddenly another. He'd always planned to care for his heirs like his family—

as his children—but knew the moment he'd laid eyes on Cate that they weren't connected in that way. Their shared power seemed more of a mutually binding correlation, and a joining that once done could never be undone.

He thought back to when he'd returned to Earth to check on Serena after her birth, and how everything was perfect. The business was running smoothly, the infant was happy and healthy, and he could sense Cate's seed of doubt about her relationship with Devin still rooted within her thoughts, despite their happiness. His plan to lure her away had worked better than he'd imagined, regardless of her refusing his advances.

Lucifer knew he'd acted coldly toward Cate in those first days back in Hell. He'd wanted her so badly he couldn't bear to punish her for denying him, and yet knew he'd have to break her will if he was going to make her see sense and change her mind. It was also the only way he knew how to handle the rejection. He'd not been able to bear Cate's thoughts and hesitations as they ran through his telepathic gift, or in those instances, his curse.

Lucifer had changed his appearance that day to try and help her cope with the changes he wanted her to make, and to distract her from what he was asking of her, but it hadn't worked. She'd stomped all over his heart that night without even realising it, and instead of combating her refusal by focussing on winning over her hesitant thoughts, he had chosen to shut them out and punish her instead. Lucifer had never dealt with not getting his own way very well. In a moment of rage, he'd thrown her into the fiery pit where she might contemplate her decision some more and left her there despite having hated every second of it.

Satan had then needed to double his efforts to remain busy while she was in there. Through their strong bond he could feel the flames burning into her as though it were his own body being tortured, and Cate's pleading thoughts she sent him while held captive in the flames had been agonising. He knew then that he loved her. He had committed his body and soul to her completely, despite knowing he would have to wait for her fidelity in return. Lucifer had also commanded for her to stop loving Devin. He'd focussed on it with all his might, and after a while he could feel her heart shutting off to him. Despite all the concepts humans had that love could not be messed with, he had managed it. Opening Cate's heart to Devin had been simple but closing it again had not been so easy. The torture had helped. The Prince of Darkness also knew that no matter how much he wanted her, he didn't want to order her to love him the way he had with Devin. He'd wanted it for real, forever.

Up on Earth, Devin had felt it too and stopped searching for her, stopped pining. Lucifer could sense that his son didn't understand why their master had kept Cate away so long or why he had banned him from coming to Hell, but he hadn't needed to know the details, and Lucifer knew he wouldn't approve of his methods to sway her resolve. He'd known nothing of what his ex-lover was going through down there at Lucifer's hands, and their master had intended to keep it that way.

When Cate had finally left the pit, Lucifer was sure she'd gotten the message, loud and clear. Her thoughts were open and honest, and she was afraid he would hurt her, but could also feel their connection growing. Lucifer had then made the mistake of letting her know the free will element of the deal, and straight away he'd known that she wouldn't give herself to him. Her thoughts gave her away, and he knew she'd exploit that pivotal rule to try and get more time to make her decision. His broken girl had been stronger than he'd given her credit for.

Although it'd pained him to allow her further suffering, he did what he'd had to so he could break her will even more and used a different approach. He'd known for sure, though, that once Cate had been broken and tortured enough, she would yield. Everybody cracked eventually.

It'd taken her longer than Lucifer had hoped, but eventually he got the *yes* from her he so desperately needed. He'd been strangely proud that she'd fought so hard and had sensed her submission before the words had even left Cate's lips. A snap of his fingers and he'd taken her away from that terrible dungeon, and despite his eagerness to claim her, Lucifer had then delivered her straight to the witches' dungeon. They'd then tended to her wounds and bathed her in that special concoction of herbs and potions that would heal her quickly, and she'd needed it.

Cate had no idea just how close she'd come to a pure death. She was half human after all, and although she was an immortal being, she could still technically die if her body was hurt badly enough. They were all susceptible to one form of death or another. She would've then ended up in purgatory for however long it took to process her soul and then, he presumed, come back to Hell. By that time, she would be just another worthless new arrival for them to torture, with no more powers or high standing than any other human essence. There would've been no place for Cate at his side if he'd allowed that to happen.

She'd been so defeated when Lucifer had come to her in the tub, a shell of her former self, and yet ever so beautiful. Even the night when they'd first made love, he could sense her fear and foreboding of him. By the time they were done, though, she'd been putty in his hands, and her heart had opened to him like he'd always hoped it would.

And so here they were now. She was finally his and would forever be. Lucifer would make damn sure of it.

CHAPTER TWELVE

"You are cordially invited to the wedding of His Infernal Majesty, Satan, and his bride, Hecate, on All Hallow's Eve. The ceremony will begin promptly at sunset," Devin read the invitation aloud to Serena, who grinned across at her lover as she listened. She clapped her hands excitedly while bouncing in her seat, and he had to warn himself against making fun of her daftness. While young, his new lover knew her mind, and Devin knew she would tell him off in a heartbeat if he let himself develop the bad habits of a humourless old man. Instead, he simply smiled back at her, and let her beauty fill his senses. Love had returned to him at last thanks to Serena's presence in his otherwise still lonely world, and Devin was glad to know that Cate and their sire were finally tying the knot. Moving on hadn't been easy, but as soon as he was with Serena, their connection had flourished, and he'd forgotten all about the sense of abandonment that'd once consumed him so entirely. They'd now been together for just a few months, but she'd already embraced their dark world with ease, just as he had. Devin knew it was because someone they'd loved and trusted had shown them both how, and he pitied Cate for having been the first of their kind. It was no wonder their master had fallen for her. After all, he'd been her one and only semblance of the family she'd craved back then, and it seemed their ties had sprung to life during that relationship without either of them being aware of it. That was how Devin always thought about it, anyway. Theirs seemed a love forged out of both right and wrong, and yet they'd made it work. The past decade had seen a new world for all of them, and a new ruler. Satan was another being entirely for having her, and all their dark dominion agreed she'd become a welcome addition beside him on the throne. It was about time they finally made it official.

Devin hadn't risked any part of Serena's transformation and had been with her every step of the way. He'd even offered to train and teach her all about her dark powers and abilities exclusively, and their master had agreed. The bright and bubbly young woman had taken everything in her stride and was the more relaxed member of their dark dynasty.

Cate seemed to love having Serena around to help ease the burden she obviously still felt when it came to having left Devin alone. He'd had hardly any explanation of what'd happened since she left, but they were friends again now, and the three of them had grown closer during the last few months since Serena had joined them in Hell. Devin had struggled with the betrayal and deceit at first but had come around soon enough and accepted Satan's decision to be with Cate. He'd also had to accept, in the end, that there wasn't really any other choice in the matter.

Many years had passed since then, and Devin had accepted his new fate and was now with his true love at last. He was truly happy with Serena and hadn't ever looked back since the day he'd finally been allowed to meet her. Devin was looking forward to celebrating Lucifer and Cate's big day. They'd become an enviable couple, and one that all of Hell revered, so he was glad he'd let her go rather than fight. His only regret was blaming her for his misery, but he'd had to hate someone, and even Cate seemed content to let his anger be directed at her rather than at their sire.

***

Cate had been bombarded with making wedding decisions and details for months, and part of her just wanted it to happen already so she could relax a little. The other part of her knew it had to be perfect, and so she gave it everything she had to ensure that every meticulous detail was planned out. Everything was black and red, of course. They had red roses and black dresses, but it was the fine detail that she obsessed over. Even if no one else noticed them, Cate sure would, and she knew that Lucifer appreciated them as well. They both needed it to be perfect—the event of the century.

When the day finally came around, Cate and the witches went up to Earth early to get ready, while Lucifer remained in Hell with his demonic groomsmen—Devin, Beelzebub, and Leviathan. The church was dressed beautifully in black decor and a dark red aisle for her to walk down, and it looked amazing. The finishing touches were already complete, and all that was left for Cate to do was to personally make sure their venue was secure, but she wasn't worried. Demons and warlocks guarded every entrance, while the witches strengthened the barriers restricting any light beings from crossing over the threshold, and she knew they wouldn't get close thanks to the immense dark power emanating from within their sacred ground.

"You ready?" Serena asked Cate as she applied her makeup, giving her soft features a delicate touch that emphasised her beautiful green eyes and red lips effortlessly.

"Absolutely," she replied, grinning back at her.

"You'll be the Dark Queen of Hell after today, Cate. Imagine the life you'll lead, and children you might have together—so wonderfully powerful," Serena added with a sigh. A dreamlike haze clouded her eyes, and Cate knew she must have been daydreaming about the future of her potential dark brood.

"I hope so," she said, thinking of the possibility. The lovers had already discussed Lucifer's desire to sire more children, and she had to hope it might work for them. She was nowhere near ready to try, however, and simply held that optimism dear to her heart with faith it might someday come true.

***

The sun began to set over the church, and the red light streamed in through the stained-glass windows as Cate walked down the aisle. She was dressed in her gorgeously flowing long black gown and felt like the most beautiful woman in the world. It had a stunning fitted bodice and long skirt, and both had blood-red roses sewn on that went all the way from the bustier top down to the long tail behind her. The dress, like her marriage, was one of a kind, and she'd chosen only the most skilled seamstress she could find to make the custom piece for her special day.

Her bridesmaids—Serena, Sara, and Alma—were dressed in black gowns as well. Their ones had stunning and sexy plunging necklines and open backs, with skirts that went all the way to the floor around their feet. The material also seemed to shimmer in the dark church, and the four women looked stunning against the black backdrop of the church. They followed her down the aisle as Cate walked the short stretch towards her groom, and each had their black rose bouquets in their hands and broad smiles on their reddened lips.

She peered down the aisle and could only see him. Lucifer was elegantly dressed, in all black except for the red rose protruding from his lapel. Devin stood beside him and wore a matching suit to his master's, watching with a huge smile as the bride and her entourage walked towards them.

Lucifer opened his *expression* to Cate as she approached, and she beamed back at him. She welcomed his offerings of warm emotion and love as they poured into her and could sense that he was eager to seal their union at last, just like she was.

The Satanic minister welcomed them, their family, and friends to the church. He then bowed to Satan as he ushered the bride and groom to join him atop the steps before the altar. Cate was sure she saw him trembling as he led them, but he seemed to hold his nerves well despite the ominous occasion. The congregation then sat down and stared up at the almighty couple in absolute silence as they turned to one another.

"Please begin," the minister said to Cate, bowing to her again in respect. They'd decided to read their own vows to each other rather than to follow the minister's lead and had written the oaths themselves. Cate took a deep breath and gazed up at her handsome groom as she recited her practised verse, and she had to fight back the tears pricking at her eyes. They'd come so far, and she couldn't deny how right it felt to be standing there with him at long last.

"From the darkness we came, and into the darkness I'll follow you.
We are like two flames, but from one force, one endless black light.
I'll never keep secrets, but share them willingly, and with love, trust, and strength in our bond.
I will love you now and for all eternity, and I promise to honour you every step of the way.
I'll follow you forever."

She felt as if her heart might burst out of her chest, but Lucifer held her hand in his and let his *expression* tell her how much he'd adored her short verse. The promises were there, as well as the acknowledgements of their past, and she knew he accepted her solemn vows.

Then it was his turn. The dark minister gestured for Lucifer to recite his vows as well, and he did so without once breaking away from Cate's loving gaze, grinning broadly at her.

"My darling. I promise to smite all who might ever try to harm you.
My love will not enslave or control you, but grasp you tight, and keep you safe for all eternity.
I will never love another. You, and only you, possess my heart, body, and soul. They are yours.
I promise you now that I will take care of you forever. Just say yes."

Cate watched Lucifer with a wide smile, relishing in his wonderful words, and she felt true happiness filling her from within. He felt it too, and she could tell he was reading his bride and taking in the wonderful thoughts and feelings she openly shared. The minister then beamed at the two of them and finished the verbal part of the ceremony.

"Remember, your love should always be more powerful than your pain, and you should strive to make one another's dreams a reality. May the moon bring you strength, and may you live the rest of your days in true love and happiness as one," he said, and then concluded the ceremony by binding their wrists in black ribbon and pronouncing them as husband and wife.

"So mote it be," the pair called together, and Lucifer looked right into his beautiful wife's green eyes before he grabbed her and kissed Cate deeply.

"So mote it be!" The crowd roared, adding their shouts of praise to Satan and his new Queen. They all then stood and clapped for them as the happy couple walked back down the aisle together, their hands still entwined and their smiles wide.

The party that followed their wedding lasted for days. The witches and demons were free to celebrate and enjoy the dark delights thanks to their master's wonderful mood, and they happily took the opportunity to let loose. The London penthouse was transformed into a huge banquet hall where the upper-level demons accompanied the royal family to celebrate their union. They toasted the happy couple and chatted loudly as the lower-level witches served them fine wine and the King's favourite aged whisky.

"Here's to the happy couple," exclaimed Beelzebub as he approached, and he gave a small bow to the King and Queen as he did. He was wearing a black and grey suit, which looked wonderful with the shoulder-length black hair that fell around his ears. His deep brown eyes stood out handsomely above his pronounced cheekbones and strong chin, and Cate could see many of the witches looking over at him far too eagerly, hoping for some attention from the powerful and ancient demon. "Now that you've finally claimed your true love, do you think you'll stop being such a miserable bastard?" he then asked Lucifer playfully, with a huge grin across his face. He spoke to his ruler in such a familiar way that still shocked Cate, but he was never punished for it. Rather than be enraged, Lucifer knew his friend's humour far too well, and he laughed loudly along with him as Beelzebub roared at his own joke. The old friends clinked their glasses, and the demon patted his king on the shoulder to show his affection. Beelzebub never was one for hugs and kisses.

"You know I'll never stop. My adoring public would never allow it. And besides, who doesn't love a grumpy old bastard?" Lucifer answered with a wink, and he smiled as Leviathan walked over and joined them. He too raised a glass to Cate, who smiled and clinked her champagne glass with his as he bowed to her. He wore a dark suit and shirt like Beelzebub, and his was a grey colour with black pinstripes. Leviathan had the same cheeky, playful look as the other two, but his blond hair and blue eyes made his appearance seem brighter than his comrades, despite Cate knowing just how powerfully dark and dangerous he truly was.

"Do you need me to remove this cretin, your majesty?" he asked, indicating that he meant Beelzebub with a cheeky poke in his ribs. "Wow, you really can polish a turd," he added, joking, and laughing with the pair of them for a moment longer as they exchanged their jibes. They stayed to chat for a few more minutes and then bowed to Lucifer and bid them farewell before heading back off into the crowd in search of women and wine.

Lucifer and Cate stayed for a few more hours, but quickly decided it was time to leave. They needed some much deserved time alone. The newlyweds sneaked away without a word and went into the huge master bedroom of the penthouse, complete with its four-poster bed and black silk sheets. Lucifer clicked the lock shut once they were alone inside and pushed Cate back against the heavy wood beam at the foot of the gigantic bed. His hand then reached up and gripped her neck to lift her chin to meet his eager mouth, and he held her tightly but didn't hurt her. In fact, the Dark King vowed to himself that he would never hurt her again. She gasped, desperate and eager for his touch, his love.

"Help me get this dress off, will you?" she asked with an impatient grin on her face. Lucifer turned her quickly so that his bride faced away from him, and his lips gently traced the line from her shoulder to her neck as his hands moved swiftly over the ribbon that tied the corset style bodice of her black gown closed at the back.

The dress fell to her feet and Lucifer ran his hands down her naked back, stopping only to slip a finger inside the hem of her black lace panties and slide them down, too. Cate turned to face her husband and pulled the clip out that'd been holding her dark hair up in a high ponytail, letting the thick curls fall to her bare shoulders. She then stepped out of her abandoned clothes, kicking off her black stiletto heels as she went, and stood before him without a shred of clothing on.

Lucifer stared down at her, his eyes hooded as he took in her beautiful body. He smiled and licked his lips. Cate reached up and ran her hand down the thick stubble on his cheek. And was glad he'd grown the short beard again. That, along with his short dark-blond hair that he had styled in a quiff at the front, was her favourite look for him. He'd completed the rock star look with a small black diamond earring and looked positively striking.

"You're gonna need to take this off," she said, running her hands down the lapels of his suit jacket.

"You do it," he ordered her with a cocky grin before he pulled Cate closer and kissed her again, allowing his hands to explore her naked body as he did. She leaned back, smiling up at her lover as she pulled the knot of his tie down and threw it aside before moving on. Lucifer's jacket and waistcoat were then quickly discarded, followed by the shirt, and then Cate ran her hands over his thickly muscled torso, biting her lip teasingly.

"I want you, now," she told him, walking backwards to the bed and climbing up onto it. Lucifer couldn't bear to keep his Queen waiting, so unbuttoned his trousers and kicked them to the floor along with the rest of his outfit. He climbed up on top of Cate and slid himself inside of her straight away, lifting her hips up to meet his as he thrust hard and deep.

Cate's body had been so ready for him and so tense with her desire that it wasn't long until she came for him. His touch sent her body into overdrive as usual, but so much more intensely now that they were finally husband and wife. She got the sense he was claiming her, a feral need instinctually telling him to mark her as his, and she let him have every inch of her body and mind. He stared down into her eyes and stroked his hands through her long curls as he continued in his pursuit of more sweet cries of pleasure, and she gave him them. Lucifer held her gaze as they moved together, and they were so in sync with one another's bodies that it wasn't long before they shared their climax. The bed beneath them vibrated as Lucifer reached his wonderful release, and he poured himself into her while roaring with pleasure.

"Choose anywhere in the world you want to go," he asked later when they were lazing on the bed together, revelling in the afterglow of their epic first lovemaking session as husband and wife.

Lucifer knew they still had a few more days he could remain on Earth thanks to their chosen wedding day and wanted to make the most of it. Theirs was a rare Halloween, which was exactly why they'd chosen it. It was an All Hallow's Eve followed immediately by a three-day full moon, and it marked the longest duration Lucifer had ever been on Earth before. He intended to use every moment to ensure Cate felt the most special woman alive.

"Paris," she answered, and smiled back at her husband. He nodded and climbed off the bed, offering her his hand to help her up before handing her a fresh set of clothes from the nearby drawers.

The pair of them dressed and then teleported away, and they arrived in the beautiful city of Paris within seconds. They dined in the decadent cafes along the river Seine and climbed to the top of the Eiffel tower that afternoon. The loved-up pair spent hours taking in the fantastic sights as they went, walking together, and unable to release their tight grip of one another. She knew none of the humans who saw them would ever suspect who they were and found she enjoyed the anonymity.

After spending the day enjoying their first stop, Lucifer asked her the same question again, and Cate answered by asking him to take her somewhere hot and all their own. He knew exactly where to take her and teleported his bride to a private island off the coast of Hawaii, where she lounged with him in the hot sun and sucked his hard cock for hours. When he came into her mouth with such intense bursts, she fell backwards onto the hot sand, and laughed when he helped her up, then returned the attention by focussing on giving her pleasure with his adept mouth. Lucifer made her climax ten times before eventually releasing Cate's sensitive clit from his strong and commanding grasp, and she was perfectly spent by the time he'd finished with her.

They lay back on the padded lounger and she nestled into him, resting her chin on her lover's chest. She knew Lucifer wouldn't allow any sleeping on this mini honeymoon, and she kick-started her dwindling energy again.

Cate climbed onto his lap and slid his ready hardness inside her wet chasm one more time before they carried on with their whistle-stop world tour.

When they were ready again, she decided on the ancient city of Rome in Italy as their next destination. They both knew the churches and holy areas would be out of bounds in the picturesque city, but they happily wandered around the ruins of the old town and dined in exclusive restaurants before partaking in a tour of some of the ancient crypts and catacombs. All the other tourists around them seemed both disturbed and intrigued by the creepy underworld of the city, but Cate devoured the historic sights. It was just the kind of gothic history she loved discovering, and they both revelled in the fear pouring out of the humans around them.

"This is so you," Cate whispered to Lucifer as they wandered the skeletal corridors and took in the dark vaults, still hand-in-hand, and he smiled down at her.

"I might've had a hand in it some time ago," he told her with a sly wink.

Before finally heading back to Hell, the newlyweds headed for their final stop on their honeymoon. They teleported to the forests of Greenland so Cate could watch the Northern Lights fill the sky for her first time. They stood atop the snow-covered mountains and watched in awe as the coloured waves hovered overhead. Cate had never seen anything so spectacular in her life and couldn't speak as she let the breath-taking view wash over her. It was fantastic, and she was happier than she'd ever been. The last few days had been the most wonderful of her existence, and in all honesty, she didn't want them to end.

Lucifer held her closer than ever and spoke quietly in her ear as they embraced beneath the shimmering colours. "I cannot read your thoughts anymore, my Queen," he told her, and wasn't disappointed to have lost that bit of power over her. He welcomed the comfortable silence and had noticed her mind slowly closing to him during their honeymoon. He didn't know how or why, but he gave into whatever higher power was driving them towards a different dynamic. "You have to tell me how you feel from now on," he added, leaning down to kiss her.

"I think I can do one better than that," she replied, and wordlessly sent him her love and emotion to him via their *expression* connection. Since she'd become the Dark Queen of Hell, Cate had slowly realised that her power had intensified, and understood why. She was becoming his equal, or at least it seemed that way.

Her power had reached the point where she thought she might be able to share that part of herself with him back through the strange link, where before it'd only ever been one-way. She'd been right. Her adoration poured out of her towards him, and they enjoyed each other wordlessly and thoughtlessly through their back-and-forth *expression*. Lucifer was lost for words. He simply revelled in her offerings of emotion and love without a sound.

Cate was glad he'd reacted so well. She felt more powerful than ever, as though he'd given her some extra omnipotence along with his hand in marriage, and she giggled at his surprised stare. It was good to know that her thoughts were her own again, as well as that her powers seemed to be increasing. While she had nothing to hide, she did enjoy the idea of being able to keep some things between them to herself from now on.

When the newlyweds returned to Hell later that night, they were greeted by shouts of hail and praise. Lucifer and Cate enjoyed the welcome, and he carried her over the threshold of the castle before wasting no time in taking her to their now shared chambers.

She undressed slowly for him, enjoying every moment and teasing Lucifer with every seductive move. When he could handle it no longer, he grabbed her, ripping off her lacy underwear and taking her swollen clit in his mouth while she groaned loudly in response to his touch. Lucifer sucked and nibbled his wife into submission and took great pleasure in feeling the throb of an orgasm pulsing through the exposed nerve as she climaxed beneath him.

He then moved his kisses up further over her torso to her tender breasts, and she yelped slightly as he bit down on one nipple but lifted her chest up to invite him to push her further. Lucifer was driven wild by her insatiable need for him and quickly moved to the other nipple. He clamped down hard and sucked the tender peak deep into his mouth while curling his fingers around her still throbbing nub. Cate came again for him, lost in the moment, and she gave into the pleasure that swept over her.

When Lucifer thrust himself inside her, she felt him deeper than ever before. She couldn't resist his commanding influence and let go, relinquishing her power and giving herself to him entirely. Her need for him was strong as his now, and her dark powers increased as time passed by. They spent weeks in bed together and basked in each other's wants and desires, climaxing together over and over.

CHAPTER THIRTEEN

A few months after the wedding, Alma knocked quietly on the King and Queen's chamber door, and Lucifer silently commanded for her to enter, having read the witch's mind. He already knew she was there to give Cate some bad news but let her be the one to do the talking. They hadn't left their bed in days and lay resting together after another lengthy few days of lovemaking, but she forced herself out of her slumber when she saw Alma's serious expression.

"Your majesties," she said, greeting them with a low bow. "I'm afraid I come bearing sad news, my Queen," Alma addressed Cate directly with a solemn expression.

"What is it?" she asked, sensing her trusted adviser's worry.

"Your human mother is old and is going to die very soon. I've just been informed of her condition, and it's very likely she'll be taken in the next few days," she added and bowed again, giving Cate a few moments to let the sad news sink in.

"Thank you, Alma," she replied, feeling wretched, and immediately guilty. She leaned up and looked to Lucifer for his guidance. "Do you think I could go and see her to say goodbye?" she asked him, requesting his permission to leave Hell. He nodded and then gave the command to Alma.

"Take my wife to Earth and stay with her while she visits her mother," he said. "And make sure she comes home safely. Is that understood?" he asked, and the frightened witch nodded profusely. She then left without a word, rushing off to prepare for their visit.

Cate was worried about Ella's condition, but also felt terrible that she hadn't been to visit her in such a long time. Her guilt showed on her face as she wordlessly got herself dressed and ready to go, and tears were close to falling already.

"I know I cannot truly understand how you are feeling, my love," Lucifer told her, looking over at his wife with a frown. "I do not value human life because I've never had any strong connection with a human. But I can sense your sadness and I want you to have the opportunity to say goodbye.

I think it'll give you closure," he told her. Cate knew it was hard for him to try to relate with her human feelings and appreciated the effort. Lucifer really didn't have a clue, so it made her smile—relieving her guilt somewhat. "I can't come with you, the moon isn't right…" he began, and tailed off when she sent him her silent understanding via their *expression*.

"I know." She leaned down to kiss him. "And anyway, I want to do this alone. I need to say goodbye properly," she added, and he nodded in agreement.

A few minutes later, Alma returned and re-entered their dark chamber after a tiny knock on the huge wooden doors.

"Everything's ready, your majesty," she told Cate, who nodded and took the witch's hand in hers. She was glad Alma seemed ready to lead the way as her mind was too fraught to concentrate on teleporting, and she bid farewell to her husband before blowing him a kiss.

"See you soon," he told her, snatching her goodbye kiss from the air with a smile, and he then watched as they teleported away.

***

When she arrived on Earth, Cate immediately aged herself so people wouldn't ask questions when she arrived at the hospital asking to see her mother. She introduced herself to the nurse and was led to the small room where Ella was resting. Inside, there were no monitors or bleeping machinery hooked up to the frail old woman. There was just a small bed and an armchair for visitors. Cate knew this was the place they took the patients who had no hope of recovery, and that the end really wasn't very far away.

She was totally unprepared for the way she felt upon seeing her, and her tears fell as soon as Ella's green eyes lit up at seeing her long-lost daughter again. Cate could hardly recognise her mother and hated that she'd abandoned her. So very many years had passed since she'd last seen her, but Ella knew Cate's face instantly, and regardless of the distance between them, perked up as soon as she went over to the bedside. She seemed so happy to see her daughter one last time and smiled at her as she sat down in the armchair.

"Cate," she said, and her quiet voice faltered. "I thought I might never get to see you again. Where have you been?" she asked, and a small tear ran down her sallow cheek as she greeted her.

"I'm sorry, Mum. I've been living far away for a long time. I can't give you all the details, but please know I am truly blessed and very happy," Cate replied. She knew there was no point in revealing her life's twists and turns to her mother, and that she wouldn't understand even if she tried. All that mattered was that she was here now.

Ella looked over at her and took Cate in. She really did seem happy and healthy, and she was so pleased to see her only child at last that she couldn't be upset. She took Cate's hand and nodded in understanding and didn't care if she wasn't prepared to be forthcoming about her life. After a long hug and a few more tears from each of the women, they chatted for hours. It was only when Ella was too tired to keep on going that they relaxed, and the frail old woman drifted off into a deep sleep.

Cate decided to get some rest in the armchair beside her instead of leaving her mother's side and was glad she had. She woke with a start when Ella reached for her hand in the middle of the night, her eyes wide, almost fearful. Her breathing was shallow, and they both somehow knew the end was close. Cate held on until her mother passed, and even caught a glimpse of an angel as it came to take her to Heaven. Despite her encompassed dark side, Cate knew that Heaven was where Ella belonged, and smiled as she bid farewell to her soul.

***

Cate and Alma stayed for a few more days while everything was put in order and Ella was cremated. The Dark Queen was in a despairing haze, but Alma helped with everything. She pretended to be a distant cousin of the family and facilitated with the preparations, along with overseeing the reading of Ella's will.

Cate decided to scatter her mother's ashes on the rocky beach where Ella would take her when she was a young child, and she sprinkled them over the rocks near the tide's edge with tears streaming from her eyes. She then watched the waves as they carried the ashes away to the ocean and hoped her mother might at last be free. Cate then used her power to alter her age again as she looked out at the sea and knew it was time to say goodbye to everything she'd once been. She was about ready to go back to Hell but waited to watch the slow tide thoughtfully for a few more minutes as a light rain began to fall from the sky, masking her tears.

Up on a wooden bench overlooking the promenade sat Alma, and she'd been sure to sit around the corner so as not to be watching her Queen directly but was close enough to be called upon when she was ready to go home.

Alma never saw the white witch coming, nor had she sensed the lightness as the woman appeared silently from behind her. A blast of light power combined with a strong spell from over Alma's shoulder sent her flying off the bench to the ground. It'd knocked the dark witch immediately unconscious, and with a sly, satisfied grin, the white witch then continued down the path towards the beach.

Wandering along the water's edge, Cate suddenly felt eyes on her and turned around. She faced the witch as she approached and recognised her immediately. The woman standing a few feet away was once her friend. Well, Cate had thought she was, but had eventually realised it'd all been a rouse to keep her under surveillance. The witch standing before her was in fact the high priestess of Dylan's coven from all those years before that'd tried to keep Cate away the night Lucifer came for her.

"Hello again, Angelica," Cate said as the witch neared her. "It's been a long time."

"Yes, Cate. It has," replied the witch. "How are you?" she asked, and she sniggered. They both knew she didn't care and was only asking to stall her.

"What do you want from me, witch?" Cate spat, not answering her insincere question. She was growing impatient and thoroughly pissed off that Angelica had dared intrude while she was saying her last goodbyes to her mother.

"*I*, don't want anything," Angelica said, pointing to herself with feigned disinterest. "But your presence is requested by my master," she added, with a nonchalant wave of her hand. Angelica had always been somewhat theatrical. She loved any and all attention, but Cate didn't care for her games anymore.

"Oh really, and just who might that be?" she asked, wondering if some angel may be trying to use her as bait to lure Lucifer to Earth. She wondered if perhaps the witches were after a fight in retaliation for her husband's treatment of Dylan a few years before, or if it could simply be about Angelica's bruised ego after her coven had failed the night Cate had been summoned to the church.

The Dark Queen waited impatiently for the witch to answer, to declare her master's name and their intentions, but she didn't reply. Angelica simply wandered nearer and when she was close enough to reach out and touch Cate's arm, she did so. She could feel her attempting to teleport her away, but her power wasn't strong enough.

The powerful Queen had to laugh. She sent out a blast of dark power that caused Angelica to wince, and she pulled her hand back with a hiss. Cate could tell she was no match for her and held her ground.

"Sorry," replied Angelica with a smirk, clearly pretending for a moment to be remorseful. She rubbed her hand as though it were still sore from Cate's blast of power, though, and the Dark Queen smiled. "Perhaps I should've said *our* master," she told her, and a sly smile curled at her mouth again. With that, another nine white witches appeared and encircled Cate. Once inside the white circle, she quickly realised that she was unable to move or teleport away to safety. She tried summoning Alma, but when she realised she couldn't sense her witch through the impenetrable circle, Cate immediately gave up trying. Even she could tell that resistance was pointless, and instead she stood tall and held Angelica's gaze, waiting for the witch to make her next move. "Check-mate," Angelica told her with a snigger.

The coven then joined hands and stepped closer, tightening their circle around her. Cate noticed Dylan wasn't with them but wasn't sure if that was a good sign or not. She was positive that her old friend was no longer her ally after what she'd let Lucifer's demons do to her in that terrible dungeon, and Cate held out no hope of finding a friend within the white coven.

The witches started chanting, and Cate could feel her head begin to spin. Their spell was taking control of her body, and a strange summoning took over her. She was then wrenched away from Earth and couldn't control her course. She tried not to panic and tried to focus her mind and power on readying herself for whatever fight might be waiting for her at their destination. The main worry she had though was that she was moving up and not down, however she guessed the good guys might not be as into torture as her husband's legion of evil minions.

CHAPTER FOURTEEN

Cate lost consciousness somewhere during the ascent and later awoke in a bright sunlit room. She was laid on a huge bed covered in white silk sheets, and she was dressed in a white satin summer dress. Her hands had been placed over her heart—like the dead—and she knew she must look ridiculous. When she stood, Cate felt strangely woozy, and regained her composure after a few seconds, but was shocked to discover she was completely powerless. The witches must've somehow taken away her powers, and she made herself a silent vow to personally see to it that Angelica was beaten and tortured to death very soon.

"You have *got* to be kidding me," she mumbled when she looked over at her reflection in the mirror. She looked preposterous, dressed all in white. After taking stock of her surroundings, she moved over to the door and gave the handle a try. It was locked, of course, so Cate decided to go over to the window and see if she could figure out where she was. A beautiful, white sandy beach stretched out before her, followed by an endless clear blue ocean and a cloudless sky. It was gorgeous, but she was starting to feel a chill down her spine that she couldn't ignore.

This place did not feel like Earth, and it was most definitely not Hell. There was no way she could be in Heaven, so she figured it must be some kind of dream, or alternate plane, that the white witches had taken her to. Cate hoped she was right about torture being a no-no with the good guys but wondered if she might be killed with kindness or something equally as pathetic.

"Welcome," a man's voice said quietly from behind her, and Cate turned to see where the sound had come from. She found that a tall, dark-haired man had silently entered the room, and already shut the door behind him. Either that or he'd teleported inside. He wore white khaki trousers with a white shirt, and was gorgeous, but not that Cate let herself notice. She had only one lover, and he seemed very far away right now.

"I suppose you're Angelica's master?" Cate asked, and the man nodded.

"I am everyone's master, Hecate," he said, eyeing her casually. "Even yours." She faked a small smile and shook her head. He seemed harmless enough, but she didn't believe he could have any power over her. White beings weren't their overseers. As Cate went to respond, though, he cut her off. "I am one of Lucifer's old friends, and his brother, of sorts. So, in a manner of speaking, that makes us in-laws. Does that sound about right?" he asked, then grinned and waited a moment for his words to sink in. Cate's face dropped.

"Holy shit," she mumbled, knowing she must be in the presence of one of the very powerful angels that'd cast Lucifer out of Heaven, and he laughed.

"Less of that, please, darling. That's no way to talk to the Master of the High Council of Angels," he said, eyeing her with a smile. The title sounded about right, and she guessed perhaps he might not be quite as harmless as she'd initially thought. "My name's Uriel, and I am an archangel. Now then, that's us officially introduced," he added, while she still stared over at him in shock and surprise.

Uriel moved towards Cate slowly, taking slow but long strides across the room, and she knew she couldn't escape him. If she was right, this plane was probably just a square-mile or so of beach that he'd created as a place to hide her from Lucifer, and also to keep her just where he wanted her.

My very own prison, Cate thought as he neared.

"Exactly," Uriel replied, answering her thoughts just like Lucifer had used to do, and Cate jumped in surprise. It'd been a while since she'd had to be careful of her innermost musings and it shocked her having them answered again. "Make yourself at home, you're going to be here some time," he then added, inching closer until her back was up against the large window.

Cate could feel his power resonating through both her and every inch of the prison around her. He radiated light, and she could feel her inner darkness trying to fight it, but it was no use. His witches' spell had blocked her dark power and trapped it somewhere deep within her. Energy couldn't die or be stolen, it could only be transferred, and she doubted any of his underlings would've wanted what was bubbling inside of her blackened heart. They'd found a way to suppress her power, and she wasn't happy about it. Cate felt an almost human-like weakness before him and wanted to curse him. Nothing about this situation gave her cause for hope, and she just hoped her kidnapper would get to the point sooner rather than later.

Uriel took a moment to take Cate in, staring at her lips and then into her eyes. He read her every thought, feeling and memory while he stood just inches away, and was entranced. Cate couldn't fight him, and she didn't even have the chance to try. His invasive examination was over so quickly it made her head spin.

"You and Sataniel are incredibly happy together," he said, and it seemed like a bemused statement rather than anything else. She knew he must have been processing the information she'd just wordlessly given him and hated how he could know entire life story so effortlessly. "But why? After everything he put you through, how could you bear to be his wife?" he asked her and was clearly genuinely confused by her love for Lucifer, and by her forgiveness for his terrible and selfish treatment of her. "Don't answer now, darling," he then told Cate before she could answer with a snarky comment. "We can discuss him in due time," he added dismissively.

Uriel placed the palm of his hand on Cate's cheek and rubbed her top lip gently with his thumb. She wanted to tell him to back off, but he advanced no more. The archangel just held her there for a few minutes before letting his hand drop, and he turned away. "Get dressed," he finally said, and surprisingly it sounded like more of a request than an order. "I want to make you dinner," Uriel added as he opened the door and went out into the rest of the house, leaving her bedroom door open and unlocked, for now.

She went to the closet and found nothing but a variety of white clothing. After rolling her eyes and giving the contents a loud "*tut*," she decided on a pair of shorts and a baggy shirt and pulled them on. Cate caught a glimpse of herself in the mirror again and sniggered. She couldn't remember the last time she'd worn white. It didn't look right on her, but with no other options left, she just had to go with it. It was wear them or else head out to dinner naked, and she wasn't prepared to play that game with her husband's greatest adversary.

She walked out into a long hallway and wandered down to a room near the end where she could hear classical music playing. Uriel was there, humming along to the aria and tossing a salad while some steaks cooked on the hob. Cate was taken aback. *Who knew?* she thought as she watched him. He caught her eyeing him and smiled, beckoning her to sit at the table before he poured them each a large glass of red wine and went back to check on his sizzling meat.

"I don't see why we can't enjoy all things in moderation," Uriel told her with a wink. "After all, my council and I created these delights, so why can't I enjoy them?"

"I suppose you're right," she replied with a shrug before she took a sip of wine. *Damn, this is good,* she thought and took another, longer swig. A stern "tsk," from him told her that blasphemous thoughts weren't appreciated just as much as her saying them aloud, however she didn't care. Those weren't her rules, and regardless of where she was being held, she wasn't about to convert and serve Uriel or his council.

Cate watched him for a while, feeling nothing if not more confused. This God-like angel was making her dinner and labelling her as some kind of extended family. But she knew that Lucifer was his greatest enemy; his angelic brother-of-sorts who was cast out of Heaven for all eternity and forced into darkness and a torturous, wholly sinful existence at this very angel's hands. She couldn't understand why he'd brought her here. Or why he was taking care of her, cooking for her, and now humming to music as if they were old friends enjoying a meal together. Surely his ultimate goal was to use her, or maybe even kill her, to make Lucifer pay? Perhaps he was about to force her to make her husband come out and fight? What did he want, why had he bought her here? Cate's head was spinning again.

"Enough with the questions," Uriel snapped sternly, and he turned from the stove to face Cate, while his face darkened angrily. He composed himself immediately, though, and set down a plate of tender steak before her. "You'll ruin this wonderful meal I've planned for us," he added calmly as he sat down opposite her and passed Cate the salad bowl. The petulant side of her wanted to push him, but her instincts told her it wouldn't be wise. Instead, she did as she'd been told, and got stuck in.

She ate everything Uriel had made for her. The steak was delicious, while the wine matched it perfectly and flowed easily as they ate together. The conversation was slow at first, but soon the two of them were chatting about everything and nothing, and they talked well into the night. Cate was confused at how easily she could relax around Uriel, and his warm nature drew her in as they chatted openly. The change in dynamic helped her overcome her grief for her mother, and Cate felt more relaxed than she thought she could be around such an intimidating archangel.

He kept the conversation light, asking her opinion on the current state of things on Earth while chatting animatedly about his hopes and dreams for the future of the human race rather than bring up her husband again. "Imagine, if you will, my idea of a perfect world. No more war, no famines, and no governments vying for power and wealth. All we need to do is create a higher race of beings that would take control. They would then rule over the humans and help to absolve them of their sins. Free will can be a nightmare, but if they are led, the humans will evolve and thrive," he told her thoughtfully.

Cate tried to fathom this potential future, but none of it made sense. After all, his God had reportedly created man to be free, so why would Uriel and the council seek to change that and control them? That would go against everything the light power dictated, commanded, and expected from their followers. "That's the next problem. How would I go about it without disturbing the balance? The council has not agreed to my plan yet, but they'll see sense soon," he told her with a slight grin curling the corners of his mouth.

Cate knew that the angel sat before her was not to be trifled with. After all, he'd managed to cast out Lucifer, and then Leviathan and Beelzebub from Heaven for defying him, and after the millennia since she was certain his power had to have increased tenfold. She wondered if perhaps the other opposing members of the high council would simply be next on his hit list and didn't envy them having to deal with his all-powerful expectations. Uriel smiled across at Cate with a twinkle in his eye that made her pretty sure she'd just hit the nail on the proverbial head.

He then moved on, quickly changing the topic, and asked her how things were in Hell.

"Over-crowded," she joked, grinning at him over the delicious soufflé pudding Uriel had just set down before her.

"Unrepentant sinners are not welcome in Heaven, Cate. That will never change," he said seriously. The mood changed then, and his expression grew sombre. She didn't like the tense silence, but also hoped that the real questions might be answered at last.

"Where are we now then, surely not Heaven?" Cate asked him in the hope he'd decided to be open with her.

"On an astral plane between Earth and Heaven," Uriel told her, confirming her suspicions. "The angels all live on plains like this so that we can watch over the humans we're charged with protecting. This one, though, is all ours," he told her and then paused for a moment. He let Cate take his explanation in, but he was simply confirming her earlier suspicions rather than telling her anything she didn't already know. "My turn," Uriel added before she could respond. He seemed to want the opportunity to ask his own questions in return for him opening up to her. "Do you really love Lucifer, truly?" he asked, watching her as he did.

"Yes," she answered without hesitation. "I gave myself willingly to him and became his wife—so I should hope so," she then added with a shy smile.

"And do you intend to give him unholy, abominable children?" he pressed on, seemingly disgusted at the possibility.

"Someday, if we can," Cate answered, forcing herself to stay calm.

Uriel sat back, seemingly surprised by Cate's answers and thoughts on the subject, but he pressed on. He leaned forward and stared into her eyes with his bright blue, intense gaze.

"I don't get it. Why would you feel that way about him when he left you in that pit all that time, only then to be whipped and tortured by his dark servants? He ignored your pleas for mercy and forgiveness, regardless of his affection for you. How is that behaviour worthy of your love in return?" he asked, seeming determined to know how she could possibly love him. "He broke you, Cate. He then manipulated you into his bed, where he possessed you. That's not love, it's supremacy and control."

Cate was red-hot with anger at his rash assumptions. If he were anyone else, she'd lash out and slap him for daring to question her so intensively while refusing to understand her loyalty. He didn't know the two of them, despite his power to read her thoughts. Cate knew full well that it'd been thousands of years since Uriel had even seen or spoken with Lucifer, so he had no idea who he now was or why he did the things he did. She knew him—truly knew him. Not every little detail. She was no fool, but she'd seen into his primeval soul, and gone far deeper than anyone else had ever been before. Cate also knew that the majority of his anger and pain came from the one rejection that'd happened a very long time before she was even in the picture. The rejection from his own dear 'brothers' had made him that way, along with his banishment and years of lonesome exile at their hands.

Uriel read her thoughts and stood from the table without another word. Cate sat in furious silence watching him, then polished off her wine and stood too, aiming to storm off.

"Time for bed," he said, without looking at her as he began clearing the plates.

"It seems so," she answered, and turned on her heel. Cate stomped back up the corridor to her room, slammed the door closed, and stripped off her disgusting white clothes. She couldn't stand them against her body and let out an enraged groan when she wandered over to the white covered bed. Climbing in, Cate knew she might've pushed it too far, but didn't care. After all, if Uriel was going to read her thoughts all the time, he had to be prepared to hear some things he might not want to.

Despite her anger, she quickly fell into a dreamless sleep, not noticing the figure that watched her from the now open doorway almost the entire night.

CHAPTER FIFTEEN

The next morning, as Cate roused, Uriel greeted her with a breakfast tray filled with bacon and eggs, served with buttered toast and fresh mango juice. Despite the events from the previous night, Cate thanked him. She didn't even shy away from the playful smile she received from her captor when she quickly covered her naked body and sat up in the bed.

She ate the entire plateful and was oddly famished despite their big meal from the night before. Once she was finished with her breakfast and had gotten dressed, Uriel took Cate outside to enjoy the view. It was beautiful out there and seemed warm and peaceful. She enjoyed the scenic tranquillity despite her knowing it was all just an illusion. The sun felt nice on her skin, too. Cate had almost forgotten how enjoyable it was to bathe in the sunshine. The heat of Hell was more like an intense pressure, and although she was perfectly happy there, she had to admit it felt good to feel the sun's rays warm her pale skin again.

Uriel watched her every move, constantly reading her thoughts and feelings as she took it all in. She couldn't keep him out but wished he would just talk to her instead. Surely he would know if she was lying, but at least they would have the opportunity to pass the time easier through conversation and interaction. He still wasn't giving anything away as far as his intentions were, and Cate wondered about those things openly in her mind, knowing he would hear her. She just hoped he might finally decide to answer her questions soon.

"What do you want from life, Cate?" Uriel asked her later that day over another delicious home-cooked dinner.

"To be happy," she told him honestly, surprising the angel somewhat. "I know it might not seem like much, but I think it's very hard to find real happiness," Cate added thoughtfully.

"It is a nice concept, but the problem with happiness," Uriel replied, taking a bite. "Is that it's dependent on your interpretation. What makes you happy, Cate? Love, power, purpose? Or even just a sense of belonging? But think what makes a serial killer happy, or a molester of children, or a rapist of innocent women. Everyone has been made to be different. They were created that way and those variances can mean a huge difference when the pursuit of happiness gets in the way."

"How do you know rape or murder doesn't make me happy?" Cate asked, with a wry grin on her lips.

"You really do forget who you're talking to sometimes," he replied. Uriel smiled warmly and reached towards her, touching her hand softly before lifting it gently into his own. Cate's whole body tingled in response to his touch, much like it did in Lucifer's strong hands, but this was a purer feeling—lighter.

"You can sense my light?" Uriel asked, seemingly surprised. Cate nodded. However, she wasn't sure what that really meant.

"Yes, I think so. Why, is that not normal?"

"Not for a long time," he said, but added nothing else. The powerful angel simply let Cate's hand drop gently back on to the table between them.

***

He watched her sleep again that night, wondering the whole time how he might persuade Cate to join him in the light. Uriel had originally sent Angelica to take her from Earth with the intention of using her to lure Satan away from his dark domain.

The plan had been that when Lucifer left the safety of Hell, Uriel and the other angels would finally finish their feud with him once and for all. He hadn't decided which way to go yet, but it'd be either by a pure death or by persuading Lucifer to join them back in the light.

A lot of time had passed since they'd last seen one another, and they'd both changed immensely, but their feuding had created a seemingly unending void between the two worlds. It was a hollowness that would take an awful lot to bridge, and one of them would surely have to concede for that to ever happen. Lucifer would have to yield or die. There was nothing else for it.

Thinking back over the past, Uriel knew he was right to become suspicious of his fallen brother's intentions when Lucifer had finally sired an heiress of his own, and he'd known he had to keep watch over the girl. He'd chosen to send a small coven of witches down to Earth so they could find out what Lucifer's plans for her eventually were, and also to try and keep Cate from going to Hell with him at all if they could. When they'd eventually failed, she'd completely gone from Uriel's reach. He couldn't know what she was doing down there in the darkness, what sinister lessons she was learning, and how she was being influenced by her evil master. Of course, he'd feared the worst.

The council had immediately assumed that she would bring about evil and death wherever she went when she travelled to Earth. They'd presumed she might bring about the apocalypse, or at the very least turn saints into sinners with every step she took—her influence over susceptible humans uncontrollable.

But no, she'd done nothing to force his hand, or even register on his radar when she came to Earth those first few times. Much to his and the High Council of Angel's surprise, she was discovered to just be living a seemingly normal life—as normal as the Dark Princess of Hell could have, of course.

Years later, when Lucifer's second heir came along, Uriel was sure they would use him for the same evil deeds too, but again, no. A few sins were committed thanks to the pair's influence over the humans that encountered them when they were later back on Earth, but nothing the council hadn't been able to handle.

Then the third child was sired, and still nothing. No war between their worlds and no attempts to contact their council. No evil massacres, rituals, or sacrifices in Lucifer's name that would add to his dark power. Uriel simply couldn't fathom his intentions back then, and he hadn't liked it one bit. That was why he decided he must kidnap one of Satan's heirs. He would then force them to give up their knowledge of their master and use them as bait to lure Lucifer out of hiding.

When Cate had reportedly left Earth and returned to Hell without Devin, they'd had no idea that she was going through such torture and manipulation at the hands of her immoral master. When Uriel had heard the news that the pair of them had married a few years later, it was clear to him that she was the one he had to try and kidnap. Uriel's servants had watched the hospice, and he'd always intended to give the order to take Cate as soon as she was by Ella's side again, but something had stopped him. When he'd descended and stood looking through the window to Ella's room, he'd felt enough compassion to let her see it through. He'd watched for a few minutes at Cate holding her mother's hand in that hospital bed and had been intrigued by her warmth and love for her human parent.

He'd been utterly captivated by the beautiful Dark Queen and surprised by the tears she shed for the elderly woman's passing. The pain in her heart she showed so openly as her mother had died confounded him. He'd seen her true nature in that moment and decided then that he would give her some time to grieve before she was to be captured.

Before returning to Heaven, Uriel had ordered for Angelica to wait. He didn't want to take her away before Cate could say a proper farewell to her mother, and he then watched from above with fascination as she'd gone through the motions and finally scattered the ashes into the ocean.

Uriel was sure Lucifer would never stand back while his wife was in captivity and was convinced that he would endeavour to find his way to her soon. However, he had no way of knowing when it might happen. One of the biggest problems that they'd always encountered, though, was that none of the angels could sense either Lucifer or his progeny while they were on Earth or in Hell. Their darkness concealed them from their reach, so he'd always needed to use other ways in which to find them. Tracking them down often took a lot of planning and forethought—and time.

The strange thing now, though, was that Uriel felt a connection with Cate that he hadn't counted on. It confused him. How could he ever plan for the possibility that after all these years he might finally sense something for another being other than the love he'd always felt for all mankind? He loved each and every human, angel, and being him and the council had created. Uriel loved Lucifer and his other fallen brothers still. He loved Cate too, but he realised now that it was in a different and strangely more potent way. He wanted to know her, to be near her and to touch her. He wanted to kiss her and make love to her. She'd somehow infiltrated his usually so hard shell, and she didn't even seem aware of the power she had to compel him and everyone else around her.

Uriel knew that there was probably a part of him that wanted her simply because Cate was Lucifer's wife, but he was sure it was more than just his ancient rivalry that made him feel the way he did. He wanted to protect her, to make her smile, and to be the one to make her happy.

Anticipation flowed through him at the very possibility of a kiss, an intimate touch, or even the chance he might get to make love to her. He could feel himself growing hard at the thought of her at his mercy, and imagined Cate lying naked before him, begging him to take her.

By morning, Uriel had sorted through his thoughts, and knew that his objective had changed. Cate was the prize now—and he was determined to win.

***

Cate awoke the next morning to the same sensation of light power flowing through her that she'd felt after dinner the night before. However, it wasn't through Uriel's touch this time, but through his *expression*, just as Lucifer would often do. In honesty, it made her feel slightly nauseous. His wave was an overload of powerful emotion and light suddenly coursing through her entire body, and it caused strange, yet not unwelcome surges to collide somewhere deep within her.

She was used to the dark, dangerous, and intense emotions she received from her husband, but this lightness was new, and far scarier to her than the darkness had ever been. Cate looked over to the doorway and took in the Adonis before her. Uriel looked astounding. He was half dressed in white chinos and nothing on top to cover up his thickly muscled torso. He was beautifully tanned and perfectly toned, and gave her a cheeky, knowing smile as she stared across at him.

"Like what you see, Queen Hecate?" he asked, turning off the *expression* as he pulled a cream t-shirt over his head. Cate was left feeling disappointed, but shook it off immediately, and felt guilty that she even let herself look that long. She was a married woman, after all. "I won't tell if you don't," Uriel told her with a chuckle. "Breakfast's ready," he then added, and sauntered off to the kitchen without another word.

Cate was hot and bothered suddenly. The energy between them had just changed dramatically, and she didn't know how to process the feelings that he'd passed to her while he'd opened that intense link. She got up and pulled on a cream dress from the closet, having given up her resistance to all light clothing now, and she then padded down the now familiar hallway to the kitchen.

She found Uriel sat at the large wooden dining table with a steaming cup of milky coffee. He watched Cate for a moment as she entered the kitchen, before grabbing the pot and pouring her a freshly brewed cup of the black nectar. He then offered the still confused Dark Queen a seat beside him.

"So, you can do *expression* too?" Cate asked, but then laughed to herself. "Of course you can." Uriel just smiled and nodded.

"All my angels can do it if their bonds with those in their charge are strong," he told her. Cate hadn't really thought about it being an angel thing before, but of course Lucifer was once like Uriel, so it made sense. "You can do it back to him now because of your marriage, but only with him," he informed her.

That made sense as well, although in all honesty she'd never tried with anyone else before.

"Does that mean our bond is strong, then?" she asked, having realised what he'd just said. Cate knew she was pushing him a little, but sensed he was finally in a more open mood this morning.

"Clever girl. I suppose you could say that," Uriel answered, but Cate could tell he'd held back. She was ready to give up when he offered her a little more clarification after a few thoughtful moments. "The reason I opened my link to you this morning is because I believe there's a strong bond developing between you and me. And well, I want to nurture that bond and see where it takes us."

"As friends, or as your sister-in-law?" she asked. Cate hoped to discover whether all the desirous emotions she'd felt coming through the *expression* earlier were a quest for family ties, or if it was about something else.

"Neither," was all he replied, looking into her eyes intensely. His deep blue irises burned into hers, and he held her gaze for a long time before he got up to fetch more coffee from the kitchen counter.

Cate knew immediately what Uriel had meant. She was scared and still more than just a little bit confused but couldn't help the rush of adrenaline and flutter of excitement thanks to his leading comments. By the time he returned with the coffeepot, the air was thick with tension between them. Cate could tell he was enjoying her response to his words, and he watched her curiously as she mulled everything over in her mind. "Don't feel guilty," he told her after a few moments.

Uriel took her hand in his and she felt the strange buzz pass through her again as their skin touched—his light somehow pouring into her through the contact. The strong and intense *expression* he then opened up to her was Cate's undoing, and she tried to pull back, but he already had her at the tipping point. She was way over that line within seconds thanks to his intense eyes on hers, and before she could even focus her thoughts, Uriel planted a deep kiss on her lips.

His gentleness kept her wanting, needing more, and Cate leaned into his touch. She allowed his tongue to delve inside her ready mouth while hers flicked back and quickly succumbed to his desire for her. Uriel then traced soft kisses down to her neck while she ran her hands through his dark brown hair and pulled him near. He placed a hand on her neck to pull her closer, which excited her while intensifying the contact, and Uriel whispered in her ear.

"All I need to hear is one little word and I'm all yours," he said.

Her eyes flicked open immediately, and she was bought well and truly back to the room with a thud. There she was, all over again. Cate could've kicked herself for falling for it. She was just another piece in another game and was angry as hell for being used so profoundly.

CHAPTER SIXTEEN

"How could I be so weak?" she cried, and she pulled away from his hold. Cate pushed back in her chair and stormed off out of the kitchen, heading straight to the front door of the house without another word. She then ran down the beach, kicking up the sand as she went, and then stopped just after she reached the line where the gentle lapping waves met the white beach.

Cate stood there for a few moments with her arms wrapped around her body, hugging it tightly. She stared out at the horizon as she let the water swell around her feet and the sun warm her body, and all the while, she wept quietly to herself. Uriel watched from further up the beach, giving her a few minutes to calm down before he went and joined her at the water's edge. He'd been surprised by her reaction but read Cate and quickly understood. The very mention of his required confirmation had brought back awful memories of her submission to Lucifer—memories that she'd pushed aside for so long.

He stepped close behind Cate and then slipped his arms around her stomach and held her close. Surprisingly, she spun around and held him back, letting her head fall on to his shoulder. Uriel could feel her emotions flood through him as he read her, but he kept quiet while she wept in his arms for as long as she needed.

***

A few days later, following another lovely home cooked meal, Cate sat quietly in the small beach house's living room. She was relaxing on the sofa and enjoying the calm quiet, but her mind was wandering, so she pushed all thought away in preference of the pleasant silence. Uriel came in a few minutes later with a cup of tea, another so seemingly normal gesture which still made her laugh, but she appreciated the effort he was going to and thanked him. They then sat quietly together for a while, and he left Cate to her thoughts as usual, but never seemed to want to physically leave her alone for too long if he could help it.

Uriel moved across and climbed behind her on the large sofa, where he embraced her as she leaned back into him, offering her a warm and loving circle of peace and safety. As much as Cate knew she shouldn't, she let him hold her. She hated to admit it, but she enjoyed being wrapped in his arms. Despite the guilt she had to constantly push away over her yearning for him, she didn't stop him from stroking her hands delicately before sliding his fingers through hers.

They'd grown closer over the last few days and had talked for hours while lying on the sunny beach or devouring more of his deliciously cooked meals together. They were slowly becoming friends, and she'd soon found herself growing more relaxed in his company, regardless of the ever-present reminder she was still his captive.

Uriel had dialled his affections back a notch though and had agreed to allow Cate some more time to make sense of this strange scenario the two of them had found themselves in before pursuing her again. He hadn't changed his mind, however, and still knew with absolute certainty just how much he still wanted her for himself. With his sights set on her rather than his plan for vengeance, he'd also heightened all security to their astral plane and commanded that more witches secure the portals, just in case. He no longer wanted unexpected visitors. Despite his original plan, Uriel now knew for sure that Cate was the only thing he wanted—the time of reckoning with Lucifer would have to wait.

"I love you, Cate," Uriel told her after just a few weeks at the beach house and her eyes widened in disbelief. She was shocked and thought for sure that there was no way he could love her. They barely knew each other yet, and she was still the wife of his nemesis. Surely he just wanted to possess her for some crazy rivalry? "No, it's not that at all," he answered her thoughts again. This whole mind-reading thing was starting to really bother her now, and she pursed her lips with frustration.

A few moments passed in silence, but eventually Uriel decided to let down his walls. "I do know you, Cate. I've seen your life from your memories and thoughts, as well as what you've told me about yourself since we came here. I listened to everything. I remember every detail. I don't love the situation we're in, where you came from, or how it is we came to be here together right now. But I do love you. I love your laugh, your smile, and your warmth. I love the way you still blush at the memory of our kiss, and most of all, I love the way all you want from life is to be happy. Not power, not money, but happiness. I know you believe you belong in the darkness, but I don't think so. I think you belong here in the light, with me." He'd finally given Cate the answers she so desperately craved, and her eyes widened in surprise at his heartfelt words.

She looked up into his intense stare and immediately felt the walls of her resistance come crumbling down. He hadn't resorted to breaking her will to make her say yes, she'd got there all on her own thanks to his patience and kind words. Cate then felt her heart fill with the light from Uriel's tender touch as he reached a hand up to stroke her cheek. Their bond was suddenly stronger than it'd ever been before, and her resolve crumbled even further. The kiss that followed was powerful and intense. Both wanted more, and Cate knew—right or wrong—she couldn't keep away from him any longer.

"Will you make love to me?" Uriel asked her when he finally pulled his lips away from hers.

It was so wrong to want him so badly, and yet she'd been slowly seduced, and knew there was no turning back now that he'd won her heart. He overwhelmed her ready and willing soul, and she let him, no matter how much her love for Lucifer tried to tell her otherwise.

"Yes," Cate replied, and giggled as he pulled her up into his arms and carried her to the bedroom.

The kissing couple burst through the door with a crash. Cate was still in his strong arms and had her legs wrapped tightly around his waist while their mouths explored one another's passionately. He shut the door and lay her down on the bed, leaning on top of his lover, and despite their eagerness, both remained fully clothed. Uriel took his time to kiss her deeply and enjoy their intense closeness rather than hurry. He didn't want to rush this and vowed to take things as slowly as she needed him to. As much as he hated it, her guilt still welled up inside of her, and he knew he had to be patient while she worked through it.

She felt so much warmth and powerful emotion coming from her angelic lover that all she could do was lie back and bask in his energy. She lapped it up and was soon desperate for more. Cate kissed him and ran her hands through his dark hair, pulling him closer, tightening their embrace.

Their bodies screamed for each other, and it wasn't too long before she felt the strap of her dress being pulled down her arms. As her breasts were exposed, Uriel leaned down to kiss each of them, taking time to caress each nipple in turn with his gentle mouth. Cate groaned, relishing his touch, and as she arched her back, he pulled her dress all the way down and flung it on the floor. His kisses then fluttered all over her stomach and down to her hips before he pulled her knickers down and threw them aside—leaving her completely naked before him.

She opened her legs, watching with a grin as he licked his lips and nestled himself between her thighs. Uriel sucked her throbbing clit into his mouth and fluttered around it, using his tongue while Cate arched up on the bed again, unable to control her intense reactions to his touch. Her body was so sensitive, tingling wonderfully, and threatening an orgasm already.

"Don't hold back," he then told her in a gruff tone. Uriel slipped two fingers inside her hot, wet opening and continued in his pursuit of her release. Having him inside her sent Cate slamming straight into an immense climax. She cried out, calling his name, and writhing on the bed as she flushed white heat throughout her entire being, and all thought was lost in that incredible moment of pure ecstasy.

When her body began to come down from the incredible high, Uriel started pressing his lips against her skin again, this time over her thighs and down to his lover's feet. He sucked on her toes for a moment and laughed at her ticklishness before finally letting her go. The sexy angel stood and pulled his t-shirt over his head and then tossed it on the ground alongside the discarded dress and underwear. He was showing off that gloriously muscular body again, and it drove Cate wild in anticipation of what was coming next.

Leaving his trousers on, for now, he climbed back on top of her, pressing his body into hers as he leaned down to kiss her deeply again. She wanted him and could feel his hard cock pushing against her core through the thin material of his chinos. His body's response told her he wanted her too, but he still didn't make his next move. Uriel took her mouth in his, and he delighted in Cate's touch and taste as he let his hand wander down her body to her breasts. He cupped each in turn and tugged on her nipples, firmly but gently, arousing her further.

She let her own hands wander down his torso as they kissed, the tips of her fingers stroking each perfect muscle before eventually reaching the belt of his trousers. She couldn't wait any longer and slipped her finger under the band at the waist and pulled the hem down, taking Uriel's hard cock in her hands. He groaned and arched himself back up, taking his weight on his knees as she began stroking up and down on his rock hard length, gently pulling back and forth, but never taking her mouth off his. Uriel then kicked off the last of his clothing and pulled Cate around.

Before she knew it, she was up on his lap, and their chests were pressed together as he cradled her. She leaned into him, kissing him passionately, still pulling up and down on the hardness beneath her with her hands. "I want you to be in control, Cate," he told her, and she obeyed, climbing up and positioning herself above his erection before gently coaxing his tip inside her eager cleft. "I'm yours. Take me however you want me," he groaned as she pushed him inside a little further. Cate's deep muscles tightened over him instantly, making her eager for more, and she flooded in readiness for the intrusion. She let herself ride down a few more inches before pulling up again, and then took all of him inside her at last. She was ready, and the thickness of him pulled every wonderful muscle within to its limit as she enveloped him greedily. She rose up, but her body was eager to have him back again, so she quickly pushed herself back down onto him. Soon she was going faster and pushing harder, welcoming him deeper with each delicious thrust, and she cried out in her pleasure.

Cate couldn't fight the orgasm that soon claimed her as she continued to cradle him inside. It lasted for so long she wondered for a moment if she could even carry on, but the wave eventually relinquished its hold of her, and she started to move again.

Sensing her fatigue, switched it so he was on top. He moved slowly while the aftershocks continued to reverberate intensely within her for a few moments, and then faster and harder as she opened up for him more. Cate could think of nothing but her angelic lover and welcomed the wonderfully intense connection they now shared. Having him inside of her was a welcome distraction from the guilty emotions that still threatened to creep in, and she let go of everything while Uriel pursued his high.

The powerful orgasms that Lucifer had while they made love did little to prepare her for the intense bursts that came forth as Uriel climaxed inside of her a while later, and she exploded along with him. She'd thought she knew what she was in for, but was she wrong? She had to cling onto him for dear life while the world around them burned with a bright white light, and their makeshift home crumbled to absolute ruins around them. The walls then magically rebuilt themselves following the earthquake-like burst that Uriel gave off, and Cate was left feeling woozy and full of light from his release.

***

The days passed quickly, and the pair barely left the bedroom. They only took breaks to make a quick bite of food, but more often than not, they just ended up making love somewhere else on their private island instead.

After months together, Uriel finally had to leave Cate alone to attend to some business in Heaven, and she decided to lie on the beach and soak up the sunshine. Her mind wandered, though, and she started to contemplate just how different things might be for her now. She knew she could never go back home after everything she'd shared with Uriel, and the love she'd so willingly given him. And yet, there was still such a strong part of her that missed her dark family, especially Lucifer. She knew that if he were to welcome her back with open arms, she would go to him without hesitation.

"This crazy love triangle is gonna be the death of me," she moaned to herself, and climbed up from the sun lounger to take a short walk along the water's edge. It was odd. She somehow felt like there was light power emanating from inside of her and could hardly sense the darkness she'd readily accepted so long before. It was as though Uriel had given her the chance to break away from the binds her master had placed on her, and the freedom to finally choose for herself. Free will, she supposed, but perhaps in its truest form at last.

She laid back down on the lounger and fell asleep in the warm sunshine but woke shortly afterwards thanks to Uriel's *expression* that was pouring into her from across the beach. He was so open with her, sending Cate his love, respect, and desire through the bond, and she had to smile.

Cate's desire for him only made Uriel want her more, and he happily gave every inch of himself to her, even though he knew she was cleverly trying to hide away her earlier thoughts of Lucifer. He'd take whatever he could get from his captivating prisoner and hoped he might find a way to turn her head fully in time.

Later, as they relaxed on the sofa together before a warm fire in the living room, Uriel decided to ask one more thing from his lover and tested the waters regarding a possible future together.

"Would you ever consider giving me a child?" he asked, and Cate stared up at him open-mouthed. She was unable to answer at first. A million reasons to say no were flooding through her head. It was far too much, too soon, and she still had a lot to figure out with this crazy love triangle she was in. She sat up and looked over at him—the gorgeous, God-like angel that'd somehow found his way into her heart. He had to know that he was still fighting an unspoken war between him and his fallen brother for her true love and affection and having a child would only complicate matters more. Cate was still torn, despite her insistence that she was happy there with Uriel. She was sure she couldn't answer definitively which powerful man she chose over the other, and hoped he'd never ask.

"No," she finally answered, but he knew anyway, having read her before she even opened her mouth. "Not yet anyway. At some point, we will have to leave this plane and go back to the real world. We need to figure out how the future will pan out for us, or if it even could. We haven't actually considered how Lucifer's going to react yet," she added, and her face dropped at the realisation. He would no doubt already be so incredibly angry with her for her betrayal with Uriel as it was, and Cate couldn't even begin to think of how awful it would be if she were to return having had Uriel's child.

The angel was furious at both her words and thoughts. He quickly stood from the sofa and lifted the wooden coffee table with one hand in his rage. Uriel threw it through the window and out onto the beach with no effort at all. The hole that it left behind was half the size of the wall itself, and then he walked over and stood staring out at the beach, his entire body shaking with anger. Within seconds, dark clouds filled the sky outside and lightning came crashing down on to the sand around them, shaking the house with the electric blasts.

Cate was terrified. She'd never seen Uriel angry before and, given his omnipotent power, knew she had to appease the situation, otherwise things could get a lot worse. Hesitantly rising from the sofa, she slowly walked up behind Uriel and placed her hands on his bare arms. His white-hot skin burned her palms, but she held on, and forced her feelings out to him via her thoughts.

Please, she silently begged him. *Please stop this. I chose you, but I cannot give you more, not yet, but maybe someday.*

After a few moments, the clouds started to retreat, and he stopped shaking. Turning to face Cate, Uriel grabbed her hands and kissed her palms, healing the burns on them instantly.

"I've just never been so impulsive before, Cate," he told her. "But with you, I want it all and I don't want to wait."

She smiled and was both flattered and grateful for his honesty. He looked down into her green eyes as he held her close and then tucked a loose, dark curl behind her ear before planting a soft kiss on her still trembling lips. "When you were more concerned with how Lucifer would react than you were about my feelings on the matter, it just made me crazy," he explained further. "I suppose you're right, though. I hadn't thought far ahead enough. The fact remains that we will have to face the outside world some time, so we'll just need to be ready for the retaliation when it comes."

He gave off nothing but love, understanding, and warmth now, and Cate was glad he'd calmed down. Seeing this powerful angel's tiny bit of wrath had made her sure she never wanted to see it, or anything stronger from him, ever again.

CHAPTER SEVENTEEN

"Would our child have to remain on Earth, like Jesus?" Cate pondered aloud a few days later as they relaxed together in a warm, soapy bath. Uriel had gone back to being his calm, wonderful self, and hadn't raised the subject again, but she hadn't been able to help contemplating how it would all work.

"Yes. The fact remains that you're still Lucifer's blood, and your offspring would bear his mark regardless of my, *contribution*, so to speak. Neither of you could ever be welcome in Heaven," he told her, and his explanation convinced Cate more that she wasn't ready to make such a commitment to him. She felt disappointed that she hadn't considered it earlier.

If she gave Uriel a child, they would both be stuck on Earth permanently. They wouldn't be welcome in Hell with her family any longer. She would be an outcast, and so would her angelic child. They wouldn't have their father around to help them grow up either and might even be persecuted by the humans who didn't understand or comprehend their existence. Add to that the undeniable probability that they'd be hunted by the dark beings her husband commanded at the same time. Cate couldn't think of a worse future for herself or her potential offspring.

As the dark thoughts washed over her, she then felt very defeated suddenly. Guilt and regret crept in more than ever since her time with Uriel had begun, and she wanted to cry.

He knew, of course, and tried in vain to distract her with his *expression*. Uriel held her closer as he sent his love and emotion to Cate through their link, but they both knew it wasn't enough. Uriel wanted nothing more than to make her happy, hoping to make her fall more in love with him, but there wasn't any more they could do while he still held her captive. She wanted more, but there was still this little niggle—a small doubt she simply couldn't shake. Cate knew for certain she wouldn't be able to clear her conscience until she was free to leave their wonderful prison, take a breath, and decide for herself what she wanted for her future.

Uriel wasn't ready to give her the freedom yet though, despite her moment of clarity on the subject. The world could just stop turning, and things could just stay as they were for now. He would deal with the real issues in time, just not yet.

Before long though, Uriel had to start leaving more often to attend to his angelic business. After they'd been in their astral plane for a few months, he knew he'd taken liberties with his time away from his charges, and reluctantly gave Cate some alone time here and there while he saw to his responsibilities. She enjoyed the quiet and usually spent the time sat basking in the warm sun. The only thing she hated about being alone was the dark thoughts that flooded her mind uncontrollably in his absence. It was as though her privacy brought with it a tidal wave of forbidden thought and emotion from deep within her, and Cate knew it was everything she'd forced aside when she was in Uriel's lucent presence. He'd promised to stay out of her head for the time being, but she'd also figured out how to guard her thoughts a little more wisely following his outburst. She'd started to use some of the diversionary tactics she'd used on Lucifer years before, focussing only on the important details while pushing her more risky thoughts aside to deal with later. As far as she could tell, it seemed to be working.

One afternoon, Cate decided to go for a swim in the crystal clear waters that surrounded their island. She kicked off her sandals and sarong and then waded into the shallow pool near her usual spot on the white wooden lounger. The warm water was lovely, and she immediately swam out into the depths. For some reason, she then decided to keep going out as far as she could, and part of her wondered if she might magically return to the beach if she kept on. She picked a faraway star and followed her line in the horizon, out of curiosity more than anything else, and didn't stop for a long time. When Cate looked back after taking lots of long strides through the waves, the island was far away in the distance. Turning back towards the horizon, there seemed to be an endless expanse of water still stretched out ahead of her, and she guessed her assumptions that she'd go full circle had been incorrect.

She pushed on through the waves regardless, but then not long later, Cate felt her foot push on a stone or some kind of rough floor deep beneath the water's surface. The ocean somehow started to get shallower as she continued, even though her eyes told her it still went on for miles. It was just an illusion, though, and she soon started to climb the odd ridge. The water got shallower until eventually just her ankles remained submerged.

"I'd stop right there if I were you," came a voice from behind her. Cate turned around to find Angelica's smug face as she walked slowly on the water's surface towards her. "You'll drop off the edge, and more than likely fall to your death. My master wouldn't be very happy with me if I let that happen now, would he?" she asked rhetorically, with an unimpressed wave of her hand.

"It'd be worth it knowing just how much trouble you'd be in for letting me fall, witch," Cate couldn't help but snap back. Angelica simply smirked, but didn't advance further, her eyes boring into Cate's as she contemplated her next move.

"If you'll please follow me," Angelica ushered Cate back in the direction of the island but couldn't hide the tiny bit of fear that flashed across her eyes. She was obviously afraid that their captive might try to do something foolish.

Cate wondered why the witch was so scared of her master, but knew she would never answer her, even if she asked the question aloud. She did as she'd been asked, though, and silently glided back through the water as her guard wandered impatiently along beside her on the water's surface.

When they arrived back on the beach, Angelica turned to leave, but hesitated for a moment. "Quit fucking around, Cate," she then said, her voice low and her eyes wide. "He always gets his way, so you'd do better to just give in now and save yourself the torment," she said, her eyes sad. It seemed as though the usually so playful witch was remembering something she shouldn't be, and the fear in Angelica's eyes scared her.

Cate froze, completely taken aback, and she couldn't respond right away. Angelica seemed to sense her foreboding and teleported away before she could find her voice again.

"Holy shit," Cate then muttered to herself, it suddenly dawning on her just how deep in it she really might be.

Uriel didn't come back to their astral plane until the next day, and by then Cate had made sure to file the previous day's events with Angelica to the very back of her mind in case he decided to take a peek. She greeted him with a smile and a kiss, while making coffee and openly fantasising about making love with him. Cate found it was an effective distraction and stopped him from interrogating her on what she'd done in his absence.

"Everything okay?" she asked, knowing he wouldn't give her any information on the goings on in Heaven, but she had to ask, hoping to find something to talk about with him. There really wasn't much left for them to discuss any more. She'd made her feelings clear about their future, and they both knew that her life there really was just a comfortable imprisonment. Nothing would change until she was free to choose her own path.

"Of course," Uriel replied, accepting the hot drink with a warm smile. Cate peered up at him and was still taken aback by his beautiful features. His hair was almost black, not unlike her own, but his incredible blue eyes still took her breath away. He wore a white shirt and jeans that framed his toned body wonderfully. It was a look she'd somehow gotten so used to now. Even her own white wardrobe was no longer quite so alien to her anymore, and she would pick out her clothes for each day without even a grumble at the white fabrics. In many ways, she felt she'd lost herself to him. But, then again, Cate wasn't sure she truly missed the woman she'd been before arriving on the astral plane either. She wondered if there even was a real person beneath all the façades, or whether she was simply another version of what once had been moulded to Lucifer's preference. No part of her life had ever been her own choice. Not once that she could ever remember.

***

As time went by at a snail's pace, Uriel was called away many more times. When she was alone, Cate often ended up thinking about the day she'd swam to the edge of their fake world. The solace gave her many opportunities to let her mind wander, and she soon found herself thinking of the various escape possibilities. It wasn't much longer before she began regularly imagining herself swimming out to the edge again. She'd envision herself fighting with Angelica before throwing herself over the edge of the plane and falling to Earth—and to her freedom. Yes, she could die in the process, but at some point wasn't that a better alternative than remaining hostage, even if her captor wasn't bad company at all?

If she were truly honest, this place was boring her, and her feelings for Uriel had started to wane. She missed her old life and began to contemplate carrying out those drastic measures if that was what it took to get back to her friends and family. More than four years had passed since she was bought to Uriel's island, and although her time there hadn't been terrible, Cate couldn't stop herself from feeling incredibly homesick.

She was also truly ashamed of herself and her actions and was unafraid of the potentially fatal consequences that falling to Earth might pose. Cate wondered if perhaps she was just bored and welcomed a change to this mundane existence, despite the dramatic and potentially life-threatening method. If and when she eventually found her way to Earth or Hell, she'd have a lot of explaining to do to her husband and could wait for that day to come around.

Weeks later, Cate awoke from another dreamless sleep to find a note beside the bed telling her that Uriel had gone up to Heaven for business again. She stretched, and started to climb up out of the bed, but was forced back down onto the white pillow as a bright wave of light slammed hard into her bare chest. She collected herself, but quickly realised that she couldn't move. A mysterious force trapped her, and Cate couldn't see or fight against it.

A few seconds later, Dylan appeared in the doorway to her room. She stood there, watching Cate intensely, but didn't say a word. There was no warmth in her face as she scowled down at her, but there had to be a reason she'd come, and Cate hoped she was there to help rather than to hurt her. She looked up into Dylan's cold hazel eyes as she approached, hoping for some answers, but the witch remained stoic. She didn't say a word until she reached Cate's side.

"Hello, old friend," Dylan said as she sat down on the edge of the bed, and there was no softness to her tone. She looked her same beautiful old self, but Cate could see that she was wrestling with herself internally. Dylan seemed undecided on how she intended to deal with the woman who was once her best friend. The woman who had no doubt broken her heart the day she'd stood by and let her be tortured.

"Hi," was all Cate could think to respond, and her voice faltered as she took in the sight of her damaged friend. They hadn't seen each other in such a long time, and their last encounter had been truly awful. The memory of it made her want to reach out and hug her, but Cate could see the hurt and anger behind Dylan's eyes even now and knew it wouldn't be welcome. She deeply regretted the treatment her friend had suffered at the hands of her husband's vengeful ire but knew there was nothing she could do to take it back. What was done was done, and it was just another burden she would have to bear for all eternity.

There was an awkward silence as they took each other in. "What're you doing here?" Cate eventually asked her, and she kept the tone of her voice soft and warm towards her old friend. Dylan didn't respond, but her eyes seemed to flash brightly for a moment, as though she'd made up her mind about something at last, and she stood. The witch's mouth then started to move over strange, whispered words, and she recited a spell that Cate couldn't hear. Her arms were still pinned to her sides, and her body felt as though it was being pushed harder into the mattress as Dylan spoke the incantation.

"Are you ready to die?" she finally asked after a few moments, and her voice was calm and steady as she reached a hand around her back and pulled something from the pocket of her blue jeans. She then raised a huge, golden dagger over Cate's chest and grinned, as though excited to finally have her revenge. Dylan held the blade high over her frozen body as she continued reciting the spell. Cate wanted to fight back, but she couldn't move. She was paralysed by both her own fear and by Dylan's powerful incantation and could do nothing but watch.

"No!" she screamed, but the witch ignored her. Dylan leaned over and began lowering the dagger, and Cate screwed her eyes shut. She waited for the pain to come, for the dagger to silence her final heartbeat, and then for her transition from life to death to begin. Oddly, she felt like she deserved it, and just hoped it'd be over quick.

The golden tip penetrated not only her body but her soul, too, as Dylan pushed the blade into her chest. She continued to whisper her spell repeatedly as she pushed the dagger deeper and deeper into Cate's body, but she didn't utter any kind of farewell to her old friend. Cate cried out and tried to speak. She even tried begging Dylan to stop. It was no use though. The dagger's sharp blade eventually went right through her heart, and she lost consciousness in seconds.

CHAPTER EIGHTEEN

"There's still no news of her, your majesty. They have the Dark Queen well hidden," Alma told Satan. She was shaking in fear as she said the regretful words again and kept her eyes on her King's feet and her thoughts full of apology. Despite her very best efforts and exhaustive searching, she still couldn't find even a single trace of Cate. They were all confused by the lack of ransom or other such stipulations by the angels but knew full well who was holding her captive.

Lucifer said nothing in response to her pointless update and stood from the desk where he'd been sat when Alma had entered. She knew without him saying so that she was dismissed and backed away slowly and made her way out of the door. The huge wooden desk then narrowly missed her small frame as it was sent flying past her in his rage and went crashing through the wall to her right.

"You mean, *he* has her well-hidden," Lucifer said to himself rather than to his high priestess. The rage seeped out of him and into the walls of his home, and he knew everyone in the castle could sense it. The mood in Hell was more than dire. It was disastrous. He didn't care enough to turn things back around, though, and couldn't concentrate on anything long enough to try. His worry for his wife and the thoughts of what Uriel must be doing to her haunted the living nightmare he was in, and he was consumed by his hatred for everyone and everything.

Lucifer was alone and empty, but he craved no companionship at all. He'd even sent Devin and Serena to Earth to live in one of their secure mansions nestled in the Yorkshire countryside rather than in one of his city penthouses. There they would be safe and secluded, and out of his sight for a while. He simply couldn't bear to look at them. Their presence constantly made him think of Cate, and he found himself resenting the pair for not being the ones Uriel had chosen to kidnap.

It'd been years since she'd been taken, and he'd heard nothing from them ever since. Lucifer couldn't sense her at all. Their connection now blocked, or perhaps broken somehow—he didn't know for sure. There'd been no demands, no declaration of war. There was simply…nothing.

Lucifer had ordered the kidnap of any white witch that his dark minions could find, but they hadn't come across a single one since she'd been taken. Alma had tried to convince Lucifer that the reason must be because the High Council of Angels would need all their witches' power combined to keep Cate prisoner. She was far too powerful for just a few witches to have taken her captive, and so their disappearance from Earth had to mean she was okay. He hoped she was right, and that Cate was just being held somewhere out of his reach. All that mattered in the long run was that she was safe and, most importantly, alive.

Even contemplating an existence without her drove Lucifer to madness, rage, and thoughts of annihilation and all-out massacre. Should the worst ever happen to her, he knew that his need for vengeance would lead him to Heaven's doorstep, even if it meant sacrificing everything, including his own existence, in the process. He'd meant every word of his dark wedding vows and would not stop until he found her again.

Lucifer's insatiable adoration for Cate never waned in all the time she'd gone, and he never even considered taking another lover. In fact, their forced period of separation told him more than he'd ever needed to know about his self and their relationship. If he'd ever had any doubts as to the extent of his love for her, he knew they were futile after this absence. Nothing mattered to him more than she, and he'd do whatever it took to have her home with him again.

***

Waves lapped quietly on the shore not too far away, while seagulls squawked, and the wind rustled through the trees. Cate started to rouse, wondering where Uriel was and why she felt so strange. For some reason, she was utterly exhausted. She tried to open her eyes, but they didn't want to work just yet, so she just lay there and listened for a few minutes to the familiar sounds of her island paradise.

"Oh good, you're awake," Dylan's voice bought her screeching back into full consciousness, and the memory of the witch's spell and her piercing dagger came rushing back to Cate's mind. Her eyes fluttered open, and she tried to sit up, but was far too weak. Her mind was racing, and her head was fuzzy, but her body was even worse. She felt terrible, worse than she'd ever felt before—even following Lucifer's strong persuasive tactics all those years earlier. Dylan laid her hands on Cate's shoulders, urging her to lie back down on the bed, and she begrudgingly did as she was silently told.

"Am I dead?" she asked.

"No," Dylan replied, with a cold edge to her voice that Cate knew she deserved. "I had to take you near to death to free you, though. It was the only way. I knew I'd need to take drastic measures to try and get you out of there, but it worked, so that's a bonus," she told her with a shrug. Dylan spoke as though she hadn't been sure her spell would've worked when she'd cast it. Like she'd chosen to blindly stab her old friend through the heart with only the vague hope she'd be successful. Cate shuddered at the thought, but then forced herself to focus her eyes on Dylan's soft face at last. She didn't look any older than when she'd last seen her, but there was a pain behind her hazel eyes that was never there when she'd known her before. It seemed a combination of weariness and a defeated sadness that Dylan just couldn't quite hide.

"Why did you do it? Why bother saving me?" Cate asked her, looking up at her from the bed. "Why care after everything I put you through?"

"Well, for one, *you* didn't put me through anything, per se. It was your dick head of a master—I mean husband—who ordered it. You were simply blinded by his affection for you. Oh, and by the way, I think you two being together is very wrong, you know?" she added, chastising her. The rant made her sound a little bit more like her old self, and Dylan giving Cate a speech about right and wrong was exactly like old times. She smiled to herself but kept quiet so Dylan could finish getting things off her chest.

Cate knew she owed her much more than just the chance to vent a little, but it seemed like a good way to start. "I truly did love you once, Cate," Dylan continued solemnly. She stared down into her face intently, and her features softened as her emotions finally came to the surface. "I don't think you ever really realised just how much. I wanted to keep you safe, to take you where the dark witches couldn't find you, and do you know what *he* told me?" Dylan asked, raising her eyes to the sky, clearly implying Uriel. "He told me no. He said you were an abomination who could never be trusted. He said that a partnership of light and dark would bring about nothing but chaos and bedlam to the Council's perfect world," Dylan told her with a bitter edge to her voice she didn't even attempt to disguise. "But, when he decided he wanted you, all those things were somehow irrelevant. He had to have you, no matter the cost. He's left the Earth unguarded by white witches for years. Subsequently, the darkness has flowed freely, and the sins soon started pouring in. He didn't care when he chose fucking you over answering the prayers and pleas of his loyal servants, whose friends and families became easy pickings for the demon's who'd been left to roam here on Earth. Innocent people suddenly started selling their souls for fame and fortune, with no-one to stop them, to help them see the righteous path," she seethed, a forlorn expression on her face.

"Dylan, I…" Cate knew there was nothing she could say, so let her voice tail off. The witch didn't seem to even hear her anyway and carried on with her rant.

"Uriel then called us to him and said that he expected us all to accept you as his lover. Just like that. Because he said so. Talk about an unholy partnership!" Dylan added. She then took a deep breath and calmed herself for a few seconds while Cate lay still on the bed. She tried to take in everything that she'd just heard her friend fume about, but the overload was exhausting her even more. After a few minutes, she decided to change the subject. Her pounding headache was making it hard to take in much more of the serious talk, despite her being glad to help Dylan and her need to offload.

"Where are we now?" Cate asked, although she was quite sure she already knew.

"Earth," Dylan replied. "But don't worry, he can't find you here. The spell I cast has hidden you from both him and all the other white witches under the Council's command. I've renounced them, so he cannot use me to find you either," she then added.

Cate gasped, but Dylan just shrugged her shoulders, looking downcast and defeated. "You don't go through everything I have and keep believing— keep trusting in just the good. I think I've honestly seen much more darkness than light in my time, and both sides are just as terrible as each other. I guess I realised that I'd rather be on whatever side you're on than blindly believing for the sake of it. I think it's safe to say I've never gotten over losing you."

Dylan then got up and busied herself with sorting out some bags of clothing she must've bought while Cate was out of it. She was grateful for her honesty and sensed that Dylan had said all she wanted to for now, so she didn't bother asking for more information. It could wait until later.

They spent the rest of the day reconnecting, and Cate was glad to find that Dylan wasn't holding too much of a grudge with her. They reminisced and talked openly about what'd happened since the night of Cate's coming of age reunion with Lucifer, and why things had ended up the way they had. The pair then talked about many things but didn't go into too greater detail about Dylan's torture. The scars still seemed too fresh for either of them to bear reopening those awful floodgates.

Instead, Dylan told Cate how she'd been misinformed by Angelica that Lucifer was keeping her in Hell by force, and that he was torturing her into submission. She said she couldn't bear the thought of him hurting her, so had acted—rashly, yes, but she hadn't been able to help it. Cate adored her for trying so hard to keep her safe and knew she'd never find another friend like Dylan in the entire world. Even after their time apart, and the fact that she had known their relationship was never going to be allowed to go any further, she'd always felt a deep void since losing her that night in the field. Cate knew she truly loved her in return, and always would. She was glad that Dylan still felt that way, and she finally opened up about what Lucifer had then gone on to do. Angelica had almost been right, just not at the right time.

"You're the first person I've talked to about it…"

"How can you love him?" Dylan asked her when she'd finished explaining what'd happened and was clearly disgusted by Cate's disturbing admissions.

"Don't, Dylan. Please," Cate answered, unable to bear an interrogation from her. "He's my home, my absolute everything. Despite the bumps in the road, we're meant to be. After everything I've endured, I still know that for sure. I couldn't stand it if you didn't accept us."

"I do, and I'll accept whatever makes you happy, Cate. That's all I want for you," Dylan told her, smiling warmly, and the Dark Queen grabbed her best friend and hugged her tight.

***

Later that night, after scoffing Chinese food and watching television in the sanctity of their hotel room, the pair finally settled down to get some much needed rest. Dylan looked over and watched Cate as she began to lull and drift off to sleep, and she knew she'd done the right thing. Despite the bad blemishes in their history, she was happy to have her back in her life, even if it meant her having to pledge her allegiance to the dark underworld in order to do so. She too drifted off after a few minutes, but her dreams were fretful and scattered despite her exhausted body. She had worries and fears for the future that seemed to be affecting her more than she'd realised, and knew she needed a definite plan.

The next morning over pancakes and fresh fruit, courtesy of room service, Dylan was back to being her playful and fun self again and wondered aloud about the current state of Cate's love-life.

"Maybe there's something about you that people cannot help but fall in love with? Everyone that knows you loves you in one way or another. Have you ever noticed that?" she asked, popping a strawberry into her mouth. "Whether they want to fuck, marry, protect, or even just be your closest friend. Everyone is drawn to you in some way. Most of the time they cannot understand it themselves," she mused, looking to Cate for her input, but all she could do was blush and shake her head.

"Surely not?" she finally answered a few moments later, but also had to wonder if Dylan might be right. What if it was all just part of some strange power she'd not yet mastered? Or some all-consuming evil influence that drew others to her? Was all her tumultuous love life her fault because of a power she'd inherited, yet even Lucifer had no idea of? Serena didn't have this problem, so why her?

As Cate sat and wondered about all these terrible possibilities her thoughts eventually settled on her husband. In all honesty, she was scared to face him, and hated the reality that she'd have to tell him of all the things she'd let Uriel do to her up on that astral plane. Now that she was away from that place, and the powerful angel, she could think so much more clearly. Cate knew for sure that she never truly loved him but had been coerced into submission by him and his powerful prowess. She hated the thought that she'd succumbed to such intimidation again, but in a different form of it this time.

Cate knew she would have to be honest with Lucifer when she saw him again. There was nothing else she could do. She was truly disgusted with herself for giving in to Uriel's advances so readily, allowing herself to be possessed by him, and giving him the *yes* so quickly. There was even a part of her that didn't want to go home just yet. She wanted to hide away for a little while, to give herself time to think about how she might explain these things to her husband, and how she might go about begging him for his forgiveness for her forced betrayal. Despite her best intentions, Cate always seemed to end up hurting either herself or those she loved, and she hated it. *Perhaps that's just another one of my fucked-up powers, too?* she contemplated, but couldn't bear to decide on an answer to her inner musings.

After a couple of days resting at the hotel, Cate felt much better. Although still not remotely at full strength, she was finally ready to get up and face the world. Things with Lucifer would be tough, but she knew she had to tackle the truth head-on. No more stalling.

She and Dylan had agreed on a plan during their recuperation time and had decided to wait a few days until she was stronger and then find a Satanic church. Once there, they intended to gain entry and travel together to Hell using the dark witches' help. Cate would then—when she was hopefully welcomed back, arms wide open—speak for Dylan and ask Lucifer to allow her safe passage to Hell. She would also request that she be able to join his ranks as a dark witch. She owed Dylan far more than a place in Alma's coven, but it was a decent place to start.

There was only one other complication. For some reason, Cate hadn't regained any of her powers at all since they'd returned to Earth. She couldn't teleport, and she couldn't sense or summon the witches or demons. There was no beacon drawing her to her husband yet either, and it made her worry that Uriel had somehow kept her powers locked away at his command. Without them, she feared she might not be strong enough to return home, but knew she had to try.

Even Dylan thought it was strange, but the pair both put it down to either the spell she'd cast, or perhaps the on-going healing process Cate might be going through. It wasn't until they tried walking over the threshold to the church later that day that it all became clearer.

Dylan stepped over the invisible line that surrounded the dark church without any resistance, and that act alone made clear her lack of allegiance to the High Council of Angels. Cate took a deep breath and then lifted her right foot, trying to follow her friend over the threshold. There was a little push back at first. It was just a small amount of resistance she barely even registered as she pushed on through, but it was mere seconds more before a strange sensation then flowed through her. Suddenly, as though a brick wall had slammed into her chest, Cate was sent flying backwards, and she landed hard on the concrete floor behind her.

"What the?" she started to ask, but Dylan came running back over and pulled her away from the church in a panic. She hurried Cate along, and both ran as fast as they could without stopping until they were well clear of the hallowed ground.

CHAPTER NINETEEN

Huffing and puffing, the pair slumped in a shop doorway to catch their breaths. Cate was shocked, and so completely baffled, she couldn't speak. She looked to Dylan for answers, finding only another perplexed face looking back at her.

"Why couldn't you cross into the church's inner circle, Cate?" the witch finally wondered aloud, and was clearly shocked and worried by the rejection of the Dark Queen from her own church as well.

"I don't bloody know. I was hoping you might have an idea!" Cate cried in response, her green eyes wide with worry. "Why did we run?"

"We don't know what we're dealing with here," Dylan told her. "What if the dark witches couldn't see you, perhaps my spell hid you from them, too? They might have only seen me wandering up like I belonged there and would've kidnapped me and zapped me to your Dark King in less than a second. You would've been left there, stranded, and with no idea how to get home, while I would be tortured for all eternity!"

Cate nodded, understanding what Dylan was trying to get at. They both quickly agreed that they needed to stick together and figure this out. Eventually, they'd try again, but for now, it seemed as though Cate was stuck on Earth. She was, however, a little relieved that she could put off the family reunion for a while longer.

There was only one problem with that. Bar the witch who had pledged allegiance to her, Cate was completely unprotected from both sides.

Dylan insisted they planned to constantly move around, only ever staying in one place for a few nights at a time. They would have to be careful which magic Dylan performed, as it would leave a small trace of them that the witches, whether light or dark, could use to follow them if they picked up on it.

The pair travelled around for a while, staying in hotels for a few nights at a time, but they never settled in longer in fear of being followed. After just a few months, Cate was exhausted. She still hadn't gotten her powers back, and the stress was taking its toll on her.

"I can't do this anymore, Dylan," she told her friend after they'd hungrily tucked into some cheeseburgers and chips. They were poor, dirty, and beyond exhausted, and Cate knew she had to do whatever it took to get back home.

"I'm going to try to get into the penthouse. Maybe Devin is there, or at least Belias?" she wondered, sipping on her sweet tea and enjoying the warmth from it as it spread throughout her body. "The moon is full tonight as well, so you never know," she added, tailing off thoughtfully.

"Maybe," Dylan replied, understanding immediately what Cate was hoping to find. "Okay, but let me come in with you," she added, stuffing her mouth with salty fries. Her lips were covered in mayonnaise, where she'd devoured her dinner so hungrily, and Cate threw her a napkin from across the table.

"Absolutely not," she replied, shaking her head. "If I find anyone there, I'll come and get you before going home. I promise." She couldn't risk Dylan's capture, even though they'd both wondered if it might be one of the only ways to get their attention. If any of the dark beings caught Dylan, she would undoubtedly be taken to Hell. Lucifer would read her mind, and he'd find out the truth at last. Dylan might have to take a beating first but had insisted it'd be worth it to help ensure they both got there in one piece. "Whoever it is might decide against chit-chat and kill you on sight. Did you ever think of that?" Cate asked her friend, who shook her head. "I'd never be able to forgive myself and would rather we live on the streets than me lose you, Dylan. You're my best friend and I would die before I let anyone hurt you ever again," she promised, and they both knew she meant every word.

They took the train that evening to the penthouse and gazed up at the gloomy building for a moment before Cate went inside, alone. Dylan agreed to wait in the tube station for her, but Cate knew she would be clock-watching the entire time she was inside.

"You've got twenty minutes," Dylan told her, tapping her black wristwatch with her index finger. "And then I'm coming in to get you. I don't care who's there."

"Okay," Cate replied with a warm smile. She pulled Dylan into a tight hug and then turned on her heel and headed off towards the huge building. A human man opened up the glass door for her on his way out, and Cate thanked him before heading inside. She was incredibly aware of the lack of resistance she felt as she entered the building, indicating that there was either no protective threshold or that she had managed to pass over the invisible line without being rejected this time.

The lobby was empty, which Cate wasn't sure was a good sign, but she wandered over to the lift and pressed the call button while her eyes darted around, looking for any sign of life. Moments later, she was making her way skywards. She felt both impatient and scared of what might be there to greet her when she arrived at the top-floor apartment she'd once lived in with Devin. Many great memories came back to her as she ascended, though. It felt like such a long time since she'd lived there, but it was also as if it were only yesterday that they'd be back and forth, holding parties and running Black Rose Industries with Devin while living their fake married lives together.

After a few minutes, Cate arrived at the dark hallway that led to the main door to the penthouse flat, and she flicked on the light switch. It was cold in there, and she noticed that no fresh flowers adorned the antique unit beside the doorway. She could hear nothing but silence, broken only by her own footsteps as she walked towards the huge, dark wooden doors. Cate pressed her index finger down onto the bell in anticipation, before waiting for a few seconds and then pressing it again, just in case.

No answer came, despite her hopes, and the realisation quickly dawned on her that the flat must currently be empty. No humans, witches, or demons were there to greet her, and most importantly—no Lucifer.

Cate burst into tears and fell to her feet, curling herself into a tight ball on the floor while she wept. She felt so desperate, so lost, and she sobbed even harder as the silence of the hallway enveloped her further. Uncontrollable tears fell onto her knees as she hugged them, and her heart broke.

Strong arms wrapped around her a little while later, after Dylan ran over to her from the elevator's open door. She didn't say anything; she simply held Cate tight and cradled her friend as she fell apart.

"It's as if God himself is trying to keep me out, as if he's trying to keep me away from him?" Cate cried between sobs and knew her despair and desperation was clear in her tone.

"I thought you didn't believe in him?" Dylan asked with a small laugh. She'd always believed in the higher powers of both good and evil that drove both sides, and had told Cate her theories many times, but her ideas were always met with a blank stare and a shrug. It was only now that Cate could fathom the idea of it all, and she had to wonder if that strange divine intervention was now forcing her into exile for some reason.

"Perhaps I'm coming around to the idea of a higher power," she eventually admitted, looking over at Dylan with a forced smile at last. She then nodded, and the pair stood and got back in the lift, going down to the empty lobby before heading back out to the street.

On the train out of the city the next day, they decided it was time to stop searching for answers. They both needed a break, and it'd only be until they could figure out what was going on, or until the universe made its next move. Cate and Dylan both agreed that they'd have to find a quiet little town where they could settle in for a while and decide how they might plan their next move.

"The use of magic will have to stop completely," Cate said, and Dylan nodded in agreement.

"Absolutely. It's the only way we can be sure there's no way for any of the witches to track us," she replied. They both knew it'd be hard, but were tired of the running, so it was worth it.

They stopped off on their way out of London, deciding to consult an aura reader as their last attempt at figuring out what was going on with Cate and her powers. Dylan had searched for a spiritual reader using her own divining power, and they decided to give one last avenue a try before they then disappeared for good, or at least for as long as it took for Cate to get her powers back. When they reached Paddington station, Dylan worked her last bit of magic on a young guy behind the desk of a nearby car rental agency, convincing him to let her take a hire car away for free. She signed the forms using a fake name and signature and then produced a couple of crumpled up receipts from her pocket that she magically manipulated him to believe were her identification and credit card.

The pair then sped off and programmed the satellite navigation system to take them to the aura reader's address just outside the city. When they arrived at the small house, the two of them were welcomed into the reader's home by his wife, a kind lady who offered them tea and a plate of delicately decorated cupcakes. Dylan scoffed some down, while Cate just nervously took a few sips of tea as she sat back in the large, throw-lined sofa.

The house was cluttered. Bookshelves lined every wall of the living room with hardbacks detailing the use of gemstones and horoscopes, along with incense burners and scented candles. The woman was dressed in a floating, paisley printed dress and leather sandals, and she gave off a faint scent of lavender when she passed close to Cate. She assumed the woman must prefer a few drops of flower's essence on her clothes rather than her wearing actual perfume, and she liked the smell—it reminded her of Ella.

When she was ushered into the back room, Cate didn't even need to speak. The grey-haired man waved his hand for her to sit with him at the crystal covered table, but then stared at her for a moment before he spoke. What he said immediately took her breath away.

"You are full of light, my dear. Many, many congratulations!" he told her excitedly. "I've never met anyone with such a strong light power inside of them. It's almost as if God himself filled you up with the most wonderful present and power to ward off evil," he cried, raising his hands to the sky with a triumphant joy she could not even begin to share. Cate found herself simply staring open-mouthed at the aura reader once he'd spoken the glaring truth, unable to say a word in response. She mentally kicked herself for not having realised it sooner, though.

"Of course!" Dylan shouted out from the other room before jumping up and storming into the back. She quickly handed the man some cash and dragged Cate away. "How did we not figure this out before? You're full of light, Cate. Get it?" she almost screamed at her as they climbed back into their rental car and sped off.

"Yuk," Cate replied, but nodded. "Okay, so I'm full of light, no darkness. There's our answer. So now what?" she asked, not able to hide her petulant attitude.

"We wait, I expect," Dylan offered. "Eeeew, I suppose you're kind of, *infected* with light then," she added, laughing even harder when Cate slapped her on the shoulder in response.

They then headed off towards the motorway in search of somewhere to call home for as long as it took for Cate to be cured of her lightness, however long that might be.

CHAPTER TWENTY

Cate and Dylan decided to spend a maximum of three years in any one place, and for the next six years, they did just that. They'd get set up, find themselves somewhere to live and odd jobs, while assuming different identities each time—just to be safe. They managed far better than they'd first thought and kept to themselves while staying under the radar. They also spent time searching for any ways in which they might try and contact Cate's infernal family but missed out at every turn.

Meanwhile, the rekindled friends grew closer over the years. They confided everything in one another, and Cate knew she would have Dylan by her side forevermore. Their friendship had somehow survived their horrific ordeals as well as the tests of time, and she had every hope they would continue working through the hardships side-by-side.

After their third move, Cate really missed home. She'd had enough of being stranded on Earth and was ready to face the music back in Hell. She still had no powers and living a fully human life was hard without them. Dylan still wasn't using her magic for fear of the watchful eyes and the keen senses of her old coven, and she would complain daily about having to carry out their mundane chores. Neither of them aged, strangely, which meant that they would've had to keep on moving anyway, but as they settled into their third new home, Cate felt lost.

Choosing a new town had been simple, and Dylan assured her that the ley lines of England would help keep the pair hidden, so they'd followed the line westwards from the capital. The ancient power reportedly interfered with the witches' magic, both light and dark, and would help keep their senses scrambled should any come close enough in search of either Cate or the absconded witch.

Regardless of the hardships, Dylan was glad she had this time to be with Cate. They really were best friends again and being by her side made her happier than she'd been in years. Helping and protecting the Dark Queen gave her a profound purpose, and she knew she'd much prefer a lifetime in her service than to ever go back under Uriel's command. They accepted each other, warts and all, and Dylan considered them to be a remarkable team. There was nothing sexual about their relationship this time either, and she was fine with that. As long as she was in Cate's life, she was happy.

Cate let her guilt overpower her desires and didn't take any lovers at all during their exile. She remained abstinent, while Dylan frolicked with many a cute guy or hot girl she found along their travels—enough to make up for both of them. She was enjoying her preparation to becoming a dark witch and had really come into her own since allowing that side of herself to flourish. Dylan had always had a fun and carefree nature and being back to her old self took her mind off the big issues she'd run from for so long. Being with Cate again brought back many memories from their days as friends, both good and bad. She often thought back to the years she'd spent being the doting best friend, all at the behest of her angelic master, but they were an amazing few years.

She'd gone willingly to the school, where plans had been made and their ages altered to match that of the devil's so-called evil heiress. Angelica was in charge, and her dominance over the rest of them was clear and unyielding. She commanded her coven with an iron fist, and Dylan had always struggled to get on with her. She'd decided to go against her orders the day she'd gone to the girls' toilets and met Cate, though. Dylan had purposely gone there to lie in wait and was in prime position for when she came in to hide from P.E class.

It wasn't long before she'd heard her silently enter and hide away in a cubicle, and within minutes, Dylan had drawn Cate into a conversation about how much she hated long distance running, making her giggle and agree wholeheartedly. She'd known at that moment that they were going to be great friends and hadn't regretted defying her high priestess.

They now knew almost everything about one another, but for some reason she still had secrets she hadn't confided in her yet. Dylan hadn't told Cate about her true family. In their many long and intense conversations about the past, she'd kept quiet, and often wondered why she'd chosen to keep the truth to herself. It was common knowledge among their kind that witches could be either created or they could be born to witch and warlock parents—like Dylan. Her mother had been the high priestess of all the white witches hundreds of years before, and she had married the chief white warlock. The powerful couple had four children, two of whom still served their angelic master's in their white covens, and one who'd died when Dylan had been four years old.

She was the youngest of the family, and the only daughter. Her eldest brother, Gabe, had joined their father's coven at only fifteen years old. He'd responded to calls for help following a demonic attack one night but had gotten home too late. Gabe had found their father curled up and alone in his bed after having been poisoned by the demon Asmodeus during a battle. He'd then died in Gabe's arms just minutes later, and the loss of their father had caused vengeful desires to well up inside her brother like he'd never felt before. Gabe had disappeared that same night, and for over a year, neither Dylan nor the rest of her family knew what'd become of him. That was, until his broken, dead body was left at their family's doorstep one crisp winter morning.

Her mother had then fallen into despair. It was a kind of depression none of her kind had ever seen before in such a strong white witch, and it overwhelmed her usually so strong prowess. Darkness had then crept into her every pore; changing and affecting her in ways she didn't even know herself until it was too late. Dylan had been told years later by her brother Mike that one night when the full moon rose in the sky, their mother had felt the darkness summon her from deep within and had gone straight to the Satanic church. She'd reportedly crossed the invisible threshold with no resistance and was then taken to Hell. She was brought before Satan to be tried, where she'd begged the Dark Prince to take her life, but he was not so merciful as to grant her the much desired peace.

Lucifer had reportedly looked down upon the broken spirited witch as she knelt before him and read her thoughts with intrigue. He'd sensed the power and strength she possessed within and had coveted it. He knew that if she could be fully turned, her power would be infallible—a dark force no white witch would ever be strong enough to thwart. Lucifer had seduced her that night, turning her anger, pain, and hate into a new and disturbing sense of love and loyalty to her evil master.

From that day on, she'd been his to command, and had then pledged her allegiance to him for all eternity. Her mother, Alma, was then promoted to high priestess of the royal dark coven, and Dylan hadn't seen her since, even when she herself had been tortured and beaten at the hands of Satan's legion of demonic soldiers. She had no idea what'd become of her, or if she'd ever see her again, but she hoped she might one day at least rekindle some kind of relationship with the mother who'd been drawn from the light in much the same way as Dylan had. She too had been seduced, but had turned away from her angelic master willingly, and knew she'd never return to him.

***

Cate and Dylan had been living in a small town called Avebury just a few miles from the infamous Stonehenge for a little over two years, when Cate finally felt things start to change for her. She had assumed the identity of Dana Williams, and Dylan was known there as her big sister, Nina.

Cate still looked every inch the twenty-year-old, fresh-faced young woman, despite her now being close to one hundred years old in official terms, and Dylan looked to be in her early twenties even though she was double Cate's age.

Just like when she was younger, Cate had taken a job working at the village pub over the last couple of years, and she enjoyed the laughs and jokes she'd often have with the patrons, no matter whether they were there to drink down their problems or to celebrate and have fun. Cate even found some of the men quite charming as they drooled over her and kept her tips generous, but she wasn't interested in any of them, of course. Her heart still yearned for Lucifer, even after all their time apart, and she knew now that she was ready to see him again. Regardless of how awkward or scary it might be at first, she was sure they'd find their way back to each other eventually. They were worth fighting for, and she had to hope he still felt the same way.

She tried many times in vain to summon her power into her. Cate meditated, prayed, and even used summoning spells to try and focus on her lost sense. She downright encouraged the humans around her to sin in the hopes that the dark doings would rid her of the light's power, but it was no use.

"Don't bother," Dylan snapped one morning when she'd found Cate sat at the kitchen table immersed in a Satanist's bible she'd purchased online, desperately looking for some kind of ritual or demon summoning spell she could try out.

"I can't just sit here waiting for my light to go so we can head home, Dylan. I need to try and push it along a bit," Cate replied, and was angered by her friend's uncharacteristically impatient attitude. They both knew that the future wasn't going to be an easy one, but she was sure that she could be happy in Hell again. She hoped she could go back to her rightful place as Queen and would make sure Dylan would remain by her side for eternity.

Cate took a sip of her hot coffee and caught Dylan's curious eyes on her over the top of the black leather-bound book.

"You're horny aren't you?" she cried and burst out laughing. She shook her head in mock disgust, and her ash-blonde hair fell loosely down her back as she did so. Cate loved the colour of it in the sunshine and thought it was a shame Dylan kept it hidden in a ponytail most of the time. This morning's bedhead look even suited the witch's round face, and Cate had to smile back at her.

"You can't blame me, it's been *far* too long!" she informed her, blushing slightly. "And anyway, what's your problem today?" she asked, wondering why Dylan had snapped at her.

"I've got a guy *and* a girl asleep in my bed right now, and I need to kick them out. Why the hell did I invite them back here?" she asked rhetorically, and Cate just shook her head with a wry grin.

"Because you're a deviant dark witch who cannot keep her legs closed," she replied, earning herself both a laugh and a slap on the shoulder from her best friend.

Dylan shrugged and headed back to her room to get dressed for her shift at a local supermarket, a job which she despised, but it bought in some cash, so that was all that mattered. Ever since they'd left London, the pair had found it much easier to find little jobs that wouldn't require too much in the way of references and identification to get a foot in the door, and they'd been all the healthier and happier for the cash they brought in. It was worth the mundane life to have food in their bellies and a roof over their heads.

Cate thought of her old, privileged life she'd led when living on Earth the last time. She'd give anything to go back to that lavish lifestyle, but guessed those days were over. After attempting to contact Devin and Serena a few times without any luck, she'd all but given up. Her emails bounced back to her every time, giving Cate the usual, *undeliverable*, message back in response. She'd even called the lobby of the London penthouse not too long ago, but it was still empty. The doorman admitted he hadn't seen anyone there in years. He told her that Mr Black's family back in Germany had inherited Black Rose industries after his death, which led Cate to believe things were being handled from afar once more. Unfortunately, the man said he had no contact information for any of them, and she knew the entire organisation was lying dormant until Lucifer was ready to let it flourish again.

***

Later that night, Cate got ready for her shift at the pub. She climbed into her favourite black skinny jeans and a red t-shirt, adding a splash of colour in an attempt at being less gothic in her choice of outfit. She'd been trying to add more variety to her wardrobe recently, but more often than not would still end up in mostly blacks and the occasional reds. She then pulled her dark brown curls away from her pale face into a high ponytail and applied her usual light makeup, before sliding on her black leather biker boots and jacket and heading out across the village. Thanks to Dylan's paranoia having rubbed off on her over the years, she'd also taken a moment to make sure the door was double locked behind her.

When she reached the pub, Cate ditched her jacket in the back room, and quickly went about taking over from the young barmaid, who was finishing up from the day shift. She kept herself busy behind the bar for the first few hours, while waiting for the place to fill up and help her pass the time more easily. Cate chatted to a couple of men who were regulars at the Lion's Head while she poured them their beers and handed over peanuts and crisps, and thanked them for their kind and generous tip, but refused when they'd asked her to join them for a drink during her next break. It seemed like a game many of them liked to play, as if they kept on asking in the hopes that someday she might just say yes. She'd always made sure the regular patrons knew that while she was happy to be warm and friendly, she wasn't flirting with them. Many a time she'd even had to avoid getting set up on blind dates by the older women from the village, all of whom seemed dead set on setting her up with someone they knew who would apparently be perfect for her.

There was only one man for her, and she pined for him rather than let any new face crumble her vow to remain loyal to him. Despite all of Cate's carefully closed-off emotions, though, she sensed a strange connection with one of her new customers who came for a drink that night. She was attracted to him as soon as their eyes locked over the pint of lager she placed on the bar in front of him, and she did a double take. Cate was careful to maintain her usual cool and calm composure but couldn't help enquiring after him when he sat down opposite two young men who were small business owners from the village.

"Do you know who that is?" she asked another regular who was sat at the bar, an older woman called Lily who was on her fifth glass of white wine. She also happened to be one of the nosiest people she'd ever met and knew everything when it came to the comings and goings in their small community.

"He's just moved here. Apparently he's going to be the new doctor, or so I have heard," Lily told her matter-of-factly. "Harry, I think his name is. Cute too, hey," she added with a wonky smile before focusing on her wineglass again.

"I suppose," Cate replied nonchalantly, and inadvertently looked over at his table. She caught him watching her as well, and quickly busied herself wiping down the bar area.

Harry looked across at his new mates over the wooden table. He'd only moved into Avebury a few days before but had already made friends with both Jamie and Marc when he'd popped into the small supermarket Jamie owned in the village centre. They'd got on well and had chatted for a while before he'd then agreed to go for a drink with them, and Harry was glad he'd said yes now. The barmaid was stunning, and he knew he had to find out more about her.

"Who is she?" he asked, gesturing over to her with a nod.

"Ah yes, we see you have finally met Dana," replied Marc, smiling at him over his whisky and cola. He owned the village bakery and was what Harry would call a little on the chubby side but was a nice guy all the same.

"She's the ultimate, unattainable woman," added Jamie with a sigh. "She's lived here for a couple of years now, and I've never seen her even go out on a date with a guy, let alone anything else. You'd think she was a prude or something, but her sister's the biggest slut around, and Dana doesn't seem to care," he added, as though that was supposed to mean something to

Harry. He shrugged and looked over at the bar again, taking in the beautiful woman as she chatted warmly with another customer, and he finished off his beer.

"Who wants another?" he asked with a grin, and the two guys nodded. Harry stood, grabbed the empty glasses, and then made his way over towards the bar, his sights set on Cate.

"He's got no chance," Marc said quietly to Jamie, who laughed and nodded in answer. Both had tried to pick her up many times too, only to have their best chat up lines and warmest smiled shot down by the mysterious and much admired girl.

"Hi, um," Harry started to say when she looked over at him expectantly from the other side of the bar. He was desperately trying to think of something cool and impressive to say, but his mind went completely blank once he was under her beautiful gaze. Those intense green eyes of hers had him mumbling like an idiot, and he forced himself to speak some words. Any words…"Can I grab two beers and a whisky and cola please?" he then asked and gave up on trying to be smooth. He peered over the wooden bar at Cate with a shy smile and was mesmerised by the woman staring back at him. As he looked into her stunning face, he was lost in her allure. When she smiled back at him before taking away the empty glasses, he was spellbound.

Cate felt a pounding inside her chest that she didn't recognise, and it took her a minute to realise it was her heart beating extra fast. She'd already noticed how his light blue eyes lit up when he laughed, but when they were locked with hers, she saw how wise they also were—as if his soul was centuries old. She had to admire the set of his strong, square jaw, and even memorised the little dimple in the centre of his chin. When he smiled, she bet all the women swooned.

"Anything else I can do for you?" she asked as she placed the fresh drinks down in front of him, and she had to remind herself to breathe when he shot her an awkward smile. Dread finally reared its ugly head, and Cate suddenly felt nauseous. Regardless of their connection, she knew it was no use getting close to anyone, least of all hot doctors with cute dimples.

Harry shook his head, handing her a twenty-pound note.

"Just one for yourself as well, okay?" he offered. His warm smile was back on his gorgeous face, and Cate thanked him.

He knew he was hot, and had been quite the womaniser in his past, but he'd decided it was time to stop looking for one-night stands any more. Harry had known for a while that he was finally ready to find the right girl and settle down, but his studies had kept him so busy he hadn't had the chance to meet the right kind of woman for the job. That was, until he'd met the unattainable barmaid. In just a few days, he'd not only met some new friends but also a woman unlike any he'd met before, and he'd been dumbstruck for the first time in his entire life.

Harry returned to his new friends with his head low and his ego dragging behind him but laughed as the guys joked with him about his lack of skill in the pickup-line department.

"You did better than me, mate," Marc said as Harry sat back down at the table. "I was in here about three times before I could even order the right drinks. I'd get so flustered from trying to talk to her, I would forget what I was supposed to order every time!" he cried. Harry laughed and shrugged, thinking perhaps he hadn't done so badly after all then.

CHAPTER TWENTY-ONE

By the time Jamie and Marc had finished drinking, it was almost closing time at the Lion's Head. Harry bid farewell to his new friends and took the empty glasses over to the now quiet bar. He was glad to have met them, and even more pleased he'd agreed to meet them for that drink after all.

"One more for the road?" Cate asked him, and Harry nodded, smiling broadly at her as she quickly went about pouring him another pint of cold beer.

"Thanks, I'm Harry, by the way," he told her, with his boyish grin firmly back on his face. His confidence was back thanks to the several pints of beer that he'd already consumed, and rather than get flustered, he let himself enjoy the beautiful barmaid's attention. He handed Cate some money and waved his hand when she offered him the change.

"Cheers," she said, eyeing him warily. She couldn't figure out why she felt drawn to him, but she felt safe in his presence, and more alive than she had in almost a decade. He confused her, but she didn't want to push him away like all the other men and women who'd dared try to get close over the years. She could tell he had a gentle soul, and she wanted to get to know him. Despite them having only just met, there was a connection there already. "So, Harry. I hear you're the new doctor?" she asked, making small talk, but she was genuinely interested in his plans.

"Soon to be, yes. I have a placement at the village practice for a year before my final exams," he told her with a smile. "It's nice to know you've been asking about me though," he added, and Cate rolled her eyes playfully, but grinned back at him.

"The name's Dana," she told him. "But I guess you already know that about me, too, don't you?" she asked him with a knowing look.

"Touché," he answered with a gruff laugh before taking a long swig of his beer.

They chatted for a while as she cleared up and could both feel their immediate kinship to one another. They didn't talk about the things she thought normal people talked of in bars, but discussed philosophy, debated religion, and he wowed her with the scientific advances that were now part of his everyday life. Cate enjoyed the attention from him, but let Harry know straight away that she wasn't looking for a boyfriend. Regardless of their connection, she would never risk her cover, her heart, or his safety. He smiled, appearing to understand, or at least to accept her wishes, and seemed even more like the most perfect gentleman she'd ever known because of it.

"Can I walk you home?" he asked as she locked up and seemed to genuinely want to make sure she got back safely. As they left the dark pub, though, Dylan's face came into view from just a few metres up the road that led to their part of the village, and she did a double take at discovering Cate wasn't alone.

"Hey sis, who's your friend?" she called, concern clearly etched on her face. She could sense he was human though and calmed down as she neared the pair of them.

"The name's Harry," he said, shaking her hand. "I was just offering to walk your sister home, but I see there's no need to worry now," Harry added with a smile, before heading off in the direction of his flat. His mind was racing with both excited and anxious thoughts of the barmaid that had already stolen his heart, and he had to literally force himself to walk away. No woman had ever made him feel that way, and he couldn't resist peeking back over his shoulder at her before she disappeared.

"He's cute," Dylan said, eyeing Cate curiously while the pair of women walked off in the direction of their flat.

"Kind of," replied Cate, but smirked over at her old friend as she did so.

"Be careful," Dylan warned, and Cate knew without her having to explain exactly what she'd meant by that. They were both at risk if she let anyone get too close, and she owed it to Dylan to make sure she never suffered because of her again. They linked arms and wandered home, chatting quietly as they went, and Dylan told her fake sister all about the man who'd shared her bed that evening.

***

Harry returned to the Lion's Head the next night during Cate's shift at the pub, and then the next. He soon became a regular and would often sit with Jamie and Marc, but eventually started heading straight over to the bar after just a few visits. He found he preferred to chat with Cate rather than hang out with the guys and guessed they didn't mind. In fact, they seemed more impressed than offended.

They quickly got to know one another well, only as friends, of course, but she honestly loved having someone else to hang around with other than just Dylan. Cate had kept everyone so far at arm's length she didn't really have any close friends of her own, and it was nice having someone new to spend her time with.

Harry was the first person she'd ever let break down some of her carefully built walls. He was both understanding and patient, despite her secretiveness towards her past, and their friendship grew incredibly stronger over the few months that followed. So much so that a year later, when Dylan raised the issue of them moving again, Cate told her no.

"I've had enough, Dylan. We've been stuck on Earth for years, and we don't know for how much longer. I couldn't bear losing everything I've made here as well," she told her best friend. They both knew she meant Harry, and Cate blushed at the admittance of just how much he meant to her.

Dylan already knew how close they were. Just because they weren't in a sexual relationship didn't mean they weren't obviously a close couple. Their connection to one another shone so clearly when they were together that everybody but the pair of them seemed to see how perfect they could be together. Most people often mistook them for boyfriend and girlfriend, mistaking how natural and easy their deep friendship was. Dylan was the only one who knew why Cate wouldn't admit her feelings for Harry, even to herself. She couldn't stand to put him in harm's way by taking things any further, regardless of the strong bond she had with him—too strong. He was in love with her, they all knew, but he'd decided to keep that unspoken truth firmly pushed to one side to make things easier on her. Cate knew it had to be hard on him, but made it clear he wasn't to push the boundaries.

"Okay, we'll stay," Dylan agreed, and seeing Cate's face light up thanks to her words was bittersweet. It seemed the tides were changing, and she desperately hoped Harry wouldn't bear the brunt of Lucifer's anger when those waves finally collided.

Cate and Harry continued spending almost all their spare time together. He kept her company during her shifts, and she took him out for long walks to try and help clear his head of all the medical terminology he'd been studying relentlessly. They often went out for meals together in their favourite restaurants, all the while chatting and getting to know each other even more. Cate regaled him with her knowledge of languages and history, while Harry taught her about sports and educated her about the movies he was shocked to discover she'd never seen. Their shared love was music, and her face lit up when he reeled off a list of his top bands, many of which were her favourites, too.

Harry was open and honest about everything. He told her about his childhood and his family, as well as his hopes for the future, while Cate had to lie about everything she'd been through in her life. It was the first time she'd ever regretted not being able to share the part of herself that was so important, yet so scary. She was positive that revealing the truth would either make him concerned for her mental health, or too scared to remain friends with her. Either way, she and Dylan would then be forced out of Avebury and she would lose him forever.

When Harry finally asked her one night about the black diamond ring she still wore despite all her years away from her husband, Cate couldn't even bring herself to look down at the dark stone that signified her union with Lucifer. Instead, she rubbed it absentmindedly with her index finger. He'd already tried asking about her previous relationships before, and she always tried to skirt around it. This time, though, she decided to tell him just a few details about her former lovers.

"Well, my first boyfriend, Devin, was a wonderful man," she revealed. "I loved him very much, but one day I fell for someone else—Luke. When he came into the picture, I just couldn't say no." She had to stifle her laugh at those words, thinking just how literal they were. "He and I were, and still are, each other's soulmates. He stole me away and turned my world upside down," she told him, and Harry's face dropped. What she'd said wasn't too far from the fundamental truth, and although she hated hurting him, Cate needed to let him know just why she was so unavailable. She'd referred to Lucifer as Luke, his normal alias from his visits to Earth, and it felt strange talking of him again after such a long time.

The way she talked about him spoke volumes to Harry, who knew she was still in love with him. This 'Luke' was the reason she and Harry weren't together. She was pining for a man who wasn't even around, and he hated him for somehow still commanding her heart. After a few moments of awkward silence, he finally asked her the one question that was burning away at his insides.

"So why aren't you together now?" he said, with a cold and bitter edge to his voice he couldn't hide, but he needed to know.

"Something, or should I say *someone*, always manages to come between two people in love," Cate told him. Her eyes were so sad, but he didn't stop her. She continued, telling Harry just a little bit about her last partner, despite how hard it was to talk of him and her most recent heartbreak. "I have no excuse for it. He seduced me and I fell for all his lies. I learned my lesson there, and eventually realised just how manipulative and controlling he truly was, but by then I'd already lost everything," Cate told him, fighting back the tears.

She then confided a little more in Harry, knowing she could trust him. "Nina and I had to move away. We needed to run from him. That's why I'm so careful now," she added, but couldn't really say any more. She'd skimmed over the fine details as much as possible, being careful not to get Harry too intrigued in the crazy history behind her sad eyes. She couldn't bear to talk about it in any further detail anyway, or risk giving too much away about her love triangle of darkness and light.

It finally seemed to register then. Harry knew for sure just why she'd closed herself off to men. Cate had always known that he liked her, and deep down she also knew that she really liked him back, which was all the more reason she couldn't let herself fall again. When the time came that Lucifer would return for her, Cate knew full well what fate would befall any human who might've dared touch her, let alone having loved her. Lucifer would want to take out his fury in one way or another and would surely not go easy on Harry if he found out that the pair of them had been together during their separation. Cate cared too much about him to let him suffer because of her foolish actions, so was surer than ever just how much she had to keep their affection for each other locked away.

A few weeks later, Dylan and her current girlfriend, a young woman named Sophie, begged Cate and Harry to go with them to a music festival. Cate still loved listening to her favourite bands. It was a passion she'd almost forgotten while in Hell, but one that she and Dylan had rekindled since they'd been living their human-like lives on Earth again.

They travelled for a few hours by car to a huge field in the countryside that'd been transformed into a massive arena with three stages. After they arrived at the site and pitched their tents, they quickly got ready and donned their boots before heading off in the direction of the loud rock music.

Cate loved every minute of it, and quickly remembered just why she loved live music so much. She crashed around happily with the throbbing crowd and sang along with the bands as the various artists played. Harry joined her in the throng and grabbed Cate's hand protectively, standing close behind to ensure she didn't get washed away or hurt by the masses that surrounded the pair of them.

Their electricity was immense, and the feel of Harry's hand in hers gave Cate a long forgotten pang in her once empty heart. He leaned closer and sang the deep and heartfelt words to a delicate acoustic song in her ear.

"I want you. I need you. Be mine," he sung, and the lyrics made her heart pound as he whispered them, while his breath sent shivers down her spine as it tickled her skin. "I'm crazy, I'm lost. Hold me, be mine."

She turned and looked up at him, suddenly forgetting about the dancing, and peered up into Harry's gorgeous blue eyes. She didn't pull back this time and knew she couldn't push him away again. Cate quickly realised that she didn't even want to anymore.

She looked into his warm face and climbed up onto her tiptoes to inch closer, before hesitantly caressing his lips with hers. Harry kissed her back with every ounce of unspoken desire he'd kept at arm's length for so long, and he wrapped his arms around her waist while hers went up around his neck. They swayed together, enveloped tightly by the heavy crowd, and they caressed each other tenderly. Cate let him hold her closer to him, and by the time he let go, she was buzzing. She was so happy and enjoyed the carefree adoration as they embraced one another and took that next step at long last. Rational thought was long gone, and she let her heart rule her head for the first time in her entire existence. What she had with Harry was unlike anything she'd known before, and yet it was somehow more terrifying.

Harry cherished every moment and held her close for the rest of the afternoon. He didn't ever want to let her go and hoped to God she would never leave him or push him away again. The rest of the first day at the festival went by in a blur, but all the while, Cate and Harry were inseparable. They simply couldn't let go of each other, not that either of them tried. He knew she needed to take things slowly, but didn't mind at all, and lapped up her affection as she allowed him in at long last. They danced for hours and didn't stop when the rain lashed down and clagged their boots in mud. She seemed happier than he'd ever seen her, and it was a thrill knowing he'd been the one to put that smile on her beautiful face. Harry knew he'd remember their day for the rest of his life.

Later that night, as the music began to die down and the crowds of festivalgoers returned to their tents, someone gave Cate a tap on the shoulder. She'd been stood talking with Harry off to the side of the now quiet stage, waiting for Dylan and Sophie to come back from a run to the beer tent, and she jumped. She turned to look at who'd interrupted them with a scowl. It was one of the burly bouncers she'd seen watching the crowd earlier, but who now stared down at her with a seemingly forced smile.

"Hi, how would you two like free VIP wristbands?" he asked her and Harry, lifting up two thick, red cotton bands, and she could make out the promised upgraded access that was embossed along it in black writing. The bands would allow them admission to the special, behind the scenes area where she knew many of the band members were now hanging out, and Harry nearly jumped out of his skin with excitement. However, Cate just smiled and shook her head. She'd been taught well by her magical best friend and was suspicious of the man's motives.

"No, but thank you," she replied, taking Harry by his arm, and starting to walk away.

"These usually only go to the band members and their entourages. You two are very lucky to have even been offered them," the man answered back teasingly, but she saw through his façade. He wasn't going to take no for an answer, and there had to be a reason for it. Cate tried to search the dissipating crowd for Dylan, but she was nowhere to be seen. She could tell Harry couldn't understand her hesitance, and so she looked inside the VIP area behind the man, where she caught a pair of dark eyes watching her from a dimly lit tent. They called to her, summoning her closer. Curious, she finally conceded.

"Okay, go on then," she said, and they put on their bands and followed the burly man through the gate into the VIP area. They were quickly led over to where one of the rock bands they'd been watching on the stage just an hour or so before we're sitting having a drink together. Harry was immediately star struck and shook hands with them all before chatting animatedly to the lead guitarist about how much he loved their new album. Cate smiled and greeted them all as well, but quickly sat down next to the band's lead singer and the owner of that intense stare she'd locked eyes with minutes before. He was none other than her old friend, the demon Berith. He looked different to the last time she'd seen him but she knew right from the moment she'd found herself in his presence, it was him. Cate didn't quite know how to act or what to say, but it was Berith who spoke first, saving her the worry.

"Well, then. Hasn't it been such a terribly long time, my Queen?" he asked her with a wry, knowing grin. He took care to keep his voice low in front of the humans he was now associating with, and she was glad he seemed intent on keeping their secret. His long dark hair fell to his shoulders messily, but he was clean-shaven now, and looked almost like a normal human, apart from his array of new tattoos and piercings. "There are an awful lot of different beings looking for you in this big wide world, and in those above and below. I can see now just why they haven't had any luck," he added, grinning broadly while looking Cate up and down, as though seeing something she couldn't. Berith's brow furrowed, and he seemed distant for a moment, but then shook off whatever memory had stirred in his ancient mind.

"What do you mean?" she asked and had to wonder what it was he was looking at. "You can see me though, and you knew it was me, didn't you?"

"Yes, Hecate. I knew it was you," Berith answered, and his dark brown eyes bore into hers as he leaned in closer. Cate could tell he was finding it hard to explain how or why he could sense her and wondered if he knew the answer himself. "I cannot see your true form. It has somehow been hidden. Those looking for the Dark Queen will not be able to find you as you are now; the spell concealing your nature is so strong they would pass you in the street. I see you today as just an ordinary human girl. The darkness that lies beneath that guise is well hidden by both magic and by light power that still courses through your veins. It's as though the combination of the two has blocked your powers and true presence from coming through, despite the passing of time," he told her with a clearly confused look on his face.

"Then, how did you know it was me?" she asked, glancing over to Harry and giving him a smile as he continued chatting away happily with two long haired, black clothed, band members.

"I never forget a pretty face, whether human or otherwise, and especially one as infamous as yours, your highness," Berith told her with a quiet laugh. "I was drawn to you instantly and liked watching you have fun.

You do know I am bound to report this back to my master when I can next have an audience with him?" he added, looking over to Harry and then back at Cate, and he gave her a knowing look. "All of this—including what I saw the pair of you doing in the crowd today." Cate's stomach dropped. She could kick herself. Of course, the one day she'd let her guard down would be the day she'd get caught. Wasn't that just her luck?

"I've not cheated on Lucifer with him," Cate told the demon quietly and calmly. Her green eyes peered over at him, pleading with him to believe her. "There would be no need to anger my husband with unnecessary bad news, not when we can finally be reunited at last. How might I convince you to leave out the part of the story that involves the human and keep my reunion with Lucifer a wholly joyous occasion?" she asked hopefully, and Berith nodded solemnly. "I've tried to gain access to the churches, and even went to the old penthouse in London, but there was no one there. Please tell him I tried everything I could," Cate implored him further. "But I couldn't get into the church. The light inside me blocked my darkness, and I couldn't cross over the threshold. The only reason I had to hide away is because the white witches would take me back up there if they caught me, and I couldn't. I…I just couldn't. Please, old friend?"

Berith pushed a stray lock of dark hair behind Cate's ear with his hand, and she looked up into his almost black eyes, feeling slightly uncomfortable beneath his gaze. He smiled and then leaned closer, whispering into her ear.

"I understand completely. I tell you what, sell me your soul and my lips are sealed," he offered, then sat back and grinned, seemingly to enjoy watching Cate squirm as she mulled over his incomprehensible proposal.

CHAPTER TWENTY-TWO

"It is not mine to give, you know that," Cate told him, disturbed somewhat by Berith's lack of loyalty to her husband.

"True," he admitted, and then pondered on it for a moment. "Okay, well, how about we just go with one good, hard, fuck?"

"You do realise you'd be tortured for all eternity by your Dark King?" she replied, smirking over at him now as she realised he was just messing with her.

"True," he replied again, and then thought about it for a moment. "A kiss?"

"Still dodgy ground, don't you think?" Cate replied with a shrug. She was so relieved he'd been kidding and gave him a playful smack on the shoulder.

"Okay, well, how about a kiss off your friend over there instead?" he asked, and Cate was surprised he wanted a kiss from Harry. She hadn't heard of him taking male lovers before. Then, she followed Berith's gaze to the opening of the VIP area, where Dylan stood glaring over at them with her hands on her hips, and she was clearly angry as hell.

***

"I'll keep your friend out of it," Berith told Cate the next morning as he hugged her goodbye. "Granted that nothing else happens between the pair of you, I will never tell. But you know he has ways of finding out the truth even in the dark corners of our minds," he added, and Cate knew she had to be careful, but nodded solemnly. She was sure the demon was adept at disguising his thoughts, and just hoped that Lucifer would be so distracted by their reunion that he wouldn't be interested in hunting Harry down. She would make sure to keep him well occupied.

Berith had gotten much more than just a kiss from the promiscuous Dylan and her open-minded girlfriend the night before and seemed more than willing to help his Queen get back to her King's arms safely. She gave him a small, folded piece of paper with the address written inside for the flat she shared with Dylan, which Berith slipped in his pocket and then he gave her a nod. Cate knew it wouldn't be long until her husband knew that his wife was safe, and how she was ready to see him. The realisation that her exile might finally be over at last left Cate feeling both scared and excited all at the same time.

"Deal," she promised the demon. "And make sure you tell him I love him."

"I will," he smiled and climbed aboard the tour bus, waving goodbye to Dylan as they drove off.

Cate heaved a sigh of relief, but she couldn't be too happy to have found a way home at last. Her body yearned for the freedom she'd discovered the day before while wrapped in the arms of a man who wasn't her husband. She felt like crying.

"Wow, how amazing was that?" Harry asked loudly as he joined them. He'd been walking on air the entire night and was still buzzing thanks to his first VIP experience. He also had no idea Berith's unwitting followers had been commanded to keep him occupied while they talked. Cate and Dylan laughed but hooked their arms in his and led Harry back into the crowd so they could enjoy the final day of the music festival. They'd been able to keep the VIP passes, so watched from just in front of the stage as a handful of bands finished off the wonderful weekend. Cate felt terrible for having led Harry on, but knew she had to push him away again. There was no doubt about it now. Lucifer would come for her soon, and she knew that Harry had to be far away from her when he did.

He could sense Cate's coolness straight away and tried not to let it show that he was bothered by it. She barely looked at him as the music played and didn't seem half the woman she'd been the day before. It was as though she was too lost in thought to even enjoy herself, and she didn't go anywhere near him, as though she was scared he might try and pick up where they'd left off the night before. Harry quickly realised she'd pulled away again and thought perhaps the tiny amount of intimacy from the previous day was all he was ever going to get from the beautiful woman he desired so very much. He wondered if maybe it was just time to let her go and save himself the torment of loving this unattainable girl. Better to walk away than get his heart broken, but he feared the damage there had already been done.

Dylan sensed their silent disconnection too and gave Cate a supportive squeeze as they watched the finale.

"It's the only way," she whispered in her ear, and she wiped away a stray tear that rolled down Cate's cheek as the realisation finally hit her. They returned to the camping area in silence, dismantled the tents quickly, and then made their way home. Cate closed her eyes all the way back and felt utterly exhausted. She slept a little, but also wanted the quiet time to think over everything life had thrown at her so far, wondering what she'd ever done to warrant all the heartache that seemed fated for her.

Dylan drove while chatting away to Sophie in the front seat, and Harry just sat in solemn silence, watching the world whiz by out the car window beside him.

***

The next few weeks were agonising for Cate while she waited for the moon to become full. She wondered if Lucifer would come for her when it did, but truly hoped he was planning on it. She was unsure whether she could even go home or not when he finally did come to take her back to Hell, but knew she had to try. Life on Earth hadn't been terrible, especially the past few years, but now she was ready to leave it all behind.

She hadn't seen Harry since the music festival, and knew he'd stayed away on purpose. He didn't answer her calls, avoided her when she tried to intercept him at the supermarket, and in the end, Cate decided to write him a letter. He needed to know that she was planning to move away again soon, and that he shouldn't try to look for her.

Dear Harry.

I'm truly sorry for my behaviour. I never meant to lead you on, and I will regret hurting you for the rest of my miserable existence. You deserve the chance to find someone who can love you and put that love above all others. I tried to tell you as much as I could about my past, but you just wouldn't have understood if I told you everything. I cannot be with you, and I cannot keep you safe or make you happy.

Nina and I are moving away again soon, and please do not try to find me. It's better if you just forget about me completely. Live your life to the fullest Harry, and I hope you find your soulmate.

Goodbye.

It pained her to push him away so forcefully, but it was for his own good. For his safety, she'd do it.

On the night of the next full moon, Cate waited at home in the hope that her husband would come to her. But for some reason, though, Lucifer didn't appear during that full moon, nor the next, and she began to fear that he'd rejected her. She tried to call to him, and to summon Berith to her side, but it was no use. Her powers were still blocked, and she had no way of knowing if or when Lucifer would decide to find her. Cate felt so lost and alone and couldn't settle her body or mind. Dylan tried to help, offering her support and comfort while never leaving her side, but nothing eased her, and she felt miserable again, just like she had in the hall outside the penthouse.

Cate reached out to Harry, foolishly she knew, but she couldn't help herself. She was so damned desperate to see a friendly face, but he still refused to return her messages. Cate hadn't received any response from the brutal letter she'd sent, or the texts and voicemails she left for him since. She'd ruined the best thing she'd ever had, and it broke her heart in two knowing he was done with her. Dylan kept on telling Cate that it was for the best, but she felt miserable knowing she really had lost him so completely.

***

When the next full moon shone in the night's sky, Cate was sick of waiting in the flat, so agreed to do a shift working at the pub. She kept busy, clearing the tables, and re-stocking the fridges, all the while dispensing with the small talk. She was so morose that she hadn't felt the shift in pressures, or the darkness that'd begun creeping in around the small village. The patrons were even gambling more readily in the bar's fruit machines as the night drew darker; giving into their greed, while others drank more than usual in their gluttony. Cate continued to busy herself with cleaning and tidying the bar area, instead of noticing the men and women who were flirting more openly in the corners of the room, so ready to commit sin as though being influenced somehow.

"Whisky on the rocks please," a voice said from just inside the doorway, and her heart immediately fluttered wildly at the oh-so familiar sound. She knew it was Lucifer before even seeing him and turned slowly to face her husband as he wandered into the pub, just like any other Friday night drinker.

He looked fantastic, dressed in black jeans and a grey t-shirt teamed with heavy military style boots and the same cargo jacket he'd been wearing the first night she'd met him. It was strange how much she remembered from that night so long ago, and how different their lives together had become since then. His blue eyes were dark and brooding, and he didn't take them off Cate's for even a second as he took her in, despite her being aware he was undoubtedly reading every mind in the room.

She could hardly breathe. Her mouth opened and closed as though she wanted to say something, but she was unable to find the words to even start their long and hard journey back to each other. Lucifer smiled across at her, taking Cate's breath away again, and she dropped the glass she'd been holding, but didn't even register the smash as it hit the ground and shattered at her feet.

"You're here," she said in a whisper, finding her voice at last.

"I'm here," he confirmed, walking through the crowd with a smile before coming around behind the bar so that he could stop within inches of his trembling wife. She still had no powers but could feel the electricity passing between them as though it were lightning, and Cate knew then that neither of them had lost their love for one another despite their years of having been forced apart. "Your housemate didn't want to give up your location, my love. She wanted to bring me to you herself, but I made her an offer she simply couldn't refuse," Lucifer told her after a couple of silent seconds. His words sent her into immediate panic, and she began worrying for Dylan's safety.

She peered up into his warm face pleadingly. "Don't worry," he told her, and a gruff laugh escaped his lips. "Berith told me everything. She's been rewarded for keeping you safe." He took her face in his hands, staring deeply into Cate's green eyes. "She's joined the dark coven. Dylan's perfectly fine."

She let out a sigh of relief, her head going fuzzy as she accepted his explanation. Her body screamed out for her lover and she stared back up at him, willing him to take her home. But they didn't go. His defeated sigh a few seconds later gave away Lucifer's frustration, and she could tell he'd just tried to teleport her away but couldn't. He looked down at Cate, seeming just as desperate to reignite their flame, and he gave away his only weakness—her.

She reached up and touched her King's cheek tenderly with her hand and revelled in his touch and embrace after such a long and lonely time.

"I'm so sorry, for everything," she said, staring up at him, and Lucifer smiled warmly back down at her. He kissed her palm and then put it back against his cheek.

"I know," was all he could reply, and then leaned down to kiss her lips tenderly at last.

"Well, if we can't go home. Perhaps we can go somewhere more private?" she asked him, and giggled excitedly as Lucifer gathered her up in his arms and carried her from the pub. None of the patrons seemed to have even noticed the dark entity that'd been among them, or the fact that Cate had then disappeared off into the night with him. She didn't care and assumed that he must've been working some kind of mind control power on all of them, ensuring they had privacy during their wonderful reunion, and was glad for it.

They walked quickly, hand-in-hand in silence, revelling in each other's company at last as they headed across the village towards the flat. In her hurry, Cate then fumbled with the keys for a moment before her impatient husband grabbed them from her, flung the door open, and pulled her inside. Lucifer wasted no more time, and he pinned Cate to the wall with his strong body. He kissed her deeply as he ran his hands through her long, dark hair. One arm came down and grabbed her left thigh, pulling her body up into his strong arms and towards him as they kissed.

Cate relished in his strength as he devoured her. She was so weak before him, but gave every part of herself to her lover, willing him to possess her entirely. He pulled her other leg up and around his waist and pushed her harder into the wall. The world turned upside down for Cate and she gasped for breath in his arms. Her body screamed for his, and she thrust her hips forwards, wrapping her thighs tighter around Lucifer and gripping him eagerly. He then carried her to her room in his arms and dropped down on the bed, allowing her to straddle him as they continued to kiss lasciviously.

She leaned back, gasping for air, and giving him access to her neck, and he kissed it eagerly, popping open her black shirt as he kissed lower and lower down Cate's chest. Her top was quickly discarded, and Lucifer moved on to unclip her bra, and sent that flying across the room also. He cupped her tender breasts, tweaking her nipples with his fingertips as Cate gasped and then lunged forward into another deep kiss.

He fell back onto the duvet, and she followed, straddling him as he lay beneath her. She arched her body over his, and began pulling his shirt up over his head, before then tossing it to the floor beside the bed. She took the time to kiss each of Lucifer's nipples, suckling gently on his sensitive peaks as he groaned. Her kisses then moved further down to his toned stomach muscles, licking and kissing every ripple that she could get to. Her hands moved to his belt, undoing the metal clasp and pulling the leather strap free, before opening Lucifer's fly and gripping the hems of his jeans and boxers with her small hands. She looked up to her lover with a grin, and then pulled down, slipping off his clothes and releasing his ready erection in the process. It'd been so long, and she was ravenous for him, ready for the pleasure, and even the pain, if that was what it took to show her husband what he meant to her.

Cate began sucking his tip gently, taking more and more of him in her mouth with each pull, but it wasn't long until Lucifer reached down to stop her. After stroking her face gently, he demanded that she remove her skirt and knickers. She stood at the bedside and obliged her King, of course, and felt sexy as hell giving him a striptease.

He sat up, watching her eagerly before ushering her to straddle him again. Cate climbed onto Lucifer's lap, but he didn't enter her right away. Instead, he kissed his wife with insatiable passion one more time before leaning back and letting his powerful guise slip a little.

"Don't ever leave me again," he told her. His tone was more of a command than a request, and Cate stopped her barrage of kisses. She stared deep into Lucifer's eyes and sensed the pain and hurt in them.

"Never," she told him honestly, before kissing his lips softly.

Lucifer grabbed Cate and lifted her up by the thighs. The opening of her wet, ready cleft was just millimetres from his hard cock, and she let out a groan of anticipation. He held her there for a few moments longer, refusing to give her what she desperately craved—what she needed. Not yet. He delighted in drawing out her pleasure, keeping her from him, while he made himself even clearer in his commandment.

"Never," he demanded again, his eyes swirling with black flecks and expression ominous. "You are mine, Hecate. Forever." Cate stared lovingly into Lucifer's gaze, holding it, and she made sure she didn't hesitate for even a second.

"Forever," she promised him, kissing the tip of his nose as Lucifer dropped her onto his hard length. She cried out as the stretching feeling of him inside created both the pleasure and pain she'd anticipated but refused to stop. She might be weak and feeble—as good as human—but it wasn't going to stop her giving her lover everything she'd just promised, and more.

He lifted Cate up and down, faster and harder, with his powerful arms. She had no control, even though she was the one on top, and lost all conscious thought as he pummelled her from below. Lucifer lifted her effortlessly and sent her crashing down onto his hard-on, again and again. Her muscles throbbed and tensed inside, enveloping her master greedily, and he grinned as he watched her come undone. She climaxed hard and intense, but he pushed her on even faster, unrelentingly, until he reached his own glorious end. The walls shook around them and Cate cried out as another intense orgasm seemed to ripple throughout not only her entire body but also her very soul. Lucifer emptied into her and held her close. He watched her as they came down from their joint high, not willing to let go of his true love ever again.

They stayed in bed together, making love well into the next day. Cate's fragile body struggled to keep up with Lucifer's powerful sexual prowess, but she couldn't stop even if for some reason she'd wanted to. They both had a lot of catching up to do, and she was pretty sure Lucifer wanted to fill her with as much darkness as he could to try and take her home with him before the moon waned. If she still couldn't travel home then, he'd have no other choice than to leave her there until the next full moon, and both hated the sheer thought of it.

"I can't bear the prospect of being alone in Hell without you again, not even for a day. Let alone another month," Lucifer told her, and Cate nodded.

"Now that I've found you again, I won't be able to survive without you, Lucifer. I need you to take me home," she mumbled, snuggling against him beneath the sheets. It felt good to be in his arms, and she knew she couldn't leave them again.

A loud knock at the door to the flat that afternoon disturbed their satiated peace, following another epic bout of lovemaking. Although Cate had said to ignore it, Lucifer couldn't help his mischievous self. He had to go and see who it was and hoped it might be a disgruntled neighbour coming to complain about all the sexual noises that he could mess with. He pulled on his jeans and slicked back his tousled hair before heading to the door, while Cate hastily tried to get herself dressed.

Harry stood in the doorway to the flat, having hoped that Cate would be the one behind the door as it was quickly pulled open. He was shocked to see the half-naked man standing before him, but immediately presumed he must be there with her sister. Lucifer stared at him expectantly, both scaring and intimidating Harry without having uttered a single word.

"Urm, is Dana here?" he eventually asked. Trying to hide the look of disgust that crossed his face when Lucifer smirked over at him.

"She's a bit, *busy*," he replied, eyeing Harry curiously. "But, please come on in." He opened the door wider, ushering their guest inside. He wanted to read him, to figure out his connection with Cate, but needed to make contact to properly read the human boy's thoughts and memories.

Harry hesitated in the doorway for a second, but Lucifer smiled insistently, doing his best to come across as warm and friendly. It didn't seem to be working. Harry frowned, but eventually went inside and headed through to the living room, where he took a seat and stared down at his hands awkwardly.

"Beer?" Lucifer asked him, standing over him still only half dressed.

"It's two o'clock in the afternoon?" Harry answered, but quickly changed his mind when he saw that Lucifer didn't care what the time was. "Actually, yeah please," he quickly corrected his attitude and smiled up at his host uncomfortably.

Cate came running in from the bedroom, looking from Lucifer to Harry and back in silent anticipation. She didn't quite know how to tackle this, and decided to say nothing, yet. She raised her hand to Harry in an embarrassed half wave, and then followed Lucifer into the kitchen, where she watched as he grabbed a couple of beers from the fridge. Cate took a tall bottle from the fridge's door, poured herself a large glass of Chardonnay, and took a big gulp. Lucifer eyed her; curious as to why she was so nervous.

"Friend of yours, darling?" he asked her quietly, with an accusatory tone clear in his voice.

"Yes, and just that," she replied, placing a hand on Lucifer's chest, and she stared him in the eye solemnly. He gave nothing away as he peered back down at her; he simply grabbed the beers and left the kitchen without another word, while Cate trailed behind him in her tracksuit bottoms and t-shirt. They re-joined Harry in the living room again, and she tried to seem relaxed as she made the introductions.

"Harry, this is Luke," she told him, and Harry understood immediately. He nodded and took a long swig of the cold beer. Funnily enough, he was now glad to have said yes to a proper drink after all.

"Her husband," Lucifer added. He watched the pair of them keenly but hated not being able to read either of them enough to know for sure if there was something he was missing. His senses were off thanks to the intense reunion with Cate, and he was struggling to tap into Harry's mind from afar. Lucifer put his hand out to him, wanting the physical contact so that he could properly search the boy's memories.

Cate had to stop herself from intercepting the connection. It was the last thing she wanted but knew that it would look much worse if she intervened. She had to let it happen and would face whatever consequences came her way once it was done. She was tired of running and remained still as Harry reached up and shook her husband's outstretched hand in his. They only kept contact for a couple of seconds, but it was enough. Lucifer knew everything.

CHAPTER TWENTY-THREE

The three of them made small talk for a little while, but when the time came for Harry to go, he was relieved. He didn't like Luke, and thought he wasn't at all the way she'd described him. He seemed the possessive, controlling type, and was a scary guy, if he was completely honest. Harry was glad he'd had the chance to make his excuses and leave and knew for sure that this really was their last goodbye. Cate saw him out and hugged him tightly. Their awkward final exchange left him feeling depressed and anxious though, rather than getting the closure he had desperately hoped for, but he left without another word or even a backwards glance. She'd made her choice weeks ago, and he'd given up fighting for her.

Cate made her way back to the living room where Lucifer sat, calmly finishing off his beer and fiddling with the paper label. She cautiously stood near the doorway but didn't say a word, waiting for his reaction to Harry's visit. She watched him closely, sensing his rage, but wasn't sure how to act or what to say. A second later, the now empty beer bottle came hurtling across the room, and it smashed just inches from Cate's head.

She squeezed her eyes shut as the shards scattered nearby, and by the time she'd opened them again, Lucifer was standing right in front of her, his face inches from hers. He pinned her to the wall with his strong body, but there was nothing exciting about his hold this time. His hand gripped her by the throat, holding on tightly, and he pulled her face closer to his as his blackened eyes bore into hers.

"You kissed him!" he growled, and Cate could feel him shaking with anger, the powerful rage threatening to burst out of him if she said the wrong thing in response.

"It was only that one day. I was just so alone, Lucifer. So desperate. It was nothing but a big mistake," she cried, and her voice sounded hoarse thanks to his tight grip he had around her throat.

"He's in love with you, Cate. Do you love him back?" he shouted, thumping the back of her head hard into the plaster, and she winced but didn't cry out. His other fist came around a moment later, and in his rage, he smashed a hole the size of a bowling ball through the wall behind her.

"No, you know that. You must've read his mind!" Cate eventually cried out, desperate to make him understand. "It was one moment of weakness, and it didn't happen again. I was never with him, ever." The tears streamed down her face as she pleaded, begging him to believe her words and trust that they were true. He might not have been able to read her thoughts anymore, but surely Harry's version of events was clear enough?

Lucifer stared at her, seemingly absorbing her words, and working over her explanation in his head. He was so still, unblinking, and unflinching, as he processed it all in his mind. Cate had to try and bring him back to her again, to calm him and to loosen his hand that still was wrapped tight around her neck. "Please, Lucifer," Cate begged, her voice quiet again. "You're hurting me." His grip on her released at once, and he backed away a few steps.

He'd read Dylan's thoughts before going to the pub to meet his wife and was aware of the friendship Cate had with Harry, but he hadn't realised just how strong the pair's bond was. Harry was completely in love with her. He was consumed by it, but she'd never realised just how strong his feelings were. She was telling the truth though, and Lucifer knew that she'd pushed Harry away at his every advance, except for that one day. The image of the pair of them together echoed painfully in his mind, though. It was one of the downsides to seeing into another person's head he knew all too well, and he had to force the shared thought away.

He knew from those memories he'd just plucked from Harry's mind that they really were only friends, and yet Lucifer couldn't help but still feel angry at their connection. Perhaps it was sheer jealousy that they were so close, he wasn't sure. He honestly didn't know how to even begin processing all the things that'd happened to Cate in the years since she'd been taken from him at the beach, but he knew for sure they needed to get her home again during this full moon. The thought of leaving her there with her 'friend' angered him further, and a flash of rage came bubbling to the surface uncontrollably.

"If I ever see that boy again, he will wish for death. He'll beg me for mercy, and you know he will not get it. Is that understood?" She nodded, the sobs escaping from her uncontrollably as she peered up at her master. His eyes soon turned back to their usual deep blue, and he smiled down at her as though nothing had happened. "Good. Now, let's go back to bed."

Lucifer took Cate's hand and led her back through to her small bedroom. She followed but was still shaken and needed some time to calm down. Cate had to sort herself out before she could even think about forgetting that whole thing had just happened and carry on as they were.

"Give me a minute, okay?" she asked, excusing herself for a few much needed minutes alone in the bathroom. She stared at her reflection in the mirror, refusing to let herself cry, despite the more than willing emotions that threatened to burst out of her. She splashed her face with cool water and then dried it with a nearby towel, heaving a huge sigh into the cotton.

Cate thought back to her wonderful days with Lucifer before Uriel had come between them. She thought of their fantastic wedding and romantic honeymoon, as well as their happy reunion just the night before, and smiled to herself again. Lucifer was her true love, and she decided then and there that she'd never dwell on her memories of Harry ever again.

Thanks to the flood of happiness that filled her soul, it wasn't long until she felt ready to face her husband, and she wandered back into the bedroom. Cate looked over at Lucifer as he lay on the bed, reading one of her magazines. He was his usual calm self once again, while she was still a little bruised by his actions, both on the outside and on the inside.

He knew she was hurting, despite her best efforts to hide it, and took her in his arms as she joined him on the bed, embracing Cate tightly.

"I love you so much, my Queen. It feels like a century since I last held you in my arms. I want to murder anyone that so much as even looks at you," he told her honestly, needing Cate to understand his anger towards her relationship with Harry.

"I know. But I'm yours, my King. Always and forever," Cate assured him with a smile. "I love you."

"I love you, too."

Rather than urge her back into bed, Lucifer then ran Cate a bath to soothe her weak and aching body. She slipped into the hot, soapy water and groaned happily, making him laugh. He joined her, sitting opposite Cate and massaging her feet as she soaked for a few minutes with her eyes closed. He took her in, watching his wife as she relaxed. She was so beautiful, vulnerable, and human-like without her powers, but mesmerising. Her dark curls spread out around her in the water, clinging to her pale skin and she still looked so young, almost innocent, and pure.

Cate reminded him of the night she'd first come to meet him in the dark church. Her features were still soft and delicate despite all the years she'd lived and the hardships she'd faced. Lucifer's mind was racing with questions, but he couldn't bear to ask her yet what Uriel had wanted of her up on that astral plain. However, he knew by the still strong light he could sense inside of her that the whole truth might be more than he could ever handle knowing and thought perhaps he'd never ask. He wanted to forget the last chapter of their lives completely, to wipe out the last seventeen years that'd been terrible for them both, but he knew there was no way. For now, he would settle for having her back in his arms, and back in Hell where she belonged.

There was only one way he thought for sure that he could rid Cate's body of all the lightness and fill it entirely with his dark power once again.

Lucifer sat forward, startling her awake, but then she opened her eyes and smiled over at him as he peered down at her with a broad grin.

"How do you feel about giving me a child, Cate?" he asked, and she stared up at him, her eyes opening wider. The dread-inspiring words brought her crashing back to Earth from her restful state, and she swallowed the lump that'd formed in her throat. Cate sat up and leaned forward so she could look into his eyes. She wanted to feel his *expression*, to understand his motives, but her lack of power seemed to be stopping their wordless connection. He had to tell her more. She needed to know more.

"Why?" she asked him, eager to know before she could even fathom being able to answer him.

"I'm ready to be a proper father, my love. You're the only woman for me, and I want you to give me a full-blooded heir. Our child would make our reunion complete, and I'm positive it'd make us whole again," he said, looking over at her with an open and earnest expression on his gorgeous face. "Also, I have no doubt that having a good dose of my darkness along with my child inside you would ensure you could travel home safely. And once we're there, you'll be able to work on getting your powers back, once and for all," he added.

"And we'd all stay there together?" she had to ask.

"Forever," Lucifer answered, and it was all Cate needed to know before she made her decision. She stared over at him, open-mouthed and completely taken aback by his honesty, but was so incredibly happy he'd opened up to her about his feelings.

She knew now that his desire for a child hadn't been because of any need to have power or control over her. It was only about his love and how he wanted to strengthen their bond. She thought back to their conversations about children from a long time ago and remembered how scary the idea of having a family was to her back then. Now, though, things had changed. She had changed, and while she wanted nothing more than to go home and be loved and happy by Lucifer's side, Cate knew that she was finally ready to give her love to a child of her own as well. She knew she needed to earn her husband's trust and respect back, but also that she wanted to rid herself of the goddamn light Uriel had forced inside of her. Cate was ready to regain her dark powers again and agreed that this had to be the best way to do it.

"Yes," she told Lucifer after settling her thoughts, looking back at him with a huge smile. "Of course, it's a yes."

Lucifer sprang towards her in the hot water, sloshing it over the sides of the bath and onto the floor accidentally as he pulled Cate into his arms. But neither cared for the mess. He then laid her back in the warm water, kissing her eagerly, and didn't care about anything other than her and their future. Sliding inside Cate's welcoming body was effortless in the warm water, and it felt so right, so natural.

She gasped as he thrust hard into her ready and willing opening and whispered her affirmation over and over again in his ear between her deep kisses. He plunged into her eager cleft repeatedly, and she was lost in his heat, his hungriness, and his desire for her.

The room span around them as they came together, and Cate cried his name as Lucifer lifted her out of the suds and emptied into her with a powerful thrust that caused her entire body to tremble beneath him. Their bodies seemed in perfect sync again, and the world around them struggled to catch up. She'd never been happier.

"I only have a few more hours left," Lucifer told Cate a while later when they stood drying themselves off, and he climbed under the sheets of her bed. It was almost midnight, and Cate knew he'd have to be gone by sunrise. She looked over at the all-powerful man beside her, taking in his darkly handsome face, and she adored the light bit of stubble that'd grown on his cheeks over just the past day. His tousled hair had lost its stylish quiff now thanks to the hours they'd spent in bed already, and the water that still dampened and darkened the usually dark-blond locks. It now fell messily across his forehead, framing the oceans in his eyes perfectly in the glow of the bedside lamp.

Lucifer looked worried, and Cate knew he was desperately hoping that she'd be able to go with him. He propped himself up onto his elbow, lying on his side so that he could look down at his beautiful wife, and she gazed up at him with a smile. She turned onto her side to mirror him, leaning in so she could snuggle into his warm, safe body. "I can help make sure you're full of darkness, if you'll let me?" he then whispered, and Cate leaned back, looking up into his face with a frown.

"How?" she asked. He didn't say anything at first, but then used his fingertip to slit open an inch of skin on his neck, which he offered to her.

"Drink of me, Hecate. Take what I willingly offer. Cate was gobsmacked, but knew it was common practice for demons to blood-share, and guessed it was worth a shot. They'd never done it before. At Lucifer's insistence, it wasn't needed to strengthen their bond like others needed, so she wasn't sure what to expect. Cate leaned toward his open vein and lapped at the blood while screwing her eyes shut to avoid having to watch the crimson flow. She tried to imagine it was tea, rather than blood, but still couldn't fight her gag reflex as she gulped. It stayed down, and she was glad. Surely it had to work, and she just hoped that his blood, along with his dark seed, was strong enough to bring life into existence within her. Lucifer was patient, and he didn't push her to drink more than a mouthful at a time, but simply reminded her why they were doing it to help spur her on.

When she could drink no more, he lifted his leg over hers and wrapped his free arm around her back, enveloping Cate tightly with his strong body while he leaned down and kissed her deeply. When he released her mouth, she snuggled against him, feeling sleepy, and he watched as she rested her chin on his chest and closed her eyes, as though drifting off to sleep.

Lucifer could sense that she was weak, but that her tired body was struggling to stay awake in his hold. He intended to let her rest for a little while, happy to keep her safely cocooned within his protective grip as she did so, but then his wife jerked slightly. She forced herself awake again and looked up at him with a smile.

"How will we know if it's worked?" she asked, automatically placing her hand over her belly as she stared up at him thoughtfully. Her green eyes seemed to shine bright even in the dim light, and they hypnotised him as he looked down into the face of the woman he loved so very much.

"I'll sense it," he answered her. "Well, I think so anyway. I did with all three of you, but it was weeks after I'd been on Earth, not right away," he added, referring to her, Devin and Serena. It was odd hearing him talk of her that way. It'd been such a forbidden connection that they hadn't acknowledged in so long and it felt strange to be reminded of her true heritage.

"So, we have to wait?" she asked him.

"No darling, we keep on trying," Lucifer replied, and grinned as he climbed on top of her. He stopped to briefly check that she was ready, aware that her frail body was still struggling to keep up with him despite wanting to keep going, and he shot her his most seductive smile.

"Yes," she said, gazing up at him as Lucifer pulled up her hips and slid himself inside her wet chasm again and again until they both reached another glorious climax.

"Okay, let's do this one more time," Lucifer said, gripping Cate's hands tightly as she stood before him by the bed. She raised an eyebrow playfully and he laughed. He didn't need to read her mind to know she was having dirty thoughts and shook his head in mock astonishment. "Not that," he whispered in reply, with a wicked smile on his lips.

He had only a few minutes left until the waning moon would begin to affect him and knew it was time to try and take her home again. Lucifer called to every ounce of his dark force to empower him and focussed his mind on his dark realm.

He held Cate closer, closed his eyes, and attempted the teleportation again. A second later, he could feel them pulling away from Earth, down towards Hell, and he dedicated all his strength on taking his wife home at long last. It worked, and as they shifted between the worlds, a tiny spark of new power came into his almighty consciousness. It was like a small flame, and Lucifer knew right away that it was the essence of a life that was just beginning.

The pair of them teleported straight into their castle chambers this time, and Cate caught her breath quicker than she'd thought she would without her powers. She then looked up into her husband's eyes with a satisfied smile and was so happy to be home at last.

He smiled down at her and pulled her into his arms, kissing her passionately. It was just seconds before he was telling her the wonderful news, and Cate broke down in happy tears that their plan had worked. She was going to be a mother, and while she was terrified, she was also ecstatic.

CHAPTER TWENTY-FOUR

The entire underworld welcomed Cate back home with joy and relief. She was at Lucifer's side as he convened his dark council, and even his closest and most loyal demons cheered loudly. They congratulated her on having found her way home at long last, and even Lilith seemed relieved to see her. The ancient demon smiled warmly over at Cate when she took her seat beside her husband at the top of the huge wooden table, and while it was a surprise, she couldn't resist grinning back at her.

The celebrations that followed her return lasted for many days, thanks to the King's good mood that simply could not be overlooked. They partied hard and celebrated without a care. As Cate reconnected with her friends and family, it was quickly revealed to her how not a single hellish being had been able to sense her existence at all during the long absence, and they were all glad to have her back where she belonged.

"He's been so lost without you," Serena told her when they were stood to one side together later that night, watching the party from the side-lines. The upper-level demons and witches all continued to party around them in the great hall of the dark castle, and the energy was electric. "He went to Earth many times to try and find you, but he kept coming back empty-handed. There wasn't so much as a hint of you, and I swear he came back a little more defeated every time. We didn't even know that you'd escaped until a couple of years ago when Alma managed to contact one of that angel's white witches, Angelica, I think her name was. She told her that you'd gotten away from that bastard a long time ago and took great pleasure in finding out that you still hadn't returned home. It took every ounce of strength Alma had not to kill the bitch for daring to mock her," she added. "Where were you? Why didn't you come home? She asked and paled as she pieced the story together. Serena smiled awkwardly over at Cate, who'd gone quiet thanks to her unwittingly harsh words. "I'm sorry, is it too hard to talk about it?" she then asked, her cheeks flushing almost as red as her hair in the dark hall when she realised how upset Cate was.

"Yeah it is. I just hadn't even thought about it from the other way around. I didn't realise how little you all knew about what'd happened to me. Dylan has given Lucifer all the details now, but I suppose I'll have to tell my side before too long as well."

Cate shook her head when Serena started to respond, somehow knowing she was about to ask for more information. She knew she had more questions but wasn't even close to being ready to answer them yet. "That stuff's definitely off limits for now. It's far too soon for me to talk about it. Part of me never even wants him to know," she admitted, looking over at Lucifer with a pained look as he chatted happily with Devin a few metres away.

Both men instinctively looked over at her, sensing her eyes on them. While Devin smiled, Lucifer frowned. He managed a supportive half-smile and Cate knew that he must've either overheard their conversation or he'd read Serena's thoughts while the pair of them had chatted. They came back over, and Devin kissed her cheek before hugging her again.

"Hey, are you okay?" he asked, and his genuine concern made her smile. She was glad they'd mended things a long time ago, and it was nice knowing he hadn't lost his affection for her after all. Of course, now it was because of both his loyalty and protective urges towards her as his Queen, rather than any of his old emotions.

"Yes. I'm fine, Devin. I honestly couldn't be any better," she answered with a wide grin, looking at each of them while a contented pang shot through her still healing heart. It was great to be home. She instinctively brushed her hand over her stomach and caught Serena's mouth as it dropped open beside her, the realisation hitting the Princess like a sudden bolt of intuitive insight. Thankfully, she didn't say anything. Serena knew the King and Queen would want to tell everyone their happy news themselves when they were ready. She just beamed over at them and bounced on her feet excitedly. Lucifer grinned down at Serena and afforded her a wink as a silent thank you.

"What I'm about to tell you is strictly between us for now, okay?" Satan asked, looking at both Devin and Serena with a serious expression, and they both nodded in understanding. "Cate's expecting our first child," he told them, reading their happy thoughts as they both smiled up at their master. Serena reached over and took Cate's hand and gave it a gentle squeeze before pulling her into a tight hug.

"Congratulations," she told them both, and she leaned up to give Lucifer a soft kiss on his cheek. He hugged and kissed her back, and then patted Devin on the shoulder, pausing for a moment to gaze upon his family with a smile.

Before any of them could say another word, Leviathan ran over to the royal brood, grinning mischievously at Cate. He bowed to Lucifer, who smiled back at his friend, and then ushered for the demon to join them.

"Hail to the Queen," Leviathan bellowed as he stepped forward, grabbing Cate and lifting her up off her feet for a few moments, as he twirled her in his arms. Devin and Serena laughed at the demon's playfulness and left the three of them to talk. They headed back over to speak with their coven but bowed to the King respectfully before they left his side.

"Get off me, you bloody fool," Cate chastised the demon jokingly. She wriggled and climbed down from his tight embrace, slapping him hard on the shoulder. After stepping back, she giggled as he feigned pain at her feeble hit, and then felt strong hands grab her waist from behind. Cate then felt Lucifer's stubbly chin rest against her shoulder as he peered over at the demon and wrapped his arms tighter around her, his hands resting over her stomach protectively.

"Hands off, Levi. She's all mine," he ordered him, but was still being playful with his friend. He knew Leviathan didn't have any ill-conceived ideas towards his Queen. He wouldn't dare.

"My sincerest apologies, sire," he proclaimed, bowing down overzealously at their feet, and making them both laugh even more. He rose after a second and they continued chatting for a while, each of them enjoying the relaxed atmosphere and long overdue calmness that'd descended over the entire castle.

***

Being back home at long last affected Cate much better than she'd ever thought possible. She hadn't realised just how human she'd become again during her forced time away. The Dark Queen had to adjust to everything all over again, especially the lack of everyday comforts.

"I'd do just about anything for a cup of tea right now," she mumbled grumpily to Serena after just a few days back in Hell. She already missed the ability to eat and drink, and was sure that it must be her cravings setting in. Milky tea with a handful of biscuits to dunk in it was all she could think about for some reason. Her companion simply laughed and rolled her eyes, but soon doubled her efforts to keep her busy. Cate knew it was all a ploy to take her mind off both the things she missed from Earth and the more unsavoury reminders of her recent past but was willing to take any distraction she could get.

They sat together in the royal quarters, working hard, and Cate tried again to summon her dark power. She wanted to bring it back as quickly as possible, but something was still getting in the way. The Dark Queen huffed, annoyed once again at her failure and still weak body, but she tried again despite the setbacks.

By the next night, Dylan had been fully initiated into the dark coven and was allowed to visit Cate and Lucifer's private living area. Alma presented her to the King and Queen, promising Lucifer that she'd completed her transition and had encompassed her dark powers fully. He stood and approached the kneeling witch, looking down at her with a stern expression on his face as he read her mind again.

Seeing the pair of them like that, Cate was reminded of the last time Dylan had been in Hell, and just how awful those days had been for her. This time, though, it was going to be completely different. The past was long gone, and their amazing new life was just beginning, and she'd help make sure of that. Lucifer nodded to Alma, who visibly let out the breath that she had been holding in anticipation.

"Rise," he commanded Dylan, who immediately did as she was bid. She didn't dare meet Lucifer's gaze, looking over at Cate instead with a longing, almost shy smile. "You may now greet your Queen," he added, walking back over to where she still sat, and Dylan followed closely behind him.

Cate stood and walked to meet them, lifting onto her tiptoes to kiss her husband when he reached her.

"Thank you," she whispered into his ear as he gripped her waist. She kissed him again before he released her and was glad he'd trusted her enough to leave the two of them alone. Alma followed the King's lead and left the living area too. Perhaps adhering to a silent order from him, Cate couldn't be sure.

Dylan's face lit up when they were finally alone, and she almost ran the last few paces to get to her friend. She quickly gathered Cate up in her arms, hugging her tightly.

"We finally did it," she said as they pulled back from their hug, beaming at her. Cate grinned back at Dylan, revelling in her friend's happiness. She was so glad they'd made it to Hell together safely, just like they'd always hoped they would, and was pleased to see she hadn't been harmed.

"We sure did. Are you okay?" Cate asked, looking across at Dylan and checking her over as she asked.

"I'm better than okay," Dylan replied, putting her at ease immediately. "I finally have everything I ever wanted, Cate. And it seems you do, too," she added, looking down at her stomach with a sly grin. Her cheeks flushed red, and she gasped, shocked at how Dylan could already know her secret.

"Can you sense it?" she asked, genuinely surprised. Her old friend nodded. Dylan knew her better than almost anyone, so it made sense that she was the first one to notice the changes in her.

"It's more like a feeling, and you smell different somehow. I only realised it for sure once I was close to you," she explained. "How fucking amazing is all of this?" Dylan then shrieked, jumping up and down excitedly, and Cate was pleased to see she hadn't lost any of her usual vulgarity during her transition to a dark witch.

Cate pulled her back into a tight hug and held her close for a few minutes. When she pulled away, she ushered for her to sit at the nearby table beside her. They caught each other up on the events from the last few days, and Dylan told her all about how Lucifer had come to the flat that night and found her there rather than Cate. "I opened the door and totally freaked out. I didn't know what to do, so I just fell to my knees before him. I opened my mind before he could even react to my being there instead of you. Somehow, it worked, and luckily he spent a few minutes reading my thoughts rather than just opting for interrogation," Dylan told her. "I let him have all of it and didn't hold anything back. All my thoughts and memories, especially my knowledge of the astral plane and the spell I'd cast up there to get you out. He knew I wanted to join his coven, and he must've read my mind to know where you were. He clicked his fingers and teleported me straight to Hell, without having actually said a single word to me."

"Whoa, well, I'm just glad it worked out that way. I know it can't have been easy for you seeing him again without me there. I guess Alma was commanded to be at the dark gates to greet you?" Cate asked, and Dylan nodded, but immediately looked away from her intense gaze.

"Yes, she met me. It was awkward at first though, because there's something I haven't told you—something else that draws me to Hell as well as my connection with you. It goes deeper than just our friendship," she told her, looking worried.

"What is it, you can tell me anything, Dylan," Cate promised, and her mind was racing as to what her friend might be about to reveal. She'd never known Dylan to keep a secret from her since releasing her from Uriel's captivity and was eager to hear the truth.

"Alma's my mother," she finally admitted, her eyes still down. "I don't even know why I never told you about it. I just never found the right moment to bring it up, and I guess I didn't really want to re-live it all. She kind of abandoned me when I was just a little kid, so I guess I was always too torn up and angry all these years to deal with it. But we've mended so much between us in just the last few days together, and I finally feel like I have the answers I needed. I'm now truly ready to serve you and the King completely, and I'll keep no more secrets from you from now on. I promise, and I understand if you can never forgive me for not telling you the truth sooner."

Cate reached over and grabbed Dylan's chin, pulling her gaze back up to meet hers. She stared at her friend for a moment and was taken aback by her worried words. Cate smiled across at her, silently letting her know she could never be angry with her, and Dylan couldn't stay sad. Her usual playful smile crept back in after a few seconds.

"It's okay, Dylan," Cate told her quietly, but earnestly. "I'm so very happy to be here at last, and it's all thanks to your hard work. You deserve to be happy, but it's a reward only you can find for yourself," she told her with a smile. "It seems that we've both been able to come home and be with our family at last, and that's all that matters." Dylan grinned broadly, seemingly unable to help herself. Cate was right; she was home at last.

The pair talked in private for a while longer, and they loved being given some time alone to process the events from the past few days. Lucifer graciously left them to it, and Cate felt more relaxed and happier than ever. It was a wonderful realisation to know that both her family and her best friend would be by her side for eternity. Together at last—and always.

CHAPTER TWENTY-FIVE

It wasn't long before being back in Hell made Cate feel so much more like her old self again. Thanks to her stubborn sessions with Serena, she quickly began getting stronger and her senses keener, and her powers soon made their way back under her control at last. It did help, of course, that Lucifer's darkness coursed through her body again thanks to their rekindled relationship, his continued blood-sharing, and his child that now grew inside of her. Those key elements all added to her recovery tenfold as the pregnancy progressed, and she felt better than she had in years.

After just a few weeks, Cate was able to teleport herself around the castle at will. And the superior strength she'd once had returned to her body, allowing her to keep up with Lucifer again as they made love for hours. She desired him with every inch of her being, and often downright demanded that he satisfy her intense cravings for him. Cate was insatiable, and her powerful husband was the one and only outlet for that passion. Lucifer was the one drug she needed, or wanted, to get her high, and luckily, he was always keen to oblige.

"Pregnancy becomes you," he told Cate one night with a sultry smile. They were lazing on their huge bed, lying on the black satin sheets while surrounded by black roses that'd been manifested as a treat for them from Alma.

He trailed kisses down Cate's already slightly swollen belly, her ready core in his sights. She groaned loudly as he sucked her sensitive nerve endings into his mouth and flicked his tongue over them expertly before sliding his fingers inside her gushing cleft, while he continued to devour her delicate, tender nub. Cate came within minutes but hadn't had nearly enough of him. She gripped Lucifer with her strong legs and pulled him closer for a kiss, sliding him inside of her within seconds of her previous comedown. He followed her lead, revelling in her increased strength and incredible sex-drive. It was hours before she'd had enough and snuggled down to rest in her husband's arms.

As the next few days passed by, Lucifer and Cate quickly realised that the pregnancy could not be hidden any longer. All the witches seemed to sense it as soon as she was within a few feet of them, and many would give her a knowing smile. They said nothing, and Cate guessed they'd been made aware that they weren't to speak a word until Lucifer had made a formal announcement, which he finally gave during their late-night gathering to celebrate the spring equinox. The news was met with cheers and praise, as expected, and the Dark King and Queen didn't stop smiling the entire time.

Following Dylan's initiation, Alma had been free to watch over Cate with increased effort, and the Dark Queen could feel the witch's presence around her almost all the time, as if she couldn't stay away. Alma still hadn't forgiven herself for failing to stop her from getting captured up on Earth and begged her Queen to punish her however she saw fit. It was as though she wanted to be tortured for her shortcomings, rather than carry her shame so heavily on her shoulders, but Cate wouldn't hear of it. She was a fair and merciful Queen, despite her dark core, and couldn't blame Alma for the unfortunate events that'd happened up on that beach all those years before.

The witch had tried her best, as always, and she wouldn't punish Alma for Uriel's disturbing doings. None of them could've ever anticipated his plans. In fact, Cate was glad Alma had simply been knocked out and then left while Angelica and the other white witches completed their mission to kidnap her. She almost certainly couldn't have taken on a whole coven of white witches alone, and Cate couldn't bear to even contemplate the possible outcomes if she'd tried to fight them off single-handed. She refused to fret on it and urged the high priestess to do the same.

Dylan had seemingly gone through her trials and initiation with relative ease, although Cate could still sense her fear and trepidation of the King when she was near him. The scars were still fresh, and although neither of them raised the subject, it was always the elephant in the room whenever she attended to them. It was nice to see that she and Alma had grown closer still, and one night, while they were relaxing together before a roaring fire in the royal living area, Dylan finally told Cate the story of how her mother had come to be at Lucifer's side. Cate listened to Alma's story intently, but there were parts of it she hated hearing. She wasn't comfortable knowing that their high priestess and her husband had once been lovers, but she chose to let it go. There were more than just a few women in his past, and she couldn't bring herself to dwell on either of their histories, especially when it came to their lovers.

Cate just enjoyed their rekindled love and happiness, while trusting that Lucifer only had eyes for her. It was good learning the truth about Dylan's past, and she opened up with her in return about her fears and guilt. Dylan was a calm and assuring friend as always, and both women enjoyed the closeness they could still share, even if it had to be in private. Lucifer's understanding of their close bond was an element of their new life she simply couldn't live without, and it felt good to have a true friend around.

Her King had also gone one step further, and appointed Dylan her official protector, thanks to her unflinching loyalty and love for the Dark Queen. She was more than worthy of the role and seeing Dylan flourish under the dark reign empowered Cate even more.

Cate strengthened more as the days passed, which in turn pleased Lucifer immensely. He was still incredibly angry at the way their marriage had been forcibly split in two, but couldn't blame his wife for Uriel's doing, nor for hiding away following her escape.

Lucifer summoned Dylan to explain the situation the other council members in greater detail one night during one of their regular meetings, having informed them he refused to put Cate through the ordeal of reliving the painful past in front of the council. After Lilith's seemingly relentless questioning, the witch was released, and they all had to agree that the Queen and her witch had done the right thing. They all knew that if Uriel had found her on Earth again following her escape, there would be no chance of her evasion a second time.

"We need a plan, just in case," Lilith advised him when Dylan had gone. "If this ever happens again, we go up there baying for blood. Do you agree, your majesty?"

"I do," he replied. "All we need to do is find the perfect pawn, and I think I know just the one." He knew Uriel would be ruthless in his seduction a second time, and he would force her to say yes to his every desire. That would never be allowed to happen again, and they all agreed the Queen should remain in Hell for the foreseeable future.

Later that night, Cate rested in her husband's arms as they lay on the large sofa together. He tried to force them away but couldn't fight Dylan's memories of her time with Cate invading his thoughts. Envisioning the sad, tender moment the pair had shared together at the empty penthouse, as well as Cate's first few days back on Earth, brought him nothing but pain. Reliving Dylan's memory was like a movie playing in his mind of the desperation Cate had faced, and he loathed seeing her so lost and afraid.

"What are you thinking about?" she asked him, looking up into his deep blue eyes. Cate could tell that Lucifer was pensive. She'd been lying in his arms quietly as he cradled her from behind, but he hadn't spoken in a while.

"You're not ready to talk about it yet, my love," he told her, gazing down into her bright green eyes adoringly as he spoke, and his meaning was clear. He was desperate to uncover the truths about what had gone on in that astral plane.

"You can still ask. I understand there are many things that have been left unsaid. If I'm not ready to answer, I'll say so," she promised, turning onto her side in his embrace so that they could see each other more easily.

"Dylan's memories, they've told me almost everything I need to know," he told her, and he twirled one of her ringlets between his fingers absentmindedly.

"Almost," she muttered quietly, but urged him to carry on.

"The spell I can understand, and see that it made you untraceable, but I just cannot seem to get past the fact that you were full of so much light? Why did he keep you so long, Hecate? What were you doing?" he asked, and his eyes speckled with black flecks as he contemplated her answer.

"I don't even know where to start, Lucifer," she answered honestly. "You won't like my explanation no matter what, and I'm so ashamed I don't think I could bear to even say it out loud. He wanted vengeance at first, but then his goal changed. He wanted…"

"You," he answered. And Cate nodded.

"Yes. Please, can you ever forgive my foolishness?" she asked, curling into a ball in his arms, afraid of his reply.

"Only if you can forgive mine, too," he told her, hugging Cate tightly.

***

"I can hear something strange," Lucifer told Cate as they lazed together in their huge bed. She was lying on her back under the black sheets, while he lay next to her with his head snuggled into her chest. His legs were wrapped around hers protectively, and she loved how close he always kept her now that they were back together. His strong hand ran up and down her stomach, and the baby continuously kicked the palm of his hand, making him laugh.

"Like what?" she asked and was delighted to share every moment of her first pregnancy with her husband. She knew he'd never been able to enjoy such moments in the past while his heirs had grown within their other mothers' wombs. She often wondered why and how it'd finally worked after his many years spent trying, but he always refused to talk about the details with her, and she had to respect his need for privacy. Cate hoped someday she'd get the truth, but for now it was just another mystery only he had the answer to, and it didn't bother her enough to pursue it.

"It's like a strong thumping sound," Lucifer told her, and climbed down to lay an ear against his wife's swollen belly. He listened hard. She was now around halfway through her pregnancy and had begun getting the frequent strong kicks and prods on her bladder that let her know the little one was bouncing around in there quite happily. Lucifer often talked to the bump, saying he could sense the energy that grew from deep within her, referring to it as a dark flame that developed and grew stronger and more powerful every day.

"Do you think it's the baby's heartbeat?" Cate asked, eager to figure it out. She propped herself up on her elbows and looked down at him, drinking in the sight of his gorgeous face and rugged beard she loved so very much with a contented smile.

"Perhaps, but if it is—that means there are two of them," Lucifer answered, grinning as he pulled Cate up out of the bed. Her eyes grew wide with surprise, and he laughed. "Come on, let's go and ask the witches," he added. They dressed quickly and Lucifer teleported them to the witches' chambers immediately, which were littered with dark spell books and bottled potions. It always occurred to Cate how they were highly organised and incredibly clean—no big cauldrons or spider webs like she'd once imagined thanks to children's stories and movies she'd pored over as a child. They had every potion imaginable, and never seemed short of an answer for whatever Lucifer tasked them with, and this request was no exception.

Alma tried her best but couldn't see into Cate's thick womb lining using her magic and informed them it was completely normal for the offspring to be too powerful for the magic to penetrate the protective layers. When two mighty beings mated, the pregnancies were often unusual, so she wasn't at all surprised that it'd happened to the Dark King and Queen. If they went to Earth, she hoped the electronic hospital equipment might be able to see, but that was still out of the question for either of them. The risks were far too high.

"Next suggestion?" Lucifer demanded, and Alma set about searching their ancient books for a spell she might try instead. After reading through the old texts and having a feel of Cate's belly for a while, she believed there to be two foetuses as well. The knowledgeable witch took a few more minutes to press on Cate's stomach, gently prodding and poking her while they chatted. All of them were incredibly excited at the prospect of there being two babies on the way, and Cate was surprised she wasn't afraid.

"Wow, imagine that," Dylan whispered as she joined them, leaning down to lay her hands on Cate's stomach. The strong kicks she received in response to her touch made both her and her closest friend laugh. "Cheeky," she told the bump playfully. They then agreed to try some other methods, as long as they didn't cause any harm to the Queen or her offspring. Sara and Dylan put together an alternative version of a chant they'd found in an old almanac, while Alma concocted a potion for Lucifer to rub on Cate's belly. The idea was that the combination of potion and a spell would hopefully allow him a glimpse of what lay beneath Cate's protective layers—almost like a second sight.

It wasn't long before the witches all began reciting the altered incantation and Lucifer rubbed the gooey potion over Cate's belly. Only he was powerful enough to try and have a look without causing harm to her or the baby, or perhaps babies. Lucifer closed his eyes, keeping his hands firmly on his wife to keep him grounded, and he concentrated on the witches' powerful words.

The Dark King soon felt his consciousness shift, somehow going out of himself and into his wife. It was like an awareness, moving down through the layers of her skin and muscle, and then into her protective womb. She made sure to lie completely still, wordlessly sending Lucifer the go ahead via Dylan, who watched her like a hawk knowing her thoughts were being read. Cate also let him know via their *expression* that she wasn't being affected by his actions in any way and to continue.

Lucifer quickly became aware of her strong body, trying to push the intruding presence away, but he pressed on. He wasn't there to harm them, and the resistance eventually halted. It wasn't long until he saw a tiny, pink-skinned baby. The arms and legs were scrawny, and he could see its veins through the thin skin, but the foetus was moving around with strong movements. Their child was opening its tiny mouth and sucking its thumb as he watched in awe for a moment, and Lucifer could tell right away that the baby was a little girl. He then urged his consciousness to shift around some more, trying to see the whole space that was available to him. He nearly withdrew after a few minutes, but then there it was—a second baby, just as he'd thought. The other one was a boy, and he was moving around just as strongly as the girl but was a little larger than his twin. The boy baby was sucking his little thumb eagerly while moving gracefully in the amniotic fluids. He was content and healthy, just like his sister.

Lucifer watched each of them for a moment longer and then retreated gently. With careful gestures, he allowed his mind to push through the layers and come back to himself, and back to Cate. When he eventually opened his eyes, Lucifer grinned at his wife.

"Twins!" he exclaimed. He was clearly in shock at the incredible news and had a mixture of surprise and excitement he couldn't seem to hide on his usually so stoic face.

"Whoa," she replied, laughing at him. Two babies. Twin flames coming into their dark world. This news was just getting better and better.

Both Alma and Dylan insisted on Cate being checked over before they left but were happy that the spell had been a success, and quickly congratulated their rulers on their fantastic news.

***

The pregnancy continued without any complications. Both Cate and the babies seemed powerful, strong, and healthy, and when the day came that her water's broke, Lucifer was by her side the entire time. He banned anyone other than Dylan and Alma from attending to his Queen during childbirth, deciding not to allow anyone else to interfere with her or their babies during Cate's moment of vulnerability.

The labour progressed quickly, and Lucifer held her hand while Cate's now strong body took over the birthing process wonderfully. She was tough, and yet still showed the same frailty as any human woman would during the birthing process. Her pain consumed her, but she pressed on in readiness to deliver their precious bundles, and he was in awe.

"I'm ready now," she called out, looking up at Lucifer from the bed as soon as she felt the urge to push, which was only an hour or so after the contractions had started. Dylan and Alma stood at the ready, watching and helping her as much as possible while her body took over. Cate's inner muscles clenched strongly as the next contraction took over and she screamed, sending their first twin, the boy, into Alma's ready hands. He cried out with strong lungs right away, and Lucifer took him into his arms immediately. He wrapped the child in a warm towel and cleaned him up while Alma cut the cord.

Lucifer then leaned down to show their son to Cate, who smiled and touched his tiny head gently, and kissed him. She let the happiest tears of her life fall onto her red cheeks, but it wasn't long until she needed to push again, and she readied herself one more time. Their little girl was born just minutes after their son, and she too cried loudly at first, just like her brother had done. She settled quickly though, already seeming relaxed, and snuggled into her own soft towel before Dylan put her into her mother's awaiting arms.

Cate was delighted and looked up into Lucifer's eyes as they held their two newborns. He seemed absolutely besotted with his son, but soon placed him in Cate's empty arm so she could hold them both close. The doting father then took their baby girl into his embrace so his wife could greet her son properly at last, and she couldn't take her eyes off his gorgeous face.

The babies soon both fell asleep, seemingly peaceful in their parent's arms, and each then groaned when Alma and Dylan took them away again. They needed to get the twins cleaned and dressed thanks to the mess of blood, but they worked quickly before handing them back to the blissful couple.

While they were sorting out the babies, Cate could feel her muscles tensing from deep within. Her body seemed to be strengthening with so much force that it felt as though a strong pulse reverberated through every inch of her, but luckily, it only lasted for a few minutes. She quickly felt her pains subsiding with each powerful wave, and by less than an hour after the birth she'd completely healed. Cate was back to her old self in no time at all and was glad her dark power had grown so strong during the last few months.

"What shall we call them?" Cate asked Lucifer when they were relaxing together a little while later. She'd just climbed out of a roaring hot shower and had to admit she felt amazing. The witches had left them alone at last, having been satisfied that both she and the babies were fine. Even the usually playful Dylan had insisted on doing numerous checks with them first, and while she'd loved having her be a part of the birth, she was glad when they'd left. Cate wanted to have some time alone to enjoy their little family in peace. It felt strange to suddenly be a parent, but she adored the sense of all-consuming pride she had for them and discovered how instantaneous her need to protect them was.

Cate also marvelled at her body's reaction to her hungry offspring. Her belly was flat, and her soreness gone, but her breasts swelled with her milk, and she fed the twins with natural ease. All the while, Lucifer couldn't take his eyes off the three of them.

"What do you think of Blake?" Lucifer answered, looking down at their son. He seemed so sure. It was as if he'd known what he wanted to call his new son all along, and she smiled. She supposed that this was the first time he'd had any control over their names and remembered how he'd wanted her to be named Hecate—a name she'd readily assumed regardless of it not officially being her full name. "And, how about Luna?" he asked, kissing his daughter's tiny forehead as she slept peacefully while suckling away at Cate's breast.

She nodded in agreement and kissed her husband when he looked up at her with a shy smile at last.

"They're both absolutely perfect names, yes to each of them," she told him, and was glad to give him this. He was so naturally warm with them, and she'd never seen his hardened façade slip so far as it had in that moment. Lucifer seemed vulnerable, and Cate was pleasantly surprised by his tenderness, but truly loved both the names he'd chosen for their beautiful dark babies. It was decided, and she whispered their names to them as Blake and Luna finished their feeds and drifted off into a blissful sleep.

CHAPTER TWENTY-SIX

By four years old, the twins were bright, powerful little dark spirits. They'd brought so much happiness and love to both Lucifer and Cate in their short lifetimes, more than the almighty couple could have ever hoped for, and life was finally good. Their unusual family was complete, and they all thrived thanks to the twins' powerful energy and strength that'd somehow connected all the dots along the way.

Despite Lucifer's initial worries for his heirs' safety, Devin and Serena were living up on Earth again. They'd wanted to continue adding to their successful following, and Lucifer had agreed, however, he'd insisted they return home regularly. The pair had agreed and brought with them gifts for their young niece and nephew each time. They regaled the twins with fun stories and strange tales from up on the mysterious realm, and the children both loved hearing all about Earth.

The twins always asked Cate to tell them stories of her old home when she tucked them in at night, and she couldn't resist. She animatedly retold her children the storylines of old movies and books that she'd read when she was younger, and they lapped them up with huge smiles she found infectious. Cate basked in their excited shrieks and eager pleads for more of the fantastical stories, so would indulge them happily. She often told them about her childhood and of their grandmother, Ella. Despite how sad it made the Queen to remind herself of her guilt, and of the awful memories that thinking of Ella's passing would summon within her, she spoke warmly of their lost grandmother.

"Don't you have a Daddy then, Mummy?" Luna had asked her one night, with such an innocent tone to her question that Cate couldn't lie. She had to laugh at her intuitiveness, though, and knew Luna was a clever little princess already.

"No, baby girl, I don't have one," she'd replied with an awkward smile, and shook her head before she kissed her goodnight.

As well as teaching the twins to play games and read, Cate had also ensured they encouraged the children to learn about their powers from a young age. Blake and Luna always had powerful beings around them, even when they were asleep, and each was there to keep them safe, as well as to teach them all about their powers and dark lineage. With the help of both their parents and the witches and demons, they'd already learned how to teleport and had also developed a strong mental link with one another, allowing them to share their thoughts via a strange psychic bond. Cate had even felt their messages creep into her dreams and thoughts at times, too, proving how powerful they already were.

She thought about their differences, and how each had developed over the years, and her heart swelled with pride when she thought how far they'd both come. Luna was a gentle little soul. She was kind and warm hearted, and she loved making her mother smile. She had soft green eyes and dark brown hair that already curled into huge lockets around her tiny shoulders, just like her mother, and Cate found staring into her face odd—as if she were looking at herself from when she was the same age. Blake had the same hair and eye colour too, but unlike his twin, he was neither soft nor gentle. He was incredibly strong though, even at such a young age, and they could sense his power swelling and extending inside of him. He was decisive and stubborn, a trait he had to have gotten from his father, or so Cate would always joke. But he too could be kind, and would show his sensitive side on rare occasions, usually only when he was alone with his mother.

Blake would also revel in Cate's affections, and yearned for more from her, eager to hear her laugh or keep her attention on him as long as possible. She loved them both so dearly she couldn't bear not to lavish them with hugs, kisses, smiles, and encouragement along every step of the way and she guessed they needed the steadiness her tenderness offered them. Her human side seemed intent on teaching them the important lessons in morality and kindness that Lucifer, unfortunately, still seemed to have no concept of, and the balance between their two sides was working wonderfully.

***

Cate winced and cried out as her head began pounding again with agonising throbs of a sharp, shooting pain. The royal living area of the dark castle began spinning around her and she swayed, unable to stay on her feet. She even had to grab the nearby wall to steady herself properly. The headaches had started a couple of months before and had been happening more and more ever since. Neither Lucifer nor any of the powerful dark witches within their premier coven could figure out what might be causing the affliction, but they all worried what the pain might mean. The strange episodes would come and go once every few weeks at first, but were happening much more frequently, and when they did, she'd be overwhelmed by blinding agony for a few minutes while each bout lasted.

This time, though, something felt different. Cate's nose felt hot and throbbed as the pain raged inside her head. She raised her hand up to her mouth, having reached up to wipe clean a trickle from just above her lip. She thought it odd to have a runny nose, but when she pulled her hand down, Cate paled nauseously at the sight of her own blood. She quickly reached for a tissue from the table before her and sat down on the nearby sofa, and Dylan ran to her side. She grabbed a towel, soaking up some of the blood with a worried expression, while Cate shooed her away.

"I'm fine," she promised weakly, and Dylan shook her head.

"Liar," she replied, but said no more, concentrating instead on ensuring Cate recovered from her moment of illness.

Alma looked over at the Dark Queen and her protector from across the room. As soon as she'd noticed the nosebleed, a shiver had run down her usually steadfast spine. Lucifer had summoned her to discuss Cate's health with him again, but he now had a sneaking suspicion he wasn't going to like her theory. He had tasked her with creating a spell or a potion that might stop these strange attacks, but without knowing the cause of her illness, Alma hadn't had any luck in providing the Queen with a solution. They were both worried, especially Lucifer, who looked forlornly over at his wife, but there really was nothing either of them could do. Together they watched as Dylan tossed the blood-soaked towels into the fire before her and grabbed another.

"My lord," Alma said, beckoning him closer to speak with him more privately. "I think I've seen something like this happen before," she told him, and it was a bittersweet realisation as it hit her at last.

"When?" Lucifer asked her tersely, urgently wanting to find out more from his high priestess and her speculations on Cate's condition.

"Many years ago, when you travelled to Earth without the moon to protect you," Alma replied, looking dejected. Lucifer hoped she was wrong but knew in his heart that his loyal servant might've finally found the key to solving Cate's malaise.

"What does this mean?" he asked, and knew the answer, but still hoped he may be wrong in his depressive assumptions.

"I believe the Queen needs to return to Earth, master. I fear she may get a lot worse if we ignore these symptoms," Alma told him, already thinking of what healing potions she could adapt. She wondered how she might use them to cure Cate in time, but for now, she worried that time might not be on their side.

"I will not let her go up there without me," he bellowed angrily, looking down at the short witch with black eyes, showing the rage bubbling beneath the surface. "She's stayed in Hell before, without this happening?" Lucifer added, questioning the worried and frenzied thoughts she was having.

"Yes master, but maybe she was stronger before, or her human side wasn't revolting against the invading darkness? She was going to Earth regularly back then as well, whether in practising her teleportation or when we went to meet Devin. She's never stayed here for more than a couple of years at a time, and since everything with the angel, the pair of you have remained here permanently for her safety." Neither one of them needed reminding about that absence, but Lucifer added up Cate's time in Hell, and knew Alma was right—she'd never been there so long before. "That was five years ago now, my King. I truly believe that her human side is protesting— or maybe dying—I don't know for sure. But I cannot know until I am able to investigate further and test out some ideas for potions. If I'm right, this could be the end of her completely if her body is too weak to stave off the death I fear has already begun creeping in." Alma stared at Lucifer's feet while she gave him her predictions, and she shook with fear before him. Even after the last few years with the wonderful twins in his life to soften him, Lucifer was still an almighty dark force that no human or demonic being would ever want to mess with. The same went for delivering bad news. He didn't respond, but stared through Alma absentmindedly, deep in thought.

"Daddy," Blake called to him from across the room, breaking the King's reverie. "Mummy fell asleep," he informed his father, pointing over to where Cate had fallen from the sofa onto the hard floor, unconscious. Alma ran to the Queen. She lifted her up in her tiny, yet deceptively powerful arms and placed her back up on to the nearby couch. Dylan went running back in, Luna's tiny, pale hand in her own as she led her back into the main living area.

"Get them out of here," Lucifer commanded her, patting Blake on the head. Dylan followed his order and led the children out into the hall, heading for their bedrooms to play a game. Despite her fears for Cate's health and her desire to be by her friend's side there was no refusing her dark master's order.

"The Queen will have to go to Earth, master," Alma told him again, and this time Lucifer knew there was no other choice.

"Hide her from him, Alma. Do you understand me? Make sure she stays within the confines of the church at all times, and as soon as she's healed, or you figure out a cure, you bring her back to me," Lucifer commanded with a stern expression. His eyes began swirling with black specks at the very thought of losing her all over again, and it took everything he had not to explode with rage. "Is that understood?" he asked again, and Alma nodded and bowed to her master. She summoned Dylan back to them, and when she re-appeared, instructed her to gather some things and come with them to Earth. The witch nodded in agreement and left, tears already welling in her hazel eyes. Lucifer took a moment to be with his wife. He leaned down and kissed Cate's soft lips, but he felt utterly useless. He then headed off to sit with the twins for a while, needing their company to help him to calm his frenzied mind.

CHAPTER TWENTY-SEVEN

Alma arrived at London's Satanic church, carrying the still unconscious Queen, and Dylan was right behind them. Thanks to the lower-level witches who'd received the silent commandment from their master, a room had already been made up for her in the back of the vast, dark church, and Alma took her there without delay. There would be no stopping to explain the Queen's predicament to them, and the others stepped aside as they passed.

Cate was immediately slid under the covers to rest, while Dylan unpacked the belongings she'd brought from home for her, but she didn't even seem aware that they'd left Hell at all. Alma then sat beside the bed and watched as her mistress slept for two solid days. She never moved from the Queen's side, nor did she let herself drift off to sleep even once. After what felt like forever to the two witches, Cate slowly began to rouse. She was drowsy, but lucid, as she opened her eyes at last. When she came to, she was shocked to find herself on Earth, and looked over questioningly at the witches beside the bed.

"How do you feel?" Dylan asked Cate and was unable to hide the worry from her usually so relaxed face.

"Like crap, but better already. Did you manage to heal me?" she asked. She tried to sit up, but quickly slumped back down on the bed weakly, and Dylan urged her to rest. "I'm guessing it's a no, otherwise why would we be up here?" Cate answered her own question, seeing Dylan's disappointed look. The witch updated her on the unfortunate build up to her necessary sanctuary, and then climbed up on to the bed with her best friend. She held Cate tightly as she began to cry and didn't begrudge her a moment of weakness in the slightest. "How long do I have to leave it before I can go back?" Cate asked Alma when the powerful high priestess came over to join the pair of them.

She sat up and felt calmer and stronger now already. She then gratefully accepted the cup of sweet tea that the witch offered her and dunked in one of the accompanying chocolate biscuits with a smile. One thing was for sure, she'd really missed the food on Earth, and she hungrily dunked in another.

Cate then laughed at Dylan when she did the same with her own cup of tea and pile of biscuits, breaking the sombre mood.

"You need to stay here until you're at your full strength, your majesty. I believe your sickness to be your human side's rejection of the long stay in Hell. When you're well again, we'll try taking you home a little bit at a time— just at first. Perhaps then we can bring you here each full moon to stave off any more illness, at least until I can make a potion for you," Alma informed her, smiling over at Cate with motherly affection. "For now, though, you need to rest. You must always stay within the church's boundaries. It's for your safety, and this is what the King wants for you." Cate nodded and trusted Alma's words were true. She knew Lucifer had to have given them the order to send her to Earth. There was no other way she'd be there without him otherwise. She also understood that as long as she stayed within the church's protective circle, she'd be safe. To step over the threshold and out into the open could render her powerless to stop the white witches from finding her again, and that absolutely could not happen. Now that Dylan's spell was no longer keeping her hidden, tracing her was a very real possibility, and Cate shuddered at the prospect of Uriel succeeding in having her taken away again.

After a few more days spent resting, Cate had to admit she already felt much better. She'd had no more headaches or any of the other symptoms since her return to Earth and felt more energetic than ever. Regardless of the improvements, Alma ensured she continued to rest. The motherly witch had played the part of the caring nurse well but had also been quite pushy whenever she thought Cate might be taking things on again too quickly. Dylan stayed by her side, both by Alma's order and by her insistence of always being close to her Queen, and Cate was comforted at having her best friend nearby.

"I hadn't been feeling right for a while, but I never told anyone," Cate finally admitted to her as they relaxed in front of the television one night. They were just tucking into a gorgeous meal of spaghetti and meatballs cooked for them by the other lower-level witches who lived at the church, Suzanne, and Bea, and she groaned in satisfaction of their amazing cooking skills. The pair had been slowly making their way through all the newest movies and television shows that they'd missed out on during their time in Hell, and had been enjoying themselves, regardless of the circumstances that'd led them here.

"We could all see that you weren't right, Cate," Dylan replied, sipping on a glass of juice as she stared over at her friend. The Dark Queen had gone noticeably paler and skinnier over the last few months and had been much more tired and lethargic than she'd been at all since returning to Hell with Lucifer years before. Despite her insistence that she was okay, Dylan had known something wasn't quite right. "I actually thought you might be pregnant again or something," she added with a shrug, smiling over at Cate's shocked face as her incredulous assumptions took her by surprise.

"I wouldn't mind if that was the case," she replied after a few thoughtful seconds, blushing at the idea. She and Lucifer hadn't discussed the possibility of having more children yet, but she was sure that she'd want more when the time finally came for them to decide. "How long until the full moon?" Cate then asked with a sigh. She'd found that thinking of them made her miss Lucifer and the twins terribly but wouldn't let it upset her. Yes, she'd enjoyed the relaxation time with Dylan, and having the human food at her disposal again, but nothing compared to having her family with her.

"A week," Dylan informed her with a sly grin, her hazel eyes twinkling playfully. "Wow, you must be feeling better if you're already planning your next fuck," she teased, and had to duck an airborne meatball that Cate then sent flying over at her. The now stronger Queen threw it with such speed that the gooey meatball hit the wall behind and splattered into a huge, brown, sloppy mark that stayed stuck there, rather than bounce off the wall and onto the floor, and the squishing sound made them both giggle. "I must be right," Dylan then added. She then laughed loudly and threw a sticky string of tomato sauce covered pasta in Cate's direction, having eaten all her meatballs already. Cate simply caught the strand in her mouth and sucked it into her pursed lips, giggling again as Dylan shook her head in mock disgust.

"You always take it to a dirty place. I think maybe it's you who needs a good sorting out?" Cate replied with a wide grin, even though Dylan had been spot on—she was incredibly horny.

"Don't remind me," Dylan replied, feigning a pained, forlorn look. "It's been *so* long," she added with a forcefully sad expression on her pretty oval face.

"What, like a week? You're such a filthy fiend," Cate cried with a wicked grin. She discarded her plate on the low coffee table and then slumped back into the cushions of the comfortable sofa she was sprawled on, laughing so hard she snorted. Dylan laughed too, and she just shrugged in response, her lack of a witty reply telling Cate she was right.

Alma came in and cleared up the empty plates and cups, but not before telling the pair of them off for making a mess with the flying meatball. Dylan climbed up from her armchair and cleaned the splattered mess off the wall, bowing to her mother apologetically before she then left the two of them alone again.

Cate had found herself watching the two of them with intrigue during their short moment together. She'd always loved watching the pair of them interact since they'd been reunited at last a few years before. Dylan was still such a strong and playful character, and she'd seemed to settle into the darker way of life with complete ease. Alma, however, was of a much quieter nature.

She'd always seemed focussed on her duties so entirely that it was almost hard to imagine the mother and daughter as anything other than a high priestess and one of the witches in her coven. Cate had often caught them talking quietly together, though. Alma's usually so serious features would grow softer as she spoke to her daughter privately, and Cate hoped they were connecting bit by bit over the years. She remembered how she'd watched with a smile one day as Alma had held Dylan's hand protectively while they'd worked a powerful spell together. Their connection, combined power, and strong will had seemed to increase the magic's potency somehow, and even Cate could sense that their bond was slowly creating a formidable duo.

She hoped the twins would be that way with her and Lucifer when they were older, but that nothing would come between them like with Dylan and Alma. She had every hope that their magic would combine and strengthen each other's as they grew, rather than them vying for more power or rebelling against their parents as they got older. Cate was sure they'd soon become quite the pair. So far, their natures seemed to be in perfect balance, and she looked forward to a future in which that steadiness would undoubtedly lead them onwards, together.

***

Lucifer came to Earth as soon as the next full moon allowed him to teleport to his wife's side safely. He appeared in the doorway to Cate's bedroom, and watched as she napped peacefully for a few moments, sensing that she was already doing much better. Dylan lay beside her on the king-size bed, asleep too, but she quickly awoke from her nap, having sensed her master's presence. She stood and bowed to her King before she hastily left the pair of them alone, and he was pleased she'd never lost that healthy bit of fear in his presence. Lucifer read the witch's mind and knew that his beautiful wife was not only well, but also more than ready for him to come to her.

He smiled and shut the door behind him, and wandered over to the bed, stripping off before climbing under the covers with her. Cate didn't even stir as he leaned up on his elbow beside her and watched her sleep for a few moments longer. With a salacious smile, he then slipped his head under the warm covers and climbed between her legs. She slept on even as he lifted her nightdress and nestled himself above her hot, wet cleft, opening her legs further so he could access her delectable core.

Cate soon started dreaming of her husband, of his mouth against places that'd gone untouched too long and devouring her with his strong mouth. In her dream, he flicked his tongue over her swollen nub and his fingers delved deep inside of her to stroke on the sensitive spot inside with expert precision, making her moan in delight. She climaxed within minutes, her body shuddering as the strong release pulsated throughout her entire body. Cate flushed with heat and jumped awake and lifted the covers to look down at her body in sleepy bemusement. Lucifer's smiling face greeted her from between her trembling thighs and she laughed, releasing the confused tension she'd felt when she first awoke.

"Well, hello to you, too," she whispered down at her husband, before allowing her head to fall back onto the pillow. Lucifer groaned in response, laughing gruffly as she twitched beneath his touch. He was still stroking her sensitive insides wonderfully, and he began lapping at her clit again. Cate writhed and gripped the covers in her hands, arching her back as Lucifer pursued another climax from her, and she soon fell headfirst into a glorious wave of pleasure.

He then gripped her hips forcefully with his free hand as he tongued her effortlessly, pulling her closer to his eager mouth and heightening her climax. She cried out his name as she trembled and revelled in the aftershocks of his deep, pleasurable gift. She was so sensitive that Lucifer's hot breath made her shudder, but he didn't pull away. Cate lay back and panted as he trailed soft kisses up her belly to her breasts, sliding beneath her nightdress so she couldn't wriggle away. He commanded her pleasure, revelling in it himself as he devoured every inch of skin he could reach, and she didn't even try to fight.

Lucifer had worried so much for his wife during the last couple of weeks spent apart and was delighted to sense how strong and well she now was. He'd take this over her frailty, even if it meant they might have to spend more time apart until an answer could be found for her illness. He knew Alma would come through for him, and that they'd soon have a solution for the adverse effects Hell had seemingly been having on Cate's human half. In the meantime, he'd gladly settle for nights like this.

She arched her back and then pulled the cotton dress up and over her head in one quick move, exposing her dishevelled husband, who was still leaning over her now naked body. He caressed her breasts one at a time with his powerful kisses, soliciting more delighted groans. Lucifer looked up at her and smiled, his deep blue eyes playful and excited in the dim light of her small room. His dark-blond hair was tousled thanks to his antics under the heavy covers, but he somehow looked even more gorgeous to her. She took in his warm and happy smile and reached down to cup his coarsely stubble-covered cheeks. Cate then pulled him up so she could kiss her beloved husband's soft lips at long last. It'd been far too long since she'd kissed his mouth, those lips, that face, and she let him know just how much she'd missed them.

The enamoured couple chose not to leave Cate's small bedroom for the duration of the full moon's time over London. They decided to enjoy one another for as long as they could, rather than worry about what would have to happen once the moon waned. Lucifer laid beside his wife, basking in her attention, and lapping up the beautiful afterglow she now radiated with following her numerous climaxes. He pulled Cate into his arms and hugged her tightly.

"I don't want to leave you," he whispered into her ear, allowing her to sense his tiny moment of weakness. She was still the only being he ever showed that small side of himself to, and while she loved that he could open up to her, she felt sad not to be going back home alongside him. His words were a reminder that their time together was only short, but at least it was only for a little while.

"I don't want you to go either," she told him, snuggling into his neck and wrapping her legs around his muscly thighs as she breathed in his musky scent. They lay there together for a while longer, but eventually she felt him pull away, and he climbed up from the bed to get dressed. He peered down at her sadly before leaning down to give her a kiss goodbye, but she simply wasn't ready to watch him leave. As Lucifer then began to teleport away, Cate sprang up from the bed and grabbed his hand, travelling down with him to their home, regardless of his orders for her to stay behind. When they arrived, he pulled off his cargo jacket and wrapped it around her naked body before staring down at her angrily.

"Cate," he groaned, but she raised her mouth to his, stopping him from finishing his chastisement by placing a deep and powerful kiss on his lips.

"I'll follow you forever," she then whispered as she pulled away, smiling up at her lover and melting his resolve.

"It's not safe yet. You need to be well," he said, stroking her pale cheek with his hand as he stared into Cate's deep green eyes.

"Okay, but can I just see them. Only for a moment and then I'll go back, I promise?" she asked, and Lucifer knew she was talking about the twins. He nodded and immediately teleported the pair of them to the children's bedchambers, where they found their dark offspring playing a game of hide and seek with the demon Berith. All three beings smiled widely at the Queen as she entered, and Berith immediately teleported away to give them some privacy. Cate hugged the children tightly and beamed down at the pair of them, taking in their happy faces. "I can't stay, my darlings," she told them, feeling her smile falter slightly as she spoke. "But Daddy's here, and I'll come back as soon as I can. Be good for him, okay?" she asked them, and both Blake and Luna nodded in agreement.

"Get better soon, Mummy," Blake said as Cate stood, seeming to understand so much, despite his young age. She smiled down at him and nodded, seeing the worry in his tiny green eyes.

"I will, baby boy. I will," she told him before she padded back over to Lucifer and kissed him goodbye. Cate then teleported back to her bedroom in the church, feeling weak after her first sneaky few minutes back in Hell. She fell into bed exhaustedly as soon as she arrived, but before she could drift off to sleep, Dylan burst into her room. She was shouting and bellowing at her friend in annoyance and worry.

"How could you be so bloody reckless?" Dylan demanded, but Cate just curled up under the covers. She began falling into a deep sleep, mumbling her insincere apologies as she drifted off. Her heart was still back in the underworld, entombed forever in the two children she and Lucifer had created together, and regardless of her illness, it'd been worth the trip so she could see them.

CHAPTER TWENTY-EIGHT

After her first visit, Cate tried teleporting again every few days. Soon she was managing to go back to Hell for a few minutes here and there, splitting herself between the two worlds for a few more weeks, before building up to longer periods of time each visit. It wasn't perfect, but it was working, and at least that way Cate got to spend some time with the twins. She hadn't been away from them at all before her illness had struck, and she missed them terribly.

Each time the moon was full again, Lucifer came to Earth to be with her. They delighted in each other's company for as long as they could, shaking the church walls around them whenever the Dark King climaxed inside his lover, but the couple of days passed by in a fast blur each time. It was over far too quickly and always left them both feeling unsatisfied, having been used to being together every day again after her return to Hell.

After a few months, they decided to let the children come up to visit Cate at the church during one full moon. They weren't entirely sure, but they presumed the twins, like their father, couldn't stay up on Earth once the moon waned. Lucifer believed that because of his full darkness and Cate's half dark heritage, the twins were surely on the heavier side of the scale. He suspected the moon would bind them just as it did him, but they didn't even want to risk trying the theory out on the pair of them yet.

Cate loved spending time with Blake and Luna for longer than just the few hours she'd built her tolerance up to in Hell before the headaches crept in, and after that first successful visit, the twins were allowed to go and visit Cate during most of the full moon's that followed. Lucifer kept them close, holding their hands as they teleported up to the church excitedly, and they didn't leave their parents' sight the entire time. Both children enjoyed the change of scenery, despite the restrictions, and they'd happily watch the world go by from behind the safety of the church's big windows.

One night, though, Blake's curious nature got the better of him and he decided he wanted to see more. He waited until his father was busy elsewhere and then sneaked out of the church's side entrance. Within seconds, he'd crossed over the sacred line and was out in the open world.

Lucifer caught his son after just a few steps and grabbed him tightly. He pulled Blake back into the safety of their hallowed ground, scolding him immediately for his careless behaviour, and his vicious temper flared at his son's foolishness. Blake ran back inside in tears and curled up next to Luna in front of the fire in the main living area at the back of the church, nursing his bruised ago. Cate knew she should be angry but couldn't bear to scold her precious boy any more than his father already had for his moment of curiosity. After all, they'd raised the twins to be powerful little dark beings who knew their own minds, and she couldn't bring herself to disparage him for having followed his curious heart.

It wasn't long before Blake became intrigued by the outside world again, though. During each of their visits to Earth after that day, he managed to sneak away undiscovered. The Black Prince had even managed to hide his thoughts from his father, cleverly figuring out how to close that part of himself off to Lucifer's mind reading capabilities, and no one even knew he was doing it. All he did at first was cross the threshold and stand in the real world for a few seconds before ducking back inside, but he soon began exploring farther each time. He'd listened intently to the stories of the terrible white witches and had paid attention when he'd been told it wasn't safe outside of the church's protection. But he still didn't understand why his oh-so-powerful father was so scared. As far as Blake could see, there was nothing to be afraid of. Devin and Serena seemed to be able to live on Earth safely, so he figured why couldn't he just explore a little?

One night, Blake and Luna were playing quietly in their room while Cate was resting in her chambers. Lucifer had gone to Hell with Alma for a short while to check out a potion she'd finally managed to concoct in the hopes of curing Cate's symptoms, and Blake had an idea. Dylan was watching over the twins and agreed to grab them some hot chocolate if they promised to go straight to sleep after they'd finished. The pair grinned innocently, and each fluttered their eyelashes, making her smile down at them, her resolve quickly disappearing.

"Okay, I will be back in one minute. Stay right here," she told them, before ducking out into the kitchen to grab some hot drinks.

"Luna, come with me," Blake quickly whispered once Dylan had gone, taking her hand, and pulling her out of the church. She obliged but trembled in fear when they crossed the quiet road and headed towards a play park he'd found around the corner. Luna tried to say no, but her curiosity got the better of her, and she soon stopped trying to pull her brother back towards the safety of the magical threshold.

"It's okay. I've played here lots of times. I know it's safe," he promised, and despite her fear, Luna joined him in the fenced play area. They swung on the swings together, slid down the slides, and span giddily on the merry-go-round—laughing loudly and enjoying their thrills as they spent the next few stolen minutes acting like real five-year-olds.

Neither of them noticed the group of women that began encircling the fenced park, moving silently and gracefully through the still night air. They drew closer, chanting quietly and tightening their circle around them as the children played on obliviously for another few minutes. Eventually, Blake looked up and noticed their presence, but it was too late. He grabbed his sister close to him, sensing her panic, but there was nothing either of them could do. He held Luna as she cried, trying to be brave, but he knew he'd done something so incredibly wrong in taking her there. A heavy sensation welled in Blake's stomach, and for the first time in his life, he felt truly afraid.

***

Cate awoke with a start and knew immediately that something was wrong. Luna had sent her a mental flash, some kind of telepathic cry for help thanks to her strong power, and it scared her to have seen the white witches through her daughter's eyes even for that split-second. She looked for Lucifer, but he was gone from their bedroom, and she remembered that he'd headed home to talk with Alma about the potion.

There was nothing else for it, and she jumped out of bed, pulled on her black boots, and ran for the church's exit, feeling her daughter's mental beacon emitting from just across from the back entrance to the church. Cate ran outside and crossed the protective threshold without a second thought. She rounded the corner, and she saw them immediately—a white coven. They were being led by Angelica, and encircled her two precious children, trapping them within.

The twins were trying to get through their wall of witches, but they couldn't penetrate the powerful white circle. Both Blake and Luna pushed at the women, kicking, and hitting them, but the witches didn't flinch. They also didn't grab at them or try to bind them in any way. Cate was confused as she watched them for a moment but kept on towards the group as she tried to figure out how to defeat them or find a way to break their circle long enough to free her children.

She was so busy focussing on them she realised too late how the real reason the white witches weren't reacting to the twins' retaliation was because they weren't there for them. They were using the children as bait to lure Cate out of hiding.

A second coven then appeared and teleported around the Dark Queen, strategically encircling her. She didn't even have time to react to their presence and felt a burst of light power course through her body, weakening her instantly. Cate clutched at her aching chest and cried out as the witches blocked her path, while each of them smirked at her delightedly. None of them spoke, but she soon felt the familiar feeling of them teleporting her skywards and knew why they'd come.

She tried to resist but knew from previous experience that she couldn't fight them, so quickly gave up. Cate couldn't see clearly in the blurry white haze that flashed past her as they travelled up and away from Earth, and she quickly realised she couldn't move at all. She gave up trying, allowing herself to be teleported away without any further resistance—it was pointless, and she knew it. Cate couldn't stop her thoughts turning to Lucifer, and her heart ached as his face flashed across her mind. She pushed the thoughts of him away and focussed on Luna and Blake instead. She hoped the witches had left them behind, but also suspected they might've preferred that their bait accompany them.

Please don't hurt them, she thought, sending out a silent plea to the master she knew must've orchestrated her abduction. Cate was also pretty sure she knew where her destination was and who would be waiting there for her once she arrived there, and her stomach dropped at the sheer thought of what she knew he wanted from her.

CHAPTER TWENTY-NINE

Cate landed with a thud in the oh-so-familiar living room of the bright beach house, and it was both reassuring and disturbing to discover that it was no different than it'd been all the years before. The smell of the ocean and the bright sunshine that streamed into the windows bought back many memories, and not all of them were awful ones if she was completely honest. Things were very different for her now than they'd been when she was last here, though, and she'd changed very much in that time—in both herself and her priorities.

She scanned around and saw that to her left sat her two clearly terrified children. They'd been left on the soft white sofa in the centre of the room in front of the large fire that was, for now, unlit. They weren't visibly restrained, but neither of them seemed to be able to speak or move, and Cate could see the struggle behind Blake's sad eyes. He was clearly trying desperately to fight whatever spell or commandment was holding them in place, but with no luck. Cate tried to go to them, desperately wanting to wrap the pair in her arms and tell them everything was going to be okay, but she quickly realised that she too was stuck, unable to move or speak despite her best efforts. She stood still as stone over her equally motionless offspring in wait for their captor—a strange and eerie sight against the backdrop of the bright beach house.

Cate began to think of the possible escape options, and anything she might use to bargain with Uriel for the twins' release. Her mind was completely blank, though, and she couldn't help but feel lost and powerless. Dylan had freed her before, and she was far away down on Earth with no hope of gaining access to his astral plain. She wondered if Dylan even knew that the three of them had been taken. Cate didn't know if or how Lucifer might try to get to them and attempt a rescue, but she very much doubted that Uriel would let his guard down a second time, and the presence of the two covens had already proven that.

A cool, steady breath fluttered along Cate's collarbone from behind her, and she felt his presence before Uriel even spoke or came into view. She was so angry, and wanted to lash out and hurt him, but was still unable to move or react thanks to his powerful commandment holding her still. With an inward curse, she let her hatred pour out of her via her thoughts, but her captor didn't seem to care at all.

"Welcome back. I've missed you," he whispered, and he inhaled her scent. "We have much to catch up on, but first thing's first. The way I see it, my love, you have two choices," Uriel said quietly into her left ear, gesturing with his hand towards the two babes who looked innocently on at them from their forced resting places on the sofa. Cate could see the tears that were running down Luna's cheeks and knew that she had to be incredibly frightened. Being imprisoned inside her own body was obviously scaring her profoundly, and she silently pleaded with Uriel to free her poor children, but he ignored her. "You can say yes, or you can say no," he continued calmly.

Uriel then stepped around to face Cate, and he looked her straight in the eye. His eyes burned brightly as he took in her memories and thoughts for a few moments, and she didn't even try and fight the mental intrusion. "And, I have two choices too," he said as he inched closer.

He pressed his torso into her statuesque frame and moved his mouth so close to Cate's that he was almost kissing her. "Leverage, or blackmail," Uriel added with a vile grin, and then watched her squirm beneath his spell. She wanted to tear his eyes out, but at the same time, she knew fighting him was pointless. It no longer mattered what she did or didn't want. She was helpless, and they both knew it. With that thought, she was released from the spell that'd been keeping her trapped in her immoveable body. Cate stumbled back slightly, but he caught her with a strong hand against her lower back.

Uriel captured her in his tight grasp again and held Cate's body firmly against his.

He didn't have to say anything more. It was abundantly clear to her what he was willing to do, and whose lives he was willing to sacrifice to blackmail her. Cate trembled against his hold, feeling defeated.

"I thought you were meant to be the good guy?" she asked him, her pained voice just a whisper, but he heard her clearly enough. He didn't answer, but pushed her back, so she stumbled. Uriel then used her moment of confusion to his advantage and pinned her to the wall. His strong body held hers tightly in place as his hands reached up her waist, over her breasts, and then to her face. He cupped her cheeks, running his fingers over her lips and then up through her dark, curly hair. In another life, she might've enjoyed the passion in his eyes or the care he touched her with, but not now—and never again.

When he planted a soft, delicate kiss on her lips, Cate put her hands on Uriel's chest and tried to push him away, but she couldn't stop him. Her strength was no match for his. The angel's mouth expertly caressed hers, and he soon felt her relax ever so slightly into his powerful kiss. Cate was giving in to him at last, despite her mind still running through her possible escape options, and he smiled against her mouth. They both knew she really had no choice anyway, so the sooner she submitted, the better.

When he finally released his hold of her soft, red lips, Uriel pulled back and searched Cate's face, taking in the beautiful Dark Queen. He'd missed her so very much since she'd been ripped from his grasp all those years before.

She looked up at him, taking in the gorgeous angel that stared back at her. His deep blue eyes still mesmerised her as she stared into them. What a paradox he was, and Cate considered it odd that beneath his light power and angelic cause, Uriel might perhaps be one of the evillest beings she'd ever known. She was terrified for her children, and of what he was willing to do, and that fear dominated her every thought as she awaited his response. Cate was unable to hide her emotions from the powerful being whose touch was already sending light coursing through her, and so stopped trying to fight.

"Do you still not realise by now, darling, that the whole *good versus evil* thing is all about interpretation? I told you about a similar concept once before, do you remember?" he asked, and Cate nodded, feeling woozy thanks to her pounding heart and the frenzied emotions that'd taken over her body. His touch also gave her that tell-tale tingle again, even after all the time they'd spent apart. Despite her indifference to him now that she was no longer under his once so seductive spell, her body reacted to him, and it annoyed her that he was still able to affect her so strongly. "Man believes us to be the good guys, so even when we do something bad it's simply seen as God's will," he went on, his sly grin still firmly in place.

Cate didn't care what he thought or how he justified his evil deeds. She could tell he was incredibly pleased with himself for getting her back here at long last, and truly despised him. Uriel didn't care and carried on with his rationalisation. "But man believes Lucifer to be evil, no matter what. Regardless of what he does, or any of you dark bastards do in his name, it is, and always will be, considered an evil deed," Uriel explained, running his hand down her cheek again.

"The road to Hell is paved with good intentions," Cate muttered, with a low laugh, despite there being nothing funny about the angel's words. He nodded, pleased that she was already getting his point. "So, no matter what we do, we'll always be the bad guys?" she asked, her green eyes looking up sadly into his as he continued to pin her to the wall.

"That's right, but don't forget that being bad is not the same as being hated. It was my will that he be cast out from both Heaven and Earth, but not by fear, and certainly not because of hate—it was for love. We love him still, and yet the council and I cast him down into that dark pit, regardless. It was done that way so that he'd thrive, become powerful, and become his own master. We needed to appoint someone as the ruler of the underworld, so had to choose one of our angels to fall, and he was the obvious choice. Lucifer was the most stubborn and headstrong of all the high council," he informed her, making Cate jump with shock at his side of the story of how her husband had been cast out from Heaven.

"So you wanted him to question your orders? Encouraged him to disagree? You probably told him to speak out, didn't you?" she snapped back angrily, and the smile that curled in the corners of Uriel's lips told her she was right.

"In order to encourage someone to reach their full potential, you do not deliver the object of their desires. You open up a world of possibilities to them and encourage them to find that power or possession for themselves. They need to earn it. Sometimes the ones we love meet our expectations adequately, other times they fail miserably, and every once in a full moon they might just surpass our ambitions for them entirely. They accomplish far more than you ever thought them capable of, and you then find yourself envying them for all that they then possess," he said. Uriel eyed Cate with a dark expression before he leaned down and kissed her again, pressing her even tighter into the wall.

"So, am I just a possession of his that you want for yourself then?" Cate asked him quietly once he pulled back again. "Hardly the pillow talk I was always so used to with you, Uriel," she added, aiming for a playful distraction from their intense conversation. It worked, and Uriel smiled down at her, the tension in his own body subsiding slightly.

"I wasn't just talking about him. I was talking about you, too." Cate was utterly taken aback by his openness, but urged herself to calm down, knowing that she needed to keep the conversation light and her wits about her. She was still desperately aware that the twins remained trapped in their seats and how she still needed to negotiate their release with their captor. Cate searched his face, but the angel gave nothing away, and she hated she had no way of knowing what his next move would be.

"I wonder," Cate pondered aloud after a few quiet moments passed. "Is there a way I can persuade you to release the children from their binds and send them home? We can then use the time alone to talk about all of these issues in more detail," she tried, and hoped he might at least give her the peace of mind of knowing that her babies were home and safe with Lucifer in Hell—even if she couldn't go with them. Cate didn't want to dwell on thoughts of her husband, especially under Uriel's gaze, but knew the number-one priority right now was the safety of her children. She would find her own way back to their father as soon as she could.

"Do you give me your word you'll stay with me?" Uriel asked, stepping back, and looking her square in the eye. "Do not answer lightly, as I will hold you to your word, Cate." He took her shoulders in his strong hands. "Do you promise to stay here with me until I release you?" he asked again, looking down at her with a stern and unrelenting expression on his face.

"Do you give me your word that they'll be delivered home safely, Uriel?" she asked, her own tone strong and demanding, and her counteroffer firmly on the table. Giving into him was the only way, but she was determined to do it on her terms.

"Blake will be delivered to his father instantly, I promise," he responded, a sinister grin creeping in around the corners of his mouth.

"And what of Luna?" Cate asked.

"She's the blackmail," he answered. The response made her gasp, but she also knew she had no other choice but to accept.

"Let me say goodbye first?" Cate asked him, and Uriel nodded in agreement.

He stepped away, releasing her from his command, and he watched as she walked tentatively over to the sofa. She knelt in front of Blake and waited as the spell holding him silent and still was quickly removed. Uriel watched them from beside the sofa with intrigue as she embraced her child tightly, and a satisfied look crossed his face as he took in the sight of her. Cate was so different now that she was a mother, but her actions only served to make him want her more. Her selflessness had brought her right to him, and now he intended to utilise that same instinct to get exactly what he wanted from her.

Both Cate and her son sobbed together as they cuddled, and Blake's muffled apologies could be heard clearly from within her tight grasp.

"It's okay. You didn't mean for any of this to happen, so you be strong, baby boy," she told him, leaning down to whisper in his ear. "Be strong for Daddy and Luna, Blake. I love you," she insisted, kissing his forehead, and fighting back her own tears. He nodded in promise.

A moment later, Blake was gone. He'd been magically teleported away right from within her arms thanks to the powerful angel, and the emptiness made her heart ache. Cate's sobs shuddered through her uncontrollably, and Uriel just stood and continued to watch her, his curiosity aroused. He was bemused somewhat at her reaction but was also pleased that she was such a maternal woman. He then decided to give her a few minutes to calm down in privacy, taking himself off to the kitchen to make them both a glass of wine, just like old times.

Despite the bright sunshine, the clock on the mantel struck six o'clock in the morning on what would've been the end of a dark, cold night on Earth. Panic quickly rose in Cate's chest, realising what that meant. The night would be over soon, and the sun would then rise down on Earth, beginning the waning process of the moon, and indicating the end of her husband and children's safe time away from Hell.

She quickly stopped her sobbing and looked down at Luna. Tears still lay on her daughter's cheekbones from where they'd fallen earlier and were almost dry after her long imprisonment in her own body. It broke her heart to see the fear in Luna's gaze, but before she could soothe her, the reaction began. Despite the spell's incredible power holding her still, Luna let out a muffled cry. Her nose then started bleeding, and she closed her eyes. Cate jumped to her feet and charged quickly down the hall to find Uriel. He was still in the kitchen, pulling the cork from a deep red bottle of wine in his hands.

"You have to send her home now!" she cried, begging him. "The moon's waning and she's already started showing symptoms. Please Uriel," she bellowed and fell to his feet. Cate grabbed his light trousers with her hands and bowed her head before him, almost as though she were praying. He smiled, enjoying watching her fall to her knees for him.

"I will save your daughter's life today, Cate," Uriel told her. "But you must say yes to me first."

She looked up at him, tears streaming down her face, but knew that there was no other choice. She nodded and rose to her feet, taking Uriel's hand in hers as she then led him back to the living room.

"Lift the spell, please. I need to see if she's okay," Cate pleaded when they were stood staring down at Luna. Uriel didn't say anything, but nodded, and Cate knelt before the child as she slumped down onto her side, moaning, and crying out as she went. She leaned forward to grab her, wanting to lift Luna off the sofa and into her arms, but Uriel reached down and stopped her from going any further. He grabbed Cate's arm and pulled her back to her feet, turned her around and pushed her forward, flattening her cheek against the wall opposite the sofa. He then pressed himself into her back, pushing her stomach and chest hard against the wall.

Cate didn't resist. She let him take control of her, and knew she was going to have to promise to be his to command now, and that she'd have to do whatever he demanded of her. Every part of her body that he pressed into the wall ached terribly, but she didn't cry out or push him away. Her strength would be no match for his, even if she had wanted to fight back.

All Cate could think about was Luna. She knew there was no other choice for her, and she had to do whatever it took to save her daughter's life.

"You reek of him, even more so than before," Uriel moaned in her ear. "Are the rumours true? Do you drink from him like some vampire from the horror stories?" She knew he was teasing her, riling her up to get a bite, and her thoughts gave her away before she could even try to fight them, so she spoke up regardless.

"I was borne of his blood and took it again so he could share his strength, his power, and more. Mock me if you must, but at least it worked in getting rid of the light you'd infected me with," she spat.

"Lapping at his vein like the good little puppet you are," he mocked her further, but Cate refused to answer back with the vicious retort on the tip of her tongue. Time was of the essence, as was Luna's life, and she didn't have time to waste standing there arguing with Uriel about the gory methods she and Lucifer had used to set her free of him the last time. She'd do it all again to get back to his side, but this time Uriel wasn't taking the time to woo her, leaving her full of light like before. Nothing about his actions this time reminded her of his once so romantic ways, and she promised herself— perhaps foolishly—that she wouldn't give up her mind so easily a second time around. "I don't need your permission to fuck you, Cate," Uriel told her, whispering impatiently in her ear. "You gave me that before. But you will say yes to giving me a child this time, or else you will watch your daughter die today." With one quick move of his ankle inside hers, he pushed Cate's legs open while still pressing her harder against the wall. He pushed his erection into the back of her thigh, running his hands down to her waist as his entire body ached for her. She gasped, finding herself both angered and aroused at his forceful desire. She knew she had to give into him and forced the words to leave her mouth even though she hated saying them.

"I am yours, Uriel. And yes, I will give you a child," she told him, and her entire body felt weak and defeated after the submission. She would give him her body to use as he pleased, but she wouldn't give him her heart or her soul. Cate had to keep something of her own if she were to survive a future beyond this realm, and he could have her body, but nothing else. "Now please, send my daughter home to her father," she begged.

"Good girl," he replied, and she could tell without looking that he was smiling. Less than a second later, the commandment keeping her child in the astral plane was lifted and Luna was gone. Cate wanted to scream.

"How can I know for sure they're safe?" she asked, in a hushed and scared voice. She remained pressed firmly into the hard wall by Uriel's immovable frame, yet she had to know for sure.

"Because I said so," he told her angrily, turning her around to face him in one quick move. He kissed her deeply, lifted her up into his arms, and wrapped her legs around his waist. She gave into his silent order and held on, allowing her new master to carry her down the hall and into the white bedroom, his mouth not leaving hers for even a second.

Cate's black clothes were ripped from her body by an unseen, powerful force, as Uriel's eagerness to dominate her overruled his usual carefulness. Once she was naked, he lay her down on the bed before him and undressed himself with a click of his fingers, watching her. "Don't fight me, Cate," he told her, and she halted in her attempt to cover her body from his prying eyes. It was fruitless, and they both knew it.

"I wouldn't dream of it," she answered sarcastically. Uriel then climbed onto the bed and leaned over her, nestling himself between her legs with a satisfied smile, and he stared down into her stunning eyes. She wasn't ready, but he refused to wait, and gave her just one more kiss before plunging himself inside with one deep, heavy thrust.

She cried out, grabbing his shoulders tightly as the tender membranes inside took a few seconds to stretch for him, and she dug her nails in hard. He didn't stop, and pushed deeper with each thrust of his thick, hard length. With her body betraying her, Cate closed her eyes and tried desperately to concentrate on Uriel and her oath to him, rather than anything else. She knew she needed to focus on anything other than Lucifer and the children but was also terrified by the very real possibility of giving him a child.

Despite her rollercoaster of emotions, Cate's physical impulses took over, and she climaxed quickly. The wonderful and still familiar feel of him inside her, along with the twinges of both anger and guilt she felt deep in her gut, quickly led to an outburst of both physical and emotional release at the same time. She didn't hold back, and lifted her hips up towards him, thrusting herself to meet his strong advances as he penetrated her deeper. Uriel groaned loudly as she tensed around him and then flipped Cate over to lie on her belly, and he grabbed her hair roughly as he plunged back inside her soaked core. He then closed her legs beneath him to wrap her tighter around him inside her hot, wet cleft as he delved harder and faster in pursuit of his own climax.

She soon began to writhe beneath him and called out as she came for him again, panting exhaustedly as the aftershocks coursed throughout her body. He'd never been rough with her before, but this time she guessed he was punishing as well as pleasuring her, and Cate couldn't deny it was a thrill. Uriel then pulled her hips up towards him, and he shuddered and gripped her tightly as he allowed his own climax to burst out from him like a wave of intense pleasure.

Their beach house practically crumbled around them as he came. The small earthquake that erupted from his body sent a shockwave that tore through the hard stone walls and rippled across the sand on the beach that surrounded the house. The powerful burst carried on out into the ocean, sending waves crashing back through the deep waters in an incredible display of Uriel's omnipotent power.

Less than a second later, the damage to the beach house was repaired thanks to another of his silent, powerful commands. Despite her frantic panting and still shuddering body, Cate didn't hesitate to obey her new master when he leaned down and whispered in her ear that he was ready to start again. She climbed on top of him as he lay back on the bed and eyed her eagerly. Cate leaned back on her heels, welcoming his hardness deep inside her again as she rode up and down on his thick length, and all the while forcing herself to fight back the tears still prickling at her eyes.

CHAPTER THIRTY

Uriel lay beside Cate, cradling her tightly as she wept. She'd turned her body away from him, but he continued to hold on, regardless. He knew she was still angry and didn't want him to see her while she was so vulnerable, but he couldn't walk away. She belonged to him again, and despite being aware that he was the reason for her tears, Uriel refused to leave her side. He'd pursued her relentlessly for three days non-stop, and she was now utterly exhausted and incredibly sensitive. Her desperation and worry seemed to be bubbling up inside her uncontrollably, and even though she'd tried to fight it, the emotion was currently overwhelming her.

Cate had given herself to him entirely and had even allowed herself to enjoy the rolling orgasms that came with the territory. But after days of nothing but sex, she needed to rest, and her body was crying out for sleep. She had a deep void inside of her that she knew was that of her tremendous loss, both of her children and her husband. She didn't know when or if she would see them again, and the sobs that came pouring out of her was her grief for them forcing its way out at last, refusing to be stifled any longer.

Uriel climbed up from the bed, snapping his fingers once again to repair the damage to the walls and furniture around them. He went to the bathroom where he ran Cate a hot, deep bath, complete with bubbles and candles. He approached the bed and stroked her damp cheek, making her jump. She looked up and took his hand, following him into the warm bathroom without a word. Cate then climbed into the red-hot water graciously and closed her heavy eyes as she relaxed in the soothing suds, trying desperately to calm down.

Uriel decided to leave her alone for the first time since she'd said yes to him again. He had to trust that she wasn't going to do anything foolish or try and escape. Doing so would only force his hand to deliver her another lesson in what he was capable of, and he had the sneaking suspicion she might not survive another punishment. She just needed some quiet time, and he couldn't deny that it brought him no pleasure to see that she was hurting. Cate looked exhausted and pale. Her pain was coming through via her thoughts and emotions she was so openly sending to him, seemingly unable to hide or mask her feelings at all, and he could tell it was consuming her.

He went to the kitchen, fixing her something to eat as he mulled over the events of the past few months in the build-up to getting her back. There was still an incredible amount of love he felt for Cate, despite all their time apart, and her escape the last time they'd been there on his astral plane together. He knew Dylan had been the instigator of her release rather than Cate herself, though. Although he knew that she'd welcomed being set free, Uriel still hoped she might find a way to love him again despite her resistance.

The anticipation had almost driven him mad waiting for her to come back, and he thought back to the night he'd eventually received word that she was up on Earth again. Angelica had sensed a shift in the balance of light and dark and had come to him immediately. She was a formidable witch, her instincts only ever having been surpassed by her predecessor Alma, and Uriel had ordered her to investigate it immediately.

She'd soon discovered that not only was Cate on Earth, but that she'd given Lucifer two children, one of whom was a curious child, and that he could be used as bait to lure her out of hiding. All they had to do was be patient and he would bring Cate to them, which was exactly what'd happened.

Uriel knew he had all the power. Although he wouldn't have willingly hurt the twins, he'd known he would have to push the boundaries of his own will to its limits in order to force hers to bend and eventually break the way he needed it to. When Cate had knelt before him in the kitchen, he'd known then that she had finally submitted to him entirely.

It'd felt so good having her ready, waiting, and willing to give him everything he desired. Being proven right was fun, and he'd enjoyed seeing her on her knees, begging. Uriel was well aware that his darker urges had stirred up in him then, and they'd spurred him on towards his only goal that night, but he'd had to have her, he'd had to win.

Uriel made Cate a cup of sweet, milky tea and a couple of slices of buttered toast, taking it to her where she still lay in the centre of the misty bathroom. She smiled up at him from her resting place in the large metal tub and gratefully sipped the tea.

It tasted good, and her stomach rumbled for the rest. Instinctually, she leaned sideways and held the toast over the side of the bath so she could eat it without getting any crumbs in the deep water and had to remind herself that she needn't care about making a mess.

The angel looked down at her thoughtfully as he perched on the edge of the sink. His dark hair fell into his eyes as he smiled playfully, feeling ready for her again, but he fought his urges. She needed a bit longer to rest first. He watched as she finished off the toast and set the plate down before lying back against the incline of the tub with a satisfied smile, and then slipped off his white linen trousers and climbed in behind her. He urged her to lie back and rest against his chest rather than on the hard metal basin and was pleased when she did as she was bid.

Cate leaned forward and pushed open the hot tap, quickly topping up the water to re-heat the warm cocoon around them, before lying back in his strong arms. Her mind was blank, and Uriel couldn't be sure if she'd forced all her feelings aside or was just becoming more numb to them. Either way, he knew she couldn't bear for him to question her on it, so he resisted. Holding his lover close for a few quiet moments, he hoped she'd find comfort in his arms, rather than just sadness and fear.

"I love you," Uriel told her after a while, knowing that Cate didn't feel the same way about him, but he didn't care.

CHAPTER THIRTY-ONE

Within a few weeks, the beach house was in absolute ruins. Uriel decided to give up on the repairs, and instead he'd simply left them a huge, white bed in the middle of the sandy beach for them to lie together on and do as they pleased. No one else was allowed on his astral plane, so there wasn't anyone around to see their antics, anyway. The beach house simply couldn't withstand the shockwaves he continually gave off due to their relentless lovemaking, and he couldn't be bothered with trying.

Despite the time that'd passed, Cate still wasn't pregnant even after his continual efforts. Uriel was disheartened but carried on enjoying being with his lover far too much to worry about the details regarding their child's inevitable conception.

She'd grown emotionally numb over the last few weeks, her mind usually blank or despondent, but her body responded willingly to her new master's orders, and her strong muscles gave him everything he craved. When she allowed herself a moment to think, Cate would quickly realise that she preferred it when her mind was blank, or they were making love. Both denial and the distraction kept her occupied and helped stop the terrible thoughts and feelings from trying to creep back in for just a little while longer.

A few days later, she stood on the beachfront, looking out at the crystal clear waters that stretched out before her—a seemingly endless ocean, although she knew it was all just an illusion. She'd been there for four weeks, and soon found herself wondering absentmindedly if the moon was full again below, and whether Lucifer was down there on Earth trying to find a way to them. Cate couldn't help but hope he might be on his way to take her home, but she also knew that it was impossible. She felt lost and couldn't know for sure where he was or what he was doing. Her connection to both him and the children was completely severed, thanks to Uriel's strong power over her once again.

Thickly muscled arms then came around from behind her and held Cate tight, and her arms were pinned to her sides as he stroked down her bare forearms to her hands.

"Feeling thoughtful, my love?" Uriel asked her, serving a reminder to his captive lover that he knew exactly what she'd been thinking about. Cate didn't reply, but pushed the thoughts of Lucifer away at once, and shook her head. He laughed gruffly and leaned over her, kissing her neck softly before trailing gentle kisses down to Cate's collarbone. Uriel tugged at the thin straps of her white summer dress, each of which then fell down her arms to her waist, exposing her breasts. He cupped them gently with his hands, trailing kisses up and down her neck and shoulder while she continued to stare blankly off to the horizon.

"Get your fucking hands off my wife," a voice then boomed behind them, disturbing their isolation.

Cate jumped. The voice had startled her, and she was scared but also desperately yearned to see the face of the man who'd spoken those words so assuredly from behind them. She wondered for a moment if she were dreaming, hallucinating, or even if it was Uriel playing tricks on her to test her loyalty. Cate knew one thing for sure though, she'd felt the angel's strong body tense from behind her, telling her she hadn't imagined it. Uriel quickly pulled the straps of her thin dress back up her arms to her shoulders, covering her naked body again, yet he kept his arms tightly around her as the pair of them turned to face the intruder together.

Standing just a few feet away was the Dark King, his eyes jet-black with his power, while anger and hatred billowed out of him towards his angelic foe. He glared over at the pair of them, and there was darkness in him that scared Cate when he looked at her in disgust for a second before focusing his attention on Uriel again. Lucifer looked older somehow, and he too, seemed numb and broken. His usually playful prowess was long gone as he took in the sight of Uriel holding onto her so protectively.

Lucifer was wearing a black shirt and jeans, both of which were splattered with red blood, and in his arms he held the body of a beaten and bloody, blonde haired woman.

"Angelica," Uriel whispered gruffly, looking to and from the lifeless witch and the monster that carried her in his arms.

"Yes," his brother-of-sorts replied with a sneer. "She tried to fight at first, but she was no match for me, of course. I promised the stupid witch I wouldn't kill her if she took me through the portal to your astral plane," Lucifer said as he dropped Angelica's clearly dead body to the ground. "I lied," he then added with a smirk.

Uriel's grip tightened on Cate's shoulders, hurting her as he pulled her closer. She was the only leverage he had, and he was determined not to let her go.

"Cate's mine now," he told Satan.

"And what makes you think you can simply have her? My blood runs through her veins, my power gives her the life-force you yourself are so drawn to, and yet you believe you can own her?" Lucifer smirked and had the gall to laugh at the angel's audacity. "I alone possess her, do you understand? Hecate is mine and always will be. She'll infect you with my darkness before I allow you to taint her with your light again. She and our children will do my bidding for centuries to come, and you can do nothing to stop us."

"You're wrong," Uriel demanded. "Cate belongs to me now."

"And what do you hope to achieve in keeping her?" Lucifer asked him pointedly. His voice was clear and his stance powerful now in the face of his long-time adversary, but Cate was gobsmacked by his selfish words. Part of her hoped they weren't true, that he was simply taunting Uriel, but she had the sneaking suspicion they might stem from a real place within him. Perhaps the second betrayal was one too many, and she began wondering what the future might hold for them once all of this was over.

"I yearn for the same as you, I suppose," Uriel replied thoughtfully. "Love, family. You have your heirs, and she will now give me mine. Cate has already given herself to me," he added matter-of-factly.

Cate paled. If hearing Lucifer basically call her his trophy hadn't wound her up enough, listening to Uriel speak of her like an object that way quickly made her downright furious. Intense rage built up quickly inside of her, and the powerful emotions that she'd tried to push away for the past few weeks suddenly burst out of her uncontrollably.

She wrenched herself away from Uriel's hold, ignoring the intense pain that flared up on her skin from the grip his hands had once had on her shoulders. Cate moved sideways and stood between the two of them and then took a step backwards. She wanted to edge away from both of them and stared angrily at the pair of omnipotent beings that fought so obsessively for her affections.

"I'm not some fucking baby maker, you know!" she cried. "Nor am I a possession for either of you to own or use at your bloody convenience." Both Lucifer and Uriel looked taken aback by her strong words, their gazes each flicking over to her anxiously before returning to one another. "I don't think either of you even know how to truly love another person, or what that word means," she added, looking down forlornly. "Perhaps monsters are real after all," she added, a whisper to herself more than to either of them, and she had to grip her gut as a pang of angst swept over her. She felt broken. Utterly and so profoundly lost, it was soul-destroying.

Lucifer looked over at her for a second, saddened by her powerful words, but he quickly returned his gaze to his adversary. He focussed his anger and pain on Uriel, rather than his wife, despite her hurtful speech. He started edging over towards Cate, but the angel took note of his movement and took a step in her direction, too.

The hate in Lucifer's eyes flared again, and he stepped forward this time. He slammed his fist into the angel's left cheekbone with a punch that would render any human dead without question, but not him. Uriel retaliated instantly, his immense counterattack sending a shockwave through the ground beneath Cate's feet, stirring the air all around the pair of powerful beings. Before she could beg for them to stop, a wave of power rushed her, and she was sent flying backwards through the air. She was thrown far away from the beach thanks to the strong blast that'd hit her and crashed into the deep water with a huge splash.

Cate broke the surface and looked towards the now far off beach, seeing the two powerful enemies brawling on the sand. Their matching strengths were giving off such blasts of power that the water's current seemed to have changed course because of it. The waves were being forced away from the beach by the shockwaves created on it by the feuding men. Pure power surged through the water, pushing Cate farther out with the tide. She tried to swim towards them, to push back through the now powerful force of the current, but it was no use. It was only a few seconds before she found her footing, just like before, and the water quickly began to shallow beneath her as she was pushed back thanks to the strong waves.

She was just about able to look above the waves at the beach, but quickly realised that she must also be very near to the edge of the astral plane. Cate began to panic that she might fall over the side and away from the protection of the realm that was, until very recently, her prison. It was now the only thing keeping her from falling the thousands of feet to the Earth below, and potentially to her death if Angelica's previous words of warning were to be believed.

When only her ankles remained covered by the water, Cate stood and stared out, trying to catch a glimpse of the fray ahead. Uriel and Lucifer were so far away. She could only just about make out a blur of quick movements along with loud cracking noises, which she assumed must be their powerful blows as they rained them down on one another. Dark black clouds began moving in overhead, and Cate could hear deep, ominous thunder that rumbled through them. A second later, a large fork of lightning shimmered across the sky all around her, landing on the beach. Cate watched as the bed she'd once shared with Uriel exploded thanks to the blast from the power, and shrieked.

She stood there for a while longer, contemplating her options, but a huge wave then sprung up in front of her, pushing her backwards. The edge of the astral plane felt as sharp as a knife's edge under her bare feet, and she immediately lost her balance. Cate toppled backwards and was soon plummeting downwards, away from the plane. The wind whistled loudly around her and enveloped her as she fell towards Earth, picking up speed uncontrollably. She looked up, trying to see back to the plane as she descended, but she could see nothing except the swirling black clouds that sparked with incredible cracks of lightning and boomed loudly with thunder from above her.

Cate fell faster, unable to control her descent, and after a few seconds, she closed her eyes. She tried bracing for the impending impact as much as possible and curled around herself. Thoughts of Blake and Luna's smiling, happy faces came to her, with the sad acceptance that her death may come soon. She hit water, and was grateful for the slightly softer landing, but still fell fast through the depths, despite the tide that pushed back against her powerful plummet. Within seconds, the deep, dark water swirled around her and blackened the view all around as she sank further down to the ocean floor. She nearly blacked out but urged herself to stay lucid in the hope she might find a way to resurface. The lack of oxygen caused her chest to tighten and the shocks of pain that coursed through her entire body made Cate jerk and writhe in agony as she yearned for a breath of air.

You don't need it, she thought, knowing it was that way in Hell. She couldn't help but wonder, or rather hope, that maybe she didn't really need oxygen while she was on Earth, too. Cate finally managed to calm herself down, mentally relaxing her tense body and easing the painful pangs that plagued her chest as she began to slow down at last.

Jagged rocks soon came up to greet her as she furthered her descent into the dark depths, and Cate winced as she slammed into them. The searing pain as another rock crashed against her head then caused her to lose consciousness at once, and her lifeless body floated away at the behest of the current.

CHAPTER THIRTY-TWO

Cate stirred and forced herself awake, ignoring the dull aches that still throbbed throughout her entire body, threatening to pull her back into the sleepy abyss. Part of her welcomed it. The emptiness would help her block it all out and let her heal a little while longer. However, she needed answers, and pushed herself to rouse. It felt as if she was breaking the surface of the dark water that had not long before swirled all around her, and she took a deep, loud breath as she sat up in the strange bed where she'd been lying.

Cate looked around her, taking in the unfamiliar surroundings. She was in a small metal room, almost like the ones she had seen before on ships and cruise-liners. After taking a deep breath, she thought back, trying to piece together the events that'd brought her here. An overwhelming barrage of memories hit her, and she lay back down in the bed, sobbing loudly as everything came rushing back. A few minutes later, the large door opened slowly, and a young man entered. Cate figured he couldn't be any older than twenty, and he tried not to look at her directly as she wept, seemingly embarrassed to have walked in on her crying. The tall, skinny young man stood beside her bed for a moment, and he awkwardly set a tray of food on the table to her left. He then made to leave silently before she stopped him, clearing her throat, and wiping her eyes with her hands as she stared up into his dark brown eyes from the bed.

"Thank you," she mumbled, and he smiled kindly down at her. "Where am I?" Cate then asked, feeling completely lost on many different levels.

"We're on an oil rig not far off the coast of Norway," he told her, his accent thick, but his English was still very good. He sat down on a solitary chair that was near her bedside and handed her a bottle of cool mineral water from the tray, which she took with a smile.

"Thanks," she said again, and introduced herself. "My name's Cate."

"Torstein," he told her shyly.

Cate was grateful for the nourishing drink, and once she'd taken a long gulp, she looked across at the tray he'd bought in. She could see that he had kindly prepared her a delicious smelling bowl of soup and some buttered bread, along with a pot of yogurt and a chocolate biscuit. She smiled over at Torstein, thanking him again before propping herself up a little bit more on the pillows so that she could eat and drink a little easier. Cate winced as she moved her still tired and bruised body, but she pushed herself on nonetheless, knowing she would heal properly in no time. "You washed up near our rig. Just appeared out of nowhere," Torstein told her bemusedly. "We weren't even sure if you were alive at first, but we fished you out of the water anyway and bought you here to the infirmary." He waved a hand around as if to motion that was where the two of them were now.

"Thank you, I don't think I would've survived otherwise," her voice faltered, and she stared intently at her water bottle.

"It was a wonder we even saw you through the rain and wind of the storm. The waves were so high it was almost as though they carried you up here on purpose," he continued, still looking at her with a confused look. Cate just nodded, understanding his bewilderment, but she couldn't even begin to explain her strange predicament or how it was she came to be in the ocean near his rig.

"Oh yes, the terrible storm. How long did it last?" she asked, wondering how many hours her two feuding lovers had continued their battle.

"It's still raging outside," Torstein told her, his eyes wide with excitement and fear. "It's some kind of freak weather phenomenon. No one can explain it. The whole world is experiencing the terrible weather, it's all over the news," he told her animatedly, seemingly excited to give her the strange update.

"How long has it been going on now, then?" Cate then asked him, her eyes growing wider as she propped herself up higher on her elbows. She was still unsure how long she must've been unconscious, but knew that this was bad news, and could only mean that the pair of them were still fighting up there.

"It's been eight days since it all began," he told her, and Cate flopped back down on the bed, exhaling loudly.

"Eight days?" she asked, wondering aloud. "Whoa, this is bad."

The young rigger didn't seem to know how to respond to her, so he said no more. He just stood and lifted the tray from the bedside onto her lap.

"Eat this before it gets cold, Cate. It will make you strong," he said with a grin, and his feeble attempt at a stern order made her smile. She nodded and saluted him playfully with one hand.

"Yes, sir," she joked, and Torstein laughed. He then nodded triumphantly and walked over to the metal doorway, looking back over at her before he left.

"I'll be back to check on you later," he promised, heading out and leaving Cate alone in the ward room with her food and her thoughts.

Another week passed by before the terrible storm finally started to ease. It was a week in which Cate rested and recuperated with the help of Torstein and the other riggers, and she finally felt more like her old self again. She didn't know what the ending of the storm finally meant, whether it was because Lucifer and Uriel had both stopped fighting at last, or if it meant that one of them had finally been defeated. Either way, Cate was worried and still full of so many mixed emotions. She didn't even know where to begin to process it all. She was glad to be alive and back to her normal strength again, especially after what she'd thought might be a fatal fall from that astral plain.

Cate tried to teleport back to Hell a few times, but every time was unsuccessful, much to her dismay. She couldn't even teleport elsewhere on Earth and could only imagine it was because of Uriel's light being inside her once again. Cate hoped she would hear news of the fight and its outcome when she finally reached home but was still unsure how to get there without being able to teleport. She knew she had no choice other than to wait and hope for the best.

When the ocean around the rig was calm again and the sun shone brightly in the sky overhead, Cate looked up at the blue expanse above. She felt full of hope and wonder and knew then that it was the right time to go in search of answers, and hopefully a way home. She packed a small backpack with a couple of changes of clothes given to her by the generous riggers and some food packs, before saying a huge thank you to Torstein and all the others that'd helped her over the past couple of weeks. Those mere humans that she'd somehow begun to take for granted in her long life had taken great care of her and had never asked for anything in return. Cate was positive they'd saved her life the day they'd fished her out of the stormy waves and vowed never to forget their kindness.

She boarded a small boat and headed for the shore, having to sleep rough in the ferry terminal for a night before she managed to talk her way onto an overnight boat headed for England. She'd met a middle-aged lorry driver who offered her a seat in his cab in return for her company for the evening, and she made it clear she wasn't about to give him more than a kind smile and some polite conversation. Cate made sure that the man drank his weight in vodka, smiling and chatting warmly with the rotund man who lapped up the attention from her with a twinkle in his eye as she poured him shot after shot of the potent drink. When he eventually passed out drunk in his seat, she sneaked away and headed for the quiet lounge to find a comfy spot in which to sleep for a little while.

When Cate arrived in Hull the next morning, she disembarked and made her way over to the nearby bus stop. She couldn't deny it was a sorry sight, and she was shocked to find the port still in such a tragic mess following the storm's damage. Cate headed into the local town and was gobsmacked to discover more destruction and ruin that'd affected almost everything in sight. The streets and homes there were either covered in branches and debris or had been boarded up and left behind while the occupants made their desperate attempts to flee the coastal areas in fear of tidal waves or flooding. The sight sickened her, but she knew it wasn't her doing. The devastation was the work of her two formidable lovers, and she hated them both in equal measure for what they'd done.

As the evening grew darker, she still had nowhere to stay and had very little money, so Cate wandered around in search of inspiration. She eventually found a small bed-and-breakfast, and talked her way inside, promising to help the old couple that owned it if they gave her shelter for a few nights. They agreed, seemingly happy for the helping hand, and Cate spent the next two days there, working hard through the day helping them recover from the storm, and all the while she was well fed and taken good care of by the elderly owners, Bob, and May. When she finally said her goodbyes, May thrust some money in Cate's hand.

"Take it. Go and find your family," she told her, and Cate was taken aback by the kindness showed to her by yet another stranger. She took the money, grateful that she could now afford her train fare to London and hugged the kind woman goodbye. Her plan was to go to the Satanic church in the capital, where she hoped to find some witches who could use their magic to send her back to the twins. She could figure out things with Lucifer later.

Cate was still disheartened that she hadn't felt any of her usual power since she'd woken up on the rig, and not even a glimmer of the usually strong beacon she'd normally felt with Lucifer. Her powers were completely gone, just like before, and she hated it. She knew it wasn't quite right but kept on going in the hope that she would find some good news once she got to the church.

That evening, Cate left the tube station and crossed the busy street. She then headed down a dark alleyway, where she stepped over the invisible threshold to the dark church without any resistance. Inside, she found the two lower-level witches, Suzanne, and Bea, whom she'd met during her time living in the church not too long before. The two of them were alone in the large central room, and were huddled around one of the warm, glowing lanterns that'd usually lined the walls, each of them looking dishevelled and dirty.

"Your majesty," Suzanne cried as Cate approached, her brown eyes wide with shock, and she smiled broadly at the Dark Queen. "You're alive!" She climbed up from her spot on the floor, pulling her dirty brown hair out of her eyes and into a scruffy ponytail in an attempt to tidy herself up.

"Well, yes, of course I am," Cate answered, and she couldn't help her impatient tone. "Has there been any word from my husband?" she asked them expectantly.

"No, your majesty, nothing," Bea told her, looking sullen. "We've had no word from anyone since the King went to retrieve you. Alma and Dylan are with your children back home, so don't worry, but he hasn't been seen or heard of ever since the full moon."

"I cannot feel his power, can you?" Suzanne interjected, looking worried. Cate wondered if the pair of them had been holding out in the hope she would bring them good news, just as she had with them, and she realised that none of them were any clearer thanks to having found each other again.

"No, I can't sense him either," Cate told them honestly. "The storm, it was Lucifer and Uriel. They had a terrible fight. I got away, but I was badly injured," she explained.

"He can't be, you know...*dead*, can he?" Bea asked, looking as though she might cry.

"I sure as hell hope not," Cate replied with a gulp. "Can you take me back home?" she asked hopefully, having had enough of their depressive conversation, but the two witches shook their heads forlornly.

"We have no powers, mistress," Suzanne told her. "We've been stuck here since the storm started."

***

Cate stayed with the witches in the cold church that night, not sure what else to do with herself now that she knew for sure she was stranded on Earth. The dark church, it seemed, offered no real protection without their powers or the invisible threshold to keep the white witches out, but there was no other place they could go. She and the witches needed to stay put, and Cate was positive that Lucifer's first instinct would be to go there, just like she had done. As she lay awake in the early hours of the next morning, cold and scared, Cate knew she might need to find herself somewhere safer to hide out until they had more news. Weeks had already passed without a sign of him, and she was unsure just how long it might take for them to hear from her husband.

She drifted back off to an uneasy and anxious sleep and woke up starving a couple of hours later. Cate leaned over and rummaged in her backpack, finally finding her last bit of food, a cereal bar, which she wolfed down in seconds. She then lay back on the hard bench, wondering to herself where Lucifer might be, but within a couple of minutes, her stomach began to churn painfully. She climbed up out of her makeshift bed and ran down the hall to the toilet, only just making it in time before she was violently sick.

"Oh hell no," she whispered to herself when it was finally over. She wiped her mouth clean and took a deep, calming breath and stared in the mirror, the realisation suddenly dawning on her. Cate placed a hand over her tender stomach and thought back over the last few days, realising that she'd been feeling woozy ever since she left the oil rig, and had just been too busy and focussed to take notice.

She knew the signs were there and wondered if the unthinkable could really be happening. It absolutely could be. She'd said yes, after all.

Tears streamed from her eyes without warning, and she put her hand over her mouth so the witches wouldn't hear her sobbing. Cate cursed Uriel, wherever he was, but also cursed herself.

CHAPTER THIRTY-THREE

"I'm going to see if I can find anyone else that might be able to help us," Cate informed the witches later that same morning. "If we gather as many of us together as possible, I hope that maybe we can combine our darkness to bring back our powers. I'll check in with you regularly, so stay here in case anyone else comes to find sanctuary at the church, okay?" she added, staying strong despite her fears and frenzied thoughts. The witches both nodded in agreement, despite them worrying for the Queen's safety, and each of them hugged Cate goodbye. She had to hide the anxiety in her own face as she left the familiar safety of the church, but she simply had to be away from all of them, especially any dark beings who might realise what was going on with her, or who could sense her suspicions regarding her *condition*.

Cate knew exactly where she needed to go, and whom she had to seek out. There was only one being on the entire earthly realm that she could truly trust—Harry. She took the underground and boarded a train heading southwest, fretting the entire way over what she'd say when she finally found him. Cate arrived in Avebury later that same day, and then headed straight for the Lion's Head pub. She hoped to see some familiar faces there from her old days as its barmaid, days that seemed so long ago now that so much had happened, but it was still a comfort seeing the village again. The same old regulars were there, and she waved over at Jamie and Marc, who'd stared at her as she entered with the same bemused faces and drunken grins. Cate then spoke with the young girl who was working behind the bar for a couple of minutes, but she wasn't of any help, not seeming to know anyone named Harry that lived in the village at all. Her face fell. She turned to leave just as her old boss, Joe, poked his head around the doorway that led through to the rest of the house.

"Blimey, Dana. Look at you!" he shouted to her, running through the entrance before grabbing Cate and pulling her into a tight hug. "My God, you don't look any different. How long has it been? Six years?" he quizzed her, smiling, and ushering her to join him through the back.

"Seven," she corrected him, grinning warmly at her old employer and friend. He'd always been a kind man, and a fair boss. She'd enjoyed working with Joe and, most importantly of all, Cate knew she could trust him. In the living room above the bar, the pair caught up over coffee and cakes, and Cate thanked him but refused when he later offered her a stiffer drink.

"I'm trying to find Harry. Does he still live around here?" she asked him hopefully.

"Yeah, but he got married about two years ago and moved to Marlborough, I think," Joe told her, and Cate's stomach dropped. She knew she had no right to be jealous that Harry had moved on after she'd left, but she honestly felt a little disheartened. "I think he moved back into his old place a few months ago when it all went wrong, though," Joe added with a sorry look as he took a swig of his beer. Cate knew she shouldn't be glad to hear of Harry's failed marriage, but she couldn't help but be a little relieved at the revelation that he was back in the village, and that he was single.

"Thanks Joe, it's been great catching up, but I'd better get going," she said, rising from her chair to leave, eager to see her old flame.

"It's late," Joe replied, and after looking over at the small clock on his living room wall, Cate realised it was almost midnight. "Have you got somewhere to stay?" he asked, and she shook her head. "Hey, why don't you just stay here tonight? You can have my room and I'll take the couch. It'll just be one night until you can get yourself sorted," he offered, and Cate had to smile, glad she wasn't about to spend the night sleeping rough. She nodded, grateful for the offer of a warm bed after the previous night's restless sleep in the cold, unguarded church.

"Thank you, Joe. You always were a good man," she said, smiling over at him. He stood and grabbed her backpack, slinging it over his shoulder as he then led her out to the hallway and down to his bedroom.

"I'll get some fresh sheets, and help yourself to the hot water," Joe added, seeming to know she'd appreciate the hospitality, and she grinned gratefully.

It wasn't long before Cate emerged from a lovely hot shower and then climbed under the freshly changed bed linen Joe had made up for her. Safe and comfortable once again, she drifted off to sleep almost instantly, dreaming of Blake and Luna as they played in the dark castle, smiling, and cheering as she watched them with a huge smile.

***

The next morning, after getting dressed and calling herself a taxi, Cate thanked Joe for his hospitality. She refused breakfast just in case and then went off in search of her old friend. After a few minutes, they pulled up to the familiar row of Victorian houses, many of which had been split into apartments that lined the wide road. The cab came to a stop outside Harry's ground-floor flat, and Cate could see the clear number thirteen inscribed on the doorway—an omen that'd always made her laugh. She paid the driver and hurried up the path. Anticipation was welling up inside her as she stood on the doorstep for a moment, hesitating for a minute before she eventually rang the bell.

It was a Saturday morning, and it was only early, so Cate wondered for a moment if he might still be in bed. She almost took a step back, thinking it might be better if she went back later, when she heard a sound on the opposite side of the door. The latched lifted, and a key turned, and Cate waited impatiently for the door to finally open. When he answered, Harry looked neat and comfortable in his black tracksuit trousers and a t-shirt emblazoned with a superhero slogan. He looked good. The pair stared at each other for a moment, and she smiled up at him, feeling happier than she had in weeks.

Harry hadn't changed a bit. He was older looking, of course, and even had a few grey flecks that speckled his brown hair to show for the years that'd passed since their last encounter. His blue eyes widened in disbelief as he took in the sight of Cate standing there staring up at him expectantly from his doorstep, and he stood motionless for a second. It seemed as if he needed a moment to process the sight of his long-lost friend—the unattainable object of his affections he'd tried to forget. Harry then burst into a huge grin and he scooped her up off her feet and into his arms. Cate gave in to his welcome embrace, needing the safe and warm protectiveness more than she'd even realised, and held him back tightly.

"What are you doing here?" he asked excitedly, finally putting her back down on her feet, but he kept her close. "It's been ages, too bloody long," he added, scalding her mockingly, with one eyebrow raised.

"I know. I'm so sorry, Harry," Cate told him. "Can you ever forgive me?" she added, and then started sobbing uncontrollably into his strong arms. He pulled her close again, shushing her, but Cate couldn't hold back the tears. She didn't want to, feeling incredibly vulnerable yet completely safe in his presence.

"I couldn't find you," he told her, his voice almost a whisper against her dark curls as he leaned his head down and breathed her in. After a few seconds, Harry leaned back to look upon her face, searching for a sign of why she was crying. "I tried to track you down, to track Luke down, but I found nothing. It was as if you two didn't even exist," he told her, and his face fell. "Did he hurt you?" Harry asked, a solemn look crossing his gentle face, and Cate shook her head.

"No, but I really need a friend right now. Are you willing to forgive me for running off on you?" she asked as she looked up into Harry's gorgeous eyes, searching them for forgiveness, and she found it, of course.

"I could never be mad at you, Dana. You know that," Harry told her, wiping the tears from her cheeks with his thumbs. He then beckoned her inside, and she gratefully accepted the invitation, following him into his small flat. It still looked the same as it had all those years before when they'd spent much of their time there together as friends, and he took Cate's bag and placed it by the sofa. "Do you want a cup of tea?" Harry asked, and a gentle, knowing smile crossed her lips as he did so.

"Always, you know that," she answered, grinning over at him, and the pair then wandered into the small kitchen to chat some more. Harry boiled the kettle and grabbed two large mugs from the cupboard, looking thoughtful.

"So, are you gonna tell me where you've been all this time?" he asked, placing teabags in the mugs and then adding the boiling water and a dash of milk. Harry then reached up into another cupboard for the tin of biscuits he knew she'd want as an accompaniment to her hot, milky brew, and set it down without having to ask. Cate wanted to laugh at how well he still knew her, but resisted, choosing to enjoy the familiarity rather than tease him about it.

"Somewhere far away, but it's kinda hard for me to explain, Harry," she answered, reverting straight back to her old diversionary tactics to stop him from asking questions. She then caught the disappointed look on his face and stopped herself from telling him more lies. Instead, Cate felt a sudden urge to tell him everything. A longing for full honesty came over her and she wondered why not? Harry was her only friend and was absolutely the one person she knew she could truly trust with her secrets. If she didn't tell him the truth, it was a real probability that Harry wouldn't be willing to take care of her and the baby she was sure was growing inside of her like she needed him to.

Cate knew it was time to reveal all at last, regardless of her old, yet necessary closed-off nature. "Okay, I'm going to tell you everything," she told him, and Harry's face lit up, clearly pleased that she'd changed her mind. He'd always known there was more to her story than she'd revealed to him in the past, and he was eager to hear it at long last. "But you're gonna need to sit down for this," she added, looking over at the table in the corner of the room.

Harry started to laugh, sure that she must be joking, but quickly stopped himself when he saw the seriousness in Cate's eyes.

"Urm, okay," he said, leading her over to the small table with its two chairs that he'd squeezed into the corner of the kitchen. After depositing the mugs between them, along with the biscuit tin, he took a seat. Cate sat in the chair opposite, staring into Harry's gorgeous eyes for a moment, taking in his handsome face. She basked in his gentle expression before she reached forward and grabbed a biscuit. After soaking it in her tea, she devoured the sweet treat whole and stared down at the hot mug she had cradled in her delicate hands.

"Well, firstly I guess you need to know that my name's not really Dana, it's Cate. And I'm not just the normal, human barmaid you once thought I was." She took a deep breath. "The girl you knew as Nina isn't my sister, she's my best friend. Luke *is* my husband, but we have what you might consider to be a rather strange relationship. We'll get to that in a minute," she said, still staring down at her hands. "Oh, and there's one other thing. I'm pretty sure I'm pregnant right now with someone else's baby," Cate added, feeling butterflies in her stomach as she finally admitted it to him, and to herself, for the first time.

"Whoa, I really am glad I'm sitting down now," Harry muttered, looking at her intently, but then stopped himself from commenting further. "Okay, go on," he added, urging Cate to continue after seeing the vulnerable expression on her face. She knew it was time. Now or never…

"I never had a father growing up, and when I was eighteen, I found out why," she hesitated slightly at the next part, taking a long swig of her tea as she thought hard how to word it. "Don't freak out or call me a weirdo, okay?" she asked, looking up at him, and Harry nodded, unsure what she was getting at. "I wasn't the same as you. I was different, and I discovered that the reason why was because I didn't have one. I was created instead. Sired by the Devil," she added finally, and his mouth dropped open. He stared at her incredulously, obviously trying not to freak out as he sat back in his chair and tried to work it out.

"No way, what?" he blurted out after a few awkward seconds of silence had passed between them. Harry was watching her intently, as though hoping she might burst out laughing and reveal the strange punch line, but she didn't. Cate remained perfectly still and watched him with a serious expression.

"It's true. I'm now over a hundred years old. That's why I don't look any older than last time I saw you," she went on and she saw the realisation hit him then. She wasn't joking.

"Yeah, I did wonder about that," he admitted, scratching his chin before swigging his tea. He then grabbed a biscuit and shoved it in his mouth.

"I lived in Hell for a while before meeting my first love, Devin, who I told you about before. Now, this is going to be strange—perhaps stranger than everything else I've already told you so far. But please try and take it in, okay?" she asked, needing him to hear her out rather than judge her and her strange family before she could explain it all better.

"Okay, but are you sure you're not having me on?" Harry asked, checking one last time, and then shrugged when she raised an eyebrow at him impatiently. "Alright, no more questions. Carry on," he said, raising his hands and then pretending to seal his mouth shut and throw away the key.

Cate sucked in a deep breath, letting it out slowly before continuing.

"Devin was like me. A Devil's heir. He wanted us to be together, but our master changed his mind. Devin's now married to another like us, Serena, and they're in Hell at the moment," she told him, talking fast to get that part out as quickly as she could. Cate then looked at Harry, checking that he was following, and he hadn't already had his mind blown before she continued to the next revelation. "Luke's the Devil, Harry. Also known as Lucifer, Satan, etcetera," Cate said, catching the shocked look as it passed over his face. She sat back in her chair, giving him a moment for it all to sink in while staring over at him from across the table as she desperately tried to gauge his reaction.

"What the actual fuck?" Harry cried, jumping up from his seat angrily before he began pacing the small room. "Didn't you tell me before that he stole you away from your first love? Seems more like he groomed you rather than wooed, if you ask me!" he bellowed, his face contorted with rage.

"You promised me you'd try to understand, Harry," Cate said calmly from her seat, watching him stride up and down. Harry stopped pacing and stared back at her for a moment before sitting back down at the table. He stared across at her, his expression a mixture of sadness, anger, and confusion.

"I'm sorry Dana—I mean, Cate. This is just so crazy; I can't get my head around it. I don't even know where to begin to make sense of it all," he told her. "I'm trying, I promise."

"I know," she said, reminding herself just how young and uninformed he really was about the world. She knew she couldn't expect him to understand all her craziness right away. "I guess I've had a lot longer to figure it all out, haven't I?"

Cate smiled. She then reached across and took his hand in hers and was glad that he didn't pull away from her touch. "I need you to know everything before I can let you ask me any more questions. Does that make sense?" she asked, and Harry nodded, staying quiet once more so Cate could continue. "Thank you. So, Lucifer and I eventually got together, and we were married. I resisted him at first, but you know what, we do work and we're happy together. I know it might seem odd to you."

Harry shrugged, but said nothing in response, his ego still seemingly bruised from that day he'd met him at the flat all those years before. "I came back up to Earth to say my goodbyes to my mother a few years after our wedding. She died holding my hand, an old lady in her bed, and I scattered her ashes at the beach near where we'd lived when I was a young girl. But, while I was there, I was kidnapped," she said, her voice faltering here and there with the raw emotion she felt at reliving the story.

"By whom?" Harry asked, unable to control his intrigue.

"A coven of white witches," Cate told him, and he gazed over at her, seemingly transfixed by her strange story. "They took me to an astral plane near Heaven where an angel named Uriel held me hostage for five years." Harry continued to stare over at her, his mouth dropping open in shock.

"Why?" he then asked, incapable of stopping himself again, but she let him off.

"At first, it was to use me as bait to get Lucifer out of Hell. I think Uriel wanted a fight, but then he changed his mind. He wanted something else," Cate said, and her face dropped.

"You?" Harry guessed, and she nodded. "Sweet Jesus," he replied, and then covered his mouth quickly.

"No more of that, okay? We only blaspheme where I come from," Cate replied with a smirk, trying to lighten the mood a little. "But seriously, no more, okay?" she insisted, and Harry nodded, a smile creeping into his lips, too.

"So, is he the one you said manipulated and controlled you, then?" Harry asked her quietly.

"More than you'll ever know," she replied forlornly, nodding, and taking a final swig of her tea.

"So much for him being one of the good guys, hey?" he asked absentmindedly, finishing off his brew. Cate chuckled darkly to herself at his poignant comment and nodded in agreement.

CHAPTER THIRTY-FOUR

Cate gave Harry some time to absorb what she'd told him so far. She made them both another cup of tea and then continued with her sad story. She needed Harry to know every detail, and it felt good telling him the truth at long last.

"Well, Uriel wanted me to give him a child, but I refused, and I managed to get away. Nina, whose real name is Dylan, used to be a white witch. She was and still is my very best friend, and she helped me to escape using a powerful spell. Since then, she's stayed by my side and renounced the High Council of Angels as her masters. She turned dark for me, Harry, to save my life and to protect me," she said, letting him know that doing so had meant an awful lot to her. "We couldn't go home when we got away though, and I know this sounds gross, but I was—how do I put it—full of light?" Cate said, pulling a face.

"Eeeew!" Harry replied, laughing at her awkward expression.

"I know, right? Well, I had to wait until it was clear, so to speak, so we moved around and that's when I met you. I had no powers, so couldn't get any messages to Lucifer that I was free. Oh yeah, I have powers most of the time, but not then, and not right now," she told him, laughing at how odd it sounded. He couldn't help but laugh with her, thinking just how strange his life had recently become, but he didn't care. He was glad to finally know her story.

"The day of the music festival, do you remember?" she asked him.

"Of course I do," Harry replied, his awkward smile making Cate think back to their wonderful kisses that day, and she blushed at the memory.

"Well," she continued, pushing herself on. "The singer that I was chatting with in the VIP area is actually a demon named Berith. He recognised my human form because we'd met years before when he was in another band. He took a message to Lucifer for me, telling him where I was, and that was why I pushed you away. I'm so sorry I hurt you, but I had to," Cate said, and she blushed at the memory of her couple of days spent in bed with Lucifer when he'd returned to her. "He would've killed you when he came to find me if he found out we'd done anything more. Lucifer was angry as hell about our kisses as it was. Imagine what it would've been like if we'd done more?" she asked, and Harry nodded. He finally understood both the strange chemistry he'd sensed between them that day, and the way 'Luke' had been with him.

"He scared the shit out of me," he told her honestly, and was glad to finally be able to tell her how he'd felt about meeting her husband. "Now I know why. Whoa, no one would ever believe me if I told them I have met the Devil and shook his hand, or that I'd kissed his wife…" he added with a cheeky half-smile. "I remember thinking he couldn't have been the love of your life you'd told me about. He just seemed so wrong for you, so moody and controlling. But then I saw the way you two were together, so in sync and obviously in love. It was a no-brainer," Harry admitted, looking down at his hands, and he'd forgotten she was holding them.

"I'm sorry," Cate said again, giving his hand a squeeze before she continued. "Well, we had to go back to Hell the next day, as he can only be up here during a full moon. One of the setbacks of being the master of all evil, is they don't want him on Earth too often," she told him. "So we tried filling me with his darkness, yuk I know, sorry again." She blushed. "We managed to get me home just in time for the waning moon, and it was all thanks to me having been pregnant," Cate added, and Harry gasped, looking up into her eyes again.

"You have a child with him?" he asked, genuinely taken aback by her remark.

"Yes, well, two actually. It was twins," she told him, knowing that full honesty was her best approach, even if it meant hurting his feelings. "They're in Hell now, being cared for by Dylan and the other dark witches."

Cate's expression grew serious then, and she looked Harry square in the eye as she braved the final part of her dark tale. "I stayed in Hell for as long as I could after they were born, but as I'm half human, I had to come back to Earth for a while. Being in Hell too long had started to make me sick. The children came to visit during some of the full moons, but one night, the white witches cornered them outside the protective boundaries of the church. I had no choice but to go to them, I had to help."

"Was it a trap?" he asked, understanding more than she'd thought she was giving away.

"Yes, and the three of us were taken back up to that damned astral plane. Uriel used the children to force my will, to make me agree to conceive a child with him. They were more than just the bait, and he called them his leverage and blackmail," she told Harry, and a tear ran down Cate's cheek as she thought of Luna's limp body when she'd reacted to the moon's power over her. Harry leaned forward and wiped the tear away with his thumb, and the delicate touch soothed her instantly.

"And so, you think you're pregnant. I'm guessing he's the father?" Harry asked, breaking the silence, and Cate nodded. "Does anyone know?"

She shook her head.

"No. Lucifer found his way to us on the plane. They started fighting, and I was thrown down onto Earth. Luckily, I fell straight into the ocean and passed out. I washed up near an oilrig and was saved by the riggers there. They were fantastic and let me rest with them until the storm was over."

"The storm!" Harry almost shouted, jumping back in his chair. "Whoa, was that them fighting?" he asked, and Cate nodded, burying her face in her hands. Harry quickly calmed himself down and sat silently again, watching her intently from across the table for a few seconds before she lifted her head back up and looked over at him worriedly.

"I don't even know the outcome of the fight, or if either of them is still alive. I managed to find some dark witches at our church, but none of us have any of our powers. I can usually feel Lucifer's presence too, like a beacon, but now there's nothing. I realised just yesterday that I might be pregnant, so I knew I had to find a safe place where I could go to figure everything out away from either the light or dark influences. You were the first—no, the only person I could think of, Harry," Cate told him, staring into her mug, feeling suddenly exhausted from her emotional re-hashing of her life's ups and downs.

Harry looked across at Cate, his soft gaze sweeping over her beautiful pale face as he stared into her sad eyes. He reached over and absent-mindedly tucked a stray dark curl behind her ear.

"I'm here, Cate. For whatever you need. And you can trust me, of course," Harry told her, his voice unwavering as he spoke his promise. "You know I love you. I've always loved you, and I won't hide it away anymore, but please know that I will never expect anything from you in return. I would never try to manipulate or control you because of my love. I want you to know that, and remember it always, okay?" he said, cupping her cheek in his palm while gazing into her eyes adoringly.

She couldn't fight the smile his words brought her and knew that it was exactly what she'd needed to hear. Cate nodded to him and leaned forward so she could hug Harry tightly, feeling safe again at last.

"More tea," she said after a moment, refilling the kettle while he raided the biscuit tin again.

He grabbed a chocolate bourbon as he watched her potter around the small kitchen, still in shock after her story. Harry knew he wanted Cate in his life, regardless of the strange sequence of events that'd led her there, or how dangerous it was for him to continue down this path. He still couldn't help but wonder if it was really happening. How could the girl he thought he knew so well be something so mysterious and powerful, while at the same time so frail and scared? Either way, there was no turning back, not that he even wanted to.

***

"So," Harry said later as they chatted over a Chinese takeaway. "You're the Queen of Hell then?" he asked, a smirk on his face at the strange title. Cate chuckled and nodded, digging into another bite of crispy chilli beef as she wrapped her legs under her on the comfy sofa.

"Well, yes. But you can call me, your majesty," she then replied with a cheeky grin, and Harry laughed, shaking his head. He sat opposite her on a matching couch, and there was a small coffee table between them on which they had laid out the delicious meal.

"Not a chance. And I won't be serving you breakfast in bed or any other such nonsense you may be accustomed to down there," he replied, and they both laughed. The whole thing seemed ludicrous in his ordinary little town and normal human life.

She didn't have the heart to explain why they didn't eat, so kept quiet. Cate simply leaned forward and re-stocked her plate with spring rolls and chicken chow mein, looking across at Harry thoughtfully.

"You got married then?" she asked him, not sure how to broach the subject of his ex-wife. "Joe told me."

"Yeah," he said, looking back at her over his own second helping of food. "We were happy for a while. I guess she kind of filled a void I had inside of me after you left," Harry told her, and Cate felt herself blush. The butterflies in her stomach made another appearance, and he smiled at her reaction, but carried on, pretending not to have noticed. "It felt good at first, but then somehow, once the dust settled, I just knew we weren't right together. We argued constantly towards the end. She desperately wanted to start a family, and I wasn't ready, or maybe I knew we weren't going to last. Either way, she ended up running off with a colleague of hers, and I filed for divorce the next day. She got pregnant straight after that with his child, and I don't think he even stayed with her in the end either."

"Whore," Cate said, smiling mischievously as she chomped down on a prawn cracker piled high with noodles. Harry laughed, but she knew he was hurting from thinking back to his ex's betrayal. She was glad to be there with him and wondered if maybe they could help each other through all their relationship woes.

"You know I'll have to go to work on Monday, so I won't be able to stay with you all the time?" he informed her as he finished up and put down his plate. "Will you be okay?"

"Hmmm, yeah. I guess I hadn't thought of all the details yet. Where are you working now? Do you think there's anywhere there or close by that I could get a job, too?" she wondered, and Harry shrugged. He didn't know for sure but was willing to pull some strings if he had to.

"I'm a qualified doctor now. Maybe I can try and get you something at the practice? It'd be great if we could work together, and at least that way I can always be close to keep an eye on you, and you'll feel safer." He stood and began clearing the used plates. "How's your telephone manner?" Harry asked as he took the empty cartons into the kitchen and discarded them by the sink, returning to give Cate a protective squeeze before he sat down next to her on the sofa.

"Not great, got anything where I don't actually have to deal with people?" she replied with a smile, but she was honestly so happy to have a plan in place so quickly that anything would do.

Later that night, Cate drifted off to sleep in Harry's double bed, while he had kindly pulled out a blanket and snuggled down to sleep on the couch. She slept deeply, relaxed, and happy for the first time in weeks. The pillow smelled of her long-lost friend, which comforted her, and she woke the next morning feeling full of hope. Harry insisted that they needed to get sorted, and he took her shopping that afternoon. He seemed eager to get rid of the unflattering clothing the riggers had given her and encouraged Cate to buy herself a whole new wardrobe, including her usual choice of dark clothes. She opted for a few pairs of black skinny jeans, grey and black t-shirts, along with biker boots and a leather jacket.

"Thank you, Harry," she said gratefully, hugging him as he handed over his bank card to the cashier. He grinned down at her and hugged her back, taking the bags. Harry then pulled her towards a nearby café, his hand in hers as they walked. They ordered two lattes and shared a brownie, chatting quietly to one another as they devoured their treat. Harry still had many questions to ask about her strange life, and Cate was more than willing to answer him honestly. She was just glad that there were finally no barriers between the two of them.

An hour later, and after a second coffee, Harry finally felt like it was all much clearer in his head. Regardless of the strange events that'd bought them here, he loved the fact that he was sitting opposite her again, and he lapped up her attention as she opened up to him further.

"There's one more thing," he said when she stood to go and use the bathroom. Harry reached into his jacket pocket, where he pulled out a small box wrapped in a paper bag. He handed it to her and Cate peeked inside, finding a pregnancy testing kit.

"Harry, I'm already pretty sure," she started to say, but stopped herself when she saw his stern look.

"I want to be absolutely, one-hundred percent sure. At least then I'll know if I get to keep you here for at least the next nine months, or whether I have to stop kidding myself that you'll be able to stay," he told her, smiling up at her from his seat.

Cate blushed and nodded, heading over to the ladies' toilets. She peed on the test strip and sat nervously waiting for the result to show on the plastic window for a minute, but she didn't need to wait. The double line showed up almost instantly, confirming her suspicions once and for all—she was pregnant with Uriel's child.

CHAPTER THIRTY-FIVE

Cate's waters broke with a huge gush eight months later while she was stood washing the dishes at the kitchen sink. Harry was at work, and she'd only just left to go on her maternity leave from the medical practice the day before. Cate had worked there as an administrator since Harry had arranged it for her after her return to Avebury, and she'd held on as long as possible before finally slowing down and leaving the job behind.

She called Harry on his mobile phone, calmly telling him that things were starting and to get home as soon as he could. They'd already agreed that he would deliver the baby himself, but Cate knew there wasn't long. She still distrusted everyone but Harry, and even he agreed that no one else should be with her and the baby while she was helpless. So, he lied. He told his colleagues he felt a migraine coming on and excused himself from work, all so that he could get away without telling anyone that Cate was in labour. He grabbed his things and set off towards home, readying himself to welcome her baby into the world.

They'd told all the people in their lives that the child was Harry's, and that it'd been conceived straight away when they'd rekindled their romance upon Cate's return to the village. Everybody that knew them both from before and after her reappearance had believed the story, and they played the besotted couple easily as there was so much natural chemistry between the two of them. Harry didn't have to pretend at all, and as he'd told her that first day, he never once hid his loving feelings for the dark girl who kept her distance.

Cate didn't need to pretend or put on an act to show her love for Harry to those around them either, but she still fought those same feelings for him when it came to their private hours. Her true allegiance was to Lucifer, and she still believed he'd return one day. When that happened, he'd come to find her just like before. If they forgave each other, life could continue as it had been. Even if they couldn't, they were still bound to one another and would have to come to an arrangement for the twins' sake. Either way, Cate looked forward to being able to return to Hell and be with her children again, but she didn't want to have the added fear for Harry's safety. Lucifer had told her already that if he ever laid eyes on him again, he'd kill him, and she didn't doubt it for a second.

It wasn't that she didn't love Harry. In fact, she adored every moment they spent together and dreaded the day she'd have to leave. She was happy and content with Harry by her side, but she knew she could never let herself forget her place, both in this world and in the underworld. She thought of Blake and Luna all the time and missed them terribly.

Cate used her thoughts of them as a constant reminder not to take her time on Earth for granted. Her little family would soon have another member, a secret member, and Cate vowed to herself that she would not put the baby or Harry in harm's way ever again. Lucifer could never know she'd even been back in touch with him.

They'd also discussed the return of her husband from another perspective, too. Both agreed that first and foremost, the baby must be hidden from him at all costs. Harry understood how much was at stake, and he was prepared to take the child and run from him—from them all—if it came to it. Cate hated the very thought of losing the pair of them but knew that someday it might be their only choice. If it meant saving their lives, she would do it. She'd prepared a backpack already and stashed it away for such a time. It was packed full of money and maps of the ley lines, along with ideas of small towns and places she and Dylan had lived in where he and her child could live safely together. Harry vowed to Cate that he'd make sure the baby was safe, and most importantly, away from the reaches of both Lucifer and Uriel. Either influence could prove to be devastating, and both Cate and Harry had made a solemn promise to one another that they would protect it, no matter the cost.

Cate clung to the kitchen chair as another contraction clenched her tender muscles, hunching over it as she concentrated on slowing her breathing. She knew she had to be careful to keep the noise down so the neighbours didn't call by to see if she was okay, but her strong body was already taking control and she had to bite her lip to stop from crying out. The few minutes she had between contractions allowed her to recover quickly from each painful episode, but the gap was shortening with every intense contraction.

Harry arrived home in hardly any time at all and dropped his things in the hall quickly before running to find Cate in the kitchen.

"Are you doing okay?" he asked, cupping her face in his hands and taking Cate in for a moment. He gave her a once over, and she nodded, smiling back at him. Harry kissed her forehead and grabbed the antibacterial soap from its wrapper beside the kitchen sink. He then vigorously washed his hands, scrubbing them with a well-practiced technique thanks to his medical training. There were clean towels and blankets already out on the kitchen side, and he dried his hands carefully.

He was trying to stay calm but was glad that they'd prepared themselves well for the impending arrival. He might be a doctor, but he'd never delivered a baby before. He'd read up on it as much as he could in preparation, though. It'd helped, and Harry was sure he would be running around like a headless chicken if everything wasn't already organised for him. "How far apart are they?" he asked, grabbing the rest of the linen.

"Two minutes, I think," Cate answered him between the contractions, before taking his hand and allowing Harry to lead her into the living room. He laid down a couple of the large blankets, covering one of the small couches as well as the floor in front of it, and she perched on the edge of the sofa, her legs open and trembling. Cate panted as another contraction took over her body and Harry took her hand in his, groaning as she gripped onto it tightly. As the pain relinquished once again, she let go and apologised.

"It's fine, don't worry. Can I check how dilated you are?" he asked, an embarrassed look on his handsome face, and Cate laughed and nodded. She pulled the hem of her nightdress up so he could check on the baby's progress and didn't feel at all uncomfortable by his presence between her thighs.

"We should've planned your first time down there much better," she told him playfully, laughing as she heard a loud "*tut*" from beneath her bump.

"It's almost time," he told her as he reappeared, smiling up at Cate excitedly. She grinned back at him, relishing in his warm smile. She was tired, but ready, and slid down onto the blankets to rest on the floor.

The next contraction came hard and fast, and Cate quickly felt the familiar urge to push. She looked to Harry for guidance. "Go for it," he told her, kneeling between her legs as she gripped her thighs and breathed deeply. She bore down, and just a few minutes later gave birth to a healthy and beautiful little girl. Harry checked the baby over quickly before cutting the cord and wrapping her up in a soft towel. She was perfect, and hardly even cried. He smiled lovingly down at her, kissing her forehead quickly before placing her in Cate's ready arms.

Less than an hour later, Cate was completely healed. Harry was absolutely astonished by how fast her body had gotten over the trauma of childbirth, and he'd barely finished clearing up the bloody towels and blankets when she came sauntering happily into the kitchen, holding the cleaned and dressed baby to her breast.

"I'm starving. What shall we have for dinner…Chinese?" she asked Harry, startling him with her nonchalant attitude.

"Bloody hell, Cate," he said, his doctor's urges taking over uncontrollably. "You should be resting."

"I'm fine," she told him with a smile. He could be so over the top sometimes, but she also loved his caring nature. "I'm all healed up and I'm bloody starving. Come on Daddy, I need some grub," Cate ordered him, grinning cheekily as she leaned over to give him a kiss on the cheek. He blushed but kissed her back and then leaned down to kiss the baby's head as she suckled gently on her mother's milk.

"I like you calling me that," he murmured, and she grinned. It was necessary for them to call him Daddy, but it'd also felt good, and right. He was going to be a wonderful father, Cate knew it. "What shall we name her?" Harry then asked as he pulled the menu for the Chinese takeaway out of the kitchen drawer. They hadn't really discussed names much in the buildup to her arrival, and they hadn't been sure if the baby was a boy or girl. There was a part of her had even wondered if it might be twins again. They'd also chosen not to go for any scans during the pregnancy, as Cate wasn't sure if there would be some strange light or unusual goings-on inside. She wouldn't be able to explain something like that away, so they opted instead for a natural approach. The pair had told their friends and colleagues that they'd decided to just wait and see. Cate lifted the now sleeping baby away from her chest and handed her to Harry, staring down at the already calm and peaceful babe.

"I really like the name Lottie, and I was thinking it'd suit her, too. What do you think?" she asked, looking to him for his opinion, and he smiled and nodded. Harry's blue eyes lit up as he stared down at the child he cradled so protectively. He didn't care that she wasn't his. He loved that baby with every inch of himself and knew he always would.

"Lottie, it's perfect. Do you know what that name means?" he asked, gazing up into her beautiful green eyes.

"No, why do you, *Mr Baby name dictionary*?" she asked, joking with him.

"I do actually, and only because a friend of mine called her daughter Charlotte, and she told me," he replied matter-of-factly. "It's actually pretty perfect, by the way. It means, free," Harry told her with a loving smile.

***

In two corners of the world, two young men lay in their hospital beds. The first, Lucifer, was unconscious in Moscow, Russia. He was in a coma, having been so for nearly nine months already, and had no signs of any brain activity or responses to the doctors' tests. He'd been admitted to the hospital the day after the freak storm had cleared at last, with no form of identification on him, and he'd been wearing nothing but bloody, ripped clothes.

All the attending doctors and nurses guessed he must've been caught in a flash flood or avalanche during the storm, and so regardless of his lack of identification, he was taken straight to the intensive care unit. Lucifer had many deep, severe cuts and bruises to his entire body, along with badly broken bones in his legs, arms, and spine. It was a wonder he was alive at all, but apart from his unconscious state, he'd healed physically in record time. His broken bones had snapped back together, requiring hardly any casting or physiotherapy to mend. Lucifer had also needed no help to breathe, or for his organs to function normally on their own, so the only strange thing was that he just would not wake up. It was as though he were simply in a deep sleep. Marvelled by his record-breaking healing, the doctor in the ER had kept a bed free in the hope he'd wake up and regale them with his story, however they'd eventually had to concede. The bed was needed, and the strange patient had been moved to a small room on a quiet ward in the back of the hospital. Since then, the unknown man hadn't had a single visitor. They couldn't find a match for him on the missing persons' database either, but his nurse, Yelena, regularly checked back for updates.

Yelena took her responsibilities very seriously. She soon began talking to him and telling him stories in the hope he might be listening to her from somewhere in his deep, dark slumber. She was a lonely woman and had immediately felt a strange kinship to the handsome man that was all alone in her care. She would buy flowers for his room and play him music or sing to him as she cleaned him up and changed his sheets. Sometimes, she sat chatting away to him for hours, as though they were having a conversation, and she'd soon created an entire identity for him in her mind. Yelena would occasionally curl up next to Lucifer on the bed, rather than go home to sleep, and she'd nestle into him as she drifted off. She often slept on his chest, listening to his shallow breathing, and regularly pulled his arm over her as though he were holding her tight. Yelena found she couldn't help herself. She had a strange attraction to the unknown patient and somehow found her darker urges came to the forefront of her mind more and more with every day that passed by.

In Rio de Janeiro, Brazil, a small local hospital housed the other man, Uriel. He was awake and physically well but had suffered with complete amnesia. Thanks to him also having no form of identification on him, he'd been allowed to stay in the hospital until they could figure out who he was, when they'd send him safely on his way. He too had been brought into the hospital the day after the storm had ended, his body battered and broken. All the staff had been working overtime thanks to a tidal wave that'd destroyed part of the harbour, so they'd all just assumed the unknown man had been caught up in the destructive wave too, and so regularly told him how lucky he was to be alive.

The doctors had helped him, tending to his wounds, and setting his bones, which had also healed impressively fast. Despite having broken bones in both legs and his neck, he'd managed to walk again after just a few weeks of bed rest and physiotherapy. The local nurses had quickly referred to him as a *miracle from God,* and they'd soon discovered how more and more of his wounds had healed each time they unwrapped them to change the dressings. The brain specialist that came to visit him after a few months could find no visible damage to his nervous system or brain function on the numerous tests he carried out and was unsure what might be the cause for the amnesia. They'd then tried hypnosis and even shock therapy to try and help him recover, but without any luck.

Both the staff and other patients in the care community he now resided in flocked around him constantly. They were drawn to him in a way none of them could really understand, and not a single one of them were in a rush to send the unknown man on his way. They enjoyed the way he made them feel far too much to say goodbye. He made them feel good and became someone they flocked to for guidance and understanding. He didn't know who he was or from where he'd come, but he knew how to bring people serenity, and did so without knowing how or why he had an affinity for bringing peace.

They all guessed he was simply a natural.

CHAPTER THIRTY-SIX

Lottie was a happy baby, rarely ever crying, and from just a few weeks old, she had a warm smile and happy nature to her that drew everyone's attention. She looked just like Cate, with dark hair that was already growing in ringlets around her ears, and she had deep green eyes the exact same shade as her mother's, too. Cate had come to suspect that perhaps there really wasn't any physical trait for the divine omnipotence that her children's fathers possessed that could be passed on to them. Thinking aloud one night, she asked Harry for his opinion, having showed him a photograph of her mother. She'd managed to find it online from the archived website for the legal firm Ella had worked at for all those years, a firm owned and run by Lucifer and his demons. Or so she had later come to find out.

"I did wonder that, too," Harry replied, handing her a freshly brewed cup of tea. "Especially when you described how the twins look the same," he added.

She looked down thoughtfully at the sleeping baby in her basinet, who rested so calmly, and Cate loved that her relaxed nature had already begun showing in her. Lottie and Luna could've been the same. Their natures were so similar and their delicate features almost identical to one another's, and Cate couldn't help finding herself thinking more and more of the twins as Lottie grew. "I know you miss them," Harry said quietly, knowing that far-off look she would get when she thought of her older children. "I have absolutely no doubt they miss you like crazy, too. But Dylan will love them like her own, and they'll always feel your love through her," he told her. She knew he was trying to offer her a little bit of his intuitive insight and a slight respite from her guilt, and as she thought about it some more, his words did bring her comfort, as always.

"You're right. Dylan loves us all so very much, and I'm sure she reminds them every day just how much I love them," she replied, her face losing its sadness at last. Harry put his mug down on the coffee table and then pulled her into a tight hug. His warm embrace was a welcome and needed comfort, as usual, and she wrapped her arms around his back, breathing in his familiar scent with a contented smile. She really did adore him, and often wished they'd met in far different circumstances.

Before long, Cate accepted it was high time she went to the church to check in on the witches. She had to hope for news of Lucifer at the same time, but, if she was honest, she'd been putting it off. She was terrified that there might, in fact, be news of his return, and if there was, it would mean she couldn't go home to Lottie and Harry.

It was something she needed to do, though. Cate owed it to them to show she still cared, and she hadn't been able to go back to London during the pregnancy because it would've given the secret away. Now that Lottie had arrived and could safely stay with Harry in Avebury, Cate knew she needed to start at least showing her face every now and then to the witches and demons that might still be sheltering there.

"I'm their Queen. I need to show them support. I cannot be selfish. They need me," she told her reflection in the mirror before heading to bed, trying to give herself the kick up the bum she so desperately needed. The rehearsed lines weren't convincing her at all, but she still repeated them over and over in the hope she'd leave her fears behind.

The next morning, she packed some clothes and toiletries in her trusty backpack, and then prepared herself to set off. She hesitated at the doorway on her way out of the flat, wanting nothing more than to just turn back and wait it out for just a little while longer, but Harry's stern look urged her onwards.

After one more hug and kiss from them both, she was finally on her way. Cate reached the city centre within a few hours and parked her hire car easily beside the seemingly derelict building that was the old Satanic church. Inside the main hall, she could see that the former aisle and seats had been transformed into makeshift beds for the many beings that were now taking shelter there. It seemed many of the others had come to the same conclusion as her after all and had flocked there to find their dark kind. She looked around, counting no fewer than ten dirty and uncomfortable looking beds, and was glad she hadn't stayed. Cate searched for Suzanne or Bea and eventually found them sat amongst some other lower-level witches and a couple of demons that Cate assumed were their new roommates.

After greeting them with a wave, she made her way over to the group and the pair of them stood, their faces lighting up at the sight of her. The two witches quickly bowed to their Queen, as did the others around them once they realised who she was. Cate hadn't met the new refugees before, and without their powers or keen senses, she could forgive them for not knowing her human form this time. Either way, all of them seemed relieved to see her.

"Do we have any more information on my husband yet, ladies?" Cate asked, addressing them casually. They both shook their heads, grave looks on their scrawny faces, and their disappointment was clear.

"No, my Queen," said Suzanne. "We hoped you might bring some news?"

"No, I'm afraid to say I've found nothing either," Cate answered, touching each of the witch's shoulders lightly with her hands to comfort them. "How have you managed?" she asked Bea.

"Not great. There's not much food, but we can keep a fire going, and as long as the doors are shut tight, the heat stays in," she answered, indicating with her hand around the large room. Cate noticed that the once magnificent windows were now boarded up and air tight. She nodded and gave Bea and handful of pound notes from her bag, instructing her to buy supplies sensibly and to hold tight.

"I'll be back again soon. But for now, I must keep searching for news of the King," she told them, and they bowed their heads, a quiet prayer to him on each of their lips.

Cate then said her goodbyes and went out towards the car. She hadn't stayed nearly as long as she ought to though. She felt bad but was grateful to be out of that dirty place and back in the fresh afternoon air again.

"My Queen," called a voice from the shadows just as she clicked the unlock button on the car key. Cate looked in the direction of the familiar sound and had to go closer to see the person who'd called to her more clearly. Just as she thought, it'd been Berith. He'd never really been a fan of sunlight, more of a night-time creature, so Cate joined him in the shadows. She even hugged him tightly as she greeted the demon and was glad he was safe.

"Long time, no see," Cate said with a smile. "I guess you're stuck here too then?"

"Yep," he told her. "I've heard no word from the King since he left, yet the storm subsided around a year ago. I must admit I fear for his wellbeing," he told her, his usual humorous and fun nature hidden behind his forlorn features, and his worry was obvious. Cate knew Berith was fiercely loyal to Lucifer, as loyal as Dylan was to her, and she also knew he was not one to be underestimated, despite him having helped her in the past.

"Me too," Cate admitted. "I'm trying to figure out where he could be. Surely we would feel something if he were on Earth, don't you agree?" she asked, trying to gauge his suspicions.

He nodded in agreement, his long, dirty hair falling from behind his ears into his face.

"I've actually been wondering about purgatory," Berith said, not finishing his sentence, but Cate knew what he meant.

"Perhaps," she agreed, looking into his brown eyes earnestly. "I would assume that if Lucifer and that bastard angel were there, we probably wouldn't be able to sense them until each eventually returns to their dominions. That would also explain the lack of powers on both sides."

"So, we wait then," he said, another statement rather than a question.

Cate nodded, and bid her old friend goodbye, feeling grateful that he hadn't questioned her further to find out where she was staying while they were all forcibly exiled to Earth.

Before she returned home, though, she decided to hold out for a little while longer and checked into a cheap hotel by the motorway. Cate wasn't sure why, but she was worried someone might've decided to follow her from the church, and her conversation with Berith was especially playing on her mind. She sent a text message to Harry, letting him know she was fine, but that she'd be home the following day. She'd decided to put some safety plans in place first and would explain it when she got home.

Later that evening, after a quick dinner, she sat at the hotel bar enjoying a glass of wine as she browsed through some web pages on her laptop.

"You come here often?" a voice behind her asked, his tone playful. It was Berith. She knew he must've followed her from London, and Cate was glad she'd trusted her gut. It proved that she should follow those same hunches again in future.

"No," Cate answered curtly, and was genuinely angry that he'd been tailing her. "What are you doing here, Berith?" she demanded.

"It's just, it occurred to me after you'd left that I never asked where it is you've been going that keeps you so busy looking for our Dark King. I wondered if perhaps you were holed up wherever it was you were living before, with that boy. What was his name? Henry?" he questioned her, and she didn't correct him, being careful not to rise to his accusations.

"And why would I bother? You know Lucifer wouldn't take kindly to me consorting with humans unnecessarily, especially men. Not that I need to explain myself to you, Berith, but I've been travelling around England, doing odd jobs for cash, and looking for any sign of my husband," she told him poignantly. "I was also thinking about getting myself a permanent base somewhere in London. I'm sure Lucifer wouldn't begrudge me a better state of living than those poor people squatting in the church. Don't you?" she asked, her tone flat and unfriendly.

"I'm sorry, your majesty," Berith answered. "I didn't mean to infer that you were up to something. You were just not very forthcoming earlier, and it made me suspicious."

"Well, maybe when your master returns you can talk to him about your suspicions, but until that time comes I'm in command, and you do not want me on your bad side," Cate replied sternly, and Berith bowed his head in respect as she stood and turned to leave. "I suggest you carry on with your business as usual, Berith. I'll see you again when Lucifer returns, and if I even get a sniff of you following me, you really will be sorry," she promised. Cate then went back to her room, furious but more determined than ever to put extra measures in place to ensure the safety of her secret little family. She then researched late into the night for any sign of her husband, or of Uriel. News of either would be something at least, but she still found nothing.

She also checked out some flats for rent near London before settling down to sleep and emailed a few of the landlords to request long-term rental options, before snapping the laptop closed and turning out the light. Cate decided she would rent a place where she could go during the full moons without Harry and Lottie anywhere nearby, assuming that when Lucifer returned to her, he might be bound by the moon as usual. She decided that she would go every month and wait there until the moon waned again. It'd be awful leaving home so regularly but hoped it would ensure that when the time eventually for Lucifer to come back to her, she'd be there instead of at the flat. Although it pained her to even think of it, Cate knew it was the best scenario. It was the only way she could leave her new family behind, knowing they were safely hidden from his all-knowing radar.

The next day, Cate found the perfect little place. It was a one-bedroom flat near Brixton, just outside of the capital city. She'd be close to the church, but to not too close to invite anyone from the dirty refuge to come to her doorstep unannounced. Cate signed a one-year lease agreement there and then, paying up front, and taking the keys from the overjoyed landlord before she got in the rented car and headed back home.

She arrived at Harry's small home later that night; having checked what must've been one hundred times that she was no longer being followed. She crept in quietly, finding Harry asleep with Lottie in the basinet beside him in the bedroom. Neither stirred as she sneaked in and gave the beautiful baby a kiss, her heart full of love for her precious bundle. Cate then stood there for a moment, watching Harry as he slept soundly in the bed. He'd been a wonderful man, friend, and father the past year, and she couldn't deny, she yearned to add lover to that list. Her heart beat for him, despite her efforts to quieten it, and she knew she loved him.

"Hey gorgeous," he whispered, startling Cate, who was so deep in thought she hadn't even realised he was awake.

"Hey yourself," she whispered back, sitting down to perch on the edge of the bed. They'd always slept separately in the flat, Harry usually sleeping on a sofa bed in the living room while she had the bedroom along with Lottie. He'd slept in there to be next to the baby throughout the night while she'd been away, and Cate felt a little naughty being in the bedroom with him. She also couldn't help herself from feeling excited as she stared down at Harry, and her attraction to him seemed to come bursting out of her all at once. She quickly realised just how much she'd missed them both over the last couple of days, and that she was incredibly happy to be home.

Cate reached over to Harry, unable to stop herself. She gently caressed his face with her hand before stroking her palm slowly down onto his lightly haired chest. He smiled up at her, not knowing for sure what she wanted, but not stopping her in the hope he might finally get a taste of what he'd coveted for so long.

She leaned down, planting a soft kiss on his ready mouth, and they both moaned in readiness for more. He grabbed her shoulders and pulled Cate closer, instantly deepening the kiss, and she let him. The unadulterated closeness with the man she truly trusted to take care of her every need was sheer bliss, and she knew she couldn't fight it any longer.

Cate climbed on top of Harry, straddling him on the bed. She was still fully clothed on top of his duvet, while underneath, she knew he was naked. Harry always slept in the nude and the thought of him so pure and exposed beneath her turned her on even more.

They lay like that for a few minutes, kissing each other passionately and intensely for the first time in far too long. Harry let his hands run through her long hair, grabbing it gently and pulling her closer, not letting her mouth come away from his for even a second.

"I need you, Harry," she eventually told him, an almost silent whisper escaping her lips between his ravaging.

"I've always needed you, Cate," he told her back, looking up at her as she leaned over him in the darkness. "Take everything, for without you, I'm nothing…"

CHAPTER THIRTY-SEVEN

Cate grinned and sat up, leaning back on Harry's lap, and she could feel the tell-tale bulge of his need beneath her thigh. He watched her with a smile, intent on savouring every moment, and didn't take his eyes off her as she pulled her black shirt off and then slipped off her bra. He wanted to resist, to hold back and let her lead, but his hands instinctively reached up to caress her breasts. Cate heaved a sigh, savouring the feel of his hands on her at long last, and leaned back down for another deep kiss, while he let out a guttural groan. She giggled but didn't stop him as Harry gently cupped them before he then carried on down to her jeans so he could unbutton them.

She then rolled onto her back beside him, pulling the black denim trousers down her slim legs, along with her knickers, which she then kicked off the end of the bed.

Harry took her in for a moment—the beautiful, dark goddess that lay bathed in the moonlight before him. He was so eager to touch her, to taste her, but he knew she was still in a delicate place and needed to be the one in complete control. It wasn't the time to pounce on his would-be lover, and he was more than willing to wait. Harry would please her in whatever way she commanded, and they both knew it. Cate smiled coyly over at him and climbed up onto one elbow to look him in the eye, while his gaze swept up and down her naked body.

"Well?" she whispered expectantly. "Your turn," she added with a cheeky grin. Cate tugged at the edge of the duvet she was lying on top of, the only thing keeping her away from his naked flesh, and grinned. Harry quickly shuffled himself free of the linen and climbed on top of the bedcovers to join her, and she took her turn to gaze upon his gorgeous body. His arousal was hard and ready, sticking out prominently against his slim body, and she wanted to touch and feel it more than anything.

"Will you make love to me, Harry?" Cate asked him, an almost shy tone to her voice as she spoke, and she looked up into his eyes in the darkness.

"Oh yes, I thought you'd never ask," he told her, never having wanted anything more.

"Then come over here, will you?" she asked him playfully, and Harry conceded. He climbed on top of her and kissed her passionately again before trailing his kisses down her neck to her breasts and then stomach. She groaned loudly as her body responded to his delicate touch, and he shushed her, laughing to himself as his kisses continued further down towards his sweet prize. Harry's mouth soon surrounded her swollen bead, taking it between his lips. He began suckling on it gently, yet firmly, and revelled in Cate's squirms of delight. She thrust her hands into his hair, urging him to continue, which he did with vigour.

Her thighs began to tense, signalling her rapid closeness to the glorious orgasm she needed and wanted. Harry took her commands for more without comment and continued his unrelenting deliverance of pleasure to Cate's aching core. His hands gripped her thighs tightly while his tongue flicked over her clit for a while longer, before he then delved it inside of her hot, wet cleft, making her gasp and moan again.

Cate came, her back arching on the bed, and she had to stifle a louder moan that threatened to escape her lips as she did so. She instead let out a quiet, satisfied groan and released her grip of his hair, revelling in the aftershocks of her first orgasm in far too long.

Harry wasted no time, continuing his kisses again as he climbed back up onto his knees and laid his mouth against her stomach and breasts as he glided back up towards her mouth. She kissed him feverishly when he reached her soft lips again, tasting herself on his tongue, but didn't care at all.

Cate stared up into Harry's eyes a few moments later, a broad smile on her lips as she reached down, running her hands over his slim stomach. When she reached his waist, she grasped his still rock-hard cock between her hands and stroked it. He gasped, delighting in her touch as she guided him towards her. Cate then lifted her hips up to meet his as he leaned down, and the tip of him finally entered her wet opening. She held his gaze as she welcomed him inside her at long last, and the world around them disappeared when he plunged inside. All that mattered to Cate was Harry, and her heart ached for him, and only him.

The pair kissed each other hurriedly as he thrust into her, neither holding back as her body opened for him. She wrapped her legs around his waist and pulled him deeper inside of her, eager for him, yearning, and yet she was desperate to please him too. She had to know it felt right for him and loved watching as his body told her everything she needed to know. He plunged deep, thrusting harder and faster in tune with her body's silent commands, while taking what he needed to reach his climax as well.

Cate called out his name as she unravelled beneath him, throwing all caution to the wind as she shuddered with the wonderful surges of pleasure that seemed to collide wonderfully with the raw emotion she felt gushing out of her from within. There was no guilt, no shame, and certainly no regret. Unlike with her previous lovers, she'd made love to him by her own choosing, and wished she could continue doing so for the rest of her seemingly endless life.

Cate slept in the bed with him after their wonderful lovemaking and had woken Harry by wrapping her mouth around the tip of his long shaft. Lifting the covers, he'd grinned broadly down at her, and gladly urged her to continue. She drank him down, and then laid kisses over his torso and up to his chest, having taken her time to suck his nipples, biting down gently as she went. Harry gasped, but his sharp intake of breath had done nothing to stop her eager mouth. She then lay in Harry's arms, each of them feeling happy and relaxed as they enjoyed their embrace.

Cate turned to gaze up at him in the morning sunshine and was pleased to find he was ready for her again. She climbed on top of him, wet, and more than ready herself, too, and slid him inside. Cate rode up and down on his lap, his long cock pressing on just the right spot inside of her. She came quickly, riding on and on despite her tenderness from the night before, and Harry sat up so he could kiss her. He cradled Cate in his arms and pressed himself even deeper into her while her muscles tensed around him. With a kiss, he brushed the hair away from her face with his hands so he could stare into her eyes as she started moving slowly on his lap again, and his own climax soon followed hers.

They lay back down, dozing happily in each other's arms until their daughter woke up, ready for her morning feed. When she eventually stirred, Harry scooped Lottie up from the Moses basket and placed her in her mother's arms. After giving them both a quick kiss, he then headed off to the kitchen, where he made some coffee and buttered toast.

Harry brought the tray of food in and placed it on Cate's lap, taking Lottie from her so she could eat while he burped her and change the baby's nappy. The three of them then relaxed in bed together for a while, Harry lying back against the pillows with a happy smile. He silently took in the wonderful sight of the two girls before him that he loved more than anything else in the world. He had a pure and contented feeling inside that he just couldn't hide, and he felt giddy when Cate looked at him, making him pretty sure he had to be the happiest man alive.

It felt to Harry as if there were a secret bond the two lovers now shared. It was like a final, utterly complete, and unadulterated connection to one another existed, and they could both finally enjoy it after being denied the freedom for so long. The intimacy they'd shared, the pleasure, and the love that'd finally flourished between them made him smile to himself as he remembered every moment, every touch. Harry wanted to shout it from the rooftops, to proclaim his love for her to anyone that would listen and beg her to be his forever.

There was still that little niggle in the pit of his stomach, though, and he knew that there always would be. There was an annoying little voice in the back of his mind that knew it couldn't last forever, but while he had Cate and Lottie there in his feeble little human life, he was determined to enjoy every minute of their time together.

Cate watched him as he lay there with a far-off look and a relaxed smile. Her feelings for him were stronger than ever, and utterly determined not to be pushed away again. She'd denied herself his love, simply because she didn't want to put Harry in harm's way, but knew it'd been pointless. Cate had convinced herself it was the right thing to do, but she realised that she'd already put him in the crosshairs for the demonic wrath that might be coming her way just by him being in her life again. No matter how her future with Lucifer might pan out, he was already ruined, already fated to burn thanks to her. It was the one thing she truly regretted most in her long and immoral life, but there was no going back, and she figured if they were both damned, they'd better make the most of what little time they had left.

"Are you okay?" he asked, catching her thoughtful look.

"I'm wonderful," she answered, making him smile.

"But," he persisted, a knowing look on his face as he placed Lottie back in her basinet.

"But, I can't help but think I'm going to be the death of you, Harry, and worse," she told him, a sad half-smile on her pale face. "Not only have I asked you to take care of me—the wife of the most dangerous, evil being in all creation. But I've also asked you to help me cover up the existence of a child that is potentially a ticking time-bomb dependent on how her future might go for her," Cate said, reaching across to stroke his cheek with her hand, and she stared into his gorgeous blue eyes. Harry's smile didn't falter. He just gazed back at her, looking into Cate's eyes with his heart on his sleeve, and his soul hers for the taking.

"The beauty of free will," he told her, covering her hand with his own, and giving it a squeeze. "Is that it's my choice, and I choose you, Cate. I don't care what he does to me for loving you, I'd rather live my life knowing I'd been fortunate enough to love my soulmate for as long as possible, than ever running away in fear. I know I can never keep you here when he returns, but until that time comes, I'm going to love you for every minute of every day. I'd sell my soul if it meant you could stay with me," Harry told her. He leaned down and gave his lover a deep, desperate kiss, sealing his devoted promise to her before he pulled her into his arms. She reached up and ran her hands through his slightly wavy hair, pulling him into her embrace as she feverishly returned his kisses—stunned by his macabre pledge.

She'd known the second she chose to find him again that she'd asked him for an incredibly dangerous favour, and at first had offered him nothing but her company in return for his protection. And yet, he'd still said yes. Cate was astounded that Harry had been so ready to take care of her and Lottie, regardless of the high risk and potentially little reward for himself. He truly was a good man, and she couldn't help but fall even more in love with her secret lover with every passing moment.

The many years of suppressed desire, love and passion had come pouring out of Cate the night before, and she refused to shut it off, run, or hide it away anymore. She wanted Harry, and had always loved him, but was blinded and consumed by the terrible love triangle she'd found herself in, twice. The devastating effect it'd had on her had meant she hadn't been able to see that he was the one for her. Harry truly was her soulmate, and she wanted to be a part of his life for as long as she could as well.

Cate cocooned herself in Harry's arms, relishing in his protective circle as they continued to kiss, neither one ready to break their connection. She finally felt free, as though she could take a step back from the situation at hand and stop being selfish. The bigger picture was most important, and she owed it to him to make the foreseeable future the best she could provide for him and Lottie. Cate vowed to herself that she would be strong and decisive from then onwards. She would dedicate herself to keeping them both safe, and no longer worry about herself or her fate.

She realised then, in a strange moment of clarity, that her own future somehow seemed set out for her. It was suddenly apparent that whatever higher power appeared to be keeping her dark abilities at bay might also be keeping her two omnipotent lovers lost in whatever abyss they'd found themselves. This higher power she'd never believed in had somehow steered her on the path to eventually having Lottie and Harry come into her life. There had to be a reason, and somehow, she believed it would all work itself out in the end. All she had to do was sit back and wait for the rest to play out. It seemed she'd found some faith for the first time in her entire life and couldn't deny it felt good to have hope.

***

The morning before the next full moon, Cate held her beautiful Lottie close. She smelled her soft, dark hair, and kissed her forehead, watching as the baby slept peacefully in her arms.

"I'll be home in two days," she told Harry, who nodded and kissed her after she'd handed over the precious bundle. They'd talked a great deal about her plans to go and stay in the flat during the moon's full phases, and he'd agreed that it was a good idea. The plan made perfect sense to Harry, but he still hated the idea—the reality—that one day Lucifer would come and find her. Just like before, he would take her away again. And just like before, there would be nothing he could do to stop them.

It made him sick with worry, knowing that at some point the full moon would claim Cate once and for all, and that when it did, she might never return home to him and Lottie. He didn't show her his fears though, urging her out the door with an understanding and reassuring smile despite his inner turmoil. His one insistence on the arrangement had been that Cate had to check in with him each night at around eight o'clock, via any means, telephone call, or text message—even an email would do if she somehow lost her phone.

If Harry didn't hear from her within another twelve hours, they'd agreed he would take Lottie and run, just in case. He'd given Cate his word that he would hide her away forever if that were what it took to keep Lottie safe, and she believed him.

Cate didn't know what the future would hold for the child, a half-breed mix of both good and evil. Perhaps they would have no choice which path she went down, or maybe she could choose her own way. Cate could never be sure until that day eventually came, but she hoped that against all odds, Lottie would thrive and ultimately be free to choose for herself.

She dreamed her child might even be able to join her in the darkness, much preferring the unholy fate to her being an outcast of Heaven. Lottie would no-doubt be shunned by the elitist angels who sat on their thrones in the astral planes above, yet she'd be expected to follow whatever path the High Council of Angels set out for her.

The only setback in her wishful hopes for Lottie's future was Lucifer. She knew he'd never allow her into their home. No pillow talk or alluring persuasion would ever win him over on that subject, she was sure. Regardless, Cate knew she had no choice but to hide her on Earth for as long as it took to figure out where their lives might end up. Lottie would be safe there, and Cate was glad that Lucifer would never be able to read her thoughts to find out about her. So, provided the light beings didn't find them either, she figured Lottie might be able to live a somewhat normal, happy life.

Cate arrived at the flat later that afternoon, with some shopping and DVDs at the ready for her couple of days away from normality. She'd intended to hide away during her short visits to the flat, and that's just what she did. She locked the doors and lay in bed, watching movies and eating junk food all day. Cate tried not to let her mind wander too much, but the quiet solace of her time alone allowed her more painful thoughts to creep up on her.

She couldn't help but think of Dylan. Cate missed her terribly, and while she was glad her best friend was with the twins in her absence, she still wished she were there with her. She knew Dylan would understand and be able to help her get through all of this, just like she'd done before.

She wondered what the dark witch was getting up to in Hell without her. Cate hoped she was with the children, teaching them, and playing games together as she'd always done before. She spent hours fantasising what Blake and Luna might look like now, and how their little personalities and characters may have developed in her absence. The bittersweet wonderings bought her both smiles and tears, and Cate curled up under the covers in the small bed, kicking herself for being so damn emotional. She grabbed her headphones and plugged in her MP3 player, opting for a diversion via some heavy metal music. Cate dried her eyes and lay back on the pillow, Berith's deep, soulful voice singing in her ears. It surprised Cate that she wanted to listen to the demon sing, but in the end, it didn't matter that he'd annoyed the hell out of her the last time. The familiarity of his voice brought her comfort and it worked to help distract Cate from her depression.

When the moon began to wane again, she grabbed her things and quickly tidied up the flat, feeling eager to leave. After a tense drive back, Cate returned to Avebury later that afternoon, and was glad to be back home with her small family at last. She was eternally thankful to walk through the doorway and back into Harry's loving arms and kissed him fervently to let him know it.

CHAPTER THIRTY-EIGHT

Cate and Harry were incredibly happy together, and as the years passed by, she couldn't help but fall in love with him more and more. He'd captured her heart forever, despite her dark vows to her King. He was the perfect friend and lover and was the most wonderful father to Lottie she could've hoped for. Harry was firm but kind in a way she'd never known Lucifer be to the twins, and she saw how Lottie loved and respected him for it.

In lots of ways, Cate couldn't quite believe her luck. She'd found love without any interfering forces or intervening fate. Her old friend had turned into someone she could rely on above any other. He'd cared for her regardless of the risks and shown strength the likes she herself had never done. He'd loved her and vowed to risk his life to show it. But Harry was still just a human. His will was strong, and Cate adored his fearlessness, but she cut no corners when it came to keeping him safe. There was no risking it this time and she was absolutely ready to sacrifice her own life for Harry and Lottie should she need to. Being a mother had changed her previously so selfish ways. Gone was the naïve girl who had let both Lucifer and Uriel control her fate. There were far more important things at stake.

The trio eventually moved out of Harry's flat into a two-bedroom house closer to his practice so Lottie could have her own room, and they made it their own. They were always together, thanks to the careful and necessary paranoia the pair of them shared when it came to their precious child's protection. They never let anyone babysit her and chose instead to spend their evenings together in front of the television rather than going out with their friends, regardless of their taunts that the pair of them were boring.

When she turned four years old, Lottie was enrolled at the local primary school, and Cate couldn't help but worry about her while she was away from their protective gaze. She quickly decided that she needed to get a job at the school so she could be close by during Lottie's days there. After a simple interview with the headmaster, Cate got herself a position working as the school librarian. It was quiet, secluded, and perfect. She could use the quiet time to check on Lottie regularly, as well as up her reading and research time as much as possible while things were slow.

One day, after having the idea to run various searches on the Internet for medical miracles and unusual patient stories, Cate happened across a strange story of a young man in Rio de Janeiro.

It was reported that the patient, suffering from amnesia, had developed quite a following from his hospital bed. He was written to have apparently healed a fellow patient's sprained ankle with just a touch of his hand, and magically cured another of his migraines thanks to a head massage. Such small miracles were enough to get the local journalists intrigued, but evidently weren't big enough to get the story into the national newspapers, so all she'd found was a small piece about the man. A quick skim through it revealed nothing of too much interest, however the picture of the patient at the bottom made her heart lurch. It was Uriel. His image on the screen was as clear as day. He was the strange miracle patient they were reporting on, a patient with apparently complete amnesia.

Bile rose in Cate's throat, but she couldn't take her eyes off the photograph. Uriel looked no different to the last time she'd seen him on the astral plane, right before the fight had started on the beach with Lucifer. His amnesia seemed, in her opinion, the only thing stopping him from realising who he truly was and coming to find both her and Lottie. She shuddered at the thought of what could happen when he eventually regained his memory and vowed to strengthen the charms and protective talismans she'd placed all around their house when she got home.

She then thought about his condition some more. Uriel was obviously weakened, even still, from his fight with Lucifer. She wondered if her husband might be somewhere close by to where Uriel had fallen as well, or if perhaps he might even be in the same hospital as the injured angel. Another glance over the faces of the other patients that accompanied him in the picture didn't reveal Lucifer's face, and she couldn't help the little bit of relief that washed over her as she stared at the small following Uriel now had in Rio. None of the friendly faces around him even had a clue just who they were associating with, and she hoped it would stay that way for as long as possible.

***

Cate and Harry did their very best to maintain a seemingly normal life with their daughter as a few more years passed. There was still no word of Lucifer, while Uriel reportedly continued to reside in the care home she'd found him in via the newspaper article back in the school's library. Cate didn't dare go to Rio to try and visit him, just in case seeing her face again bought his memory back somehow, and instead kept an eye on the local newspapers. She checked regularly to see if he was featured again, but thankfully there'd been no further reports on the so-called 'miracle patient.'

She and Harry remained vigilant though. The still loved-up pair carried on as usual and enjoyed their quiet life, just them and their precious child. They eventually decided to raise Lottie as strict atheists too and instructed her school not to involve her in any prayers or religious studies of any sort. Cate was worried that her thoughts and any schoolwork on the subject, or involvement during mass, might end up being heard by some of the other angels, or maybe even Uriel. It wasn't unusual to choose a non-religious path, anyway. Many humans practiced different religions, both celestial and demonic, and there were always going to be those who didn't find any comfort in faith at all so wanted to live their lives away from the binds of religion.

Harry and Cate chose to steer clear of either side of the powerful balance, despite them knowing the truth about their existence. Atheists usually got quite a shock when they passed on and ended up in purgatory. Cate knew from experience that those souls often became the demonic playthings for the dark creatures in Hell because of their sins in life—sins they didn't believe they'd been committing the entire time. Business had been booming thanks to their non-repentant lives.

However, Cate knew that Harry was still a good man. She adored him and never wanted their time together to come to an end, but still had no doubt that when his time came, his soul would go up to Heaven and she would never see him again. It was an insight that brought her both comfort and pain, but one she never shared with him. He had to remain pure when she left him, rather than be tempted into the darkness in the hope of finding her in the abyss.

As the time went by though, Cate needed to start trying to look older. She still looked like a twenty-year-old thanks to her lack of powers again. When to keep in sync with Harry and their supposed age gap, she should be closer to forty. She'd decided to wear older styles of clothing and dressed like their friends of the same age. She also chose more grown-up hairstyles and makeup to make herself naturally look older, and thankfully, it seemed to be working.

Human Harry had naturally grown older the last few years, but Cate always thought he looked more and more handsome as he aged. The more pronounced grey flecks in his brown hair just made him look more distinguished, yet he didn't look all that much older in the face. His boyish good looks and charming nature still managed to attract him a lot of attention, even though he hated it. The women he worked with and the other mums at Lottie's school would flirt openly with him, but Harry only ever had eyes for Cate. Whether friends or strangers, everyone around them could see it. She didn't even get jealous of the lonely women who would swoon over him, knowing he'd always been hers, and always would be.

***

Five more years passed by in a flash for Cate, Harry, and Lottie, and the three of them continued to live happily together in Avebury as a family. Their small unit were still secretive and private, and Cate and Harry were immensely protective of their young daughter. They'd also slowly learned to trust Lottie's instincts over the years and had quickly realised she had an intuitive and clever prowess all her own. Cate had sensed a curious strength within her from a young age, and was sure now that she would always find her own way in any of the three worlds she might eventually end up in. Regardless of the lack of magical power she possessed, Cate was stronger than ever thanks to Harry's unending love and support, and she cleverly put more plans in place to ensure his and Lottie's safety.

She'd gone to visit the witches many times over the years, always without any further news, but she periodically stopped by the deteriorating church anyway, especially during her full-moon visits to her flat. Cate delivered food and blankets to the refugees there each time and worked hard at cementing her alibi for her time on Earth while she was at it. She told them fake stories of the countries she'd supposedly visited, looking for others of their kind and seeking out news of Lucifer. They all believed her cleverly thought out tales, and never questioned Cate whenever she went on her way again. She continued to stay in her small flat during the full days of the moon's phases, but thankfully without any sign of her husband, so she'd returned home safely to Harry and their daughter each time.

On a sunny Sunday morning when Lottie was nine years old, Cate and Harry lay relaxing in bed together. They were wrapped tightly in each other's arms while they listened as Lottie got up and went downstairs to the kitchen to prepare herself some breakfast.

"Coffee?" Harry offered with a smile as he gazed into his lover's eyes and planted a light kiss on the tip of Cate's nose. She smiled, groaning as he pulled away and grabbed some tracksuit trousers to wear as he climbed up out of bed.

"Oh, yes," she answered after stretching her arms and legs sleepily, grinning as she fluttered her eyelashes at up him. "But after another five minutes of sleep, okay?" she asked.

Harry just smiled back down at her, rolling his eyes in mock frustration. He then kissed her cheek softly before heading out to see what tasty breakfast Lottie had dreamed up downstairs. She'd developed a particular flair with food, putting together strange combinations that somehow worked brilliantly though, such as her herby flapjacks and banana butter biscuits.

Cate snuggled into Harry's pillow, breathing in his scent as she dozed for a few extra minutes, her mind wandering as she relaxed. She suddenly found herself thinking of Lucifer, his face coming to the forefront of her mind out of the blue, but then she quickly realised it wasn't just that she was thinking of him—she could sense him somehow.

It was only a tiny feeling that seemed to be emanating from deep inside of her. More of a suggestion of his presence somewhere far away than a strong beacon like it usually would've been. But sure enough, and to Cate's utter dismay, it was there.

She jumped up out of bed, dressed quickly and then ran downstairs to find Harry, her eyes wide and her need for sleep completely replaced by a fearful, ominous feeling.

***

In Moscow, the unnamed patient that'd been in a coma for ten years finally opened his deep blue eyes. He looked around, needing a few minutes to figure out his strange surroundings, and took in the brightly lit room and the wilting flowers that were in a crystal vase next to the hospital bed. Lucifer was stiff, weak, and powerless, but he was glad to finally be awake after so long. He tried calling to his power, willing it to return to his battered body.

Nothing.

He cursed his feeble bones, but hoped it was only a matter of time until he could go home. For the time being, he had to figure out what was going on, where he was, and how he was going to get back to Hell.

A nurse came wandering into his room, and she jumped at the sight of her patient awake in the bed. She shrieked and dropped the vase of newly picked flowers she'd been carrying on the hard floor but didn't care when it shattered at her feet and the water inside spilled across the tiles. She spoke to him in Russian, asking if he knew his name, or where he'd come from. Lucifer understood the language but replied in English. His mind was too foggy to respond in her native tongue.

"Luke," he managed to say, and his dry, gruff voice was almost a whisper after such a long time without use. He started to sit up but felt his weak muscles strain feebly in response as he did so. Yelena ran to his side, quickly pulling an extra pillow out from under the bed and sliding it beneath his shoulders to help prop him up some more. She stared at him in shock for a few moments longer before filling a glass with water, popping in a straw, and holding it for him to take a sip. He gulped it all down, eager for the nourishment, and then looked over at her from the bed.

Lucifer felt as though he'd been in a stifling haze for years, lost in his own thoughts, and unable to sense any of his family or followers during his imprisonment inside his own body. He was grateful not to have ended up in purgatory after he'd fallen from the astral plane yet couldn't help but feel anxious that it'd been so long. He also didn't understand why he was still so weak, and it worried the Dark King that the moon's usual power over his evil force wasn't affecting him, nor had it seemed to do so during his comatose state. "How long have I been unconscious?" he asked the nurse, looking into her brown eyes as he spoke.

"Ten years," she replied with an awkward smile, seeming nervous under his intense gaze. Her thick Russian accent made Lucifer hope for a moment he'd misheard her, but he knew, or rather felt, that her words were true. His face dropped and paled.

"Has anyone ever been here to visit me?" he asked, hoping Cate might've survived as well and that she would've found her way to him some point during all that time.

"No, never," she replied, staring into his handsome face.

He nodded in understanding, not sure whether that meant she too was powerless and couldn't find him, or if she'd already returned to Hell. He hoped with every ounce of positive thought he had that she'd not purposely chosen to stay away. Her broken words from the beach had haunted his dreams the entire time he'd been unconscious, as had his own foolish taunts he knew had hurt her deeply. He didn't want to dwell on the details though, and instead decided to focus his efforts on getting stronger. Then, he would travel home, hopefully finding her and the twins there safe once he did.

***

An hour had passed since Cate had felt the strange pull, but the far away beacon that was her husband's power still lingered within her consciousness, consuming her thoughts entirely.

"You need to go," Harry told her, trying his best to stay calm as he held her close, but she could feel him trembling. "For Lottie's sake," he said, reminding her of her solemn promise to her child and to herself. Cate was packing up some things, getting ready to travel to the flat. Lottie was playing computer games in her room when he'd appeared with the emergency supplies and encircled her in his strong arms. She knew Harry was right, but now that the time of reckoning was finally upon them, she couldn't bear to go.

"I know," she said, her stomach churning at the prospect of leaving the pair of them for good. "But," Cate started to say, desperate to find some loophole in her own careful plan.

"No buts," he interjected, being the strong one, and she needed him to be. Harry took her phone out of her bag and slipped it into his pocket.

They'd agreed she would leave it with him in case anyone found it and used it to find him and Lottie. In imposter could easily send a text message pretending to be her, using his weakness for the Queen to find and trap both him and her illegitimate child. The gesture also meant that the time really was up for their little family. It was a symbolic moment that saddened Cate to her very core, but she stifled the sobs that threatened to explode out of her, knowing she had to stay strong.

Cate went into the other bedroom and hugged Lottie goodbye, having decided against putting either of them through the ordeal of a big farewell. She just pretended to be going away for a few days like she normally would, and then she left their home without another word to her darling daughter. Cate stopped for a few seconds to kiss and hug Harry goodbye before tearing herself from his arms and gazing up at him, seeing her pain reflected in his eyes.

"Don't go looking for me," she told him, knowing he knew not to, anyway. "I'll come back for you when, or if, I can."

He nodded, tears welling up in his own eyes as she started to walk away.

"I love you, Cate," he called after her. "I'll keep her safe."

"I know you will. Thank you for everything, Harry. I love you, too," she told her paramour, forcing herself to walk away. Her body was trembling and she struggled to breathe as her grief hit her like a hammer to the heart. Tears streamed down her red face, sobs forcing themselves out of her uncontrollably as she drove away. Her world had ended, and she felt empty. Pain consumed her, and it was unyielding and uncaring. Regardless of her hardships in the past, Cate had never felt anything like it in all her life and she cursed everyone and everything. It was no comfort at all to know she was doing the right thing. She simply felt dead inside when she knew she should feel strong.

When Cate finally reached the flat in Brixton, she curled up in the cold, empty bed and cried herself to sleep.

CHAPTER THIRTY-NINE

The next day, after an overwrought night's sleep, Cate went to the church, and found it fuller than ever with refugees. None of the dark beings she spoke with, however, had sensed any change. She quickly decided not to tell anyone what she'd felt the day before. Cate wasn't sure how or why she was the only one to have sensed the shift in the air, which was still just an awareness of their leader rather than a strong urge, but she was sure there had to be a reason for it. Either way, she was determined to act on it alone.

Cate caught up with the witches, warlocks, and demons there for a little while, acting as normally as she could. She then gave some money to Bea and bought them food and water before heading out again, doing her best to give nothing away.

Fake it till you make it, she told herself.

Berith was there, and he caught her eye as she left the church. She nodded and smiled at the demon, who bowed respectfully over to her, but didn't come over to chat, and she was glad. Their relationship had been much less familiar since her stern talk with him when he'd followed her after that first visit, and although she hated being estranged from her old friend, she knew it'd been a necessary step in ensuring Lottie's safety.

Cate returned to the flat and waited, unsure what else to do. Two more weeks passed by, and apart from the small awareness of Lucifer's flame that she still felt, nothing else had changed. After another day of angry solace, she lay in bed and checked the clock on her nightstand. It was nearly midnight, so she turned out the lights and quickly slipped into that strange place between being awake and asleep.

She was awoken again within just a few minutes as the clock turned to zero, not having realised that it signified the start of Halloween on Earth. The lightning bolt that surged through her out of nowhere quickly made Cate aware that the darkly powerful day had begun, though, and the deluge of power coursed through her entire body in seconds. Her arms and legs grew heavy, while her fingers and toes prickled with a static-like shock. She levitated off the bed by about a foot, unable to move as the power seeped into her and coursed through every muscle—a demonic-like possession occurring as she somehow reclaimed her strong, dark force once again.

Within a few seconds, it was over, and she knew instantly that her powers had fully returned. Cate could feel her physical strength heighten incredibly within seconds, while the full extent of her powerful gifts was at her command again at last. Most importantly, she could now completely sense the presence of her husband on Earth. She saw him in her mind's eye, lying in a hospital bed far away—fast asleep and incredibly frail.

A second later, Cate was by his side, having teleported straight to him. She looked down in surprise at the feeble man as he slept. She'd never seen Lucifer sleep. He was taking small, shallow breaths, and resting peacefully as she looked on for a few moments, shocked to see him in such a bad way. Cate reached out and laid a hand on his shoulder, rousing him instantly with a start.

"Cate?" he asked, his voice just a whisper.

"Yes, Lucifer. I'm here," she told him, sitting down on the edge of the bed as she took in his skinny frame and the exhausted look in his eyes. "It's All Hallow's Eve, my love. My powers have returned to me at long last," she told him, reaching down to stroke his face.

She looked at him questioningly from her perched seat, but Lucifer just shook his head in response, indicating he hadn't been blessed with the same gift of his power. She shrugged, and climbed on the bed with him, sliding herself into her husband's embrace. Despite her sadness at having left Harry and Lottie behind, Cate couldn't deny there was a part of her that felt pleased to see him at long last.

She felt she needed to show him she still loved him, perhaps to prove it to herself as well as to him, but it felt awkward. She could sense that he was still weak, but lifted his chin with her hand, leaning down to place her mouth on his. He responded, of course, having missed her too. Lucifer kissed her lips as passionately as he was able, his hands going around her waist as he held her tightly.

The pair of them let their mouths linger on one another's for a few minutes, relishing in their mildly re-kindled romance. Cate ran her hands down to his pyjama shirt and began unbuttoning it, finding herself eager to prove her allegiance.

"No," he said, pulling his head back and taking her hands in his. He looked up into her face, almost hidden in the dark light.

"No?" she asked, watching him in bemusement.

"No," Lucifer said again, sterner this time. He stared up into her eyes and Cate could see the dark circles underneath his usually mesmerising irises and understood just how weak he must really be. She nodded, lying down on the bed beside him instead, and she then rested her head in the ridge between his chin and shoulder. It was the spot that'd once been her most favourite place in the world to rest, but now felt like the wrong fit.

"It's okay. It's all going to be okay," she said, snuggling into him before they each fell into a deep sleep.

Cate woke the next morning to the sound of a woman frantically screaming and trying to pull her off the bed. She was talking in Russian, but Cate could understand every word.

"What are you doing, how did you get in here?" the woman demanded, still grabbing at her jacket.

Cate climbed up from the bed and was furious. She felt powerful and commanding and looked down at the small woman with a scowl. The nurse cowered slightly as Cate gazed down the foot or so of height difference between them.

"This man is my husband," she replied, speaking in perfect Russian, and using her body to block the nurse from seeing to Lucifer. She could see the woman's nametag and addressed her directly. "It's time he was discharged, Yelena," she ordered her, turning to him before she began to pull the covers away from Lucifer to get him ready. The foolish nurse grabbed Cate's arm again, attempting once more to yank her away from him. As she did, she made contact with her skin and Cate got a flash of a memory in her mind's eye—Yelena's memory.

She was in love with Lucifer after all his years spent in her care, despite not even knowing him. Her dark urges had overcome her as she'd watched over the unknown man, and she'd begun fantasising about a life she hoped to have with him when he awoke. Cate could see that Yelena had not only curled up in the bed to be close to him over the years, but she'd also touched him sexually, and tried in vain to make him hard for her as he'd lay comatose in the bed some time ago. She'd put his hands on her naked body too, cupping her breasts with his palms and even thrusting his fingers inside her cleft when her urges had taken over completely.

Yelena's memory was as clear to Cate as if she were watching it in a television screen, both surprising and disgusting her all at once.

The Dark Queen's face clouded over, and her eyes speckled with black flecks. Yelena pulled her hand away from her arm, fear flashing across her face instantly. "So, you think you have a chance with him? Shall I tell my husband just how *personal* the care is in this hospital?" she asked the nurse in a whisper so Lucifer couldn't hear her, raising a knowing eyebrow as she did so. Yelena stepped back, obviously alarmed. She was shaking her head quickly, not being able to comprehend how Cate might know her guilty secrets, and she took a stride forward, closing the gap between her and the nurse with ease. She pushed Yelena against the brightly coloured brickwork behind, staring down at her as she spoke.

"No, please…" she mumbled.

"We'll see each other again, but not anywhere you might expect," Cate told her, knowing she would end up in Hell once her time came. Then the deviant nurse would then know the Queen's wrath, and she would enjoy every moment of it.

She then reached down and pulled up the right arm of the shaken woman, where she traced an inverted cross onto the inside of Yelena's right wrist with her index finger. The mark burned black for just a moment before disappearing again, and she gasped and tried to pull her arm away, but it was no use. Just before Cate released her, she couldn't resist threatening the disgusting woman some more. "For now though, you'd better get the fuck out of my way," she added menacingly, and Yelena ran for the door without so much as a backwards glance. Lucifer laughed gruffly from behind Cate, and she turned to see him rising slowly and cautiously from the bed.

"Jealous much?" he then asked, a satisfied smile on his lips. She didn't know if he was aware of what'd gone on with Yelena during his long sleep, but knew it wasn't the right time to reveal all. Cate just smiled back across at him, shrugging nonchalantly before she wandered over and helped Lucifer get himself changed.

Less than half an hour later, Cate teleported the pair of them to the flat. She didn't want him to be bombarded quite so soon by all the eagerly awaiting beings in the church, so she put off a visit for the time being. He absolutely wasn't strong enough to face the masses. Lucifer leaned on her for support and Cate helped him over to the black leather sofa, where he rested while she made him something to eat. When she came back, he devoured four slices of jam-covered toast in seconds. She'd never seen him so hungry before but urged him to eat as many as he wanted.

"Where have you been, Cate?" he asked her at last, finally full after another two slices. He watched as she slipped down on the opposite end of the couch, curling her legs underneath her as she settled down, and casually pulling his feet onto her lap.

"Back and forth between here and the church, mostly," she replied. Cate didn't want to go into too much detail, but she knew he'd need more to curb his suspicious nature. "I searched around for you for a long time, but I had no powers myself until midnight last night, so I couldn't find you. I'm sorry, my love. I had no idea where you'd landed."

"And, what about, *him*?" he then asked. She could sense his distrust in her, knowing she must obviously be holding something back, and she tried to appease him as much as she could, not hesitating with her answer.

"The same as you, injured badly. I believe him to be in Brazil, suffering with amnesia rather than in a coma like you were. As far as I know, he hasn't yet recovered," Cate told him, and Lucifer nodded, but continued to look at her expectantly, urging her to continue. "I haven't been to see him if that's what you're wondering? I never want to be near him ever again. I found an article on the Internet of a miracle man who had amnesia in Rio. He was somehow healing fellow patients of small ailments. It was him—his photo was in the article, but I would never go to him. Please trust me when I say that," she told him insistently, eager to explain herself.

Lucifer stared across at his wife, feeling far from close to her. He was confused and felt vulnerable and frail as he lay before her, his weakness bringing him nothing but suspicion and distrust. He could see that there was pain behind her eyes but couldn't read her to know what was hurting her so much. He wanted Cate to tell him everything she'd gone through and how she felt, but for some reason, she was holding back. There was also a tremendous amount of desperation in him to regain their once so easy connection, and to know she hadn't meant the cold words she'd said to him and Uriel that day on the astral plane.

She looked different to him somehow, although physically she was the same as always. Cate had a different energy to her, and a strange newness he couldn't comprehend. It wasn't the lightness he'd sensed in her last time, but a closed-off indifference she was trying too hard to mask.

They took each other in, and an awkward silence passed between the two of them for a moment, before Cate finally broke it. "I've missed you so much," she told her master as earnestly as she could, and Lucifer hoped he'd been wrong to doubt her—suspicion clouding his judgement. He wondered if the emotion he was sensing hidden behind her eyes was all for him, or for the time together they'd lost while he was unconscious. He wanted to believe her. "I haven't been able to go home since the fight," Cate added, looking down at her hands forlornly. He realised then that she must've been missing the children terribly, and that would explain her pained look.

Lucifer calmed his fraught mind, trying his hardest to let go of his own pain, desperate to learn to trust her again. "None of us have been able to travel back to Hell. The witches and demons have had no powers either," she continued. "Vast amounts have been living in the churches awaiting your return. I found them there after I fell from the edge of the astral plane."

"I remember now, were you injured?" he asked, thinking back to the moment on the beach when she'd been thrown backwards into the water. He hadn't been afforded the opportunity to follow her, thanks to the barrage of blows that'd then rained down on him from Uriel's fists, but vividly remembered watching her disappear.

"Yes. I was out cold for a few days, and then I needed a couple of weeks to heal. After that I was fine physically, apart from the lack of my powers. But like I said, I soon found out that it was all of us who no longer had any, not just me," Cate told him, taking his hand in hers. "It must've been a terrible fight?" she asked, looking into his eyes with a sincere, warm smile.

"Yes," he said, thinking for a moment before going any further. "I was so enraged. I couldn't and wouldn't stop. I wanted him dead. Knowing that he'd been with you again was torturing the hell out of me. It still does. And, after he'd taken the children and used them to force you into his bed again, I was completely consumed with rage and my need for revenge. I didn't care if I died, as long as I took him with me," Lucifer added.

He took a deep breath, lulling the anger that threatened to bubble up inside him at the thought of it all again, and guessed it was time to tell her how he'd found them. "Alma had put a plan in place years before for if you were ever taken again. She'd placed a secret charm on Angelica so she could always find her, and we tracked her down within minutes of her return to Earth—she had no idea. The fool was such a bitch when we caught up with her, and she even tried to fight me, but she eventually did as she was told and took me up to that astral plane where you were. I promised I'd spare her life in exchange for her taking me to you, but I couldn't help but beat her to a pulp once she had, relishing in taking her life. I didn't care, all I wanted was you back."

Cate was shocked, but lifted his hand, kissing the palm and placing it on her cheek, leaning into his touch as he continued his dark version of events. "After the lightning began, I knew you'd fallen, but that there wasn't anything I could do to stop it. I couldn't feel your presence once you'd gone over the edge either, so had no idea what'd even happened to you. Uriel and I fought for days, neither of us giving up or giving in. I think we both needed it after all our history, but each blow was deafening, and so very powerful. Eventually, we felt the floor beneath us start to crack, and it shattered like glass. We each went plummeting downwards, but I lost sight of Uriel before I hit Earth. I lost consciousness instantly, and other than some hazy dreams, the next thing I remember is waking up in that hospital bed a few weeks ago," he told her, tailing off. Lucifer seemed exhausted from his storytelling, and Cate urged him to rest for a while, leaning over and curling up on the sofa next to him as he drifted off. His story added up, and while she hated they were so estranged, she was glad they'd cleared the air a little.

CHAPTER FORTY

Lucifer slept deeply for hours, but Cate was wide-awake and struggled to rest. As she lay on the sofa curled up next to him, she watched the sunset through the window and couldn't help but think of Harry and Lottie. She got up from her spot and looked down at him, taking in the frail sight of her usually so strong and powerful husband before her. She watched him for a moment, with emotions that were so mixed and fraught she wondered how on Earth she might overcome them. Cate still cared for him and knew she could live by his side like before, but also knew she didn't love him the way she once had. She also knew that it'd take a very long time for her to get over the deep and terrible void she currently felt for Harry, but that she would never get over the loss of her beautiful daughter.

She headed into the kitchen to busy herself and stop her mind from wandering beyond the point of no return. The scars were still far too fresh for her to hide them from Lucifer if he questioned her further, and she couldn't bear to let herself dwell too much on the two people she missed so terribly.

After tidying the small kitchen, she sat at the dining table and played around on her laptop for a while, listening quietly to some music as she tried to curb her boredom. Cate then slept alone in her bed that night, having decided against joining Lucifer on the sofa again, and then didn't rush to wake him the next day. In fact, he remained fast asleep until well after midday.

Earlier that morning, as she'd lain in bed, Cate had made the decision to bypass the church reunion entirely. Lucifer was still too weak, and she knew she needed to take him home as soon as possible, opting for a return straight to Hell instead. He devoured half a loaf of bread's worth of toast again when he awoke and was famished but seemingly stronger. After he'd finished, he chatted to Cate at the kitchen table, and both felt far more relaxed than they'd been the night before.

"How have you managed to survive here alone, Cate?" he asked her, smiling at his wife warmly over his hot cup of tea before taking a big sip, finally understanding what all the fuss was about. She peered back at him, laughing at his messy blond hair, but relishing in his relaxed and happy look. She, too, let go of her guilt and pain, welcoming the time to talk.

"I had to beg and borrow to get money at first," she told him. "But eventually I found work here and there for cash, bar work mostly. I couldn't bring myself to live in the dirty church. It was awful there. After one night I quickly realised that I am not the kind of girl who does well with sleeping rough," she added, and Lucifer laughed.

"Well, I could've easily guessed that," he replied with a cheeky grin, teasing her. "I wouldn't want to hear of it anyway," he then added, his expression serious again. "You should never have to suffer like that. It's not right for the Queen to have to live that way, no matter what was happening. I hope Berith took good care of you?" he then asked, angered somewhat that she'd been seemingly left to fend for herself while also being expected to provide for the refugees at the church. Cate just nodded, unsure how to respond or explain her now estranged relationship with the demon he was so close with.

"Shall we try and go home?" she then asked, eager to get back to their family and friends, and to move the conversation along. Lucifer nodded and took her hand, but she was the one who needed to do the teleporting this time around. Cate focussed all her efforts on home and pulled the still weak King down with all her strength.

It worked, and within seconds they arrived at the dark gates of Hell, where the familiar change in pressures and heat hit them both instantly. Lucifer coughed and fell to his knees, choking on his human-like gasps while his body seemingly struggled to cope with it. He regained his composure after a short while, but Cate was gobsmacked as she watched his body's reaction to having come home. She'd never seen him struggle before, not even for a second.

Cate, however, didn't react to the changes. She stood tall as she took in the familiar sight of home with a wide smile and had to bite her tongue when she almost asked him if he needed her assistance. It went without saying he didn't want her to draw attention to his weakness. The dark castle was towering over the red city ahead, and she couldn't wait to get inside and see her family. Cate focussed on the presence she'd felt almost instantly of Blake and Luna somewhere deep inside herself. She called to her children telepathically, somehow finding a power within to summon them to her, and she marvelled at how wondrous it was having her powers back again. In the blink of an eye, the twins appeared before the pair of them, both wide-eyed as they took in the sight of their parents.

"Mum, Dad!" Luna shrieked, running over to them and throwing her arms around Cate's neck, while Blake went to Lucifer and offered him an arm to lean on. They looked so different since the last time she'd seen them, and Cate did a double take. Now fifteen years old, they were both as tall as their mother, although Blake was actually a good foot taller than her, and they looked like young adults already. Luna hugged her tightly before pulling back, her green eyes searching Cate's face, taking her in.

"You look exactly as I remember you," she said, smiling warmly. Luna had her long, dark brown curls pinned up in a high ponytail that reminded Cate of how she used to wear her own hair as a teenager, and she had to smile at their likeness. She drank in the sight of her beautiful daughter and stroked her cheek with her index finger.

"Well, I can safely say you don't look the same at all," she told her in reply, laughing as she took in the young girl who could've easily been mistaken for her sister rather than her daughter. "I've missed you both so much. I'm so sorry we couldn't come back sooner," Cate added, giving Luna a kiss on the cheek before pulling back to look over at Blake with a smile.

He caught her eye, allowing himself a moment to bask in her warm gaze before dropping his eyes to the floor, guilt overshadowing his joy. She wanted to go to him, but instinctually knew he didn't want her to, and she sensed a closed-off vibe from him. Cate didn't know why Blake resisted her affections, but she was sure they just needed time to get to know each other again. She knew they'd soon figure out the best way to get him to open up about their sad past and to help him deal with his dark emotions. Their incredible bond could be strained, but never broken. Cate was absolutely sure of it.

The four of them then teleported into the main entrance of the castle, where they were instantly welcomed with applause and cheers from the dark witches and demons who were inside. Alma appeared within seconds and hurried over, pulling Cate into a tight hug as a crowd began to form around them, everyone eager to speak with the lost King and Queen.

"Welcome back, your majesty," Alma said, tears welling in her eyes as she gazed up at her. Cate smiled back at the witch, feeling genuinely happy to be home, but she got straight to business, and was careful to speak quietly when she asked Alma to help.

"I need you to take the King away and try anything you can to help. Do whatever it takes to get him his strength back," she commanded, and Alma took her first proper look at her master. She could see instantly that Lucifer wasn't well and nodded to Cate. She then hurried him away to the witches' dungeons, while Cate made excuses for his disappearance, and then chatted animatedly with the beings that still crowded around her.

Dylan then came hurtling through the welcoming committee and threw her arms around the Queen. She gripped her as tight as possible and sobbed in her embrace, much to the annoyance of some of the upper-level demons around them. Neither of them cared about the disgruntled elitists, though. Both women held firmly to their long-lost friend, and their circle was impervious to anything other than the love and warmth they each felt for one another.

"I've missed you so much," Cate whispered in her ear, holding back her own tears. "Please tell me you haven't turned my children into raving lunatics in my absence, Dylan?" she then asked as she pulled away, mocking her friend's naturally fun nature. Her motherly worry showed, despite Cate having trusted Dylan completely all these years.

"Well, Luna is a raving lesbian, and Blake's into bestiality, does that count?" Dylan answered, joking with Cate in response, and she relished in the loud laugh she got as a reply.

CHAPTER FORTY-ONE

"Don't let your guilt get in the way of your happiness, Blake," Luna said, chastising her brother later that evening. He'd remained quiet and grumpy the whole afternoon, while the rest of the kingdom had openly celebrated the return of their parents—his twin included. Luna knew he was just happier playing the dark and broody teenager rather than address his real feelings, but wished he'd give it up for at least one afternoon. Their mother had tried to speak with him a few times, to tell him that everything was fine and not to dwell on the past, but he just hadn't given her the chance to get beneath his icy exterior, and Luna wanted to scream at him for refusing to let her in.

Cate watched them, and she truly hated that she felt like a stranger to her beautiful children. She had a lot to make up for and hoped that time would help her heal those wounds.

"That boy is a troubled soul, your majesty," her witch and old friend Sara told her when she caught the hurt look in Cate's eyes as she attended her. "But it's all his own doing. He's happy in his misery, content even, and has been for many years. Blake believes he deserves it after his actions resulted in the loss of both of his parents following that terrible night outside the church. He's blamed himself ever since and won't listen to reason. But now you've both returned at long last, and perhaps together you can help him find his own forgiveness," Sara added, and then she smiled and hugged Cate tightly, happy to have her friend and mistress home again at last.

Devin and Serena had hoped to throw a proper party for her and Lucifer to celebrate their homecoming, but Cate insisted they put it off until Satan was back to his full strength again, assuring them it wouldn't be long, even though she had no idea if what she'd promised was true. They agreed, and instead presented their three children to her later that evening, much to her surprise. She'd had no idea that the pair of them even had one child, let alone three, and was eager to meet the new additions to their brood. Despite the absent years that'd passed them all by, she still felt close to Devin and

Serena, bound together by the blood of their ruler, and they seemed to feel the same way. The love she and Devin had once known was so long gone it didn't cause any animosity between any of them, and in fact it was getting easier to forget the times that'd changed so drastically for them all.

The trio of children were a perfect mixture of their parents. Their eldest, Braeden, was nine years old and looked very much like Devin. He had his father's dark blond hair, light blue eyes, and tall frame, yet he had the quiet nature of his mother. Braeden introduced himself politely and then hugged Cate before bowing to her, evidently knowing to address her formally as his Queen.

The middle child, and the couple's only daughter by the name of Leyla, was seven years old. She was very much like Serena, with her red hair and blue eyes, yet she had a fiery nature to her and a strong will that Cate could sense as she gazed into the young girl's eyes. She also had to laugh at her body language, noticing Leyla's stance and the way she poked at her youngest brother with her elbow as they stood before her. He didn't react to her attempts at a fight, obviously used to her irritating taunts already, despite being so young.

He was just a small boy and seemed somewhat shy towards Cate as he gazed up at her. His name was Corey, and he was just five years old. Corey had blond hair that had a few red flecks growing through it, and deep blue eyes like Devin's. He appeared gentle and sweet, but his eyes seemed to burn with a desire for knowledge and power. There was either great potential or dire penalties destined for his future, Cate couldn't tell which, but she hoped he would choose to go for the path of greatness.

Cate looked up at their parents after the introductions were over with a big smile. She congratulated the pair of them, pulling Serena into a tight hug before giving Devin a kiss on the cheek. She forced away all pain of the past and felt genuinely happy to be among her dark family again at last. It was wonderful to have discovered that their small group had expanded so much in the few years since she'd last been with them, and Cate spent the rest of the evening laughing and playing as they cemented their relationship again.

***

Only the royal family, upper-level demons, and Lucifer's coven were later told the truth about his frailty, and they were all understandably concerned for his health. However much they tried though, no one knew how to help him, and so the King hid himself away. He was angry and dismayed that he could possibly be so weak, and Cate found it impossible to connect with him. Her husband seemed furious that she'd gotten her powers back, but he hadn't, and he didn't seem bothered enough to hide it. To say they were estranged was an understatement, but she kept up her doting façade in the hopes that someday things might change.

Cate couldn't deny she was also surprised by her influx of power. Somehow, she felt stronger than ever, although she didn't dare tell Lucifer the truth about how strong she'd suddenly become. Cate used her power to reopen the portals between the worlds again, welcoming back the dark beings that'd been awaiting their master's return in the churches on Earth. Dylan and Sara helped them when they arrived back in Hell, dispensing potions to heal their ailments or replenish lost nourishment. The Dark Queen also rewarded their loyal underlings with lavish gifts and slave souls for them to torture, abuse, or simply enjoy to their hearts' content. Their celebrations would last for weeks, Cate was sure, and she didn't begrudge them all letting off some steam.

Cate went to visit Lucifer in the witches' chambers when she could get away the following afternoon, finding him lying in the disturbingly familiar tub of black goo. She'd needed that treatment all those years before, thanks to her time spent in the pits and dungeons at the behest of the powerful man who'd eventually won her heart. The sight of the thick, black liquid, and the strong, musty smell brought back many memories of the years of torture she'd suffered, and Cate couldn't fight the surge of anger the reminder of those times stirred up in her. She peered down at him as she stood beside the bath, and Lucifer just laid still. His eyes were closed, and he was seemingly unaware that she'd even come in. Alma then approached and bowed, giving Cate's hand a squeeze, and she gave her an update on her husband's health.

"He is in a bad way, your majesty. There's death in every inch of him, and his powers are not returning remotely as quickly as they ought to be. I don't know what else to do, except give him time," she said, looking down at the hand that still held on to Cate's tightly.

"Then we shall give him time, and hope to see a change in him soon, Alma," Cate replied, offering the witch a warm smile. She was disappointed that there was nothing more Alma could do for him but knew there was no use in adding to the witch's already guilty conscience.

Cate teleported away, returning to her chambers where she climbed up on the huge bed and tried to make sense of everything that'd happened. She concentrated on her power, feeling her own strength growing inside of her as she called to it, harnessed, and controlled it. It gave her vibrancy and a malevolent prowess from somewhere deep within—a seemingly never ending vat of incredulous power that was hers to command. Cate felt amazing, but she still couldn't understand why she'd been blessed with the return of her dark force, while her almighty King was still frail and powerless. The situation made her think back to her previous musings about the possible presence of a higher power. Her mind was alive, considering the need for balance to the forces of good and evil, and she couldn't help but wonder if it was a sign. Cate thought that their malaise could even be a kind of punishment for Lucifer and Uriel's abuse of their own omnipotent powers, whereas she'd followed the path set out for her faithfully, never asking for more, but gaining it anyway.

***

Cate spent the entire night working out what she wanted to do next. Dylan joined her in her chambers for most of it, having felt the Queen summon her like a bolt of lightning to her spine. It'd shocked the witch to have Cate call to her this way, but she'd teleported to her friend's side in an instant, regardless.

"Hey, how did you?" she began, never having felt the Dark Queen summon her so forcefully before, but then she saw Cate's determined expression and decided against asking questions. She perched on the bed, ready to hear what her mistress had to say, and gave her a much needed ear. Dylan stayed quiet while Cate ran through the possible options with her, asking for her friend's advice here and there on how best to proceed, but fundamentally she knew what had to be done.

"The realm needs you Cate, you already know what has to happen," Dylan eventually told her, curling up next to the powerful Queen on the bed, giving her the reassurance she needed. There was nothing else that could be done, and they'd both known it.

Cate convened the dark high council in the private meeting chamber the next morning, and they came to the meeting room as soon as they were summoned, however the demons were shocked to find only Cate at the head of the table as they entered. They'd assumed their orders had come from Satan himself and were all eager to see and hear from their master in the privacy of the council meeting at last. None could hide their disappointment upon realising he still wasn't well, but Cate didn't care enough to nurse their egos. She stood, peering down at them with a stern look as they took their seats.

"Thank you all for coming. It brings me great sadness to inform you that your King isn't well enough to rule our realm now, or for the foreseeable future," she told them honestly, their faces growing solemn at her words. "I will take control of Hell in his stead, but only until he's better, of course," she added modestly.

"And does the King agree to this?" asked Lilith from her chair, her face thunderous as she glared up at Cate. She'd been in control of the realm while both the King and Queen were in exile and had hoped to continue doing so for as long as she could, even though they'd returned. Cate couldn't be angry at her desire to remain in charge. She'd heard from Dylan just how much the demon had enjoyed her role of interim leader, and that she'd been a worthy choice in Lucifer's absence. But they'd returned, and Cate was going to take what was rightfully hers. Lilith clearly didn't believe that Cate was strong enough to lead the entire underworld, and she didn't bother to mask her displeasure at being pushed aside by the inexperienced Dark Queen.

"Yes, of course," Cate replied angrily, staring Lilith down. "And you'd better learn not to question me, otherwise I can see us falling out." Her eyes turned black, and she felt the familiar buzz of dark power course through her stronger than ever. Her heightened force stirred from within, and she suddenly yearned for ultimate control in a way she'd never felt before. The powerful demon backed off immediately, sensing the change in Cate, and she then stayed quiet for the remainder of their meeting.

As the days, months and eventually years passed by, Lucifer remained too weak to lead his dark kingdom. Cate, however, flourished and grew stronger every day. Dylan was by her side, encouraging her and helping the powerful Dark Queen make informed decisions and issue her orders, as well as still being her best friend and most loyal servant. She gave her mistress updates on the King regularly, but there was never much to tell. Cate barely saw him as she was so busy, and the times she did go to sit with him in his chambers, Lucifer only seemed slightly better. He'd hid himself away and was vastly becoming a recluse as he was ashamed of his fragile form, but she couldn't blame him, especially given her impressive transformation. After three years, he was finally able to teleport, but only short distances, and his body was still skinny and weak, which only angered him further.

The royal couple hadn't made love to each other at all since before the ordeal with Uriel, and Cate wasn't sure if it was his body or his mind that resisted her love whenever she attempted to rekindle their romance, but she was glad of their lack of sexual connection—it no longer felt right, anyway. She also couldn't fight the guilt that rose up as she thought of her infidelity with Harry, stirring her fraught emotions. She wondered if Lucifer might somehow know she'd been unfaithful with someone other than Uriel, but if he did, he never said a word.

Before too long, she gave up on trying to win back his affections. Whenever she was horny, Cate wouldn't bother to demand satisfaction from her husband like she would've done years before. Her thoughts went instead to her secret lover during her moments of self-gratification, and imagining Harry's hands, lips, and body against hers always satisfied her need for release. She was embarrassed that she would think of Harry instead of Lucifer but didn't bother to stop herself as she enjoyed her memories of him time and again in the privacy of her bedchambers. Safe in the knowledge that no-one could read her thoughts, she was glad, otherwise she knew she'd be in trouble for more than just her adulterous revelations.

CHAPTER FORTY-TWO

Cate slowly grew close with the twins after her return but worked hard to revive their relationship. Even Blake allowed her love and forgiveness to eventually break through the dark walls he'd built so high, and their bond soon flourished. His stubborn and dominative nature had developed into a hard armour, but she'd soon gotten around it. Cate managed to soften those rough edges and encouraged that kind side of him to thrive again in her company, much to the delight of both her and his twin sister. Blake was still very closed-off emotionally, but she hoped that in time he would open up and let his feelings back in. She guessed only time would tell.

Luna accepted the temporary change in leadership with ease. She relished in Cate's love and warmth, and all the while she ruled Hell with such strength and wisdom that ensured they all thrived. Even Lucifer seemed better for having such a resilient Queen taking the reins. Her relationship with Luna effortlessly grew and blossomed over the years, and Cate often found herself staring thoughtfully at her eldest daughter. She would think of Lottie and hated knowing she was fast growing up without her on Earth. Cate wondered if she still resembled Luna, just as she'd always done before. Her heart pined for her, but she threw all that passion into nurturing the twins and showing them all the love they too, had missed while she'd been gone. Cate would never claim to have been the perfect mother, but she was trying her hardest to ensure they knew how much she adored them.

When they turned eighteen, she threw the twins a huge party, and the entire kingdom joined in with the celebrations. Lucifer managed to come and sit with his children to enjoy the celebrations and watched with a smile while the pair received their presents. The twins celebrated with their friends and family and participated in a special coming of age ceremony their parents had put together for them. They were then given their own covens, and each seemed shocked but delighted by their wondrous gift. It was a surprise that Cate had commissioned for them with the help of Alma, who'd handpicked their magical followers to create the perfect coven each. Cate knew it was time they were taught how to command their own forces, and even the cool and closed-off Blake had one of his rare smiles when he was presented with his new group of cohorts.

Later that night, once the celebrations were over, Luna and Blake sat with the witches and warlocks on the sofas in their royal chambers of the castle. They spent time getting to know their new friends in private, and each began deciding on their roles right away. They each knew that time would be the most important lesson, but that together they would learn how best to lead their magical assistants, and the experienced witches and warlocks were tasked with helping them every step of the way. Cate thought the twins looked powerful and strong, surrounded by their covens, and both she and Lucifer were already extremely proud. They were both on their way to becoming leaders and had already shown it by effectively asserting their command over the four members of each new coven.

One night, Lucifer called Cate to him in the council chamber. She felt a subtle pull, more like a request than an order, but she was glad he could finally send for her. It was a new development in the strengthening of his power, albeit slowly, but was an improvement nonetheless. She entered the dim chamber, where Lucifer sat at the large table, looking up at her expectantly. He had some pictures in front of him on the dark wood but had covered them with his hands so she couldn't see what they were.

Berith stood to his right, glaring at Cate. A smirk seemed as if it was threatening to show on his lips, and the vibe was far from right in the room. It all made her instantly uncomfortable.

"Tell me again where you were while I was in Moscow, Hecate," Lucifer said, getting straight to the point, and there was no emotion in his voice as he addressed his wife—not that she expected it anymore. The pair of them had remained estranged, and they barely spent any time alone with one another. A part of her still loved her husband, and knew she always would, but Cate couldn't find her way back to him. Their once strong connection seemed stretched too thin to be mended, and she guessed she'd gotten used to being in a loveless relationship.

"Searching for answers, and for you. I've told you this many times," she replied in an equally emotionless tone as she stood opposite him.

"Don't fucking lie to me!" Lucifer bellowed, taking the top photograph and thrusting it across the table, his eyes black as he glared at her. She looked down and gasped. The photo was of Harry. He was much older than when she'd last seen him, and by his side was a teenage girl. She had long, dark-brown curly hair and deep green eyes—the very image of Cate. She knew instantly it was Lottie and suspected the picture couldn't be more than a few weeks old, or maybe even just a few days.

"I see," she said, aiming for a nonchalant tone as she tried to plan her next move.

"You see?" Lucifer demanded, slamming his palms down onto the dark wood angrily and shaking the table beneath him. "What do you see? You see the face of your human, piece of shit, lover? Do you see the child you had with him while I was badly injured from trying to save your goddamn life?" he shouted at her, and the spite in his voice was clear as he questioned Cate further. His face was contorted with rage, while his usually blue eyes still burned black thanks to his wrath.

She had to stifle a gasp at his words, trembling as she took in her scary, masterful husband. He thought Lottie was Harry's child. Cate hoped it might help matters slightly if she kept up the pretence, not sure if it might just be a better alternative to the reality. She searched Lucifer's face, hoping to find compassion or mercy there for her long lost daughter, but she found neither.

"She was an accident, nothing more," Cate told him quietly, holding his dark gaze. "I left them and came home with you as soon as I found you again, as you well know."

"So, they mean nothing to you?" he asked, an eyebrow cocked as he tried to read her.

"They're of no importance," she replied, feigning disinterest.

"That's not the same thing, Cate," Lucifer growled as he climbed up from his seat. Despite the years that'd gone by and his still weak self, he could still stir fear in her, and she knew it was making him stronger. She grabbed the back of the chair in front of her, tightly gripping the wood with her strong hands to hide her trembling, and she desperately tried to think what move to make next.

He lifted the next photo in the pile, staring at Cate's illegitimate child thoughtfully for a few seconds. Suddenly, realisation began to show on Lucifer's face as he took in the girl's features properly, and he sighed. "She's Uriel's child," he said quietly and then looked over to Cate for her reaction. "Isn't she?" he bellowed across the table at her. Cate didn't respond verbally, afraid her voice would falter, but she shook her head.

Lucifer's eyes somehow turned an even deeper shade of black—a vortex of nothingness—and he regarded her with pure disgust. She knew then and there how there was no love between them anymore. They could never find their way back to one another after this, and she feared for both hers and her children's safety. Cate tried to move. She wanted to go around the table to him and beg for his forgiveness but was rooted to the spot in fear. She was unable to even speak to try and calm him or reason with the powerful Devil before her. "Berith," he said, commanding the demon that Cate had almost forgotten was even there. He stepped towards the Dark King in response, bowing to him. "Do you know where to find them?" Lucifer asked him, not once breaking his eye contact with Cate.

"Yes, your majesty," the demon replied, consternation clear in his voice.

"Then go," he ordered him. "And kill them both."

CHAPTER FORTY-THREE

"No!" Cate roared from across the table, her heart pounding in her ears as he spoke the terrible command. Her entire body burned as the fear within turned to rage, and she truly hated Lucifer for giving the order. She summoned all the strength, anger, power, and darkness she could muster, calling to it with every ounce of commanding prowess she could find. Cate felt the ancient power come to her, following her command willingly. It began seeping into her pores from all around the underworld, filling her very soul with pure darkness before she harnessed and channelled it further into herself. She could feel her soul opening up and fully accepting the wonderful, dark gift, and suddenly felt empowered beyond her wildest imaginings.

Cate then felt a silent command burst out of her like a wave. Her rage drove the blast and shattered the table between her and Lucifer into a million tiny pieces. He was sent flying back into the wall behind, his strength waning after her forceful blow.

Berith watched Cate intently, fear crossing his demonic face as he tried to make sense of the scene before him. "You stay right there, Berith," she commanded, and he found himself routed to the spot, unable to move, somehow having to follow her order. She grinned. It felt good to finally be in full command.

Cate then walked across the scattered debris that was once the huge table. She watched as Lucifer tried to steady himself, and grabbed his frail arms with her strong hands, pulling him up to face her. As she stared into his still, darkly speckled eyes, his thoughts washed over her uncontrollably. His memories flooded through her in their wake, and then even some of his most hidden feelings started pouring in, too.

Cate gasped as they bombarded her senses, but opened herself to them, and she laughed maniacally as Lucifer tried to prevent them from escaping him. He couldn't stop it, and as his mind opened up further, she realised that not only his, but the entire kingdom's thoughts were hers to listen in on. Not a single thought was safe from her immense new telepathic power.

She could hear Berith's as well, and she heard him wrestling with the commandment she'd just given him. He couldn't understand why he was forced to follow her order, and she smiled again.

The Dark Queen could even make out Blake's thoughts as he toyed with his witch, Lena's affections in his bedroom. She could also hear Alma in her dungeon as she pondered the best approach to inflict a dark plague on some poor soul that'd annoyed her. Nothing was sacred, nothing was secret. No one's thoughts were safe from her reach, and it took her a moment to focus back on the matter at hand.

"Touché," Lucifer whispered, looking up at Cate, and her attention snapped back to them and her intimidating embrace. Even he could sense her increased strength, and it sent him into an internal frenzy of fear and worry. He did his best not to show it on his face thanks to the years of practice, but his thoughts gave him away. Cate could also sense a small amount of pride and respect for her that he couldn't hide. He'd underestimated his wife profoundly and was oddly impressed. Lucifer peered up at her, his eyes blue again as he succumbed to her immense power at last. It took a few seconds for the realisation of what'd just happened to sink in, but Cate understood at last. She was in total control, and Lucifer was the one at her command.

"Indeed," was all she said, a wry smile curling at her red lips.

"All hail the new Devil," he said in a mocking tone. He was trying to anger her, yet his thoughts gave away his admiration of the woman she'd become while his back was turned. "So, now that you've stolen my power from me, what do you intend to do with it? You aren't strong enough to rule, Cate. Everybody knows it," he added, taunting her. She smiled at him and knew with every fibre of her being that he was wrong.

"I didn't steal anything, Lucifer. It chose to come to me. I should've realised it when my powers returned to me all those years ago, and yet you remained weak, powerless, and pathetic," she told him, spite clear in her tone as he wilted before her. Cate continued to smile down at him, sensing Lucifer's fear. It did nothing but strengthen her even more. "You asked me, no, forced me to love you. I did. I really believed we were meant for each other, but you continued to push me. Well, I guess you didn't count on my love for my children being stronger than my love for you, did you?" she replied. "Arrogant until the end, my darling."

A snap of Cate's fingers set alight the photographs, which now lay strewn on the floor with the shards of wood that were once the great table. They were gone within seconds. She then reached up and placed her hands on her King's cheeks, taking him in for a moment before deciding his fate. She knew exactly what she had to do to keep Lottie and Harry safe and grinned at the sweet irony.

Cate teleported Lucifer with her to a fiery pit, despite his attempts to pull back. She then stood with him in the flames for a few minutes, watching with a sinister smile. The intense heat didn't hurt or even make a mark on her skin, but they burnt away at Lucifer's clothes and singed his skin instantly. He cried out, grabbing Cate's arm when she stepped away from him and leaned against the red-hot wall that had no effect on her at all.

"Don't leave me here," he pleaded, but she knew his remorse was fake.

"My child will be free to choose her own path," she said. "We're over," Cate added, and pulled the black diamond ring from her finger. She tossed it to the ground in front of him, an evil grin on her face as she relished in her freedom at last. "And you will stay here until I can be sure you are of no threat. Maybe you'll stay here for eternity. We shall just have to wait and see," Cate told him with an even wider smile.

She then teleported away, leaving Lucifer alone and burning in the pit with no hope for escape. He called to her with his thoughts and screamed her name as the flames licked his skin, but she ignored his telepathic pleas for mercy. The powerful Dark Queen understood at last that it was both a blessing and a burden being in ultimate control, but she was willing to bear them if it meant her family were safe.

CHAPTER FORTY-FOUR

All of Hell soon knew they had a new mistress. Lucifer was no more, and Hecate had taken complete control of the realm. Berith was thrown into a torture dungeon after Cate had him whipped and beaten for his insolence. His treacherous tongue was cut out, and his lips were sealed with magic thread so he could never tell another soul her secret.

Cate went to him following his incarceration. A cruel smile on her face as she took in the broken sight of one of her ex-husband's most loyal subjects. His thoughts called out for her mercy and told her just how awful the ordeal had been for him, but she didn't care. He silently begged for forgiveness, promising never to speak of Harry or Lottie again, but Cate just laughed darkly at his promise, knowing he wouldn't have a choice whether to speak of them.

"I'll lift your punishment in due time, Berith," she told him calmly and evenly, and without a shred of guilt. "When I decide you can be trusted again. This is, for the most part, to do with Harry and the girl. I will keep them safe from now on, make no doubt about it," she promised, and then stepped closer. She read him and relished in his fear—absorbing it.

Cate understood then how it made her stronger, and she lapped it up. "Your punishment is also for your betrayal, to me and to my realm. Despite my every effort to protect our kind on Earth and then to rule fairly in Lucifer's absence, you continued to be distrusting. In doing so, you turned my husband against me. He's rotting away in exile now too, and it's all thanks to you." She then left him to his thoughts, imprisoned in his dungeon until further notice.

Cate's mind raced as she headed back to her chambers, and she knew she needed to have a plan. Her youngest daughter would eventually be found, and she wanted to be the one in control of how things would go when that day finally came. She decided to wait, to hold back until Lottie came of age before she went to her. It was the only time she could effectively act, and she was determined to bring her straight home. Cate was sure that if she made contact before then it'd be foolish. She even wondered whether a trip to Earth might set off a new war between the powers of light and darkness, and if perhaps the High Council of Angels might sense her presence again. Cate didn't know whether Uriel had regained his memory, or when he might find out that she'd taken the throne. If she could hold off, for just a little while, she would happily do so, even though that meant not seeing Lottie for longer still.

Cate also wondered if Uriel would try to take her away again if he found her, or if he'd give into his dark urges and simply kill her. She could never really know for sure how he'd react to her betrayal, so remained patient. She waited for the day to come when she and her secret family could be together again, regardless of her gut-wrenching desire to go back to them sooner.

In the meantime, she busied herself with her new role alone atop Hell's throne and revelled in her new almighty strength. Cate welcomed the immense power with ease and made a commitment to always respect the sacred gift that'd somehow found its way to her. She'd already started to enjoy the command she had over the dark dominion, and finally felt as though she had control over herself and her destiny at long last.

***

A few more years passed by, and Cate ruled Hell with natural strength and skills that no one had ever thought possible in one so young. The stronger, darker power had possessed her entirely, and even she continued to be surprised by her extra strengths and abilities. Dylan was her chief adviser and kept her grounded, remaining her best friend and protector even after her transition. She was by her side day and night and never blocked her thoughts to the Dark Queen. Dylan was always honest whenever Cate would ask for her opinion or help, brutally so at times, but it was exactly what she needed.

Cate knew she could trust her with the revelation about Lottie's existence, and when the day came that she felt her daughter come of age on Earth, she knew the next full moon would be the right time to finally visit them. She and Dylan would go together, and Cate was sure Lottie would return with them. Her child belonged in Hell with her family, and Cate hoped she wouldn't need much persuasion when the time came.

Lottie's beacon called to her strongly through the divide between their worlds, and she knew it was time to act at long last. She refused to believe in anything other than a future in which she and her three children would be together.

"I need to speak to you," Cate said quietly to Dylan when she sat at the top of the new council table. "In private," she added, and stared into her hazel eyes as she read her friend's quizzical thoughts.

"Of course, your majesty," the witch replied, bowing her head respectfully as she addressed the Dark Queen. Dylan was always sure to show the highest regard to her mistress in the company of others but had always been allowed to speak freely when they were alone. Cate had wanted a true friend around to talk things through with, and Dylan was the only one she could be sure would never betray that trust.

The pair stood, and Cate said her goodbyes to the demons and witches she'd summoned to discuss the possible espousal of her twins to the two youngest children of Devin and Serena. However, Cate didn't like the idea of forcing them into a relationship like her master had done with her and Devin so many years before. She wanted them to choose for themselves, and while the pairings made sense, she'd commanded that it would ultimately be their own decision who they decided to marry. Her vote was the only one that mattered, and she was glad the decision had been made. There would never be betrothals like that again during her reign.

Luna could be a good match with Corey, even the Queen could see that, but she stood by her verdict. It was also argued that Blake could be perfectly matched with their fiery daughter, Leyla. The pair of them possessed strong wills and powerful natures, and although it was thought by some that perhaps the pairing might prove too destructive, Cate disagreed. She'd already seen them together and heard their thoughts and knew there was already a strong kinship between them. With the right encouragement, she guessed Blake and Leyla might be the perfect balance for one another, and that they could bring out each other's best qualities.

That just left Braeden, their eldest son. He was a free spirit who, while a quiet boy, had hopes and dreams beyond the imagination of anyone else around him in their dark world. He daydreamed constantly, and Cate would often listen in, enjoying his creative vision and open mind. She couldn't help but wonder if he and Lottie might be the perfect fit for one another in the future but knew that topic would come up in due course. But first, there were much more pressing matters to figure out.

"I have an issue with my daughter," Cate told Dylan once they were alone in her chambers.

"With Luna?" Dylan asked, looking up at her with a puzzled expression.

"No. My *other* daughter," Cate clarified, reaching over to place a hand on her friend's shoulder as she spoke. Dylan's mouth dropped open slightly as she took in what the Queen had just said. Cate smiled back at her friend, listening in on her thoughts as she tried to work out how, when, and where. "She lives on Earth," Cate said, replying automatically to Dylan's thoughts. "With Harry," she added with a wide grin.

"Oh, really?" Dylan finally managed to say in response, her lip curling at the edges. Cate listened in on her thoughts as she quickly wondered if

Harry was the father, but she didn't dare ask.

Her eyes darkened, but not in anger. A combination of fear and panic flooded Cate's core, but she knew she had to reveal all. It was important that Dylan knew the whole truth for her to understand the complexities of the situation, and to properly be able to help in bringing her child home safely.

She pointed her index finger skywards, shaking her head, but didn't dare say the words aloud. "Oh really?" repeated Dylan, her voice a quiet whisper.

The playfulness was gone, and the enigmatic witch's face paled as she quickly came to the realisation of the girl's heritage. It suddenly hit home. Cate's words were true, and after all her years of secrecy, she was finally able to tell her most trusted friend the truth about her time spent exiled on Earth.

She spent a while explaining how everything had happened, and how she and Harry had spent those few blissful years together. It felt good to reveal all, like a heavy burden had finally been lifted from her shoulders. Cate was ready to face the truth and couldn't wait to see them both again.

CHAPTER FORTY-FIVE

As the next full moon rose on Earth, Cate, Dylan, and a now up-to-speed Alma landed silently at the end of a short garden path. It led to a small house in the old British town of Winchcombe. The town was situated directly on the ley lines, and just as Cate had told Harry to many years ago, he'd continued to live in the towns along the ancient powerful lines during his time without her.

Harry had harnessed the ley lines' energy and combined it with the knowledge she'd given him of runes and ancient wards to keep the child of both light and darkness safe from discovery. She'd purposely given him wards and talismans that kept all light beings away, yet only the dark beings that sought to harm the child would be kept out by their magical barriers. Those from the darkness who knew of her existence and wished her no harm could easily sense Lottie's little flame. That clever detail had only been for Cate to know and use to her advantage when the time came—and it was finally that time. She didn't need it, though. It was Cate's strong link to Lottie that'd helped them find her so easily.

And so, there she stood, staring out into the dark night, and she could sense her daughter inside the house that stood just metres away. Lottie was so close, and yet there was a part of Cate that was afraid to go to her. She was convinced that Lottie would be angry, hurt, or maybe even ashamed of her mother for having left her without a word when she was just a small child. She would explain all in due time, but she still feared that Lottie might not give her the chance to try, and knew she deserved it after leaving her without a mother all those important years. She was also very aware they had only the two days the moon would allow her to be on Earth. There wasn't much time in which to convince Lottie to return home with them, but she had to. Only then would they truly be safe from the angels' reach. Cate gave herself a mental kick up the backside and stepped forwards.

Dylan and Alma followed her lead and walked slowly behind their Queen as she moved towards the small townhouse. After a sharp knock on the door from Cate, it was quickly opened, and she expected to see her daughter on the other side. Instead, a middle-aged woman answered, her head peering around the door expectantly. She eyed the trio cautiously, struggling to see them properly in the dim light. Her grey-blonde hair was in rollers pinned to her scalp, and she wore a long nightdress that reminded Cate of the ones her grandmother used to wear when she would visit her as a child.

The woman pulled her fleecy robe tighter around her, as though a cold draft suddenly caught her by surprise, and a shiver ran down her spine as she continued to look at them expectantly.

The three women hadn't aged themselves, so were much younger looking than the woman staring at them from the doorway, when in fact Cate guessed she was probably double her age. She'd opted to look just as she had the last time Lottie had seen her though, despite knowing it would confuse her somewhat at first, but how it was necessary in ensuring she listened to the stranger aspects of her heritage.

"Can I help you?" the woman eventually asked, looking out at the women who were shrouded in darkness on the front step, and Cate could tell that she felt uncomfortable. She tried to read the woman's thoughts, and wanted to figure her out before she spoke, but was having trouble. She knew her fraught emotions had to be playing havoc with her powers, and that she needed physical contact to make a better connection but didn't want to scare the woman by trying to touch her.

She concentrated harder and heard a name, *Lola*, as it flittered across her consciousness. Cate guessed that might be the new name Lottie was going by there but couldn't be sure. She decided to give the friendly approach a try, and failing that, she was willing to just barge in if she needed to— nothing was going to come between her and her child.

"We're looking for Lola, please," Cate said, hoping she was right about the name.

"It's late, she's up in her room," the woman replied curtly. "We've got a busy day tomorrow. Maybe you should come by another time," she added, and went to close the door, but was stopped when a young woman's voice called to her from an upstairs room of the house.

"Who is it, Jenny?" the voice asked, and Cate could hear soft footsteps approaching the front door. Her heart fluttered as she heard the voice's owner approaching and knew it was Lottie. The light above the three dark beings then flicked on, illuminating the porch at last. The woman still blocking the door—presumably Jenny—gasped when she looked properly at Cate, and stepped back, clearly shocked and surprised.

Lola, who was quite clearly Lottie, then arrived at the hallway and pulled the door open fully, taking in the sight before her. She gasped and her hand went to her mouth in shock as she stared into the face of her long lost mother.

Dylan and Alma both jumped as they saw her and stifled their own mutters of amazement upon seeing Cate's double as she stood there before them. She was clearly the child that neither had known about until just a couple of days before, yet was unmistakably their Queen's daughter.

"Mum?" Lottie asked quietly, and she had tears in her green eyes as she reached out and pulled her into a tight hug. "Are you really here?" she asked, her voice a muffled sound from within their embrace. Cate read her thoughts, sensing that Lottie was wondering if she might be imagining her mother's return at long last, and she knew she had to put her mind at ease before saying anything else.

"I'm really here, my darling," was all she could reply, hugging her back tightly. She took in her daughter's memories as she held on to the contact with her, smiling as the pictures of Lottie and Harry's life together flooded her mind. She was happy, healthy and had been well looked after by her father over the years, just as Cate had always trusted he would.

"I think this means we can come in now, don't you?" Dylan asked the still bewildered Jenny as she stepped forward. "Where's her father?" she added, cocking her eyebrow as she took in the woman before her. Jenny took a step back and went into the hallway, ignoring Dylan's last question as she headed back into the house, seemingly bewildered by the sight before her.

The enraptured mother and daughter pulled away from their embrace at last, and then Cate followed Lottie into the living room. She sat next to her on the brown leather sofa, and the pair took each other in silently as they gazed into the other's identical emerald eyes.

Dylan followed them and sat on the couch opposite, drinking in the wonderful sight before her with a wide smile, while Alma ushered the still bemused Jenny into the kitchen. She silently promised Cate via her thoughts that she'd work her magic on the human woman while they were alone, and the Dark Queen knew her high priestess had come prepared with sleeping potions and memory cleansers in case of such events, so let her get straight to it.

"Dad's at the hotel," Lottie told Dylan after a few quiet moments, but the witch's confused expression spurred the girl to tell her more. "Urm…he and Jenny are getting married there tomorrow," she added, not looking at her mother as she spoke. "He went there to get everything ready, and then he's staying the night so he doesn't see the bride before the ceremony. You know, in case of bad luck," Lottie added, an awkward look on her still happy face.

Dylan snorted, and then did her best to compose herself when she saw the forlorn look on Cate's face, a look she'd tried to hide, but Dylan knew her far too well.

"Which hotel? Where is it?" she then asked, and Lottie told her, giving the witch directions to the Manor House Hotel on the outskirts of the small town. Dylan was then careful to pretend she was going out to her car to head off to get him, but instead teleported away as soon as she was outside.

"Where have you been, Mum?" Lottie asked Cate when they were alone, a serious look on her beautiful face, and she took her hand. There was a strange power that seemed to come from her mother's touch, and she knew that something unusual was going on, but was eager to hear her story at long last. Lottie could tell right away that her mother hadn't aged at all since she'd last seen her nearly nine years before, and she could sense the darkness she'd brought with her into their home, too. It was as if a shadow had descended, but she didn't fear it. In fact, she was drawn to it. Lottie didn't know how she felt all those things, but she somehow knew them all to be very real.

"I had to go back to my home for a while," Cate answered her, choosing her words carefully. "I had no other choice."

"And where is your home? You can tell me," Lottie said, looking into her eyes as she silently pleaded for answers. Cate knew she was already a curious and intuitive young woman, and already felt both her presence and power deep within her. Lottie's untapped strength and dark force reminded her of her own at the same age, and Cate knew she had to be honest.

"Hell," she said, keeping her eyes on Lottie's to let her know she wasn't kidding. "I had to return there to keep you safe. You had to be hidden from both my kind and from others who may wish to hurt you or use you for their own selfish means. Harry and I loved each other once, and he promised to keep you safe for me." Cate's cheeks blushed slightly as she thought of him, and she looked down at her hands. She hated that he'd somehow managed to move on without her, and part of her wanted to storm into that kitchen and rip Jenny's throat out for daring touch what belonged to her.

"Why? Who would want to hurt me?" Lottie asked, seemingly unfazed by Cate's revelation, and her question pulled her out of her sad reverie.

"Well, the latter is unfortunately a conversation that'll need to wait for another time, my darling," Cate told her, reaching up and stroking Lottie's dark, curly hair with her hand before she continued. "But the other one is a slightly easier question to answer. My husband at the time of your conception was Lucifer, the Devil. He's not your father, though, Lottie, and I knew he would kill you if he ever knew you existed. He and I are no longer together, so I can finally come back to you without worrying about your safety," she told her honestly. Lottie's eyes grew wide, a hundred questions filling her mind, following Cate's explanation.

"How do you know that I'll be safe now?" she finally asked, her voice trembling slightly as she feared the repercussions of her mother's betrayal of her ex-husband.

"Because I'm the leader of Hell now, Lottie. I am the Devil. It's only because of this change in leadership that I can come here and be with you today," she told her with a grin before she added. "And I want to bring you back home with me where you belong."

Lottie stared open-mouthed at Cate as her words sunk in. She believed every word, though, having suspected for a while that she was no ordinary girl. The change of name and new home every few years had been enough of a clue, but there had been more. She'd found the runes and warding symbols her father had used on their home a while ago and had been researching their meanings in secret ever since. Harry completely refused to answer her questions, so had avoided the subject whenever Lottie had tried to bring it up, advising her to drop it and forget all about them. But she hadn't been able to.

Cate eavesdropped on her thoughts and marvelled at her intuitiveness. Lottie also wondered about Hell, and what it'd be like to go and live there with her mother. She was scared but knew that she wanted to be with her. She wanted to know the real story of her life and learn the truth about her long-lost family. Lottie could feel the powerful buzz that came from her mother's touch, and felt it course through her as she deliberated.

She also knew she wanted more. She wanted to know what that power might mean for her, too, and let her mind wander, thinking of the power she might already have inside of her and hoping that it might be utilised and controlled. "Yes, of course," Cate said, replying to her daughter's thoughts without even thinking. "You have your own powers already and can be taught to harness them. You'll thrive in Hell, and then we can spend eternity together where it's safe."

"Whoa," Lottie replied in a breathy whisper, astounded at both the prospect of having powers of her own, and the realisation that her mother had just read her mind.

***

Dylan reached the Manor House Hotel in seconds and went straight inside. She found the event hall immediately and burst through the doors with a powerful shove that sent them flying open.

"I object!" she shouted, laughing at her own joke as she made her strange entrance, while everyone inside stopped what they were doing and stared at her in annoyance.

Harry was stood over by the makeshift altar, talking and laughing with another tall man as they drank a beer together. He turned to look at the rude intruder, and nearly dropped the pint glass in his hand when he realised who stood before him in the doorway. He put the drink down onto a nearby table and spilled the amber fluid across the wood, apologising profusely, but left the mess behind him as he made his way over to Dylan. The shock on his face at seeing her again after such a long time was utterly clear as he approached, and he blinked as though gazing upon an apparition, rather than the woman he knew was an immortal witch.

"What are you doing here, Dylan?" Harry asked, remembering her true name from Cate's long talks of her and their relationship all those years before. She didn't look any different than she had back when he knew her, and it was strange seeing her after such a long time.

"I came to get you. Duh," she answered, making him smile. She was still the same fun natured free spirit she'd always been, and Harry shook his head jokingly, the glimmer of hope igniting in his chest at what her presence might mean. "Wow, you got old," she added, giving him a cheeky smile before she wrapped her arms around her old friend and hugged him tightly.

Harry hugged her back, feeling confused and surprised to see her, but he hoped it might mean her best friend was finally on her way as well.

"Where's Cate?" he asked when they pulled back from their embrace, looking down into her eyes with a shy smile.

"She's at your house, with Lottie," she told him, raising a dark eyebrow at him.

"You know about Lottie?" he asked, jumping when she spoke his daughter's real name.

"I do now. She's here to take her home, Harry," Dylan replied, and his face dropped. His expression turned somewhat fearful as the prospect of losing his daughter hit him like a hot poker to the chest. "Come with me?" she then asked him, a warm, gentle smile on her lips as she took in his sad face. "She'll explain everything."

Dylan and Harry arrived back at the house a few minutes later, finding his fiancée Jenny asleep at the kitchen table thanks to Alma's strong potions. Lottie sat curled up with her mother on the sofa, with the powerful Dark Queen's arms wrapped around her child as she cradled her in her lap. They were talking quietly, Cate eager to hear all about Lottie's school, love life, dreams, and hopes.

She climbed up from the chair, sensing Harry immediately as he and Dylan came in the house. Cate greeted him with a huge smile when he walked into the living room; taking in the face she'd dreamed about for years before saying or doing anything.

He was older and seemed to have aged so much more since she'd last seen him. His hair was almost completely grey, and Harry had kept his good looks and fresh-faced charm but had much more of a distinguished look to him now.

The air between them was thick, and neither spoke as they moved forward to greet each other. Harry had a smile on his soft lips as he gazed lovingly at her, and neither seemed to know what to say. A moment of awkwardness hung threateningly in the air, but Cate pushed it away and stepped forward again. She moved to within inches of his face, and then immediately took his mouth in hers.

She pushed Harry back against the wall behind, and he responded to her without hesitation. He kissed her back with a deep longing and finally allowed the love to come pouring out that he'd tried so hard to suppress since she'd left. He'd never stopped loving her, but had forced his broken heart to try, and in that moment, it all came rushing back.

"Let's give them a minute, shall we?" Dylan said to a shell-shocked Lottie before leading her out into the kitchen, and the young girl nodded.

Cate continued to pin Harry to the wall with her strong body, their kisses deepening and becoming more passionate. She could sense how much he'd missed her and read his thoughts as they kissed. His memories and thoughts of her came flooding back through his mind, and his desperate desire for her took control of him all over again. Harry still loved her with all his heart, Cate knew for sure, and he'd been lonely without her. He'd missed her terribly, despite having had her doppelgänger there to keep him company. If anything, she now knew that'd made it harder. She pulled back, staring into his deep blue eyes for a moment. They were the eyes she'd dreamed about for years, that she'd fantasised about countless times while they'd been forced apart.

"Well, hello to you too," Harry said in a whispered voice that faltered with excitement, and a coy smile curled at his lips as he took in the dark goddess standing before him.

Cate couldn't help but smile back. A giggle escaped her red lips as she thought about how their greeting must've looked to Lottie and Dylan.

"So, you're getting married tomorrow?" Cate then asked Harry with a serious edge to her tone as she gazed up at him. Her powerful body was still pinned against his, and she didn't want to let him go, despite knowing they needed to talk.

"Well, recent events *might* have affected that decision somewhat," he replied. Harry watched with a grin as she backed away a few steps and sat down on the sofa. He stepped forward, looking down into her sad face, and needed her to understand, even if it meant hurting her. "I was so lonely without you, Cate. Then Jenny came along, and she made me smile for the first time in years. She's a good woman and, besides—I'm an old man now. I can't have a twenty-year-old on my arm anymore." A dry laugh escaped his lips, but there was no smile in his eyes.

"I know," she replied, reading his thoughts. She really did, and he was telling her the truth about Jenny. No matter how much she wanted to hate her, she seemed to have been good for both him and Lottie for the past couple of years. "I can't stay here anyway, Harry," Cate told him, peering up at him from the couch. "I'm bound by the full moon now." He looked down at her, clearly confused by the moon's restrictions on her.

"But I thought you could stay as long as you wanted? The moon thing's just for him, isn't it?" he asked, a hint of jealousy in his voice when he spoke of Lucifer, and she had to smile. Harry then moved toward the sofa to join her.

"That was before. I've changed. I'm not the same woman I once was," she said, staring at her hands.

"Well, what are you then? Where's your husband?" he demanded, needing answers.

"Ex-husband. He's gone, I'm the Devil now," Cate told him calmly, and Harry flopped down next to her on the couch with a thud. He was grateful to have had a seat close by when she'd dropped that little bombshell. "Lucifer isn't in control anymore. I took the throne from him," she added, looking across at Harry with a smile. "I'm finally free." Tears welled in her eyes. It was the first time she'd admitted it to anyone, but in all honesty, she was glad he'd forced her hand.

"You control the entire underworld?" he asked her incredulously, smiling back at her. She read his mind and knew that he was in shock, but also in awe of her. He was impressed by the strength and power she'd encompassed but wasn't surprised. He'd always known she could do it.

"Yes, but as well as that, I control every other dark being. I'm their ruler now, and what I say goes," she told him, her smile widening.

"Oh, so will Lottie be safe in Hell now?" Harry asked, suspecting that although their reunion had been wonderful, Lottie was Cate's real reason for returning.

"Yes, she can now take her place at my side with Blake and Luna," she replied, watching Harry as he swallowed hard at the prospect of being left alone. After dedicating his life to raising the beautiful child he'd sworn to protect—the child he loved with all his heart—he couldn't imagine being without her. Harry could already feel his grief for Lottie creeping in, threatening to drag him down into a dark despair. The heartache for Cate he'd pushed aside for years rose up in him too, and he struggled to force it back down, suddenly feeling overwhelmed.

"I wish you could come with us, Harry. We'll have to wait until your time comes, if you know what I mean?" she asked, and he nodded, knowing that Cate was talking about his death. "I can claim your soul, mark it now as belonging to me, and then when you pass on from this world, it will automatically go to Hell?" Cate offered weakly. "But I cannot guarantee anything. You would just be another human soul, technically nothing more than a toy for the demons, witches, and warlocks to play with. You'd need to prove yourself worthy and then climb the ranks." Harry couldn't hide his foreboding fear at the sheer thought of that future coming true. He shook his head. Every inch of him felt defeated and lost.

"Just take her and go," he replied, slumping back in the chair, and not daring to look at Cate as the tears welled in his own eyes.

CHAPTER FORTY-SIX

"I have an idea, your highness," Alma's voice filtered into Harry's living room. She poked her head around the corner and took in the sight of her all-powerful Queen looking into the face of the human man beside her. He was her soulmate, and the man she truly loved with all her heart. Alma could see it so clearly now. She'd always wondered why Cate and Lucifer had been so distant when they'd returned from their exile on Earth. There was no disguising that he'd been disgusted with her for letting Uriel seduce her again, and he'd confided in Alma that he couldn't get over her betrayal a second time, despite knowing she'd been forced. Alma had always assumed that Cate had felt ashamed for her part in the seduction, and she'd never even considered that the Dark Queen might've fallen in love with someone else during their time of separation and powerless existence.

"Let's hear it, Alma," Cate said, desperate to hear any ideas the powerful witch might have.

"A demon could sire him, my Queen," she offered, sending her thoughts to Cate about an ancient ritual in which a demon would participate in a blood-sharing ceremony with a human. They would share their dark essence with them, effectively killing the human and turning them into a new demon. They'd bypass the centuries of torture human souls normally had to endure before they reached the same position—effectively jumping the queue. Lucifer had outlawed the ritual many years before, mostly because he hadn't wanted demons to be created so easily. Part of what he considered their essential makeup had been the pain and suffering they'd endured at the hands of their peers since death. It made them hateful, and far more susceptible to becoming puppets for his dark whims. He also preferred to choose worthy souls himself for the honour of a place in the demonic hierarchy, rather than to allow human candidates to cross over into the dark ranks.

Cate took it all in for a moment, and jumped up from the sofa, understanding immediately.

"Yes!" she cried, excitement bubbling up inside of her at the sheer thought of Harry completing the transition and becoming a demon. "We'd need to find a willing demon to donate their blood for the ritual, and of course, they'd be responsible for him from then onwards. But this way he could come home with us and stay in Hell forever," she said to Alma, who nodded in agreement and smiled.

Cate peered down at the still forlorn man before her, hoping he would give her one more yes. She wanted him to choose to share a dark and terrible existence with her over a human life with Jenny. It might be selfish to want it, but she didn't care. "If you do this, you could be by my side for eternity," Cate offered, looking to Harry for his understanding.

His thoughts told her he was willing. That he'd do anything it took to be with her and Lottie, and she carried on. "We'll have to turn you into a demon. You would then join my demonic ranks and serve me along with the others, but in private, we could be together. It might have to be in secret at first, but eventually you'll climb higher, and then we can make our union public." She blushed as she contemplated a long and happy life with her soulmate by her side at last, a life she'd never thought was possible until Alma had jogged her memory.

The demonic rituals had been forbidden for many years, but Cate knew she could finally change that. She had the throne, and therefore the power to alter the rules for her benefit.

"And I just so happen to know of a demon who owes you big-time, my Queen," interjected Alma one more time. "Perhaps this is the perfect way in which Berith might compensate for his past misdemeanours?" she asked, bowing when her mistress gave her an approving nod, and then leaving her and Harry to talk some more.

Cate climbed down onto her knees and perched before where he still sat on the sofa. He'd stayed quiet, his head bowed as he thought about all that she'd said, trying to make some sense of her offer. She reached up and put her hands on his knees, drawing his attention back to her. Harry gazed into her beautiful eyes intently, mesmerised by the powerful woman he still loved so very much.

"I love you, Harry," she told him with a warm, shy smile. He smiled back at her and laid his own hands over hers while she still knelt before him.

"I love you too, Cate. I always have, and I always will," he replied, caressing her hands in his before stroking them up her arms to her face, holding it in his palms. "I cannot ever imagine a time or place in which I won't love you. I'm willing to do whatever it takes," he promised, kissing her red lips softly. Cate deepened the kiss. Grabbing Harry, she thrust her hands into his hair and pulled him closer. She was ready to let herself open up again and finally felt as though her future might not be quite so lonely as she'd once thought.

"This is the only way we can be together. It isn't easy, and you'll no longer be human afterwards," she told him again, making sure he understood the repercussions of what they were about to do. "You'll be a demon, but it'll mean we can be together, forever. You'll be able to alter your age, be young again. Be with me?"

"Yes, I had already made up my mind. Of course it's a yes," Harry added to his earlier promises, but it was all she needed to hear. He knew, remembering well, the stories she'd once told him about free will. Harry remembered how the object of the powerful being's affections had to give themselves over to them willingly and say the words aloud. He had done it without hesitation and meant every word. He was ready to do whatever it took to be with Cate. Having lived without her the past nine years had been torturous and had proven to him how he didn't want to be without her ever again.

A quick click of Cate's fingers bought a beaten and bedraggled man into the living room with her and Harry. He was bowing low, concealing his face, but the man eagerly stood to greet his Queen after a few moments. Harry couldn't hide his disgust at seeing Berith bound, beaten, and silenced so horrifically. He was far removed from how he'd been that day he'd met him at the music festival.

With a nod, Cate removed the magical thread that sealed the demon's mouth shut and healed his tongue with an effortless, silent commandment. Berith brought his hands up, touching his face gently to check on his healed lips before eventually speaking. He fell to his knees and bowed before her, looking up at Cate adoringly as he spoke.

"My Queen, I am shocked and awed by your mercy. How might I serve you?" he asked, looking at Harry briefly, but focussing his every ounce of attention and admiration on Cate.

"I need you to sire a new demon for me, Berith," she told him calmly, and he remained on his knees before her. He couldn't help but glance again at Harry, knowing immediately what she wanted from him. The ancient demon nodded and raised his arms, offering her the demonic blood in his veins before lowering his head in submission.

"Of course, your majesty. Anything for you," he said.

"That's the right answer. Well done," she told him with a smile.

Alma returned from the kitchen with a dagger and metal bowl at the ready. She slit the demon's wrists, one at a time, allowing each to gush black-red blood into the awaiting vessel. When enough had been gathered, Berith slumped back against the wall and cradled his arms to his body while the wounds magically healed.

Harry was horrified, and his mouth hung open as he took in the gory scene around him. Alma said nothing but gathered up her things and went back into the kitchen with the blood, in search of Dylan with whom she'd combine their knowledge and magic to put together a spell inciting the ritual's ancient power.

Cate stood in the centre of the small living room, still standing there from when she'd summoned Berith to Earth. She regarded the pale demon with no mercy in her stare, or a hint of regret for almost bleeding him dry, but Harry felt terrible for him, and wondered just what Berith had done to deserve her wrath.

"This fucking rat," she suddenly shouted, pointing to Berith, and making Harry jump in his seat. "He's the one who told Lucifer all about you and Lottie. He was ready to kill you both for the love of his old master. I took the throne thanks to him, my hand being forced by his betrayal. Do not pity him for even a second longer," she bellowed, and the walls seemed to shake with the sound. Her eyes then turned black as she peered down at him.

Cate sat down next to Harry on the sofa and put her head in her hands, her anger vibrating the air around her as she sat and tried to compose herself. Berith stayed silent, having curled up in a ball as she spoke, as though shielding himself from her. The fear in him showed on his face as he continued to stare at her feet, while Harry looked at them both in shock. He wondered how she'd thwarted Lucifer, and how much she'd had to change in order to take his ancient power from him. He knew Cate would never have hurt another unnecessarily, and Harry trusted she was still the same now that she'd come out the other side. He believed in her and told her so via his thoughts.

Cate calmed down, and she ignored the weak demon in the corner as she peered into the warm eyes of her lover apologetically. She reached up, taking Harry's cheek in her hand, and then planted a kiss on his lips. He kissed her back, giving in to his need for her again. Harry wasn't afraid of her, and she was glad, having been worried her outburst might've scared him.

"We need to tell Lottie the truth first," Harry said when they broke away, and Cate knew he was right. She nodded and kissed him again, relishing in the feel of his mouth on hers for a few moments longer.

"Yuk, you two at it again?" Lottie said, joking with them as she came back in from the kitchen with a broad smile. She looked over at Berith in the corner, but quickly turned away. She realised he must be where the blood had come from she'd just seen the witches working with in the kitchen but didn't want to enquire as to how or why. Cate bound him again in an instant, an unspoken order demanding the demon to stay silent and still until she released him. He didn't even try to fight her command, and she was glad to see he was making progress at last.

"We need to talk," she said as she climbed up from the couch, Harry's hand firmly in her own. Lottie could tell it was important, and nodded, silently letting her mother know to lead the way.

The three of them headed out into the back garden and having Harry's hand in hers bought Cate a great deal of comfort, as if she felt at home in his presence. "There's more to our story, Lottie. You need to know the full truth before you can truly decide which path you want to go down. We both need you to know," Cate said, looking to Harry as she spoke. The three of them sat down in the chairs by the small wooden garden table and stared at each other for a moment. Harry wanted to be the one to tell her Cate could read it in his thoughts, so she stayed quiet and let him take the lead.

"Lottie," he said, looking at her intensely through the darkness. "I've taken care of you since the day you were born, and I'll always be here for you, as whatever you want me to be. However…" He hesitated but took a deep breath and forced himself to continue. "I'm not your real father." He held his breath as he waited for her response.

"I know," Lottie replied. She reached forward to take Harry's hand in her own. "I think I've always known."

"How?" Cate asked, both confused and worried about how she could've possibly known.

"I don't know, I just feel it. I always have," Lottie said, her thoughts turning to her friend Claudia and the times she'd spent at her house after school and on the weekends. Claudia's parents were devout Christians. They'd once told the girls about the terrible battles that'd raged between Heaven and Hell. Lottie had been scared stiff, never having heard much about God and the Devil before because Harry had continued to raise her as a strict atheist. Claudia had assured her there was nothing to worry about. She'd said it was all old tales and scripture that people like her parents used to scare their children onto the straight and narrow path of righteousness.

Lottie couldn't help but wonder, though, and the stories had played on her mind. She'd then decided to investigate it all further and had used her free time at school to do some research on the different religions and prophecies, as well as the historical evidence behind their claims.

Cate could sense that Lottie was well educated on both the good and evil sides of the story, and she'd somehow suspected for a while that she was more than just a normal human girl. She'd eventually found an old book in the library, a supposedly fictional story telling of a child born out of half darkness and half light, and who was doomed to hide their true nature for all time and wander the Earth alone and in fear. The novel was just an elaborately fictionalised version of the Christian bible, and Cate realised Lottie had almost figured out her own story all by herself. She'd even felt a strong kinship with the last child of Heaven, and the only other of her kind—Jesus.

"I would never let that happen to you, Lottie. Harry wouldn't either," Cate assured her, and Lottie nodded, knowing her mother had read her thoughts again.

"I know, and that's why I waited. I always trusted Dad, knowing that you'd never have left me with him unless you knew I was safe. I never told anyone about my suspicions. In all honesty, I thought they'd throw me in the nuthouse for thinking up something so crazy, so I just ignored my fears and pushed it all away."

"So, do you suspect you know who your father is then?" Harry asked, not knowing what psychic exchange the two women had just shared, but he was desperate to finish off their tough conversation.

"Yes," Lottie answered, looking skywards, and Cate gasped. A quiet sob then escaped her uncontrollably.

"Has he ever come to you?" she asked, scared to know the answer, but needing to ask the question just in case.

"No, Mum. Never," Lottie assured her, smiling warmly. "And even if he did, I would always choose you," she added, calming her worried mother at last.

Cate smiled back at her, and she sensed herself opening up to Lottie. Her *expression* started coming through uncontrollably, and it gave her daughter a deeper sense of her love and emotion through the strange and silent connection.

Lottie gazed back at Cate, staring into her face as she basked in the warmth that flowed into her with a broad, loving smile. "And anyway, I don't need another father, because I already have the perfect one right here," she added, making Harry smile for the first time since before they'd come out into the garden.

Alma and Dylan then joined the small family on the dimly lit patio area.

"Everything's ready, your majesty," Alma told Cate, bowing as she addressed her mistress.

"Sorry Harry, but we kinda had to mess up your living room," Dylan added, shrugging her shoulders, but there wasn't even a hint of an apology in her playful tone.

"How very dare you?" he cried in response, throwing his hands up in mock disgust and making them all laugh. They each stood and went back inside, ready to begin the dark and scary ritual. Dylan patted Harry on the back as she wandered in behind him, thinking that it was going to be fun having him around again.

Inside, a giant pentagram had been drawn on the wooden floor in black paint, and the furniture been discarded in readiness for the rite of passage Harry would have to take to make the transition.

"You don't need to stay, Lottie. You can go and wait with Jenny if you'd like? Don't wake her up, though. Alma has wiped her memory, so she won't know who you are," Cate told her, unsure if Lottie would be scared for Harry's safety, but she shook her head and stood firm.

"I'm not going anywhere," she replied, making her father smile. Cate understood and held onto her hand as they took their places in the corner of the living room. She just had to let the witches and Berith do their magic, overseeing the ritual rather than being part of it. Cate released the demon from his invisible restraints, and he crawled over to the pentagram, where he took a seat inside of it. Berith instinctually knew what was expected of him, and she was pleased he was ready to serve his Queen however she saw fit. His days of going against Cate were well and truly over now, and she read his thoughts with a satisfied smile.

Harry joined him, kneeling inside the pentagram tentatively. Berith sat opposite him inside the ancient symbol, and the demon's drawn blood sat in a large glass between the two of them.

"Are you ready?" Alma asked Harry, standing before them outside the pentagram.

"Yes," he answered, and despite his fear, he knew he'd never been surer of anything in his life.

Alma reached down and grabbed his right wrist, slicing it open with a quick swipe of a dagger she held firmly in her hand, and then she fed his blood directly to Berith. The demon drank it down eagerly, holding onto Harry's arm as he sucked on his open vein. Alma looked up at Cate before she carried on, who nodded, urging her to continue.

"Before the almighty Dark Queen, and in the presence of demons and witches. Do you renounce all other allegiances and pledge your soul to your Mistress, Her Infernal Majesty, Hecate?"

"Yes, I do," Harry replied, woozy from the blood-loss, but still clear and level-headed. Alma then reached back down and took his arm away from the demon's mouth. She then wrapped his wound quickly in a bandage she'd held at the ready, before lifting the blood-filled cup to his mouth.

"Then drink of your demon, share his blood and become his progeny," she ordered him, and Harry did as she asked. He gulped down the thick liquid as quickly as he could, not stopping to let himself think what was now filling his stomach and coursing through his veins as Alma and Dylan stood over him.

"So mote it be, hail to the Dark Queen," Alma finished the ritual, and then they all repeated the last line, Cate and Lottie included.

Within seconds, Harry started to feel his bones grow heavy and his muscles begin to tighten. He slumped down onto the floor, joined by Berith, who grabbed both of his wrists and held them tightly in place. It was essential neither of them left the pentagram during the rest of the ritual and Cate was glad Berith was doing his job to ensure the ritual worked correctly. A strange and ominous black mist then came up as though out of nowhere and shrouded the pair of them, as if they were inside a dark snow globe that'd just been shaken.

It made it hard to watch them, and difficult to notice the transition, but Cate could see clearly through the haze while Lottie and the witches seemed to be having trouble.

The darkness enveloped Harry. It clung to him and then disappeared, seeping into his skin. He called out an incoherent shout, but it wasn't from pain. His cries were from the overwhelming power that surged into him so quickly and forcefully. It engulfed his senses while giving him no respite from the flow of the dark forces that'd been sent to claim him. It was all or nothing, but he let it infiltrate his body without a fight. The dark power was drawn to him at the behest of the Dark Queen and her witch's focussed ritual, and Cate thought it beautiful as she watched him transform.

Every part of the ritual had its purpose and worked to alter her soulmate before her very eyes. The demonic blood that now coursed through him was a gift from the higher power, and a symbol of Harry's worthiness. Cate smiled to herself as she saw those dark gifts empower her lover and immortalise him, and she silently promised never to take that power, or him, for granted.

CHAPTER FORTY-SEVEN

A few moments later, the strange dark mist settled, and Harry and Berith stood up inside the pentagram. Cate could sense them both. She felt Berith's usual demonic presence inside her mind, and felt too the manifestation of a new entity, a dark flame emanating from deep within Harry's soul.

The ritual had worked. He was a demon. He'd have to be taught about the demonic world, as well as all about his powers and responsibilities. Harry would also need to complete the various initiations to climb the levels of demonic hierarchy and reach the top, but it was Berith's job to prepare him for them. As his demonic master, he was expected to teach him and ensure that Harry excelled. Any neglect or bad teaching from his part was punishable by death, if their mistress saw fit. Berith knew he had an epic task ahead of him, but he welcomed the opportunity to win back Cate's affections.

Both demons bowed to her respectfully as she approached. She could already feel Harry growing stronger by the second, the darkness empowering him. She also knew they had no time to waste, and he needed to go to Hell right away and continue his transition.

"Berith," she said, and he looked up at her respectfully.

"Yes, mistress," he replied.

"Take your demon progeny to our realm. I will see you both there in due course," she ordered, and Harry looked up at her too, scared to leave without her and Lottie safely beside him. Cate stepped closer and touched his face gently. He could feel her immense power course through him, and her omnipotence overwhelmed his senses, but he lapped it up. His body savoured her powerful touch. He could see her true form too, and while her usual human-looking self was still there, he could make out the extra-dark matter that seemed to surround her formidable body as Cate stood before him. She was even more beautiful than ever.

Harry's love for her was tenfold following his demonic re-birth, and he wanted nothing more than to serve her, please her, and love her—forever.

A true disciple already, Cate had to smile at his instinctual admiration. She stared into his eyes, reading his thoughts as she spoke quietly to her lover.

"This is how it has to be, but just for now. Lottie and I will see you soon, my love. We can truly be together now, Harry, and it will be forever," she told him with a broad smile, laying a soft kiss on his still bloody lips. Lottie joined them in the pentagram, leaning up to give her father a kiss on his cheek. She was proud of him as well and wanted him to know.

With a click of her fingers, Cate then sent the two demons away, but she knew they'd be fine. Despite his previous incarceration, Berith was still a level one demon in the hierarchy of Hell, the highest and most prestigious classification in her dark ranks. She knew it might be a long time before Harry could join his demonic master at the top level, but she would wait for as long as it took, and then she would make him her immortal husband at last.

Harry's initiation would require many tests and challenges before they were complete, but she would do everything in her infinite power to ensure he progressed quickly and knew that Berith would be an excellent teacher and mentor for him.

Cate also knew that she could depend on and call upon each of them at any time, as well as her other loyal demons such as Leviathan and Beelzebub. They'd fast become some of her most trusted demonic companions, and she knew they would take Harry under their proverbial wings when she asked it of them.

She could sense Harry, like a presence deep inside of herself, and a beacon. His was a consciousness she could call to at will, just like any other member of her dark service, however their connection was more potent than any other outside the dark royal family. She could sense that he was already safely in their dominion, his new home, and could even hear his thoughts from afar as Berith began his teachings. Cate felt his soul join her dark ranks, albeit at the bottom of the demonic levels, but it was better than the alternative.

"Mum, is it time for us to go too?" Lottie asked, pulling Cate from her thoughts.

"Yes, if you're ready?" she replied, wanting to check her daughter's wellbeing before doing anything else. Lottie had just witnessed a strange and ominous ritual only minutes after finding out a great deal of information about herself and her family. Yet, she seemed unfazed by it all. Cate read her daughter's mind, and her thoughts were of her new home, the possibilities for her future, and her hopes for what it might be like in Hell, exactly as Cate had desperately hoped they would be. She looked up into her mother's eyes with a knowing smile, aware that she was reading her.

"Yes," Lottie told her decisively, and Cate smiled.

"It'll feel strange at first, as though you can't breathe. The heat and pressure down there are something you'll have to become accustomed to, so don't worry if it feels weird at first. Calm your breathing and stop it. You don't need to breathe there. Does that make sense?" she asked, her thoughts immediately turning to when Lucifer had given her the same speech so many years before. How funny that times had changed so dramatically.

"Urm, I think so. I suppose I'll just have to give it a try," Lottie replied, and took her mother's outstretched hand.

Cate held her tight and pulled her daughter away, teleporting them both downwards towards their true home. When they arrived, Lottie gripped her hand tightly. She managed to stay standing as she slowed her panting breath, caught it, and quickly steadied it. Cate was immensely proud of her, and by the time Dylan and Alma teleported to their side, Lottie stood tall and proud. Cate watched as her youngest child looked out at her new home with an excited flutter in her belly. She couldn't wait to start her new life there, the darkness no longer hiding secrets from her. Lottie gazed up at her mother and absorbed her *expression* as she opened it up to her again.

"Welcome home. I suppose I'd better show you around your kingdom. Oh, and I need to introduce you to your big brother and sister," she told her with a smile, and Lottie grinned back excitedly at her Queen. She held her hand tight again as they headed off towards the dark castle and knew she'd never look back.

***

Warm sunshine streamed in through the open window. The gentle rays hit the man's cheek as he stirred and started to wake. An extra bright ray of light, invisible to the human eye, came shining in through the opening along with the regular dawn light, and it shone brightly onto the man's bare chest. It filled him, bursting through the bloody layers of skin, muscle, and bone, and emanating deep inside. He could feel the light making him stronger and making him more powerful again.

Uriel sat up in the hospital bed, grateful for the slight return of his powers, but most importantly, for his recollection at long last. His memories came back to him like a sharp detonation that'd gone off inside his mind. He groaned, the thoughts of Cate and Lucifer both angering and paining him as they flooded his thoughts.

The angel then sensed a dark change, a shift of power both in this world and in the other realms he and the angelic council had created so very long ago. It was a perverse altering of the very balance of light and dark powers that he could not control, much to his utter distaste.

"Oh Lottie, what has she done," Uriel sighed, whispering sadly as the awareness hit him of his daughter's existence, and the terrible realisation that he didn't have the power to go to Hell and be with her, or bring her back from her mother's evil realm.

He then began to vanish, rising skywards and teleporting home at last, defeated and alone. He would have his revenge, but first, he was determined to do whatever it took to get back the child who had been so cunningly stolen from him.

The end of book one in the Black Rose series.

A Slave to the Darkness

Book #2 in the Black Rose series

By
LM Morgan

2021 Revised Edition

PROLOGUE

Fifty years had passed since Lottie, the child of both light and darkness, had left Earth forever and gone to Hell so that she could be with her long-lost mother, Cate. A mother who had every reason to have been absent from her daughter for so long, and Lottie forgave her for all of it. Cate had come back to her strong, commanding, and free of the ties that once bound her mind, body and soul to her ex-husband, Lucifer. She had overthrown him and taken his place as the ruler of Hell, and finally come to Earth to claim her secret daughter as the all-powerful new Devil.

It was fifty years in which Lottie had also seen her adoptive father Harry adapt to his new life as a demon following his willing transition from his human existence to becoming an immortal, dark being. As a human, Harry had given Cate his heart many years before Lottie was even born, and when she'd called upon him in her hour of need, he had taken on her burdens without any hesitation, fear, doubt, or care for his own safety. Harry had chosen to love his soulmate no matter what fate might befall him because of that, and when the time had come for Lottie to go home with her mother, Harry too had pledged his soul to the Dark Queen. He'd then performed a gory, ancient ritual that'd transformed him into a powerful demon so they could finally be together for all eternity.

Cate's older children, twins Blake and Luna, had welcomed their new family with open arms and open hearts. They each followed their own paths, but they were paths that led to one another's sides, and which made them grow stronger and closer as the years passed them by.

These fifty short years had also given Cate the time to nurture her almighty prowess and embrace her powerful position as the fierce and omnipotent Dark Queen. She knew it was thanks to the warmth and love of her family, and she was now both loved and feared by all who served her. Hell's immortal royal family knew their dark reign would last forever. They were strong and whole at last, and yet the powerful beings remained ever grateful for every gift they'd been given along the hard and grisly road. They grew, they lived, and they loved each other with every ounce of power that they possessed. While their bodies remained unaffected by the passing of time, their minds adapted, each of them growing wiser and more commanding with every year that passed them by. They had all changed and adjusted to the new world around them, but most importantly, they'd stayed together, and knew they always would.

Each member of the Rose family protected their Queen as their first and foremost priority. It was a real danger to grow too comfortable, as there would always be those who lived in the light who would rejoice in her demise if they ever let down those protective walls around her.

Her ex-lover and Lottie's father, an angel named Uriel, wanted nothing more than to lure Cate out of hiding, but she was clever and cunning. She had the entire underworld at her command and constantly strengthened their portals and thresholds to keep herself and her family safe. The bitter, unsatisfied angel watched from his heavenly home and waited. He hoped one day that he might sense his long-lost daughter's presence on Earth again and would try and take her away from her mother at long last if he did. But he was never satisfied in his search for Lottie, and Cate would give her life making sure that he never would be.

CHAPTER ONE

Matilda Mayfair, or Tilly as she was better known, and her two best friends Renee and Gwen, took their seats excitedly a few minutes before the show began, she had never been to the circus before and had only gone along tonight on the assurance from Renee that this was going to be the most spectacular show she would ever see. The infamous 'Diablo Circus' were performing tonight for their second night in Coventry, England and had been a hit across the world, selling out in London, Paris and even as far afield as Tokyo and New York as they had toured over the past few years. The gloomily dressed performers were critically acclaimed and renowned for their skills and death-defying feats that wowed the crowds and kept the audiences coming back night after night.

The main performance hadn't even begun yet and Tilly could already see what Renee had meant. It was fantastic inside the huge tent and the air was thick with excitement and the expectation of what was to come. Some of the circus performers were out amongst the audience, wooing the crowd and going between the tightly packed benches, doing tricks, and showing off for the eager public to small bursts of praise and applause. As Tilly scanned the crowd, a tall juggler caught her attention right away. He was gorgeous, even behind his shadowy makeup and even blacker clothes. He grinned and lapped up the attention from the women before him as he speedily flung their donated bracelets and watches up and down before them as they gasped and giggled excitedly. She guessed he was in his mid-twenties, far too old for Tilly as she was only eighteen years old, but she couldn't help but window-shop for a few moments, watching him intently for a short while before Renee nudged her, breaking her reverie as she asked if Tilly wanted any popcorn.

"Yeah, go on then," she replied, paying, and then thanking the vendor as she passed her a warm box of the sweet, fluffy corn. When she looked back towards the crowd again Tilly jumped, the juggler she had been watching was now standing right in front of her, a cheeky grin on his handsome face as he reached down and stole a handful of corn from her box and then plucked the black hat she had been wearing from the top of her head. It was a warm summer's evening, and she had still been wearing her trilby from when they had been stood in the bright sunshine waiting to be let into the huge tent earlier that evening. She had dressed comfortably for their night out in a floral printed maxi dress and denim jacket, and she couldn't help but feel as though she looked garishly casual before him in his all-black tuxedo. Tilly blushed as he watched her for a moment and ate his stolen popcorn, seemingly intrigued by her for some reason, and her friends giggled as they watched their moment from beside her on the bench. She assumed that the man would start tossing the hat like he had just done with the other peoples' things, but for some reason he didn't. He looked down at her, smiled widely and then popped her hat on his own head before he wandered off back to the centre of the large tent without a word, looking back at her from the stage with a wicked grin as he gathered up his juggling balls and began showing off to the crowd once again.

"Whoa, what was that?" Gwen asked from Renee's other side, bewildered at the gorgeous man's actions but also excited by the attraction they had all sensed pass between them. Tilly just shrugged; unsure herself what he was playing at, but hopeful that she was not imagining things.

"I'm thinking he wants you to go and get it back later," Renee told Tilly, her blue eyes wide as a cheeky grin crossed her tanned face.

"Maybe," Tilly answered her thoughtfully, hoping she might just get the chance to find out whether Renee's theory was correct later.

The show was amazing, each of the various acts and performers having some time in the spotlight to show off their personal talents as well as some groups of them performing together, demonstrating their incredible skills and fearless routines before the gasping, elated crowd. The three girls sat silent and utterly mesmerised by the night's eye-opening entertainment, taking in every fantastic act, and applauding loudly along with the rest of the crowd when the impressive finale signified the end of that night's show.

Once the performers had taken their last bows and left the stage, Tilly and her friends hung around for a little while to try and find the gorgeous juggler who had stolen her hat earlier. He had worn it throughout his entire performance and had even given her a cheeky wink during the show's big finish when he tossed it high up in the air and it had then landed perfectly back on his head.

She had been sure he was interested in seeing her again after their brief encounter earlier, but now she was having absolutely no luck in finding him. She didn't want to come across as some pathetic groupie or stalker but couldn't resist hanging around the entrance to the huge tent for a little while with her friends, trying not to be too obvious about it. After a few more minutes Tilly checked her watch, realising that her curfew was coming up, so she decided to call it a night and started to make her way over to Renee's car, disappointed that she hadn't gotten to meet the handsome juggler properly after all his flirting.

"Hey, aren't you forgetting something?" a voice called from behind the trio of girls after they had taken just a few steps away. They all turned instantly, and Tilly could see the voices' owner clearly as he stood propped against a post just a few metres away from them. It was the juggler. He was even more gorgeous now having changed out of his carnival costume into black jeans and a t-shirt, his long, dark-blonde hair was pulled back into a ponytail and his light blue eyes stared over at the three of them as the girls approached. He had a broad smile and perfect teeth, and he spun her hat on his index finger playfully before throwing it in the air as Tilly neared him. It landed on her head perfectly, and she couldn't help but giggle, mentally kicking herself for being so girly but she was in awe of this gorgeous boy and couldn't understand why he had chosen to flirt with her out of all the women there tonight. She smiled coyly at him, not really knowing what to say.

"I hope you didn't mind me borrowing it for a while?" he then asked, putting out a hand to introduce himself as Tilly reached him. She shook it, swooning slightly as he gave her another dazzling grin. The bright lights of the circus around him illuminating his handsome face and bright blue eyes.

"Tilly," she told him before adding, "and no, I didn't mind at all."

"My name's Brent," he replied, keeping a firm grip of her hand as he took her in, and she smiled up at him shyly. He knew Tilly must only be young, but there was something about this girl that he had liked from the moment he had caught her watching him from the audience. Her dark-blonde hair and blue eyes matched his own, but her features were innocent and beautiful, whereas he had always looked older than he was, having been hardened and weathered by his years of hard work at the hands of his father and circus master, Lucas McCulloch.

Brent was usually very emotionally closed-off with the women he would normally flirt with and, more often than not, go on to take home with him after the shows. He had always made a habit of having one-night-stands and then kicking the women out the next morning full of empty promises and fake excuses, telling himself he was too busy for a real relationship. Tonight, though, it was somehow different. For some reason, he looked at Tilly differently. He wasn't interested in the short-term, and even after such a small amount of time, he knew he wanted to get to know this girl.

Renee and Gwen's mouths dropped open in shock as they watched the pair of them in absolute amazement; their spark was undeniable.

"It's been lovely to meet you, but I'm afraid I have to go home now, Brent. It's almost past my curfew," Tilly told him, blushing slightly, and looking down at her hands, ashamed of her childish restrictions.

"It's okay," he said, smiling warmly at her. "We are here for two more nights. How do you fancy coming back tomorrow about noon and you can help me practice? You can bring your friends, too," he added, looking over to the two girls behind her and Tilly looked back up into his bright eyes and smiled.

"Yes, yes, yes!" cried Renee in response before Tilly could even say another word. "We'll be here."

"Good, see you then," Brent replied, grabbing Tilly's hand and then planting a kiss on the back of it before letting her walk away with her friends.

The girls swooned and giggled quietly with each other as they made their way over to the car once again. When they were inside, they all screamed with excitement. Even Tilly couldn't control herself and she jumped up and down in her seat as she let the wonderful, warm feelings wash over her following her tiny bit of time with the incredible man who got her all hot and bothered despite her having only known him for a few minutes.

CHAPTER TWO

The next day Tilly, Renee and Gwen arrived outside the huge circus tent just before noon, as per Brent's instructions from the night before. It was strange seeing the place as it was now, so empty and quiet, after seeing the busy and hectic crowds there the night before, and it felt odd to the girls as they approached. Brent stood at the entrance waiting for them, dressed in a dark t-shirt and cropped trousers, and he beckoned the girls inside after they climbed out of Renee's car and wandered over towards the gigantic tent.

"Hi," he said, giving Tilly a smile and taking her hand in his before leading her into the huge arena.

"Hi," was all she could reply, feeling shy and quiet thanks to this gorgeous boy's affectionate gaze as it swept over her in the bright sunshine. She had opted for black shorts and a red strapless bandeau top, suffering with both the heat from the summer sunshine and from her excited blush at seeing Brent again, so she had dressed for comfort as well as coolness, and had pulled her dark-blonde hair up into a high ponytail, not able to bear the feel of it against her sweat-dusted skin. Brent led the way, laughing when the girls gasped in awe as they took in the men and women that were practising their talents inside, each of them smiling welcomingly at the group as they passed by. Two more young men came over and joined them once they were inside, and Brent quickly made the introductions. They were his two younger brothers, David, and Jackson, who both eagerly shook hands with the girls with broad and warm smiles on their faces. Renee swooned and soon wandered off with the eldest of Brent's two brothers, David, while Gwen took Jackson's hand and followed him over to the fire-breathing station where he had been practising just a few minutes earlier.

Tilly followed Brent to the main stage where she then met his father, Lucas, whom she guessed must be around forty-five years old. He too had dark-blonde hair and deep blue eyes, just like Brent and his brothers, and he had a once thick Scottish accent that was now dulled down thanks to having moved around for so long but was still very clearly recognisable as he chatted to her for a few minutes.

"Welcome to our humble little enterprise," Lucas said modestly, taking in the two of them with a satisfied grin as he wrapped his hands in bandages and powdered them with chalk in preparation for his acrobatic practice session.

"Thanks for having me, it's amazing to be allowed to come and see behind the scenes," she replied, genuinely excited to be there.

"No problem at all, but I do hope you're prepared to give Brent a good workout for me?" he asked, a sly smile curling at his lips, and Tilly just giggled in response while Brent rolled his eyes and laughed to himself. "Well, one piece of advice either way, don't watch the batons when he gets going, you'll get dizzy, keep your eyes locked on his and you'll be fine."

"I'll bear that in mind, thanks," she replied.

"Well, I had better get practising too, it was lovely to meet you Tilly," he said, smiling down at her warmly. She had the sense that Lucas was a genuine gentleman, leading her to hope that Brent, too, had inherited the same qualities. She had never felt so excited and optimistic about a boy before and wanted to believe in the way he and everyone else at the circus was making her feel safe, happy, welcome, and, in Brent's case, horny as hell.

"It was lovely to meet you too, Lucas," she replied politely, watching him as he climbed the steps to the trapeze until Brent's rough hand in hers broke her gaze and she followed his lead towards a small stage. The pair of them then spent the next couple of hours messing around with the juggling balls, batons, and bowling pins she had seen him use the night before. His skill and speed were truly amazing, and she watched in awe as he spun them around before her and urged Tilly to throw more into the fray. She followed Lucas's advice and kept her eyes on Brent's as he practised. His moves really were mesmerising yet dizzying. Staring into his gorgeous blue eyes for so long soon made Tilly feel a little overwhelmed by her own giddiness though, becoming genuinely hot and bothered as he stared back into her blue eyes intensely with a gorgeous, knowing grin curling at his lips. By the time Brent finally let the batons crash to the floor, he was panting and dusted with a light layer of sweat, so welcomed Tilly's suggestion to take a break, needing both a drink and a moment away from her bewitching gaze too. They talked for a while as they sat with a can of cola on one of the now empty audience benches, Tilly telling him all about her parents' farm where they lived in the rural quietness of the Warwickshire countryside, yet she enjoyed the liveliness and opportunities that having the cities close by gave her. She loved to cook. Out of her school time she baked cakes and tarts to sell in the family's farm shop that her mother ran, and where she worked on weekends and the odd afternoon if it was busy. As she told him about herself Tilly couldn't help but feel as though her quiet, simple life seemed so small in comparison to Brent's, she was envious of him travelling the world and couldn't imagine that he thought her little existence on the farm was very interesting, and yet he listened intently as she spoke, smiling and asking her more about herself as she went, seeming genuinely interested in her. Tilly carried on, chatting away animatedly about her first memories of the farm and she told him the story of how she had to help deliver a foal at the age of six with her father, a horse that she had named Raven as he was jet-black, and who was now hers thanks to the kind nature of her father, Robert.

"And what about you? What do you do for fun?" she eventually asked him, aware that she had been talking away for a while, and Brent actually had to think for a minute before answering her.

"Well, aside from the obvious," he said, indicating the circus. "I suppose I don't really get much downtime, but when I do, I like to read. Boring I know, but when you travel around as much as I do there's not much you can take with you as you go, but a good book can always fit in your backpack, and a good imagination will take you anywhere, even small farms in the English countryside," he told her with a sheepish grin, surprised at his own honesty. He had never told anyone that before. Tilly smiled up at him with an understanding look, and he knew right away that he was smitten with this girl. He wouldn't push her, knowing she was so young, but he was sure about one thing, this girl was going to leave her mark on him, but he didn't care, he wanted her, and he had no doubt that she wanted him too. Tilly was worth risking everything for, and for the first time in his shallow life, Brent was finally ready to sacrifice the life he once had in preference of a place at her side.

CHAPTER THREE

Tilly and her friends stayed with Brent and his brothers at the circus site all afternoon, and she felt comfortable and happy there the entire time, her connection with the gorgeous juggler both thrilling and terrifying her as she fell more and more under his sensuous spell.

She and Gwen sat together on one of the benches a few hours later, squealing excitedly as they watched Brent throwing Jackson around effortlessly as they practised their new routine that combined a mixture of acrobatics and thrilling displays of their strengths and perfectly honed skills. The two boys just laughed together as the girls shrieked, using their reaction as an indication that the new routine was going to be a hit.

By the time the large group of performers had eaten some delicious home-cooked chilli, a huge bowl of which was given to each of the girls without them even having to ask, it was nearly time for the preparations to begin for that night's show. Tilly half expected them to ask the girls to leave, but Lucas wouldn't hear of it. He and his wife Lily treated them like friends already and quickly enlisted Renee and Gwen to help in the ticket booths for them while Tilly handed out flyers by the doorway. Lily, the beautiful, warm and young looking woman Tilly had liked instantly, had promised free entrance to the three girls as a small thank you for their help, much to their instant happiness.

"Yes, of course!" Renee cried, eager to stay just as much as Tilly was. She and David had shared a kiss behind the ticket booth already that afternoon, and she wanted to stick around in the hope that she might get more from the handsome middle brother. Renee, with her long-blonde hair and tanned, pretty face, was the more promiscuous of their small group of friends, and she knew how to wrap any man she wanted around her little finger. David was nineteen years old, just a year older than she was, so it seemed like a good match, as there was much less of an age gap than there was between Tilly and Brent. She felt like he was so much older than she was, despite it only actually being a few years' difference, and Brent seemed to feel the same way. He was being on his best behaviour with her, although she knew he must have women throwing themselves at him every night and was no stranger to the games men and women would play while vying for each other's attention. Tilly could already sense that he was no novice in the bedroom, as well as him clearly knowing how to turn on the charm, but for some reason he wasn't doing that with her, or at least it felt that way. He kissed her cheek and turned to leave, needing to go and change his clothes and apply his dark makeup before the crowds arrived, but then turned back, staring down at Tilly for a moment. Her heart pounded in her ears as he reached down and grabbed her chin before planting a deep, urgent kiss on her lips. As he pulled away, she was sure she heard an almost silent gasp come from his parted lips, but then he let her go and walked away, a cheeky, gorgeous smile on his face as he backed away into the shadows.

The late summer evening settled over the site as Tilly, Renee and Gwen watched from beside the main stage as Brent and his extended family all performed their well-rehearsed acts with ease and skill again, the crowds roaring and calling for more as they took their bows, so Jackson and David performed one last fire-breathing routine, taking everyone's breath away once again before the audience finally dispersed and the tent became quiet once more. Tilly then wandered off in search of Brent after the last of the cars had left the parking area and she helped tidy up some of the scattered leaflets from earlier on her way, bumping into Lily as she made her way through the empty lot. The woman was not tall but was somehow commanding. Powerful in her own way. Tilly had learned that she was not Brent's mother, but his stepmother, but that he and his brothers loved her like they were her own, and she felt the same way about them. They chatted for a couple of minutes before Lily directed her towards Brent's mobile home with a warm yet sly grin on her face as she sauntered off in search of her husband.

Tilly thanked her and then went inside, feeling awkward despite Lily's encouragement, and found herself face to face with a half-naked, surprised yet relaxed Brent, still wet from his shower with a towel wrapped around his waist. He dripped water onto the hard floor as he dried his hair with a second towel.

"Hey," he said, calm and steady while Tilly blushed and turned away.

"Oh my god, I'm so sorry! Lily said you would be in here and I just," she tailed off, embarrassed and shy. She had never done anything more than kiss a boy before and she didn't know where to even begin processing the half-naked image of him that was now well and truly engrained in her skull, an image that made her body tingle at the memory and she desperately wanted to see more.

Brent reached out and gently grabbed her arm, pulling her around to face him again despite him still being just barely covered by the towel.

"It's okay, really," he said, laughing at her coyness. He was obviously much more used to women seeing him naked than Tilly was to seeing muscular, gorgeous men dripping wet before her. "I know you're, how should I say this? *Inexperienced* Tilly, but you don't need to be ashamed. I won't ever expect you to do anything you don't want to do, okay?" he added, looking her in the eye with a genuine smile.

"Okay," she managed to reply, and Tilly could feel herself relaxing slightly already.

"Good," he said with a cheeky grin, before, without another word, he leaned forward and planted a deep kiss on her lips.

Tilly relished in his soft yet strong touch and didn't hold back. She let her hands go up to his wet hair and then she ran them through his shoulder-length locks as she kissed him back passionately. He pulled her up into his strong arms and then sat down on the small sofa that was built into one of the walls of his small motor home, their mouths never leaving each other's. She straddled him on the chair and could feel the hardness of his thick cock pushing up from underneath the towel. Tilly couldn't help herself and in a moment of hormone-fuelled confidence, she reached down and grabbed it, pushing the towel aside and gripping his length tightly with her small hands. Brent gasped but didn't stop her as she began pulling up and down, gently at first and then harder and faster, as they continued to kiss each other intensely. He came quickly, the hot, thick wetness bursting out onto the damp towel as she finished her pulls and finally let go. Tilly giggled as she planted one more kiss on his lips and then climbed off his lap, and then Brent just smiled over at her as he stood completely naked before her, wiping himself and then bunching up the dirty towel before throwing it into his hamper. Tilly blushed again as she found her eyes uncontrollably drawn to his glorious body, and Brent lapped up her attention for a moment before he padded over to his small chest of drawers and slipped on some black tracksuit trousers. He then returned to the sofa and grabbed her again for more kisses, not taking his lips off hers until it was eventually time for Tilly to go home, but not making any more advances, he didn't want to move too quickly despite him being more than ready for it.

CHAPTER FOUR

The girls were invited to spend the next day with Brent and his brothers again too, and they couldn't wait to get back to the site, Renee having had sex with David the night before and Gwen having shared a kiss with the younger brother, Jackson, so they too were completely besotted with the three handsome McCulloch brothers.

Tilly hadn't been able to sleep once she had gone home the night before. She was so horny following her wonderful day with Brent and she had needed to pleasure herself before her body would calm down and eventually let her drift off to sleep. Her hands had travelled down inside her panties as she thought about him and his deep kisses. She imagined his long, thick cock inside her as Tilly stroked her tender clitoris and slipped her fingers into her wet cleft, moving her hips up and down eagerly while imagining his mouth, those hands, and that glorious body on hers. It wasn't long until she reached her climax, the aftershocks reverberating throughout her entire body for a few minutes, and she had then drifted off to a relaxed sleep at last.

The three of them all lied to their parents the next morning, saying that they were sleeping over at one another's houses for them to all stay the entire night on the campsite for the circus's final show in their area. Tilly knew she was old enough to just tell her parents the truth about staying overnight with her new crush, but she had always lived a sheltered life; her parents were quite strict, and she couldn't bear the conversation that she knew they would put her through if she told them she was planning on staying out all night with a boy.

This day bought with it a bittersweet anticipation for them both. She already hated the thought of Brent leaving, and she was even having wild ideas of running away with the circus to be with him but knew that she would never actually have the guts to do anything quite so crazy. She hoped they would try and stay in contact once the circus moved on, but for now, the last few days had been the most wonderful of her life, and Tilly wanted to enjoy her last bit of time with her gorgeous juggler without worrying about the future.

Brent welcomed her with a deep, wanting kiss the instant she climbed out of the car and the pair quickly went off to his motor home to be alone, while the other girls did the same with their suitors. Lucas had given Brent some time to relax rather than practice hard again that afternoon, and the pair loved having some time to themselves properly. They kissed and chatted quietly for a while, opening up more and more as they gazed into each other's eyes while perched on his motorhome's sofa.

"I've never had to worry about leaving anywhere before, Tilly," Brent told her honestly as he made her a cup of tea. "But this time, I don't want to go. I want to stay here, I want to stay with you," he said, blushing slightly himself as he let his feelings show for the first time ever. Tilly smiled, basking in his attention and loving his sudden coyness.

"Me too, but you have to go, Brent. This is your life, and I can't take you away from it. I've got nothing to offer you here," she said, standing and accepting the tea he had made but then looking down into the mug forlornly as she said the words. He reached across the small counter and grabbed her chin, pulling her gaze up to meet his.

"You have everything to offer me Tilly, don't you understand, that's the problem?" he asked, leaning closer and then kissing her gently. She didn't really understand in all honesty, and she could not let herself hope he was feeling the same way about her as she was with him. She smiled up at Brent and kissed him back, allowing his loving words to wash over her. Tilly then felt the air between them change and knew that he had felt it, too. He stared at her thoughtfully for a moment over his strong tea. His father had given him some advice that morning, urging him to follow his gut with Tilly and take the next step but not lead her on, and he knew Lucas was right. Brent wanted her with every fibre of his being but couldn't bear the thought of hurting Tilly the way he was so accustomed to do so with other women. He vowed to himself that he would take care of this sweet, gorgeous girl; he was desperate not to hurt her.

There were only a few moments of tense silence before the tea was discarded and the pair resumed their position from the previous night on the sofa, Brent having pulled Tilly onto his lap while they kissed one another feverishly. She wanted him to be her first, but was scared and unsure of herself, still feeling self-conscious despite her conviction. He sensed it, and expertly guided her, knowing she could do with a helping hand, someone to take the lead. He didn't say a word and started by first taking off her white t-shirt and bra. He then took the time to kiss her small breasts, sucking on each nipple gently as she groaned with pleasure atop him. Brent then lifted her up in his strong arms and moved Tilly over to his double bed, laying her down on the dark sheets before pulling off her denim skirt and knickers in one quick move. She blushed as he swept his smouldering eyes over her naked body. She was a curvy girl, neither short nor tall, but had always been self-conscious about her wide hips and small breasts that she prayed would grow some more but didn't hold out too much hope. Despite her insecurities, she couldn't help but smile up at him when she saw his hard erection that was already threatening to burst out of his jeans.

"It's only fair," he said with a cheeky grin, leaning down on top of Tilly to kiss her again, his clothes staying on for now. "Seeing as you got to see me completely naked last night," he added, trailing soft kisses down her chest to kiss her nipples again. She groaned her affirmations as he kept going, reaching her navel, and then expertly sinking his mouth into her wet nether lips, enveloping her clitoris quickly and sucking on it as she writhed beneath him. Tilly arched her back, forgetting all about her shyness, as she felt ready and willing for him to take her further. Brent pushed open her thighs with his hands and then plunged two fingers inside her wetness, sensing her readiness for him.

She gasped and moaned loudly again, twitching slightly as she soon came for him, her body hot and more than ready for what she hoped would come next. Brent then rose from between her thighs and pulled off his black t-shirt, followed quickly by his jeans and boxers. Tilly watched him with a smile, still buzzing from her orgasm and wanting him so much. She nodded, giving him that silent confirmation he craved, and then he grabbed a condom from a drawer to the side of the bed.

Once sheathed, he climbed on top of Tilly and pulled her hips up to greet his, sliding himself inside of her with ease and opening up her tender muscles as he pushed deeper inside of her gloriously inviting cleft. The pain flared deep within her for a moment, but she urged him to continue, relishing in his desire for her and wanting him to reach his climax, needing him to enjoy his own release too. They thrust together wonderfully until Brent reached his own glorious end, gasping as he came and all the while kissing her passionately.

Tilly lay in his arms afterwards, content and happy as she revelled in the afterglow of her first time. It was perfect, Brent was perfect, and although she was feeling too sore to do anything more, Tilly was glad she had decided that today was the day, and she was looking forward to doing more with Brent later that night after the show.

CHAPTER FIVE

The girls watched their lovers perform again later that evening for the third night in a row, relishing in the tantalising and thrilling feats of the show with even broader smiles after their wonderful second full day spent at the circus. Tilly watched Brent with an excited glint in her eye, catching his deep blue eyes on her many times over the evening and laughing to herself as the other women in the crowd, both young and old, fawned over him and tried to get his attention. Tonight, though, he was not interested in them. His attention reserved for her alone. The three friends loved every minute of their last show, their shrieks and applause just as loud and genuine as they had been on the first night. Renee and Gwen laughed raucously along with the crowd as David performed his hilarious one-man clown act before the big finale, and Tilly slipped away, heading outside the great big tent as the encore began inside with a sly grin on her face.

Brent almost ran out of the tent once he had finished his part of the finale and had ducked inside his motor home before the show was even completely over. He was hoping to find Tilly waiting for him inside, having noticed her sneak away, but was even more pleasantly surprised when he found her naked and soaking wet from having just helped herself to a hot shower in his motor home. She smiled at his shocked and impressed expression, towel drying her hair for a moment before rubbing the soft cotton down her torso as Brent watched her hungrily. She then wrapped the damp cloth around herself, covering her body teasingly before folding it under her armpit, securing it with a simple knot.

"Oh no you don't," he told her with a cheeky grin, dropping to his knees in front of Tilly and then pulling on the edge of the towel, which quickly dropped to the floor, exposing her naked body once more. Brent grabbed her hips and pulled Tilly towards his ready mouth, taking her throbbing nub between his lips before he then began sucking gently on it. Tilly reached down and ran her hands through his long hair, gripping onto Brent tightly as he pursued her climax effortlessly and with an expert touch.

She came quickly, the glorious pulses resonating around her body as she stood woozily before her lover. Brent looked up, watching as she relished in the aftermath of her climax, his face still covered in his black and white makeup, some of which he had inadvertently shared with her freshly washed nether lips.

Tilly couldn't help but giggle as she took in the dark and sexy man that still kneeled before her, and Brent shrugged his shoulders and laughed, too. He then stood up, pulling off his own clothes eagerly as she watched him, biting her lip in anticipation when his hard length sprung loose from its restraints. Brent pulled her back into the small bathroom, taking her hand and leading her back under the hot shower as he washed off the makeup, sweat and dirt from himself before gently rubbing the smeared, now greying face paint from her thighs and mound with a soap covered hand. Tilly groaned as he touched her sensitive nerve endings again, and then pushed herself up against Brent's muscular body under the hot water, pressing him into the tile covered wall behind. They kissed passionately and eagerly, their want and need for one another so very clear and unrestrained. His hard length stroked against the tender inner folds between Tilly's thighs as she rocked back and forth against him for a while longer, neither one ready to release their grip on each other until they were forced out of the shower by the quickly subsiding warm water thanks to the rapidly emptying hot water tank of the motorhome. The pair then grabbed two fresh towels and wrapped them around their trembling bodies as they dried themselves, but then Tilly quickly pushed Brent against the edge of the sofa. She knelt before him and he smiled down at her, gasping as she leaned forward and sucked the tip of his thick shaft before he could even finish drying it from his shower, slowly gliding up and down as she took more and more of him in her eager mouth. Brent muttered his affirmations and groaned as she went, urging her onwards until he eventually came into her mouth. She spat out the salty wetness, unable to swallow it down for him, but he didn't mind, laughing to himself as she tried to hide the deposit into one of the nearby towels.

It was not long until Brent was ready for her again, and he was pleasantly surprised to find her ready for him, too. He lifted Tilly onto the bed, kissing and sheathing himself again in preparation for the rest of their night together. She lifted her hips and wrapped her thighs around him tightly, urging his thick length inside her wet cleft, and this time she was able to enjoy his hard and heavy thrusts without the pains she had experienced earlier, thanks to her inexperienced inner muscles. She stared up into his deep blue eyes as he made love to her, relishing in his wonderful closeness and soft touch that drove her crazy.

Tilly slept in Brent's arms that night following a final and gloriously exhausting orgasm thanks to his gentle yet skilled body. Brent wrapped his arms around her, thinking that today was a day of many firsts. Tilly was lightly dozing as she lay with her head on his chest, listening to the thumping of his heart and the rhythmic sound of his breathing, her body still buzzing and her mind unwilling to switch off. She knew she would miss him so much after the circus moved on again. Even after just a few days together, their connection was so strong and she would feel very alone in bed without Brent there to share it with her now.

CHAPTER SIX

Tilly jolted awake in the early hours of the next morning, having heard a crash from somewhere in the camp, and then what sounded like Renee giggling from somewhere not too far away. She quickly assumed that David and her loose friend must be up to some sort of mischief somewhere, and she quickly decided that she was not interested in leaving Brent's warm embrace in order to check it out. Tilly soon found that she couldn't seem to fall back to sleep after being awoken so close to morning though, and lay back down, snuggling into her lover's arms in an attempt to shut out the morning light, but it was no use. A quick glance at the clock on the bedside table told her it was now five o'clock in the morning, but her body was already trying to persuade her it was breakfast time. Tilly's stomach rumbled loudly, and she eventually gave in, climbing up out of Brent's arms and sliding on her skirt and blouse from the night before. And then she went looking in the small kitchenette for any sign of substantial food. There was nothing in the fridge but cola cans and beer bottles, while the cupboards held only dry pasta and stale cereal. Tilly decided to head out of Brent's mobile home for a quick dash to Renee's car, grabbing the car keys from her bag as she went. She knew there were some cereal bars in the back seat she had made and left there the day before, and she was ready to eat at least two or three thanks to her rumbling stomach.

Thanks to the summer sunrise, it was already very light outside as Tilly made her way over to the small blue car and grabbed the bars from her backpack. She unwrapped one and took a big bite, devouring it in seconds before putting another in her pocket and then locking the car door behind her, quickly heading back towards Brent's warm bed. She then heard another giggle as she neared the caravans again, her mouth full of chocolaty muesli, and Tilly looked over in the direction of the sound, catching the sight of Lily as she disappeared behind the huge main tent's entryway. She turned to follow her, intrigued as to what she might be up to but quickly decided against it, knowing that nothing here was any of her business and not wanting to taint her wonderful experiences from the last few days by potentially finding Brent's stepmother up to mischief or possibly even worse so instead she took another step in the direction of her lover's warm beacon.

Curiosity soon got the better of her though when a second giggle broke the silence, followed quickly by another crash and the sound of a man laughing, too. Tilly tiptoed forward, swallowing down the last of the bar before heading silently towards the circus entrance in search of an explanation of the early morning wakeup call.

She reached the big tent and looked around to check that no one was watching her before stepping inside the doorway, the dim light obscuring her vision for a moment until her eyes became accustomed to the darkness. She could see two figures on the stage after a couple of seconds and could tell that it was Lily and a man, and that she was bouncing up and down quickly on top of his hard cock as he lay beneath her, her mouth on the man's neck. Thankfully, Tilly soon realised that the man Lily was riding happened to be her husband Lucas, so she made to go, embarrassed to have caught them in the throes of passion, but she then stopped dead when Lily sat up and she saw her face properly in the dim light. Her once soft, pale features were now dark and her eyes seemed almost black as she looked down at Lucas from atop his lap, continuing to thrust up and down on him eagerly. His hands were bound above his head with rope that was tied to one of the metal joints and Tilly could see blood dripping down Lily's chin, as though she had been drinking it from him. She then noticed a small cut on Lucas's collar that told her that her suspicions were right.

She turned and crept away, feeling sure that she hadn't been spotted, but then as she rounded the doorway, Lily was somehow stood directly in front of her. Tilly looked back over her shoulder for a second and saw Lucas still lying on the stage, his naked body and hard erection left exactly in the same place and position as they had been just moments before, but his wife was now inexplicably over by Tilly in the doorway, stark naked and blocking her exit with a dark and menacing look on her pale face.

She was back to looking like the same woman Tilly had first met just a couple of days before, apart from the blood that still dripped down her chin, and she eyed the young girl for a moment as though unsure how best to proceed. Lily then stepped forward, closing the gap between them, and pinning her to the heavy wooden beam behind, taking in the sight of the scared girl before her with a satisfied smirk. She then leaned closer and sniffed Tilly, smiling as she pulled up and peered into her blue eyes knowingly.

"You smell like sex, my dear. Tell me, did my stepson suitably sort out your little virginity problem?" she asked her with a wicked grin.

Tilly couldn't answer. She was utterly disgusted and shocked by the woman's strangeness and filthy words. Lily continued to stare deep into her eyes as though waiting for a response, but then reached down and grabbed her right wrist, pulling it up and twisting it slightly so that she could see the inside of Tilly's forearm.

"May I?" she then asked, and Tilly nodded, unsure what she was agreeing to as Lily then delicately traced an inverted cross in the soft flesh there with the tip of her index finger, which burned hot on Tilly's skin and flared red before somehow sinking away as though it was never there.

With a devilish smile, Lily then raised the same finger up to her lips and bit down on it, drawing a tiny drop of blood to the surface, which she then deposited into Tilly's mouth without a word. She could not fight her. Tilly was completely mesmerised by the woman and controlled by Lily within seconds of the blood touching her lips. As the dark drop seeped down her throat, the memory of what Tilly had just seen and experienced magically drifted away, and she then wandered back to Brent's motor-home having completely forgotten the last few minutes of her strange morning, believing that she had just wandered back from Renee's car. Tired and dazed, Tilly climbed back into bed with her lover and fell into a deep sleep.

CHAPTER SEVEN

A year had passed by since Tilly had last seen Brent, and he had been on the road with the circus ever since those first few glorious days they had spent together had come to an end. The two lovers had stayed in touch, talking almost every day on the phone and via web chats on Tilly's laptop, and she would send Brent books to read in his downtime while he sent her strange gifts and foods from around the world with postcards from all along the whistle-stop tour Lucas had planned for the thriving performers.

The pair of them had agreed not to be exclusive to one another, neither one wanting to tie the other into a long-distance relationship. But still, neither of them had been seeing anyone else in the time since they had first met. Tilly had not met a man since Brent that had made her feel the way he did, and he too had stopped his womanising ways in preference to holding out until he could be with Tilly again, a fact that both surprised and brought happiness to the usually so casual lover.

During the past year, Tilly had enrolled at a local college during Brent's absence, choosing to follow her dreams of being a chef rather than work full-time on the farm once her mandatory schooling was over, and she was enjoying every minute of it. Renee and Gwen were both studying different courses to Tilly at the college, but they all still saw each other every day and would go out drinking together in the bars and nightclubs in the city most weekends and during their end of term holidays.

When the circus finally finished their eastern European leg of the tour and came back to England again, Tilly couldn't wait for them to be closer and quickly set about arranging a road trip with Renee to see Brent and the others while she had a few days off from her studies before the summer break. She couldn't wait to see him, and the two young women chatted excitedly as they drove down the motorway, off to spend a few days with him and the others in London while the circus performed at a huge indoor arena there, a very welcome upgrade from the huge tent.

The show had continued to be a huge success since they had last seen it, and Brent promised the girls VIP access into the arena. They felt like celebrities as they approached the security guarded doors, walking past hordes of queuing young girls and poster bearing fans, all of whom hoping for autographs and to have their picture taken with the performers. She and Renee gave their names to the bouncers and, after receiving their VIP, all-access passes, were shown straight over to the backstage area by the darkly dressed guard.

Brent ran over as soon as he saw them walk in and he scooped Tilly up in his arms, embracing her tightly as they greeted one another. Neither of them could hold back and they kissed each other deeply, their want and passion for one another obvious to all that was around them.

"Brent," his father and boss, Lucas, called over to him from the stage area after watching the besotted couple be re-united at long last, beckoning with his hand for his son to go and see him. "You're excused for today. Take the night off, son," he told him with a wide smile and a slap on his back. He nodded to Tilly and waved, giving her a welcoming smile. She couldn't help but grin back at him over Jackson's shoulder as he, too, scooped her off her feet and into a huge hug in welcome.

"Thanks Dad," Brent replied, grateful for the time to be with the woman he had missed so very much, and he made no effort to hide his affections for her now.

Renee and David hadn't bothered to stay in touch with each other during the circus' touring time, each of them having been perfectly happy with their short and sweet love affair the summer before, but they too snuck away after the show that night, leaving Tilly's conscience clear when she and Brent checked into a nearby hotel and holed up there for the next twenty-four hours straight, surviving on room service and the contents of the mini bar between their passionate love-making sessions.

The next few days passed by in a blur, and all far too quickly before the team had to pack up and move on to their next venue in Bournemouth on the south coast of England. Tilly hugged Brent goodbye, hating to have to let him go again, but was glad that they were staying in England for a while now so around college and work they would be able to see each other as much as they possibly could.

Renee drove the two of them home after the goodbyes were finally over, regaling Tilly with stories of hers and David's sexual exploits from the last few days and demanding to know how hers and Brent's passionate reunion had gone. Tilly just laughed but retorted that her lips were firmly sealed and for Renee to keep her nose out. She couldn't help but give her nosy friend a sly grin, though, letting her know just how wonderful it had been being back in his arms after such a long time apart.

Tilly then travelled back and forth between various venues for the first few weeks of the circus' tour, but soon ran out of time and money once they had moved on to perform in cities that were further away than she could travel to using the trains and buses so easily. She hated reverting back to their old, long-distance style relationship, each of them having known for sure now that they were well and truly an item, despite their previous resistance.

A couple of months later, a quiet knock at the door of her converted barn made Tilly jump as she relaxed on her sofa with a book. She had recently turned the farm's guesthouse into her own private little home with the permission of her parents, as she was nearly twenty now, and had wanted some space of her own, but she never had visitors, especially ones that knocked; Renee and Gwen would always just wander in unannounced when either of them stopped by. She rounded the corner of the living room and pulled open the frosted glass door to find Brent stood in the doorway, a huge smile on his face and a dozen dark red roses in his hand. She almost jumped for joy at the sight of him, but managed to stop herself, keeping her cool, and she opted instead for a passionate kiss to welcome him to her home.

"What are you doing here?" she asked excitedly, ushering him inside. He held up his right wrist, which was bandaged and in a splint.

"Accidents in the workplace," he said with a smile, but winced slightly when he let it fall back down to his side. "It was David's fault, he fell on me while we were trying to put together a new number, which obviously is not gonna work anyway, and I've ended up out of the show for a week or so while I rest my sprained wrist," he told her, his smile telling her he was not all too upset by David's foolishness. "And, well, I figured, where better to come and rest, than here with you, if you don't mind, that is?" He then asked, hoping she wasn't going to turn him down.

"Hmmm, now let me think," Tilly replied, tapping her chin with her index finger and trying to fool him into believing that she might not be up for it, but failing miserably. "Okay, I suppose so," she then added, and Brent smiled, scooping her into his arms for another deep kiss despite his sore wrist. Inside the doorway, they finally released one another, and Tilly took the flowers off to the kitchen to find a vase while he put down his backpack and looked around. This tiny home had her touch all over it and Brent knew Tilly must have decorated it all herself. The living room was only just about big enough for a television unit topped with a large flat-screen and one small sofa, but the black and white damask covered walls were adorned with different sized black shelves that showed off her ornaments and photographs of her friends and family. He even saw one of her and Brent backstage at one of the London shows, each of them smiling and staring in each other's eyes, so obviously in love, even if they hadn't known it themselves back then.

CHAPTER EIGHT

Tilly and Brent's week alone together was wonderful. The besotted pair made love for hours every night, talked until the small hours of the morning, and went out on dates for meals at Tilly's favourite restaurants, to watch movies at the local cinema, or they went out in the town for drinks with Tilly's friends, Brent wowing them all as he showed off some of his circus skills, being careful not to put any stress on his bad wrist. He even had time to get to know Tilly's parents while he was there and the pair of them really responded to him, liking him instantly and quickly accepting Brent as being a big part of their daughter's life. She had spoken with her mum, Bianca, about him many times, but she could now finally see what all the fuss was about and could not deny having seen their strong connection for herself during his visit.

When his wrist was healed, Brent stayed one more day, not ready to leave her just yet. The next morning Tilly was sad to say goodbye to him, but she knew they would see each other again in a couple of months when the circus came back to Coventry, so she didn't mind as much this time around. She and Brent kissed each other deeply on the train station platform, and each of them finally said, "I love you," for the first time to one another before he boarded his train to Glasgow to meet up with his family there before the circus moved on to an arena in Edinburgh.

When she got home, Tilly sat staring sullenly at her photographs from the last few days, missing Brent terribly, and then her mobile phone rang in her handbag. She reached for it and answered just in time before the voicemail kicked in.

"Hello?" Tilly said to the unknown caller as she lifted the receiver to her ear.

"Hi Tilly, it's Lily here, Brent's stepmother," a soft voice on the other end replied.

"Oh, yes, hello Lily, how are you? Brent's on his way up to meet you guys now, if that's what you were wondering?" she asked, unsure why Lily had rung her out of the blue.

"Thanks, that's good to know, but no, that's not why I called. We are having a ceremony in Edinburgh on Halloween night to celebrate mine and Lucas's wedding anniversary, and I was just calling to ask if you would like to come up and join us, as a special surprise for Brent?" Lily asked her, and Tilly smiled, her blue eyes lighting up at the prospect of seeing Brent again so soon.

"What a lovely idea, thanks Lily. Yes, I'll be there," she answered, pleased that Brent's parents considered her important enough to invite her along to such a big family event.

"Great, I'll send you your tickets and all the hotel information, etcetera, via email now, and don't forget, not a word to Brent about this, okay? I want it to be a surprise," she added excitedly.

"Sure, my lips are sealed. Thanks Lily, see you in a few days."

They hung up the phone and within seconds an email arrived confirming her train timings and telling her that a car would be waiting for her at the train station in Edinburgh to take her to the ceremony's venue, which was also their hotel.

"Wow, she works fast," Tilly said to herself, printing off the information before heading over to her parents' house to tell them the exciting news.

Two days later Tilly boarded her train and travelled first-class to Edinburgh. It was very comfortable in the spacious car, and she loved the feeling of travelling in style. She had picked a stunning red dress to wear for the occasion, assuming that there would be a party or something following the ceremony, but she hadn't been given any other details by Lily so had taken a suitcase with plenty of options along in case she changed her mind on the red one. A few hours later, she arrived at the station and found a driver in a black, crisp suit waiting for her, her name printed on a card that he held high. Tilly blushed and followed him out to a posh black sports car that was parked just outside the station. She smiled and relished the admiring looks she received as he held open the door for her and then climbed in the driver's seat, setting off towards Lucas and Lily's ceremony as the sun began to set over the old city. Less than an hour later, they pulled up at a huge dark-bricked building, ancient and ominous, as it dominated the sparse skyline outside the city. There were no signs or directions outside the iron gates or on the huge wooden doors that led inside, but the driver seemed to know where he was going, grabbing her bags and leading Tilly inside. It was a magnificent old castle, probably hundreds of years old, and it was decorated with stunning black and red motifs and drapes, adding to the ancient, dark theme Tilly admired as she stood and took it all in.

"The ceremony is through there," the driver said, pointing to a closed set of doors a few feet away. He checked his watch, and added, "they have just started, but if you go in now, you should be fine. I will take your bags to your room, Master Brent has the key." Tilly nodded to the man, surprised by the way he had called Brent 'master', and she made her way over to the huge wooden doors and hovered outside them for a moment, worrying that she might be going to barge in at exactly the wrong time. She leaned close and listened, and heard lots of muffled voices, which indicated to her that there were no speeches or anything going on inside just yet, so she clicked open the door and quietly snuck into the hall.

She looked around the large room, seeing many people inside, but all of them were dressed in black and it was so dimly lit that she couldn't make out whom any of them were. There were no seats inside, just a large black altar in the centre of the room, in front of which kneeled Lucas. He had his head bowed, with Lily stood over him and despite her petite frame she looked somehow tall and commanding. She was smiling down at her husband as the crowd encircled them, each of them talking quietly while the couple spoke in whispers to one another, ignoring the others nearby. Lily looked beautiful, dressed all in black with her dark-brown hair pinned back from her delicately featured face with hairclips adorned with large black roses. Tilly suddenly felt like she had made a huge mistake. She didn't understand what on Earth was going on, and she didn't like the way this strange ceremony made her feel. It was dark, ominous, and she sensed evil all around her. She turned to leave, but then she saw the pair of wide, blue eyes that were watching her from across the room, just to the side of the altar. The scared gaze was from Brent, his face pale, and his mouth open as he stared at her, his fear obvious on his usually so handsome face. He looked up to Lily, who peered down at her stepson with a wicked grin and eyes that seemed shrouded in black shadows, but Tilly had to assume it was just a trick in the dim light. Lily then looked through the crowd directly at her, a sinister look on her satisfied face as she took her in.

"Come here, dearest Tilly. You're just in time," she called to her, her personal request making the entire group of dark followers turn to look at the new arrival. There must have been twenty or thirty faces now watching her, curious about the new girl yet far from welcoming, seemingly unfriendly in their grim gazes as their many eyes swept over Tilly and her bright dress.

She stepped forward without a word, feeling like she had no choice but to join them beside the altar, taking a wide birth around the dark steps and joining Brent at his side. He peered down at her, anger and fear very clear on his sullen face. The surprise for him, it seemed, had worked exactly as Lily had hoped.

"What are you doing here?" he asked Tilly a few seconds later, his voice an urgent whisper.

"Lily invited me, she paid for me to travel up here and everything, she said it would be a nice surprise for you," Tilly said, looking up at him. She was feeling very afraid now and couldn't understand what was going on. She looked around at the strange gathering, realisation starting to dawn on her. "Are you in some sort of a cult, Brent?" she asked, her voice a whisper now too as she looked again at the other people all around them. David was by the altar with them too, but Jackson was over by the back wall with some of the other younger members of the group, and she didn't know why they stood separately to the rest of the crowd but assumed it might be that they either weren't initiated yet or were too young to participate in whatever ceremony was about to commence.

Brent didn't respond for a moment, looking up at his stepmother questioningly as his father stayed rooted to his spot at the base of the dark altar, his eyes still only either down at the floor or on his wife.

Tilly continued to look around for a few seconds, completely bemused by it all. The other attendees were no longer interested in her, though, and she was glad the spotlight was off her again. They were all gazing up towards the altar once more, watching Lucas with expectant, excited stares. Brent looked down at Tilly, not knowing where to start to explain it all to her, and he took a deep breath.

"It's much, much more than that, Tilly. I didn't want to tell you about it yet, but," he began.

"But I forced his hand," Lily interjected before he could finish, climbing down from the altar and flashing the pair of them a wicked grin, stepping closer so that she was now just inches from Tilly's face. She reached up and brushed a lock of blonde hair out of the human girl's eyes with intrigue and a satisfied look on her face that Tilly could just not understand. Lily then ran an index finger down her cheek, peering into Tilly's eyes as she made contact. The strange woman's touch somehow made the inside of Tilly's right wrist suddenly burn red-hot and she lifted it up, looking at it in confusion as it glowed red and a shape began to form there. Brent gasped beside her, seeing the inverted cross rise from underneath her skin.

"You marked her, Lilith?" he asked his stepmother, his voice just a gruff whisper, but she could hear him clearly in the quiet room.

"Yes, she is mine, just as you all are. Be grateful, my son, for I have decided to let you keep her, for now," she told him with an air of frustration at having had to explain herself, but Brent just stared back at her angrily. Tilly couldn't understand what they were saying, their unusual wording and dark meanings completely lost on her. Before she could ask them to explain, a sudden twinge of pain hit her temple, making Tilly wince for a moment before it disappeared again just as quickly. In its wake, the memory of what she had seen that night in the tent came crashing back to her. She looked up again at the woman before her and trembled at the remembrance of Lily's actions that early morning the summer before, and then gasped as she saw her true dark face in the shadows before Lilith then turned and wandered away, climbing back up the steps to her husband's side.

CHAPTER NINE

"Brent, what *is* going on?" Tilly demanded as Lily stood back atop the steps that were obviously the centre-point of the ceremony that was due to start, and which was clearly going to include Lucas in some way. The scary woman looked out at her dark congregation as though she was about to begin a sermon, her smile firmly on her face as she took in the faces of her loyal subjects.

"I will explain everything later, Tilly, but for now just stay close to me, keep your mouth shut and your head down, do you understand?" he demanded in a harsh whisper, and Tilly nodded. "I mean it, this is no joke," he added, looking forlornly at his lover. She took his hand and held it tight, eager for all this to be over, but knowing deep down that it was only the start.

The group soon hushed, and Lilith began to speak.

"Welcome to you all, my most loyal and devoted followers. Tonight, we have gathered to carry out the final challenge in my husband's demonic trials," she said, calling out as the group stared up at her, no one saying a word as they absorbed her speech. "We are in for a rare treat indeed, my friends. His Royal Highness the Black Prince, Blake, has graciously agreed to come and be his adjudicator for the proceedings, tonight is all Hallow's Eve after all," she added happily, and the followers all gasped, then mutters began among the crowd, whispers of excitement and frenzied admiration, some even shouted their affirmations as they looked up at her lovingly.

"Who's Blake?" Tilly whispered to Brent, looking at his pale face as he stared up at Lilith deep in thought, and he inhaled sharply at her words, his face screwing up into a scared and pained wince as he peered down at her.

"That would be me," a deep and omnipotent voice boomed from across the room, the sound seeming to come from inside her head as well as her hearing it in her ears. Tilly looked around behind her but couldn't see where the voice had come from. She then turned back to look towards Lilith at the altar, afraid to say anything more, but was startled to come face to face with a man who had appeared to have come out of nowhere and was now standing just inches away from her.

He was tall, powerfully built, and gorgeous. His dark-brown hair was short but curled slightly at the ends and he looked to be in his mid-twenties, however something about him made the man seem much, much older and wiser, all-powerful and extremely dark and sinister. Tilly stared into his deep green eyes for a moment, utterly mesmerised by him. He stared back into her eyes too, seemingly deep in thought as he took in the sight of the foolish girl that stood before him.

In their moment of shared intrigue, Tilly had failed to notice that every other person in the room had dropped to their knees before this ominous new arrival, and some of those around her shook in fear while others buzzed with excited anticipation in his presence. Even Lilith had knelt before the young man, her head bowed in respect to him, but Tilly just stood there awkwardly for a moment and then started to kneel, hoping to join the others in their respectful poses but he stopped her, grabbing her arm tightly, pulling both Tilly's body and her gaze back up to meet his own.

"Well, well, well," he said quietly, his voice deep and stern. "I see Lilith has marked you, and that she is the one who invited you here tonight, and yet she has not given you proper instructions on how to behave in the presence of royalty," he said, breaking his eye contact with Tilly for a moment to look scornfully at the woman at the altar, who bowed lower to her master in response to her admonishment.

"I'll tell you what," he continued, staring back into Tilly's wide blue eyes. "I'll let you off this once, but the next time you see me, I suggest you get on your knees and worship me, just like your friends here. Is that understood?" he asked her, gesturing to Brent and his brother along with the rest of the crowd, and Tilly nodded, too scared to speak.

"And don't you ever say my name again, or else I'll have your tongue," he added, his deep green eyes speckling with black as he threatened her, sending Tilly's mind into overdrive. She whimpered slightly, trembling, and nodding again at his fierce order.

She hoped her telling off was over with, but the Black Prince eyed her for a few moments longer, looking Tilly up and down with intrigue and taking in the red dress that made her stand out so prominently in the otherwise black filled room. He then lifted her wrist up so that he could inspect it for a moment, and then covered the area with his own hand where her red inverted cross had not long ago appeared from nowhere, showing Lilith's claim on her. She felt it burn beneath his touch, but didn't dare pull her arm away, too afraid to move a muscle.

"I'm sure she won't mind," he told her with a wink, and Tilly stared again up into his deep, suddenly all black eyes, mesmerised again by the powerful man before her. He let her hand drop back to her side and moved over to the altar without another word to her, speaking quietly with Lilith as she rose to greet him.

Tilly looked down at her arm and saw that the inverted cross Lilith had previously drawn on her had now turned from red to black after his burning touch, but she still had no idea what it all meant.

"Whoa," David whispered from behind her, staring at the black mark as he climbed to his feet with the others. Brent gave him a stern look, and he said nothing more to her. Her lover didn't say a word, however Brent couldn't help looking very afraid as he stared into Tilly's eyes from beside her.

CHAPTER TEN

The final trial Lilith had spoken of was soon ready to begin, and Tilly and Brent watched from the side-lines in fearful silence with David and the others as Blake addressed the crowd.

"This human has conquered all in order to win this demon's heart, as well as her hand in marriage and now she seeks sponsorship in order for him to complete his demonic rite of passage," the Black Prince said to the crowd, who all gazed up at him lovingly from the floor below. Tilly could see his darkness, sense his power, and feel the omnipotent buzz in the air all around them, and his words were finally starting to sink in. Talk of demons and royalty filling in some of the blanks in her mind at last. She, too, stared up at her new master as he spoke, feeling herself getting hot and bothered under his gaze as it swept across the crowd while he continued to address them.

"He has completed the first two trials, and bears their marks on his chest," he added, pointing down at Lucas, who removed his shirt and showed what looked like two tattoos on his chest, both in the shape of the number six. The crowd roared and cheered, while Lucas smiled and fist-pumped the air happily.

"Settle down, we still have one more trial, and this one is the toughest," Blake commanded, and the group was instantly quiet again. "I will now take him to the brink of death and back six times. If he survives, his trials are complete and his soul will be considered by my mother for the ultimate prize: an eternal place at Lilith's side, as well as the gift of immortality and true demonic power. So, what are we waiting for? Let's begin!"

"Hail Satan, hail to the Dark Queen," the crowd roared, following his motivational speech, including Brent. Tilly repeated the strange words quietly to herself, catching the green eyes that watched her from atop the altar as she did so, along with the slight curl of Blake's mouth as she continued to flounder in the black sea of followers around her.

They all watched in horror, or fascination for some, as Lucas was then beaten, poisoned, and hung from his neck before them by the Dark Prince, who gave him no mercy and showed no remorse in any of it. Lucas would come back to life again each time, a little darker and less human with every one, but back again all the same.

He then had his still beating heart ripped out of his chest by Lilith's bare hands which she then proceeded to shove back in the cavity she had left behind, dark forces somehow healing Lucas's wounds inexplicably before them, and Tilly's stomach turned as she watched. Brent was then called upon by the powerful Prince and ordered to stab his father through the only just healed heart in his chest with a black dagger, all under the watchful eye of the dark adjudicator and his eldest son carried out his order without question or hesitation. Blake brought Lucas back just in time again, healing the wounds, but it was obviously blackening his soul one little piece at a time too, a thought that scared the hell out of Tilly.

Before long, the sixth and final challenge of his death trial was due and Blake roused the crowd, welcoming their suggestions on how best to torture Lucas one last time and relishing in the depraved and sadistic ideas that were called out to him.

"No, no," he then shouted, silencing the crowd once again. "I am thinking of a good one, let's see if any of you can guess it," he said, playing with the group and egging them on with a cunning smile. There were shouts from the followers as they made their suggestions: hot pokers, suffocation, drowning, beheading and mutilation, however none of them were correct, much to the disappointment of the Dark Prince.

Tilly then let her mind wander, thinking of the many terrible ways to die. She suddenly thought of fire, flames licking the skin and burning off the flesh, and she shuddered, remembering the stories she had been told as a child of a poor boy who had played with matches and set his clothes alight. She had seen him a few years later, barely recognisable thanks to his awful scars.

"Got it!" Blake suddenly shouted, pointing his finger at Tilly, and breaking her from her reverie as the crowd silenced and stared in her direction again. More disturbingly, though, in that moment she realised that this Black Prince had just read her mind.

"Care to share it with the rest of the class?" Blake questioned her, stepping closer to Tilly as he spoke, an edge of appreciation and admiration in his tone.

"Fire," she said quietly as he neared her, not releasing her from his gaze for even a moment, she then cleared her throat and quickly added, "your Majesty," as she bowed and he moved back towards the altar with a satisfied smile.

"Good girl," he said, staring up at Lucas again and, with a click of his fingers, set the poor man alight. He writhed in agony and screamed as the flames licked every inch of his skin. Tilly flinched and covered her nose as the smell of burned flesh filled her lungs, but thankfully it wasn't long until he stopped fighting the flames and the crowd watched eagerly as he lay there, seemingly dead, before coming to just a few minutes later, his body healing one last time before their wide eyes.

With the trial finally over, Lucas rose feebly to his feet and was greeted by cheers and applause from those who had watched over his dreadful challenges. Blake then stepped forward, laying a hand on his chest for a moment before stepping back again, having left a new black mark on Lucas's skin, another six, which sent a shiver down Tilly's spine as another realisation hit her.

"Six, six, six," she whispered to herself.

"Exactly," Brent said, moving his hand to take hers in his own, wanting to comfort her, but then he changed his mind and pulled it away again.

CHAPTER ELEVEN

The trial was finished, and, after cheering loudly along with the crowd in recognition of Lucas's achievements, Blake then shushed them again and silence fell within less than a second.

"I shall take my news to the Dark Queen, and she will make her decisions. In the meantime, though, drink, fuck, sin aplenty and relish in your dark delights, my friends. So mote it be!"

"So mote it be!" the crowd all cried in response to his highly motivational closing speech, every one of Lilith's loyal followers grinning with pride at their mistress's husband's achievements. Blake then stepped down from the altar, and they all kneeled before him one more time. Tilly being mindful to follow the lead of the group this time and kneeling quickly before him alongside her friends. She expected the crowd to stand again after a few moments and for her to find the Black Prince gone again, but this time, they didn't move. Everyone stayed exactly where they were, as though frozen in place, the silence around her pressing like a stifling force. She risked a peek to her side at Brent, but he was completely still, his eyes unblinking and his breathing had slowed considerably and unexplainably.

A hand on her shoulder caused Tilly to jump and look up, bemused, and she found Blake looking down at her with a sly smile. He was every inch the dark and dangerous god, demon, or whatever he was. Either way, he both excited and terrified her.

"That's better. This is just how I like you, on your knees," Blake told her, his eyes dark again as he peered down at her.

"Rise," he commanded her, and it was then that Tilly realised he had either stopped time or frozen the rest of the dark congregation to speak with her a moment alone. She did as she was ordered, having to crane her neck to keep looking up at him even after she was standing at her full height, as he was a good foot or so taller than she was.

"I'm going now, but before I do, here are a few ground rules," he said, lifting a hand and cupping her cheek, pulling her towards him and leaning down so that he was just a few inches away from her face. Tilly could hardly breathe, his touch sending powerful shockwaves throughout her entire body. He laughed, a deep, gruff sound, and then continued.

"Firstly, educate yourself adequately so that the next time I come, you are much better prepared to receive me. Get yourself a Satanist's Bible, and ask your friends here to help you, but either way, I want you up to speed next time," he added, pulling back slightly to look at her expectantly.

"Yes," she replied, her voice faltering thanks to her excitement and fear.

"Secondly, you call me master, your Highness or your Majesty at all times, Tilly. You are never to utter my name again, otherwise you will be punished, severely. Is that understood?"

"Yes," she answered, and then quickly added, "master."

"That's better. Thirdly, you belong to me now Tilly. Do you understand what that means?" Blake asked, commanding her eyes on his so that he could properly read her.

His mother, the Devil, had given him and his siblings access to higher powers over the years, he could heal himself in an instant, age himself if he chose to and teleport anywhere he wanted, but Blake could also read the mind of any being in his company, he had the physical strength of one hundred men and he could control the body of any being he pleased, such as the crowd that were now frozen before him.

Tilly shook her head in response to his question, realising she really didn't know what it meant.

"Is it like what Lily, I mean Lilith, has here, a sort of following?" she asked him cautiously.

"No," he answered, "because you are the only human who bears my mark, Tilly. You are, quite simply, to obey my every command and order without hesitation, and do not ever keep me waiting. You may live your life how you see fit, but you are to always put me first and follow the rules I am giving you now."

She gasped, both scared and excited by his explanation. Tilly understood him clearly and couldn't disguise the little flush of pride she felt upon realising that she was the only human in his following, however she also couldn't help the twisting of her gut at the realisation that he now owned her, in more ways than one.

"I am sure that Lilith will not object to you staying as a guest in her circle. You already have friends here and they can help to teach you," he said, looking down at Brent. "But know this, you are mine, entirely. Mind, body, and soul. Whatever affections you once had for this boy are done. Do I make myself clear?" he asked sternly.

"Yes master," she said, stifling a sob at the realisation that her love for Brent had to be over with now thanks to her new allegiance to Blake.

"Good, because I do not like to share, Tilly. So if he, or any other man, woman or beast touches you sexually, I will slit their throat as you watch and then make you bathe in their blood," he told her, staring into her eyes without even flinching as he delivered his sinister promise, both turning her stomach and sending a deep throb to her cleft as he did so.

"I don't even want you touching yourself. Your pleasure is mine to command now, and only I will deliver it when you have served me well and pleased me adequately. Let yourself succumb to me, and I will take you places you have never dreamed of before," he promised, a sexy smile curling at his lips.

Tilly was aroused by Blake's firmness, drawn to his dark pursuit of her, yet still truly afraid, and she vowed never to underestimate him. He was not joking, and this was all very real. She knew without a doubt that her life was no longer her own, and that thought scared the hell out of her. Blake read her thoughts for a moment, and then reached down from her cheek, laying his hand over her chest as she trembled before him.

"Stop thinking with this," he said, indicating her fast-beating heart, before trailing the same hand down to the hem of her dress and expertly splaying his fingers up her thigh and to her panties, rubbing her clitoris beneath his fingers gently. She felt weak at his touch, almost faint, but his other hand reached around to secure her back and pulled Tilly even closer, his body now pressing into hers.

"And start thinking with this," he finished, planting a deep and delving kiss on her lips. Tilly swooned, the pleasure and the fear bubbling up inside of her as he continued to rub her and kiss her expertly in sync. Blake then stopped suddenly before she could reach her climax and pulled back from their kiss. He kept her pinned to him, his hand still gripping her back and pushing her into his hard body, but the other hand stopped its rubbing of the now swollen and ready nub between her thighs.

"Do you want me to make you come?" he asked her, a sly grin on his face as he spoke.

"Yes master, please," she begged, desperate for her release.

"Then you've learnt your first lesson, my darling," he told her, bringing his hand away from her throbbing nerve endings, leaving her panting and weak in his arms.

"*My* pleasure comes first, then yours, but only if I have been fully satisfied first. That is your top priority from now on, satisfying my every desire," he said, steadying her and then releasing Tilly from his strong hold before stepping back. "You need to earn your rewards," he added with a wicked grin.

Blake then looked her up and down once more, licking his lips and smiling darkly as though he were contemplating many wicked things for her, but Tilly could not be sure what they might be as he gave nothing away.

"One last thing, you are only ever to wear black clothes from now on. However, I do like you in red. You may occasionally wear red underwear, which will be for my eyes only, of course, Tilly," Blake said, giving the final commandment for now to his new slave, or minion, or whatever it was that she would be referred to as from now on. She still didn't know for sure. Tilly nodded her understanding and bowed slightly as he left, still feeling woozy and horny as hell thanks to their intense encounter. The crowd then began to stir and rise once Blake had gone, their commandment lifting. Brent and David stood and joined her, which was lucky, as Tilly quickly felt too weak and lightheaded to stand, and then fainted, falling right into Brent's strong arms.

CHAPTER TWELVE

The brothers carried the still woozy Tilly out into the main hall and then up to the room, placing her down onto the bed she had been due to share that night with Brent before things had been changed dramatically for the two of them thanks to Blake's new claim over her. David quickly left them to it, knowing they needed to talk and eager to get away from the tense atmosphere between them.

As she refocused, Tilly gratefully drank a large glass of water and then laid her head back on the pillow, wondering for a minute if she had imagined the entire thing, but one look at Brent's forlorn face told her it was all very real. She had to fight back the tears as she peered up at him, still not quite able to accept the fact that they had to be over.

He looked back down at her, eager to know if she was okay, but he also kept his distance rather than hug her or hold her hand as he would have before, and Tilly knew he would have to be on his best behaviour around her now or else face Blake's wrath.

After a few minutes, she started to feel much better and sat up against the pillows, taking in the small room around her for a moment, still deep in thought. She remembered her early morning back at the circus so clearly now, replaying the strange and bloody scene she had witnessed between Lucas and Lily in her mind's eye. It almost made sense now, whereas at the time she had not been able to comprehend their creepy actions at all.

Tilly lifted her arm, looking inside her wrist for the inverted cross that Lilith had drawn on her that same morning, but it was gone again.

"It's still there, but only *they* can see it. Demons and witches will know you belong to one of the royal family the moment that they are near you, and because I bear Lilith's mark I can kind of sense it on you, too," Brent said quietly, sitting down on the opposite end of the bed and staring across at Tilly with a sad, defeated expression.

He knew she had many questions and decided to get right to it, needing her to understand so that they could both just move on. She needed to accept that there was no fighting her master's orders, no matter their past or what she might still want. "Lilith's followers and others like us that have been marked by our demon masters can sense another marked Satanist in their company. It is up to the follower whether they wish to declare whom their master is, but it is an honour Tilly, you must wear it with pride," he told her earnestly. "I thought something seemed different about you. I guess Lilith blocked me from sensing her mark on you until she wanted me to know," he added, looking down at his hands.

The door of the bedroom then opened, and in walked Lilith, without knocking or having been invited. She looked down at the two of them on the bed with a stern expression but was quickly satisfied that they were not up to anything that they shouldn't be.

"Tonight did not go as I had planned for the pair of you, but plans change, and we too must adjust in order to suit our almighty masters' wants and needs," she told them matter-of-factly, quickly dismissing their past love as though it were nothing. "You have been given a great honour, one that is not to be thought lightly of, Tilly. Your master has never marked a human before, so you had better be grateful," she added, staring at her fiercely.

Tilly went to respond, but Lilith raised her hand to command her against it, and she followed the order, knowing that this would not be the last time she would be ordered around, so she had better start getting used to it.

"Your master wants me to watch over you, and it is my absolute pleasure to do his bidding. You will be taught our religion, our history and our expectations of you as his devoted, loyal follower," Lilith continued, her tone softening as she spoke of the Black Prince so lovingly. "The two of you will remain up here for the rest of the evening. Brent will now be your teacher, a friend, and nothing more. Is that understood?" she asked sternly, her eyes dark and ominous.

"Yes mistress," Brent answered, and Tilly copied his response but was quickly silenced by Lilith's disgusted reaction.

"I am not *your* mistress. Your only mistress now is the Dark Queen. You may address me using my full name," she corrected her and then left without another word.

"I've got a Hell of a lot to learn," Tilly said quietly as she slid off the bed and made her way to the bathroom to change into her nightwear, eager to get out of her tight dress.

"You have no idea," Brent told her with a scowl, staring out the window.

"Shit, I need some black clothes!" Tilly then shouted to him from the en-suite, tossing aside her blue pyjamas with a huff and then Brent threw her a black hoodie and some tracksuit trousers from his bag to wear instead.

"You're gonna need to go shopping tomorrow," he told her with a scowl.

They were soon brought plates piled high with food by David and Jackson, who disappeared again within seconds, both eager not to get involved in their depressive conversation and rushing in case they missed the festivities in the hall below them.

Tilly and Brent thanked his brothers and then the two of them sat crossed legged at opposite ends of the king size bed as Brent began telling her about the history of the Dark Queen.

"We need to start with the Devils," he told her, chomping on a breadstick.

"Devils, as in plural?" she asked, a puzzled look on her pale face as she pulled her plate towards her and started munching on a spicy chicken skewer.

"Yes, there was the old one and now the new one. Let's just start at the beginning, okay?" he asked her impatiently, and Tilly nodded, keeping quiet so that Brent could begin telling her the strange tale. He reached over and grabbed a small notepad from the bedside table and a pen, and then began writing a list while Tilly watched him quietly, making her way through some more food from her plate.

"I suppose I should say, first and foremost, that we are not worthy of speaking their names Tilly. The royal family are beings far above us and our lowly human status, and we will be punished severely for doing it, even accidentally. I have seen it, and trust me, you don't even wanna know, or ever go through, what they might do to you for the insubordination. He was incredibly lenient on you tonight, whether it was because of your lack of knowledge or because of his want for you, I do not know. But either way you were very, very lucky," he stressed, his blue eyes staring across at her intensely, and she paled at the thought of what her master might have put her through had he been in a less jovial mood earlier.

CHAPTER THIRTEEN

Brent looked down and pushed the notepad towards Tilly on the bed. He then pointed to the first name that he had written on the pad, *'Lucifer'*.

"He used to be the Devil, I'm sure you've heard the name before?" he asked her, and Tilly nodded. "He is your new master's father, but no longer is he the Devil. Most humans have no idea that everything changed in Hell. According to Lilith, it happened around sixty years ago, but only our new bible makes it known. As far as movies and literature go, he's still in charge and they are happy to let most humans believe so. Anyway, over to your master, we are permitted to call him the Black Prince. He has a twin sister, whom we can call the Black Princess," he said, pointing to the name, *'Luna'*, on the paper.

"The pair of them are incredibly powerful. Your master is heir to the dark throne now, and he is the most powerful of all the dark beings below the Queen. The twins do not come to Earth together if possible because their combined dark power brings about nothing but chaos, war, freak weather occurrences, and other such catastrophic events to mankind and our existence. They are bound by the moon and can only come to Earth during its full days, or on all Hallow's Eve, like tonight."

Tilly nodded, trying to take it all in.

"They have another sister. She is younger. We may call her the Unholy Princess and I do not know her real name, no human does," he told her, pointing to the line below Luna's name where he had written her sister's chilling title.

"But it is rumoured that she is a child with no paternal father, only a mother, the Dark Queen. She is the fabled death bringer, Tilly. You want to hope that you are never taken before her as she is famed to be merciless, cruel and the epitome of all her family's dark powers combined. No human has ever seen her face or knows her true story, and we do not ever dare ask for it from our demonic masters. All we know is that she can never come to Earth. She would bring about the end to all humanity, the fabled, 'end of days', Tilly. Does this make sense?" he asked her, stressing this point so hard that Tilly knew she would never forget it. She nodded, looking pale again and then pushed what was left of her food away, feeling as though her last mouthful was now stuck in her suddenly dry throat. She took a large gulp of cola instead and looked down at the next name he had written on the page as Brent took a deep breath and continued, pointing down at the name, which read *Hecate/Cate*.

"The new Devil. You may call her the Dark Queen, as well as Satan or the Devil, as she has adopted both of those titles too. She is their mother, the all-powerful ruler of Hell and our almighty mistress," he said, a deep affection towards her so clear in his voice at the very thought of the Dark Queen, a devotion that Tilly could not quite understand, not yet anyway but she was sure she would learn about it all very soon.

"She was once married to the old Devil, gave him their children and then went on to dethrone him. No one knows why, how, or where he is now, only she knows the truth and you can guarantee her lips are well and truly sealed. Not even your master knows what happened to his father, Tilly," Brent added, every ounce of seriousness in his tone now.

He leaned forward and wrote a few more notes on the page but then closed the notebook and passed it over to her to keep rather than continue telling her, knowing that Tilly might be glad of the notes to jog her memory later.

"There are more of them, the Queen has siblings that live on Earth together, but it can get complicated from here, so I suggest you take one of the bibles home with you to read, and I urge you, read it thoroughly for your master knows every word by heart and he will surely test you. I also suggest you think about performing a commitment ceremony, Tilly. Cleanse your soul of your old life and beliefs, and then embrace the new and your master will no doubt be very pleased with you," he said, looking sad as he contemplated her future with Blake instead of him.

She nodded, thinking of her master and his gorgeous green eyes. She knew she would do anything it took to please him, to feel his satisfied gaze fall on her again and to reap the pleasurable rewards for her submission. Tilly could feel her once deep emotions and love for Brent already waning, as though having dulled a little bit at a time over the past few hours thanks to her master's new commandment that they were no longer allowed to be together. She looked across the bed at her friend, who was, until incredibly recently, her boyfriend and lover. He looked back at her too, seemingly thinking the same as she was, a dark look of regret on his face, although he didn't dare say the words to express his loss or anger at losing the one woman he had ever truly cared about.

Tilly jumped, realising that she was staring at Brent a little too longingly, and she then busied herself with writing notes next to the names he had written in the notebook, adding little annotations to explain who they were and a brief version of their story. When she was done, it was still only early and, despite the strange events of the evening; she was not tired. Her head was swimming with far too much information to rest, yet full of too many scary thoughts and dark memories to let her settle down to sleep.

"Any questions?" Brent asked once she had finally closed the book and looked up, careful not to stare into his blue eyes too deeply this time.

"Just a couple. How come we can say Lilith's name but not Bl, the Black Prince's? And why is it she *is* allowed to say his name?" she asked, glad she had managed to stop herself in time before saying his name again.

"She is a level one demon, just below the royal family in the hierarchy of Hell. Only level ones can speak the royal names, having earned their positions at the top of the ladder after years of evil service and unwavering loyalty. Many of them are the Queen's most trusted advisors that took centuries to rise to their powerful positions. They are the only ones who know the royals closely," he explained, and Tilly was shocked to realise that the so seemingly human Lily was actually a very powerful demon, much more so than she had previously imagined. "It is only the royal family that we are forbidden to say the names of. Demon classification does not affect humans. If we know their name we can say it, that's kinda the rule. It seems old-fashioned, but that's because it is. The rule goes back thousands of years. A human may consort with demons and pledge allegiance to one or more of them, but you must be willing to ask them for their name to earn their respect. Some will give it willingly, especially if they want you as a follower, but others will make you work for it first, which can be fucking scary as they don't always want to tell us. The stories of demonic possession are largely exaggerated, but somewhat true. By knowing their name, you have a hold over them and they don't give that up too easily. You should be fine though; you bear the Black Prince's mark so there is no reason for any demon not to want you to know their name. They are always on the lookout to progress higher up their levels and might use you to gain favour with your master. You can tell a demon's classification level by the colour of their mark when called to the surface. Red means level one, green is level two, and then I think it's blue for level three. After that I can't remember them off the top of my head but it's in the books, and after level three they don't really get to have human followers anyway, so you won't need to worry," he said, giving her a moment to jot all of that down. Tilly knew she had a lot to think about. All this stuff about classifications of demons and dark royal families were so new and unnatural to her, and she knew it would take her a while to get used to all the terminology and unusual rules. She quickly realised that she could do with a break from all this studying already.

"Okay, I could do with stretching my legs. Do you think we've finished our lesson for this evening?" Tilly asked him, hoping to get out of the small room and to break the awkward silence that had descended after she had finished taking her notes. Brent shrugged, checking the clock quickly.

"Yeah, I suppose so. We can get you your books and some new black clothes tomorrow. I'm guessing that was one of his orders while we were frozen?" he asked her, seemingly understanding Blake's control over the crowd without question and knowing her answer already. Tilly nodded, realising then that she had always seen him wearing black too, but had never thought about it before.

"Yep, and nothing but black. I might as well throw out half of my clothes now," she replied with a pout, and Brent smiled. Despite the changes in her, she could still feel that spark lingering between them, and decided that they really didn't need to be alone in a room, talking and smiling at each other like old times right now.

"Do you think Lilith will let us join the party?" she eventually asked, hopeful that they could head back down to the crowd and join in on Lucas's celebrations, eager to clear her mind and have some fun.

CHAPTER FOURTEEN

Brent grinned over at Tilly and then grabbed his jacket from the hook behind the door, reaching in the pocket for his mobile phone. She watched eagerly as he gave David a quick call, asking him to speak to Lilith and seek permission for the two of them to leave the upstairs room, hopeful that his younger brother might have the chance to use Lilith's good mood to their advantage.

"Yeah, let me go and ask if," David began, but was quickly silenced and then ordered to immediately pass the phone to his mistress while Brent winced, knowing that he and Tilly were pushing their luck after just a couple of hours on their own.

"Do you mean to tell me you feel as though she has learned everything already, son?" Lilith asked him, in a stern but slightly softer tone, as she addressed the boy she was so closely linked with. She had always called him her son and considered him and the other two boys as such. Lilith had even offered him her support if he wanted to attempt the demonic trials someday too, a rare gift that countless other followers would give anything to receive.

"Yes, well, what I mean is," he mumbled. "She has learned enough for now mistress, I have taught Tilly the basics and while there is much more for her to learn I feel she may benefit further from the group experience, from enjoying the party and speaking openly with my father about his experiences rather than us hiding away up here all night," he replied, hoping she would be lenient on them.

"Very well, has she changed her clothes?" Lilith asked curtly, and Brent smiled.

"Yes," he replied, crossing his fingers hopefully.

"Then you may come," she told him and hung up the phone without another word.

Brent turned and smiled at Tilly, letting her know they had been given permission to go. She jumped off the bed and checked her suitcase again, remembering she had packed some black items after all and she soon found a black skirt and tights that she paired with Brent's black hoodie, feeling much more comfortable than she had done in the track suit trousers.

Within minutes, the pair then made their way down the stairs and into the great hall, being quickly enveloped by the darkness inside as they made their way through the crowd towards what was once the altar. It had now been transformed into a kind of bar area and a variety of drinks had been lined up for people to help themselves to. Lucas was there, chatting away animatedly to some other men, all of whom Tilly had seen in the dark crowd earlier that night, and he downed shots as he relished in their congratulatory toasts. He smiled happily to his friends, seeming just like the same man Tilly had met so many times before, and he continually planted kisses on his wife's dark-red lips, who also still appeared just like the same woman Tilly had met all those times at the circus too. They seemed so happy together, and she couldn't help but watch the pair as they interacted so comfortably, surprised that a demon and human could be so in love with one another.

"It is possible, strange as it might seem at first," Brent's voice said quietly from behind her. He had seen her watching them and somehow knew exactly what she was thinking. "But they have had many years together now and in that time, their goal has always remained the same. Each other," he told her, looking over at them fondly. Tilly smiled, hoping she may truly understand or possess a bond that strong with her master in the future, but it seemed very hard to even attempt to predict what that future might be like. She hated the idea that it was scarily out of her control right now. She was just a puppet in whatever game Blake wanted to play. Love might never come into the equation.

"What's with the blood sharing?" she then asked him, looking up into his dark blue eyes in the dim light and remembering back to that night in the tent.

"Demons can use their blood to control humans, like she did with you that night so that you'd forget both what you saw and the fact that she had marked you. But that's not what *they* do it for. Their true love allows for the sharing of blood between them without control or power being the reason behind it. It is a sharing of one another's essence, a mutual understanding and a sign of both their individual strengths and their strong bond as a couple," he replied, and she could hear the admiration and respect in his tone as he watched them for a moment beside her.

"So, they make each other stronger?" she asked, and Brent nodded before taking her elbow and gently leading her on through the crowd once again. They made their way over to them, Brent receiving a tight hug from his father and brothers before he bowed to Lilith and kissed her hand in respect. Tilly watched them all interacting as though this old-fashioned approach was so normal to them and she couldn't help feeling awkward, like an outsider. After a few minutes, she made her way towards Lucas when he beckoned her over to his side. Brent staying to talk quietly with Lilith, and she was glad to have some time away from the scary demon.

"Congratulations," she told him as he embraced her, making sure to look especially impressed at his new tattoo-like mark that completed the three sixes on his bare chest. He smiled and thanked her, looking Tilly up and down as though seeing her for the first time, and she realised he was sensing something different in her. She wondered if perhaps it was the change in her thanks to her new black mark and smiled back at him coyly.

"And congratulations are in order for you too, Tilly," he replied, excited for her but seeming to understand her reservations and fear at her new gift. He watched her for a moment longer, his expression softening and then he looked at her like he would do his own daughter, with a warm and gentle smile and understanding eyes.

"You have a lot to learn, and I understand you have your fears, but if you take advice from no one else, please listen to me, for I have been where you are now," he said, and she looked up into his deep blue eyes, seeing the darkness in them now that she was sure was not there before, thanks to his completed death trial. But she wasn't scared. She could sense that he was still the same man, a good man, and she thought that perhaps the darkness that was now inside of him was not just to be feared, but it was to be embraced and respected as well.

"I was once just a man, with a wife and three young boys. I was not a Satanist back then, not even religious at all, and then when Jackson was five years old, my wife left us, saying she had found another. It turned out she had fallen in love with my only brother, that they had been having an affair since Jackson was just a baby. I was furious, enraged, and betrayed, so I prayed to the gods above for vengeance. They did nothing, and then, as though by some unholy intervention, I crossed paths with the mesmerising and beautiful demon that I am now truly honoured to call my wife," Lucas told Tilly, looking over admirably at his demonic lover.

"She and I helped each other. She was lost too, but she showed me a world I had had no idea about before, a life I never knew I could have, and she also taught me how I could punish those who had crossed me. With Lilith's help, I destroyed them both, relishing in their misery and never once feeling an ounce of guilt for my dark actions. I finally got my vengeance, and I loved her for showing me how. My brother eventually went crazy and killed my ex-wife. He then tried to take his own life but failed. He is in prison now, rotting away like the coward he is and when he eventually does die, Lilith will make sure that his soul is tortured for all eternity," Lucas finished, his eyes seeming sad for just a moment, but he quickly shook it off, regaining his composure, and then he offered her a shot of whisky from atop the bar with a sly grin. Tilly smiled back at Lucas and accepted the small glass, nodding in understanding and gratitude for him having shared such an intimate story with her.

Although he was now very dark, damaged, and obviously still burdened by the memory of his ex, Lucas could still show her a warmth and kindness she wouldn't have thought could exist in this strange world that she had just joined. He brought her comfort and Tilly happily clinked his glass with her own and then drank down the strong alcoholic shot to celebrate with him, reaching for another at the same time as Lucas, which made him smile even wider.

Later, as Brent escorted her back up to their room and grabbed his things, intending to share a room with Jackson instead now, he hovered at the doorway for just a minute and turned to look at Tilly, leaning against the frame thoughtfully.

"I'm truly sorry about all of this. I never intended for you to get involved in this part of my life. But I guess it was never going to be my choice, was it? I should've known Lilith would find a way to mark you, whether I was ready for her to or not," he told her, looking forlorn, but as though he needed to get it off his chest once and for all. Tilly stepped closer and slapped him across the face as hard as she could manage. Brent took the hot, stinging pain as though he felt he deserved it, without any anger in his eyes towards his ex or even a hint of a flinch.

"You should have always known she would do it. Of course she would, don't make up excuses, Brent. I love you, or should I say *loved* you," she said, tailing off and having to stifle a sob at the finite words, but she had already begun to accept the fact that they were over. It was one of Blake's first orders to her and there was no way she would not follow it. "There would have always come a day that you would have had to tell me about all of this, but in the end, you were just too busy being a fucking coward to do it yourself," she snapped, angered by his sad eyes and she refused to let him play the martyr; after all, it wasn't his life that had just been changed forever. Brent chose this dark life years ago when he willingly became Lilith's follower. He had always planned to live the rest of his life under her rule, but Tilly had been forced into their world without ever having been asked if she even wanted it.

One thing was for sure, Tilly was already undeniably excited and attracted to her new master, despite only having been with him for a few minutes and she felt the flutter of butterflies in her stomach at the sheer thought of what dark delights might be in store for her under his rule. But she was also truly terrified by Blake and all the evil and darker things he might also decide to do to her and vowed never to make it easy on Brent for having forced her to become his plaything.

CHAPTER FIFTEEN

The next morning Tilly, Brent, and his brothers went into the city centre to do some shopping. She picked out some black dresses, skirts, and jeans before also treating herself to a biker jacket and boots to complete her dark new look. She felt amazing in all of it, gothic, sexy and confident. Tilly didn't take too long with the shopping, much to the boys' delight, and they stopped by an old church on the way to the train station afterwards. It was a hidden building that no one would even know was there without being shown to it, but she wondered if perhaps that was precisely the point. Brent grabbed her some books from the back room and gave the church a large donation in return for them before introducing her to one of the dark ministers whom she could sense was marked as well. She somehow knew that his mark was black, a royal ownership just like hers. The human ministers wore long, black robes embroidered with black roses and they had hoods that covered half their dark faces, concealing their eyes, but the few she met were kind and warm despite their sinister uniforms. They had started out as devout followers to the Satanist religion, and the Dark Queen herself had handpicked each to climb the human ranks to become her ministers. Each one wore his mark with so much pride that Tilly couldn't help but smile to herself and rub the inside of her right wrist with a strange sense of anxious pride too as she stood there, feeling special and blessed, or perhaps it was cursed, she could not yet be sure.

An hour later, after saying goodbye to her friends, she boarded the train, glad to be able to slump down into the comfortable first-class seat once again, and grateful for the time alone at last. Tilly was tired but couldn't seem to rest, so after polishing off a tall coffee and a bagel she picked up her new reading assignments, flicking through the pages of the Satanist's bible for a quick skim first before settling down to read it more thoroughly with her second cup of coffee in hand. By the time she got home, Tilly was well versed in the dark texts and rules surrounding her new world. She popped in the main house to quickly greet her parents, informing her mother that she and

Brent had decided to split up, that their long-distance relationship was to blame, but she didn't say any more, knowing that she would have to get used to concealing her dark life from her parents from now on. Robert stayed quiet, but after a little quizzing Bianca seemed convinced enough, and after giving her a tight hug, Tilly excused herself then went out to her little nook to be alone. She was exhausted and fell immediately into bed and into a deep, dreamless sleep.

The next morning Tilly awoke and she then quickly proceeded to throw out all her colourful clothes, slipping them into bags ready to give them away via the charity collection bins in town. She then continued to study the books Brent had given her, absorbing everything she could about the Satanic world while making notes and researching online for more information and rituals, pouring over every piece of information she could find. Tilly soon found out that Brent had been right about Blake's extended family; that his aunt, uncle, and cousins were powerful extensions of the Dark Queen's brood, but who lived on Earth rather than in Hell and ran a secretive order by the name of the Crimson Brotherhood. She couldn't find anything else on them so would have to wait until she would be allowed to know more, presumably by Blake himself when she was deemed worthy of the knowledge, as she was sure that delicate information like that would not be given out to just anyone. Tilly just made a note about it in her book and then carried on researching the many other aspects she needed to educate herself on to feel more comfortable in Blake's following, adhering to yet another of his orders without hesitation.

Tilly searched the internet some more, and she eventually came across a commitment ceremony the next evening. She remembered Brent's advice and decided that she might as well do it sooner rather than later; she knew Blake could only come Earth during the full moons but could not be sure when the next visit from her master would happen and she wanted him to be pleased with her progress when he did. Tilly knew that the next step was to commit herself: mind, body, and soul, to both him and to his mother.

She set up a small altar on her desk as per the website's instructions; complete with a black candle and small knife she had had to sneak out of the main house. Tilly then drew a pentagram on some paper and lit the candle, before pricking her finger and dripping the blood onto the page as she prepared to recite the dark text. She took a deep breath and spoke the binding incantation, meaning every word of the powerful spell.

"I call upon the darkness to hear my call. I hereby renounce all others and pledge both my allegiance and my soul to the Dark Queen," she said, before setting fire to the bloody page with the candle.

"So mote it be, hail Satan," she finished, then blew out the candle and cleared up the mess before heading off to get changed for bed. Tilly didn't feel any different following the ritual, but she hoped it had worked, or that at least it was appreciated that she had tried. She climbed into bed and fell straight into a deep sleep again.

Tilly was stood before the huge mirror in her small bedroom, dressed in a beautiful, long black gown that was made up of a boned corset on the top and a layered skirt underneath that covered her all the way down to her feet. Her dark-blonde hair was pinned back in a side-bun that was wound with black ribbon and she had dark, smoky shadowed eyelids and long, black lashes. Her inverted cross was now clearly visible on the inside of her right wrist for some reason, and she couldn't help but think that it looked almost like a tattoo. The mark looked amazing at her side beside the black dress that clung to her hips alluringly and Tilly felt wonderful, as though she were a princess ready to go to a dark ball. She gazed at herself for a few moments, taking in the gothic look she had now so easily taken to with a satisfied smile.

Two hands reached up her bare arms from behind and held her shoulders for a second, one of them then moving around inside her left arm to her torso and gathering Tilly around her stomach as the other reached over her right shoulder and grasped her neck softly, yet powerfully. A set of bright green eyes then appeared over her shoulder and Blake's face materialised from within the shadows, looking sultry and incredibly sexy. She smiled, leaning into his strong hold and succumbing to him, staring back at her master through the reflection in the mirror.

"You're here," she said, her voice almost a whisper, and she found herself genuinely pleased to see him.

"Yes, Tilly," he answered, kissing her neck softly. She groaned, feeling the excited tingle course through her at his touch.

"Is this real?" she asked him quietly as he trailed his lips up and down her exposed collarbone, his gentle touch making her tremble before him with both anticipation and nervousness.

"No," he answered with a gruff laugh. "You are dreaming, but your body will respond to any stimulation I give you in your dreams as though it were really happening. You will feel everything I do to you as if I am really there," he told her with a wicked grin before lifting his head up and looking into her eyes through the mirrored reflection.

"Tell me what you desire from your life, Tilly, what you crave. Show me," he said, and then the mirror before them seemed to blur and darken, and soon their reflected image was gone from it completely. Moments later, it was as if a video was showing through the large framed screen a clip of her, and she was just a few years older than she was now. Tilly was a famous chef. She had made it at last and was running an award-winning restaurant, signing her recipe books, and making television appearances as her adoring public watched on. Fame and fortune, being desired and respected by all that watched from the audience, that was her dream.

"Yes, this is what I want, master. I want to be successful, rich, famous and adored," she told him, ashamed somewhat at her shallow aspirations, but he was completely unsurprised by it. Power and fame were what everyone wanted, what almost all the humans he and his demons encountered along the way sold their souls for.

Blake smiled down at her as the image before them changed again. Tilly couldn't control it. It was as though he was showing her what was inside her own head, and she had no idea what nuggets of truth and desire he might pluck out of her next. The following scene was that of her and Blake, naked and lying in bed together, making love and he was staring into her eyes, telling her he loved her. Tilly blushed at the image and gasped as he tightened his hold on her, silently commanding her to keep her eyes on the screen.

"And this?" he asked, whispering in her ear, and she nodded. She blushed harder but ignored her embarrassment and lifted her own hands, covering his as they held her in his still strong grip.

"Are you sure it's not *this* that you want?" he asked, altering the image to replace himself with the image of Brent's naked body, his blue eyes looking up into Tilly's as he too spoke the same words of love that Blake had just done in the previous, matching movie. She stiffened at the sight before her, but knew that it was not true, that she wanted the first variation of that image now, more than ever. The look on his face as Blake had proclaimed his love for her was all she wanted, needed, and Tilly knew she would do anything to have it.

"No master," she said, turning to face him, wanting to get away from the image of her and Brent so intimately together. She dropped to her knees before him and looked up at her Black Prince as he stood towering over her. He looked gorgeous, like a beautiful statue of her dark god that belonged in a museum somewhere rather than here in her tiny bedroom. He was wearing a perfectly tailored and entirely black suit, with a matching waistcoat, shirt and tie, every inch of him exuding the powerful force she was now so drawn to.

Blake looked down at Tilly, a smile curling the edges of his lips, and she could see that she had satisfied his curiosity on the subject at last.

"Good, you may rise," he ordered her, and then pulled Tilly close and planted a deep and fierce kiss on her lips when she did so. She could feel his grip on her as though he were there, feel the pressing of his lips against hers as he took possession of her mouth and she kissed him back fervently. His hands slid behind her as they kissed and he then unzipped the black dress she was wearing, causing it to fall immediately to her feet. She realised then that she had been completely naked underneath it, but she didn't care.

Blake eyed her for a moment and then lifted Tilly up into his arms and took her over to the bed, laying her down on the duvet before lifting himself over her trembling body. She was utterly naked before him while he remained in his perfect suit, and Tilly was positive that he had absolutely no intention of removing it this time. His mouth found hers again, and they kissed lasciviously, his touch and the taste of him sending her body into overdrive and she found herself desperate to run her hands through his dark curls, but she didn't dare reach up to grab them and instead gripped the duvet beneath her tightly.

"I know what you did," he whispered in her ear between their kisses, and Tilly couldn't help but tense up, wondering if she had done something wrong. Blake immediately laughed though, letting her know she was not in trouble with him, and he lifted himself up on his hands to look down into her eyes. "You committed your soul to my mother, and to me," he told her, smiling down at Tilly as he cupped her cheek with one hand and she was instantly mesmerised by his deep green eyes again as he spoke to her quietly, his tone much softer than when he delivered his stern orders at the castle.

"You are to be rewarded Tilly," he then added with a wry curl of his lip, and without another word he started laying his mouth on her now so sensitive skin again, trailing kisses across her chest and to her breasts before sinking lower on the bed and opening her thighs before him. Tilly gripped the duvet beneath her even tighter in her hands and gasped as he kissed her nether lips and began caressing her tender nub with his mouth. Blake then delved his tongue expertly inside her cleft and then slid it out and upwards to flick over her already swollen clitoris. His fingers filled the wet crevice, rubbing her skilfully inside as his tongue pursued her climax from above. She cried out, being careful not to say his name as a wonderful orgasm rippled through her, the shockwaves strong and mind blowing as they reverberated throughout every inch of her being. Her body continued to pulsate even as he pulled away and stood over her, smiling down, before disappearing into the darkness again.

Tilly woke up from her wonderful dream with a start, gripping the bed covers tightly while drenched with sweat and with her core still tensing wonderfully from her climactic release. She lay back and revelled in the afterglow, panting, and feeling so delighted.

"Whoa," she whispered to herself before falling back asleep, and she was disappointed that Blake was not there to greet her this time, having already delivered Tilly with her sublime reward.

CHAPTER SIXTEEN

Blake's eyes flew open, as though he had just awoken from a deep sleep, too. Being inside Tilly's consciousness was strange, but fun, and he looked forward to spending more nights in her dreams in the future. The powerful Prince quickly found himself eager to strengthen their already amazing connection, but he was willing to wait until he saw her in the flesh before joining Tilly in bed properly, wanting nothing but the real thing from his new endeavour. The link between them was stronger than ever now thanks to her having performed the commitment ceremony, and he had been very impressed that she had decided to do it without him having to order her. Blake had high hopes for this intriguing human, and he expected nothing less than complete submission, obedience, and loyalty from her from now on. He lay back on his bed, thinking of her and her delicious body for a moment with a satisfied smile.

His twin sister, Luna, then came bursting into his room, disrupting his wonderful daydream without a care, and he glowered across at her.

"Hey brother," she said, ignoring his scowl as she flopped down on the bed next to him and eyed him curiously. The two of them had always stayed close friends as well as siblings despite their many years in Hell together, and they still shared a strong bond regardless of their age, power, and the individual strengths and responsibilities that they had developed along the way. She had sensed it instantly when he had marked Tilly, having felt it somewhere deep inside of her, and she had been excited for him to finally share that part of himself with someone. He had insisted that it meant nothing, but Luna knew him better than that and while she had chosen not to tease him about it, knowing better than to push him, she had still given him a knowing smile in return.

Luna had only marked a handful of humans in her lifetime, but she had shared strong bonds with each of them and had taken them all as her lovers at some point, whether male or female. She used to visit each of their dreams quite frequently while she was stuck in Hell, as well as going to Earth during the full moons to be with them properly, and it had been wonderful having her own small following to both command and love in one way or another. She had eventually granted one of them, a man she now truly loved, called Ash, entrance into her coven. He was not strong enough to complete the demonic trials, so had instead settled for eternity by her side as her servant. He had been granted his magical powers and immortality by her mother and had then gone on to quickly become her chief warlock. The two of them were inseparable and Ash would beg Luna to marry him daily, but only proclaiming his love to her in private due to his lowly status when they were in the company of others. She wanted to say yes, to allow him a more respected position in their dark hierarchy, but it was too soon. They had only been together twenty years and had many more to come yet. She never understood why he wanted to rush it all when they had eternity together to do all those things. Ash would just smile knowingly and bow to his mistress, and then fall to his knees before Luna and ask her again the next day.

Her mother, the Dark Queen, had smiled when she moaned to her about his proposals with a pout. She told her daughter that it was simply because Ash loved her so very much and couldn't bear the thought of not calling her his wife. Luna knew Harry had felt the same way towards Cate and had asked her to marry him the moment he had made it to the highest level of the demonic hierarchy all those years ago following his transition from man to demon at her request. Cate had said yes to him immediately, of course, and they had been married before the day was over. They had been together in secret for years before that, her mother having returned home with Lottie, their surprise little sister, and having made the first new demon in centuries. It was very much to everyone's surprise, but they had soon figured out why she had done it, that this young demon was the missing half of their mother's heart. After years of her trying to ignore the loss, Cate had finally found it again and admitted all to her eldest children. Blake and Luna took to Harry instantly, and their newly discovered sister, Lottie, spoke so highly of him that the five dark beings soon became a formidable and very close family.

Cate had then lifted the ban on making new demons, but all willing candidates had to complete the almost impossible demonic trials first and she could still turn them down if she did not deem them worthy for the highly coveted powers. The final ritual could only be carried out in the Queen's presence as well, and while her time was deemed too precious by some to spend on human matters, it didn't take too long anyway as almost all who tried didn't even make it to the council table for her consideration. Harry had been the only new demon for many years, followed eventually by a second, Eliza, but she had only made it to a level four position in the demonic hierarchy, much to her new father, the level one demon Asmodeus's despair. He had fallen in love with the human while she was in his following on Earth and wanted her to be his demonic bride, which she immediately became after her initiations were over, but the pair were not welcome in the company of high-ranking demons thanks to her two failed attempts to climb higher in the initiation arena. They would have to wait centuries for her to try again, and in the meantime, Asmodeus would have to attend the higher-level gatherings alone.

Listening in on his sister's thoughts, Blake just could not understand how a powerful demon such as Asmodeus would settle for a lower-level existence just so that he could be with the woman he loved, there was no way he would ever give up his high status for something as foolish as love.

"Why are you so horny? I thought you just went into her dream?" Luna asked Blake, pulling him out of his thoughts. She could sense his frustrations at only having given Tilly her pleasure in the dream rather than having had his own release, too. He had wanted more, wanted to gratify his own needs too, but he had decided against it. He would never tell Luna, but there was a strong part of him that wanted to wait until he could be with Tilly properly, in full physical form when they could make love for hours, gratifying both their needs over and over.

"She woke up," he told her dismissively with a nonchalant wave of his hand. "And I owed her one after leaving her hanging on Halloween."

"You need to work on that then, she's not meant to wake until you release her," she replied with a smirk.

"Did you actually want something?" he asked Luna impatiently, sick of her leading questions.

"No, I just wanted to figure out if you had finally fallen in *love*," she teased, nudging him with her elbow and fluttering her eyelashes, but she teleported away before he could even answer her. Luna knew Blake thought himself incapable of love, he had told her many times that he would never let himself fall in love, and she really hoped that this human girl might just break down those incredibly high walls of his, or at least make a decent dent in them before he discarded her and moved on to his next distraction.

He sneered and lay back down on his dark pillows, then closed his eyes and focussed, mentally closing himself off to everything and everyone around him, which was his usual mind-set. This was how he had always managed to keep his walls so highly built and his darkness so strong, he kept his emotions at arm's length, which was easy, you just had to become numb inside, a cold, closed-off shell fuelled by power, strength, and purpose rather than by love or emotion. He had learned how to many years ago thanks to his father's teachings, and those terrible lessons just could not be forgotten no matter what the female romantics in his family wanted for him.

By never letting anyone else invade his little bubble, Blake had maintained his ominous strength and incredible power perfectly, never allowing nonsense such as love affect his decision-making abilities or cloud his renowned judgement. If he was horny, he would fuck, and he had plenty with whom to do it with, but right now he just wanted to sit and be melancholy for no reason other than that he wanted to, and he did not have to explain himself to his twin sister.

CHAPTER SEVENTEEN

Home and work life continued as normal all around Tilly, as though everything was still the same as it had always been. She supposed that to everyone else, life still was the same, but nothing was as it had once seemed for her. The world had become a new and scary place ever since her life-changing night at the castle, and Tilly knew it would only get crazier as her time as Blake's follower went on. The following week she returned to college, her new wardrobe attracting negative comments from Renee, who called her a Goth and then rolled her eyes when Tilly told her just where she could stick her opinion. In the food hall later that week, Tilly felt a strange little beacon from somewhere deep in her gut and couldn't understand what it must be. She couldn't help but look around the large room to try and figure it out and that was when she saw a girl dressed entirely in black, watching her from a small table in the corner. She sat alone, and beckoned Tilly over with a wave, smiling and eager for her to join her once they had made eye contact.

"Hi there, fellow follower," the girl said as Tilly sat down opposite her, and she was gobsmacked. That must have been what the strange little feeling was. She could sense the girls mark even from across the room.

"Hi," she said back, instinctively rubbing her wrist where her hidden mark was. The girl saw and realised that she must be new to all of this, so helped her out.

"Are you new?" she asked excitedly, her dark-brown eyes wide and her black hair bobbing up and down on her shoulders as she talked enthusiastically. Tilly nodded and smiled, looking all around her at the other people milling around in the hall to check they weren't going to be overheard. "Well, don't worry, okay. I am not gonna start shouting about it in the dining hall." She laughed, making Tilly smile and instantly drop her guard.

"My name's Sapphire, and my master is the demon Belias," she informed her formally, and then waited for Tilly to do the same in return.

"Well, my name's Tilly," she said, but hesitated as to what she should say next. "And urm."

"It's nice to meet you Tilly. You don't have to tell me who your master is if you don't want to. It is our choice whether to divulge the details or not, it's okay if you don't want to say it yet," she said with a warm smile as she rose from her chair and offered her a cigarette. Tilly shook her head no but joined Sapphire outside to chat to her some more as she smoked, grateful to have a friend at college who knew all about her secret world. They became friends right away, and Sapphire never pushed Tilly to find out who her master was, seeming to understand and respect her privacy much more than her other friends would ever do if she kept anything so important from them.

A couple of weeks later Tilly and Gwen were informed that they were all going out to celebrate Renee's birthday in Coventry, the plan being to hit the bars and end up at one of the huge nightclubs there to dance the night away and get insanely drunk. She said yes, eager to let her hair down and thinking that, after all, Blake had told her she could live her life however she wanted while she was not given any orders to follow. She was certain that she would behave herself while she was out and maintained that she would just have a few drinks with her friend, not intending to get too drunk and disappoint her master quite so soon. Tilly also had no idea when she would see her Black Prince again and had not heard from her master since that wonderful dream, so could do with the distraction that a night out with her friends would give her. Gwen agreed to come too and the three of them happily bar-hopped their way up the high street before drunkenly making their way into one of the busy nightclubs. Tilly had decided to wear her dark-blonde hair in a high ponytail with dark eye makeup and she had gone for a black skater style dress with fishnet tights and very high-heeled black boots. She topped it all off with a thick silver necklace and cuff bracelet, and along with her biker jacket, she looked amazing. Not even one of them noticed the bright and very full moon that had risen in the sky above them as they made their way along the busy high street and then hurried excitedly into the bars for their next round, the energy of the night calling to them. Tilly was having a great time, laughing, and joking with her friends as they made their way through far too many cocktails and shots while Renee flirted wildly with many a handsome barman or fellow drunken comrade on a night out too. By the time they had gotten to the club, Tilly had had more than enough to drink, thanks to the two-for-one deals in the bars that had lined their path there. She headed straight towards the bustling dance floor once she was inside rather than to the bar with Renee. Gwen joined her and they happily throbbed with the heavy crowd, keeping hold of each other as they were thrown around a little when the music picked up speed. The loud bass hurt Tilly's ears, but she didn't care. She hadn't been out dancing in such a long time and was enjoying herself far too much to worry about having ringing ears for the next day or so.

Renee appeared at their side after a few minutes with drinks in her hands, which she passed to Tilly and Gwen.

"Thanks," Tilly shouted as she took the cool drink and greedily downed a large gulp, whisky and cola, her favourite.

"I didn't buy them," Renee told her with a sly grin, and had to lean in closer and shout over the music for Tilly to hear her better. "I met three totally gorgeous guys at the bar. They bought them for us," she said with a pleading look. "I promised we'd go over after this song has finished. They are so hot, trust me!" she shouted with excitement, and Tilly shook her head.

"Nope, not interested Renee," she said, looking at Gwen, but her friend's big brown eyes were looking at Tilly pleadingly too, and she groaned in defeat.

"Just because you're not interested, doesn't mean we can't pull some hotties. Come on, for me?" Renee asked with a smile and a flutter of her long eyelashes. Tilly smiled and nodded in agreement, finishing off her drink with a large gulp before she then followed Renee over to the bar in search of these so-called, 'hot guys,' that her friend had promised would be waiting for them there.

She caught Blake's green eyes watching her from across the room before seeing him properly in the crowd by the bar and she nearly squealed with excitement as she neared him, catching the sly grin curling at the corners of his mouth as he watched her approach.

CHAPTER EIGHTEEN

"There they are," Renee said, pointing in the direction of Blake and his two friends, but Tilly had already known that they must be the guys she was talking about, and she could somehow sense that his two companions were demons. Renee led the way and a few seconds later the trio were stood beneath the terrifyingly seductive gaze of the three dark and powerful beings.

"Tilly, Gwen, this is Luke, Bob and Levi," she introduced them with a satisfied smirk, eying her as if to say, *'I told you so'*.

Blake couldn't take his eyes off Tilly, and she felt her knees go weak under his gaze. She smiled, reaching out to shake his hand while the other two men focussed on obtaining her friends' attentions, and she wondered if they had been ordered to keep the two girls busy so that Blake could have her to himself.

"Pleased to meet you," she said, performing a small and unsuspecting bow to her master and graciously accepting another whisky and cola that he offered her. He hadn't even needed to ask what she might like to drink. Tilly knew he could read her like a book so was not surprised he would know what to get her, but she loved the gesture, anyway.

"Well, if it isn't the girl of my dreams," he said quietly, smiling as he watched her sip the drink, tipping the glass higher to try and hide her blushing cheeks.

"I suppose I can't say you're the *man* of my dreams, but perhaps the master of them," she eventually managed to reply quietly, smiling up at him sheepishly. He laughed gruffly and grinned back before he then took her hand in his and pulled Tilly away without another word, only stopping when they reached a dark corner where he then pinned her up against the wall and kissed her deeply. She swooned in his grasp and kissed him back with a passion and need for him she hadn't even realised she had built up during his absence. He finally broke their intense kiss and pulled his head back to stare into her eyes, a flicker of surprise in his gaze too.

"Ready to get out of here?" he asked, looking around to make sure no one was watching the two of them.

"Of course, your Majesty," she replied in a whisper, panting, and trembling before him, having completely forgotten all about her friends and the busy club around them.

In less than a second, they teleported away from the club and arrived in a dark foyer, and Tilly had to give herself a second to find her feet. The whisky and cocktails coursing through her system weren't helping matters, though.

"Did we just," she started to ask him.

"Teleport, yes," he answered her, laughing as she shook her head in bemusement and gripped the nearby wall to help steady herself.

"Cool," she then said to herself as Blake moved over to one of the walls, turned on the lights and then unlocked a huge set of wooden doors that were before them. The lights inside had flicked on now too, and Tilly could see into a huge penthouse flat that stretched out before her. It was darkly decorated in blacks and reds but was lavishly furnished and the walls each held dark, erotic, and ominous art. She had never seen anything like it before and stood for a few moments, taking it all in and she couldn't help feeling common and unrefined in this luxurious home fit for nothing but millionaires and socialites. He shook his head, reading her, took her hand and then led her inside, locking the doors behind them so as not to be disturbed, and Tilly felt her heart flutter with excitement at being here alone with him.

Blake then led her over to a small bar area near the lounge, where she sat down on a stool and watched him intently as he poured them both some whisky over perfectly square cubes of ice.

"Any chance I could have some cola with that please, master?" she asked timidly, hoping not to annoy her powerful companion. He smiled but huffed and shook his head again as he pushed the glass towards her.

"This is a ten-thousand-pound bottle of whisky Tilly, you absolutely do not mix it with cola," he told her authoritatively but with an edge of playfulness about him.

She had not seen him so relaxed before. His cold, business-like manner from the night of Lucas's trial was gone now, giving way for his more playful and fun side to shine through. She liked this side of him and smiled in gracious defeat as she picked up the crystal tumbler and swirled the ice around in the thick, dark spirit for a moment, coating the ice with the strong drink, which helped to water it down slightly. Tilly then raised it to her lips and took a small sip as he watched her intently. The whisky really was lovely, and she couldn't help but concede to his triumph in this matter, shrugging and nodding with a coy smile before she took another sip.

"Good, you'll soon learn to just trust my judgement without question. Now, let me give you the tour," he said, taking her hand and pulling her close.

"It must be nice always being right," she murmured, smiling up at him and he couldn't help but grin back down at her, taking her in silently for a moment before leading the way around the huge penthouse flat. There must have been six bedrooms, each of which was stunning and lavishly decorated, just as the lounge had been. Along the corridors revealed a library, office, huge television room, home gym, and finally the master bedroom. That final room was almost as big as the lounge, with patio doors that led out onto a shared terrace with the living room, and it had massive windows on the other side that had huge black curtains over them. In the centre was a gigantic bed, with four black-curtained posts on each corner and black satin sheets covering it. Blake led her inside and placed the whisky glasses on a chest of drawers beside the patio doors. He then turned on a music system that also sat atop the wooden unit. Acoustic rock music immediately filled the room, seductive guitar riffs along with the deep, yet gentle voice of a man singing. It was beautiful and Tilly couldn't help but close her eyes and let the sound wash over her. This was much better than the thumping club music they had been listening to less than an hour earlier. Tilly listened intently, the lyrics suddenly speaking volumes to her.

"I'll follow you forever, through the darkest nights and darker days.
No need to compromise. Join me in the shadows.
Your darkness is no burden. I'll carry its weight in my soul.
Never apologise. Just make sure your soul obeys.
I'll follow you forever, just say yes."

"I'm glad you like it," Blake said, breaking her dreamlike reverie, and Tilly opened her eyes to find him standing just in front of her, his face only a few inches away. He reached up to cup her face gently in his hands, staring down into her eyes as he read her thoughts.

"You didn't mind me going out to the club tonight, did you, master?" she asked him; suddenly worried she might have needed to ask his permission or something.

"No, I told you before, you may live your life as you wish. All I ask is that you follow my rules and orders, and that you come to me when I summon you," he said, still staring into her blue eyes alluringly.

She couldn't help but laugh, thinking that even if that was all he wanted from her, it was still an incredible amount for her to have to take into consideration, but she knew she would do so willingly if it meant more nights like this.

"Did you summon me tonight?" she wondered aloud, hoping she hadn't accidentally ignored his commandment in her slightly drunken haze.

"Trust me, you'll know it when I do. I read your thoughts while I was in Hell Tilly, so I knew that you and your friends were planning this night out. Why did you think I bought along some 'hot guys' to help distract your friends for me so that I could get you alone?" he asked with a fiendish grin, confirming her earlier suspicions on the subject.

"Ah, I thought that was quite a happy coincidence," she replied with a smile, her eyes lighting up as she peered up at him.

"There are no coincidences, you should know that by now?" he asked, however he didn't wait for an answer and pulled her towards him, capturing her mouth again with his, and they kissed deeply. Tilly had to grip Blake's shoulders to stop herself from falling, so woozy from his wonderful kisses, weak from his powerful prowess and commanded by his omnipotent power that she nearly forgot to breathe. His hands reached down to support her, pulling Tilly even closer into his embrace.

"Strip," he then commanded, just a whisper, but so incredibly clear and powerful that it was as though she heard him in her mind as well as in her ears.

"Yes master," she said, understanding now that there really was a big difference between him asking and him telling her. Tilly reached down and began pulling off her dress, slipping it down and then throwing it onto a nearby chair. Her tights soon followed, and then her underwear. She stood before him, naked and trembling with anticipation, and looked up into his satisfied green eyes and she smiled, sensing his pleasure with her.

"Déjà vu," she whispered, looking him up and down, taking in his complete outfit and remembering her dream where she was naked before him then, too. He laughed and reached down, scooping Tilly up into his arms and then pulling her legs up to wrap them around his waist as he carried her over to the bed.

"This is not going to be like anything you've had before Tilly, I absolutely guarantee it," he informed her as he placed her gently on the sheets and stood back, pulling off his black shirt before unbuttoning his jeans. She sat back and crossed her legs, gazing up at him; her dark, sexy, God-like master, and she almost drooled as she finally got to take in his perfect, half naked body as he stood before her. His arms and torso were so muscular, so defined and sexy, and his open fly showed off those sexy hip muscles that made Tilly feel wet at the thought of what was to come next. Blake laughed, almost coyly, as he read her and her wicked thoughts about him and his glorious body. She just grinned and climbed up onto her knees and sat before him on the bed, licking her lips and silently pleading with him to continue undressing for her. He obliged, pulling off his jeans and boxers, releasing his hard cock at last as he did.

"Come here," he commanded, and Tilly shuffled forward, eager to touch him, to feel his flawless skin against hers. Blake leaned in and kissed her, grabbing her lower back, and pulling her closer, pressing his hard body into hers. He then lifted one thigh up and wrapped it around his waist, opening her up for him as they continued to kiss passionately. He finally pulled his mouth away, needing to ask her just one last question before they could proceed.

"Are you ready to fuck me Tilly?" he asked her, his gorgeous green eyes staring at her intently.

"Yes," she whispered back, her voice trembling with anticipation.

In less than a second of her response, Blake pulled her closer with one strong thrust and he was inside her in an instant. She gasped as she enveloped him, her muscles tightening wonderfully and her body moistening for him instantly. He pulled her back and forth, commanding her body with his. The wonderful strokes he delivered to the tender spot inside of her making her succumb to him without hesitation or fear. His kisses grew deeper, more intense, and eager as he moved harder and faster inside her hot and welcoming cleft. She came quickly, unable to contain the pleasurable release, no matter how much she tried to slow it. He didn't care though and carried on, enjoying her climax but also intent on continuing in his pursuit of his own release.

After her body calmed down, Blake laid Tilly back onto the bed, but she continued to tremble in his strong grasp thanks to the most satisfying and intense orgasm of her life. He turned her over onto her stomach before him with a satisfied smile. Finally, joining her on the bed, he then climbed over Tilly and slipped inside her from behind, his strong body pressing her fragile frame into the huge bed as he thrust hard inside of her. She groaned with pleasure as he continued his strong and deep thrusts, grabbing at the sheets with her hands and pushing back to welcome him even deeper inside her, eager to give him every inch of room she was able to open for him. She came again, deep and breathtakingly intense, as he pushed even harder inside her and cried out for him.

Blake flipped her over again, this time to face him before he sat up, pulling Tilly onto his lap so that she could ride his long length while he watched. She happily obliged, climbing atop her Adonis and slid him back inside her still wet, ready, and willing opening. Blake watched her with a wicked grin as she rode up and down, and then grabbed her hips and deepened the thrusts, unable to help himself.

He sat up further, cradling Tilly in his arms and taking her mouth in his again as she continued to pleasure him, eager as he was for him to reach his climax. She was desperate to give him his gratification and pushed her body way beyond its normal limits to satisfy her dark master. She cried out uncontrollably again as a third orgasm rippled through her, the aftershocks making her weak, and her human body finally started to struggle to keep up with his relentless lovemaking.

Blake pulled her closer to him, stopping his thrusts for a few moments as he kept still and enjoyed the feeling of her inner muscles as they clenched around him from deep within. He looked up at Tilly, and kissed her gently, staring into her blue eyes as he revelled in her pleasure, basking in her satisfied glow. She was dusted with sweat, red-faced, and truly beautiful. There was no way he could stop now.

Blake then laid Tilly back onto the bed; his strong body lifting her easily before he then wrapped himself inside her trembling thighs. She looked up into his gorgeous green eyes again as he continued to slide in and out of her still moist opening, slower now and less urgent but still hot and hard for her as he leaned over Tilly and gripped her thighs with his strong hands, lifting her hips to meet his. She ran her hands up his shoulders and then through his dark-brown hair, smiling up at him through her woozy haze of emotion, lust and even love. She was falling for him. She could already feel it and knew she couldn't control it.

They continued for hours, and eventually Tilly was left panting and exhausted after her sixth orgasm, while Blake grabbed her tight and pulled her closer one more time. The bed beneath them shook slightly as he came, his hot bursts throbbing inside of her as he reached his powerful climax and cried out, kissing her feverishly as he revelled in his glorious release at last.

Tilly lay in his arms afterwards, relaxed, and wonderfully exhausted, while she watched the sun stream into the bedroom through the open curtain as she rested her head on Blake's chest. She was too exhausted to talk, yet still too buzzing to sleep, and so she just let her mind wander, knowing he would be listening in. Blake lay silent too, smiling, and caressing Tilly's bare back with his hand as she draped herself over him and he wrapped her protectively in his arms, working hard to push away the feelings that were threatening to creep into his heart for her too.

"I can't give you what you want Tilly," he told her later that morning after she had managed to drift off for a couple of hours' sleep. He had stayed with her but hadn't let himself fall off to sleep beside her, his mind running through every possible scenario for the pair of them and their future together.

"What do you mean, master?" she asked, confused by this sudden, bleak statement.

"The image of us you showed me in your dream," Blake told her, and her face fell. "I can never love you. Don't live in hope that I will ever say those words to you, Tilly. I am not capable of love," he added, quiet and sombre, but he wanted to be honest with her. Blake knew that she was falling for him, and he wanted her to be his. He wanted to control and possess her entirely and have her at his every command, but that was all he could ever offer the innocent young girl. Possession was all he knew. Love was something long forgotten, and he knew he could never love Tilly back, never give her the love she deserved and wanted so desperately.

"Will you hurt me?" she asked him, leaning up on one elbow so that she could look into his hooded green eyes properly. Her response surprised Blake, having expected her to cry out or try to reason with him, or even beg him to reconsider. This was an unanticipated reaction. For some reason, she accepted his harsh words. He could sense it in her calm, decisive thoughts. Tilly took his dark words like a strangely profound promise, and was willing to live with them, even if it meant loving him for the rest of her life and never having him love her in return.

"Yes," Blake answered, knowing that in all honesty he most likely would hurt Tilly eventually, both mentally and physically. He was bad news, no matter how either of them looked at it, and Blake knew he would probably just end up using her to satisfy his needs and then leave her once he had had enough. That was just his way. He had always blamed his black heart for it, despite knowing that his siblings and mother did not suffer from the same aversion to emotions that he did.

He had never had a relationship with a woman that did not involve fucking them and then leaving, calling on them again only when he was horny. His witches and lower-level demons had seen to those needs perfectly well in his almost eighty-year existence. He did not stick around for the declarations of love, cuddling or date-nights and knew he never would.

Tilly stared into his eyes thoughtfully, trying to read him but was not able to understand the true motives behind his words or properly sense the emotion he was fighting so hard to keep hidden behind his stoic features. She just smiled down at him and kissed Blake's lips gently. She knew she was already far too close to being in love with her master, and she couldn't bring herself to care that he might never love her in return. After all, she was his possession now and if he never saw her as anything more, she would just have to get used to it.

"Well, I'm sure you know just how much I can take, whether physically or emotionally, and still be able to come back from in one piece, so do it. I'll take it. I made a vow to you and I will honour it, regardless of what I have to go through to do so," Tilly told him, and Blake knew she meant it. Her body was weak from their lovemaking, sore and tired, but she was strong in other ways and knew her mind, so spoke it confidently without fearing him now, not in this moment.

It was the most truly honest anyone had ever been with him, and Blake couldn't find the words to respond, honestly taken aback by this beautiful girl and her incredibly strong nature.

CHAPTER NINETEEN

They rested together for a while longer, and then Blake rose from the huge bed and pulled on his black jeans. Tilly had been dozing in his arms again and groaned as he moved away. He laughed and kissed her cheek, heading off through the penthouse in search of some coffee. She forced herself to wake up too and, after a quick shower, joined him in the large kitchen. She had found his shirt folded neatly in the bedroom and pulled it on, but with nothing underneath, and plodded into the heavily coffee scented kitchen with a smile as she pulled her still damp hair into a ponytail.

She caught sight of his perfectly toned back as he stood at the kitchen counter, his flawless body already making the butterflies return to her belly.

"Oh really?" he asked her with a grin as she joined him and grabbed a mug. Tilly smiled and shrugged as he filled it for her, and she sipped it after inhaling the delicious scent dreamily.

"My clothes were all crumpled and dirty. I didn't think you would mind your Majesty?" she replied with a cheeky smile. "But I think I might be in trouble wearing this shirt in particular," she added playfully, taking another sip of the dark drink.

"And why is that?" he said, turning to look her up and down as she stood before him, her bum only just about being covered by the dark cotton.

"Because my master is a naughty boy and I'm pretty sure this is dark grey, not black," she said, looking up to him as she spoke, hoping that she wasn't pushing her luck.

"You're right, good girl. You had better take it off this very instant," Blake commanded her, smiling down at Tilly as she unbuttoned the shirt and then draped it over the back of the stool next to her. He took in her stunning, naked body as she stood before him while he sipped on his hot, black drink and then reached into the drawer beside him and pulled out a small knife. Tilly looked on in shock for a moment, unsure what he was planning to do with it and watched as he poked his finger with the tip of the blade, drawing a small drop of blood to the surface, which he then offered to her.

"You'd best have this then Tilly, because I need to fuck you again right now and you're gonna need the strength," he told her with a wicked grin, relishing in her brazenness and groaning with pleasure as she stepped forward without even a moment's hesitation and willingly sucked the blood from his fingertip. Within seconds, she felt its effect on her, immediately soothing her soreness and delivering her with the energy and strength to start again. After just a few seconds, Blake pinned Tilly to the kitchen side as he kissed her deeply, pulling her legs around his waist and then ripping open his fly and forcing himself inside her as she gripped his shoulders and groaned loudly, eager and ready to please him again.

A couple of hours later, Tilly stood at the large living room window that overlooked the city, still naked following their second round of fantastic lovemaking and her core still trembling thanks to the wonderful memory her muscles just could not let go of. Blake came up behind her and pressed his rippled torso into her back as he grabbed and embraced her in his strong arms before pulling her chin up and back so that her lips could meet his. He needed to taste her again.

She wondered to herself about the blood she had drunk from him, thinking back to her conversation with Brent about how demons used their blood to control humans. She didn't feel like he had used it that way, though, and couldn't figure out what had passed between them in that little drop.

"Demons do use their blood for control you're right, unless their bond is strong, which you already know from your experiences with Lilith and Lucas," he said, replying to her thoughts. "It's my choice what I use it for, Tilly, and my blood is incredibly powerful, so just a drop at a time will do. I used it today to heal you, to rid your body of its tenderness and fatigue. That's all," he told her, and she smiled up at him, grateful for the explanation.

"Thank you," she replied. "Are we in London?" she then asked him, looking back out at the skyline.

"Yes," he answered, keeping his arms around her. "We keep this penthouse as a base for when we come to Earth. Luna and I often come up during the full moons. Our mother rarely comes up anymore, but she has been known to throw a party or two here over the years. My other family are not bound by the moon so can come whenever they please. They live on Earth permanently now though, so don't need to use this as a base," he told her, opening up a little bit about his family.

Tilly looked back at him, and then turned herself around to face him and looked up into her master's eyes.

"Do you mind me asking, why is it you cannot come here whenever you want?" she asked him hesitantly. Blake looked at her thoughtfully for a moment but was not angry. This was not the sort of information his family would readily give out to the masses, and it most certainly wouldn't have been in the books she had used to help her learn about him and his unusual family.

"My Uncle Devin and Aunt Serena are half-human, and so are their children, my cousins Braeden, Leyla, and Corey. This allows for them to travel freely between the two worlds and stay as long as they wish in either one. My mother was once half-human too, but since she took over the throne, she has been transformed and is now one-hundred percent pure darkness," he said, pausing to check that she was following. "Luna and I were born while she was still half-human, but our father's full darkness made us only one-quarter human, so we are bound by the moon just as he was," he added, and his face fell. Blake hadn't spoken of his father in a very long time. Tilly reached up and touched his cheek gently before placing a light kiss on his lips.

"I'm sorry. Thank you for explaining it to me," she replied, quickly breaking his sad mood. She thought about the family he had just told her about and the children that were born into their powerful brood, panicking for a moment about whether she needed to worry about contraception with him. Blake laughed to himself, shaking his head as he read her thoughts.

"There's no need to worry Tilly, I'd have to ask you to bear my offspring, and you would have to say yes first, free will and all that. Plus, we would most likely need my mother's permission, too. It doesn't just happen like with humans, it all takes a bit of, *planning*," he told her, putting her instantly at ease.

He then smiled down at her and kissed her deeply before finally releasing his hold on her and heading back to the kitchen. Tilly followed him and found Blake pulling on his black jeans again. He picked up the shirt from the stool where she had put it earlier and handed it to her.

"You'd better put this back on," he told her with a wide, knowing grin.

"Why?" she asked, just as a knock at the door made her jump.

The two demons she had briefly met the night before, Bob and Levi, entered a moment later, only just as Tilly had finished buttoning up the dark shirt. She still felt exposed, knowing that she had nothing on underneath it and that the hem of the shirt was so very high. She leaned back against the side of the kitchen counter to cover her backside and smiled warmly at the two demons as they entered.

"Good evening your Majesty, you're looking buff tonight," Levi said with a cheeky smile as he took in the sight of his half-naked master, but he still bowed to his Prince respectfully, and Bob did the same.

"Hey guys," he replied with a grin, flexing his biceps jokingly to break the formality and he then slid them both a mug filled with steaming black coffee. He handed one to Tilly too, and she smiled, thanking him quietly. It was strange for her to see him with his friends, joking around and having fun, and she liked it.

"Did you have a good time after we left last night?" Blake then asked them with a wink.

They both sniggered and Levi spoke first.

"Yeah, that Renee girl was certainly a fair bit of fun. She couldn't handle me all the way till the end though, so I had to finish in her arse, but you know I'm never against a harmless bit of anal," he said, laughing. Tilly gasped and blushed, which only made the others laugh even harder.

"Gwen was a real nice surprise, too," Bob told Blake. "Rode me for hours," he told him with a wink and Tilly buried her face in her mug, not wanting to hear more intimate details about her friends. "Seriously though, I was pleasantly surprised with her. I'm thinking of marking her now that I'm due to stay here on Earth for a while. What do you think, boss?"

Blake looked at Tilly, reading her reaction for a second before answering him. She was shocked but liked the idea of having a close friend who knew the truth and she could talk with her about all this demonic business. They could help each other get through the transition.

"Good idea, but mark Renee as well, it'd be good for Tilly having her friends in the upper circle of followers as well," he told him, a commanding order to his friend and servant, who nodded in agreement. "Speaking of Tilly, don't you have something you need to ask these two?" he said, reminding her of the rules when it came to associating with demons.

"Yes, I guess I'm supposed to ask you both for your names, right?" she asked, ashamed that she was still so new to all of this. They both smiled patiently over at her, and Levi spoke first.

"Well, my name is Leviathan, but you can call me Levi if you'd prefer," he told her, reaching out to shake her hand and eying her bare legs as she stepped forward to take it. A dark scowl from Blake stopped them both in their tracks, and Tilly jumped back as Levi stopped his flirtatious, wandering eyes and held up his hands, a silent apology passing between him and his Black Prince.

"Keep your hands to yourself and your eyes up Leviathan," he warned him, and the demon bowed in apology. Tilly remained still while the air around them seemed to buzz, Blake's ominous power emanating from him for a few seconds before he noticeably calmed himself down and took another sip of his coffee.

"I'm Beelzebub, or Bob if you prefer," the other demon told her with a grin, and Tilly smiled back at him, glad that he had broken the tense silence.

"So why do you go by the name Luke?" she asked Blake, forgetting her place for a moment, but being reminded instantly as he turned cold, almost black eyes on her, and the two demons slunk back noticeably. He stared across at her, his eyes growing darker as she sent him silent pleas and apologies through her thoughts as she tensed up, ready to take his punishment and mentally kicking herself for being so foolish.

CHAPTER TWENTY

"Luke is an alias my father always used to use, there's no real way to alter mine, so I thought I'd use it last night so that you had something to call me in front of your friends," Blake told Tilly coldly, but then suddenly switched back to his playful self as he locked away the feelings that threatened to bubble over and forced away the darkness that had crept into his eyes. She stood still as she watched him, desperate to take back her foolish words, but he thankfully moved the conversation on rather than dwell on her mistake.

"I think we should have a party tonight. What do you think?" Blake then asked them, and the two very much relieved demons turned to their master with wicked grins.

"Absolutely," said Leviathan excitedly.

Blake then nodded and grabbed Tilly before turning her and leading her away from the kitchen, her body still tense and he almost had to move her arms and legs for her as he led her away.

"Get the word out boys, upper-level demons and their hand-picked followers only, oh and get those two girls down here as well," he said, another order to the two demons as he and Tilly made their way out into the living room. She looked up at him, trying to read her master, but he was giving her nothing, so she pushed her fears aside and followed his lead.

She then heard the main doors to the penthouse open behind them just a few seconds later and turned to see a group of women enter through them. She assumed Blake must have sent out a silent order for them to come to him, awed by his power once again. He left Tilly's side for a moment and went over to welcome them, talking first to a tall and beautiful, dark-red haired woman as the others began fussing about with the décor and moving the furniture around in the main living room.

The young woman gazed up at him with lust and want, but Tilly could tell that Blake was not even bothered by it, perhaps far too used to being looked at that way by his devoted minions. He gave her his orders and then led her over to meet the still scantily clad human.

"Tilly, this is Selena, she is the high priestess of my coven," he told her, and waved his hand around to indicate the other women that had arrived with her. Selena smiled at Tilly and bowed her head to her master respectfully.

"Hi," was all Tilly could think to say to her, unsure of how to address the witch just yet. She could sense the woman's incredible dark prowess and suspected that she must be very powerful if she was his high priestess.

"Selena will help to get you ready. There is a selection of clothes and shoes for you in the main bedroom now, as well as products and makeup for you to use. I want you ready in half an hour," he ordered, and the two women bowed and left him, rushing off to go and get Tilly ready in time. Selena barely said a word as she led Tilly away, but then tersely told her what to do once they reached the bedroom.

"Get in there and take a shower, shave every inch of your legs, armpits and pussy then apply a generous layer of moisturiser to every bit of your skin as quickly as possible," she barked, making Tilly feel uncomfortable, but she quickly did as she was told.

In his office, Blake chatted quietly with his old friend, and loyal demon, Leviathan. They discussed his current orders and Levi's plans, the powerful demon hoping, as always, for a coveted place on Blake's dark council, but the Black Prince refused him again.

"You're not right for it, too mischievous. I need dark and brooding," he told him.

"Fair one. I never was any good at that. I prefer the lure, the seduction and then the attack," Leviathan admitted, grinning broadly at his master.

"Don't get me wrong, I like that too," Blake admitted.

"Like with that girl?" his friend asked, one eyebrow raised.

"I suppose. She's a good girl, Levi. So sweet and pure, and you know what that means?"

"Oh yes," the demon replied, a satisfied smile curling at his lips. "Good girls turned bad are always the most tantalising of trophies."

"Exactly, and I have this girl exactly where I want her," Blake said, an evil glint in his eye as he smiled wickedly at his friend before heading back out to the lounge.

When Tilly emerged from the bathroom, having done as Selena had asked, she wore just a black robe with a towel that she had wrapped around her head, and the witch was at the ready with a hairdryer and brush.

"He prefers curls and likes hair to be left down not up in a ponytail," she informed Tilly matter-of-factly once her hair was dry and she then began twisting hot irons around her long, dark-blonde locks.

"No," a voice boomed from the doorway as Blake joined them, making

Selena jump. "Put it up, in a side-bun, and she is to wear this," he said, taking a black corseted dress from the wardrobe that flowed beautifully down to the floor from under the boned top. He smiled at Tilly in the mirror's reflection, and she blushed and smiled back at him, knowing that he was thinking of her dream, and that he wanted her dressed in the same way she had been then.

Selena nodded and immediately began working Tilly's hair up into a neat bun instead, letting just a couple of curls fall by her face before applying some dark makeup. Blake stripped and Tilly couldn't help but look at his gorgeous form as it was reflected in the mirror, but she also noticed Selena's eyes dart up to look at his reflection too as he wandered naked into the walk-in wardrobe. The witch then caught Tilly looking at her, and quickly composed herself again, working on the finishing touches silently.

Blake emerged from the wardrobe a few minutes later, fully dressed in a perfectly tailored black suit, with matching waistcoat and with a crisp black shirt and tie, the perfect match to the outfit that he too had worn the night she had dreamt of him. She blushed again, the two of them sharing their little secret as the witch finished off the last of Tilly's makeup.

"Good, you may leave us now, Selena," Blake ordered, barely even looking at her.

"Yes, master," she said quietly, leaving the two of them alone in the bedroom. Tilly stood and took in the sight of him before her. Seeing him in that suit sent all kinds of wonderful messages around her body. He smiled and grabbed the belt of her robe, pulling her towards him for a deep and passionate kiss before he untied the knot and pulled the robe off, leaving Tilly standing naked before him again.

"Déjà vu," he said with a sly grin, and Tilly heard a faint *click* from behind him that told her that the bedroom door had just been magically locked shut.

"Lay on the bed," he ordered her, and she followed his command immediately, eager to please her master in the hope of the reward she prayed might come next. Blake kept his gaze on her as he lowered himself down, kissing her breasts and stomach before slowly making his way lower. Tilly gasped and gripped the covers tightly as his mouth took hold of her ready nub and began caressing it, delicately at first, then harder and stronger. His hands pulled her thighs apart further, opening her cleft to him as he began stroking his strong tongue up and down her tender lips. Two fingers slid easily inside, and he pushed down on her g-spot, making Tilly gush, and come for him almost instantly. She groaned loudly, gripping the covers beneath her tighter as she rode the wonderful waves of ecstasy that her master had given her.

Blake pulled her legs closed and stood, watching as she came down from her high with a satisfied grin. He grabbed some red panties and a matching strapless bra from one of the drawers and passed them to her.

"Put these on," he commanded with a wink. "No one will know but me," he added as he ducked into the bathroom to freshen up while Tilly slid on the underwear with trembling hands, her body still reeling from her climax.

He returned to the bedroom a couple of minutes later and helped her into the beautiful dress. Blake then stepped back to take her in. She was still flushed from her orgasm and looked amazing, just like in the dream with her smoky eyed makeup and side-bun. He came around behind her in front of the huge mirror and gripped her the same way that he had in the dream, trailing kisses along her collar as she stared into his deep green eyes through the reflected image.

"Wow don't you two just make the most gorgeous couple?" asked a woman's voice from behind them, and Tilly jumped before turning to look at who had broken the silence. A young woman stood before her, with long, dark curls that fell by her beautiful face and she had deep green eyes that bore into Tilly's skull as she stared over at her for a moment. She then dropped to her knees instantly, realising at once that this must be Blake's twin sister, Luna.

CHAPTER TWENTY-ONE

"What are you doing here?" Blake asked her, stepping forward to embrace his twin and kiss her cheek in greeting.

"I just thought I'd pop up and see what this party's all about, don't worry, I won't stay long," she joked, eying him thoughtfully. She looked down and took in the sight of the young woman that kneeled before her.

"You can stand up Tilly, I don't want to get you in trouble for ruining that beautiful dress of yours," she added, reaching down to help her up. Tilly took her hand gratefully and bowed to her as she climbed to her feet, not sure how to act or what to say to the powerful, beautiful woman.

"Thank you, your Majesty," she then said, feeling uneasy under the Black Princess's intense scrutiny.

"You may wait for me out in the hall Tilly," Blake then ordered her, and she left the siblings to talk, bowing to them as she ducked out into the hallway and closed the door behind her, grateful for a moment to herself.

"She seems nice," Luna said to her brother once they were alone, and Blake raised an eyebrow at her.

"What are you *really* doing here, Luna?" he asked impatiently.

"I felt a change in the air, in you, so I thought I would pop up and see what was going on. You two seem really happy, close, but I sense some hesitation from you, dear brother, and you know I cannot keep my nose out," she told him, and he tensed, prickling angrily in an instant.

"You would be wise to keep your curiosity to yourself Luna. I am sick of you trying to interfere in my life. We are having fun, that's all. Don't try to push me," he said, his features mashing into an angry stare.

"I'm only here because I love you, hard as it might be for you to hear, Blake, but I do love you. We all do. And yet, I know that you're thinking of him, remembering him fondly and using his alias. Why? Why would you choose to think of him over our mother?" she asked, getting angry herself now. "Did you know he was a tyrant? He forced his will on everyone and tortured those he was supposed to love and protect?"

"You know as well as I, just how well I know all of those things, Luna.

Who told you to say that to me? Mother?" he snapped.

"You know she would never speak of such things. I have listened in on other's thoughts, Blake. Alma, Dylan, and even Devin opened up to me. She knows I have quizzed them and has not tried to stop me. She wants me to know the truth and for you to learn it, too. Stop trying to pretend that you don't care what happened to her, what happened to them both after she was taken that night in the park. Stop blaming yourself for his dethroning. He deserved it Blake, and you will never be King if you continue to be like him: cold, manipulative, black-hearted and cruel," she bellowed, her eyes turning dark as she too grew more and more angry.

Blake looked down at her, his eyes becoming completely black now too as he absorbed his sister's harsh words. The floor beneath them started to shake, an earthquake seemingly beginning from Blake as he stood stone-like and cold before her.

"Who the fuck do you think you are, Luna?" he shouted in her face, the anger pouring out of him uncontrollably.

"Get out of here right now before I do something I might regret!" he bellowed, and Luna teleported away, not wanting to have this out with him on Earth, her beautiful face forlorn. This was not how she had expected their conversation to go.

Out in the hall, Tilly grabbed at the doorframe as the shaking building jostled her around uncontrollably in her high-heeled shoes. Selena came running down the hallway towards her, going to the door with the aim of going inside and finding out what was going on, but Tilly blocked her path.

"Stop," she shouted to her. "He's in there with his sister, you must not disturb them."

"Well, that explains it, then. Get out of my way," Selena shouted, shoving Tilly aside as she burst into the bedroom.

"Master, there's an earthquake. Send your sister away," Selena began to say, but was cut short as Blake turned to look at her, his eyes still black and his anger further fuelled by the unwelcome presence of his witch. Invisible hands gripped her throat and pulled Selena off her feet. He stared at her coldly as she writhed in panic and fear, and then with a flick of his head she was tossed across the room where she slammed into the wall and fell to the floor, limp and seemingly dead.

Blake stared at her for a moment and then looked up and out the open doorway where Tilly stood staring at him from the hallway. She was rooted to the spot in fear, her mouth open and he stormed towards her. Her breathing was fast and shallow, terror pouring out of her after seeing his dark features and what he had just done to his high priestess.

She couldn't help but let out a small scream as Blake reached her and grabbed Tilly by the throat, lifting her off her feet and then pinning her against the wall behind her. He then pressed himself into her with such force that her back ached and she winced as he pushed her harder into the cold brick.

Tears flowed uncontrollably down Tilly's cheeks as he pinned her there, but for some reason he didn't say a word to her or squeeze her throat any tighter. Blake just held her there, his forehead against hers and his eyes closed. He too breathed fast and hard against her skin, and Tilly could somehow sense that he was trying to calm himself down. She slowed her own breaths, holding back her tears with all her might as she reached up and touched his face, gently cupping his cheeks with her palms.

"Please, please," she begged, imploring him to calm down, to regain his usual composure again. Blake opened his eyes slowly, the green returning to them a little at a time and he loosened his grip on her neck, then pulled his hand down and placed it over her heart, feeling the beat slowing beneath his touch as she took control of her panic. It calmed him, as did just having her close, and breathing in her scent had somehow helped to lull his rage. He kissed her, deep and passionate, eager to release some of his emotion. When he finally broke away and placed her back on the floor, she slipped her arms under his, wrapping them around his ribs to his back, pulling Blake into a tight hug and resting her head against his chest. "Please," she begged again, feeling him slowly coming back to her.

Blake wrapped his arms around Tilly too and held her close for several minutes before breaking the embrace. He then looked down at her and smiled at last.

"Thank you, Tilly," he whispered to her, kissing her on the lips softly and wiping the tears from her cheeks with his thumbs. Her heart was no longer pounding in her ears, and she suddenly realised that the earthquake had long since stopped and that there was now music playing from the main lounge of the penthouse.

"Let me just sort myself out and then we can go in, okay?" she asked Blake, smiling up at him before heading into the bedroom once again. She couldn't help but look down at the floor where Selena had dropped, but she was gone.

"I sent her back to Hell. I will deal with her later. She isn't dead, don't worry," he told her, having read her thoughts, and the news was a welcome relief to Tilly. "I know you tried to stop her, well done," he added, watching as she re-applied her makeup and checked herself in the mirror. Her eyes were a little red, as was her neck, but other than that she looked fine, so shook it off, took a deep breath and then headed back over to her master. She checked his suit, smoothing the front where she had leaned into him and accidentally left a tearstain. A click of his fingers and the suit was perfect again, as was her dress, giving nothing away of the anger and pain that had just been pouring out of him minutes before and its destructive power over him and everything in his vicinity. She didn't dare ask what his sister had said or done to incur such a devastating outburst.

"Let's forget about all of this and go have fun, okay?" Blake asked her, taking Tilly's hand, and leading her towards the doors that led to the living room.

CHAPTER TWENTY-TWO

"Ground rules first," Blake said as he stopped in front of the huge doors for a moment before he and Tilly went inside. "You are to stay by my side unless I release you. You do not speak unless you are spoken to, just smile and nod, okay?" he asked, and Tilly smiled and nodded, eager to bring the playful Blake back and he couldn't help but smile down at her. She knew he was testing her, but Tilly was more than willing to play along if it kept her in Blake's favour.

"Good. And I'm gonna need a lot of alcohol tonight thanks to my dear sister's visit. You are in charge of making sure that I always have a glass of whisky in my hand, Tilly. Fill it just two fingers deep, with one ice cube. When I start to get low again, tell me with your thoughts that you need to get me another glass and I will let you go to the bar, got it?" he asked, gazing down at her with a cheeky grin and she nodded, reaching up on her tiptoes to plant a kiss on his cheek.

"Anything you need, master," she whispered. Tilly then took his arm and let Blake lead her into the now busy living room of the huge penthouse.

All eyes turned their way as Blake and Tilly made their entrance. Smiles and gasps greeted the gorgeous couple along with the demons and other dark beings that moved towards them, eager for a moment with their Black Prince.

She slipped away once inside, instantly grabbing Blake a drink and then returning to his side as quickly as she could. He talked animatedly to many of the guests, introducing some of them to Tilly and she smiled and shook their hands or nodded along to their stories and anecdotes just as her master had ordered. She disappeared to grab her master another drink quite a few times, but she soon realised that she was not missed when she did. The dark beings only really wanting Blake's attention. When they eventually had a quiet minute to themselves, he leaned in to whisper in her ear.

"Once everyone feels they have had their moment with me, they will all chill out and we can have some proper fun. You just wait," he told her with a wicked grin, and she couldn't help but smile back.

"Your Highness," said a familiar voice from over Tilly's shoulder. It was Lilith, and she had Lucas and their children with her. She looked Tilly up and down, somewhat taken aback seeing the two of them whispering and smiling at each other so intimately but regained her composure again almost immediately.

"You remember my husband?" she said, bowing as she ushered towards him with her hand.

"Yes, of course. Hello again Lucas," Blake said, shaking his hand and then looking over to the three boys beside the pair of them as they also bowed to him. Brent didn't dare look at Tilly, who continued following her orders to stay quiet and she simply smiled up at Lilith as she spoke with Blake. Before long, it was Lucas who broke the strange silence, pulling Tilly out of her submissive, quiet state.

"How are you?" he asked her, much to Lilith's obvious distaste, but neither she nor Blake stopped them from talking freely. Lucas smiled across at her, the same warm smile that had always made her feel safe and loved in his company, and she couldn't help the affectionate pang that shot through her heart for him.

"Wonderful. Thank you for asking Lucas. Things could not be better," Tilly replied, but then saw Blake gulp down the last bit of his whisky and eye her cautiously. "Would you please excuse me for just a moment?" she asked, ducking away and almost running to the bar to grab another whisky for her master. She returned just in time to see Blake deposit the empty glass onto a passing waiter's tray, and handed him the new one with a smile, while he winked down at her in thanks.

Lilith was going on about some new plans for the circus, having pulled Lucas into their conversation now and their boys all stood looking at their feet anxiously. She chanced a glance at them and could immediately sense something different about Jackson. Tilly realised he must now be fully initiated into Lilith's following. He had to be otherwise he would not be here with them tonight. She was happy for him and smiled over at Lucas again when he caught her watching his youngest son.

Later, once everyone had bent Blake's ear and Tilly had bought him his twentieth glass of whisky, the mood began to lighten, and the strong alcoholic drinks started to work their magic on the partygoers. Blake handed Tilly a glass of champagne at last, her first drink of the evening, allowing her a moment to relax as the crowd bustled around them.

"You can have something stronger later, but this will do for now. Can't have you getting drunk can we," he told her, and she nodded, taking the glass from him with a smile.

"Anything you say, master, thank you," she replied with a bow, making him beam again. She loved it when he did that and relished in his warmth towards her, finding her cheeks flushing red as her thoughts gave her away. Blake then pulled her to a dark corner where he planted a soft kiss on her lips, his hands cupping her still burning cheeks. Tilly's heart fluttered wildly in her chest, the anticipation of what might be in store for her after the party driving her on. She could taste the whisky on him though, so looked up at her master questioningly, hoping he wouldn't be the one getting too drunk.

"Don't worry, it takes a lot more than this much to get me drunk," he informed her with a cheeky grin, his green eyes alight and his handsome features playful.

"It's true, I once saw him go through an entire crate of that posh whisky before he even started slurring," came a voice from behind them. It was Beelzebub, and he had Gwen on his arm, dressed all in black with an elegant gold chain around her neck and her brown hair had been cut into a short bob. This new look suited Gwen and while she felt guilty for having brought her into this world, Tilly was glad to have her here. She could sense Beelzebub's mark on her and smiled at her friend.

"Gwen, this is Blake, the Black Prince, and Tilly's master. Remember what I told you?" he asked, and she nodded and quickly fell to her knees before him. Tilly could see that Blake was reading her, and she saw the tell-tale inverted red cross come to the surface of the skin inside Gwen's right wrist.

"Hello again, Gwen," he said, ushering for her to stand. "It seems you have picked up the whole bowing formality much quicker than Tilly did, but I'll let her tell you that story later," he told her with a laugh, putting Gwen at ease a little although she was trembling before him, having obviously been informed by Beelzebub of his status. Renee soon joined them too, following orders and bowing before Blake immediately, who smiled and read her quickly, before he ushered for her to stand beside her demonic master as well.

"Tilly, you may go and speak with your friends for a few minutes while I make some arrangements with Beelzebub here, I will get my own drinks from here onwards," he told her, releasing her from both his order and his side, for now. She smiled and thanked him, then made her way over to the bar area with her friends, where she ordered a whisky on the rocks for herself this time.

"Well, are you gonna tell me what the fuck happened to you Tilly?" demanded Renee, her hands on her hips. She looked great in her black dress. Her blonde hair was pinned up in a messy knot and she gave off her usual, effortless sex appeal, even in these strange new surroundings.

"I'm sure you know everything by now, Renee. I am marked by the Black Prince, and you two belong to Beelzebub. That is it. We just need to live our lives and figure out where to go from here," she answered impatiently, not sure what kind of explanation Renee had wanted from her.

"I think what she means is, how did you even get here Tilly?" Gwen asked, reaching over, and taking her hand for a moment before giving it a gentle squeeze. She always was the calm, sensitive one of the group and Tilly was glad to see the understanding and affection in her deep brown eyes as Gwen stared at her.

"I know, it's just I'm still getting used to it all myself and I don't need you telling me off, Renee," Tilly grumbled before telling them her story. "Okay, well, you all know Brent," she said, and both girls smirked and nodded. "Well, his stepmother that we met, Lily, she is a demon, her real name is Lilith. She marked me that first night we stayed at the circus, but then wiped my memory so I didn't even know she had done it. When I went up to Scotland on Halloween after she invited me, it was for a Satanic ritual, not their anniversary party. She invited me up to surprise Brent, to let him know I had been marked and I think she had intended to initiate me into her following, but things went very differently than she had planned," Tilly told them quietly, feeling eyes on her and looking over her shoulder to see Blake watching her from the other side of the room. She smiled at him, knowing that he was reading her, and she was eager to get to her point quickly to satisfy the other girls need for information and let him know she was not dwelling on that part of the story. They sat down at the huge dining table and Tilly continued her tale, her friends silent and eager to hear the rest.

"She made a kind of speech about him, about the Black Prince, and she said his name. I didn't know I wasn't allowed to, so I just said it. I didn't even think about it until he was stood before me with a face like thunder. The rest of the crowd then bowed before him as well, while I just stood there like an idiot because I had no bloody idea," she said, laughing at her foolishness now while her friends gasped in horror, having been warned against saying the royal names by their new master, and told about the consequences for accidentally doing it.

"He was lenient on me though, and in that moment of stupidity saw something about me that intrigued him or something, because next thing I knew, I belonged to him instead of Lilith," she said with a smile, finishing off her drink and placing the empty glass on the table before her.

"And him alone," said a voice from behind her, and she knew without looking that it was Blake. Tilly hadn't even realised that he had made his way over to her, but she was happy to hear his voice and feel him near her again. He placed a fresh glass of whisky before her on the table and plopped in an ice cube, licking the stray drop of water from his fingertip as he peered down into her deep blue eyes.

"I thought you might like a new one, don't want you going empty," he said, and she thanked him before he headed back off towards his friends. She laughed to herself, thinking that they were developing quite a few inside jokes now, and she liked it.

"Whoa," said Gwen, looking at Tilly as she sipped the fresh drink. "You two are intense together. So, last night at the club, was that the first time you had seen him since Halloween?"

"Yeah, I didn't even know he was in there until I saw him at the bar. Then he brought me here," she told them, indicating the penthouse and blushing as she thought of their first night together.

Brent, David, and Jackson appeared then and plonked down a tray of shots on the table, joining Tilly and the other girls.

"Hey ladies, who's up for some fun?" David asked, and Renee grabbed one of the shots and tossed it back without even checking what was in it.

"Oh yes!" Renee replied, grinning wickedly.

"Hell yeah!" David cried, smiling at her, and grabbing a tequila shot, which he then knocked back in one gulp. They all helped themselves, Gwen taking a milder shot of liqueur while Jackson opted for the rum, leaving Tilly and Brent to fight over the last couple of drinks, a shot of either vodka or whisky.

"I'll take the vodka," he said, pushing her the other one, even though she knew it was his first choice of drink too.

"Cheers," she said, supping it back in one go.

"So, are you two still friends, then?" asked Renee, breaking the awkward silence that had descended around the table.

"Of course," replied Tilly, and then mentally added, *'and only ever that,'* just for her master to listen in on.

CHAPTER TWENTY-THREE

"You girls do realise you can't celebrate Christmas from now on, don't you?" Brent asked them later that night, following their third round of shots. He grinned down at Renee as she swooned drunkenly beside him. She was all over him and had been teasing and flirting wildly with him all night. Tilly still couldn't decide if she thought her friend was trying to make her jealous or if she was just after a thrill of her own now that he was a free man, but either way she decided she was just going to leave her to it, he was not on her mind that way anymore and never would be.

"Oh no!" Gwen cried, looking sad. "That's always been my favourite time of year."

"Sorry girls. We have a gathering every year instead, run by our stepmother. Speak to your masters, you never know they might have something similar planned for you too," offered Jackson with a bemused smile, they hadn't celebrated the holiday since he was tiny, and he didn't care for the garish, colourful and strange tradition of it at all now.

"Either way, I'll have to get away. My parents will make me celebrate it if I'm there. It's always been a big deal in our house," murmured Tilly, mentally trying to figure out when the next full moon was and hoping that it fell over the festive period so that she would at least have Blake's visit to look forward to.

"Look Tilly, just say, hey Mum, hey Dad, I worship the Devil now, so I do not want any of your stupid presents, okay?" Renee blurted out, her slurs making them all laugh thanks to her clearly drunken state. "What, it's the truth, isn't it? Oh, and do you think Beelzebub will let me wear normal clothes again? I can't believe I have to wear black all the time. When have you ever known me to wear black?" she rambled on, only adding fuel to their laughter as she went.

"No Renee," Beelzebub's voice said authoritatively from the crowd, appearing behind her and Gwen a second later. "You absolutely cannot wear colourful clothes again. Any colour is a sign of disrespect to our Queen, so watch your mouth or else I will punish you," he told her sternly, silencing her immediately. Tilly thought about the red underwear she was wearing beneath the dress, and a moment of panic rose in her at the thought that she could be deemed as disrespecting the Dark Queen by wearing even that tiny splash of colour beneath her black gown.

"Time to go," Beelzebub then told them, taking Gwen's hand to help her up and then grabbing Renee's arm to steady her. He rolled his eyes at the state she had gotten herself in to, and Tilly could tell she would have to be careful to keep from being disciplined. She made a mental note to have a serious word with her friend soon.

"Tilly?" called a voice from behind her as she finished her drink, thinking of going to find her master now that the other girls had gone. She had not seen Blake in a while and was starting to wonder where he had gotten to, but also felt like he might not appreciate finding her sat drinking alone with the three men, regardless of their friendship. Tilly had been careful not to drink too much, but the strong whisky was still working its magic on her and it took her a moment to find where the voice had come from. A smiling face then appeared from the crowd behind her.

"Sapphire?" she asked, and the girl she had met at college just a couple of weeks before nodded and hugged Tilly tightly as she made her way over to her.

"Yeah, how are you? I didn't know you would be here tonight!" she squealed excitedly. "Where is your master, are you ever gonna tell me his name?" she asked, joking with Tilly as she joined her and the boys at the table and introduced herself. The three brothers welcomed her and laughed, realising that this girl really had no idea who Tilly's master was, but they sat back, letting her be the one to try and tell her without being able to.

"I'm great, thanks Sapphire," she replied. "My master is here somewhere, but I still can't tell you his name. I'm sorry," she added, with an awkward expression that just made the boys laugh harder.

"Why?" Sapphire asked her, looking upset now thanks to the laughter that was obviously directed at her.

"Because she would be in serious trouble for doing so," boomed Blake's voice when he appeared, as if out of nowhere, from the crowd and Sapphire practically fell off her seat to kneel before him when she realised who it was that had spoken to her. He sat down next to Tilly, smiling, and taking her hand in his as he peered down at the crumpled heap that was Sapphire and then nodded to the three brothers in greeting, his calm and casual demeanour taking them all by surprise.

"You can get up," he told the still kneeling girl after a few seconds, and she climbed back up to her seat in a flustered mess.

"So, what were you talking about?" he asked them, knowing, of course, that the answer was him. Tilly just smirked and gave him a wink but squeezed his hand and couldn't help but feel her heart beating faster in her chest thanks to his touch.

"Come with me?" Blake asked Tilly a few minutes later, leaning in to whisper seductively into her ear. "I want to do a lap of the crowd again with you on my arm," he told her as he stood and took her hand in his.

"Of course, master," she replied, and Sapphire swooned as she watched the two of them. Tilly bid the group farewell and followed Blake's lead, his hand never letting go of hers. The gorgeous pair made their way towards the centre of the crowd, where most of the people there were drinking, talking, or dancing to the thrum of the rock music that played from speakers somewhere that Tilly could not see. As they reached the centre of the throb, the track changed and the familiar rifts from the night before filled her ears. It was the same song that Blake had played for her in the bedroom, and she smiled to herself, instantly thinking of their wonderful first night together as he turned and pulled her into his arms. They danced slowly together for a moment before the entire crowd around them then came to a halt as he magically froze them, just like he had done to the crowd at Lucas's trial on Halloween. She peered up into his eyes and smiled, kissing her master deeply as he held her close, and they moved gracefully together while the rest of the song played just for them.

"What am I going to do with you?" he asked her as the song finished and he let Tilly go while the partygoers began to unfreeze around them.

"I have a few ideas," she whispered to him with a sly grin.

CHAPTER TWENTY-FOUR

Without another word, Blake pulled Tilly off to a dark corner and pinned her against the wall like he had done earlier in the hall, but this time much more gently and without his hands around her neck. They kissed feverishly, Blake delving inside her mouth with an urgency she hadn't felt from him before.

"All I can think about are those little red panties, and how I want to rip them off of you," he whispered in her ear once he pulled away, planting kisses on her neck and collarbones as he pressed her even harder into the wall. She felt dizzy, giddy even in his passionate embrace, and then happily followed him through the doors and back to the master bedroom just moments later, without him even saying goodbye to any of his guests.

Blake locked the door behind them and quickly unzipped her dress, which tumbled to the floor and revealed Tilly's half-naked body and her somehow now black lacy underwear. She looked up at him, puzzled, but he just smiled and laughed to himself.

"My mother works in mysterious ways," he told her with a deep sigh, and Tilly couldn't help but panic again that she might be in trouble for having dared to wear the red underwear he had given her earlier.

"Don't worry, she won't punish you. It was my idea, remember?" he added, putting Tilly at ease instantly.

"Oh yeah, you're the naughty one. I remember now. A real life bad boy," she told him, a cheeky grin curling at her red lips and his eyes sparkled in the dim light as he took her in, completely mesmerised by her yet again.

Blake grinned wickedly and then took off his suit, one beautiful piece of clothing at a time as Tilly stood before him, awaiting her next order, watching him strip for her. When he was finally naked, she dropped to her knees before her master without needing to be told and took the tip of his thick cock in her mouth. Blake gasped, relishing in her unexpected yet breath-taking move. She sucked for a few minutes, taking his long member as far back as she could before he then commanded her to lie on the bed. Tilly quickly did as she was told and unclipped her bra as she climbed up onto the huge bed, removing it and then throwing it down onto the floor before lying back and relishing in Blake's gaze as his eyes swept over every inch of her almost naked body. He then climbed up on top of her and gripped the lace panties in his hand as he planted kisses on her stomach, suddenly pulling the material taught and then ripping them off her hips before pulling her up to meet his ready cock and then slipping inside her wet opening with ease. Tilly cried out as he pushed hard and fast inside of her, gripping his shoulders tightly and staring up into Blake's stunning green eyes as he moved so expertly inside of her. It was not long before her first orgasm claimed her body, weakening her for a moment but also delivering her the wonderful response to his fantastic thrusts she craved so much. He pulled her up onto his lap and lifted her with his strong arms up and down onto him as she cried out, feeling the next climax building already from her inner nerve-endings. She came again and again for him as he unrelentingly carried on, delighting in her pleasure as well as needing to find his own release.

Tilly weakened again before him after a while; begging him to slow down and saying that she couldn't bear to have another orgasm. She felt so weak and feeble compared to his almighty strength and almost didn't feel as though she could carry on. She hated it and vowed to be stronger for him next time. He kissed her, listening to her exhausted thoughts, and slowed, but did not stop, knowing that she could still handle more. Blake held her tight in his arms and kept her there, slowly dipping his thick length in and out of her wet, hot opening before a final, intense orgasm claimed her as he too reached his glorious end, and she felt his body tense beneath her.

Tilly couldn't help but fall into a deep, exhausted sleep following their extensive lovemaking, her body and mind both wonderfully exhausted from having spent the past two days mostly in his bed. Blake held her as she slept, watching her, and allowing Tilly to snuggle into him as she rested. He knew it would not be long until the moon waned, and that for some reason this time he was not happy about leaving, there seeming to be nothing back home to go to other than an inevitable row with Luna and a potential telling off from his mother about the red underwear. Although he still tried to fight Tilly's feelings for him, he knew that the reason for his regret at leaving was the one thing he had kept telling himself meant nothing to him, Tilly.

CHAPTER TWENTY-FIVE

They said their goodbyes the next morning and Blake teleported back to Hell, leaving Tilly at the penthouse to rest, Beelzebub having promised to stay with Renee and Gwen for a while with her and then he would teleport them all back home later that afternoon.

Blake teleported to his chambers and lay down on his bed, immediately feeling Luna calling to him through their strong psychic link. He gave her his silent acceptance to join him, and she immediately appeared in his chambers, sitting on the bed next to her twin with a sorrowful look on her face.

"I'm so sorry," she said, peering down at him with tears in her eyes while her brother remained cold, his face void of any emotion. "I don't know what came over me. Saying those things, going about it that way. But, please believe me, and read my thoughts. You will see for yourself that what I said was true," she implored him earnestly. Blake looked up at her, sensing just how true her words were, and he decided to do as she asked. He softened at last, taking Luna's hand in his and then opening himself up to her memories as she lay down next to him. Luna snuggled into her brother's embrace on the dark sheets, glad that Blake had forgiven her foolishness.

She focussed her mind and showed him the memory Alma had shared with her. It was of their mother as a younger woman, so frail, innocent, and completely broken. It was in the days following the torture Cate had suffered in the fiery pit, whipping chamber and torture cage. Alma had told Luna how the demons and witches involved were tasked with breaking her will, by any means necessary or else suffer themselves. This one vision showed the twins just what Lucifer had put Cate through to make her compliant to his dark desires at last, despite her clear resistance. She barely even looked like the same person they now knew so well as she lay in the black goo bath with a blank stare while the witches fussed around her, staving off the death that Lucifer had almost let claim his conquest rather than admit defeat in this matter of the heart.

They continued to watch as the image then changed slightly before them, Blake gasping as Alma had then shown Luna the sight of Cate, healed now but forcibly stripped naked and shaking with fear at the prospect of being in Lucifer's bed chambers that first time. He remained calm but was grateful when Luna changed the vision again, his anger towards his father burning brighter in the depths of his soul. Dylan's memory was next, showing them the torture she had suffered at his command for trying to contact her friend while she was still a white witch.

Her awful ordeal disgusted and dismayed Blake; he had only ever known Dylan as a dark witch and closest ally to Cate. Even when Lucifer was still with them, she served him without any question of her loyalty and the twins never realised just what awful past their father shared with her. Dylan's memory was then followed by Devin's, a rarely shared vision of himself and Cate together, happy, and young. They were living in the same penthouse Blake had just been in with his own lover, but then she was taken away from him with barely a word of explanation. Next, he had shown Luna the moment he first saw Cate again. It was many years later; she was a cold shell of herself, broken and manipulated, but there was nothing he could do about it.

Berith's memory was the final image, showing them the scene in the council chamber the day that Cate had finally taken the throne from Lucifer. Blake shuddered when he saw his father command that the ever loyal demon was to kill Lottie and Harry, he saw as Cate snapped and summoned her full power at last, his father cowering before her yet still mocking his wife's new found omnipotence right until the end.

It was more than Blake could handle, and he finally pulled away from Luna, coming back from her thoughts as quickly as he could. Despite his cold nature, the visions couldn't help but pain him. The truth of his family's history finally unravelling in his mind. Blake's green eyes speckled with black spots thanks to the anger that spiked from within, as was usual for all the dark royal family during times in which their ancient power rose from deep inside of them. They all experienced the uncontrollable show of darkness at times, whether through pain, anger or even the overwhelming surge, thanks to using their dark powers when marking a soul as theirs or performing primeval rituals.

"Okay, I get it," he told her, his voice a harsh, pained whisper. "But it doesn't change me, what I did and who I have become because of it, Luna. You just need to accept that I won't ever change and move on," Blake said, rising and teleporting away from his chambers without another word to his sister. He had business with Selena to take care of and teleported into the prison where he had delivered her broken body to the night before within a few seconds.

She immediately pleaded with her master for forgiveness, bowing to him and promising him never to be so careless again. Luckily for Selena, he was not interested in punishing her further this time. She had already been on the receiving end of his rage at the penthouse and had learned her lesson, but he did not mask his distaste with her.

"Do not step out of line again Selena, you are on your last warning," he ordered, looking down at her darkly.

"Yes master," she promised as he released her and they both teleported back to the castle.

CHAPTER TWENTY-SIX

Tilly went home that night after spending a lazy day in the quiet penthouse with her friends and their new master Beelzebub, chatting with them and learning more about the royal family from the warm and friendly demon she would never have pegged for an evil servant of Satan if she had met him in other circumstances. She was exhausted and weak but still buzzed from the amazing couple of days she had just spent with Blake and thought back to their intimate moments with a shy smile. The dark and scary few minutes from the hallway after Luna's visit still played on her mind though, but she endeavoured to try and understand her master's pain as much as he would let her, even with his usually cold nature towards his emotions always keeping her at arm's length. Tilly thought back to that moment and could not be happier that Blake had chosen to use her closeness to calm him, rather than her having been the one to cause him more anger during his overflowing and uncontrollable dark rage.

She couldn't help but feel sorry for Selena, wishing that the witch had just listened to her warning rather than barge into the bedroom unannounced. And yet, she couldn't help but be glad that Selena had been the one to take the full brunt of his rage instead of her. The powerful witch was much more able to withstand the punishment in that moment thanks to her magic powers. Tilly knew that she could have been really hurt if Blake had turned his black gaze on her frail human body instead.

She returned to college the next morning, still feeling tender, but she didn't care. He was worth it. Tilly studied hard, working tirelessly on recipes, and perfecting her cooking and preparation methods, wowing her mentors, and soon becoming the top student in her class, her passion and skill becoming apparent very quickly. She even received a letter telling her she had gotten a much-coveted spot in a young chef's internship program in the new year. She had been invited to re-locate to London and cook under a highly decorated and famed chef named Andre Baxter for the next stage of her career development. Andre had received many prestigious awards over the years and had a fantastic reputation in the food industry for excellence and impeccable taste; he would be the perfect mentor for her budding career. Tilly was incredibly excited to start the next phase of her career under his expert tutelage, so said yes immediately, ready to start the next chapter in her life.

As the days passed Tilly found she missed Blake terribly and cursed the tiny sliver of moon in the sky above for keeping him away from her. He made small appearances in her dreams here and there, sometimes just coming through as a set of deep green eyes that watched her from afar as her subconscious took over the scene around them, but other times she would find herself stood before the large mirror in her room again, dressed in that beautiful black gown as he peered over her shoulder, his arms wrapped around her in that same way she now loved so much. She had always been independent and strong-willed but knew now that she was willingly submitting to him. She relished in his possession of her and would find her celestial self leaning back into his embrace as he held her tighter and kissed her neck softly, wanting to be dominated.

The following week, Beelzebub came to sit with her in the college lunchroom with Gwen on his arm. Renee was not with them this time as she was in trouble with her demonic master again and so was being punished. While Tilly felt bad that her friend was learning her lessons the hard way, she could not deny that Renee most probably needed the stricter approach. She had not been at college for the last few days, and Tilly didn't dare ask what she was going through to appease her new master, but just hoped that he was being fair. Despite his darkness, Beelzebub seemed to be the least scary demon she had come across yet and considered him a friend already. She trusted him and his judgement, believing that he would not harm her friend unnecessarily.

Tilly bought them coffee and then opened a plastic box from inside her bag, serving up some lemon and poppy seed cupcakes she had just made in class while the three of them sat chatting at the plastic table for a few minutes before the bell rang.

"Gwen, Renee, and I are going to spend the holidays at a lodge in the Swiss Alps with Lilith and some of the other demons, along with their followers," Beelzebub told her. "Tilly, you are invited to come along too, of course. Blake will join us there during the full moon around halfway through the break. You can tell your parents whatever you want, but you are all expected to come. Is that understood?" he asked, more of an order than a request.

"Yes master," said Gwen, and Tilly nodded.

"Yes sir," she said, addressing him playfully, and the demon smiled across at her, giving her the thumbs up as he took a large bite of his cake and groaned appreciatively, letting her know how tasty it was. "How are we getting there?" she then asked, trying to figure out if she had the money for airplane tickets.

"You will teleport with me Tilly, as per your master's wishes," he answered once he had finished his mouthful, and she laughed to herself.

"Of course," she answered him, but she was glad that they now had a plan in place for the dreaded holiday season. Their non-Satanic friends were already going on about their plans for Christmas and what presents they were buying for their families, whereas Tilly and her marked friends actively had to avoid the subject at all costs.

After college Tilly went straight over to the main house to speak with her parents, telling them she had decided to go skiing with her friends for Christmas this year rather than spending it at home with them, which was the only plausible excuse she could think of for being away over the festive period. It would be the first time she would ever spend the holidays without them, and she knew they would not be happy about it. Her quiet-natured father, Robert, stayed silent, but her mother was disappointed and angry, immediately chastising Tilly for her cold, closed-off attitude recently.

"It doesn't matter if I'm not here. I don't want any presents anyway, so just let me do what I want. I'm not a child," she cried, eager for them not to question her on it further. Bianca had already tried having words with Tilly about her new dress code and darker behaviour following her disappearance to the penthouse. Tilly wanted to be honest and hated lying to them, but she just couldn't talk to her about any of it until Blake gave her permission to and so pretended that she wasn't interested in her mother's opinion of her dress sense or attitude.

She stormed out of the house and stomped over to her small nook, grateful for the solace. In all honesty, Tilly knew she had been closed-off with them recently, but her only care other than her career now was Blake, and she spent most of her time thinking of him and how best to please her master. Tilly had even been working out in the college gym, hoping to be stronger and more ready for him the next time they were together, she desperately wanted to keep up with him better the next time they made love and sizzled inside at the sheer anticipation of it.

CHAPTER TWENTY-SEVEN

Tilly packed her bags and made her way over to Beelzebub's flat on the night that she, Gwen, and Renee had broken up from college for the two-week Christmas break, ready to head off to the mysterious lodge where they would all be staying for the holidays. It was reported to be completely snowed in, access impossible by both car and foot so they could all go and have lots of dark fun, safe in the knowledge that they would not be bothered by any outsiders. They all took each other's hands and teleported away, arriving within seconds outside a huge, snow-covered building that looked as if it was quite possibly used as a hotel or could perhaps even be a monumental landmark during the summer months.

It was absolutely freezing outside, despite all of Tilly's prepared layers, and she was glad once they got inside the warm and colossal building that had been completely under-sold to them by Beelzebub. It was enormous and had been completely modernised inside, with over one hundred rooms and several fully stocked bars and restaurants. There was also a vast hall, cinema, gym, and a spa for them all to use as much as they wanted during their stay. The girls' jaws all dropped as they made their way inside, taking in the lavishly furnished main hallway that led to the huge hall. Tilly was lucky enough to have been allocated a master suite, complete with private Jacuzzi and terrace, and she couldn't help but think how she could quickly get used to all this preferential treatment thanks to her black mark and royal master.

Blake had not visited her dreams again in the last couple of weeks, but Tilly felt his presence around her somehow, somewhere deep within herself, and she knew he was keeping an eye on her from afar. Beelzebub was still being very helpful and kind; always making sure that she was happy, comfortable, and well taken care of in Blake's absence. She assumed it was all at the behest of their Black Prince, but in all honesty she didn't mind. She was much happier with Beelzebub as her interim demonic guardian rather than having to deal with Lilith too much. Tilly presumed that Blake was more as ease with him watching over her too, keeping her away from Brent and his brothers under Lilith's leadership.

The rest of the demons and their groups of followers soon joined them at the lodge, and then the partying and promised fun well and truly started the next evening when everyone was invited down to the main hall for the welcoming party. It was a night planned for initiating the new followers into the mixture of human acolytes, as well as welcoming back the demons that were now returning to Earth for their demonic tours of duty. Some of the partygoers celebrated by participating in all sorts of depraved and sinful acts with one another, and nothing was off limits to those who were without prior orders from their demonic masters. Tilly knew without having to ask that she was to stay well away from those groups.

Most of the other followers just relaxed together while chatting and getting drunk, having fun rather than getting into anything too intense, and Tilly joined in with that group, along with her friends. She only drank a few whiskies that night, having fun but being careful not to go too crazy or get involved in anything that she knew Blake would not be happy with. Her new follower friends and the demons she met did not push her or make any advances in their drunken hazes, though, knowing all too well that she was spoken for by one of their highest and most feared leaders.

As the first week passed by, she spent her days relaxing, working out in the gym, and watching movies with her friends, staying warm rather than going out in the snow too much as the cold never really was her thing. Tilly eventually tried her hand at both skiing and snowboarding after Renee's constant pleas for her to participate in the outdoor activities, but after having fallen on her bum more times than she cared to admit she quickly crossed them off her list of things to do for the rest of their stay in Switzerland. Her master would not be happy with her if he came and found her sore and bruised instead of ready and waiting.

Lilith and her large group of followers took up almost an entire wing of the huge lodge and Tilly had found herself genuinely happy to see them all when they arrived, hugging Lucas with a cheerful smile before she greeted each of the circus members she had grown to know so well over the years. She openly enjoyed the three brothers' company too, and they all had a lot of fun together, whether it was swimming lengths with Jackson in the pool, helping David and Brent to practice their routines in the gym or settling down in the warm cinema-style room, propped up on cushions and blankets with them while they watched movies on the big screen and ate vast amounts of popcorn and ice-cream.

Tilly had worked hard to find her way with Brent again, feeling like she could finally put aside all the emotions she had once had for him, and in those relaxed few days they both learned that they could still be friends as long as neither of them ever brought up any reminders of the past. It was still there, they both felt it, but somehow, they each effectively pushed away their history in their efforts to remain friends. Tilly knew Blake would never let her even be around Brent if he posed a threat, so trusted that his thoughts and memories of his relationship with her must be safely locked away in his mind, and she hoped, for both of their sake's, that they would stay there.

CHAPTER TWENTY-EIGHT

A few days after Christmas, the full moon rose overhead and Blake arrived at the hotel, teleporting straight into Tilly's room to bypass the crowds that might try to take away his attention; after all, he was not interested in them. All he wanted was her. He had decided to stay out of her head while in Hell, as he couldn't stop thinking of Tilly. The temptation to visit her dreams was strong, but he knew he would not be satisfied until he saw her properly and had physical contact again. Blake knew he was opening up his soul to her more and more as each full moon bought him to Earth, but he still fought his feelings, closing himself off to his aching heart each time the turmoil from his past tried to creep in with the love he felt brooding from within. He wasn't ready to deal with it all just yet; he was not equipped to feel and to love and was not sure if he ever would be.

Tilly was ready for him, sitting naked in an armchair by the fire, eagerly awaiting Blake's arrival in their suite. When he appeared before her, she felt the instant flutter of her heart as it sped up and the immediate moistening of her cleft as it ached for him. He, too, was overcome with need and, in just a few seconds, he had stripped off. Blake then wasted no time in gathering Tilly up and into his strong arms, sliding his hard length inside her whilst pinning her against the wall beside the huge fireplace. His kisses were powerful, eager, and deeply passionate and she willingly gave in to his every desire, wanting every inch of his body against hers and delighting in the delicious taste, touch, and smell of the lover she had missed so very much these last few weeks. They moved down onto the thick rug that lay in front of the roaring fire after a few minutes, both thrusting hard together before finally enjoying a shared climax and then falling into one another's arms as they revelled in their joint highs.

"You can greet me like that any time, Tilly," Blake told her, leaning over her as they lay on the warm rug and kissing her neck as he whispered into her ear. She smiled up at her master, taking in his gorgeous face and smouldering, sexy green eyes. He was so strong, so dark, and even though she somehow knew he was damaged and broken, she was still so drawn to him, just like a moth to a flame. She didn't care how much she could get hurt in the process. Wearing his mark meant everything to her now, and she wanted things to stay like this forever.

"I have a surprise for you," he told her, climbing up off the rug and wandering over to grab something out of his jacket pocket. He looked perfect in the dark shadows, his naked, muscular body catching the light from the fire at just the right angles, and she enjoyed the view very much. Blake quickly returned and bought with him a small box. He had a huge smile on his face as he looked at his stunning, innocent yet dirty girl in the flickering light from the bright flames and enjoyed his view as well.

Despite his doubts he had been trying to open up more over the last month, he had been attempting to let the emotions sink back in after the dust settled following his educating experience with Luna and the memories she had shared with him the night after his last visit. His twin hadn't left his side, having sensed the change in him, and they had talked for hours almost every day. She opened up more about the information she had pieced together and showed him some more of the old memories that she had coaxed from their owners, all of them loyal servants and friends of theirs, and so Blake knew that their shared visions could be trusted.

"It's just a little something to make you think of me when we are apart," he told her, and an almost shy look crossed his gorgeous face. Tilly sat up on the rug and folded her legs underneath her, completely taken aback by this unusual display of affection from her usually cool master.

"Thank you, your Highness. I did not expect to get a gift from you. I didn't get anything to give you in return," she told him, leaning forward to give him a soft kiss before accepting the present.

"You are welcome," he said, eying her with a boyish smile. "It is not a Christmas present, if that's what you were wondering, so there is no need to get me anything in return. I have everything I need," he added, stroking her cheek with his index finger, and Tilly swooned.

"Can I open it now?" she asked eagerly, and he nodded.

"Of course."

Tilly pulled the lid off the small, black velvet box to reveal a stunning thick, black metal ring with a dark green stone set in the centre that just so happened to be the exact same shade of his gorgeous eyes. She immediately put it on, grinning up at Blake as she stared back and forth from his eyes to the green gemstone.

"It's absolutely perfect, thank you so much," she said, feeling like a lovesick teenager as she stared down at his wonderful gift.

Blake shrugged nonchalantly and said nothing more; he just pulled her closer and planted a deep, wanting kiss on her lips. Tilly immediately climbed onto his lap, eager to have him again despite her tenderness from their first lovemaking session. He slipped inside her wet opening naturally again, hard for her at once and just as eager. She moved up and down on him gently, her eyes on his as she rode him and opened herself fully, both physically and mentally. She planted kisses on his mouth and neck as she continued her pursuit, leaning back and crying out as her first orgasm claimed her, grateful to the hours spent at the gym for her new found vigour and strength.

Blake then let Tilly fall back onto the warm rug, climbing between her legs as he pushed himself even deeper inside her delicate tenderness, the soft strokes of his hard cock urging her to continue, and she peered up at him, her hands running through his dark curls as she succumbed to him entirely, willingly. Blake groaned, smiling down at her, and basking in her clear submission to his dominant side. He plunged himself hard inside her welcoming cleft at first and then began slowing his thrusts after a few minutes, the two of them staring into one another's eyes as they kept up the softer, more passionate pace.

When he had found his release, the pair lay side by side on the thick rug, satiated and satisfied beyond anything either of them had felt before. She curled into his embrace, enjoying the warmth of him, his scent, and the gentle buzz she still felt from his touch. Her body was tired, but her mind was alive, awakened thanks to the pleasurable hormones released during their lovemaking.

As she lay there in his arms, Tilly suddenly had an urge to say the words, those three little words she knew she felt so strongly but had to fight, knowing that he was not ready. She tried to push the thoughts away before Blake realised what had just welled up inside of her but felt him tense beside her instantly and knew that he had read her thoughts before she had been able to push them away.

"Please don't," Tilly asked Blake in a whisper, desperate not to lose the closeness they had just shared. He smiled down at her, but the smile did not reach his eyes and she could feel him already pulling away, growing colder thanks to those unconquerable high walls.

"I'm not worthy of those words Tilly, don't ever say them to me," he said, looking slightly forlorn yet decisive as he uttered his terrible admission. She couldn't help but feel both angry and sad at his depressive statement, and her response came pouring out of her before she could control her tongue.

"Don't you do that, not to me," she cried, leaning up on her elbow to look at him. "You are more worthy of love than anyone I have ever known. You are warm, kind, merciful, and even a little shy underneath that hard exterior, but all you have to do is let me in. Just let me love you, Blake," she begged, and then covered her mouth in shock, trying to take back both her daring words and the name she had accidentally just spoken, but it was already too late.

CHAPTER TWENTY-NINE

Tears welled up in Tilly's eyes as she gazed fearfully at her master, not sure what he might do to punish her for the lapse in etiquette and her presumptuous outburst. She flinched and pulled back, but Blake gripped her tight and then leaned over her, staring down at Tilly with eyes that began to churn with black specks, and she trembled in fear. She could sense his anger and venomous rage as it began to boil over uncontrollably and she flinched as he leaned in close, whispering into her ear.

"Don't ever say anything like that to me again Tilly, I have given you more than enough warnings, yet you still think you can treat me like your little pussy-whipped boyfriend? Trust me, your cunt isn't that sweet," he whispered, his tone deadly and full of rage while his face mashed into a sinister, truly scary mask. Every inch of Tilly's body shuddered in fear and tears already welled in her eyes.

"You will now learn to keep your mouth shut Tilly, not to say a fucking word, and don't say I never warned you," he commanded, and she could hear his powerful voice inside her head as well as in her ears. She knew she must follow the order but still tried calling out anyway, to beg his forgiveness, but she quickly realised that she couldn't talk, that she was somehow not able to even open her mouth. Instinctively, Tilly reached up and touched her lips, finding them magically sealed closed, her body adhering to his command even if her mind wanted to disobey. An evil smile spread across Blake's face, his eyes still black as he watched her begin to panic, finding satisfaction in her fear. Tilly sent him pleading thoughts, begging him to calm down, desperate for forgiveness.

Blake said nothing more as he climbed up and kneeled over her, still staring angrily into her eyes and then reached his hands up to her neck, grabbing her tight with both hands as he wrapped them around Tilly's vulnerable windpipe, and she just peered up at her master regretfully. She didn't grab at his hands or try to fight his hold over her. She knew she deserved to be punished and closed her eyes, ready to take whatever terrible lesson he chose to teach her.

After a few moments, she opened her eyes again, and found that he still hadn't moved. His hands were still firmly wrapped around her throat, but he had not proceeded any further in his punishment and Tilly hoped he was fighting his urges, not wanting to taint this wonderful day, but she just could not be sure.

She shuddered beneath him uncontrollably with fear, suddenly feeling cold despite the warm fire beside her, and Blake jumped as though she had interrupted him from a daydream. He pinned her tighter into the floor with his body, staring into her eyes as he reached across and placed one of his hands directly into the burning fire beside them. The flames didn't hurt him, of course, but when Blake pulled it back out again Tilly could see that his fingertip was now glowing red-hot thanks to the thick flames. She stared up at him in fear and tried to cry out, her voice getting held captive behind her sealed lips, her pleas unheard.

Blake then lifted her left wrist with his free hand and he quickly drew an inverted cross on the soft flesh inside Tilly's forearm with his burning fingertip, giving her a matching mark to the one that Lilith had first drawn on her opposite wrist and he had taken over the night they met, however this one was going to remain permanently visible thanks to the instant searing of her flesh as Blake traced his finger along in two perfect lines.

Tilly cried out in pain as he branded her, the screams muffled by her closed lips and tears fell instantly from her eyes as the skin burned and singed painfully beneath his touch. She tried to pull away from him, but he still held her there, staring down at her with black, unforgiving eyes and watching as she could do nothing but cry.

"I told you I would hurt you, didn't I?" he then asked her coldly, climbing up from the rug and getting dressed quickly. "Perhaps you might want to rethink your last statement about how kind and merciful I am now," he added before going out into the main living area of the suite where he made himself a large glass of whisky in silence. Blake's eyes still burned black as he struggled to lull his rage, his body continuing to tremble with anger despite his efforts as he down glass after glass of the amber liquid.

The commandment sealing Tilly's lips was lifted as soon as Blake had left the bedroom and she lay on the rug for a moment, writhing in pain and sobbing silently as her wrist continued to burn. She then screamed into the fur beneath her, grabbing her arm tightly and pulling it close to her body protectively, but there was nothing she could do to soothe it, and the warmth from the fire only made it sting harder.

Tilly climbed up off the floor and ran into the en-suite, holding the wound under the cold water, her tears still flowing down her red-hot cheeks. She fell to her knees weakly, holding her arm up in the sink to ensure the cool water still flowed over her burn, easing it just the tiniest bit, but she was grateful for the slight respite from the scalding pain and desperately needed the soothing coolness from the ice-cold water. Tilly sat there on the bathroom floor and cried as she continued to hold her arm under the faucet, the sobs escaping from her uncontrollably for almost an hour, while Blake stood out on the cold terrace drinking one large dram of whisky after another, desperately trying to calm his temper.

He knew he had acted rashly, but there was no going back now. Blake had been considering asking his mother if he could give Tilly permission to use his name when they were alone together, but for some reason he had still reacted so strongly to her saying it tonight. He had been enraged by both her audacity and by the fact that she had dared speak to him of love, despite his many warnings on the subject during their previous conversations. Blake wondered if perhaps it was the very insinuation that he was such a good man underneath his cold, devilish shell that made him punish her so much harder. He knew he had felt an overwhelming urge in that moment to prove to Tilly just why she should never love him, that he was still a heartless monster despite her high hopes for him. His instincts had taken over, teaching her a terrible lesson as he acted on autopilot despite her words still cutting him deep.

Blake could feel Tilly's pain, hear her scared and hurt thoughts through their bond right now, but he knew he had to see it through. He could not show her any weakness. The Black Prince, no matter his affection for her, did not trust himself to let down his walls around Tilly, and despite his regret, he was sure that this punishment would finally prove to her he had never lied about his unwavering dark nature.

CHAPTER THIRTY.

Once she had calmed down, Tilly got herself showered and dressed, and then wrapped her wrist with a wet cloth to soothe it and keep it cool. She sat on the bed, looking at herself in the large mirror. She looked like she felt, terrible, but applied some makeup and brushed her dark-blonde hair before pulling it into a high ponytail. She was angry, hurt, scared and full of regret, but she thought back to the words she had spoken to her master, and still meant them despite the awful punishment that had followed afterwards. She also couldn't help but think back to what she had said before about him hurting her, and she endeavoured to keep that promise to him regardless of what had just happened. Tilly looked down at the swollen bandage on her arm, vowing to shed no more tears over the wound and then she headed out into the living room area where she poured herself a large glass of whisky and then joined Blake on the terrace. Neither of them said a word as they both stared out at the beautiful scenery before them. The snow-covered mountains and huge forests all around the lodge were breath-taking and she downed her strong drink with trembling hands before placing the empty glass down on the frozen table.

She went to him, moving round to stand before her master before falling to his feet to kneel before him and then bowed her head, feeling ashamed and embarrassed. She stayed there for a few minutes, Blake stood over her, his expression still cold and distant, and his eyes black as night. Tilly kept her head low, too scared to look up at her omnipotent master, waiting for him to make the next move. After a few minutes, he unexpectedly turned on his heel, and sent the glass in his hand hurtling to the wall next to the patio door, shattering it instantly. Blake then reached down and grabbed Tilly by the arm, dragging her back inside with him before effortlessly throwing her onto the huge bed. He then climbed up on top of her, pushing her arms up over her head forcibly as he pressed down on her with his strong body. Tilly winced as he brushed against her sore forearm but said nothing to try and stop him, keeping the promise she had just made to herself. She then felt cold metal in her hands, and Blake closed her grip around the thick bars of the bedframe.

"Don't let go, not even for a second," he ordered her, turning Tilly over onto her stomach and then pulling down her skirt and knickers. Blake undressed and hovered over her, his face buried in her hair, breathing in her smell in an attempt to stop himself, but it was no use.

"Do it," Tilly whispered, lifting her hips up off the bed in an oddly inviting way. She braced herself for what she knew would be his unfeeling, unloving thrusts, but silently reminded her master that she was ready to keep her promises and he pushed himself inside her hard and deep. Blake pulled her hips higher, pushing her thighs closed tight as he did, and he pushed her harder than she had ever been before. She gripped the metal frame as tight as she could with her throbbing hands as he pressed her firmly into the mattress, his relentless thrusts delivering Tilly both pleasure and pain as he continued his carnal punishment.

He came quickly, pulling out of her without another word and then heading off for a shower, leaving Tilly trembling and sore in his wake, feeling used and more than ever, like she was a possession rather than his lover. She continued to grip the bed frame as he showered, realising that he had not yet released her from that order, and so she lay there, sobbing quietly into the pillow. He emerged from the bathroom looking just like his normal self again a few minutes later, his eyes green again, but he could not hide the sadness in them. He ordered her to take a bath and then left Tilly alone in the bedroom, still trembling and screaming her emotional torment into the pillows beneath her.

"Stay here. I'll be back later," Blake called from the living room a little while later as he grabbed his jacket and left their suite. Tilly didn't respond. She was already laying in the warm bath, resting her sore body, and nursing her bruised ego. She just could not understand where all this had come from, and Blake was so closed-off and distant towards her now that she knew there was no point in trying to talk to him about it today. He had punished her far more than she had ever thought he would, and over such a tiny mistake. She suspected that his anger was probably more down to her foolish words of love rather than her mistake at saying his name, but Tilly had certainly learned her lesson and knew never to take their relationship for granted again.

She lay in the deep, soapy water and stared at the ring on her finger, the beautiful present that Blake had given her to remind Tilly of him during their weeks apart between the moon's full days. It really was the perfect match for his eyes, and she had to take it off and place it to one side. She just couldn't bring herself to look at it right now. Tilly glanced down instead at her sore wrist. It had started to heal already, but she was sure it would scar and then undoubtedly show the burned inverted cross clearly against her pale skin even once the redness had gone. It would be her very own brand as a permanent reminder of this awful day.

Blake left for Hell the next day with hardly having said another word to Tilly, but she too was sulking and tried not to be too obvious about it but was glad when he had gone. Gwen came to her room, checking if she was okay and Tilly lied, saying that she was just exhausted so needed some rest and would re-join the fun the next day. Gwen didn't believe her, but left her friend to it, Beelzebub having ordered her to keep her nose out. Blake's business was none of hers despite it involving her good friend.

It was three more days before Tilly eventually emerged from the huge suite. The despair that had overpowered her had been awful. She had cried, slept feverishly, screamed, and even smashed up some of the crystal tumblers and vases from the room in a bid to rid herself of the terrible, overwhelming emotions that would burst out of her uncontrollably as she processed the events from those awful few hours. Tilly had cried herself to sleep each night, barely resting as the nightmares crept in and she would soon wake again, weeping uncontrollably into her pillow.

Eventually her hunger got the better of her though and Tilly made her way out to the dining room to join the others, remaining silent and sombre as she devoured her huge mound of hot chicken curry and fragrant rice. She then did her best to take her mind off everything for the duration of their stay, grateful now for the cold weather so that she could wear long jumpers and cardigans for the rest of their time at the lodge to cover the new mark Blake had left on her. Gwen remained her usual cheery self, eager to perk up her grumpy friend. However, Tilly noticed Beelzebub watching her with a sad look every now and then, especially when he caught her scratching her arm gently as the scab began to clear a few days later. She suspected that Blake's old friend must know what had happened, perhaps her master having gone to the demon for advice following her punishment that day, but she could not know for sure and wouldn't ever ask him.

She quickly turned away from his warm gaze, feeling the tears well up in her eyes once more, so she took herself off for a walk in the snow covered gardens instead, not feeling the cold this time, feeling nothing but numb and emotionless.

Tilly was glad when it was time to go home again a few days later and hid herself away once she got there, nursing both her still sore arm and her bruised ego for a few more days before setting about making plans for her move to London, intent of focussing on the happier elements of her dark new life.

CHAPTER THIRTY-ONE

The new year brought with it lots of changes for Tilly, and she immersed herself in keeping busy with perfecting her recipes and organising her move to the big city. It was insisted upon her she move into the penthouse rather than find her own flat in London, and as much as it annoyed Tilly to have to accept Blake's hospitality while she was still sulking, it was a welcome gift as it stopped her having to worry about finding the money for rent or needing to procure furniture and appliances for a place of her own. She left the farm with tears in her eyes, having wanted to feel grown up and independent, but she couldn't help but feel so unsure of herself and her place in the world around her. Tilly would never tell a soul, not even Gwen or Renee, but she was terrified of going it alone with all the changes she now needed to come to terms with and hated not being able to talk to her mother about any of those fears.

She was still angry and upset with Blake, but there was a part of her that missed him terribly, her body ached for his touch and if she stopped and let herself think about him too long, her anger quickly waned and was soon replaced by the love she still fought hard to try and suppress for him, but she refused to let it get the better of her.

After a couple of days getting settled into the penthouse and learning her way around, Tilly felt much more like her usual happy and confident self again. She made a conscious decision to leave the terrible day in Switzerland behind her as she focussed instead on the future, pushing on towards her selfish goals of fame and fortune as a chef. She was eager to start doing what she wanted to do from now on, and what would help get her closer to that shallow dream she had shown Blake in the mirror just a few months before.

She worked hard in Andre's kitchen and learned many new skills while welcoming every challenge he set her, loving being in both the kitchens and out in the main dining area of the contemporarily designed, critically acclaimed, 'Innov-ate restaurant' near the centre of London. It was modern and very posh, with new and impressive takes on classic foods that had won over the clients and earned Andre a reputation as a truly inspired chef and teacher. Tilly soon settled into her role as an entry level commis chef with relative ease. Andre had been very impressed with her portfolio and was even more amazed with her fantastic recipes and skilled hands, as she worked tirelessly in the kitchen for ten or twelve hours a day with no complaints.

The next full moon came around very quickly thanks to her busy days, but Blake did not come to her during it. Tilly had stopped sulking now and was eager to sort things out with her master, and she hated not knowing what he was doing, or what his intentions were for her now, and his absence brought her nothing but dread and anxious butterflies to her stomach. Despite this terrible bump in their road, Tilly still cared for Blake and hated the fact that she had not seen or heard from him since their time at the lodge, not even in her dreams.

Tilly made plenty of new friends at Innov-ate, and another chef at the restaurant, Trey, had taken an obvious liking to her. He kept on asking Tilly out for a drink or for coffee with him, making her feel slightly uncomfortable despite how cute and friendly he was, and how lonely she felt in Blake's absence. She kept telling him she was unavailable, saying that she had a boyfriend who worked overseas, and she didn't see him very much, but that they were completely faithful to one another. Tilly would never be honest with her new colleague. She didn't want to admit that she was unsure what was happening between them right now, not wanting to even admit it to herself.

"All the more reason to come and fill your quiet times with me," Trey had answered with a wink over the salad preparation one lunch time after his fifth attempt to woo her. She couldn't deny that he was handsome, tall, and slim with black skin and deep brown eyes that were warm and kind, but she was just not interested, there was no part of her right now that wanted anything to do with the hassle of entertaining his advances at all. Tilly was sure it must be that she was still getting over that exhausting and scary day with Blake, and her plate was well and truly full anyway, so she finally put her foot down, telling Trey once and for all to stop pestering her.

"No Trey, I've told you more than enough times. Please don't make this uncomfortable, okay?" she asked him with a stern look, and he conceded, nodding his head and holding up his hands in defeat before reaching over for another pack of tomatoes to chop from the centre of the table between them.

The next few weeks passed by in a blur again thanks to her incredibly busy days and before long, the full moon lit up the skyline over London again. Tilly stood on the penthouse's huge terrace wrapped in a heavy coat with a large glass of whisky in her hand, enjoying the cold night air while looking up at the bright moon overhead thoughtfully. This was the second night of its fullness, and she was now convinced that Blake was not coming to see her again. She couldn't help but feel sad, lonely, and angry that they had not sorted things out. In all honesty, she was pissed off more than still hurt, feeling like he couldn't even be bothered to fight for her. Tilly rubbed her arm instinctively as she thought of her master. It had healed a while ago and the scar wasn't as bad as she had thought it might be. Her cross was still noticeable, and she had to wear either jewellery or long sleeves to cover it, but it was manageable, and she had gotten used to seeing it there now. Tilly had even started wearing her beautiful green ring again too and her hand instinctively moved down to it as she absentmindedly ran her fingers over the soft gem. Tilly soon finished her whisky, placing the tumbler down on the cold stone before her as she peered up at the stars, wondering what to do with the rest of her lonely evening.

"Care for another one?" asked a voice from behind her, and Tilly spun around to see Blake standing in the terrace doorway, his body language playful and a smile on his lips, looking just like he had that first night that they had shared together in this same penthouse. Tilly walked over to him slowly, taking him in in the darkness. Blake wore black jeans and a jumper, looking casual and relaxed rather than in his usual formal gear, and his green eyes twinkled sexily at her in the dim light. He was gorgeous. She still could not deny that, but there was an awkwardness that hovered between them now, the elephant in the room that shuffled around them awkwardly and left them both on edge. Tilly nodded and handed him her glass, bowing low as she reached him, never forgetting the formalities that would still be expected of her.

"Yes please, master," she said, and he turned, wandering off to the bar without another word. She followed him inside and then closed the glass doors behind her before then discarding her coat and shoes. Tilly then flopped down on the sofa next to the fire, watching Blake as he walked over to her with two large whiskies in his hands. He joined her on the sofa, eying her intensely, his sexy green eyes boring into hers as he read her thoughts for a moment, a knowing grin curling at his lips. 'Go to hell,' she couldn't help but think, hating that he could access her forgiving thoughts so easily and Blake laughed but said nothing in response. After a long, tense silence, he smiled across at her, rapidly causing Tilly's cold demeanour to thaw a little piece at a time. He could melt her mood in a second and they both knew it, but she was determined to make Blake work for it just a little bit and he didn't mind at all. He admired her strength and would play her game if it made Tilly feel better.

"So, firstly, I need to tell you I am truly, truly sorry. I tried to stop myself, I really did, but sometimes the power utterly consumes me and I'm no longer in control," he eventually said, staring into her beautiful blue eyes earnestly as he spoke. "But I promise you now that I will *never* do anything like that again," he added, taking her hand in his and removing the large silver cuff bracelet that she had worn to cover her burn mark. He looked down at the brand for a moment, his eyes speckling with black spots, but he said nothing else, placing the cuff back around her forearm and stroking his hand up to her neck where he left it there, staring at her thoughtfully. Tilly trembled before him, fear and hurt seeping out of every inch of her despite every one of her senses going crazy for him. Blake sensed her fear but continued his apology; eager to regain the closeness he had so foolishly destroyed during his last visit.

"You deserve so much better than how I have treated you, and I should never have lashed out like I did. I'll remember everything about that day for the rest of my sorry life," he said, cupping her cheek with his hand gently. A small sob escaped from Tilly's chest uncontrollably as she peered up into his eyes, and he wiped away a tear that rolled down her cheek and onto her top lip.

"I thought you were here to tell me we were finished," she admitted, not hiding how lost she had felt during his absence.

"Not a chance in Hell," Blake replied, smiling down at her. "I am trying to control my emotions better. I have been letting them back in, learning to handle how they make me feel. All of it I have done for you," he told her, and Tilly couldn't help but let go of all the tension she didn't even know she had been holding so tightly in her stomach, the butterflies in her abdomen fluttering away wildly at his strong words while her battered heart suddenly beat again in the hope that she and Blake could still have a future together. Perhaps all was not lost after all.

Tilly smiled up at her master, desperately wanting to regain some of their strong bond again, but in that same moment she quickly came to realise that it had never left them at all, it had just been dulled by the raw emotions neither of them had been able to control following their last bit of time together.

"Forgive me?" Blake asked, his face full of regret.

"Of course, yes," Tilly replied, her pain numbing with every moment that passed.

The pair of them spent the rest of the night sitting on the sofa together, chatting and drinking the last bottle of Blake's expensive whisky, while they found their way back to each other again. Blake did not ask her to join him in the bedroom or make any move towards her sexually this time, remaining understanding to Tilly's unspoken pain. This visit was all about rekindling their emotional relationship anyway, not their sexual chemistry, as both knew that that was not the problem.

His heartfelt words worked, and by the time he left for Hell again the next morning, she was smitten with her Black Prince all over again, each of them vowing to one another that they would get over all the tough emotions and move past the terrible day at the lodge before the next full moon.

CHAPTER THIRTY-TWO

Working under Andre continued to keep Tilly incredibly busy, but when her working day was done, she would finally have some time to think, to work through the last of her fraught emotions, and she moved on from Blake's snowy visit at last. He would come into her dreams most nights, eager to show her his much more open emotions thanks to his twin sister Luna's help, and she quickly became far more willing to have an early night than ever before, eager for the sexy, dark god of her dreams to visit. They soon found themselves opening up more and more to each other during their nightly exploits, feeling as though they really were there together in whatever scene Blake had put together for the pair of them in her mind.

The full moon that followed brought with it the chance for the pair of them to be together properly again at last, and Tilly was anxious but excited to see Blake, ready to give herself to him entirely just like they had been before. He arrived at the penthouse almost as soon as the full moon rose in the sky over London and was greeted by Tilly waiting patiently with her hip resting against the arm of the sofa. She had her arms folded, going for her best dominative look, and was wearing her sexiest black negligee, fishnet stockings and some killer stiletto heels.

"Strip," she ordered him, in a playful tone and he couldn't help but relish in her confident prowess, so obliged her command with a wicked grin, removing his black shirt and chinos without a word. Tilly took him in with a smile, the beautiful, dark, and dangerous being that she was still figuring out how to be with, how to love, but she knew she was ready to give herself to him again, she needed it, desperate to feel closer to him.

She kicked off the heels and walked towards him, looking up into his deep eyes with a satisfied smile as he gathered her up in his strong arms and wrapped her legs around his hips. He then kissed her deeply as he held her there, wanting Tilly just as much as she wanted him. Blake then carried her to the bedroom and laid her down on the huge bed, his mouth never once leaving hers as he pinned his lover there with his powerful body. She relaxed into his embrace, breathing him in, desperately wanting to touch and kiss every inch of his muscular body. Blake then suddenly rolled sideways, and she followed his lead. Tilly climbed up onto his lap, straddling her lover as she ran her hands down to his chest and perfectly rippled abs for a moment, savouring the sight.

Tilly then stood up on the bed, towering over him as Blake laid back on the pillows, watching her every move, and he bit his lip expectantly, thoroughly enjoying the show. She took off her lace camisole and then slipped down her panties, moving slowly and sexily before throwing them to the floor but she left on the black, netted stockings and then climbed back down onto his lap, sliding Blake's hard shaft inside her very ready cleft as she did. He sat back, allowing her to be in full control as she slid up and down over her dark lover, taking him deeper and deeper as she thrust into his powerful hips. When she came, Blake sat up to kiss her deeply, pulling Tilly down harder onto him so that he could press deeper into her wonderfully pulsating muscles. As she came down from her high, he then turned her, lying on top of Tilly as he then began thrusting into her again, slow and softly at first and then harder as she opened up for him, his mouth never leaving hers and his heart opening as her wonderful thoughts flooded through him.

They continued to make-love for hours, staring into one another's eyes and kissing each other deeply and intensely as they moved together so effortlessly on the dark bed. Just before the sun began to rise, Blake leaned over her and held Tilly close while he cupped her face in his hands, staring down at her in the bed, his intense green eyes warm and full of emotion for the first time in his long, cold life.

"I love you," he told her, looking into Tilly's deep blue eyes through the dim morning light. She gasped and kissed him, gripping Blake tightly with her thighs when she then began to feel the bed shake beneath them as he reached his climactic end, emptying into her forcefully before slowing down and sinking into her loving arms.

"I love you too," she told him as he held her tightly in his strong embrace, but she knew he had already known it for a long time.

CHAPTER THIRTY-THREE

The next day Tilly had arranged to take Blake across the city to Andre's restaurant for lunch. Her boss had heard all about her infamous, long-distance boyfriend and had agreed to give her the day off while he was visiting, as long as she promised to stop by so that he could meet him at long last.

"Blake Rose," he said, introducing himself and reaching out his hand to shake Andre's with a warm smile. He seemed so formal, so refined, and even Andre was taken aback by the young but so commanding man before him. Luckily, and much to her delight, Blake hadn't taken too much convincing to go with Tilly to meet her boss. As well as being interested to meet the mentor she spoke and thought so highly of, Blake also knew just how important Andre and her career were to Tilly. He was mindful to be friendly, courteous, and warm with him, making every effort to come across as a normal, friendly guy, and the two of them seemed to get on well, much to Tilly's delight. She had loved hearing him say his full name too and had not really considered him having a surname before now.

Blake took the chance to charm Andre while they were chatting, luring him in with a mesmerising gaze and then planting a harmless little seed in the back of his mind, a dark spell that would ensure that in the future Andre would either instinctively give Tilly the days off during his monthly visits or plan her shifts around the moon without even realising he had done it. Andre had no idea what Blake had done, but the Black Prince was glad to know that going forward, he would not have to sacrifice any of his precious time with Tilly. He didn't care about being selfish with this order, her work was too important to always have to take a sick day or beg to take a holiday day, and this way he could be sure that the restaurant wouldn't be getting in the way of his time with his lover again.

After the delicious meal that Andre had cooked especially for them, the two lovers then took a walk around the centre of London, seeing the sights for a while before Blake then treated Tilly to a shopping spree in one of the posh boutique's they found along the way. The entire day was wonderful, they walked hand in hand as they wandered and Tilly felt nothing but love and happiness pass back and forth between them as they spent what would seem like a very normal day together if she wasn't walking along with the Prince of Hell, not that any of the humans around them knew that dark truth, of course.

They returned to the penthouse later that afternoon and were greeted by Beelzebub and his followers that had let themselves in while they waited for Blake and Tilly to come home. The demon had now recruited three more humans into his following, and much to Tilly's happiness Renee had found her place with the group at last, no longer questioning her master or his rules and Tilly guessed his punishments had worked on her after all. Renee held hands with a new boy in Bob's group, a dark-haired boy with a grungy style and a cheeky smile named Jared. Tilly learned from Gwen that the pair had fallen quickly in love over the last few weeks, that they were absolutely smitten with one another and she couldn't help but smile at them as they kissed and swooned over each other while snuggled together on the sofa.

Beelzebub and Gwen had officially become an item now too and seemed happy together. Gwen's genuine smile and affectionate glances towards the ancient and very powerful demon proved more than enough to Tilly, and she was thrilled that her friends had found their place in this new life, too. They completed their circle of couples nicely, and Tilly thoroughly enjoyed spending her time with them. Both she and Blake enjoyed their company as they all relaxed together and had fun, feeling natural and just like any other group of friends as they chatted for hours.

That evening, they ordered in some Chinese food and popped open some champagne as they all relaxed together happily. Tilly kept catching Blake watching her with a sly grin as she giggled excitedly with Renee and Gwen about their amazing weekend, and couldn't help but smile back at him, fluttering her eyelashes coyly but enjoying his attention. He genuinely enjoyed seeing as she chatted away with her friends animatedly in the kitchen and listening in on her happy thoughts was a welcome treat, far nicer than the ones he had had to endure not so long ago. Tilly then effortlessly showed off her cooking skills for them all, whipping up some puddings and cocktails for them to enjoy, much to her friend's delight and praise. Tilly had also caught Beelzebub watching her a couple of times over the evening too, and he eventually plucked up the courage to talk with her quietly after Blake had taken himself off to another room to sort out some music.

"Are you two okay now?" he asked as he helped her clean up in the kitchen, looking slightly uncomfortable and maybe out of his depth, asking her such a personal question, but he still had a smile behind his warm brown eyes.

"Yeah, we're good, really good actually," Tilly told him with a grin, and she patted him on the shoulder, truly grateful to have someone around to keep an eye on her, someone that she knew she could trust to have her best interests at heart as well as his Black Prince's.

"Good, because I know he's made a really big effort to try and sort out those sides of himself that he has kept locked away for far too long, Tilly. You've made him question everything he thought he knew. It takes a huge adjustment. Just promise me you'll be patient with him, okay?" Beelzebub replied, taking Tilly aback, but she was glad he could be so honest with her.

"I will, there's nothing I want more than to carry on this way, to be everything he wants, and needs me to be," she told him honestly.

"Good," said a voice from the doorway, it was Blake, and Tilly wondered for a moment if they might be in trouble for talking about him, but he was not angry with them at all and was still exuding his relaxed, easy attitude and playful nature so neither Tilly nor Beelzebub panicked they had been caught discussing their master.

"Speak of the devil," she whispered playfully, and relished in the wicked grin he shot her in return.

"I'll leave you guys to it," Beelzebub said, slipping past Blake with a bow and then he headed back out to re-join the group. Tilly looked up at her lover with a smile, rising onto her tiptoes as he came closer to kiss him. Blake grabbed her waist, lifting her up onto the counter as he deepened the kiss and pulled her closer. She could feel his hardness through his black jeans and instinctively reached down to unbutton his fly, knowing he could command the others to give them some privacy.

"No," he told her, breaking their embrace, and stepping back with a grin.

"No?" she asked playfully, climbing down from the kitchen side with a pout.

"No," he reiterated more forcibly, but still with his wicked, sexy grin in place before he grabbed her hand and pulled Tilly back into the living room. Their friends were all sat on the sofas as they approached, and Beelzebub's other two new followers quickly moved from the couch onto the floor so that the pair of them could sit in their favourite spot.

Once she was safely cocooned between his legs, Blake then grabbed a small remote control from the coffee table and hit play. The acoustic rock song that Tilly had not so long ago dubbed as their song then began playing through the unseen speakers. She snuggled into him, smiling, and leaning her head up to kiss her lover gently as the song played and bought back wonderful memories of both their first time in the penthouse together and the moment they had stolen while the partygoers froze in place around them during the last party. She hummed along, knowing every word by heart now.

Blake let himself enjoy their closeness now rather than pushing it away, and had chosen this song purposely, feeling the same way about this one melody that both haunted and comforted him as he relished in her thoughts. He smiled and cupped her face with his palm, pulling her chin back up to his for a deep kiss before he then leaned forward and poured her a glass of their favourite whisky.

CHAPTER THIRTY-FOUR

Bright sunshine poured in through the huge bedroom window the next morning as Tilly and Blake made love one more time before he had to go back to Hell, the waning moon treacherously close but he didn't care, eager to stay with her for as long as he could. The early sunrise brought with it the promise of warmer, spring days and the weather had already begun to turn for the better, as well as the days getting longer, and Tilly couldn't wait for the summer to come, she had always loved the heat. She thought back to the night of her dream when she had shown him her desires through the mirror's image and looked up at Blake as he held her in his strong arms, wondering just how it had all come true despite his many warnings to her. She kissed him, allowing her master to pull her up onto his lap with his strong arms as he thrust harder into her pulsating muscles.

"I love you," he told her, reading Tilly's thoughts, and she smiled, laughing quietly to herself before she said it back to him, and then gripped his shoulders tightly as a shared climax claimed them both.

The next week of work at the restaurant was a hectic schedule of planning and playing with recipes in preparation for the following weekend. Andre had been asked to provide an elegant banquet for a charity event, complete with fine dining services and some of the more unusual, bespoke requests from their fussy clients. He had agreed to do it, but quickly informed Tilly and the other chefs that they had better get used to not sleeping until it was all over and done with. He worked them hard, encouraging them to give it their full attention and then praising the chefs for their good work before choosing from his protégés' best dishes to serve the guests on the night. Tilly was lucky enough to be chosen to make both a starter and dessert for the elaborate event, and she was over the moon. She thanked Andre for the opportunity and then quickly got to work on putting together her plans for the dishes to ensure that she was more than ready to wow both her colleagues and the banquet attendees with her decadent food.

When Saturday came around, she was well organised and raring to go, eager for her first opportunity to properly shine as an accomplished chef. Trey helped her with the preparations, plating up the starters for her as she checked each piece of her signature first dish, a seafood medley with beautiful mixtures of fresh shellfish and sea vegetables combined with perfectly balanced spices and herbs. Every one of the guests' plates came back clean, and Trey gave her a high-five as they celebrated for a moment before getting to work on the pudding.

The rest of the evening continued to be a huge success and ended with Andre being given a standing ovation following the last cleared plate of delicious food, and he then insisted that the other chefs join him in the hall, ushering them to bow to the crowd while letting them all know that he couldn't have done it without them.

"Get cleaned up, then I'm taking you all out for drinks!" Andre shouted to them as the many chefs returned to the kitchen and quickly set about clearing up their workstations. Tilly breathed a sigh of relief and smiled over at her other new friend, another young intern named Jessica, and they did a little happy dance, wiggling their bums as Trey laughed from behind them and shook his head. The girls then got straight to work, hurrying so that they could get out of there and have their well-earned alcoholic rewards.

"Why do you always wear black clothes, Tilly?" Jessica asked her absentmindedly as they finished cleaning, catching her off guard. She looked across the bench at her friend; Jessica was a chatty, friendly girl, short and skinny with black bobbed hair and grey-blue eyes. She was a genuinely kind girl and Tilly knew she was only asking out of intrigue rather than to pry into her personal choices.

"Because I'm a goth, didn't you already know that?" she replied, playfully teasing her friend as she wiped the countertop and cleaned the oven.

"Oh. You don't really look like a proper goth to me though, well, apart from your black clothes. And you don't seem the type of person to hang out in graveyards and dance naked under the full moon?" Jessica replied, laughing as Tilly shot her the best attempt at a menacing look she could manage.

"Well, for one, that's witch's, dur. And how do you know I don't hang around in graveyards? Are you my stalker?" she joked but was glad when Jessica just shook her head and laughed to herself before changing the subject.

"You up to anything tomorrow?" she asked, and Tilly shook her head.

"Sleeping all day sounds good. I think I've only had about ten hours' sleep all week," she replied.

"Me too, it will be good having a well-deserved drink tonight first though," Jessica told her with a wicked grin and Tilly nodded in response.

They soon finished up and got changed out of their work clothes. Tilly quickly changing into black skinny jeans and a sparkly top, pinning up her dark-blonde hair and then applying a little red lipstick before joining her colleagues outside the banquet hall. The group then made their way to a nearby bar, their spirits high as they celebrated their success and Andre went straight to the bar to buy the drinks while the rest of them slipped into the booths and tables, chatting away and revelling in the comments received from the evening's guests.

Tilly had just three glasses of whisky and cola, careful as ever not to get too drunk, but more so because she was with her work friends who did not know about her secret life outside of the kitchens and she didn't want to inadvertently say something she might later regret. Trey came over to join Tilly at the table, sliding her another drink as he congratulated her again on her tremendous pudding.

"Oh my God, you were amazing tonight, Tilly!" he exclaimed, waving his hands around animatedly, making her laugh and she blushed but performed a small bow, complete with twirling hand gestures, proud of herself for having done so well with her dishes too. She thanked him and then clinked her glass with his before she took a big sip. Jessica joined them a few minutes later, polishing off her own drink as she plonked herself down in the chair next to Tilly.

"I've just pulled," she told them excitedly, indicating over to the bar where a handsome man sat looking over at them with a smile. "You don't mind if I head off, do you? He's invited me to go to a nightclub that his friend owns for some cocktails. Cool or what? Unless you want to come with us too, Tilly?" she asked, her voice a high-pitched squeal. She was obviously excited by her handsome prize, but Tilly was feeling tired, ready for her bed and so shook her head.

"No thanks, Jess, but you go ahead. Just be careful, okay?" she replied, giving Jessica a hug before her friend took off towards her hot new friend and waved them goodbye from the doorway. Tilly took another swig of her drink then stood up, determined to head off home for some much needed sleep, but then fell back in her seat as a woozy head rush hit her.

"Whoa, I don't feel too great," she told Trey, who helped her up and took her arm. Tilly hadn't thought she had even had that much to drink but put it down to her tiredness and took Trey's arm gratefully as he helped her stand, keeping a tight hold of him as she swayed unsteadily on her feet.

"Come on, let's go and get you in a taxi," he told her, rolling his eyes at Andre as they left, the look telling their boss he was happy to help her get home, and Andre smiled and waved them goodbye from the bar.

Trey hailed a cab, slipping Tilly inside and giving his address to the driver. She heard him and tried to say no. She wanted to go to the penthouse, but no words could escape her lips. Tilly was quickly starting to lose consciousness so was not able to tell Trey to just take her straight home. Her arms and legs grew incredibly heavy somehow as well, and her eyelids began to droop within seconds of the taxi setting off from the bar. She was in a deep, dreamless sleep almost instantly but tried to wake herself up, not feeling comfortable sleeping in the back of a taxi, but it was no use.

After the short car ride, Tilly was vaguely aware of being carried down some steps towards a dark basement flat, and she knew for sure that she was not at her penthouse. She tried to move, but her body was still too heavy and unresponsive, so she slumped back into the strong arms that held her, feeling nauseous and worried.

"It's okay, I've got you," she heard Trey say quietly and then she felt herself being placed on a comfortable, flat surface she assumed must be a bed before she dozed off uncontrollably again for a few more minutes. She hated feeling so powerless but hoped that a good sleep would sort out her foolish drunkenness and then she would head home in the morning.

Tilly stirred again a short while later when she heard a strange clicking noise by her ear. She opened her eyes to find Trey leaning over her, his dark-skinned face close to hers as he fiddled with something above her head, his expression calm but focussed. She was much more lucid this time and managed to figure out her surroundings a little more. He had laid her down on a small bed, just like she had thought, but her arms were pulled up above her head for some reason. She tried to move, but quickly realised that the clicking sound that she had heard had been Trey locking a pair of handcuffs closed over her left wrist, restraining her arm above her against the metal bed frame. A second of which he was now securing over her other wrist, ensuring that it too was firmly held in place on the top right-hand corner of the bedframe.

"Why would you do that to yourself Tilly?" Trey wondered aloud as he stroked his hand over her burn mark, shaking his head as though disappointed in her for some strange reason. "You could've been so perfect," he added, murmuring to himself.

Tilly looked up at him pleadingly, fearing the worst and suspecting that he did not have the most honourable of intentions towards her, bile rising in her throat as she contemplated what to do next.

"Trey, what are you doing?" she asked, her speech slurring in her haze as she tried to question him.

"Ah, good, you're awake," he said with a smile, sitting beside her as he leered over at her. "I hope you're comfortable?" Trey then asked with a sly grin.

"You drugged me," Tilly replied, suddenly remembering the drink he had bought her from the bar.

"Yeah, sorry about that," he replied unashamedly, clearly not sorry at all, leaning closer and stroking her cheek as he continued to smile down at her darkly. She shuddered, his touch making her want to wretch.

"You really are a very beautiful woman, Tilly. I can tell that you make yourself out to be such a good girl, but underneath that seemingly normal exterior, there's a bad, dirty girl just dying to come out and play. You hide it well, but I know you can give me what I crave, what I need, and have always looked for in a woman. I have been watching you for a while, wanting you so badly, but I am a patient man, so I have just been waiting for the opportune moment to take you. And here we are at long last," he told her, and Tilly flinched, both scared and angered by his disturbing little speech.

CHAPTER THIRTY-FIVE

Tilly tried focussing every ounce of energy she had on Blake, calling to him in her thoughts. She knew that the full moon was still two weeks away and that he would not be able to come and save her himself tonight, but she hoped and prayed that perhaps he could get an order to one of the other demons who might be able to come and help her. Tilly closed her eyes and prayed to her master, desperate for a saviour.

When nothing happened, Tilly looked up at the man she had thought she knew so well, the man she had believed was her friend, and decided to try a different approach.

"I wouldn't do this if I were you, Trey," she told him, coming to a little more as the drug he had given her continued to wear off. "You don't know who you're messing with. Just let me go now before something bad happens to you," she said, looking up at him with determination and her most threatening stare.

"Oh really?" he asked, laughing off her threat with a genuinely amused look on his face. "What? Do you think you can kick my arse Tilly, or have you got a secret I need to find out? Don't tell me, I'll find out for myself just how sweet you taste, and I don't mind if you wanna try fighting me off, I get much more of a kick out of it anyway if you squirm," he joked, sliding one hand down her body and cupping Tilly between the thighs, his palm lingering over her mound as a delighted smile spread across his face. She squirmed away, groaning with disgust as he just laughed harder from beside her. Trey then reached into his pocket and pulled out a small vial of clear liquid, which he held up for Tilly to see.

"Don't worry darling, you'll be nice and relaxed again in a minute, and then I'll have my fun," he told her, and she shuddered. After peering up at the vial in his hands for a moment, Tilly then had a manic laugh uncontrollably escape her lips, coming up from deep inside of her, and Trey looked down at his captive in surprise.

"Fucking try it," she warned, still laughing. "My master is gonna make your life a living hell, your afterlife, too. You have absolutely no fucking clue.

446

You think you like it bad and dirty now, you just wait and see what's in store for you, Trey."

He seemed genuinely confused by her strange threat, but carried on regardless and leaned over her, grabbing her chin, and then dribbling some of the sour liquid into Tilly's mouth. She immediately spat it back at him and Trey slapped her across the face, hard, and she cried out as her cheek burned red-hot. He grinned, seeming to have enjoyed that, and poured more of the drug into her mouth, before then holding it closed along with her nose until he was happy that she had swallowed it. Tilly gasped for breath once he released her and tried to make herself sick, but it was no use, the medicine worked quickly and she drifted back off into a forced sleep, the dark haze bearing down on her uncontrollably despite her efforts to fight it.

Trey stood from the bed and wiped his face clean before he made his way over to a chest of drawers to the side of the room. He pulled out a large, sharp knife from the top drawer, lifting it to his eye to check the blade before he placed it on the top of the unit and headed off to the en-suite to freshen up.

He didn't notice Tilly's still body twitch ever so slightly as he wandered off, nor did he see as she opened her eyes and looked around the room, taking it all in for a moment with a dark, powerful stare. She somehow had deep green eyes now instead of her usual blue, and a strange darkness enveloped her on the bed, the shadows seeming to cling to the air around Tilly as though drawn towards her. Blake had possessed his lover from his home in the underworld, his dark power now coursing within her human body as her own consciousness slept on thanks to the drug Trey had forced into her.

There were two loud snaps of bone as Blake broke Tilly's thumbs to slide her hands out of the cuffs, he did not feel the pain of the break, but knew that Tilly would suffer when she woke up, however there was no other choice right now and he knew she would be grateful for his help in the long run. Her possessed body then stood and walked over towards the wooden unit, moving slowly and carefully before grabbing the knife just as Trey emerged from the bathroom.

"What the fuck?" he blurted out in surprise as he took in the sight of her. "What happened to your eyes?" he asked, staring into them in shocked bewilderment for a moment as he watched her weak hands tighten around the handle of the blade.

A deep voice that was not Tilly's answered him, sending chills down Trey's spine.

"I am going to enjoy this," she said with a wicked grin. "And then you will be mine to torture for all eternity, you foolish little shit. You should've just listened to her warnings, Trey," she told him, and his eyes opened wide in shock.

"Who are you?" he asked, his voice a trembling whisper as he peered fearfully into the eyes that did not belong to Tilly.

"You do not know me now, or what I can do to you, but you will know soon enough. When you reach the gates of Hell, my friend, be sure to tell them that your soul belongs to the Black Prince," Blake told him as he stepped forward, using Tilly as his conduit.

Trey tried to run towards the doorway, but one final step forward and a slash from her possessed body slit his throat with the knife in her hands with one swing. Blood spurted forwards, covering Tilly as Trey fell onto his knees before her and then bled out in seconds. Blake watched for a moment, sensing the angel of death as it claimed Trey's soul, but he soon felt himself begin to weaken.

He couldn't hold on, and although he hated to, he knew he had to leave Tilly behind. His consciousness slipped away, and she fell to the floor next to the dead body of her would-be rapist and murderer, fast asleep once more.

CHAPTER THIRTY-SIX

Tilly came to a few hours later, the agony of her hands bringing her round in record time. It still took her a few moments to properly wake up, her panting breath and trembling body in shock. She held up her throbbing hands and inspected them, finding her thumbs completely immovable, hanging limply in their sockets. She stifled a gag as the pain flooded her system and then tried to remember what had happened, but the agony reverberated through her again, shooting pains travelling up and down her entire body before the realisation finally kicked in.

Fear then added to her adrenaline-fuelled strength and made the pain subside suddenly, the memory of what Trey had done coming crashing back to her in an instant. Tilly blinked, clearing her blurred eyes as she ran one of her hands down to her hips, feeling that her clothes were still on, that her jeans had not been pulled off. She quickly and gratefully realised that she didn't feel as though she had been sexually abused despite what Trey had been promising to do to her before she had drifted away again, thanks to his foul-tasting drug.

Tilly sat up, looking down at herself; her clothes were clinging to her skin, seemingly soaked in blood. She could see it everywhere and even taste it, so she spat on to the floor to her left, which was when she finally saw Trey's dead eyes boring into her from a foot or so away and she screamed.

Only when she was hoarse from screaming and exhausted could Tilly finally calm herself down long enough to take in the bloody scene around her, still confused and scared, but she somehow knew she would be safe now. She was lying in the pool of blood that had seemingly come from Trey's neck wound, and she was covered in it from head to toe, a thick spray had covered her torso and face and then the pool of darkness had surrounded her as she had lay next to him unconscious.

Tilly shivered with both shock and the cold. The wet blood had already started to dry on her skin and the thought of it made her shudder even harder. She looked down at her hands again, realising that they were now thankfully free from the cuffs he had put her in, but they still throbbed painfully and were swelling more and more thanks to her attempts at movement. She was still utterly confused, unsure how she had managed to stop him, but was relieved that he had not succeeded in abusing or killing her. Tilly was positive that Blake must be to thank for her safety, that perhaps he had heard her prayers after all.

She crawled over to her handbag where Trey had left it by the door the night before and searched for her mobile phone, her broken thumbs making it very difficult to dig around in it properly. She eventually found it, covering the screen in blood as she tried to unlock the handset, her thumbs completely refusing to work. Tilly eventually dialled the police, managing to say to the call handler that she had been attacked and needed help right away, and she was grateful for the GPS tracking function as she then passed out again. She fell backwards onto the cold ground, her phone skating across the floor beside her, but it thankfully stayed connected to the concerned woman on the other end.

When she finally came to again, it was two days later and Tilly was laid in a hospital bed, both of her thumbs having been operated on, and each hand was now encased in a large, heavy plaster-cast. She opened her eyes and listened to Gwen and Renee as they sat beside her, chatting quietly to one another in two armchairs. Renee screamed when she saw Tilly watching them, and then jumped from her seat excitedly. Gwen grinned and grabbed a glass of water for her along with a straw, which Tilly gulped down, eager and grateful for the nourishment. She peered up at her friends, feeling safe and thankful for a moment before she then laid her head back and cried uncontrollably, the tears flowing from her in hot currents as her friends' arms enveloped her, both crying too.

Later, once she had calmed down, Beelzebub came in to see her. He smiled down at Tilly as he sat down beside her but could not hide his pain at seeing her this way. She had been cleaned up by the nurses, so was no longer covered in blood, but Tilly was sure she could still taste it in her mouth, or maybe that was just in her mind. He held her thickly plastered hand and tugged at her white hospital gown with a smirk, remaining playful as ever, desperately trying to cheer her up.

"I'm pretty sure you are going to be in trouble for wearing this," he joked, making her smile. She had wondered the same thing herself, but vaguely remembered Blake coming to her in a hazy dream to tell her he loved her and not to worry about anything. He would handle it.

"Well, I'm assuming that my master is somehow to blame for my broken thumbs, so I think he'll have to let me off this once," she replied with a grin and Beelzebub nodded, confirming her suspicions, but then looked down at her seriously again.

"The police are going to need to talk to you Tilly, but just say you don't remember anything, okay?" he told her. "We've got friends on the inside that will brush this all under the carpet. Not that you'd be in trouble for finishing that guy off, anyway," he said, looking down at the hand he still held, seeming thoughtful.

"So, it was me who did it then. I killed him? Surely *he* must have helped with that somehow, though?" she asked the demon, and he nodded, looking back into her blue eyes, his dark-brown ones soft and warm, yet protective and fierce.

"Yeah, he possessed you. It really took it out of him, that's why he had to leave you there like he did, but he knew he had to do something and there was no other choice. None of us could track you down. We realise now that Trey lives, well lived, next door to a fucking white church, that'll be why our radars were scrambled. Fucker," he added, and Tilly nodded in understanding, knowing that the church's threshold probably covered the flat too, cloaking her to the dark beings.

"They found videos of him with other women, raping and then killing them Tilly. There was a camera recording you too," he tailed off, seeming as though he felt like he had said too much. Tilly slunk back onto her pillow, disgusted but annoyed at herself that she had never had a clue, never realised what Trey was up to. She had had no idea and had trusted him as both a colleague and a friend.

"Why is it I'm nearly always surrounded by demons and yet it's the humans who are the evillest?" she wondered aloud, and Beelzebub shook his head, unsure how to answer that.

The next day, the police came to talk with her, but they were very understanding and didn't question her too much. All they needed from her was an official statement.

"All I remember is falling asleep on the bed after he handcuffed and drugged me, and then I woke up in a pool of his blood on the floor," she said, which really was the truth. They nodded, wrote in their notebooks, and then left, one of them giving a nod to Beelzebub as he went. Tilly knew she wouldn't have to worry about the backlash, but when she put on the television, her face was plastered all over it and she winced. Reporters had picked up on her terrible story and were camped out at both her parents' house and at the hospital. Luckily, they couldn't get to her room though, or into the penthouse so when she was discharged later that day Beelzebub teleported them straight there. The reporters would find another story to tell soon enough and, in the meantime, Tilly desperately needed her rest.

Tilly rang her mum and after a frenzied explanation to Bianca about it all she quickly set about giving her an update on her hands, but told them not to come to London, to stay put at home and she would call them every day to check in. They weren't happy but agreed, knowing that Tilly was a headstrong girl and that she had become incredibly independent now. Jessica also rang her mobile phone, having been refused entry to both her hospital room and the penthouse by her demonic guards. Tilly answered but was tired and just told her not to worry, that she would be in touch soon but could do with some space right now, which was actually very true.

CHAPTER THIRTY-SEVEN

Tilly tried to rest, but her fearful dreams kept waking her up, dripping with sweat and shaking uncontrollably in fear, no matter how hard she tried to reason with herself that Trey was gone. Blake tried to come into them at times, attempting to control her nightmares and calm her down, but he just could not keep the awful visions at bay and Tilly soon began forcing herself to stay awake instead of letting herself drift off for her much needed rest. She would watch television all night or jog for miles on the treadmill in the penthouse's gym in an attempt to keep herself awake. Her friends stayed there with her, never leaving her alone as she needed the company as well as some help to dress and wash herself, but even with them there by her side, she still could not rest easy.

Blake came to Earth as soon as the moon was full again, finding Tilly locked away in the penthouse bedroom, fear and lack of sleep almost driving her crazy. She jumped on him, attempting to seduce her lover the instant he arrived, wanting nothing more than for him to take her mind away from all the terrible memories and thoughts that she just could not shake. While happy that she wanted him so desperately, Blake refused her advances. He immediately helped Tilly get washed and changed and then he teleported her to a tall office building somewhere in the city, and the night guard led them straight into the dark foyer. Blake placed a strong hand on her back, leading Tilly inside and up to a small room without a word, and she followed his silent orders without question. He then stopped at the doorway, letting her enter alone, but she hesitated, not wanting to be without his strong, reassuring hold on her.

"This is where I leave you, for now. I will be here when you have finished," he said, guiding her forward with a gentle push on her back. A kind-faced woman had been sat waiting for her inside the room, and she rose and bowed to Blake formally before addressing Tilly directly, ushering her to sit down on the sofa opposite. He stepped back and shut the door behind him, leaving the two women alone.

"Hello Tilly, my name is Daisy," the woman said, her voice soft and calm. "Your master cannot enter this room, nor can he hear your thoughts while you are in here. This is a private and safe place, and you can be truly open and honest without having to worry about anyone listening in. He has asked me to help you to get through your fears and worries, and to help you overcome the terrible incident that recently happened to you."

Tilly felt herself instantly relax in the comfortable armchair, taking the woman in silently for a moment. She must have been around forty years old, with long brown hair and soft brown eyes, and she seemed genuine enough.

"So, are you a witch or something?" Tilly asked, and Daisy shook her head.

"No, I am human. But I have been marked by the demon Astaroth for almost twenty years, and in that time, I have learned a lot about the Satanic world. I am a psychiatrist by day, so I can help you to deal with everything that has happened to you with insight, knowledge of the human psyche and the simple fact that you can be open and honest with me about the demonic areas of our world without worrying or hiding the details like you must have had to with your human friends and family. I have warded this office with talismans and runes to ensure we have privacy, and your master has agreed to my terms," she said, reassuring Tilly and immediately putting her at ease. She looked at Daisy, surprised but glad that this woman was sitting before her right now. She hadn't realised just how much she needed to talk with someone about it all. Tilly was already grateful that Blake had bought her here and was soon ready to get started.

"So," Daisy continued, sensing her relax even more. "Here is what I already know about you. I know your name is Matilda Mayfair, that your master is the Black Prince and that you recently suffered a traumatic experience that has stopped you from being able to function properly, both mentally and physically," she said, waving a hand to indicate she meant her broken thumbs and Tilly nodded. "I'd like you to tell me about it, Tilly, but I'm going to need all of it. Let's start with the first moment you became aware of our world," she said, smiling over at her as she grabbed her notepad and readied her pen over it.

They spent a little while talking about the night that she had first met Brent, and the feelings she had previously had for him. Tilly started to tell Daisy that she no longer felt the same way about him, but she shushed her, telling her that there was no need to feel like she had to explain. They moved on, discussing the strange night that she had been marked by Lilith, and the big reveal on Halloween, along with Blake's reaction to her that night before, he then replaced Lilith's mark with his own. Tilly also opened up about her feelings for him and how they had grown stronger and stronger until the day in the Alps, his punishment that day and the distance she had felt afterwards before Blake finally had let himself show his true feelings for her.

Tilly was completely honest with Daisy, and it was a weight off her shoulders to talk about his mood swings and the harsh punishment he had put her through with someone at last. She had not been able to talk things through with anyone before, not even Gwen or Renee, and it was very soothing. Daisy let her do most of the talking, asking Tilly questions along the way to help her open up further, but not taking over the flow of her thoughts and memories at all. She finally caught up with the most recent events and talking about her night in Trey's flat was tough. The scars were still so fresh, but Daisy helped her understand the strange night a little better, explaining the possession and helping Tilly sort through her scrambled thoughts. By the time she came away from Daisy's office, she felt drained but much more level-headed.

Blake was waiting for her when Tilly left the small room, and she felt her last few hours lock away in her mind, shielded from him magically, and she was glad. Despite having nothing to hide from her master, she still appreciated the chance to have some privacy. She and Daisy had arranged to meet again in a few days and would keep on doing so until she felt she no longer wanted or needed her help. Blake thanked her and then quickly teleported Tilly back to the master bedroom of the penthouse without another word, and then kissed her deeply, sensing the calmness in his beautiful, yet damaged lover now, thanks to her session with Daisy. She smiled up at him; glad to be in his warm and protective embrace again at last. Just having him close soothed her so very much.

"Bed," Blake told her with a sly grin, but then walked over to the chest of drawers and pulled out some black cotton pyjama trousers, which he changed into and then climbed under the thin sheets rather than instigating anything sexual with her. Tilly smiled, she wanted more than just sleep thanks to the closeness and deep kisses that had stirred her hormones wonderfully, but she knew better than to disobey even his more playful orders, understanding why he wanted her to rest, and she could already feel the fatigue starting to well up inside of her again.

She moved over to the drawers and pulled open one of hers before sliding into a black nightdress and climbing into bed with him, snuggling next to Blake who pulled her closer, pressing her into him as he turned and faced Tilly while lying on his side.

One arm went under her neck to support her head and then cradled her around the shoulders while he slid the other around Tilly's ribs to her back and cuddled her into him even more. He also pulled his top leg up and placed it over hers to cocoon her, pulling his lover closer, wanting nothing more than to keep her safe and make Tilly feel warm, protected, and snug in his tight grip. She fell asleep almost instantly, relaxing deeply and feeling safe as she drifted off.

CHAPTER THIRTY-EIGHT

Tilly stood at the door to Trey's flat, looking in at the bloody scene before her. She trembled; scared stiff, and she desperately wanted to run away, yet she felt as though a mysterious and powerful force was pulling her inside uncontrollably.

"No," said a voice behind her, breaking her panicked silence and Tilly turned to see Blake looking down at her from the top of the steps which led down to Trey's basement flat from the street. He put his hand out, looking her in the eye, urging Tilly to take it, and she eagerly pushed herself towards him, up the steps and she then took his outstretched hand in hers, noticing that her hands were healed in her dream, which felt wonderful.

"Good girl," he said, squeezing her hand slightly as he pulled her up the final step. "Now, where do you want to go?" Blake then asked her, happy to follow her lead as the view before them changed from the busy London street to a black, blank canvas for Tilly's subconscious imagination to imbue. She wasn't sure where she wanted to go, so she just tried to think back to her times of having fun with her friends, focussing her mind back to before the permanent sense of fear had become all too familiar inside of her.

The Diablo Circus suddenly came into view before them, lit up brightly against the night's sky and music was blaring from inside the tent. She looked down at her feet, embarrassed by her choice, but Blake took her chin in his hand and lifted it, looking into her blue eyes as she raised them to meet his.

"I don't mind, but I assume there won't be any memories of your private time with Brent, okay?" he asked, only half joking but remaining playful as he peered down at her, his green eyes full of warmth. She nodded and led him inside, linking her healed fingers through his as they moved through the crowd. They took two seats near the front and watched as her memories of the amazing and death-defying feats by the performers flashed by, Brent with his fast-paced and exciting juggling show, Jackson's fire breathing and David's acrobatics before Lucas and the others took to the stage and performed various other tantalising routines too. Tilly gasped and laughed along with the other imaginary people in the crowd, a huge smile on her face as she focussed all her energy on the show, visibly relaxing with each passing moment. Blake set aside his jealousy and enjoyed watching her, glad that she was having a nice dream again at last.

Tilly slept for half a day, only actually waking up when the bright sunshine streamed in through the huge window and hit her face, making her flinch. The pressure she then felt on her bladder forced her even quicker into consciousness and she blinked awake, surprised to find that Blake was exactly where he had been when she had fallen asleep in his protective embrace the night before. He hadn't left and more than that; he was fast asleep in front of her, his arms and legs still wrapped around her tightly. Blake never slept, not on Earth anyway, and she was shocked to see him there, snoring quietly and seemingly dreaming too as he rested. His handsome, relaxed features were soft, and he looked like the age he portrayed himself to be, young and almost human-like.

Tilly gazed at him for a few moments before pulling out of his grasp and heading into the bathroom, surprised that he didn't wake up when she moved away, but she was glad to have a few quiet minutes to herself as she used the toilet, brushed her teeth, and then ran a hot bath. She checked the bedroom again, finding him still snoozing in the bed, so she stripped off and slipped into the hot, soapy water, having quickly put plastic bags over the casts on her wrists to ensure they didn't get wet. She lay there for a few minutes, smiling as she relaxed and enjoyed her clear mind at last, remembering their fun dream together as she rested her aching muscles.

"Ha-hum," came a fake cough from the doorway, making her jump and Tilly looked back to see a smiling but bleary eyed Blake looking down at her.

"What? I needed to pee," she told him with a small laugh.

"So you ran a bath? Strange girl," he replied with a smirk, laughing, and shaking his head. He came into the bathroom and leaned against the sink, watching her intently.

"Mind if I join you?" Blake then asked, slipping off his pyjama trousers and sliding behind Tilly in the wonderfully hot water. She lay back on his warm chest as he cradled her in his strong arms, making sure to hold her waist and let her arms stay on the bath's sides as she lay in between his open legs.

"Feeling better?" he enquired, and she groaned an almost inaudible confirmation in reply.

"Rested?"

"Yes," she answered, more clearly this time.

"Happy?"

"Yes."

"Hungry?"

"No."

"No? Hmm, how about, horny?" he asked finally, reaching down to cup between her thighs with the palm of his hand.

"Yes," she replied, gasping as he quickly opened her legs and slid his own closed beneath her so that Tilly straddled him backwardly. Blake then lifted her up and onto his ready cock in one quick move. She leaned into him, arching her back to welcome him deeper and letting her master move her up and down in the hot suds on top of him.

Tilly soon groaned and stiffened as her first climax swept over her and Blake gripped her tighter to him, pushing harder as her deep muscles clenched over his hardness. He continued to move her like that until he neared his own glorious release, cradling Tilly in his strong arms as she revelled in her intense climaxes repeatedly until the tub shook around them and he finally came.

The pair then hopped out of the bath and straight into a hot shower, Blake helping Tilly to wash her hair and still trembling body, before dropping to his knees before her and taking her swollen clit in his mouth. She cried out as she came for him again, the wonderfully intense release sending her over the edge one more time.

CHAPTER THIRTY-NINE

The pair relaxed on the sofa together later that afternoon after devouring a huge pizza and an entire tub of ice cream while wearing baggy tracksuit trousers and t-shirts as they lazed and just enjoyed one another's company. Blake was sat upright with his back against the thick sofa cushions as Tilly laid lengthways, her back on the arm of the sofa and her feet in his lap as they chatted.

"I was wondering, if you don't mind, what do you do while you're in Hell?" she asked him, eager to know more about her lover. He smiled, happy to answer her questions, and he was glad that she had still been thinking of him during their times apart. Her question had caught him slightly off guard at first though and thinking back Blake was sure that she was the first person ever to have asked him about himself, the first person he had known in his long life that didn't just automatically know all about him, and yet he loved she wanted to know, that she was genuinely interested in him and his dark life.

"Well, there's loads I have to do on an official basis, boring stuff really, like council meetings and helping to initiate the demons and welcome new souls," he told her, rubbing her feet absentmindedly.

She laughed, not being able to help but think that those responsibilities sounded anything but boring to her. "My main role is simply being the Black Prince. All our orders come from my mother. Luna, Lottie, and I pass them down the chain of command and at least one of us are always with or near to her. I also have my own dark council, it is our responsibility to give the demons their classifications, and it can be a long process at times because we have a set of tasks that the demons must complete to progress higher up the chain of command. If they want to make it up the levels, they have to come through me and succeed under my council's watchful eyes. We oversee the trials for humans who want to become new demons too, like I did with Lucas, not that there have actually been many," he told her, and Tilly's mind was racing, trying to imagine him sat at an altar beside the Dark Queen, issuing orders and ruling by her side. He smiled over at her, his green eyes ablaze as he read her thoughts, enjoying her intrigue and imagination. Tilly realised after a few seconds he had mentioned another name, Lottie, and as she pondered over who that might be her mind was suddenly drawn back to the first night that they had met, Brent's explanation afterwards of Blake's royal family, and his other sister, the Unholy Princess. She opened her mouth to ask him, but he had read her mind already and shook his head sternly, stopping her in her tracks.

"You don't need to know Tilly, forget I ever said it. I should never have said her name up here," Blake said, looking worried at his accidental slip up.

"I won't tell a soul," she promised him, smiling gently. "Please, carry on," she insisted, and he took a deep breath, trusting her as he shook off his unease.

"Okay. Well, I have my coven as you know, they do my bidding and assist me with pretty much everything, so they need me there to give them orders and instructions too," he added, making Tilly think of Selena and the way she had looked at him so lovingly that day at the penthouse.

"And what do you do for fun?" she then asked him, hoping that he was not going to say, "*Selena.*"

"If I'm being honest, I sometimes did used to fill my quiet hours with teleporting to one of their chambers for a quick fuck," he said, having read her jealous thoughts. "But not anymore," he added, looking over to her solemnly as he spoke. "I would fulfil my urges and then just pull out and teleport away, not ever giving a shit about staying for cuddles and romance. But I have not been with anyone else since I marked you Tilly, I want you to know that," he said, and she smiled, taken aback slightly, but completely reassured. "There is another side to my duties Tilly, I sometimes have to deliver punishments too, but only if it is someone from my own coven or one of my followers, otherwise there are others who are required to take care of it. Demons with, how should I say it? *Specialities*, in certain areas," he said, looking back down at her feet thoughtfully.

Tilly detected a note of sadness in him then, like a hard truth that was trying to surface, but she didn't dare ask any more of him. She knew he might be thinking of the day he had punished her at the lodge and didn't want to talk about it now either. She wanted to push away that awful memory. He looked over into her eyes, reading her reluctance to talk about the subject, but he needed her to know, and Tilly could sense that he wanted to open up about it despite it being painful for him too.

"I am not ever going to let myself lose control of my anger with you again Tilly," Blake promised, needing her to hear it. "I will just teleport away next time, if ever, I feel that way. The burn I gave you was too much, let alone the way I treated you like a cheap fuck afterwards. I just couldn't control myself that day, but there's no excuse. I have been working on it, Luna has been helping me, but my cold nature is just too easy to keep hold of. I know my darkness. I don't fear it, but I have feared change for so long simply because I knew that I would have a lot to deal with once I did. I'm slowly letting down my walls, but it's not easy for me. I have been this way for a very long time and it's all I know. This jet-black heart of mine needs time to change," he told her, massaging her feet and calves as he spoke, finding comfort in the contact. Tilly appreciated his honesty and smiled but said nothing. She didn't want to interrupt his thoughtful admissions and was just glad he felt as though he could finally open up to her.

"I know how it feels to be punished severely Tilly, and I never, ever wanted that for you. Being controlled by someone that way can be so lonely and trying to be what they expect you to be does nothing but diminish the real you until you cannot be sure who that person even is anymore," he continued, looking at her again and Tilly nodded, trying to understand. She couldn't help wondering when or how he had been punished or had suffered so much in the past, though, thinking to herself that surely his mother would have never allowed him such a torturous upbringing? He read her quizzical thoughts and then Blake took a deep breath, as though steadying himself in preparation for his hardest admission yet.

Tilly opened her mouth to speak, wanting to tell him to stop, wanting him to know that he didn't need to tell her if it was too hard, but he raised a hand to quieten her and shook his head, needing to let go of it at long last, to keep on going with his dark confessions.

"Many years ago, when Luna and I were children, just four years old, I did something foolish and terrible. I was a stubborn child, headstrong, disobedient, and strong-willed. My mother was half-human then, and she had to come to Earth for a while because she was getting sick. You must never tell anyone this story, okay Tilly?" he asked, and she nodded, understanding that what he was about to tell her was not information that would be given out to just anybody.

"I promise, you can trust me," she told him, and whole-heartedly meant it.

"I know. The moon bound our father, Luna, and I even then. We were strengthened by our time in Hell, but she was not. Her human side suffered, and my mother became ill. She had to stay here on Earth until she was strong again, so we came to visit her each time that the moon was full. We had to stay within the Satanic church's protective threshold for our safety. But I couldn't ever understand it, I was blind to the truth, and didn't want to hear it or care for their explanations," Blake continued, looking sad.

"My all-powerful father was somehow scared to set a foot outside, to take me out into the big wide world I so craved to see. I felt as though he was a fool, as if I knew better and I pitied him for his weakness. I repeatedly snuck out, despite their warnings and even persuaded Luna to come along one night," he said and then stopped dead, his eyes blackening slightly. Blake then took another deep breath, as though the memory was hard for him to think about, let alone actually say aloud.

"We were cornered, trapped by a coven of white witches, and then kidnapped. I soon realised that my parents had been right all along, but by then it was too late. It quickly became apparent that the witches didn't actually want us though, they just wanted her."

"Your mother?" Tilly whispered, and Blake nodded, his eyes swirling with more black specks as he peered over at her, but he remained calm and in control.

"She came to rescue us, not that she could even do anything as she was vastly outnumbered, but she left the safety of the church to find us, anyway. They used her motherly love to lure her out of hiding, knowing we were the only things she would sacrifice herself for. It was a trap, and she knew it, but came anyway." Blake paused for a moment, thinking back to the witches in the park and their awful imprisonment in their own bodies all that time ago. Regardless of the years that had now passed, the memory of that night still festered like a deep well of regret that he somehow could not stop adding to. Tilly was the only being that had made him feel as though that pool might slowly diminish; strangely even his mother's forgiveness had not lessened the pain.

"It was all my fault. We were taken away, and they used us to blackmail her. I was sent back to our church not long before the moon waned and my father took me straight back to Hell with him, questioning me about it for hours. He wanted to know every detail of where she was and who had taken her, but I was just a boy. I had no idea. When I didn't give him good enough answers to satisfy his frenzied mind, he hit me across the face, hard, so hard that I flew across the room and slammed into the wall. I begged for his forgiveness, but he just grabbed me up off the floor, bellowed at me and beat me repeatedly, screaming how I was to blame for her capture, and that I had to be punished for my insolence. He took out all of his frustration and anger on me, and I was powerless to stop him," Blake told her, his hands still on Tilly's legs, pushing harder and harder into her skin, bruising her slightly as he continued to rub them while he spoke, but she didn't say anything or try to pull out of his grasp, she was in too much shock at hearing his awful story to feel the bruises yet.

"Luna was sent back to Hell soon afterwards too, but she was sick because the moon had begun to wane while she was there, so our high priestess Alma immediately had to take her away to heal her. But our mother did not come back. Her powerful captor had got what he wanted, we were just the loose ends, the leverage to get her to succumb to him," Blake added, letting go of her at last and then pulling his hands up to his face, running his fingers up through his dark hair as the painful memories flooded back to him.

"I suffered greatly for my impudence and for the repercussions of my actions. As punishment, my father sentenced me to endure all kinds of torture in the dungeons and fiery pits of Hell. Everyone involved was given an order of eternal silence by him, their minds magically forgetting all about what I had endured and by the time the next full moon came around, my body was broken, along with my resolve, my stubbornness, and my will. I was just a tiny child, and he broke me so very easily, I even thanked my father for the lessons that he had taught me, and ever since then I have been that way Tilly, cold, closed-off and emotionless. I was so young when I learned those lessons, and they are very hard for me to try and forget now. My father left for Earth as soon as the moon was full again, while Luna and I stayed behind. He was consumed with finding her, with saving my mother and he never looked back."

"That's terrible, truly awful, that he could do that to you. You were just a child. Where was she? Did he find her?" she asked, hoping that he wouldn't mind her questions, but she was enthralled and was desperate to know more.

"I cannot tell you where she was Tilly, but yes, he did find her. The aftermath was awful, though, and I did not see either of my parents for another ten years. The ancient powers of dark and light were forced out of balance by a battle between the two, and the portals between the worlds were all closed, we were stuck in Hell while they were stuck on Earth and we had no idea if or when they would ever return to us. Eventually they did come home, in the interim we had been raised by my parents most trusted witches Dylan and Alma along with our Uncle Devin and Aunt Serena, but I was still the same broken, closed-off boy that my father had left behind, content in my misery, feeling as if I had earned it, as though I deserved it and only my father and I ever knew the real reasons why. I carried on that way even after she finally returned, refusing to change even then, as I didn't feel worthy of her forgiveness. I knew I was to blame and that I could never make amends for my actions, so I didn't bother trying any more. My mother never learned the truth until she took the throne, her full power opening up every truth my father kept hidden from her over their years together. She disappeared for days, her rage phenomenal and I can only assume she went off to dispose of my father once and for all, to make him pay for his many misdemeanours, but I might not ever know for sure," Blake added, reaching down to rub her feet again, but gently this time.

Tilly let his powerful words sink in for a moment and then jumped up from where she had been laying on the couch and climbed over to Blake, straddling him, and looking down into his gorgeous green eyes tenderly.

"I'm sure she made him sorry for ever laying a hand on you, and too bloody right. Thank you for telling me. I know it is hard for you to open up, especially over something as intense as this," she said, kissing him deeply as she peered down at him lovingly.

"No, thank you Tilly. I would still be that dark, broken boy if it weren't for you. My black heart never cared for anything or anyone before you came along, you've opened up something in me I had pushed away for so many years," he said, kissing her back and holding her tightly in his arms. "And not just that, I've finally been able to realise just why he punished me so harshly, why he was so scared. When you have something you love so very much, it's like a part of you belongs to them. But it makes you weak when you lose them, or if you ruin the bit of them they gave you in return. Being in love means that you then suddenly have something, everything to lose and you will do anything to protect it. You scared the hell out of me. Love was never on my agenda, but somehow you gave yourself to me, anyway. I will never break it again, I will protect your love, protect you, forever, Tilly."

"I will always be here, master, ready and willing to do whatever it takes to protect you as well. I won't fight you ever again, but I will fight *for* you, for us. Nothing will ever come between us again, I promise," she said, so assuredly and she meant every single word. "You are my very own beautiful tragedy, and I want to be the one person you can truly trust, the only one who can soothe every one of those old wounds, Blake," she told him as she cradled him in her arms, and then jumped, realising what she had just accidentally said. This time, though, he didn't care that she had spoken his name, and he just looked up at her frightened expression with a smile.

"What am I going to do with you? Naughty girl," he said, without a hint of anger behind his eyes as he laughed quietly to himself and pulled Tilly closer for another deep kiss.

CHAPTER FORTY

The pair of them relaxed on the sofa for a little while longer, neither talking as they let each other's deep and powerful words sink in for a while. Tilly couldn't help but imagine Blake as a small boy, being tortured and beaten by his father and she shed tears for that boy, cradling the man beside her as tightly as she could in the hope that the broken child he once was might be soothed somehow as well. Blake buried his face in her hair, desperate not to fight his feelings as her thoughts spread through him and he too let a few tears fall, no longer ashamed to admit his past, wanting to move on at last.

Tilly eventually started to feel her hands throb beneath the casts again though and rose from the sofa to go and grab some painkillers and a cup of water from the kitchen, she wanted to numb the pain that despite her improved mood continued to serve as a constant reminder of what had happened, and she couldn't help but start uncontrollably thinking of Trey again while she was alone in the kitchen. She had done well to push it all aside and overcome the terrible ordeal as much as she had thanks to Blake's support and Daisy's therapy session, but the memory was still too fresh, too raw and would often still sneak into her thoughts here and there.

Blake looked up at her as she came back through to the living area, looking thoughtful.

"I have the video Tilly," he said, looking over to her with a worried expression when she stopped dead halfway between the kitchen and the sofa. He had been wondering for a while if she would want to see it but didn't know when the best time might be to ask, he had the only copy of it now and was more than willing to destroy it if she asked him to but had read her mind and he knew she had been thinking of the attack again, and part of him just wanted to get it over with so he decided to be forward.

"Put it on, I want to see," Tilly replied, stepping forward again, her face pale as she sat back down on the sofa and he raised the remote to the television screen, clicking it on before selecting the file from the memory stick he had put in the side of it while she was in the kitchen.

An image quickly appeared on the huge flat screen, showing a wide view of Trey's bedroom, empty at first, and then the two of them came inside. She watched as her so-called friend dragged her limply across the room and then laid her down on the bed and began securing her wrists with the handcuffs. Tilly was surprised to hear her own voice as she pleaded with him quietly after a few minutes, scared and trembling at first, then followed by the strange and disturbing laugh that came shortly after when she had tried to threaten him. It was hard to watch, especially when Trey ran his hand down over her body, his disgusting perversion urging him onwards despite her pleas, and all with that dark and sinister smile on his face that Tilly knew would haunt her forever.

Blake watched her rather than the screen. He had seen it a couple of times already, the macabre show only forcing forth his acceptance of his love for her as he remembered how he had felt at the thought of losing this girl, his girl. He read Tilly's responses to the video to make sure it wasn't all too much for her, but he could tell that she was doing fine, if anything she was intrigued more than upset by it, especially when her unconscious body then jerked slightly and opened its eyes on the screen.

"Green eyes," she whispered, looking at herself intently as she watched Blake take control of her unconscious body. She could see the darkness surrounding her on-screen image, a strong blackness that seemed to be drawn to her possessed form in the dim light. Tilly winced as she saw the face that was no longer her own look up at her cuffed wrists before leaning up on the mattress, pulling the metal at first as though testing the bed frame for a sign of weakness but then pushing down hard on first her left, then right thumb before wriggling them free of their restraints. The noise of the crack from each thumb was sickening, but Tilly didn't even flinch. She knew it was the only way that Blake could free her quickly enough.

Tilly's body then rose from the bed, moving slowly and jerking peculiarly as she grabbed the knife from atop the unit. She gasped and covered her mouth when she saw Trey emerge from the bathroom, hearing the deep voice that was not her own so clearly as she spoke to him, and then slid the knife quickly over his exposed skin. Her body then dropped to the floor along with Trey's as he bled out, and then they were both perfectly still, lying side-by-side on the floor drenched in his blood.

"Wow, you weren't kidding about the whole 'slit their throat and make you bathe in their blood' threat, were you?" she said with a gruff laugh, and Blake couldn't help but laugh too, remembering his dark orders the night that they first met. She then looked over wide-eyed at him on the sofa. She had thought she knew, but Tilly had had no idea just how dark things had gotten in that bedroom. She sat back against the cushions, trying to make sense of it all, unable to understand just how Blake had managed to possess her all the way from Hell, but she was so grateful that he had.

"It's very difficult to possess someone Tilly, not at all how they make it out in the movies," he whispered, trying to explain the strange image to her as he switched off the television. "It was only really possible because of our strong bond, without that and the extra power Alma had to summon for me with my mother's permission, you would not have survived his assault. I'm sorry that I had to leave you straight away once he was dead, I was too weak and could not stay to help you escape the flat, but I knew you would wake up once the drug wore off and was absolutely certain that you would then be safe," Blake told her, seemingly angry with himself for not having been stronger for her.

Tilly stayed silent for a few more minutes, letting what she had just seen and heard sink in.

"Thank you. I guess it was just so weird to watch and I can't think what else to say. Other than that, I hope you make him pay. I hope he is gonna suffer?" she finally asked him, not sure how else to respond to seeing the video or what to say to her master about it all, and he nodded. She was grateful that he had acted, knowing that it was not easy for him to have done so and she focussed on his protective urges instead of the strange and sickening scene she had just witnessed. Tilly then sat back deeper into the cushions, pulling her legs up underneath her protectively, and she was glad when Blake pulled her into his strong arms again. She was so appreciative for what he had done and pushed away all her questions and fears, knowing he had and would always take care of her, no matter what it took.

"He will do nothing but suffer for all eternity, my love. Make no mistake about that. I could have lost you to him and his depraved fetish. How could I not do something? You are mine, Tilly. My friend, my lover, and my future. No one will ever come between that again," he promised, kissing the top of her head affectionately.

CHAPTER FORTY-ONE

Tilly stood pouring two fresh glasses of whisky at the kitchen counter a little while later that day, feeling strange and still thoughtful following her having watched the awful clip, yet she was still more relaxed than she had been in weeks thanks to her clearer head and full heart. Blake joined her in the large room, grabbing her from behind and kissing Tilly's neck as he cradled her with his strong arms and pressed his muscular body into her back. She groaned quietly, the small sound a simple yet effective trigger that sent his kisses trailing faster and harder on her skin while his hands caressed her breasts and she reached her hands behind her to try and run her fingers through his dark curls, being hindered by her casts somewhat.

"Save it for the bedroom, will you?" said a voice from the doorway, making Tilly jump but Blake turned around immediately to face the voice's owner with a broad smile, and he walked over to greet the visitor, whom Tilly could somehow tell was his mother, Cate, the Devil.

She was stood in the doorway, looking every inch the powerful, forceful looking creature that Tilly would have expected her to be, and yet she was warm, beautiful, and so human-like that it was a confusing sight. Tilly took one look at the stunning goddess with her long, dark-brown curly hair, bright red lips and her intense green eyes and she fell to her knees, hitting the tiled floor with a loud thud as she did so, and she blushed to herself for her very ungraceful reaction to the Dark Queen's presence.

"Hello mother," Blake said as he kissed her cheek with a warm smile. "To what do we owe the pleasure?" he asked, standing almost a foot taller than she did and yet seeming somehow smaller and much less powerful than his omnipotent mistress, who effortlessly dominated every inch of space around her.

"I was just thinking that it has been far too long since my last visit, darling, and you know I love England in the springtime," Cate told him with a wry smile, and Blake knew that there was more to her visit than for just the weather.

"You may stand, Tilly," she then added as she made her way over to the counter and then grabbed one of the whisky filled glasses and took a long swig of the strong drink.

Tilly did as Cate commanded and stood but did not dare make eye contact with her Dark Queen. Despite her warm appearance the human girl was ever so aware that she was in the presence of the all-powerful ruler of Hell, the Devil. Cate looked misleadingly young, beautiful, and elegant despite her many years of existence, and Tilly was already in awe of her. She wore a long, black maxi-dress with sandals and had a black leather jacket placed casually over her slim shoulders. Tilly admired her casual style and loved how she had accessorised with lots of silver and gunmetal grey jewellery. Her favourite pieces were the exquisite pair of large diamond earrings that sparkled brightly through her dark hair and the long necklace Cate wore around her neck, which had a large, ornately engraved locket on the end of it. The pendant was old-fashioned but truly stunning and showed off her figure beautifully; the chain creating a long V-shape between her impressive breasts.

Cate finished off her glass of whisky and placed the now empty tumbler back down, licking her lips and watching Tilly as she peered down at her feet awkwardly. She then moved closer and took the girl's face in her hands, finally forcing her gaze up to meet hers. She stayed like that for just a moment, reading every one of Tilly's thoughts and taking in her short lifetime's worth of memories as she did so, and Tilly did not resist her powerful prowess for even the slightest second.

Blake stood to the side, watching the two of them with interest, but he did not dare to say a word as his mother read his lover's mind. He knew far better than to interrupt her, and was not worried about what she might discover there, as she most likely knew everything she needed to about Tilly from his own thoughts, which he knew she read quite regularly.

"It's a pleasure to meet you Tilly," Cate eventually said, her voice soft, and she smiled warmly at her. "My name is Cate Rose, but of course, you may call me your Majesty," she added with a wicked grin.

She read Tilly for a moment longer, her thoughtful green eyes boring into hers as she delved a little deeper into her psyche and enjoyed the loving thoughts she found there of her and Blake, and of the mistakes they had made that had almost ruined that love she held so dear.

"You truly love him, don't you, Tilly?" Cate asked her seriously, not releasing her from her grasp or pulling away from her at all just yet.

She pinned Tilly to the counter with her tall, strong body and she was glad for the support as she thought she might fall over if the Queen let her go right now. Her touch was sending powerful waves of sensual emotion and love through every inch of the human girl, making her woozy and she could not fight it, but she didn't want to either.

"Yes, your Majesty, I do," Tilly replied quietly, she was uncontrollably trembling in fear before the dark and powerful Queen, she could feel the immense and omnipotent power in the air all around her, but she was also in wonder of this incredible woman, this forceful entity that stood before her, that had graced Tilly with her coveted presence.

"Then say his name to me, now," Cate ordered her with a smile.

"Blake," Tilly said without hesitation, but she was still unsure why the Dark Queen was asking her to do it.

"And again."

"Blake."

"Good, now tell Blake exactly how you feel about him," Cate commanded, stepping back to release Tilly from both her grip and her commanding gaze. She looked over to her master, smiling as she made eye contact with him, his green eyes alight and happy as he watched the two of them with intrigue.

"I love you, Blake," she said, still nervous at saying his name aloud, and the Queen's smile widened even more.

She walked back over to her son, giving him another kiss before wandering back to the doorway, hesitating for just a moment as she turned to watch him again, her green eyes sparkling brightly too.

"Good, that's settled then. Oh, and I have decided that we are going to have a gathering here tonight, an orgy, so you two might want to go and get ready," she informed Blake with another wicked grin.

"Really?" he asked, smiling back at his mother. "It's been a very long time. Well, at least it'll be fun now that I have Tilly to participate in it with," he added, looking over to the still pale, trembling girl.

"My sentiments exactly," Cate replied, before ducking out into the living area.

CHAPTER FORTY-TWO

"Whoa, your mother really is something else," Tilly managed to say, slowly calming down once Cate had left them alone again in the kitchen. She grabbed the other whisky and took a large gulp, eager to steady her nerves. Blake padded over towards her with a contented smile, immediately gathering Tilly up in his arms for a passionate kiss when he reached her. He then lifted her up onto the kitchen counter and wrapped her legs around his waist, pulling Tilly closer.

"Yeah," he said, laughing gruffly when he pulled back from their deep kiss. "She's kind of intense when she wants to be, but did you even realise what she meant by all of that?" he asked, having read her confused thoughts and he knew Tilly had had no idea what his mother had just done to her. She shook her head, one eyebrow raised as she gazed into his gorgeous eyes.

"She gave you permission to say my name, Tilly," he informed his lover, a huge smile on his lips and she couldn't help but grin back.

"Oh, of course, and that's a good thing, right?" she asked, wanting to double check with him.

"Yes, it's a very good thing," he told Tilly, cupping her face, and leaning forward to give her another deep, passionate kiss.

"Yuk, save it for later, will you?" called another new voice from the doorway, but Blake did not let Tilly go straight away this time, instead he finished his kiss before stepping back and looking over his shoulder to smile at the other new arrival.

"Hi Dylan," he said, walking over to greet the witch he had told Tilly about and he embraced her tightly. Tilly could sense their closeness and greeted the powerful woman with a warm smile too as she hopped down off the countertop.

"Tilly, this is Dylan, my mother's right-hand witch, protector and best friend," he told her, a happy grin on his relaxed face. Dylan laughed at his formal introduction but smiled over at Tilly as she approached, patting Blake on the shoulder affectionately. The two women shook hands carefully around Tilly's casts and chatted for a few minutes about the dark boy they both loved so very much. Dylan was everything Blake had told Tilly she would be. She was warm, funny, and kind, while always maintaining an unwavering loyalty and protectiveness towards her infernal family.

"The party is going to start at nine o'clock tonight Blake, but you don't need to do anything because the witches are all here to ensure everything is done properly, we don't trust anyone else to do it right," she informed Tilly teasingly and Blake just rolled his eyes at her with a knowing smile. Tilly got the impression that Dylan had become like a sister to him over the years rather than a wise elder to be respected; she seemed far too playful and fun-natured for all of that.

"You could do me a favour, though, and get the guest list together. She wants upper-level demons and their choice of partner, plus any new blood you might want to invite along too. Set me up as well, yeah? One of each, at least," she told him with a wink before she left. Tilly assumed Dylan must have meant that she wanted both a guy and a girl to have her fun with, and Blake nodded to her with a sly smile.

"Welcome to the family," he told her, laughing as he took Tilly's hand and led her from the kitchen into the living area of the penthouse. They were greeted by smiles and waves from the witches who had all teleported in with Cate and who were now busy clearing the furniture from the large main room of the penthouse and setting up some sort of gigantic bed in the centre. It consisted of huge black satin cushions that were spread out across a few square metres of the floor and it had a thin, floating mesh curtain all around it. Tilly couldn't help but wonder just how many people would be sharing it later during the so called, 'orgy'. The very thought of it both scared and tantalised her.

"Don't worry, it's gonna be fun," Blake told her with a smirk, wrapping his arm around her back protectively and eying her as she took it all in. He then led her over to a corner where a scruffy looking man was messing around with the entertainment system.

"Hey Berith," he said, greeting the man, who then rose and bowed to Blake in respect. Tilly could tell right away that he was a demon and smiled at him, sensing his strong bond with Blake.

"Hello there, my Dark Prince," he said warmly, embracing him and then smiling down at Tilly. "And this must be the infamous Matilda?"

"Tilly's fine, thanks. You're not my mother," she told him playfully and with a huge grin, making them both laugh.

"I like this girl," Berith replied with a wide smile, reaching out his hand to Tilly and she shook it carefully but was then pulled in for a tight hug too.

"Me too," Blake agreed, grinning happily.

"Well then Tilly, I'm very pleased to meet you, my name is Berith," the demon told her as he released her again, negating her need to ask him for his name.

"Hey there guys," called another voice from behind Blake as another man walked toward the three of them in the corner. He was a handsome guy, who looked like he was in his late twenties with brown, slightly curly hair and deep blue eyes. He smiled widely, exuding affection and warmth towards them all as he neared. Tilly could tell that he was a demon, too. She saw Blake's eyes light up when he greeted him, and he immediately hugged the man tightly. Tilly started to bow as she took in the sight before her, realising that the demon must be Blake's stepfather and Cate's husband, Harry.

"There's no need for that Tilly," Harry said as he realised what she was doing, reaching out and hugging her after pulling away from his stepson's arms. "I'm just a demon. The name's Harry," he told her with a smile, also saving her the necessity of having to ask for it formally.

"But I thought you," she started to say, but Blake interrupted her.

"Harry is my step-father, yes, but unfortunately he is not worthy of our royal status thanks to his human heritage and the fact that Berith here sired him, in a demonic way obviously," he said, ushering to the two demons who stood shoulder to shoulder, nudging each other like schoolboys and laughing as though they were close friends. "Well, that and the fact that he is as common as muck," Blake then added jokingly, but he had still made his point clearly enough. Despite him being married to the Queen, Harry was still just classed as a level one demon, just as Lilith and the others were. He was part of her council and was afforded many benefits by the Queen and her children for his high demonic status, but he still served her just as any other demon was expected to do so, especially in public where he would always be seen to bow before her and address his wife formally along with his fellow demons.

"Yeah, yeah," Harry retorted, smiling at Blake with genuine affection and warmth, not having to worry about the formalities while in private, without the hordes of other demons around watching their every move. "Hey, aren't you meant to be organising the guests?" he reminded Blake, who jumped and nodded, grateful for Harry's prompt. He immediately summoned Selena to his side, who appeared and bowed, swooning up at her master once she fell under his gaze with a look that made Tilly's gut flare with jealousy.

"Come," he said, ushering the two women away to let the others get on with the arrangements in the living area. Tilly smiled and said a quick goodbye to the two demons before following Blake's lead, glad to have met some more of Blake's family at last and she was pleased that they seemed to like her.

Cate watched them from out on the terrace where she had been giving orders to one of the other dark witches, Sara, who took notes and nodded quickly to her mistress as she spoke. The powerful Queen gave the pair of them a smile and a nod as they left the main living room, her warm look making Tilly's butterflies return to her stomach just a little.

CHAPTER FORTY-THREE

Tilly followed Blake and Selena into the study, where he quickly began giving his high priestess her orders along with a list of demons for her to invite to the party. Tilly watched them for a few moments while leaning on the doorframe thoughtfully, enjoying seeing her master in his official role and glimpsing for the first time this business-like way he had about him when it came to the duties that he had told her about earlier that same day. She checked her watch. It was only six o'clock, so she wasn't going to panic about getting ready just yet, but she started to wonder about the guests, thinking if there was anyone else that she could bring into their dark life. Gwen and Renee seemed quite happy now that they were fully initiated and committed to Beelzebub, and she was sure that new followers were always appreciated in the dark followings. Just then, her new friend Jessica's face popped into her mind. Tilly felt guilty that she hadn't rang her back since that quick phone call when she had gotten home from the hospital, and she had been quite hermit-like the last couple of weeks so thought she really should make the effort to catch up with her friend now that she was feeling better. Tilly was also thinking of her because she had always thought Jessica seemed like quite a lonely girl, and she wondered if maybe she would do well in this dark yet close and protective circle of beings, too.

"Good idea Tilly, go and get dressed into something a little less casual and I'll teleport you there before I too go and deliver my personal invitations to my Earth-based family. Give me five minutes to finish up here," Blake called to Tilly from across the large wooden table, breaking her train of thought, and she smiled back at him.

"Yes master," she replied automatically as she began backing out of the study.

"Blake," he corrected her with a smile, and Selena glared over at Tilly, seemingly shocked to discover he was allowing his human to call him by his name, a name that she was still forbidden to say despite all her years of service in his coven.

"Yes, Blake," she said, smiling over at him and then she plodded over to their bedroom, quickly changing into some black skinny jeans and a figure-hugging vest, opting for easy choices thanks to her casts. She also applied a bit of makeup and pinned her dark-blonde hair up in a high ponytail, making a little extra effort regardless of her impaired dexterity as she couldn't help but feel so plain amongst all these beautiful god-like creatures, demons and witches that were now in her home.

A few minutes later, Tilly was teleported across the city to Jessica's doorstep in Blake's arms.

"Just let me know when you are done," he said, tapping her temple to remind her to just think of him. "But don't forget you haven't got too long," he added, and she nodded and kissed him goodbye before knocking on the heavy metal door. Jessica answered and squealed in excitement when she saw Tilly standing there. She threw her arms around her and ushered her inside, chatting animatedly to her with updates from the restaurant and telling her how everyone there was thinking about her, disgusted, and appalled at what Trey had done. Tilly followed her in quietly, taking in Jessica's flat as she did. It was small but cosy, and it reminded her of her own small nook on the farm. Jessica was wearing pyjamas, which made Tilly wonder if her friend had even set foot out of her home yet today, but it wasn't any of her business, so she followed her into the living room, smiling to herself as Jessica pulled back her greasy hair and checked her unwashed face in the mirror for blemishes. She was a pretty girl, always smiling, but Tilly knew she wasn't happy with the lack of social life she had since moving to the city. Despite her seemingly never-ending chatting, Jessica seemed as though she was a very lonely girl. Tilly could always feel it in the air somehow.

"Where the hell have you been?" she finally demanded, looking Tilly over thoughtfully, but she didn't give her the chance to speak. "Well, I suppose you look like you're okay, apart from the casts. Is it true that you broke both of your thumbs to get out of the handcuffs? Hard-core or what!" she cried, still not actually letting Tilly get a word into the conversation. When she finally quietened down, it took Jessica a few deep breaths to stop panting, her chatting seeming to have been put before her need to breathe. Tilly smiled warmly at her friend, though, grateful for the affection she sensed behind her chatty ranting.

"I'm much better, thanks, and yes, apparently I did break them, but thankfully I have no memory of it. Can we please change the subject now?" she replied, making Jessica jump as she realised it might just all be too raw for Tilly to talk about and she nodded eagerly, her eyes gazing back at her apologetically.

"Are you up to anything tonight Jess?" Tilly then asked her friend and Jessica shook her head no. The two of them took a seat on the small couch, and Tilly looked down at her hands thoughtfully. "Well," she said, an awkward smile on her lips. "I was wondering if you wanted to come to a kind of party at my flat? It is the full moon after all so it's time to get your goth on," she told her with a cheeky smile, joking with her friend but knowing that she had to get onto the subject somehow so she used their old conversation in the restaurant to ease them towards her explanation as quickly as she could. Tilly still had no idea where to start to tell her about the secret life she had been living. This was the first time she had needed to do this so she struggled with how best to broach the matter.

"Sure, count me in, but you know I was kidding about the witchy stuff. Yeah, unless are you really a witch?" she asked, her eyes widening as she took in Tilly's serious expression.

"No, I'm not a witch, but I am a Satanist, Jess. Do you know what that means?" she asked, not wanting to scare her but needing to get to the point. Jessica shook her head, visibly pulling back from Tilly as she stared into her blue eyes.

"Well, anyone can be one, like any religion, but I am actually involved in it, properly, as in forever. My boyfriend is very high up the chain of command, and we were wondering if you wanted to come and check it out, to see if it's for you."

"Your boyfriend? As in the guy you always talk about but won't even say his name, and I have never even met? I actually assumed he didn't really exist in all honesty Tilly, so he is real?" she asked, ranting again because she was confused as to Tilly's agenda. She even seemed a little standoffish, but Tilly just hoped it was the shock, so she smiled and shrugged, unsure what to say but opening her mouth to respond, anyway.

"Yes, of course I am," Blake said, appearing in Jessica's living room suddenly. She jumped, almost out of her seat at the sight of the magnificent man before her and stared at her open mouthed as Tilly stood and wrapped her arms around his waist and he planted a gentle kiss on the top of her head affectionately.

"Whoa," Jessica said, and Tilly just smiled and shrugged.

"So, are you up for trying something completely different then?" she asked, and Jessica nodded. Tilly could sense that Blake needed to head back, and she took Jessica's hand, gripping her tightly as he teleported the three of them back to the penthouse's main bedroom.

When they arrived, he took Tilly to the side, asking her to get Jessica cleaned up, into some black clothes and for Tilly to bring her up to speed on as much as possible, especially his family and their expectations of her in their presence. She nodded and gave him a quick kiss before he headed back off to the living area, his business-like head back on again.

Tilly then proceeded to tell Jessica everything she could in the short time that they had while they helped each other get ready, applying their makeup and Jessica helped tie her hair up into a bun. Tilly's explanation was not far from the one Brent had given her on Halloween, and just like he had done with her, she left the finer details for another day, but Jessica seemed happy and surprisingly relaxed when she followed Tilly down the hall and into the busy living area later that evening. She had borrowed a short black dress and high heels for the night, and Blake had told them to both wear some sexy black underwear, ready to show off when the orgy began. Both girls were nervous but excited, and Jessica scanned the room with anticipation as she took it all in with a happy smile.

CHAPTER FORTY-FOUR

Tilly locked eyes with Blake as soon as she was inside the large living room and he smiled over at her, taking in the stunning, tight black dress and high heels she was wearing, along with her dark makeup, bright red lipstick, and delicately wound bun. He nodded his head in the direction of Berith, giving Tilly her silent order to deliver Jessica to the demon and she immediately followed her master's unspoken instruction, taking her friend over to Berith's side to introduce her to him. He was due to move up to Earth again for a little while so was looking for new followers, and seemed quite taken with her naïve, innocent friend, so Tilly didn't mind leaving them alone together after a few minutes. The two of them seemed quite happy in one another's company and when Jessica gave her a wide smile, Tilly knew it was safe to leave them to it. She instantly felt a strong pull from somewhere deep inside herself, urging her through the crowd gently at first and then more forcefully after a couple of seconds. Tilly knew it was Blake summoning her to his side. The feeling was unmistakable, and she quickly made her way through the crowd, not even needing to check where he was in the room.

She took Blake's side in less than a minute as he chatted with Harry and Beelzebub, cuddling into him as he gave her a sly grin and kissed her in greeting. She felt as though she was both welcome and wanted at his side now, and it made her so happy to be a part of this strange group. The others smiled and greeted her, Harry beaming at the two of them with an almost paternal warmth as he watched them interact so effortlessly. The four of them chatted for a few minutes before being joined by Gwen too, who immediately took Beelzebub's side and smiled over to Tilly, looking relieved and sensing her calm happiness again at last.

"So, are you guys all ready for tonight?" Harry asked the two couples with a cheeky grin, knowing Tilly and Gwen were both very new to all of this. Blake and Beelzebub exchanged knowing looks and laughed, but the two girls grinned up at Harry shyly.

"Absolutely," Tilly answered, feeling brave and excited despite her inexperience with their open-minded parties. "I just hope Blake can keep up with me," she joked, making Harry laugh loudly, almost coughing on his beer as he shook his head and peered at her as though genuinely intrigued by this girl. He had a soft twinkle in his gorgeous blue eyes; a benevolent spark, and Tilly could see why everyone seemed to adore him so much. Despite being a demon, she knew he was once just a human too, a human that had also fought hard to win the heart of the dark woman he loved so very much, and she couldn't help but hope that someday she would be where he was now; immortal and powerful, and with the hand of his soul mate firmly in his for all eternity.

Dylan came over after a few minutes and chatted animatedly with the group as they all interacted with each other effortlessly, even Gwen seemed right at home with them all now and joined in the happy, relaxed conversation with a new-found confidence that Tilly thought could only have come from the having the love of the demon beside her. Blake still held her close, his strong hands caressing her shoulders gently and she could feel his whole body shake as he laughed along with Dylan as she joked and shared her silly stories. He had an easy, carefree nature to him that Tilly enjoyed being privy to as he chatted along with the group and the banter flowed between them all so naturally. The room soon started to fill even more, eager guests arriving for the event of the decade, and it quickly became apparent to Tilly that Cate really did not visit Earth very often, so her being here now was already cause for celebration, let alone the added excitement of the promised orgy that would soon commence.

Music started playing after a few minutes, thanks to Berith's earlier expertly set up mixture of small but powerful speakers which echoed the sound around the room wonderfully as the guests chatted happily and some even begun to dance as the melodic rock music enveloped the crowd. The conversations continued all around them, but Blake soon led Tilly away without a word to the others, following Harry towards the centre of the room, both clearly having been given a silent order from their Queen. All the other attendees around them peered at the two powerful men longingly as they moved, watching them as though mesmerised when the three of them passed by, no one seeming to even notice Tilly. She watched them with intrigue, the other women in the crowd, whether demonic or human, seemed besotted with Harry as much as with Blake and she wondered if perhaps that in knowing he had the Queen's heart it made him the ultimate, unattainable man, and therefore highly desirable to them, a beautiful prize and perhaps a forbidden desire.

Blake stopped in the centre of the crowd for a moment and pulled Tilly around so that she was in front of him, where he then cradled her in his strong arms just as he had in that first dream, with one arm across her stomach and the other on her neck as he leaned down and kissed her collarbone softly. They were lost in their moment for just a few seconds before his mother's silent order quietened the crowd and she stepped into the room from the open terrace doors. He then stopped his kisses and took her hand again, urging Tilly forwards through the group which parted for them and Harry, the three of them stopping only once they had reached Cate's side.

"Welcome," the Queen then called to the partygoers, and apart from Blake, every single one of them fell to their knees before her, including Tilly and Harry. She soon released them from their respectful bows and grinned around at her gathering with a beautiful and ominous gaze, taking in each and every thought from her devoted attendees. Her powerful prowess surrounded each of them somehow and Tilly could feel herself staring up at Cate adoringly, unable to control herself, but she didn't care. She wanted to please her mistress in whatever way she commanded.

"We will be starting in just a few minutes, so everyone, if you would like to begin undressing and then we can get ready to have some fun," she told them with a wicked grin, her beautiful green eyes ablaze. Every one of the adoring faces smiled back at her, sensing the sexual tension and promise of dark pleasures hanging in the air all around them. And none of them could wait. Tilly looked up at Blake, who was smiling down at her thanks to having already been listening in on her desire driven thoughts. He licked his lips anticipatively and then leaned closer to whisper into her ear.

"The royals take the lead Tilly, meaning that my mother and Harry start off the proceedings, followed by us and then the level one demons can bring in their partners, and so on," he informed her, reaching behind his lover to unzip her tight dress. She couldn't help but gasp at his words and looked over her shoulder into his deep green eyes nervously.

"So they *watch* us?" she asked, feeling slightly uncomfortable at the prospect of being the centre of attention.

"Yes, but it's not in a dodgy way and you won't even notice them Tilly, I promise to keep you well and truly distracted," he assured her with a quiet laugh as he tugged her dress down her arms and to the floor. She absentmindedly stepped out of it and then reached down to pick it up and place the dress on the back of the armchair beside her, too thoughtful to even care if anyone was looking at her half naked body just yet. Tilly then reached up and slowly unbuttoned Blake's shirt for him, taking some time thanks to her cast, but carefully sliding her fingers over the small plastic as she whispered back to him.

"Do other people join us as in, join in?" she questioned and was glad when he shook his head firmly.

"No, absolutely not," he replied sternly. "Not unless we invite them to, which, of course, we will not. In all honesty, most demons are not faithful to one lover, but those that are monogamous still participate and do not invite others to share their personal space with their partner. My mother and Harry will be cloaked and will not be touched by anyone else at all thanks to their sacred union, and our bond will be recognised and respected too. It is one of the strictest rules for the orgy," he told her, pulling off his black chinos and placing them on the chair along with their other discarded clothing before cupping her face in his hands and planting a soft kiss on her lips. As he pulled back Tilly took a moment to appreciate his half naked body for a moment, this sexy as hell, dark god-like being that stood before her and she smiled up at him, ready and willing for whatever was to follow.

"I'll follow you forever," she whispered, her voice a soft hum mimicking their song while their lips remained just inches apart and he still cupped her cheeks affectionately, staring into her hooded eyes lovingly.

"Just say yes," he whispered back, his lip curling as he planted another soft kiss on her lips. Tilly could then feel the air suddenly begin to shift around them even more, darkening, enticing, and seducing her somehow. Blake smiled as he pulled back to watch her, sensing it as she began openly embracing the dark power all around her, succumbing to its pull, belonging to it, to him.

This was all part of their fun; the lure, the seduction and he couldn't wait for the feelings he would soon sense in her when she begged for his body against hers and would finally surrender to him under the eyes of his Queen.

CHAPTER FORTY-FIVE

Cate and Harry climbed into the makeshift bed as Dylan lifted the veil that had surrounded the huge, black, padded floor area. They reached the top edge, which was slightly higher than the rest of the bed and kneeled before one another as they began kissing passionately. The crowd then watched on in enthralled silence as a second thin black veil fell around the pair of them, encircling them and giving the omniscient couple a tiny bit of privacy in the otherwise very open area of the huge bed. Cate slid off her underwear and then laid back as Harry leaned over her and nestled himself between his wife's thighs eagerly, their years of love and lust combining to provide them all with a wonderful glimpse into their powerful union, the proverbial forbidden fruit barely hidden so enticingly before the crowd. Tilly couldn't help but stare up at them, mesmerised and feeling hot and horny as she did so. She could also feel herself opening up to the naughty, sexy thrum in the air around them as their Queen commanded all eyes on her, along with their thoughts and their desires. She felt dirty, but she didn't care, it was as though she was being seduced by the sight before them, rather than her feeling embarrassed to be watching such an intimate moment and she thrummed inside with a dark desire while eagerly awaiting her chance to join in.

Blake moved forward after a few minutes, breaking Tilly's reverie as he grasped her arm at the elbow and pulled her into the large bed with him. They shuffled upwards on their knees, moving to their spot just below the Queen, where he gripped Tilly tightly and kissed her deeply before removing his boxers without even a hint of insecurity at showing off his magnificent body. She heard the mumbled words of appreciation for his gorgeously toned muscles and huge erection from the women in the crowd behind her, but she didn't care about them; he was all hers and she wanted him, needed him. Tilly realised at last what Blake had meant by her not caring about the others around them, she quickly zoned out the sounds of the crowd and the feeling of being watched, all her focus on Blake and no-one or nothing else.

He laid down on the soft floor, pulling her over to him with a smile while leaning up on his elbows and nodding as Tilly leaned down and took his thick tip into her mouth. She let herself go, sucking hard on his stiff length for a few minutes before he suddenly sat up and grabbed her forcefully, pulling Tilly onto his lap in less than a second thanks to his unadulterated want and powerful strength. He cupped her face in his hands and stared deep into her blue eyes with a wry smile before reaching his hands down and grabbing her hips as she straddled him, kissing his lover fervently before ripping off her black lace panties with ease and then sliding inside her wet, ready cleft. Tilly's deep muscles gripped him tightly, and she gasped, as did a few members of the turned on crowd, and then she moved her hips back and forth on top of her master, relishing in his touch and the still thick air around them as Cate and Harry did the same above them.

The upper-level demons and their lovers then joined in, eagerly taking their dark masters' lead, and there were soon bodies moving all around them. Tilly heard many cries of pleasure and need as they all throbbed together, a collective throng of pleasure and power that reverberated through each and every participant in this darkly erotic experience. She could hear other women around her crying out in pleasure as they came, along with other men as they groaned their releases and basked in the aftershocks that followed, but her attention remained fully on Blake. Tilly had no need to care or even consider who might be close by on the huge bed, or whether they were watching them as she and the man she loved with all her heart made love so intensely.

A couple of hours later following a second shared orgasm of the evening for the hot, young couple, Tilly knelt before Blake on the bed, her body pressed into his as he kissed her deeply, neither one ready to start again but also not ready to call it a night just yet. As they kissed, Tilly suddenly felt a pair of powerful hands caress her shoulders from behind and immediately stiffened in shock. Blake had assured her that no one would try to join them on the bed, but when she looked up into his face, she quickly realised that this not an unwelcome presence, his shy smile putting Tilly immediately at ease as she gazed into his gorgeous green eyes. The strong and commanding hands then moved to her chin, gently pulling her head around to face their owner, which, of course, was the Queen. She knelt beside Tilly and Blake, completely naked except for the beautiful locket that still fell sexily between her cleavage, and her body seemed to be reverberating with a combination of her immense power and a calm throb, as well as a glow that could only be the aftermath of the very recent orgasm they had all felt tremble the ground beneath them.

Cate pulled Tilly's face closer to hers, and she leaned towards the beautiful Queen while Blake held her tightly, keeping himself pressed into her torso while his hands gripped her hips, giving his weak lover some much needed support. Without a word, the powerful Queen then kissed Tilly's red, tender lips with a soft and intoxicating touch that sent an array of spine-tingling, sensuous shockwaves throughout her entire body and she felt like she might faint. Cate held her there for a few more seconds, though; her powerful mouth on Tilly's for just a little bit longer before pulling away. She climbed back up and ducked under the veil to join her husband, who stared up at her adoringly as she climbed onto his lap and began riding his ready cock again.

Tilly couldn't help but watch them, confused, and mesmerised for a moment, until Blake's mouth on her neck made her turn her attention away from the royal couple and back to her master. He kissed her lips too and then lifted one of her thighs up around his waist before he then thrust himself inside her again, laying Tilly down on the satin padding while pulling her hips up to meet his. She came quickly, a long and intense release that sent her body into overdrive and her happy heart beating faster in her chest. She felt the tell-tale shuddering begin as he climaxed again too and gripped the sheets beneath them with her few exposed fingers as the powerful waves claimed them both. He pulled out, trailing kisses down her breasts and stomach as she lay before him, taking her swollen nub in his mouth to deliver her one more burst before he pulled her into his arms and kissed Tilly deeply, waiting for her to be ready for him again, knowing she could still take a lot more pleasure from him yet.

CHAPTER FORTY-SIX

A few hours later, just a few lovers remained on the large bed-like area of the living room. Cate and Harry were still passionately enjoying one another's company, along with the attention they were getting from atop their padded throne, while Blake and Tilly revelled together in their final shared orgasm. Dylan was relishing in a threesome with two male demons below them, her playful smile still firmly in place as she commanded her own little following. The crowd around them were tired, lusciously exhausted and had been ducking in and out of the shrouded area between getting drinks and replenishing their energy or swapping partners. Tilly had never been able to carry on for so long with Blake before, her body responding to his touch so readily tonight somehow and she had loved every second of it. She hadn't felt tired, thirsty, or hungry the entire time, but was now starting to weaken thanks to their wonderfully exhausting and intense night.

"Ready to call it a night?" he asked her, rising from their embrace and pulling Tilly to her feet. He nodded to his mother, who smiled down at her son, watching them while Harry kissed her neck and embraced her from behind, his hands exploring her body lovingly.

Tilly weakly followed Blake's lead, glad of the strong hand on her back as they made their way to the bar and slipped on two fresh black robes that had been handed to them by a very sour-faced Selena. Blake ignored the witch completely and handed Tilly a bottle of water, smiling as she hungrily drank it all down. Her hands soon felt itchy in the casts, and she grabbed a straw from the bar and slipped it under the tight plaster to scratch at them, wondering if perhaps she must be sweating under there or something as they didn't normally feel this way.

"Let's get rid of these now, shall we?" Blake then asked her with a knowing smile, leading Tilly to the kitchen and grabbing a pair of strong scissors from the utensil holder on the countertop. She went to tell him no, that they had to stay on until she had healed, but he insisted and clipped away at the right wrist's protective casing. The cast broke open, and she wriggled her hand free of the bandage, suddenly realising that there was no pain there now, not any resistance at all from her somehow healed thumb. She looked up at Blake, who grinned and took her other hand, proceeding to cut off the cast and gave her other thumb a wiggle too. He then turned her hand over, exposing her forearm as he did so and revealing to them both that the burned inverted cross he had so foolishly given her was gone too. Her skin healed, unscarred and soft once again. She stared at it for a moment, completely taken aback by the perfect skin.

"It seems my mother's kiss really does heal all," Blake whispered thoughtfully, running his hand over her forearm as he leaned down to kiss her. Tilly stood on her tiptoes to reach him, quickly throwing her arms around his shoulders, and deepening their kiss before pulling away.

"I was wondering what that was all about," she told him a few moments later as she washed the plaster residue from her hands in the kitchen sink. "I thought she was trying to flirt with me for a minute. I guessed she didn't know I'm not into girls," she joked.

"You never know," he replied with a wink, but then laughed, letting Tilly know he wasn't being sincere. "In all seriousness, though, she does not do that for just anyone. Only those that are truly worthy of her powerful gifts are blessed this way. You have received a very rare favour from her Tilly, twice actually," he added, referring to their moment in the kitchen earlier when she had released her from the ban on saying his name, a sign that she had actually been deemed more worthy than any other human Blake had ever known before. Tilly nodded in understanding and gratitude. There was no doubt that she was feeling darkly blessed by the Queen right now, and by her master who had also shared a rare favour with her too in opening up the way he had.

"I don't doubt it, and I will not forget her belief in me, Blake. I am, however, quite sure that this all has much more to do with the changes in you than it has to do with me," she said, reaching up to touch his face gently once she had dried her remarkably healed hands.

"So intuitive, aren't you?" he asked, peering down at her as he kissed each of her thumbs. "You are probably right though, my love," he admitted, smiling as he leaned in for another kiss.

"Hey, I just thought," she said as they pulled back. "Why didn't you just heal me yourself, Blake, like when you gave me your blood before?" she asked, suddenly wondering why he had not helped her again.

"Because I was not completely honest with you, Tilly. Yes, I healed you, but I also found myself asserting my control over you. I couldn't resist and found myself automatically following the same path of many that came before me, including my father. I just couldn't help it; I swayed your choices and put myself in your favour. I realised afterwards just how foolish I was to do it, how I would never be sure of your affection and loyalty while I controlled you and I vowed never to give you my blood again, at least until you and I can share it equally," Blake said, reminding her of the blood-sharing she had witnessed between Lilith and Lucas. Tilly thought back to Brent's explanation of the sharing of power rather than the demon taking control of their lover, understanding the concept now.

"How do you think my father got his way with so many women throughout the years? They would all magically forget it all though thanks to his power over them," he added.

Tilly smiled up at Blake, understanding his hesitation at giving her his blood and she was glad he had decided against asserting his control over her too much, it would have been so easy for him, but he chose not to, and she loved him even more for it. There was still so much she had to learn about her dangerous Black Prince, but Tilly knew for sure now that she would endeavour to carry on learning these lessons forever. Blake read her thoughts and stroked her now unmarked flesh with his index finger absentmindedly, looking down into Tilly's blue eyes with an almost shy expression.

"A clean slate," she said, relieving his guilt, and he smiled, leaning down to give her one more kiss before they headed back out to join the party in the living room.

CHAPTER FORTY-SEVEN

The next morning, after everyone had finished their frolicking and had had their fill of drink and sex, the partygoers dispersed, the demons heading home with their lovers and followers in tow while the dark witches took care of the cleaning up.

Blake and Tilly relaxed on the sofa together, her tired body still buzzing thanks to the wonderful and eye-opening night before. Even after a few hours' sleep in the master bedroom, she couldn't help but smile to herself about their amazing and sensuous evening the day before. Both had gotten changed back into some comfortable clothes, Tilly was wearing one of Blake's black jumpers and a pair of leggings while her lover wore black tracksuit trousers, and a t-shirt, and she lay wrapped in his arms as the witches bustled around them. They had both had such an amazing evening, and she curled up lazily on his lap, their hands interlocked with one another's as they chatted with their friends some more before he and his mother would have to head off home with the waning moon.

Harry had been sat with them while his wife was busy, but he was used to that, so he, Berith and Dylan had joined the smitten young couple to relax with them and enjoy the calm afterglow of the incredible night. None of them could deny that they were all quite taken with Tilly now too, and chatted along with her happily, already sensing that she was swiftly becoming a permanent part of their dark family. When Cate was finally able to join the relaxed and cheerful group, she plonked down in one of the armchairs and took in the sight before her with a contented smile. Her family were all so precious to her, they meant everything to the Dark Queen and having Tilly around was doing wonders for her son, even if it had taken him a bit of encouragement and a lot of patience to get him here. She had enjoyed watching them together last night and could hear Tilly's happy thoughts running through her mind now as she snuggled in her lover's arms. Blake caught Cate watching him and rewarded his mother with a big, bright smile, which were once so few and far between but had become a regular occurrence now that this girl was in his life. They had had their struggles, but they seemed to have made it through everything relatively unscathed, with a little push here and there from her, of course, but she was more than happy to help if it made him thrive and be happy at long last.

Cate had been busy that morning, having spent a long time saying goodbye to their guests, and she had also decided to keep Lilith and her husband back for a moment. Having read both Tilly's fond memories of him and Blake's excellent report on his capabilities in the demonic trials, Cate had decided to give Lucas his much-desired prize, his true and eternal demonic power. He was a more worthy human than she had seen in a long time and had been kind and warm to Tilly when she had needed it, which had proven to the Queen that there was a place for him in her now far more balanced underworld.

She and her family still firmly believed in the idea of a balance for their powers and had done so for many years following the events that had brought her to the throne. Her commandments had always come from a much more steadfast mind-set ever since the ultimate dark power had chosen to bless her rather than Lucifer all those years ago, and Cate remained loyal and firm to her beliefs in that balance as well as upholding their darker ways of life.

The Dark Queen had watched Lilith and Lucas last night at the orgy with interest. They were passionate and very much in love, and Cate knew that they regularly shared one another's blood. She also knew that it was not for Lilith's control over him but a sign of them as equals, which surprised her, as Lilith had never had a bond with another being as strong as she had with her human lover, not even with Lucifer.

Despite her loyalty to Cate now, she knew Lilith had struggled more than any other demon with her master's demise. Her fierce loyalty to him had been hard to break through and so Lilith had been sent to live on Earth because, at the time, Cate had not been sure she could be trusted. But Lilith had found her way and had found a love stronger than any she had felt before in all her years of existence, a love that reminded Cate of her beginnings with Harry and she admired the usually so ruthless demon for letting down her own walls and opening her heart to him.

And so, she had called the couple aside and gave them the news before they left the party. Lilith had bowed her head and thanked the Queen profusely for her promised gift while Lucas fell to her feet and uttered a silent prayer to her and a, "Hail Satan."

"We will perform the ceremony on All Hallow's Eve," she had then told them, so that they could make the necessary preparations for the ritual, and the pair then thanked her again and left, huge smiles on both of their faces.

Alma came over and deposited a tray piled with mugs, tea bags, milk, and sugar on the coffee table before them along with a hot water urn and then a thick glass jug full to the brim with steaming hot and delicious smelling coffee. Harry poured Cate's tea first, of course, and passed her a hot, milky cup along with a handful of biscuits. Tilly couldn't help but watch as the Queen, ever so human-like, dunked her biscuits in the tea and devoured each of them with a satisfied smile. She seemed so normal to Tilly at times, like an everyday wife and mother when she had seen her fuss over Blake the night before and how she kissed her husband gently in thanks now, and she found herself growing more and more in awe of her almighty mistress. Cate caught her watching and gave Tilly a wink, making her look away, ashamed to have been caught, but when she looked up again, Cate was still looking at her, a warm smile on her lips that put Tilly at ease again instantly.

Tilly smiled back at the beautiful Queen and then leaned forward to pour Blake a mug of coffee. She handed it to him before making herself a sweet mug too and grabbed a biscuit off the plate in the centre of the coffee table and then sat back into Blake's warm arms, careful not to spill either of their drinks as she did so.

"I could do with some air," Cate said after finishing her drink, and then she stood from her chair and gave Harry a quick kiss before looking down at Tilly. "Would you care to join me?" she asked.

"Of course, your Majesty," Tilly answered, jumping up from Blake's lap and following Cate to the terrace. He gave her hand an encouraging squeeze as she rose, putting her at ease but she was still a little scared to be alone with Cate in case she accidentally said or thought the wrong thing in her presence, something that Tilly was aware she had a bad habit of doing all too often.

CHAPTER FORTY-EIGHT

Cate and Tilly stood together on the terrace in the late-morning sunshine. It was a warm and already clear day, and Cate closed her eyes and took in a deep breath of the fresh air. Tilly watched her, mesmerised by her dark beauty as the sunshine hit her skin, but she could tell it was not warming Cate like she wanted it to. It somehow didn't touch her like it did a human, as if it couldn't penetrate the dark air around her, and Tilly wondered if perhaps her powerful dark force wouldn't let it. She shook her thoughts away, desperate not to let her quizzical mind lead her into trouble and she caught the slight smile that curled at Cate's lip, the exact same way her lovers did when Blake was trying to hide a knowing smile from her.

"I do miss it up here sometimes. I have to admit that," Cate said, turning to look at Tilly. "It has been a very long time since I was last on Earth, and whenever I do come, I cannot just roam where I please. I must stay where it is safe. But that's a story for another time," she added, looking back towards the sunshine again.

Cate ushered for Tilly to take a seat with her at the patio table, a comfortable cushioned rattan set that Tilly had moved from one side of the terrace to the other so that it was now in the perfect spot in which to enjoy the view over London, and Cate agreed with her decision, it really was a wonderful view. They sat down next to each other and Tilly watched Cate for a few moments as she continued to gaze out across the city thoughtfully. The shadows fell on her face beautifully and Tilly couldn't help but feel such admiration for the stunning woman, but also so very small in comparison to her.

"What do you think of me, Tilly?" Cate asked, stunning her for a moment. She read her shock and couldn't help but laugh, smiling at Tilly, and then she shrugged apologetically. "Hmm, okay, how about I rephrase that? How do I compare to your own mother?" she then asked, letting Tilly see she was just as insecure as any mother, wanting to know that she had done the best by her children as seen through another's eyes. From what Blake had told her, Tilly knew that his upbringing had not gone the way any of them would have wanted, especially as he seemed to have ended up being worse off than any of them, thanks to his father's dictatorship. She couldn't help herself from thinking back to Blake's story from the day before, how he had become Lucifer's literal, and emotional, punching bag during those dark days, but she also knew that none of that was Cate's fault.

"You have my permission to speak freely here," Cate then added, reading her thoughts and reassuring Tilly to answer her honestly.

"Thank you. Well, that is quite hard for me to answer, your Majesty. My parents are nice, normal, boring people who have never thrown wild parties, lived for hundreds of years, and they most certainly have never been to an orgy," she told Cate with a grin. "I think any comparison of you two would be unfair, simply because of the very different lives you have led. But I will say that you are not at all what I thought you would be like," she added, looking over at the Queen, checking that she was not talking out of turn, but Cate seemed genuinely relaxed and ready to talk openly. "I understand I do not know the entire story of Blake's childhood, but it seems to me that you have had a pretty rough time of it. You have done your very best to love and protect your children every step of the way, though, putting them first and never knowingly let them come to harm despite your own hardships along the way. Blake talks of you with such love and pride, and despite the terrible lessons he was forced to learn I don't think he ever lost that affection for you, he just hid it all behind those high walls of his," Tilly said, talking slowly and carefully, desperate not to upset Cate.

"I never thought I would actually ever get to meet you, but if I did, I expected you to be a truly scary, powerful and unfeeling being, if I can be completely honest. I just assumed that the Devil would be that way, and I suppose that was just me stereotyping you rather than having any basis for that assumption. But then I met you and I learned for myself the way you make me feel, the way you make everyone feel in your presence. I feel loved and protected. It's like I can do anything, be anything. Until yesterday, I could not fathom a dark world without an evil dictator at the top, but now I see how it might just all be down to interpretation and a person's free will. Don't get me wrong, you still scare the shit out of me, but I also think that you might just be the strongest person I have ever met," she said, finishing her little speech and staring at her hands awkwardly.

Cate raised an eyebrow, taking in Tilly's kind and honest words with a smile.

"Thank you, Tilly, well done for being so brave. I admire that. You have no idea just how strong I have had to be over the years, and to stay strong that sometimes has had to include an evil deed or two, so don't give me too much credit on that one just yet," she said, a guilty smile crossing her lips before she continued. "I appreciate your kind words, though. You have an open mind and warm soul. I hope they are never quashed under the many burdens you already carry and the even darker world you must encompass as your life by my son's side goes on," Cate said, eying her seriously now.

"Thank you, your Majesty," Tilly said with a small bow, trembling as she took in Cate's omniscient words. "I have really enjoyed meeting you, and I don't think I can ever show you how much I appreciate the gifts you chose to give me during your visit," she added, looking at her hands again. Cate smiled and reached across, taking Tilly's once burned arm in her hand.

"The pleasure has been all mine," she said, stroking the freshly healed skin with her index finger thoughtfully. "I want the two of you to keep on moving forward rather than to be constantly reminded of the hard path you've had to take to get here. You are the only person he has ever let in, Tilly, and I want you to keep helping him to learn and to grow. I promise to keep a closer eye on Blake too, and will intervene if I ever see fit, but you will have to do me a favour first," Cate added, looking into Tilly's eyes seriously. "Wear my mark. Our bond will make you stronger and it will also act as a direct link to me should you ever need my help. You only narrowly escaped that disgusting boy and his perverted plans for you, and I do not ever want things to get so far out of our control again. There are many dangers you might have to face thanks to your chosen allegiance to us, Tilly. Many people and other beings are opposed to us and our way of life that you cannot even begin to understand. You cannot be naïve now, question everything and everyone, and don't trust anyone except Blake, his family or our demons," she told her, looking at Tilly with a serious stare, holding her gaze as she continued to hold her arm in her hands.

"So, are you ready to make a deal with the Devil?" she then asked, her beautiful green eyes bright in the morning sunshine and her red lips smiling wickedly at Tilly.

CHAPTER FORTY-NINE

"But I am already marked, your Majesty, would that mean I am no longer Blake's?" Tilly asked, not comfortable even contemplating saying no to the all-powerful Queen but also not wanting to lose her connection with Blake either.

Cate took in her frenzied thoughts and laughed, pleased that Tilly's loyalty to her son was so strong.

"No, of course you would still be his, my dear," she said, her smile broad as Tilly still looked uncomfortable under her powerful gaze. "I am, of course, no ordinary demon, nor am I just a god. In a way I *am* God, your ruler, Queen and mistress, Tilly, all the above. My mark would not come to you as an inverted cross on your forearm, but as a permanent blackening of your very soul itself."

"Whoa," Tilly replied, scared but intrigued by her fierce explanation and she was also excited at the prospect of being chosen by the Queen to wear her mark too, the mark she had only known her ministers to bear.

"These crosses," Cate continued, and Tilly watched as her familiar black cross rose to the surface inside her right forearm in response to Cate's summoning. "They are a sign of your dark possession, a mark of your ownership, if you will, and nothing more. The symbol itself is an ode to my reign, a powerful talisman and sign of your allegiance both to me and to whichever master gave you it."

"Oh, I'm so sorry," Tilly said, realising she may have inadvertently offended the Queen.

"You were not to know," Cate replied, putting her at ease slightly. "You have already completed the first step by performing the commitment ceremony, this would just be an extension of that, a binding of your soul to me and in return you would become stronger, more respected in our world and you will have a direct link to me. One silent prayer and I could answer your call at any time, in one way or another. There's just one more step we would have to take."

"Let me guess, sell you my soul, right?" Tilly asked, laughing even though there was nothing funny about that prospect. Cate nodded, taking in the girl before her, she really was very intuitive and Cate liked it, she could understand just why Blake had chosen to mark her after only knowing her for a few minutes, and she wanted that clever prowess to be at her full command too. Despite Cate's still kind nature, she had completely embraced the dark power inside of herself and lost her human side a long time ago. She was every bit as powerful, commanding, and formidable now as her ex-husband had once been, only she chose to use and show that power using very different methods and so ruled in her own way. However, she still could not help herself from admiring, desiring, and demanding every bit of strength and love from her loyal servants in return for the gifts she had bestowed on them, and the girl that sat before her now was no exception. Cate knew that Tilly just needed a push in the right direction, and then she would succumb to her request. They always did.

"Perhaps you might prefer a different approach, my dear," Cate said, staring into Tilly's blue eyes with a kind smile. "What do you want from your future with Blake? Will you grow old and live a human life as his follower, then die and come to Hell where you will have to suffer at the hands of the lower-level demons? Are you ready to then prove your worth and work your way up to be a demon and then finally, hopefully, make it to level one many years later?" she asked, and Tilly took her words in, honestly not having thought too much about it all before. "Or do you take this next step now, and then eventually complete your demon trials as a human before joining the demonic ranks and earning your place at Blake's side, just as Harry did with me?" Cate asked her, clearly intent on selling her the latter option.

"Either way, I get to choose Blake?" Tilly asked, making Cate smile again. She nodded.

"Of course, I would never deny my son a thing," she said, leaning closer to her before continuing. "Loving him was never going to be easy, Tilly, but you must choose now. Do you live your life as normal, or do you commit yourself to him entirely and follow the path I just told you about that will lead you to his side? Only then would you be free to love him for all eternity."

"Then, of course, I choose him, and I choose you, my Queen. What do I need to do?" Tilly asked, looking up into Cate's eyes. She had never been so sure of anything in her life as she was of her love for Blake, and she would do whatever it took to be with him.

"Just say yes," Cate told her with a smile.

"Yes," Tilly replied, taking a deep breath.

CHAPTER FIFTY

Cate smiled and lifted Tilly's hand up to her face. She inspected her inside forearm for a moment without a word and then slid her finger across the veins at Tilly's wrist, slitting open the skin in an instant. Tilly gasped but didn't pull back, stifling her squeamish gag as Cate pulled her bloody arm closer and started to drink from her.

Tilly could feel herself becoming woozy, unsure just how much blood she was required to give in offering to her Queen, but she remained calm, focussed, and determined. Her prize was firmly rooted in Tilly's mind's eye, Blake. She steadied her thoughts, imagining herself as a demon with a place at his side. Cate finished and pulled away after a few minutes, placing a quick kiss on the wound to close it instantly, a sinister smile on her lips. Blood dripped down the powerful Queen's chin and her eyes were black as she looked up into Tilly's wide ones.

"Do you renounce all others and pledge your soul to me, Tilly?" she asked, licking her lips with a satisfied grin.

"Yes," Tilly replied, and then Cate bought her own index finger to her lips and bit the tip, drawing a small drop of blood to the surface.

"Then drink of me," she told her, offering Tilly the bloody fingertip to drink from. She reached over and held onto her mistress's hand, pulling the finger closer and sucking the tiny drop of blood from Cate's already closed bite wound. She felt her wooziness subside instantly, strength and power resonating inside of her in its place. Tilly panted, looking up into her Queen's still dark eyes as she caught her breath and steadied herself.

"Whoa," she said, making Cate smile. Her eyes went back to being the deep green she was so used to staring into on the face of her master, yet Tilly saw the darkness within them now, the power and the control, but she did not care, she wasn't scared anymore and wouldn't ever fight it. Blake joined them on the terrace a few minutes later, watching the two of them with a serious expression and taking in the sight of his mother's chin as it dripped with Tilly's blood.

"Wow, I leave you two alone for five minutes," he said, producing a tissue from his pocket and handing it to her. He sat down opposite Cate at the table next to Tilly, looking between the two of them thoughtfully as his mother wiped at her mouth.

"You didn't think to run this by me first then, mother?" he asked her, but Cate just shrugged in response. Tilly looked from one of them to the other; they looked more like brother and sister than mother and son, Cate's young appearance playing tricks on her as she took them both in.

"It makes no difference, my darling," she told him. "Tilly would have come to me eventually, I just thought why not get it over with now. She will be stronger and more powerful in every way thanks to my many gifts, and it won't be long now until she can begin her trials. You should be thanking me," she added with a playful pout.

"Yes, of course. Thank you," he said, bowing playfully and then grinning at her cheekily over the table. "So, she has your permission to attempt it?" Blake asked, and Cate smiled broadly back at her son. She then revelled in his playful demeanour and happy nature for one more moment before she decided to give them a few minutes alone.

"Yes, of course. I'll leave you two to talk, but we must go soon, my love," Cate told them as she stood up from the patio set. "Farewell Tilly, I shall see you again soon," she added with a smile.

Tilly bowed to her with a smile in return. She couldn't help but still feel a little strange following their blood-sharing but was glad she had gone through with it. Tilly was already feeling stronger thanks to her Queen's tiny offering and began to think about her dark new life and how strangely at ease she was with all of it.

Blake then reached over and took her hand, breaking Tilly's reverie and he pulled her up out of her chair and over onto his lap. She straddled him and peered into his gorgeous green eyes, mesmerised in an instant. Blake reached up and brushed her dark-blonde hair behind her ears as he gazed back into her blue eyes and then kissed her deeply. The sun hit his face as Tilly pulled back and she noticed that the dark barrier she had sensed around Cate was not surrounding him, as though the small part of him that was still human allowed the sun's rays through and he basked in it just the same way as his mother had tried to do.

"You continue to surprise me Tilly," he then told her with a smile. "So strong and courageous. There will be no stopping you, will there?" Blake asked, catching her off guard slightly.

"Is that a bad thing, my love?" she asked him, looking down into his warm face.

"Not at all, it's just that most humans have to wait many years before they are given the opportunities you have already been blessed with. Take Lucas McCulloch, for example. He and Lilith have been together for twenty years and he has only just completed his trials. He was only allowed to pledge his soul to my mother ten years ago, having spent the ten before that proving himself worthy of her blessings," Blake told her.

"Whoa. Well, despite what your mother just said, I'm not in any rush, Blake. I don't think the trials are in my near future. If anything, the very thought of going through what Lucas has still scares the hell out of me, so I'm happy to wait," she said, being honest.

"I don't blame you, they are very tough challenges. Has anyone told you about the other two trials?" he asked, and Tilly shook her head.

"Well, the first one is relatively simple, but not easy, it is a sign to the Dark Queen that you are willing to undertake any cunning deed, to lure humans into doing your bidding and to prove that your conscience is ready to be ignored. You have to de-flower six virgins," he said, a wicked grin on his face as her mouth opened in shock.

"What? No, I couldn't do that. You would be furious for a start," she said, not understanding how that could even work.

"Exactly," he replied. "For if you simply fucked them yourself, you and I would be over and the poor boy would be dead before he even finished his first time, of course," Blake told her, his face dark. "The idea is to lure, to seduce, and to force the will of susceptible innocents, but not actually take care of the virginity problem yourself. There is always a way," he told her with a smirk.

"Ah, I see," Tilly said, still feeling highly uneasy even with his explanation, but then she jumped as the realisation dawned on her about her own first time, and the words Lilith had said to her afterwards. She looked down at Blake, hoping not to anger him with her memory, but he read her mind anyway, understanding why she had suddenly chosen to think of it.

"Yes, you were one of Lucas's de-flowered virgins Tilly. You helped him to complete his first trial without even knowing it," he told her, his eyes speckling with black spots at the very thought of her and Brent together.

CHAPTER FIFTY-ONE

"I'm sorry," Tilly said, cuddling Blake tighter, not wanting him to be angry with her.

"It's okay, I'm the one who raised the issue of the trials, so I have to be honest, even if it makes me crazy with jealousy," he said, kissing her gently, his eyes going back to their usual green.

"Yours and Brent's feelings for each other were real. Lucas just provided the much needed encouragement for the two of you to go ahead with it. He made you feel at home in their company and convinced Brent to take the next step when he had second thoughts because you seemed so sweet and pure," Blake told her, obviously uncomfortable talking about it with Tilly but still wanting to put her mind at rest. She nodded and smiled awkwardly at her lover.

"Gross, remind me to give Lucas a slap the next time I see him. Can we change the subject now?" she asked him, eager to get away from this subject, and Blake nodded, seeming just as keen to move on with his explanations.

"Yes, absolutely," he replied, the smile returning to his soft face. "Your second trial would be one of pure evil. It shows my mother just how much you would be willing to do to others to cross over into the demonic world. You would be required to kill six innocent people," Blake said, and Tilly's eyes widened in shock.

"Whoa," she answered him, feeling sick at the sheer thought of taking another person's life. She had technically killed Trey but felt like that didn't count because Blake had been the one that did it. Neither her consciousness nor conscience were involved that time.

"And not just that, you don't have any control over who you kill. A demonic adjudicator would make the decision for you, just like how I was given the choice of deciding how to torture Lucas on that final trial. If Lilith did it, she would have no doubt gone easy on her lover to help him succeed, and we can't have that," he told her, and Tilly absorbed the information, even more glad that she was in no rush to complete the trials herself.

"And what if I failed?" she asked him, her own eyes dark at the terrible prospect of her not being deemed worthy of a place at Blake's side.

"There are other choices. Luna's lover Ash became a warlock for her when he failed, which is fine for them, and they are happy with the choices they made. They get to be together forever as he is now blessed with immortality, but he is and always will be her servant Tilly, not her equal," Blake told her, and she knew that while it was an option, she did not want that.

"For now, I think I'll settle for just being your follower, lover and human," Tilly told him, kissing his soft lips. "We can figure the rest of this stuff out later."

Blake nodded, wrapping her in his arms for a deep embrace.

"Absolutely. And I think you can call yourself my girlfriend now Tilly," he said with a laugh, sending wonderful tingles throughout her entire body and she looked over at him again with a wide grin.

"I like the sound of that," she replied.

Tilly and Blake had to say their goodbye's a short while later and then the royal family, along with their demonic servants and covens, teleported away from the penthouse, leaving Tilly alone for the first time in days and she hated it.

The next week passed by slowly. Tilly threw herself back into cooking and tested out recipes on her friends when they stopped by to check in on her. She went to see Daisy a few more times too and felt happier than she had ever been thanks to the woman's help, her once jumbled thoughts now clear and focussed again at last. Tilly then went to see Andre the following week, deciding that she was ready to get back to the restaurant, not wanting to be left at a disadvantage with her career thanks to Trey's attack.

"Oh my God!" he cried as she came into the bustling kitchen, rushing over to her and ushering Tilly into his office with him after barking orders at his right-hand man, Leo, to take over the kitchen. Andre looked her up and down, checking her over and looking down at her hands. She had anticipated some attention on them and had decided to wear thick bandages so as not to attract too much attention to their incredibly fast healing time. Andre seemed happy that she looked well enough to be out and about but couldn't look Tilly in the eye once they were alone. He perched on the edge of his desk, staring at the floor as she took a seat in front of him.

"I can't believe what he did, or nearly did to you, Tilly. How did I not see what a monster he was? I let him take you home that night thinking you'd be safe, that he was a good guy," he told her, opening up about his guilt.

"No one knew Andre, don't blame yourself, okay?" Tilly asked him and he finally looked up into her warm blue eyes with tears in his own. "Like you said, he was a monster, and monsters have a way of hiding in plain sight. Look, I was hoping to come back, if you'll have me, of course. I need to get back into a routine," she added, making him smile.

"Of course, I wasn't sure when you'd be ready, though. I heard you had broken your thumbs. How are they?" Andre asked, looking at her hands again.

"Well, it was more of a dislocation than a break, really. They are nearly better already," she lied.

"Great, well yes I definitely want you back, however I'm afraid your intern's slot has been filled already," Andre said, making Tilly's face drop. "But," he quickly added with a smile, "I do need a new Sous Chef if you're interested?" he asked, and she grinned up at him.

"Absolutely yes," she said, and then laughed. "That's a little fucked up though, don't you think? I don't want to be accused of killing off the competition," she added, taking Andre's breath away with her dark joke.

"No, oh shit, I'm sorry, how inconsiderate of me!" he cried, staring at her wide-eyed. "I was planning on giving you the promotion, anyway. Everything that happened just got in the way, and you are not filling his spot on the team, I promise."

"Don't worry, I was just joking," she said, realising that her darker humour was not necessarily to Andre's taste and making a mental note to dial it down a notch in the future.

He smiled, taking her in. She really did seem to be doing better and looked happy and strong to him. Andre shook off his hesitation, deciding to give Tilly the benefit of the doubt.

"Okay, I guess I'm still a little raw on it all and I hadn't expected you to be ready to make jokes," he told her, which was true. Andre had always prided himself on being a good judge of character and being intuitive. It pained him to realise just how grossly mistaken he had been with Trey.

"I'm still raw, too. I just hide it with jokes, however inappropriate they might be," she replied with a shy laugh. Andre nodded and then reached behind him to grab her a new uniform, instinctively knowing to give her the black outfit rather than the white ones. Tilly grinned as she peered down at the new kit, running her hand over the embroidered restaurant logo with the words, 'Sous Chef,' underneath it.

"Take the rest of the week though Tilly, I'll see you on Monday," he told her, and she nodded in thanks.

"See you next week, boss," she said as she left.

Tilly bumped into Jessica on her way out and hugged her tightly before pulling her over to the corner to talk in private. She could sense her friend's new mark and was glad to have someone at work that she could talk with about all the Satanic side of her life.

"So, I gather it went well then?" she asked Jessica, not having had the chance to catch up with her properly since before the party.

"Hell yeah!" Jessica cried, making Tilly laugh. "It was such an amazing night, Berith marked me, and we fucked for hours on that big bed thing," she said, blushing at the memory.

"Whoa, that's great. I'm sorry, I didn't even realise you had joined in. I was kinda engrossed in other things. So, have you been learning about everything in more detail since the party then?" Tilly asked with a grin, wanting to make sure she was up to speed on the etiquette and her demonic master's expectations of her for the future.

"Yep, he gave me a bible before I went home and I've been researching ever since," Jessica told her. "And anyway, I'm not surprised you didn't realise we were there. You and your gorgeous master were well and truly in the zone, if you know what I mean?" she asked Tilly with a wink.

"Yeah, we were feeling it," she admitted with a sly smile.

"Understatement much? You two were all anyone could talk about, well apart from the Queen, obviously. I can't believe I was in the same room as her. Best night ever!" Jessica said with a smile, making Tilly glad she had decided to invite her along.

She hugged her friend goodbye, telling her to pop by the penthouse any time with her master. It was fast becoming a centre for the Earth-based demonic social scene, and she didn't mind at all; she was glad to have everyone around to keep her company. Tilly couldn't help but be envious of her friends for having their masters with them every day. It was becoming harder and harder only seeing Blake once a month and she missed him so much in between them it hurt.

CHAPTER FIFTY-TWO

Tilly decided to go and visit her parents for the rest of her week off before starting back at work, feeling guilty for having been so closed-off the past few months. She sent a silent prayer to Blake, asking for his permission to leave the safety of the penthouse, and immediately got a knock at the door. It was Beelzebub. The demon looked casual in his black polo shirt and jeans, but the posh brand names embroidered on them gave away the demon's expensive taste. He smiled at her, his dark-brown eyes warm, and she couldn't help but smile back.

"I'm here to take you to your folks," he told her, as an almost immediate answer from her master and she smiled, ushering him inside while she packed some bits for her stay.

"That was fast," Tilly replied as she checked her handbag to make sure she had her mobile phone and purse.

"Our Black Prince is not one to hold back when it comes to giving his orders Tilly, and anyway, you know I am always more than happy to help. So, what's the plan?" he asked.

"I'm just gonna go up and stay for a few days and then come back for work on Monday," she replied, making him smile even wider.

"Work? That's great, so you feel ready to go back then?" Beelzebub asked, not able to help being cautious and protective of her. He and Tilly had become genuine friends over the last few months, and he had promised Blake that he would keep a closer eye on her in his absence.

"Definitely, I got a promotion too. I'm a Sous Chef as of next week," she told him with a grin.

"Whoa, that's great, you gonna kill the boss next to take his place too?" he asked her jokingly, and she giggled loudly, struggling to catch her breath thanks to laughing so hard.

"Ha-ha, yeah I know, right? Now I know where I'm getting my new darker sense of humour from. I told a similar joke to Andre, and he looked at me like I was crazy! I will keep those kinds of comments for our circle of friends in future," she said, still laughing as she finished getting her things together.

The two of them then teleported to a hidden alcove down the road to her parents' farm a few minutes later. Tilly thanked him and then popped straight up and into the shop to greet her mother after he left. Bianca shrieked and threw her arms around her daughter straight away, only pulling back to take her in and check that she looked okay. They had still been estranged somewhat thanks to the huge number of secrets between them, but Tilly was glad to be there, hoping to regain some of their closeness again if they could.

She helped in the shop for the rest of the afternoon before heading to the main house to cook her parents some dinner. She elegantly arranged a three-course meal for them all, showing off her new-found flair and techniques. In the few days that followed, Tilly and her parents reconnected wonderfully. She told them about her new boyfriend and promised to bring him up to meet them when he was visiting sometime, much to Bianca's delight. She was sad to say goodbye when Sunday came but was also looking forward to getting home and smiled warmly when Beelzebub came to collect her from the alcove again that afternoon.

Once she was back at work again, the time flew by for Tilly. She didn't care though and was happy working such long days, often falling straight into bed at the end of her exhausting shifts for much needed rest and dreaming of her gorgeous boyfriend. The next few full moons brought a more relaxed and intimate time for her and Blake, the pair of them happy and content in their little bubble, making love and talking all night long, growing closer and closer every time. She was truly happy and finally felt settled and safe with him, as though they had found their way together at last. Her human friends all thrived thanks to their dark lovers' influence too and still came to the penthouse most nights to keep her company in between Blake's visits.

When Halloween came around again, Tilly teleported up to the old castle in Edinburgh with Berith and Jessica the day before to join in on the celebrations for Lucas's final demonic ritual, eager and excited to see Blake the next day. Only those close to the royal family and to Lucas could be present during the ritual, but the rest of their friends and the other demons were free to join the party that would then follow Lucas's fantastic transformation. Tilly was led to her room in the old castle by one of Lilith's darkly dressed followers, and then she immediately got changed into one of her beautiful, figure-hugging black tube dresses that Blake had bought her when they had gone shopping in London, which she accessorised with high-heeled ankle boots and chunky black jewellery before she then headed downstairs to join the others for dinner. Lucas and Lilith were buzzing and chatted excitedly with her and their sons over whisky shots until just before midnight. They knew that the Queen and Blake would come to Earth just after the clock struck twelve, thanks to their divine loophole on that day each year, and so the small group made their way into the great hall, awaiting their arrival excitedly. The large clock tolled midnight and Cate immediately appeared beside the altar that had been set up for the ritual, just like it had been the year before when Tilly had first learned about this dark world. Tilly peered up at her with a loving smile, happy to see the Queen again and she revelled in the smile Cate then gave her in return.

"Happy anniversary," a deep voice whispered in her ear, and she turned her head to look into Blake's deep green eyes.

"And what a year it has been, my love," she whispered back, leaning in to give him a kiss in greeting. By the time she had pulled back from his kiss, Tilly realised that the small crowd around them had fallen to their knees before the royal family, except her, again. She awkwardly fell to her knees too, grateful that Blake just chose to laugh at her forgetfulness. A few seconds later they all rose, and he took Tilly's hand, leading her over to the side of the altar where they joined the now quiet Brent, David, and Jackson. He left her there, going up to join his mother by the altar, who smiled down at Tilly again and then gave her a wink as she kissed her son's cheek.

"Welcome," Blake said, addressing the small crowd, who remained silent as he spoke. "We are all here to celebrate the gifts our almighty Dark Queen has agreed to bestow on this human. Kneel."

They all did as he commanded while Lucas and Lilith moved over to the large pentagram that had been drawn on the wooden floor and kneeled inside. Lilith lifted her hands, turned them palm side up and bowed before her Queen to indicate that she was ready to begin. One of Cate's dark witches Tilly recognised from the night of the orgy then appeared and came over from the other side of the altar with a large goblet in her small hands. She slit Lilith's offered wrists without a word, pouring a large amount of her blood into the vessel. Tilly watched as the demon wobbled slightly, seemingly woozy from the loss of blood, but steadied herself immediately, eager to continue. Both knew exactly what was expected of them and so Lucas then raised his arm to the dark witch too, which was also slit, and he then placed it directly over his wife's mouth, and she quickly sucked on his vein, eager to replenish her lost life-force.

Jackson let out a tiny yelp as he watched, doing his best to stay quiet, although he was clearly feeling squeamish and worried for his father. He was the most inexperienced in their group thanks to his age, and Tilly knew it must be hard for him to understand it all. Brent immediately reached across and took his brother's hand, offering him as much comfort as he could in the quiet darkness of the old hall. And it made Tilly smile as she watched them.

"Before the almighty Dark Queen, and in the presence of demons and witches, do you renounce all other allegiances and pledge your soul to your mistress, Her Infernal Majesty, Hecate?" The witch, who Tilly remembered was called Alma, asked Lucas.

"Yes, I do," he replied, panting and obviously a little woozy himself now thanks to his demonic wife that still sucked on his bloody wrist. Alma reached down and took his arm away from Lilith before she then held the blood-filled cup to Lucas's lips for him.

"Then drink of your demon, share her blood and become her son." She told him, and Lucas did as he was ordered, gulping down the thick liquid quickly.

"So mote it be, hail to the Dark Queen. Hail Satan!" Alma proclaimed and then turned to bow before Cate as she presided over the ritual silently from the altar. Tilly too looked up at her, taking in her dark expression and the almighty power that resonated all around her in the darkness and they all called out in respect to her, repeating the words Alma had just spoken.

"So mote it be, hail to the Dark Queen. Hail Satan!"

Darkness then quickly enveloped Lucas and Lilith in the pentagram, making Tilly's eyes blur as she tried to see what was going on inside, and she soon gave up. Just a few minutes later, it was over, and Lucas climbed to his feet, hand in hand with his wife. Tilly could sense his power, his strength and darkness just as she could when in the presence of other demons and knew that the ritual had worked.

"Wow," she whispered to herself, wondering if one day that would be her and Blake standing there like them. That was when she caught the two sets of deep green eyes that were watching her intently from beside the altar, reading her thoughts, and she looked up to find two matching dark smiles there for her, too.

CHAPTER FIFTY-THREE

It wasn't long before the debris from the ritual was cleared away and the party really started. The other attendees joined them all in the hall and each congratulated the new demon as they entered. Lucas was strong and eager to show off his new abilities, and Lilith was happy to give him his day to celebrate before they had to go to Hell and start his proper training and initiation into the demonic hierarchy, both eager to get him to the top as soon as possible.

Lucas immediately made himself look younger, around thirty years old, and he exuded a dark prowess now that drew everyone to him. The whole thing fascinated Tilly more than she had thought it would and she was keen to find out how he was feeling now that he had made the transition. She joined him for a drink at the bar; hugging and congratulating him for his successful demonic transformation while Blake continued to watch her from his mother's side with a smile. He had to wait until she released him from his duties before he could join her, but he could still listen in, and enjoyed her curiosity on the subject.

Brent and his brothers joined Tilly and Lucas at the bar with drinks in hand and they too toasted their father's success. All three of his children beamed up at him, genuinely pleased that he had obtained his desired power and demonic status at long last. Tilly chatted openly with them, absorbing the fun and carefree atmosphere as they all interacted effortlessly, and she was glad that these four men had stayed her friends despite all the ups and downs of this past year. A young girl then approached and joined the brothers, along with two of her friends, and Tilly introduced herself with a smile. The first girl bounced around, giggly and energetic, as she stood with them at the bar.

"Are you new?" Tilly asked, although she was pretty sure she already knew the answer.

"Yeah, we were marked by Lilith a couple of weeks ago," she said, and Tilly couldn't help but cringe a little at her bouncy attitude. "I'm Juliet, and these are my friends Tara and Chloe," she said, indicating to the two other girls she had appeared with using a wave of her hand. Tilly smiled at them all politely and shook the girls' hands, watching as David then put his arm around Tara and Chloe slid her hand into Jackson's. She then looked up at Brent, who smiled back at her and shrugged as Juliet leaned up on her tiptoes and gave him a kiss on the cheek.

"By any chance has your stepmother been match-making?" Tilly asked him teasingly, genuinely not bothered by his new arm-candy. If anything, she was glad to see that he had moved on, grateful that he had gotten over their break-up without resorting to his old womanising ways again.

"Yep, I think she's trying to make sure we stay busy while Dad's away learning and doing his initiations. We've put the circus tour on hold for a while too, so we're gonna settle here in Edinburgh. I might even give college a go," Brent told her with a shy grin.

"Wow, that's fantastic. You should study English literature or something, I'm sure you'd be great at it," Tilly replied with a genuine smile, remembering his love of reading.

"Yeah, and I'm moving in with him," Juliet added with a satisfied smile, eying Tilly curiously and holding Brent tighter as though laying her claim on him. "He's never even had a serious girlfriend before me. Lilith is hoping I'm the one," she added with a romantic sigh.

Tilly couldn't help but feel a little uncomfortable, but in a way, she was glad that they had decided a long time ago not to make a big deal out of their history, so she couldn't blame Juliet for not knowing the truth; if anything, it made it easier. Tilly could not have handled it if there was an awkward silence following that last comment. She simply smiled back at the girl and took a sip of her whisky, honestly hoping for the best for the pair of them while Brent just stared at the floor, seemingly eager for the conversation to move on.

A few seconds later Blake suddenly appeared at her side and Tilly looked up with a wide smile to greet him, but then her face dropped when she quickly realised he was standing eerily still instead of wrapping an arm around her in his usual calm way. He was seemingly vibrating with anger and stared down at Brent with cold, black eyes.

The partygoers around them began to slow down and freeze in their places, their eyes turning blank and silence descending in seconds while Blake continued to stare down at the trembling boy before him with a menacing look. Invisible hands then seemed to grip Brent's throat, and he fell to his knees, grabbing at his neck and choking, gasping for air. Tilly didn't dare move or say a word, knowing that Blake might punish her if she did, or that he could inadvertently turn his anger on her and do something that they would both regret. She couldn't help but stand and stare, helpless and trembling with fear, but she also knew that he hadn't frozen her along with the others for a reason; he wanted her to see this.

Blake then reached down and grabbed Brent by the neck with his actual hands; lifting him off the floor as he trembled and continued to choke, fear in his eyes as he stared into Blake's dark, blank face pleadingly.

"You don't ever think of her," he bellowed loudly at him, although their faces were only a few inches from one another. "You hear me? If I ever catch you remembering her like that again, I will rip your fucking throat out!" he ordered before dropping Brent to his knees and walking away, releasing both his physical and invisible grip on the boy's windpipe. Tilly turned to follow him but caught Cate's eye from across the room as she did and saw her give a tiny shake of her head, stopping Tilly's approach immediately. Cate took her son's hand as he reached her and teleported them both away without a word. The crowd around them then slowly began to unfreeze, no one even realising what had just happened except for Tilly and Brent.

CHAPTER FIFTY-FOUR

Everyone around the bar suddenly dropped to their knees to help Brent, who shooed them away, saying he was fine.

"My drink just caught in my throat," he said to his father, but a quick look at Tilly's pale face told Lucas a different story. He whispered in his son's ear as he helped him up.

"Don't ever be so foolish again," Lucas chastised Brent as they walked away. Tilly watched them for a moment and then had to fight back her tears as she wandered off in a daze too, trying to piece together the events from the last few minutes. She plonked herself down onto an empty stool at the bar, cradling her head in her hands as she fretted over what had just happened, and wondered if Blake was okay, hoping that he would come back to her again.

"Don't worry, Blake will be fine, Tilly," a voice said from beside her, and she lifted her head to see Luna sat there, smiling sweetly at her and then she took a long swig from Tilly's drink, finishing it off, and ushered at the waiter for two more. Tilly started to climb out of her seat to bow to her, but Luna shook her head.

"Don't even think about it," she said kindly, ordering her to stay on her stool.

"Is he coming back, your Majesty?" Tilly asked, hoping that the day was not spoiled for them.

"Yes, our mother took him home so that he can calm down before heading back up here. She stands by her promises," Luna told her, and Tilly smiled, thinking back to the deal she had made with Cate on the penthouse terrace. She took a long swig of the fresh drink the waiter delivered them and then took in the beautiful Princess before her for a moment. Luna was wearing black skinny jeans, and a purposely ripped rock band t-shirt that showed off her black bra and slim stomach underneath, looking cool and relaxed, yet still so powerful and fierce. Her long, dark-brown curls were pulled back into a high ponytail and cascaded beautifully down her back, accentuating her curves even more. Luna truly was a stunning woman. She looked so much like her mother, but she also had something about her that made her different. The Black Princess possessed kindness and a loving nature that exuded from her without her even speaking, her affectionate gaze alone putting Tilly at ease. She enjoyed her company immensely and hoped that they might become good friends in the future.

"Thank you," Tilly replied. "I didn't even know what was going on with him at first, but I assume Brent was letting his mind wander. Am I right?"

"Got it in one," Luna replied, shaking her head. "Foolish boy. Blake hates it that Brent has been with you, that he was your first. I think he would've killed him if it wasn't for our mother summoning him away."

"Whoa. So she can do that with you guys, too?" she asked, but then shook her head and smiled apologetically. "Of course she can, she's the Devil," Tilly added with an awkward laugh. Luna just smiled sweetly and reached her hand up, taking Tilly's chin in her palm and then sliding her soft thumb over her lips as she took her in.

"You really are very beautiful Tilly," she said, making her blush. "There's something about you, isn't there, something different. Has he ever told you that?" Luna asked, and Tilly nodded.

"He says I intrigue him," she replied, unsure if that was what Luna had meant.

"We each have our gifts Tilly, I can sometimes see things in others that my family cannot, and I see something in you. I don't know what it is yet, but we can all sense it in you. I think it's an energy that's kind of ancient, wise, and maybe even lucent. Beautiful. I know he doesn't like to share, but perhaps one day," she mused, tailing off before finishing her thought.

"Would you share Ash?" Tilly asked her, feeling slightly uncomfortable thanks to Luna's affectionate comments, so she tried to bring the conversation around in a different direction, to the Princess's lover that Blake had told her about.

"Hell no," Luna replied with a sly grin. "I suppose it's probably just sibling rivalry, or perhaps it could be mine and Blake's strong twin bond, but I am drawn to you," she said, planting a soft kiss on Tilly's red-hot cheek.

"Thank you, your Highness, but," Tilly began to say.

"But, she belongs to me, as you well know, dear sister," spoke a deep voice from behind them. It was Blake, his eyes the normal deep green and his expression gentle and calm once again. Tilly jumped, but Luna just smirked at him, a playful glint in her own matching green eyes.

"Took you long enough," she said, standing and giving him a kiss on the cheek before waving to Tilly and teleporting away.

"Ignore her, my love. She was just trying to get me back here quicker, knowing that I would sense her advances towards you. You'll get to know Luna better in time and she's ever the playful, yet annoying one of the family," he said, sitting on the stool where his twin had just been. Tilly bowed to him slightly and leaned forward, planting a passionate kiss on his ready lips and she was grateful to feel his urgent need for her in return.

"Blake, I didn't," she began to say, wanting to explain that she hadn't led Brent on or thought of him the same way he seemed to have been thinking of her, but he shook his head, stopping her.

"I know Tilly, it's okay. He will not be punished, but you don't realise what it's like for me. I not only hear the thoughts of others, but I can also see their memories like some sort of movie that's playing in their mind, like the image you showed me in the mirror that night of your dream. And he was remembering a very intimate time with you, only for a second or two but it was a time that he absolutely should not have been reminiscing over in my presence," Blake told her, his anger welling up again but he pushed it away, shaking himself off and then changing the subject.

"So, my love, what are we going to do with the rest of our day?" he asked her, a wicked grin on his lips. Tilly grinned back at him and took her master's hand and then led him from the party without another word, only stopping when they reached their suite to open the door. Blake grew impatient as she fumbled with the key, so he lifted her up into his arms and pushed Tilly against the closed door as he kissed her deeply and then took the key from her, slipping it into the lock with ease and then carrying her over the threshold as he began ripping Tilly's clothes off her very ready body.

CHAPTER FIFTY-FIVE

Well after the sun rose the next morning, Blake and Tilly emerged from their room, giddy, happy, and glowing following a few hours of wonderful lovemaking. He lifted her onto his back and playfully carried her back towards the party. There were still a few drunken partygoers going strong and the castle's staff members were busy laying out breakfast for them and the few early risers, or in Blake and Tilly's case the ones who had gone to bed but hadn't been to sleep. Tilly got stuck into a large plate of bacon and eggs straight away and refilled her mug of coffee three times, eager to stay fuelled and refreshed. Sleep was not an option today. She had dressed in a long jumper and leggings, feeling frumpy, but it was the warmest clothing she had brought along, having forgotten just how cold the old castle could get. Even with her insatiable boyfriend there to keep her warm, the cold air still chilled her to the bone.

Berith soon joined them with Jessica, who looked exhausted but happy and eagerly helped herself to some coffee and food as well. Tilly noticed that Berith had made himself look younger now, more polished, and much more presentable than when she had first met him in the penthouse. His dark-brown hair was shorter, and he had swept it casually to one side in a stylish quiff. He had even trimmed his beard so that it was shorter and much more flattering on his pale face. She wondered to herself what Berith would do with his time now that he was staying on Earth for a while, hoping that he was intending to keep the adorable smile plastered on Jessica's face.

"Berith's first mistress is rock-and-roll, Tilly," Blake joked with her, reading her thoughts as usual. "But his scruffy days are over now. Rock stars are much more polished and preened these days. You're putting a new band together, aren't you?" he then asked the demon, who smiled and nodded.

"Yep, and I've already started writing our first record, going back to the acoustic stuff, I think," he replied with a grin.

"I didn't even know that you were a musician, Berith?" Tilly asked him, realising she hadn't really had much chance to get to know him better over the last few months due to her being so hectic at the restaurant and him being so busy with Jessica and his other new followers while establishing his presence back on Earth.

"Yeah, I had a few bands when I was back on Earth a couple of hundred years ago. It's kind of in my blood," he replied nonchalantly, as if it was nothing. Tilly laughed, genuinely impressed, and hoping that one day a couple of hundred years would mean so little to her, too.

"There's a song of his that you particularly like Tilly. I have played it for you a couple of times I think, it's called *'follow you forever'*. Do you remember it?" Blake asked her with a cheeky smile, knowing all too well that he was talking about the track that she had dubbed as their song, the song they had first made love to. She blushed and nodded, grinning over at Berith.

"Wow, I wouldn't have thought you would have such a soft voice, even without the scruffy exterior. You will have to sing it for me sometime, if you don't mind, that is?" Tilly asked, and Berith smiled at her and bowed slightly.

"Of course I don't mind. I tell you what, I will play it at your demonic rebirth after-party," he promised with a sly grin, clearly expecting her to follow in Lucas's footsteps.

After breakfast, Blake took Tilly's hand and told her to close her eyes.

"Don't open them until we get there," he ordered her, and she nodded with an excited smile. She felt the tell-tale pull of being teleported away and then suddenly felt hot sunshine on her skin, the bright light streaming in through her closed eyelids. Tilly was desperate for a peek but followed her master's orders and waited until he gave her the go-ahead to open them again.

"Open up," Blake said after a couple of seconds, and she eagerly did as she was told, taking in the beautiful view around them. They were on their very own private beach. The pure white sand, clear blue ocean and cloudless sky were more perfect than anything she had ever seen before.

"Beautiful," she said, taking in the breathless view and stripping off her jumper and boots, suddenly feeling very hot.

"It is now. Don't stop there," Blake commanded, reaching down to grab the waistband of her leggings and he pulled them down, throwing them onto a small table next to a large hammock that swung between two huge palm trees. Tilly peeled off the rest of her clothes, basking in the hot sunshine as it warmed her pale skin.

"Where are we?" she asked him, following him to the water's edge and looking up into Blake's sparkling green eyes that shone thanks to the strong, bright rays that reflected off the water into them.

"A small island near Bali," he told her, undressing himself as he spoke. "Don't worry, it's all ours," he assured her as he pulled off the last of her underwear and then his own. He then lifted Tilly up into his arms and carried her into the warm water as she wrapped her legs tightly around him and kissed him passionately.

He carried on deeper, taking the two of them straight into the crystal clear waves and then slipped his hard length inside her with ease. They made love, thrusting together powerfully along with the waves as they bobbed up and down in the deep water, Blake delivering her pleasure eagerly and staring into Tilly's eyes as she came for him over and over again. She gripped his hips with her thighs and locked her ankles behind him, never wanting to let him go.

When he had reached his own climactic end, Blake lifted Tilly back out of the water and carried her over to the hammock, where he lay her down and the hot sun dried them almost instantly. Blake climbed on top of Tilly and kissed her deeply as he ran his strong hands down her still trembling body. She groaned loudly, ready for him, and he slid inside her hot cleft again, thrusting hard as she cried out for him, desperately wanting him to take possession of every inch of her willing body and soul.

"Well, that was a lovely surprise," Tilly whispered to him a little while later, exhausted but still revelling in their last shared climax as Blake laid with his arms and legs wrapped around hers in the hammock. They were so strong together now, their connection so deep that Tilly was surer than ever that she wanted to stay like this forever, to stay with *him* forever.

"Well, I still have a few more things planned for us to do today, my love, so you'd better think about getting dressed," Blake told her, grinning down at her as he stood and tossed Tilly her clothes. She scowled and groaned, but did as she was told, eager to find out what the next treat might be.

CHAPTER FIFTY-SIX

"Close your eyes," Blake told her again when they were ready to go, and Tilly quickly followed his orders. They teleported away again, and this time she felt the icy sting of freezing cold wind on her face when they arrived at their destination and wrapped her arms around herself as she waited for Blake to release her closed lids.

When Tilly was permitted to open them again, she looked around and took in the beautiful sight before her. She could tell right away that they were in New York, overlooking the city from a gorgeous penthouse garden. It really was a beautiful place, and it looked exactly like it had in pictures Tilly had seen in books and on television before, a city that she had always wanted to visit. Blake stood behind her and wrapped her in his arms to warm Tilly up, giving her a few moments to take it all in before leading her inside the huge apartment. It was lavishly decorated in blacks and reds, just like the other flat in London, and was obviously another of their families many bases when they visited Earth.

"There are some coats in the closet there," he said, indicating for her to choose one and Tilly grabbed a warm looking fur-lined coat in black, of course.

"Hungry?" Blake then asked, and Tilly nodded, realising that she was famished thanks to their both relaxing and active morning on the island. Without another word, he took her hand in his and, after giving Tilly a kiss, led her out through the main doors towards the lift. They went down and out through the lobby into the cold, busy street, where a limousine waited at the curb to take them to their secret destination. She could hardly contain her excitement, and Blake loved watching her as Tilly peered out the window, taking in the bustling city as they made their way to his chosen venue. He had arranged to take her to lunch at a fantastic and very posh restaurant run by one of the world's most famous leading chefs, Maximilian Dante. He was also a member of the Crimson Brotherhood, a secretive group of dark beings and their followers that was run by Blake's uncle Devin, and Tilly was eager to hear more about the mysterious order but had still not been granted permission to know more about them yet. Tilly stared open-mouthed as they pulled up outside the impressive building and Blake took her hand, leading the way into the empty restaurant. The entire place had been reserved just for them, and they feasted on a fantastic five-course meal that had been specially prepared for them by Maximilian himself.

After their meal was complete, he came out to greet his prestigious guests, bowing to Blake formally and then shaking Tilly's hand. She was star-struck at first and could barely find the words to speak with him about her hopes and dreams of becoming a famous chef herself. Blake helped her out, doing most of the talking while she stood awkwardly and laughed embarrassingly at herself, but then Tilly gave herself a mental kick up the bum and found her voice, knowing that these experiences didn't just happen to aspiring chefs in real life. She knew she had to make the most of it and before long she chatted comfortably with Maximilian about how her career in the food industry was going so far, and how she was getting on working under Andre.

"Andre Baxter is a very good chef, and will be a fantastic teacher for you, Tilly," Maximilian told her with a gracious smile. "But should you ever choose to relocate to New York, don't hesitate to contact me. We are always looking for talented young chefs to join us and if Andre says you're his up-and-coming protégé, I will gladly relieve him of you if I get the chance," he added, making Tilly smile and blush timidly as she absorbed his kind words.

They left the restaurant a little while later and walked along the busy avenues together for a while before Blake took Tilly shopping for more treats and then they took the limousine around the city to see the sights for their last few hours in the beautiful metropolis, the time whizzing past too fast for Tilly's liking. She didn't ever want this wonderful day to end.

"There's still one more surprise," Blake told her with a smile as they deposited her shopping in the penthouse, ready for one of his witches to collect and teleport back to London for her. He took her hand again and Tilly instinctively closed her eyes, knowing that it would have been his next order anyway, and he teleported the pair of them away for one last treat. When they arrived at the next destination, they were indoors, and Tilly could feel the warmth of an open fire on her skin. She could smell the logs burning in it, as well as the musty smell of old wood and pine needles.

"Open up," Blake told her one more time, and as she did so, a beautiful log cabin came into view. It was quaint and beautifully decorated with warm, earthy colours and had two large, brown leather sofas draped in heavy quilted throws in the middle of the room before the huge fireplace and there was a thick animal-skin rug beneath her feet making her feel cosy and warm already.

"Wow, where are we?" Tilly asked, looking up at Blake and relishing in his happy smile.

"Greenland," he told her, walking towards Tilly, and then turning her around so that she was looking out the window behind her at the jaw-dropping scenery outside. The sun was just starting to set, and a colourful haze filled the sky above them, a truly stunning and beautiful sight that instantly took her breath away.

"Whoa, is that the Northern Lights?" she asked, and he nodded. "Wow," was all she could add, completely mesmerised by the colourful show that played out before her.

Blake watched her rather than the sky. He didn't care about the lights that shimmered above them. Tilly was the only thing in this entire world he wanted to look at, nothing compared to her. He had loved reading her mind today. Every happy thought and experience she had had thanks to his careful planning was a welcome presence in his mind. He had wanted to give her the perfect day, a lovely mixture of tantalising treats and fantastic experiences to create a wonderful memory of their first anniversary together, and it really had been perfect.

CHAPTER FIFTY-SEVEN

Blake pulled the fur coat off Tilly's shoulders, tossing it onto a hook near the door before heading over to a small cabinet and pouring them both a drink. She smiled graciously and accepted the dark whisky, taking a small sip as she continued to watch the breath-taking illuminations in the sky before her.

"Thank you, this really has been the most wonderful day, Blake," she told him honestly, smiling over to him as he wandered over to a set of drawers and pulled out two black bathrobes.

"And it's not over yet darling," he told her, unbuttoning his shirt. "Strip," he then commanded with a cheeky wink, and Tilly immediately did as she was ordered, delighting in his gorgeous gaze as he watched her strip naked with a satisfied grin. Blake then stepped forward and handed her the robe and she smiled, unsure what he was up to, but she pulled it on and then followed him out the front door of the cabin and down a set of icy stairs that led around to the back of the frozen hut. They soon reached their destination, a steaming pool of water that was illuminated in the darkness by small spotlights that had been set into the ground underneath the blue water. Blake untied his belt and deposited the robe, showing off his gloriously muscular naked body in the dim light for a moment before he slipped down into the water, ushering for Tilly to follow his lead. She watched him for a few moments, gliding through the water gracefully before she threw aside her own robe at the pool's edge too and gasped as the cold air hit her naked skin, making Blake laugh.

"Hurry up and get in then," he said, and she quickly stepped down into the hot pool, letting out a delighted sigh as she submerged her cold body in the soothing water.

"It's so warm," she said, treading water as he swam over to her.

"Yeah, these are naturally hot springs, Tilly, nature at its best," Blake said, enveloping her in his arms before kissing her deeply, the natural saltiness of the water keeping them afloat effortlessly and the pair then laid back and watched the sky for a while, taking in the stunning show above them as they relaxed together, their hands entwined.

Later, when they were back in the cabin, Blake lay Tilly down on the thick rug that was sprawled out in front of the still roaring fire. The rug absorbed lots of the heat from the flames, making her hot and restless, and Blake didn't help matters as he expertly caressed her moist nub with his tongue and his fingers rubbed the tender spot inside of her cleft as he pursued her next climax.

"Blake!" she cried out uncontrollably, running her hands down through his dark hair as she came and she could feel her heart pounding in her chest, her body completely at his command. When she calmed down again, Blake trailed kisses up her stomach to Tilly's breasts, taking each of her nipples in his mouth in turn and sucking gently on them before moving up to her neck. She panted slightly, feeling hot and wanting more from her dark master as his lips pressed into every inch of her skin, delivering her with a sweet and sexy tingling feeling thanks to her heightened sensitivity.

"Are you ready for more?" Blake asked, his voice a husky groan against her neck.

"Yes, always," she whispered back, completely lost in their passionate moment.

He pressed himself into her naked body even harder with his own, his hands coming up to her throat to lift her chin so that he could kiss her deeper, commanding her silently as she willingly surrendered. Tilly then felt a burning, hot sensation on her neck as he leaned over her, followed by the strong and powerful lips of her lover as he covered the stinging area with his mouth.

She was confused at first, but soon became aware that Blake was sucking gently on her neck, his tongue flicking over the spot that had just been burning seconds before, and she quickly realised that he must have made a small cut on her skin. Tilly gasped as she felt him draw out a mouthful of her blood and then he swallowed it down, but she was not scared. She had promised to give him every part of herself willingly, and she had meant it.

Blake leaned up over her, a tiny bit of her blood still on his lips as he bit down on his own finger and placed it in Tilly's mouth, giving her a few drops of his blood in return for the small amount that he had just taken from her. She realised straight away what he was doing, that he was blood-sharing with her, and she smiled as she sucked his fingertip clean. It was just seconds before the wonderful partaking of strength, power and love washed over her, without there being any hint of control in it at all.

He leaned down to kiss her again and Tilly could taste her own blood on his lips, but she didn't care. The sharing of blood between them had been intense and they both could feel its power as it strengthened them and their already powerful bond. Tilly reached down and grabbed Blake's hips, cupping his bum-cheeks with her hands and pulling him inside of her, needing to feel him, having to have him inside of her in every way she could imagine.

A couple of hours later, they teleported back to the old castle in Edinburgh, signifying the end of their perfect day together. They arrived just in time for Blake to drop Tilly off at her bedroom and kiss her goodbye, unable to stay even a minute longer, otherwise he would quickly react to the harsh restrictions the Earth and moon held over him.

"See you in four days," Blake whispered, checking the clock.

"I can't wait," Tilly told him, leaning up to peck him on the cheek. "Now go," she then ordered him with a smile, and he teleported away just seconds before the clock struck midnight. Tilly did her best not to get upset this time, knowing that she would see him again in just a few days, so gave into her tiredness when it finally hit her once she laid down in the bed, and she drifted off to sleep almost instantly.

The next morning Tilly joined Jessica and Berith for breakfast in the castle dining hall again, most of the others all having left the city already, but the pair of them had stayed to take Tilly home after her day with Blake was over.

"Wow, you look like you had an amazing day. Did he take you somewhere nice?" Jessica asked her when Berith was out of earshot, taking in the bags under Tilly's tired eyes but also the content, relaxed smile she couldn't help but wear.

"Oh yes," Tilly told her with a romantic sigh and told her friend all about their whirlwind world tour the day before. She couldn't help but exude happiness after the wonderful day she had shared with her master, and she couldn't wait to see him again in a few days' time.

"Ready ladies?" Berith asked them as he returned to the girls' side, and they both nodded, each taking one of his hands and then feeling the familiar pull of the teleportation as they set off towards London.

On their way, Tilly somehow felt as though she had slammed into a brick wall. A strong, painful feeling swept through her and Tilly felt as though she was then being pulled downwards towards Earth. She fell to the ground with a hard thud, which winded her instantly. Tilly coughed and sputtered, trying to catch her breath and struggling to figure out what on Earth had just happened. When she could stand, she looked around, trying to take in her surroundings and hoping to figure out what was going on. She was in a field; definitely not at the penthouse where they should have landed, but neither Berith nor Jessica were anywhere to be seen. Tilly stepped forward, trying to head off in search of her friends but felt resistance in the air around her, light at first but then a force that felt like a kick to the gut sent her flying backwards onto the floor. The wind was knocked out of Tilly for the second time in just a few minutes and she lay there for a while, feeling confused and sore, before a voice called out to her from a few feet away.

"Well, well, well," said a woman's voice as she approached slowly. "Look what we have here, it seems I have caught a rat in my little trap," she said, looking down at Tilly with disgust when she reached the weak human that was still lying on the dirty ground gasping for breath. "I just knew it would work. I caught you in my invisible net while you teleported overhead. How very clever of me," she added, clearly pleased with herself.

"Who are you and how did you trap me?" Tilly asked, rising to her feet but standing still this time to avoid being thrown around again by the strange force field.

"I set up my wonderful little trap here that is specifically designed to ensnare dark beings and their followers who might be teleporting overhead, unfortunately your friends got away from the lightning-like hands that tried to grab at their ankles, but one out of three isn't bad I suppose," the witch replied, eying Tilly thoughtfully. "My name is Beatrice, I am a white witch, and my master is the angel Michael," she then told Tilly, and she even added an over-dramatic bow and a swish of her hand as though enjoying herself. "Your turn," she added, staring at Tilly expectantly.

"Go to Hell," she answered, not wanting to give this witch any information about herself or her master. Tilly could not sense any commandments coming to her from Blake or even a connection to Cate right now and assumed that the witch must be somehow stopping their links to each other with her white magic.

Beatrice stepped over the invisible circle that entrapped Tilly, unrestricted by the threshold, and slapped her hard across the face, sending her flying across the dirt once again. She rolled onto her front and tried to stand, but suddenly felt herself being teleported away from the field, her body unable to move as though invisible ropes had now wrapped themselves around her.

They arrived at an old white church within seconds and Tilly was thrown straight onto the floor where she lay before the dusty old altar. Beneath her was a large pentagram, painted with white lines and she could feel herself growing woozy and weak thanks to its light power as it seeped into her and tried to take hold of her senses, as though trying to force her cooperation. She soon felt her body being released by the unseen ropes, but it didn't matter. She was already too frail to even try and fight back, the powers of light and dark seemingly having a battle inside her own skin.

"You feel it already?" Beatrice asked her, staring down at Tilly in amazement while she still lay inside the powerful mark. "Who *is* your master?" she asked her again, scowling at her from outside of the pentagram.

Tilly laughed, a deep and maniacal laugh that reminded her of the same one that she had heard escape her lips just once before, in Trey's sinister embrace.

"You are going to get your throat ripped out, witch, and I cannot wait to see it," Tilly replied, venom in her weak voice when she peered up at Beatrice as she approached. She looked young, but Tilly knew she was more than likely hundreds of years old and had bright blue eyes and blonde hair that was almost white in the dim light of the old building. Beatrice stared down at her, her cold eyes boring into Tilly's as she trembled and started coughing uncontrollably.

She tried to sit up but was thrown backwards onto the floor without another word from the witch, her body being pressed into the hard wood while her arms were stretched out to her sides, mirroring the iconic figure that stood on the cross nearby. Beatrice then spoke a quiet spell that Tilly could not understand, the words neither English nor any other language she had ever heard before and she could do nothing but lie there, powerless to fight back.

The black inverted cross on her right arm rose to the surface following Beatrice's incantation and Tilly tried to twist her arm over, wanting to cover it, but she was unable to move even an inch.

"Bingo," Beatrice said when she looked down at it, a wicked grin on her face as she took in the black mark on Tilly's arm, a knowing twinkle in her eye. She stepped inside the pentagram and climbed over Tilly, straddling her on the floor and looking down into her wide eyes as she spoke.

"So, let me work it out and you can tell me when I get it right, yeah?" she asked, mocking Tilly's resistance to her questions openly.

"Luna's followers were all killed except her warlock boyfriend, so I know you aren't hers," she said, and she began ticking off her fingers as though working through a list.

"Blake doesn't have any that we know of and neither does Serena, nor her filthy offspring, so you must be Devin's, am I right?" she asked, leaning down to cup Tilly's cheeks with her hands.

"But then again, you stink of darkness, reek of it even. Your master has fucked you very recently, hasn't he, or else you are the coven slut? Hmm, this is a conundrum," she mused aloud, sitting back upright and tapping her index finger against her chin thoughtfully. Tilly could see she was enjoying being overdramatic far too much, so stayed quiet, not giving Beatrice the satisfaction of an answer.

"Oh well, I guess I'll just have to let you go then if you aren't gonna tell me," Beatrice then added, tilting backwards on her heels as if she was going to stand, and Tilly felt a small glimmer of hope come up from somewhere deep inside of her but she pushed it aside instantly, knowing that this witch would not let her go, not just like that.

Beatrice could see that Tilly didn't believe her and smiled as she sat herself back down with a hard thump and knocked the air out of Tilly's lungs.

"Okay, you got me," she admitted, and then she pulled a long, rune embossed dagger from her boot and slid it straight into Tilly's abdomen, all the while with a very wicked and satisfied smile on her face.

CHAPTER FIFTY-EIGHT

Tilly gasped, the pain searing through her instantly as her body fought against the intruding blade and her mind threatened to lose consciousness.

"Don't you go anywhere just yet, little girl. I need you to take a message to your master, whoever it might be, and to your Dark Queen," Beatrice said, leaning down closer to Tilly's face, demanding that she stay conscious, yet pushing the dagger deeper into her body as she did so.

"Tell them that the angel Uriel demands that Cate delivers the child she stole from him before the next All Hallow's Eve, along with his fallen brother, Lucifer. Failure to do so will result in the High Council of Angels raining white fire down from Heaven. She will know what all of that means, my dear," Beatrice informed her, withdrawing the blade and standing over Tilly again, watching with a wicked smile as she finally passed out.

Black, complete, and totally engulfing darkness enveloped Tilly. She was neither falling nor floating, and it was as though it was suffocating her, seeping inside her body uncontrollably. She tried to scream, to shout out, but there was nothing but endless night all around her and her body was no longer whole or real. She was a mere shell of her human self, a soul; already marked and claimed, and now on its way down into the dark abyss below.

She felt a throb from somewhere deep inside of her chest, almost like a pulse that sent her consciousness into overdrive as two distant lights came into focus from somewhere seemingly very far away. As they grew closer, Tilly realised they were not lights, but eyes, green, gorgeous eyes. She urged them closer, prayed for them to come to her faster, and in a blink, she was kneeling inside a black pentagram, surrounded by hooded figures and dark shadows. Before her stood her master, his eyes sad as he took in the sight of his lover before him. She choked, trying to catch her breath, but soon realised that it was useless.

"Master," she managed to cry out, looking up at Blake pleadingly, desperate for answers or an idea of what was going on, but she was already coming to the terrible realisation by herself.

"Leave us," he said, commanding the rest of the demonic greeting party forcefully. He needed to speak with Tilly alone. They did as they were told and then Blake kneeled to gather up Tilly's frail form in his arms, kissing the top of her head as he cradled her.

"Am I dead?" she asked, sobbing into his dark cloak.

"Not just yet, but almost," he informed her. "I have sent Alma up to help you. She will do everything she can, but you need to hold on, Tilly. Do not let yourself linger here. Fight your urges to stay with me now, for if you stay, that means you have chosen to die, and I cannot allow that. Fight the darkness, fight me," Blake told her, looking down into her face seriously and forcing her to stay lucid.

"If you die now, you will be nothing more than a weak soul thanks to that fucking witch, you will have no place at my side Tilly," he told her, and she sobbed harder but nodded, understanding his words, knowing that she had to go back, to force herself back to her broken body. First, though, she had a message to deliver.

"She told me to tell you, to tell the Queen," she managed, eager to pass on the strange yet terrible information and Blake stiffened.

"What? Tell me everything she said, Tilly," he urged her, pulling her gaze up to meet his.

"She said to tell your mother that the angel Uriel wants the child she stole from him, and he wants Lucif, he wants your father," she said, realising in time not to say his name but Blake didn't care, his eyes growing wide at her words.

"He wants them before the next All Hallow's Eve, otherwise the Council of Angels will rain down white fire from Heaven," she finished. "Does that make sense?"

"Yes, Tilly. It makes sense, she means all-out war," Blake said, his face suddenly pale thanks to her dark words, but he did not say any more. He kissed her gently and then placed a hand over her chest and pushed hard over Tilly's heart, she felt the heavy throb burst out of him and reverberate through her forcibly, and then he did it again and again until she felt herself pulling away.

"Hold on Tilly, don't you die, okay?" he told her as he delivered one final burst into her chest and she lost consciousness again, her soul returning to a body full of nothing but pain and suffering. But she had already promised him long ago to take whatever pain Blake thought she could handle, and he knew Tilly could deal with it for him just one last time.

Blake then turned and teleported away from the antechamber. He knew that time was not on his side, Tilly was fading fast and in order to save her, he might have to strike a deal with his mother first. For the first time in his long and lonely life, Blake truly knew how it felt to be afraid. Losing was not an option now. He would do anything, give anything, if it meant saving his lover's life, but the Black Prince was also extremely aware that he had a very grave and sinister message to deliver first.

The end.

About the author

LM Morgan started her writing career putting together short stories and fan fiction, usually involving her favourite movie characters caught up in steamy situations and wrote her first full-length novel in 2013. A self-confessed computer geek, LM enjoys both the writing and editing side of her journey, and regularly seeks out the next big gadget on her wish list.

She spends her days with her hubby, looking after her two young children and their cocker spaniel Milo, as well as making the most of her free time by going to concerts with her friends, or else listening to rock music at home while writing (a trend many readers may have picked up on in her stories.)

Like many authors, LM Morgan has a regular playlist of tracks she enjoys listening to while writing, featuring the likes of Slipknot, Stone Sour, Papa Roach, Five Finger Death Punch, and Shinedown. If you'd like to listen along with her, you can find her playlist on Spotify under 'writing dark romance'.

LM Morgan also loves hearing from her fans, and you can connect with her via www.lmauthor.com

If you enjoyed this book, please take a moment to share your thoughts by leaving a review to help promote her work.

LM Morgan's novels include:

The Black Rose series:
When Darkness Falls: A Short Prequel to the Black Rose series
Embracing the Darkness: book 1 in the Black Rose series
A Slave to the Darkness: book 2 in the Black Rose series
Forever Darkness: book 3 in the Black Rose series
Destined for Darkness: book 4 in the Black Rose series
A Light in the Darkness: book 5 in the Black Rose series
Don't Pity the Dead, Pity the Immortal: Novella #1
Two Worlds, One War: Novella #2
Taming Ashton: Novella #3

And her contemporary romance novels:
Forever Lost (gangster/crime)
Forever Loved (gangster/crime follow on from Forever Lost)
Rough Love (MC crime/mystery story. Can be read as a stand-alone)
Tommy's Girl parts one and two (dark psychological thriller)
Ensnared – A dark romance
Sins of the Brother – a dark torture themed short story
Cinders and Ashes – a fairy tale retelling
Fly Away – a short romance story
Dark Nights and White Lights: A collection of short stories, flash fiction and poems

LM also writes YA Science Fiction under the alias LC Morgans:
Humankind: Book 1 in the Invasion Days series
Autonomy: Book 2 in the Invasion Days series
Resonant: Book 3 in the Invasion Days series
Hereafter: Book 4 in the Invasion Day series
Renegades: Book 5 in the Invasion Day series

LM also writes dark vampire fantasy under the alias Eden Wildblood:
The Beginning: Book 1 in the Blood Slave series
Round Two: Book 2 in the Blood Slave series
Made of Scars: Book 3 in the Blood Slave series
Even in Death: Book 4 in the Blood Slave series
Tortured Souls: Book 5 in the Blood Slave series

Printed in Great Britain
by Amazon

29885999R10300